S0-ACT-050

DEC   2019

HAZARD BRANCH LIBRARY
1620 W. Genesee St.
Syracuse, NY 13204

THE
LIGHT
OF ALL THAT
FALLS

By James Islington

THE
LIGHT
OF ALL THAT
FALLS

The Licanius Trilogy: Book Three

JAMES ISLINGTON

www.orbitbooks.net

This book is a work of fiction. Names, characters, places, and incidents are the product of the author's imagination or are used fictitiously. Any resemblance to actual events, locales, or persons, living or dead, is coincidental.

Copyright © 2019 by James Islington

Cover design by Lauren Panepinto
Cover illustration © Dominick Saponaro
Cover copyright © 2019 by Hachette Book Group, Inc.
Map © 2016 by Tim Paul

Hachette Book Group supports the right to free expression and the value of copyright. The purpose of copyright is to encourage writers and artists to produce the creative works that enrich our culture.

The scanning, uploading, and distribution of this book without permission is a theft of the author's intellectual property. If you would like permission to use material from the book (other than for review purposes), please contact permissions@hbgusa.com. Thank you for your support of the author's rights.

Orbit
Hachette Book Group
1290 Avenue of the Americas
New York, NY 10104
orbitbooks.net

First Edition: December 2019
Simultaneously published in Great Britain by Orbit

Orbit is an imprint of Hachette Book Group.
The Orbit name and logo are trademarks of Little, Brown Book Group Limited.

The publisher is not responsible for websites (or their content) that are not owned by the publisher.

The Hachette Speakers Bureau provides a wide range of authors for speaking events. To find out more, go to www.hachettespeakersbureau.com or call (866) 376-6591.

Library of Congress Cataloging-in-Publication Data
Names: Islington, James, 1981– author.
Title: The light of all that falls / James Islington.
Description: First edition. | New York : Orbit, 2019. | Series: The Licanius trilogy ; book 3
Identifiers: LCCN 2019017386 | ISBN 9780316274180 (hardcover) | ISBN 9780316274173 (ebook) | ISBN 9780316274166 (library ebook)
Subjects: GSAFD: Fantasy fiction.
Classification: LCC PR9619.4.I85 L54 2019 | DDC 823/.92—dc23
LC record available at https://lccn.loc.gov/2019017386

ISBNs: 978-0-316-27418-0 (hardcover), 978-0-316-27417-3 (ebook)

Printed in the United States of America

LSC-C

10 9 8 7 6 5 4 3 2 1

For Eirielle and Taliesin.

I look forward to sharing this world with you one day.

SEA OF
STORMS

Tacin Rada

Narutav

NARUT

Deilanr

Ildora

Menarsh
Mountains

Lantarche

ISLES
OF
CALANDRA

DESRIEL

Thrindar

Devliss

Malacar

Tasidel

Talmiel

ANDARRA

Variden

Caladel

VASHIAN OCEAN

N E S K

N

W E

S

Shal
Terom

N

Ilshan Gathdel Teth

Tawwas
Eryth Mmorg

T A L A N   G O L

The Boundary

Gahille
Menaath
Mountains

Ilin Illan

A N D A R R A

Alsir

Naminar

Lake
Tyria

Prythe

Mountains of Alai

A R Y T H   O C E A N

Jais

N E S K

Caldiarre

Ishai

O T H Y N N E

©2016 by Tim Paul timpaulmaps.com

The following is meant only as a quick, high-level refresher of the events in *The Shadow of What Was Lost* and *An Echo of Things to Come*, rather than a thorough synopsis. As such, many important occurrences and characters will be glossed over during this recap, and some—in a few cases—are not mentioned at all.

THE ANCIENT PAST

More than four thousand years ago, the wedding of Tal'kamar Deshrel *ended with* Elliavia, *his new wife, being brutally and senselessly slain. Mad with grief, Tal'kamar drew for the first time on a dark power called* kan, *killing all those in attendance as he took their life force—their* Essence—*in a vain attempt to bring her back to life.*

Burdened with sorrow and guilt over both Elliavia's death and his own actions, Tal'kamar soon found that he was unable to die: even when beheaded, he would simply wake up again in a different body and a different land. Worse, he eventually discovered that not only had he failed to save Elliavia, he had inadvertently allowed a creature from the Darklands—*a place of unimaginable pain and suffering—to enter the world through her body. This creature was a shape-shifter named* Nethgalla; *having retained Elliavia's memories, she began pursuing Tal'kamar in an obsessive attempt to be with him once again.*

Rejecting Nethgalla, Tal'kamar traveled for hundreds of years, eventually meeting other people who, like himself, could not die. One in particular, Gassandrid, *claimed that their long-lived nature was a gift from* El, *the god who had created the world—but that contrary to most people's beliefs, El was currently imprisoned within the bounds of time, and it was in fact the great enemy* Shammaeloth *who had set into motion the inevitable chain of events that now shaped the world.*

Gassandrid went on to explain that their immortality was an attempt by El to change the course of these events, using the last of His power to bend the path upon which Shammaeloth had set fate. Gassandrid also asserted that if they were able to change things enough, they would ultimately be able to go back in time, undoing all that had been done under Shammaeloth's rule and living in a world where true choice was possible.

As proof of his claims, Gassandrid provided Tal'kamar with detailed visions of the future: evidence of the predestined nature of the world, and therefore the invisible chains in which each and every person was enslaved.

Tal'kamar, eventually convinced by his inability to change the events that had been foreseen, became the final immortal to join the group who would become known as the **Venerate**. *This group consisted of eleven men and women: Tal'kamar, Gassandrid,* **Alaris, Andrael, Wereth, Tysis, Asar, Meldier, Isiliar, Diara,** *and* **Cyr.**

The Venerate worked together for hundreds of years, using the visions El provided them to enact justice and do great good in the world. After a time, though, their work became increasingly focused on what El said was necessary to bend fate toward their goal, finally culminating in Tal'kamar being asked by El to destroy the legendary city of **Dareci.** *Though this act would kill millions of people, El assured Tal'kamar that it was an awful but necessary step toward freeing the world—one that would force the Darecians to flee to* **Andarra** *and begin working on the time-travel device known as the* **Jha'vett.**

Tal'kamar, sickened but choosing to believe that everything he did would ultimately be undone, agreed. He changed his name to **Aarkein Devaed** *and followed El's instructions to create the* **Columns,** *a weapon that ultimately leveled Dareci and killed everyone living there.*

This horrific act split the Venerate, many of them refusing to believe that El had truly asked Tal'kamar to perform it.

Hundreds of years passed as the Darecians, despite their incredibly advanced weaponry, were slowly driven from the **Shining Lands.** *Many of the Venerate returned to assist Tal'kamar, finally accepting that he had been acting at El's behest. However, Andrael in particular remained unconvinced, having suspected* even before Dareci's destruction that the "El" the Venerate were serving had been lying all along—and was quite possibly Shammaeloth himself.

As Andrael continued to research the consequences of what El was trying to achieve, he came to believe that it was the Venerate's unnatural ability to manipulate kan that was at the root of the Darklands' connection to their own world—a cause, as well as an effect, of the rift between realities. He eventually concluded that if that breach was widened by the Darecians as El wished, it could pose an extraordinary danger: one which, should El then be allowed to reach it, could potentially unleash the full misery of the Darklands upon the world.

Determining that the only solution was to close the rift entirely—and that the only way to do so was to eliminate the aberrant connections to the Darklands that were holding it open—Andrael reluctantly set about creating a weapon that could kill the Venerate.

To this end, he finally succeeded in making the blade **Licanius**.

Despite Andrael's warnings and the new threat that Licanius posed, the remaining Venerate continued to follow El's instructions to push the Darecians to Andarra; there, the surviving descendants of Tal'kamar's near genocide created **Deilannis**, a great city with the Jha'vett at its heart.

Tal'kamar, upon hearing that the Jha'vett was complete, forged ahead of the Venerate's army in order to sneak into Deilannis and travel back in time, believing that his doing so could end the war quickly and prevent further bloodshed. However, this only caused the Darecians, forewarned of his approach, to panic and attempt to use the Jha'vett themselves.

The result was a dire miscalculation by the Darecians, their use of **Shackles** reacting with the Jha'vett to strip them of their natural resistance to kan, turning them into beings of nearly pure Essence. Only Tal'kamar's decision to save them by sending them to **Res Kartha** allowed them to survive; effectively imprisoned there, they would eventually become known as the **Lyth**.

Tal'kamar himself then attempted to activate the Jha'vett, discovering too late that it had been damaged. After the ensuing explosion, a young man calling himself **Davian** appeared, *claiming to be a friend of Tal'kamar's from an inevitable future. Davian accused Tal'kamar of willfully ignoring the evils he had perpetrated and avoiding taking responsibility for his actions, warning him that nothing in the past could ever be changed— including the death of Elliavia.*

Enraged, Tal'kamar killed Davian.

Davian's words lingered as El and the Venerate's army drew closer to reaching Deilannis, though, and doubts began to fester in Tal'kamar's mind. Frustrated in his attempts to convince the other Venerate to investigate further, he was ultimately forced to ally with Andrael to help him complete and activate the **ilshara:** *a massive wall of energy that surrounded the entire northern third of Andarra, separating it into a new area that would eventually become known as* **Talan Gol.**

Though Andrael had been working on the ilshara for centuries, Tal'kamar only ever meant it to be a temporary measure, a way of delaying the invasion until he could be certain of El's intentions.

In the end, it would stand for more than two thousand years.

THE RECENT PAST

A generation ago, the **Augurs**—*men and women with the ability to wield kan and see an unchangeable future*—*ruled Andarra, as they had for almost two thousand years since the creation of the* **Boundary.** *Assisting them were the* **Gifted:** *people able to manipulate a reserve of their own Essence to physically affect the world around them.*

Although outwardly everything appeared to be well, one of the Augurs—*a man named* **Jakarris**—*became increasingly concerned about the worsening state of the Boundary, and worried that the traditionally warned-against uses of kan that his peers had recently been experimenting with were responsible for its decay. He spent many years attempting to prove this theory, coming close to finding conclusive answers, only for his research to one day be completely destroyed.*

Suspecting his fellow Augurs of sabotage but not having any proof, a disgruntled and disheartened Jakarris was eventually recruited by Nethgalla, who convinced him that the only way to delay the imminent collapse of the Boundary was to overthrow the current generation of Augurs. Nethgalla also explained that their downfall would enable her to introduce **Vessels** (Augur-made devices, created to use Essence in specific ways) into Andarran society, which, ultimately, could prove decisive in resisting the forces beyond the Boundary.

Jakarris proceeded to assist Nethgalla in undermining the Augurs' rule, using his position to create a series of embarrassing public mistakes that cast serious doubt on the Andarran leaders' ability to see the future. Refusing to openly admit that there was a problem, the Augurs withdrew from the public eye as they tried to determine what was happening, tasking the Gifted with controlling an increasingly nervous populace. Public unrest soon turned to anger as some of the Gifted began overstepping their new mandate, often violently. A schism in Andarran society quickly formed.

Eventually things came to a head and a shocking, bloody rebellion overthrew the Augurs and the Gifted, the uprising instigated by **Duke Elocien Andras**—a member of the previously token monarchy—and fueled by the proliferation of new weapons provided by Nethgalla that were designed to target those with powers. Jakarris slew the other twelve Augurs, and of the five original Gifted strongholds (called **Tols**), only two—**Tol Athian** and **Tol Shen**—held out against the initial attack.

After spending five years trapped behind their Essence-powered defenses, the Gifted finally signed the **Treaty** with Duke Andras and the monarchy, officially ending hostilities. The cost to the Gifted, however, was high. One of the Vessels Nethgalla had provided was used to create the **Tenets**: four magically enforced, unbreakable laws that heavily restricted the use of Gifted abilities. Commoners were also allowed to become **Administrators** of the Treaty, giving them even more legal and practical control over those who could wield Essence.

Furthermore, any Gifted who broke any terms of the Treaty not covered by the Tenets were forced to become **Shadows**, permanently stripped of their abilities and horribly disfigured in the *process. This happened most often to the unfortunate Gifted students who lacked the skills to pass their graduation Trials, and who were therefore not vouched for by the Tols as able to adequately control their powers.*

This was another of Nethgalla's contributions to the rebellion; unbeknownst to the Andarrans, every Gifted who became a Shadow was in fact being linked to a Vessel called the Siphon, which allowed Nethgalla to use that Gifted's Essence as if it were her own.

Thus the Gifted, while technically free again, remained heavily policed and despised by most. Meanwhile, the powers of the Augurs were condemned under the Treaty. For any who were discovered to have such capabilities, a death sentence at the hands of Administration awaited.

THE SHADOW OF WHAT WAS LOST

Sixteen-year-old **Davian** is an intelligent, hardworking student at the Gifted school at **Caladel**—but as his Trials approach, he still cannot figure out how to wield his powers, despite having the **Mark** on his forearm that both binds him to the Tenets and indicates that he has previously used Essence. To make matters worse, Davian can unfailingly tell when someone is lying—something that only an Augur should be able to do. His closest friends, **Wirr** and **Asha**, are the only ones he has told about this unusual skill.

When **Elders** from Tol Athian arrive early to conduct the Trials, Davian is approached in the dead of night by one of the newcomers, a man called **Ilseth Tenvar**. Ilseth claims to have been a member of the **sig'nari**, the group of Gifted who served directly under the Augurs before the rebellion twenty years ago. He admits to knowing that Davian is an Augur, and urges him to leave before he fails his Trials and is turned into a Shadow. Ilseth also provides Davian with a mysterious bronze box, which he explains will guide Davian to a place where he can be properly trained.

Confident the Elder is telling him the truth, Davian leaves the school that same night; Wirr, after discovering at the last second Davian's plan to flee, refuses to let him go alone and accompanies him.

Unaware of these events, Asha wakes the following morning to find that everyone else in the school has been brutally killed. In shock and not knowing why she is the only one to have escaped the slaughter, she realizes that Davian's and Wirr's bodies are not among the dead. However, when Ilseth discovers that Asha has been left untouched, he reveals himself to have been complicit in the assault. Assuming that Asha was deliberately left alive by his superiors (and being unwilling to kill her himself as a result), Ilseth instead turns her into a Shadow, thereby erasing her memory of everything she has seen that morning—including the knowledge that Davian and Wirr may still be alive.

Davian and Wirr head north, avoiding trouble until they are captured by two **Hunters**—the Andarran term for those who track down and kill the Gifted for profit. However, they are rescued by another Hunter, **Breshada**, who despite her profession mysteriously lets them go again, saying only that they owe their thanks to someone called **Tal'kamar**.

Continuing to follow Ilseth's instructions, the boys cross the border into **Desriel**, a country governed by a religious organization called the **Gil'shar**, who believe that all human manipulation of Essence is an abomination. In Desriel, the punishment for even being born with such an ability is death.

Navigating several dangers, Wirr and Davian are led by Ilseth's bronze box to a young man named **Caeden**, a prisoner of the Gil'shar. They set him free, only to be attacked by a creature known as a **sha'teth**. Caeden saves them from the sha'teth in a display of astonishing power, despite being physically weakened from his captivity.

Meanwhile, Asha is brought to Andarra's capital **Ilin Illan** by Ilseth, who continues to pretend that he had nothing to do with the slaughter at Caladel. The **Athian Council**—the group of Elders who lead Tol Athian—come to believe that Asha may hold the key to finding out more about the attack, but do not wish to share this information with Administration, who are also looking into the incident. The Athian Council decides to keep her at the Tol, hiding her true identity from everyone else.

After a traumatic encounter with a sha'teth that mysteriously refuses to attack her, Asha meets **Scyner**, the man in charge of a secret underground refuge for Shadows known as the **Sanctuary**. Scyner recruits Asha to find out why Duke Elocien Andras—head of Administration and enemy to those in the Sanctuary—is showing such great interest in the attack on her school.

When Elocien hears that Asha is a survivor of the attack, he uses Tol Athian's need for a new political **Representative** in the ruling body of the **Assembly** to have Asha assigned to the palace. Asha soon learns that Wirr is Elocien's son; not only may he still be alive, but if he is, thanks to his birthright he will one day be able to single-handedly change the Tenets. Despite Elocien's reputation as the driving force behind the rebellion twenty years ago, Asha also discovers that he has secretly been working for the past few years with three young Augurs—**Kol, Fessi,** and **Erran**. Knowing this, she realizes that she cannot betray Elocien's trust to Scyner, despite the deal she had previously agreed to.

In Desriel, Davian, Wirr, and Caeden meet **Taeris Sarr,** a Gifted in hiding who believes that Caeden is somehow tied to the recent, worrying degradation of the Boundary. Taeris also reveals that Ilseth Tenvar lied to Davian during their encounter at the school, and so exactly why Davian was sent to Caeden remains a mystery. Concerned that Ilseth's motives are sinister and that his bronze box may trigger something undesirable upon contact with Caeden, Taeris recommends that the box be kept away from him until they know more.

Davian and Wirr soon discover that Caeden has been charged with murder by the Gil'shar—but has no memories of his past, and does not even know himself whether the accusations are true. Taeris determines that they need to head back to Andarra, to Ilin Illan, where Tol Athian has a **Vessel** that may be able to restore Caeden's memories. However, with the Desrielite borders so carefully guarded, they decide that their best course of action is to enlist the help of **Princess Karaliene Andras**—Wirr's cousin—in order to get home.

When they finally meet with Karaliene, she recognizes Caeden as an accused murderer and refuses to risk a major diplomatic incident by smuggling him out of the country, despite Wirr's involvement. Their best hope dashed, Taeris determines that their only other option is to leave Desriel through the ancient, mysteriously abandoned border city of **Deilannis**.

In Ilin Illan, Asha forges new friendships with the Augurs, soon discovering that they have had unsettling visions of a devastating attack on the capital. Not long after, rumors begin to circulate of an invading force—christened the **Blind** due to their strange eye-covering helmets—approaching from the direction of the Boundary.

As she and Elocien try to determine how best to defend the city without exposing the Augurs, Asha makes the astonishing discovery that the Shadows are still able to access Essence, if they do so by using Vessels. This, she realizes, means that their abilities are only repressed when they are made into Shadows, and not (as commonly believed) completely eliminated.

After an abrupt, strange message from a seemingly older Davian, Asha becomes suspicious of Ilseth's version of events surrounding the attack on the school at Caladel, and she has one of the Augurs restore her lost memory. When she finds out that Ilseth was complicit in the slaughter, she fools him into revealing his lies to the Athian Council, who subsequently imprison him.

As Davian, Wirr, Taeris, and Caeden travel through the eerie, mist-covered city of Deilannis, they are attacked and Davian is separated from the rest of the group. He is caught in a strange rift, barely surviving his journey through the void; when he emerges back into Deilannis he meets **Malshash**, an Augur who tells him that he has traveled almost a century backward in time.

Disbelieving at first but eventually convinced of Malshash's claims, Davian spends time in Deilannis's **Great Library**, a massive storehouse of ancient knowledge. Under Malshash's guidance, he quickly learns to use and control his Augur abilities. Though Malshash's exact motivations for helping him remain unclear, Davian realizes that his teacher has been studying the rift in the hope that he can change something that has already happened.

Back in the present a devastated Wirr, believing Davian is dead, continues on to Ilin Illan with Taeris and Caeden. As they travel, they come across horrific evidence of the invading force from beyond the Boundary—strengthening their belief that they need to find a way to prevent it from collapsing entirely. Concerned that Caeden's memories may hold the key to exactly how to do that, they hurry to Ilin Illan before the Blind can reach the city.

Once they are in Ilin Illan, Taeris attempts to convince the Athian Council to help them, but the Council—having heard the accusations of murder leveled against Caeden, and also influenced by their combative past with Taeris—refuse. With nowhere else to turn, Taeris and Caeden take refuge in the palace, where Wirr is able to convince Karaliene that Caeden is a central figure in what is happening.

In Deilannis, a training accident results in Davian experiencing Malshash's most traumatic memory: the death of his wife Elliavia at their wedding, and Malshash's desperate, failed attempt to save her afterward. Malshash, after conceding that this is one of the main reasons he wants to alter the past, sends Davian back to the present.

Davian heads for Ilin Illan but is briefly waylaid by another Augur, **Ishelle**, and an Elder from Tol Shen, **Driscin Throll**. The two attempt to convince Davian to join Tol Shen, but Davian has heard about the invasion by the Blind and is intent on reaching the capital in time to help.

Davian arrives in Ilin Illan, enjoying an all-too-brief reunion with Asha and Wirr before the Blind finally attack. Meanwhile Caeden and Taeris, understanding that the Athian Council is never going to help them restore Caeden's memory, plan to sneak into Tol Athian and do so without their permission. However, before they can use the Vessel that will restore Caeden's memories, Caeden instead activates Ilseth's mysterious bronze box, a flash of recognition leading him to leave through the fiery portal it subsequently creates.

As Wirr and Davian help with the city's defenses, Asha convinces Elocien to give Vessels from Administration's stockpile to the Shadows, as they are not bound by the Tenets and thus can freely use them against the invaders. After Asha and the Shadows join the fight, the Blind's first attack is successfully thwarted.

Despite this initial victory, Ilin Illan is soon breached, and the Blind gain the upper hand in the battle. Elocien is killed as the Andarran forces desperately retreat, and Asha realizes to her horror that he has been under the control of one of the Augurs all along. She decides not to tell a grieving Wirr, who, with Davian's help, hurries to Tol Athian and changes the Tenets so that all Gifted can fight. Even so, it appears that this new advantage may come too late.

Caeden finds himself in **Res Kartha,** where a man seemingly made of fire—**Garadis ru Dagen,** one of the **Lyth**—reveals that Caeden wiped his own memory, setting this series of events into motion in order to fulfill the terms of a bargain between the Lyth and **Andrael.** This bargain now allows Caeden to take the sword **Licanius**—but it also stipulates that he may keep the sword for only a year and a day, unless he devises a way to free the Lyth from Res Kartha.

Concerned about what he has agreed to but even more concerned for his friends, Caeden returns to Ilin Illan, utilizing the astonishing power of Licanius to destroy the invading army just as defeat for the Andarran forces seems inevitable.

In the aftermath of the battle—having revealed himself as an Augur during the fighting—Davian decides to take Ishelle up on her offer and head south to Tol Shen, where he believes he will be able to continue looking for a way to strengthen the Boundary against the dark forces beyond. Asha chooses to remain in Ilin Illan as Representative, while Wirr inherits the role of **Northwarden,** head of Administration.

Still searching for answers about his past and determined to help his friends fight whatever is beyond the Boundary, Caeden uses the bronze **Portal Box** again. He this time finds himself in the **Wells of Mor Aruil** and meets **Asar,** another former member of the Venerate.

To Caeden's horror, Asar restores a memory that indicates not only that Caeden was responsible for the murders in Desriel of which he was accused—but that he is in fact Aarkein Devaed.

Caeden, after weeks of wrestling with the knowledge that he was once Aarkein Devaed, reluctantly accepts the truth of his identity. Asar assures Caeden that he switched sides and in fact renounced the name Aarkein Devaed long ago; despite this, Caeden continues to struggle as Asar tries to help him restore his memories, catching only glimpses of his former life.

Their efforts are interrupted when Nethgalla, in the body of Elliavia, arrives in Mor Aruil and mortally wounds Asar, claiming that she is Caeden's wife and is there to help him. Confused, Caeden heeds Asar's dying warning about Nethgalla and flees using the Portal Box. In doing so, he remembers to his horror that his plan is to seal the rift in Deilannis—which will necessitate the killing of each and every one of both the Venerate and the Augurs.

Meanwhile, near the major southern city of **Prythe**, Davian and Ishelle train in Tol Shen, protected by the newly declared **Augur Amnesty** but also unable to leave because of it. Davian becomes increasingly frustrated as the Shen Council continue to disregard the threat of the Boundary collapsing, seemingly content to keep the Augurs at the Tol and showing no desire to properly prepare them to fix it.

In Ilin Illan, Asha, continuing in her role as Representative, risks reprisals as she makes multiple secret trips back to the Sanctuary—despite the orders of both the Athian Council and the Assembly—in order to investigate the mysterious disappearance of the Shadows. At the same time, Wirr grapples with his new position as Northwarden, navigating the fraught political consequences of the new world he has created by changing the Tenets. He also attempts to help Asha by looking into the mysterious origins of the Vessels used to create Shadows, trying to determine where his father obtained the weapons that facilitated the overthrow of the Augurs twenty years ago.

Rumors of a threat to Wirr's life prove true when, during dinner with the **Tel'Rath** family, an assassination attempt is made upon him. Only the intervention of Scyner, who has been watching Wirr and Controls the assassins before they can do him any harm, enables him to survive. After saving him, Scyner tells Wirr that the information he has been looking for is in his father's journal, hidden at Wirr's family's estate in **Daren Tel**.

After burying Asar, Caeden finds himself in the **Plains of Decay** and inadvertently frees Meldier from his imprisonment in a **Tributary**: a device that has been draining his Essence for centuries in order to supply energy to the Boundary. Meldier, unable to take action against Caeden for fear that it will result in the bargain with the Lyth remaining unfulfilled, shows Caeden that he was responsible for the destruction of Dareci—insisting that Caeden is on the wrong side of the fight, and pleading with him to reconsider his current course.

Asha, during one of her secret trips into the Sanctuary, stumbles across a meeting between a clearly disturbed Isiliar, the sha'teth named **Vhalire**, and an **Echo**. Believing that she might be able to uncover important information, she risks following the Echo into the catacombs beneath Tol Athian. However, the Echo realizes that it is being followed, leaving Asha lost underground.

Asha keeps her nerve, waiting until she is eventually able to follow Isiliar and Vhalire again. She witnesses Isiliar's attack on Vhalire with the blade **Knowing**; when Isiliar leaves Vhalire severely wounded, Asha speaks briefly with the sha'teth before killing it. She escapes and hides Knowing elsewhere in the catacombs, having been warned by Vhalire that Isiliar will be able to track her otherwise.

Davian, believing that he is being followed by an Augur in Prythe, discovers that Erran and Fessi have been tailing him in the hopes that Scyner—whom they wish to bring to justice for Kol's death in Ilin Illan—would eventually approach him. The two newcomers are reluctant to submit themselves to the Augur Amnesty; not only do they mistrust the Shen Council, but they are concerned about the existence of what appears to be an Augur-proof area at the center of the Tol.

Davian agrees to ask the Council about this mysterious area, but returns to find that **Rohin**—a newly arrived Augur—has achieved instant popularity within the Tol. It quickly becomes apparent that Rohin's talent is a form of Control, causing everyone who hears him to be convinced of the truth of his words. Davian alone, his natural ability to see lies directly conflicting with Rohin's power, is able to resist.

Rohin imprisons Davian in a kan-proof cell within Tol Shen; Davian, needing kan to be able to draw Essence from his surroundings to survive, desperately manages to create an artificial **Reserve** of Essence within himself before being sealed in. Despite the dangers supposedly inherent in using kan within his own body, Davian does not appear to suffer any ill effects from the act.

Wirr, advised by the king to leave the city for a few days after the assassination attempt, travels to his family estate in Daren Tel in the hope of finding his father's journal. There he receives a cold welcome from his mother, **Geladra Andras**, who informs him that everything from his father's study has already been handed over to Administration. Not bothering to temper any of her strongly anti-Gifted sentiment, it is immediately apparent that Geladra does not believe Wirr should be Northwarden, showing both suspicion of and disdain for her son's recent decisions.

Later, at Daren Tel, Wirr is approached by Breshada, the Hunter who helped him and Davian in Desriel. She has been following him since recognizing him in Ilin Illan, desperate for assistance after discovering that she has somehow become Gifted herself, and having been branded an Andarran spy by her own people as a result. Wirr reluctantly agrees to find someone to help her control her new ability.

That evening, Wirr's sister **Deldri** reveals that their mother lied to him, and that the contents of his father's study have in fact not yet left the property. Deldri assists him, and he eventually finds both his father's old journal and an **Oathstone**: a small Vessel used by Administration to bind Administrators to the Tenets. Furious at how Geladra has been treating both of them, Deldri asks Wirr to take her back to the capital; Wirr is reluctant but, after Geladra forcibly attempts to stop them from leaving, agrees.

Fessi and Erran rescue Davian from his cell in Tol Shen, having become aware that something is wrong after Davian failed to show up at a scheduled meeting. Davian explains what Rohin has done; the three then intercept Driscin Throll as he returns to the

Tol from traveling, warning him of Rohin's ability and enlisting his help in stopping the Augur.

Driscin tells them of an amulet in Tol Shen's vault that will prevent Rohin from being able to touch kan; the four of them break into the Tol, retrieving the amulet and ultimately imprisoning Rohin.

When Davian questions him, Rohin says that he has foreseen the utter destruction of northern Andarra; he also claims that the leadership of Tol Shen knew of the Blind's devastating attack on Ilin Illan well before it happened. After **Reading** him, the Augurs discover that he was sent to the Tol by Scyner, though for what purpose is unclear.

Caeden, continuing to trust the Portal Box to take him where he needs to go, arrives at the snow-covered city of **Alkathronen**. He soon discovers Isiliar's destroyed Tributary; Isiliar, who has evidently been driven mad by her time in the device, has been lying in wait and viciously attacks him.

Alaris saves Caeden from Isiliar; after Caeden heals from his extensive injuries and wakes, Alaris does his best to convince him that he is fighting for the wrong side. Caeden learns that he needs to find Nethgalla again, as it appears that she has taken the final Vessel he needs to satisfy Andrael's agreement with the Lyth. Alaris tells Caeden that he will most likely find Nethgalla in Deilannis. Caeden returns to Ilin Illan, briefly reuniting with Karaliene before heading to Deilannis to confront Nethgalla.

After turning Rohin over to the Shen Council, Davian, Ishelle, Fessi, and Erran head north for the Boundary, defying the Council's wish to keep them in the Tol.

In Ilin Illan, Wirr begins reading his father's journal, gradually uncovering the truth behind the origins of the rebellion against the Augurs. **Aelric** approaches Wirr and asks for an excuse to be sent south, wishing to deal with a personal matter that he doesn't want anyone else—including **Dezia**—to know about. Wirr reluctantly agrees.

As a group is organized to travel to Deilannis, Asha volunteers to go, hoping to uncover more information in the Great Library about the origin of the Shadows. At Karaliene's urging, Wirr sends Breshada as well, with Asha agreeing to try to teach the former Hunter how to control Essence.

Not long after they leave, Isiliar violently attacks the palace, believing Caeden to be hiding there. Many are killed in the mad rampage, and Deldri, among several others, is injured. Only Alaris's appearance and subsequent subduing of Isiliar eventually puts a stop to the unchecked violence.

After the attack, Dezia inquires after Aelric, and she and Wirr realize that he has gone to deal with his financial backers for the **Song of Swords**, who were angered after he deliberately lost the final match of the tournament. Dezia, deeply concerned for her brother, leaves to go after him.

On the road to the Boundary, Ishelle is ambushed by flying **Banes** called **eletai**, which leave her all but dead until Davian arrives and is able to revive her. Though she is quickly healed and able to continue on their journey north, it is clear that the severe injuries she suffered during the attack have taken a toll.

Asha and Breshada, along with the rest of their party, arrive at Deilannis to discover that the bridge is guarded by snakelike Banes known as **dar'gaithin**. They attempt to enter the city, but in the ensuing fight Asha falls from the bridge into the river **Lantarche**. She is miraculously saved by Breshada; together they find a way back up into the city and then to the Great Library, where Asha discovers an ancient account describing the Siphon and its connection to the Shadows.

As Wirr prepares for Geladra to officially challenge him for the position of Northwarden, he discovers that while holding an Oathstone, he is able to force anyone who has a Mark—either Gifted or Administrator—to follow his instructions. Despite Taeris's urging him to use this newfound ability to consolidate his position, Wirr resists doing so, determined to find a way to remain the leader of Administration without resorting to such objectionable measures.

Davian, Ishelle, Fessi, and Erran reach the Boundary, dismayed to discover not only that it is steadily weakening, but also that the kan mechanisms governing it are complex beyond anything they could have imagined. To their surprise, they also find what appears to be a potential way through the massive barrier of energy and into Talan Gol.

Caeden arrives at Deilannis, reaching the Great Library and finding Asha and Breshada already there. Breshada immediately reveals herself to be Nethgalla; after handing Caeden the Siphon in order for him to bind the Lyth, she tricks Asha into using the sword **Whisper** on her, effectively transferring the power of the Siphon—and thus the responsibility of powering a Tributary—over to her.

Healed of being a Shadow but now condemned to a worse fate, Asha returns to Ilin Illan, intending to immediately use the **Travel Stones** to go north and find the Tributary that Caeden had once intended to use himself. Wirr, upon learning of this and seeing an opportunity to prove the threat of the failing Boundary to Administration, persuades Geladra to come north as well—agreeing that if she returns to Ilin Illan unconvinced, he will step down from his position voluntarily.

Caeden, now finally in possession of the Siphon, returns to Res Kartha and explains his plan for freeing the Lyth to Garadis. Though furious that they will be forced to give up their extraordinary strength, the Lyth reluctantly accept that Caeden's proposal still upholds Andrael's deal. They allow themselves to be bound, transferring their collective power to the Siphon, and thus to Asha. As part of the deal, now that they are able to once again leave Res Kartha safely, Caeden agrees to send them to their ancestral homeland of the Shining Lands.

At the Boundary, Davian, Asha, and Wirr are briefly reunited. Despite Geladra's insistence that the Augurs remain under Gifted supervision, Ishelle, temporarily not in control of her own actions, uses the gateway they previously discovered in the Boundary to enter Talan Gol. Davian and Fessi follow her in an attempt to bring her back, only to have the entrance seal shut behind them, trapping them in enemy territory.

Asha and Erran also defy Geladra and leave to find the final Tributary, which Asha is able to locate thanks to her ability to sense the whereabouts of the Shadows. They find their way to an island that has been completely hidden by kan, just off the coast and within sight of the Boundary itself. There she and Erran again meet Scyner, who has been waiting for Asha to arrive.

Erran recognizes that the amulet Scyner now possesses is the one they used in Tol Shen to subdue Rohin. Scyner admits to killing Rohin and taking the amulet from him.

An attack on the island by a group of **tek'ryl**—massive, scorpion-like Banes—is repelled when Asha intervenes, unleashing her full power for the first time and annihilating the threat. Meanwhile Erran returns to where they last saw Ishelle, Davian, and Fessi, hoping to uncover what happened to them before Asha uses the Tributary and potentially seals them in Talan Gol.

The three Augurs in Talan Gol find themselves in a nest of eletai, Ishelle's strange behavior clearly driven by a link to the creatures resulting from the Banes' previous attack on her. Discovering a set of **Telesthaesia** armor and realizing that one of them might be able to make it back to Andarra while wearing it, they return to the Boundary, reaching it just ahead of a large army.

Wirr, Geladra, and Karaliene witness the Boundary beginning to fail, a terrifying horde of Banes breaking through. The three of them take shelter, assisted by Erran, as a devastating surprise attack by the eletai crushes the insufficient Andarran defenses. As they hide from the Banes, Geladra and Wirr realize that Erran is the one who had been Controlling Elocien over the past few years.

Through Erran, Asha is able to see that the Boundary needs reinforcing immediately, despite her now knowing that Davian will be trapped on the other side as a result. Ishelle is able to make it through the weakened wall of energy thanks to the protection of Telesthaesia, but Davian and Fessi are sealed in Talan Gol as Asha is forced to enter the Tributary and restore the full strength of the Boundary.

Despite having survived the initial attack by the Banes, Geladra is shockingly killed when the corpses left by the eletai eventually mutate and revive, becoming eletai themselves. Horrified and heartbroken, Wirr and Karaliene burn the remainder of the bodies, ensuring that no more eletai are created.

Caeden finally travels to **Ilshan Gathdel Teth** to confront the Venerate; a fight with Meldier and Isiliar results in Isiliar's death, but Caeden is ultimately captured.

Davian and Fessi are brought to Ilshan Gathdel Teth as prisoners, having been seized after the Boundary was sealed. Fessi, panicking as she recognizes her surroundings, flees; Davian, forced to run as well, discovers that Caeden is being held nearby and is being tortured for information about Asha's location by Meldier.

When Davian intervenes, Meldier tells him that Caeden was once Aarkein Devaed, which Caeden himself ashamedly confirms. Despite his shock at this news, Davian chooses to stand by Caeden; when Meldier attacks, Davian takes him by surprise and kills him with Licanius. Caeden then convinces Davian to behead him with a regular sword—the only way to guarantee his escape from Talan Gol. Caeden promises that he will return soon to set Davian free.

Having woken up in a new body and shape-shifted back into his preferred form, Caeden then relives a final, devastating memory—discovering that, in a fit of rage, he killed a time-traveling Davian almost two thousand years ago.

THE
LIGHT
OF ALL THAT
FALLS

Prologue

The blizzard howled around Caeden, shading the world a merciless, freezing white.

He scraped icy flakes from his vision and bowed his head, trudging onward and downward against the ferocious gale that raged up the mountainside, each lungful sharp and every step sodden. He had been walking for what felt like hours; it couldn't be far now. Impossible as it was to make a portal directly into Alkathronen—and though the Builders' last city was hidden even to kan—he felt confident that he had opened his Gate close by.

Fairly confident, anyway.

He focused, filtering out the knifing cold and briefly extending a shield of Essence around himself, creating a bubble that sluiced through the snow ahead in a brief, hissing cloud of steam. Using even that much of his power was a risk. He needed as much time in Alkathronen as possible before anyone knew he was here, and the Venerate had taken a fresh Trace from him during his torture in Ilshan Gathdel Teth a year ago.

Caeden shook the grim memory from his mind, shrugging the heavy coil of rope more securely onto his shoulder and leaning hard into the cutting wind as he let his Essence shield drop again. A few more steps and a hazy glow began to reveal itself in the white; a minute later he was stumbling into the abrupt calm of the canyon, the sound of distantly crashing water finally reaching his ears as the flakes in the air became distinct, their movement easing from diagonal slash to gentle downward drift.

Two enormous, parallel waterfalls resolved themselves, one on either side of the path ahead, bolts of blue energy streaking along their perfectly sheer, shimmering facades. The road itself was mercifully dry, snow dissipating in tiny puffs of steam wherever it touched the stone surface. Caeden felt his body relax slightly as the reprieve of warmth began to press against his frozen cheeks.

He reached up and pushed back his tightly drawn hood, allowing the gentle heat in the air access to the rest of his face as he looked around warily. This was the central hub for the Builders' works, the point from which they had built portals to each of their wonders. Alaris had needed to remind him of that, the last time he was here, but it was clear in his mind now as he studied the symbols inscribed on the edges of the road. Recognized them. Understood their purpose.

Knowledge like that didn't surprise him anymore. He had recovered much during this past year of isolated observation and planning—almost all his memories, he thought—even if his mind still shied away from reliving the specifics of his history as clearly as it once had.

The latter, he had to admit, pleased him almost as much as the former.

He pressed forward, quick now that the deep drifts no longer hampered his progress, sensation returning to his limbs with a sharp prickling as he walked. The glow of Alkathronen up ahead formed a shielding dome against the blizzard, even as it exposed the city's utter emptiness.

Caeden slowed as he passed the symbol marking the portal to Ilin Illan, pushing down another shudder of doubt over his decision to come here. It was a risk to expose himself like this, rash, even, and yet...it was time. Davian had been a prisoner for a year now. That meant he was about to be sent to Zvaelar.

Which, by all estimates, gave Caeden less than a month to prepare.

He pressed on. The remaining Venerate had not been idle since his escape: Davian had warned him of Gassandrid's idle boast, so as soon as he'd remembered, Caeden had chanced sneaking into the Andarran capital to see if it was true. Sure enough, a disturbing number of the people he had observed there were showing the subtle mental markers. Hundreds had been Read, now. Maybe thousands.

Gassandrid, Alaris, and Diara were leaving no stone unturned in their scouring the country for him—or, more to the point, for Ashalia's whereabouts.

He'd anticipated that, of course, and had done what he could to make sure that there were no clues to find, removing even the memories of his presence whenever he did have to venture away from the Wells. Unfortunately, it had also meant not risking any contact with his friends in Andarra. The Venerate almost certainly knew of them now, would be watching them closely.

He cast another longing glance back at the Builders' symbol for Ilin Illan. That enforced isolation, in the face of what he knew was coming, had been hard...but it also meant that Karaliene, Wirr, and the others were relatively safe. The Venerate might have come within a breath of breaching the ilshara, but they were nothing if not patient—and would be even more so now that Caeden's brief capture a year ago had handed them Licanius. They would not attack their own bait.

Not so long as it was bait that they believed served a purpose, anyway.

The uneasiness of that thought clung to him as he came to a halt in front of the massive white archway that marked access to Alkathronen itself. He closed his eyes and focused on it. Sure enough, the subtle, crisscrossing lines of kan were there, blocking the only path inside.

He stood for a moment longer, hesitating.

Then he stepped beneath the towering stone, disrupting the near-invisible strands, the air shivering around him in response. Alaris would know that he was here, now.

The only real question was whether he would tell the others.

He stared in absent worry at the burbling fountains that adorned Alkathronen's entrance, then shook his head and started toward the east-facing cliff.

Either way, he had little time remaining and much still to do.

Caeden fed more Essence into the heatstone, clenching his teeth to keep them from chattering.

He held his hands out toward the waist-high cylindrical Vessel and seated himself atop a low white wall, finally allowing himself to rest. Several of these heatstones dotted the city, perfectly integrated into the aesthetics and yet somehow always easy to spot. Stoked with a little Essence, they emitted warmth well beyond that which Alkathronen already provided—an especially welcome function right now, given Caeden's groaning muscles, rope-burned hands, and snow-sodden clothes.

He could have fixed all of that quite easily, of course, but he also knew that he would need every bit of Essence in his Reserve soon enough.

He stared absently over at the eastward edge of the city, where the soft glow of Essence held back the thrashing white that raged just beyond. The storm had worsened since he'd arrived. That hadn't made his work over the past five hours any easier, but it would be to his advantage if it kept up now.

He shifted to warm the other side of his body, switching his gaze to the arrow-straight road leading into Alkathronen's center. He could see where the snow failed to melt, the flickering and waning Essence in the distance revealing a steadily deepening white.

He shivered as he watched that unsteady illumination, not wanting to think about the last time he'd been here. It was rarely far from his mind, though—still impossible to ignore both what he had learned then, and what he had done since.

Isiliar had been his friend, and he had knowingly left her to be driven insane.

And then—after she had finally been set free—he had killed her.

"You look unhappy, Tal'kamar."

Caeden started at the voice. Then he steeled himself and stood, turning and nodding a greeting to the tall, chiseled man who was standing across the street from him.

"You're not wrong," he conceded to Alaris, the quiet words carrying easily in the dead hush. He didn't smile, but he made certain not to appear hostile, either. "I am glad you came, though."

Alaris's blue eyes were locked on him. The other man at first glance looked relaxed, but there was discomfort to his stance. Wariness.

"A promise to a friend is a promise that cannot be broken," said Alaris. He studied Caeden. "And I want very much to believe that we are still friends, Tal. Despite."

"As do I." Caeden meant the words. Still, he couldn't help but let his gaze flick to the silent streets behind Alaris, processing just how quickly the other man had come. "I wasn't expecting you for a while yet."

Gassandrid was the only one of the remaining Venerate who could make a Gate, and there was a strict code of accountability for all trips outside the ilshara. For Alaris to have kept his word to Caeden and not told the others about this meeting, he would have needed an excuse to leave—a very convenient one, to have employed it at such short notice. Caeden had planned for having mere hours before Alaris's arrival, but in truth had expected days.

"I am alone," Alaris assured him, noting the glance. "Gass was already expecting to send me out for...something else. The timing simply matched up."

Caeden frowned at that—what business did Alaris have that would bring him so close to an Alkathronen portal?—but he knew the other man well enough to believe him. He slowly, carefully unbuckled the blade at his side, then tossed it onto the ground between them. "Good. Because I am here to talk."

Alaris nodded as he eyed the steel thoughtfully, but did not discard his own weapon.

Caeden gestured to the bench on the opposite side of the heatstone; when Alaris was seated, the two watched each other mutely before Caeden finally blew out his cheeks, trying to find the right way to start this conversation.

"The last time we were here," he began, "you said to come back when the Lyth had been dealt with. You said that if I wanted to understand both sides of this fight, you would be willing to have that discussion." Alaris leaned forward with something like hope in his eyes, but Caeden quickly shook his head. "I wish to be up front, my friend. I have remembered enough now to make that discussion unnecessary. I am not on your master's side of this, and I never will be again."

Alaris's expression twisted. "I am...saddened to hear that. Unsurprised, but...still." His shoulders slumped, a bitter note

5

entering his tone. "If you are no longer interested in my perspective, Tal, then what is this about?"

The disappointment in his friend's voice hurt, but Caeden pressed on. "An offer. An exchange."

Alaris snorted. "If you are talking about Licanius—"

"Of course I'm not." Caeden spoke the words softly. He already knew exactly where Licanius was, anyway. "I want you to free Davian. In exchange, I will tell you where Cyr's Tributary is, and I will not stop you retrieving him from it."

Silence greeted the statement, Alaris's brow furrowing as he considered what Caeden had said.

"Why?" He shook his head bemusedly. "I know you need both Cyr and Davian dead to close the rift, and Cyr is by far the harder of the two to kill. Even more so if you set him free."

Caeden kept his expression smooth. Cyr had gone to his Tributary willingly—had been convinced of the truth about Shammaeloth and had volunteered—but the other Venerate didn't know that. They assumed that he was a prisoner, as Meldier and Isiliar had been.

"Because I made a promise to Davian," Caeden replied firmly. "And I cannot rescue him—not from Ilshan Gathdel Teth, not with you standing against me. I am not as strong as you. I never was." He said the words simply, without self-pity or false modesty.

Alaris gazed at him. "A smart man might take this to mean that Davian is more important than Cyr, in some way that we are not currently aware."

"A smart man would realize that I would never have proposed such a trade if that were the case. This is about me trying to keep my word, Alaris—that is all. I'm trying to be the man I aspire to be, rather than the man you knew." Caeden leaned forward. "We both know that I kill Davian—that is not something that can be undone, regardless of how long you hold him." The thought still turned his stomach, even a year after his learning the fact, but he made sure not to show it. "On the other hand, neither of us knows Cyr's fate. So it is a good offer, Alaris. One that I will not make again."

Alaris stared at the heatstone for a while, obviously considering.

"Can you hear yourself, Tal?" he asked suddenly. He looked up, and there was a haunted aspect to his gaze as he stared at Caeden. "You say you did not come here to talk about this, but... the man you aspire to be? You want to exchange one friend— whom you imprisoned for two thousand years—with another, and your argument for my accepting the trade is that I already know you will kill one of them anyway." He gave a tired, bitter laugh. "Yet you are so certain that you are the one on the right path, and that the rest of us have been misled."

Caeden scowled. "I suppose you think that you and the others are less stained, somehow?"

"Yes." Alaris said the word matter-of-factly. "We act knowing that all that is done will be undone, Tal—that our actions against others do not matter, *unless you succeed.* We are not the ones bent on protecting a broken, imprisoned world and killing the people we love."

Caeden opened his mouth to retort, then stopped himself with a weary shake of his head.

"No," he said quietly. "No more, Alaris. No more trying to sow doubt. No more dredging up arguments that we have already had, or distracting me with questions to which I gave you my answers centuries ago. Shame on you for that. Shame on you for trying to take advantage of my ignorance." He stared at the other man steadily, letting him see how heartfelt was his own disappointment. "The fact is, I know what I believe now. I remember why all of this is necessary. I remember that you refuse to consider that the creature we know as El has been deceiving us. I *remember.* So let us just... skip this part, this time."

Alaris's expression twitched, and Caeden saw that his rebuke had struck home. Good.

There was silence.

"It really is you this time, isn't it, Tal," Alaris said ruefully. He rubbed his face tiredly. "Davian for Cyr, then. Let me... think a few moments on it."

Silence fell again; Caeden studied Alaris, loath to ask but too concerned not to. "How is he?"

Alaris hesitated.

"Well enough," he said. "He has created some... unique politics,

7

though, as I am sure you can imagine. Gassandrid wishes to educate, while Diara…Diara wishes to punish. Knowing who he is and what will happen to him—what he will do—has made some of their arguments quite compelling." He held Caeden's gaze. "But he is still under my jurisdiction. And for now, as far as I am concerned, he is simply one more person who needs protecting from you."

Caeden felt his jaw tighten at that, but said nothing.

Alaris watched him thoughtfully. "While we are being civil…"

"If you have things to say, then I am happy to listen."

Alaris just nodded to himself, evidently having expected no less. He reached into a pocket and drew out something small and thickly wrapped; the cloth was white but as Alaris began to remove the covering, Caeden saw the inner layers were sodden with some kind of green, viscous liquid. Soon the last piece fell to the ground with a damp slap, but it still took Caeden a few moments to realize what Alaris was holding.

"Where did you get this?" Alaris tossed the ruined remains of the Portal Box to him. "Clearly none of us made it."

Caeden's heart skipped a beat as he caught the Vessel, and he barely avoided displaying his relief as he examined it; getting to confirm its destruction was a gift, though Alaris couldn't have known that. The cube's once-bronze surface was now a slick black, the inscriptions worn off, a piece of the metal oozing away even as he held it.

Caeden had remembered early on that Talan Gol would corrupt the Vessel, as it did almost all such devices trapped for any length of time within the ilshara. But the Portal Box had been especially powerful. Unique. He hadn't been certain that it would decay in the same way.

"The Lyth," said Caeden, seeing no advantage to lying. "I stole it from them." He shrugged at Alaris's raised eyebrows.

Alaris gave a chuckle at that, shaking his head. "That is a story I would very much like to hear one day."

"One day," agreed Caeden. He let his gaze return to the rotting Vessel in his hand, regret heavy in his chest. Another reminder of just how badly he had used his friend. As Malshash, Caeden had linked Davian to the Portal Box, manipulating him into delivering it after Caeden's memories were erased—all because Davian was the only one Caeden had been certain would live to do so.

He'd drawn Davian into all of this, knowing that he would ultimately die at Caeden's hand. *Because* he would die at Caeden's hand, and therefore not any sooner.

He pushed both the thought and the decayed box to one side, carefully wiping his hands, tempted to again try to convince Alaris of why it had been corrupted in the first place. The other Venerate believed that the degradation of Vessels in Talan Gol, and in fact the very barrenness of the land itself, was an effect of the Boundary: something built into its machinery to make it a more effective means of imprisonment.

It wasn't. Caeden himself had allied with Andrael to devise the ilshara, and its purpose had only ever been to delay El's march to Deilannis, to force the other Venerate to stop and join him in questioning whether their faith had become blind. And yet, even when they'd believed that Caeden was still on their side—that he'd been an unwilling participant in Andrael's machinations—Alaris and the others had been quick with their excuses. They'd claimed that Andrael must have added to the ilshara's anchoring Vessels before handing them over to the Darecians, or that possibly the Darecians themselves had modified them.

The Venerate were intelligent men and women, and yet somehow unable to even entertain the possibility that the ongoing, contained presence of their god was the true problem.

Such was Shammaeloth's nature, though. Those who were most steeped in his corruption somehow had the hardest time seeing it—something for which Caeden could barely blame them. He knew that myopic haze all too well.

Alaris abruptly shook his head.

"My answer is no, Tal."

Caeden stared blankly, then breathed out heavily as he understood. Alaris had chosen to reject the deal for Davian's release.

"Why?"

Alaris gestured helplessly. "Because you only came here after you realized that you couldn't beat me in Ilshan Gathdel Teth. Because I cannot see the upside of this for you, which means that you must be concealing it." He paused, sounding desolate now.

"But most of all? Because after Is...I know that you are not the man you once were. You may have the memory of our friendship, Tal'kamar, but I am no longer convinced that you are my friend."

Caeden felt his heart wrench, and he struggled to find the words to respond.

"You cannot know how sorry I am to hear that," he said finally, not bothering to conceal the pain in his voice. "But you are making a mistake, Alaris."

Alaris's expression didn't change. "I will exchange Davian for the location of *Ashalia's* Tributary. Nothing less."

"No."

"Then we have nothing further to discuss." Alaris stood stiffly. "I gave you my word that I would let you leave Alkathronen, Tal, and I meant it. But the moment you are gone from this city, we are enemies. There will be no other parleys like this."

Caeden stood, too, then walked over to his blade and stooped, picking it up off the stone with a slight metallic scraping.

Then he slowly, deliberately leveled it at Alaris.

"I know," he said softly.

Alaris stared at him in indignant disbelief, and Caeden hated the guilt that look stirred in him. The two men remained motionless; then Alaris was shifting smoothly, giving himself room as he reluctantly drew his own sword.

"I suppose I should be grateful that you didn't wait until my back was turned," said Alaris, holding his blade at the ready. "At least that much of you remains." He sounded more tired than anything else, though his eyes were hard. "Whatever advantages you think you have here over Ilshan Gathdel Teth, Tal, you've miscalculated. I have no doubt that you have been busy laying the groundwork against me, setting your traps, but you said it yourself—you expected to have longer. Mere hours was never going to be enough."

Caeden didn't acknowledge the statement, keeping his blade up and cautiously beginning to circle. Alaris matched the motion.

"One last chance, Tal. Walk away. You do not have one of Andrael's Blades, so even if you have some other Vessel I don't know about, you cannot hope to win. And I will not let you escape this time." When Caeden still didn't respond, Alaris sighed, looking stuck between melancholy and frustration. "Then answer me one last question, before we end this and you are locked away forever."

Caeden kept pacing. "Ask."

Alaris's gaze never left Caeden's as they continued their slow, cautious dance. "I know that shape-shifting is simple enough for you, after all that practice a century ago—and I know that most of your memories must have come back by now, too. So why return to *this* body? Why not your own?"

Caeden almost hesitated at that. He'd asked himself something similar, in the days after Davian had decapitated him to free him from Ilshan Gathdel Teth. Wondered why he had felt so driven to change back, despite the accompanying pain. Despite his other options.

He had eventually found the answer, though.

"Because it's who I am now," he replied.

His blade flashed down toward Alaris's right arm; there was a blur and then the clash of steel as Alaris slid aside and parried, the sound echoing through the silence of Alkathronen. Caeden swayed smoothly back as the counter came, swift and clinical, slicing the air where his shoulder had been a moment earlier.

Caeden pressed the attack with a flurry of quick, light strikes, nerves taut as he kept his breathing steady, quickly assessing his best course of action. Alaris's Disruption shield was already in place, just as Caeden's was, preventing kan attacks almost entirely. Each man had stepped outside of time, too; the snow that had been drifting gently downward was now frozen in place, suspended between them, glittering ethereally as each flake refracted the Essence-light of the city.

He broke off, exhaling hard, his frozen breath drifting outward and then gathering in place as it left his time bubble. This was an even match where kan and Essence were concerned, bringing it once again down to a physical contest.

A contest in which Alaris was invincible.

Alaris didn't give him long to think; the muscular man was suddenly pressing forward, the wicked edge of his blade flashing in a mesmerizing, fluid dance of motion as it blurred at Caeden again and again and again, each strike whispering past skin or barely turned aside by desperate, flicking parries. Alaris wasn't as talented as Isiliar, not as creative or unpredictable in his attacks. But he was still very, very good.

Caeden flooded his legs with Essence and propelled himself forcefully backward, skidding hard to a stop along the perfectly smooth white stone street almost fifty feet away. Alaris was already in motion, stalking toward him and closing the distance rapidly; Caeden extended his time bubble wide, tapped his Reserve and sent a torrent of Essence at the nearest building, wrenching a large portion of stone from the facade and hurling it into Alaris's path. Alaris leaped high, clearing the enormous piece of masonry easily as it embedded itself in the road where he had been about to tread, continuing his approach as if nothing had happened.

"This is pointless, Tal," he shouted over the crumbling roar of the collapsing building to his left.

Some of Alkathronen's Essence lines had broken open; Caeden used kan to snatch energy from the air and then twisted it tight, hurling a brilliant ball at the oncoming man before launching himself forward after it, low and hard. The Essence dissipated as soon as it struck Alaris's Disruption shield, but it had served its purpose; Alaris slashed blindly at the air, anticipating the follow-up attack but not where it would strike. Caeden skidded swiftly past the other man, shielding his body against the ground with Essence and slashing hard across Alaris's knee as the other man's steel carved through the space just above his head.

Alaris snarled as Caeden's blade ricocheted off the Venerate's impenetrable skin, sending a shiver down Caeden's arm even with his Essence-enhanced strength. A small blow, almost petty, which was why Alaris hadn't anticipated it—but it was the sort of thing that would irritate him, frustrate and cause hesitation. Slow him down just a fraction and keep him distracted.

Alaris barely faltered at the strike, spinning and unleashing a furious burst of flashing, whisper-thin Essence attacks. Caeden scrambled to his feet and flung up a solid layer of kan just in time, absorbing the strikes; though Caeden's Disruption shield was tight, it was always shifting, and some of those near-invisible golden needles would likely have slipped through.

The ground beneath Caeden's feet trembled and he threw himself backward just in time; the road where he'd been standing ripped away in a shower of rubble and fine white dust. He rolled, the shattering sound of stone against stone painfully loud in his ears as Alaris used the chunk of street like a hammer, leaving a crater five feet wide in the spot where Caeden had just been.

Caeden scrambled to his feet, gasping, and launched himself forward once again.

Everything was a miasma of running and dodging and thundering destruction after that.

Twice Caeden completely lost track of where they were, the buildings around him disintegrating in massive, terrifying, roaring clouds as one or the other of them ripped shreds from the structures, then used the freed Essence that had been flowing through Alkathronen to tear away even more. Each time he managed to reorient himself, though, diving in for an exchange in steel and then flinging himself away so that the battle gradually, painfully drew closer to where he needed it to be. He fought as defensively as he could without being obvious, but still his body began to accumulate deeper and deeper cuts, ones that required more and more Essence to heal. With every agonizing blow he absorbed, he could feel his Reserve steadily dwindling, and it simply wasn't enough to snatch more from the city around him.

Alaris was winning.

An Essence-enhanced leap over a shattered fountain finally brought him within sight of the low wall that marked the eastern edge of the city. Normally the view would be breathtaking, but beyond the wall the blizzard still raged, nothing but driven white snow against black night past the near-invisible protective dome that lay across Alkathronen.

Caeden forced Essence into his legs again and ran parallel to the barrier, lungs burning and breath coming in short, sharp gasps, skidding and angling down an alleyway as stone screeched and roared and shattered in his wake. If he were stronger, if he had had more time to prepare, he might have been able to make this trap less obvious.

But that wasn't an option, now. He was dangerously close to spent.

When he finally reached the long public square that ended at the eastern wall—probably a marketplace once, undamaged as yet and perfectly lit—he slid to a stop, turning and raising an Essence shield against another barrage of stone. The shield flickered; pieces of rubble cut through it, striking Caeden in the chest and leg, breaking bone and piercing deep into muscle. He snarled in pain, stumbling back until he was leaning against the waist-high wall that marked the edge of Alkathronen's dome, then dropping his shield and snatching Essence from a nearby illuminating line. He forced the energy into his wounds, flinching as more streaking stone pierced the cloud of grit that blanketed the open space, flying perilously close to his head.

The veil of dust eventually cleared to show Alaris at the opposite edge of the square, obviously favoring one leg and looking tired, but otherwise no less determined than when they had started. The air was acrid with the smell of shattered masonry; Caeden gave a racking cough and wiped sweat mingled with grime from his brow, his hands slick and smeared with gray. The two men's gazes met.

There was a pause, a silent acknowledgment. Caeden let his shoulders slump, even as his pulse quickened.

"It was always going to end this way, Tal," called Alaris, limping forward into the square. "You need to—"

Caeden activated the endpoint of his Vessel.

The outline of a wolf's head—something he'd been compelled to add despite the extra time it took, thanks to the binding all of the Venerate had agreed to millennia earlier—sprang to life beneath Alaris's feet across the breadth of the square, instantly draining every other Essence line and plunging the surrounding area into pitch blackness.

There was a deep cracking sound, and Caeden had only a moment to see Alaris's face illuminated by the wolf's head on the ground, the other man's eyes wide, before the ground caved beneath him and the buildings that rose on all three sides smashed inward.

Even expecting it as he was, Caeden sagged back against the wall as the square exploded with a painful and disorienting roar; Alaris vanished as chunks of stone thundered at terrifying, dizzying speeds toward where he had been standing, as if drawn by some unthinkably powerful vortex. Within moments a pile of debris two stories high and just as wide had formed a tightly packed mound, barely visible within the eerily lit roiling clouds that now surrounded it.

An uneasy peace descended. The wolf's head—what was still visible of it—faded as quickly as it had appeared, shrouding the scene in darkness for a few seconds before the illuminating lines of Essence sprang back to life, regaining their access to Alkath-ronen's deep Cyrarium.

Caeden painfully hauled himself up to sit atop the low wall, letting his back rest against the net of Essence that prevented any-one from falling over the edge. He knew that if the blizzard were not obscuring the view behind him, he would be able to see the dizzying, sheer drop, though not where it ended more than three thousand feet below. Like the walls of Fedris Idri, this cliff—and the others surrounding the peak upon which Alkathronen was built—was perfectly smooth, glass-like, impenetrable by steel and impossible to scale.

He caught his breath as he gazed at the wreckage in front of him. The kan machinery had worked exactly as he'd hoped.

But he knew it had been rushed. Crude.

Obvious.

Some of the smaller stones atop the mound began to trickle down the sides, shattering the silence with their skittering.

Caeden watched wearily, not moving as one of the larger boul-ders began to tremble and then fall away, crashing aside as those beneath it steadily, impossibly lifted upward. Flashes of golden Essence shone through the cracks, brighter and brighter until the steadily expanding dome of energy pushed aside the final mas-sive chunks of stone, the man in the center of it climbing out of the sinkhole Caeden's Vessel had created and then limping toward him.

"Here is what I do not understand," said Alaris calmly when he was within hearing range, letting his Essence shield drop as the last pieces of rubble slid off it and to the ground with a dull, clink-ing rattle. "Even if the kan lines hadn't been thick enough for me to spot them. Even if this had worked and I was buried beneath all that stone. Forced to sleep for, what—a week? Two, maybe, before I healed? What were you hoping to do? Mount an assault on Ilshan Gathdel Teth straight away while I lay there?" He shook his head, moving stiffly but advancing inexorably toward Caeden. "It stinks of desperation, Tal. Sloppiness. You are reaching the end of your ideas, and I think you know it."

Caeden said nothing to that, the ache of the fight still deep in his bones. From his position atop the wall, he could see the slowly dissipating clouds of dust highlighted by wildly flickering Essence, like lightning in the clouds of a fierce storm.

Through it all was just…destruction. A full quarter of the Builders' last city, gone.

Sadness settled heavy in his chest at the loss.

Alaris saw Caeden's expression as he limped to a stop, perhaps twenty feet from where Caeden was sitting. His voice softened, though it still held accusation. "A pointless demise," he agreed quietly. "The oldest, most perfect city in the world, and we have erased it. All of its beauty, its history. I never understood why the Builders did not lay better protections against such destruction. El knows they could have."

"Asar once told me that they did it because nothing is truly beautiful unless it can be lost," said Caeden idly as he gazed out over the rubble. "We forget that sometimes, Alaris."

Alaris suddenly frowned, eyeing Caeden as if only just realizing where he was sitting.

"Don't be a fool, Tal. We both know that your head needs to be cut off," he said, tone suddenly cautious, stretching out a hand as if to pull him back from the edge by will alone.

"From this height, without using Essence to protect myself? Same thing," Caeden assured him. He smiled wearily at his friend. "So I guess this one is a draw."

Icy wind and driving snow whipped the nape of his neck as he used kan to dissipate a small section of Alkathronen's dome; the expected thread of Essence stretched outward to save him but he cut that off with kan, too, feeling more than hearing Alaris's cry of frustration as he did so.

He rolled backward.

Chill hands immediately ripped at his skin, the protection of

Alkathronen vanished. The wind roared in his ears, and every-thing was white.

As his stomach lurched he closed his eyes, forcing himself to push through kan despite the dizzying sensation of plummeting. The thin net of kan he cast back up toward Alkathronen revealed nothing for what seemed like an eternity.

And finally a figure leaping over the wall and arrowing after him, wreathed in Essence.

For an odd moment, Caeden felt a sense of melancholy at the sight. His friend, trying to save him one last time.

Then he twisted, looking for the kan mechanism he'd spent several hours hanging on the cliff side to build.

Activated the endpoint.

The Gate glowed to life directly above Caeden's plummeting body, between him and Alaris. A heartbeat later it flashed as Alaris's suddenly flailing form was flying through it; Caeden gritted his teeth and reached out again, severing a section of the mechanism. Within the space of two seconds, the Gate had opened and had been destroyed.

The whistling air around him was suddenly strangely peaceful as he fell, his sense of relief overwhelming. Alaris couldn't create a Gate himself, and there was no other way to escape from the Wells. No way for Alaris to communicate with the others in Ilshan Gathdel Teth from there, either.

He would need to be dealt with eventually—there was no doubt about that—but for now, there was one fewer of the Venerate to worry about.

Caeden forced himself to focus amid the gale and poured every ounce of Essence he had left into his body, strengthening each limb. Alaris had been right; Caeden had no idea if this fall would kill him, or merely result in catastrophic injury. If there had been time, he might have made a second Gate somewhere lower. But there hadn't.

Closing his eyes against the biting wind, he braced himself for the impact.

This was going to hurt.

Chapter 1

Wirr stepped through the portal and into a thick tangle of branches and brush, every nerve taut, the old scar across his stomach aching from tension.

He forced his way forward as quietly as he could, breaking into a small clearing and exhaling in relief at the emptiness of the surrounding night. The reflected moon in the babbling stream ahead glistened through the thick forest undergrowth, its stark silvery glow revealing no sign of danger. No waiting ambush.

Behind him, he heard Taeris's deep voice curse softly as one of the shadowy, damp-leafed branches Wirr had just pushed through snapped back and slapped him across the face. Wirr turned just in time to catch a glimpse of his father's old office through the hole in the air, the empty room in the Tel'Andras estate completely dark in order to minimize its visibility from this side. Swathes of foliage quickly covered the view.

"Thank you for that, Sire," Taeris growled as he wiped dew from his cheek, the encroaching gray in his sandy-blond hair catching the moonlight. The scarred man turned, nodding in satisfaction at how well hidden the portal was. Not even the faint glow of Essence from the black Travel Stone on the ground was visible. "We should have a couple of hours before the Essence in those stones runs out, and the portal closes. I assume we're alone?"

"Seems so." Wirr oriented himself by the moon, then peered through the forest both eastward and westward. "If Laiman's put us in the right place, we should be out of sight from both the road and the walls. Well away from any patrols."

"It will be the right place," said Taeris confidently. He gestured to the west. "I'll gather some kindling while you figure out directions."

Wirr made to protest, then let himself feel the bite in the southern night air and relented. They could be here awhile, and a fire was a small risk.

He hurried off, moving cautiously through untamed forest until he reached the moonlight-dappled road. Completely empty in both directions, much to his relief. He fetched four large, smooth stones from the stream that ran alongside it, then placed them carefully in a stack by the roadside.

He stepped back and considered his handiwork, nervous despite himself. Were they obvious enough? Too obvious?

He forced himself to calm. No one would miss the marker but it wouldn't mean anything to a patrol; there was probably no need to worry, even if he knew a little apprehension couldn't be avoided right now. If word got out about this meeting—or even of Wirr's mere presence here—it would cause . . .

Well. People back in Ilin Illan wouldn't be happy about it, that much was certain.

He made his way back to Taeris, who was already working on getting a fire started by the time Wirr arrived. Wirr settled down against a fallen log, feeling the Oathstone hanging around his neck as he closed his eyes.

"Driscin," he murmured, picturing the Elder from Tol Shen. "When you can do so safely, go to the road directly west of Tol Shen. Follow it and look for a pile of four large stones. As soon as you reach that, cross the stream and head directly into the forest, back toward the Tol." He chewed his lip. "After a minute or two of walking, you'll reach another, smaller stream. You should be able to see our fire from there. Make sure it's actually me before revealing yourself."

When he opened his eyes again, Taeris was watching him. The Gifted gave a short nod and immediately returned to building the fire, but Wirr couldn't help but note the unease in his motions.

"They should already be out via the Augur entrance Ishelle told us about," said Wirr, choosing to ignore the other man's discomfort. "We won't have to wait long. And Laiman shouldn't be far away, either." The king's adviser should know the area well, now; he'd spent much of the past year here in the south, embroiled in negotiations. He was the one who had left the Travel Stone in position, too. There was no reason for him to be late.

Taeris dipped his head again, blowing gently at the smoldering twigs and not making eye contact. The forest was hushed around them, dark and looming; it was too small for an official name on any map, but what there was of it was densely packed. More than enough to fully shield them from the illuminated walls of Tol Shen, which Wirr knew couldn't be more than five hundred feet away.

"Do you think anyone on the committee will notice I've left?" Wirr asked idly, watching as small flames appeared in front of Taeris.

Taeris snorted. "Given that we will have been gone for two days? I would hope so, Sire." He rolled his shoulders. "But they know as well as anyone that you need to keep your schedule quiet, and there are plenty who recognized you on the road to Daren Tel. So long as you're not seen here, no one will dream that you've been this far afield. And fates know they're still unaware that you have *that*," he added, indicating where the teardrop-shaped black stone hung around Wirr's neck, concealed though it was by his tunic. "They have no reason to be overly concerned; if anything, your absence for a couple of days will probably be a welcome relief. And we'll be back before that feeling wears off."

Wirr nodded in absent acknowledgment, though he'd really only asked to fill the apprehensive hush. The committee assigned to overseeing him—a group of twelve men and women from the Houses, six appointed by Administration and six by the Gifted—believed that they could account for all the Oathstones in Andarra. The one Wirr had found in his father's safe, however, appeared not to exist in any official records. Wirr had worked hard over the past year to keep it that way.

"Do you think I made a mistake, not telling them about it?" he mused, touching the chain that held the Oathstone in place.

"I think you have made several mistakes, Sire, but that was not one of them."

Wirr grimaced; Taeris's words were honest more than rebuking, but they stung nonetheless.

Especially as Wirr still couldn't decide if he agreed.

Time passed in a companionable, if anxious silence until the cracking of twigs and rustling of bushes reached Wirr's ears. A few moments later a voice called out, low and clear.

"It's Driscin Throll, Sire."

The tension in Wirr's muscles eased again, and he signaled toward a clear patch of ground to his left. Two figures emerged from the trees, their faces partially obscured in the dim light.

"Driscin," said Wirr politely as the Elder stepped closer to the fire, giving Wirr and Taeris each a cheerless nod before seating himself.

Driscin's companion hovered at the edge of the clearing, reluctance emanating from every inch of his posture.

"Come on, Dras," growled Driscin, casting an impatient glare back across the fire. "You know you don't have a choice."

Dras Lothlar—former Representative for Tol Shen—finally shuffled forward and joined Driscin in sitting, expression dark.

"This will not end well for you," he said without preamble to Wirr, eyes flashing. He turned to Taeris. "And as for you—"

"Be silent, Dras," said Wirr calmly.

Dras's mouth opened, then snapped shut again. He looked to the side, face contorted and bright red in the firelight.

Wirr turned to Driscin, dismissing Dras for the time being. "Were there any problems?"

Driscin shrugged, brown eyes appraising. "Not really, but we don't have much time. As I told Master Kardai, everyone on the Shen Council has been assigned people to check on them every couple of hours. If someone realizes that Dras is missing, they have his Trace and a Vessel to track it. This could become very messy, very quickly."

"We're on a tight schedule, too," Wirr assured him.

The Tol Shen Elder acknowledged the statement, then glanced around at the surrounding forest. "Where is Ishelle?"

Wirr shifted uncomfortably, but it was Taeris who spoke up.

"She tried," he said gently, "but it was too much. She barely lasted half a day on the road."

Driscin's jaw tightened, and he studied Wirr's and Taeris's expressions.

"That's why this was delayed until night? You saw her back to the Tol?" When Taeris nodded, Driscin exhaled. "Thank you for that." He stuck out a hand toward Taeris. "Driscin, by the way."

"Taeris," said the scarred man, not moving to shake it.

Driscin left his hand extended. "You're upset about Davian, but I only told him the truth. You were keeping things from him."

"For good reason. You set him against me, and you did it for petty political reasons."

"I am obviously past that now." Driscin held Taeris's gaze, arm still outstretched. "As I hope my presence here, and the fact that I am no longer on Shen's Council, proves. It was a mistake."

There was a moment of silence until Taeris finally clasped the other man's hand, much to Wirr's relief. Taeris had been grumbling about their working with the Shen Elder since Driscin's name had first been mentioned; when Driscin had first met Davian, he had gone out of his way to sow distrust—and it had worked. Davian had barely spoken to Taeris since.

It didn't help that when the Boundary had been restored just over a year ago, Taeris's mental link to Davian had been severed. Though they all had faith that he was still alive—Alchesh's visions foresaw Davian stopping Aarkein Devaed, after all—worry for his well-being had been wearing on them all.

Wirr shifted, gesturing to Dras. "Did he give you any trouble?"

"Quite the opposite. Aside from the constant muttering, he was helpful every step of the way." Driscin's gaze traveled involuntarily to the chain around Wirr's neck. "What did you tell him to do?"

"Whatever you said, and nothing to jeopardize what you were trying to achieve."

Driscin nodded thoughtfully. "Clever. Though next time, if you could add for him not to open his mouth at all, that would be wonderful." He ignored Dras's poisonous glare. "What about me?"

"I didn't tell you to do anything." When Driscin gave him a dubious look, Wirr sighed. "I meant what I said in the message, assuming that Laiman gave it to you properly. I only bound you to secrecy with your permission, and I won't do anything else unless you agree to it. I cannot expect people to trust me if I will not trust them in return."

23

Driscin stared at him, then flicked a questioning glance at Taeris.

"He's absentminded on the small things sometimes, but it's the truth. For what it's worth," Taeris added, a touch drily.

Driscin's lips curled upward at that, though Wirr had to hide a flash of irritation. Taeris liked to prod at him like this occasionally, probably just to see whether he still could—it was fine, and better than with most of the Gifted and Administrators, who could barely even look him in the eye.

Still, it was a stark reminder that no one with the Mark truly felt comfortable around him anymore.

"It's worth enough," said Driscin eventually. "Knowing that you're friends with Davian...fates, I'm even tempted to believe you mean what you say." He stretched, glancing sideways at Dras, who had been glaring silently into the fire during the entire conversation. "Shall we begin?"

"Master Kardai is coming, too," said Wirr. "I wanted someone without a Mark here."

Driscin glanced back toward the walls of Tol Shen. "Wise, but...if he is not here soon, we will have to begin without him. We have an hour, two at the most before someone notices Dras is missing."

Wirr grunted in agreement, the beginnings of a knot of worry tightening his chest. Even disregarding Driscin's concerns, he absolutely couldn't afford to let the portal back close again without going through: it was a three-week trip from here to Ilin Illan, and even if he somehow made the entire journey unrecognized, an absence of that length would raise far too many questions.

All of which, Laiman knew. He should have been here by now.

Driscin picked up a stick and poked absently at the fire. "I take it that the final Augur still hasn't surfaced?"

Taeris shook his head. "Not even a whisper of another one," he admitted. "You're certain..."

"Yes." The former sig'nari's tone was confident. "There are always thirteen with the potential to manipulate kan at any one time, though any who have been born in the past ten years won't have the ability yet." He began ticking off fingers. "Ishelle, Davian. That fates-cursed scum Rohin. The two who helped

24

bring him down, Erran and Fessiricia. The friend of theirs who was killed in Ilin Illan—Kol—and the man who killed him—Scyner. The girl that mob killed in Variden almost a year ago. Plus the four that Duke Andras apparently found and…dealt with." He flicked a vaguely apologetic glance at Wirr. "That leaves one still unaccounted for."

Wirr pushed down the complex, disquieting mix of emotions that surfaced whenever his father was mentioned. "We'll keep looking," he assured Driscin.

Driscin stretched, nodding. "So how is everything else in the capital, since the withdrawal?" He shrugged at Wirr's raised eyebrow. "I was able to spend a grand total of thirty seconds with Master Kardai before we had to stop talking for fear of being noticed. Don't forget that those of us in Tol Shen need special dispensation just to go outside the walls, these days—and I'm not exactly popular with the Council. I've heard plenty about Ilin Illan this past year, but none of it is what I would consider reliable."

Wirr exchanged a look with Taeris, who shrugged.

"Life…went on, after it all happened," Taeris said, turning back to Driscin. "It was a mess at the beginning, of course; even after the emergency vote kept Prince Torin in his position, nobody expected Shen to follow through and formally withdraw from the Assembly. And then when they took that fates-cursed group of southern Houses with them…"

Driscin snorted. "I imagine that didn't sit well."

"It did not," agreed Wirr, picking up the thread. "Aside from the embarrassment of the public spectacle, the taxes those Houses were almost due to pay for their seats in the Assembly—troops and supplies in particular—were badly needed in the north. Some places still hadn't recovered from the Blind when the Banes came, and they were desperate for aid. But of course, all the southern Houses could see was that they were paying to solve other people's problems."

Driscin looked unsurprised at that. "How close did it come to violence?"

"It was a near thing," admitted Taeris, which Wirr confirmed with a bleak nod. "The legal justification wasn't there, though.

25

Participation in the Assembly has always been voluntary, with Houses usually considering the extra taxes a small price to pay for the power and prestige that come along with them."

"Not to mention that the north started the split years ago along exactly the same lines," added Wirr darkly. "The south has always had to contend with both Nesk and Desriel, and the north took advantage of that—pressed back on taxes, maneuvered for more power in exchange for their aid—for far too long. The southern Houses were practically *begging* for a chance to retaliate."

"So now, everyone is just trying to figure out what Tol Shen offered them that was enticing enough for them to actually go through with the withdrawal. And what in fates it means they're planning," finished Taeris.

Driscin winced. "You...know as much as I do about that," he said apologetically. "Within the Tol, the Shen Council still insist that they recognize the authority of the Assembly. That they'll happily rejoin, should Ilin Illan provide what they consider an 'acceptable' working environment." His tone indicated his cynicism. He glanced at Dras. "I think we all know at least one reason behind the split, though."

Wirr just nodded, though as always the discussion of these events left him feeling queasy. After the chaos and blood of the Boundary almost collapsing, he and Karaliene had fought and sneaked their way back toward the capital along roads that held Banes more often than other people; only the relatively early, near-miraculous appearance of Erran and Ishelle—who had tracked them for days after the attack—had allowed them to make it the entire way safely. Even with the Augurs' help, it had taken almost six weeks to return. The distinctive sight of Ilin Tora in the distance had never felt so welcoming.

Then they had entered the city.

Everyone from Tol Shen had already departed by the time they arrived; nobody knew how the Gifted had found out about Wirr's ability to command anyone who bore the Mark, but it had been announced as fact weeks prior.

The political response, perhaps predictably, had been a mixture of hysteria and opportunism for months after.

Driscin watched Wirr with a thoughtful frown. "What about Administration?"

"Still functioning." Wirr rubbed his face, not wanting to have to think about it. "I suspect we can thank your people for that, actually. The Shen Council drew a line, and they put both myself and the Administrators on the other side. Administration didn't have enough political capital to break off in a third direction, so it was either stay in the Assembly and implicitly back me, or become completely irrelevant as an organization."

"You don't sound particularly enthused."

"I'm not." Wirr saw no reason to hide the truth. "We've lost a good number of our people and more leave every week, though at least the deadline to resign passes soon. Most are defecting to Desriel, apparently, despite the Gil'shar knowing what I could potentially do with them."

"And you just... let them go?" asked Driscin in surprise.

"I had to give them the choice. Say what you will about their motivations, the Administration they chose to join looks very different from the one it is today." Wirr kept his tone dispassionate; he'd had to go through this explanation many times before. "I can't ignore my ability now that it's public knowledge, so those who stay must in some way be subject to it. And those who resign are allowed to do so only after I've bound them to secrecy—the Gil'shar will not benefit from these defections. But I refuse to turn people into puppets. Anyone who stays gets my pledge that I'll only use this ability when necessary, never against Administration's directives, and only with the approval of an oversight committee."

"Even so. I'm impressed you've convinced anyone to stay," murmured Driscin.

"The vast majority still despise me. Fear me, even," Wirr conceded bluntly. "They just believe in Administration's purpose more—especially with the Shen Gifted striking out on their own as they did. Near half of the remaining Administrators live in Prythe these days. They're doing what they believe is necessary for the good of the country, more than following me."

Driscin grunted. "Yes, the Council have made us *well* aware of just how many Administrators are in the area." He turned to

27

Taeris. "What about Tol Athian? I cannot imagine that they were enthusiastic about any of this, either."

Taeris shifted, the dark shape of the forest undulating behind him as a breeze caressed the trees. "There was some panicked talk of trying to destroy the Vessel responsible for the Tenets, assuming that that would stop Prince Torin's ability…but leveler heads prevailed." He shrugged at Driscin's look. "They're not *happy*, obviously—but when have they ever been? Prince Torin has given them the same options and the same guarantees as he has given Administration. It is simply the reality we live in, now."

Driscin sighed. "Yes. Well. Of course, the Shen Council have their own version of what would happen if everyone believes those guarantees." He glanced at Wirr. "They're telling anyone who will listen that if we leave the jurisdictional protections of the Tol, there is nothing to stop you—and therefore Administration—from legally Controlling us. They've all but promised that's your plan, in fact. Most people are afraid to go outside, even to patrol. It's not unlike how it felt twenty years ago in there," he concluded grimly.

Wirr's heart sank at the news, though he'd had similar reports from Laiman. In fact, it was a large part of why he was here. The law was clear that while inside Tol Shen, Dras—like any Gifted—answered only to the Shen Council. And the Council had made a formal, public declaration that Dras Lothlar did not wish to leave the Tol, ensuring that Wirr could not force him to do so without it being painfully obvious that he had acted illegally.

Even with Dras suspected of treason, Wirr couldn't have risked that. It would place him at the mercy of an Assembly already more than wary of his newfound power—as well as revealing that he had his own Oathstone. The committee set up to oversee his ability-related decisions would in turn look like a sham, completely destroying the fragile trust he had worked so hard to nurture.

"So we can expect no resolution to this anytime soon," he concluded heavily. "I had hoped—vainly, perhaps—that Shen might be convinced to help fight the Banes in the north."

"Is that even needed?" Driscin asked, a surprised note of concern in his voice. "The Council have been telling us that the Banes which made it across the Boundary were all but eliminated. Not that I trust them, but it seems a strange thing to lie about."

Wirr couldn't help but scowl at that. "There were many more than have been accounted for. *Thousands* more," he emphasized, not looking in Taeris's direction. "They're still out there. Waiting for…something." He let his frustration seep onto his face, knowing exactly how it sounded.

Driscin glanced for confirmation at Taeris, who hesitated.

"I trust Prince Torin," the older man said eventually.

Wirr rolled his eyes. "It's fine, Taeris. Just say it."

Taeris gave him an apologetic look. "I am also…mindful of how hundreds can seem like thousands in the midst of chaos and death. I'm not saying that's what happened," he prevaricated quickly, "but we have had every available man scouring the countryside for a full year, and no one—*no one*—has been able to find any hint of a hidden force. There have been only pockets, groups of ten or twenty dar'gaithin and eletai, surviving by picking off isolated farmers and unwary travelers. Still very dangerous, of course…but mostly dealt with now."

"Everyone who was there agrees with me, though," added Wirr to Driscin, trying not to sound defensive. "Including Ishelle."

"Which makes four of you," pointed out Taeris gently. "You know you have my support on this, Sire. But in the absence of corroborating evidence, it would be remiss of me not to at least consider the possibility that you all overestimated the numbers in the heat of the attack."

Wirr felt his jaw tighten, but nodded sharply and said no more. It was a point not worth arguing again right now, and worse—he knew that Taeris was right. No matter what Wirr, Ishelle, Erran, and Karaliene had seen, there were simply no places left for such a large group of Banes to hide. It was as unsettling as it was frustrating.

A snapping of twigs somewhere beyond the fire made everyone hush; there was quiet, and then the skittering patter of light paws across the ground as some small creature or other scampered away. Wirr felt the muscles in his shoulders relax again.

Then there was a crashing through the undergrowth; Wirr

leaped to his feet along with the other men as Laiman burst into the clearing, his eyes wide and his breath coming in ragged gasps.

"Patrol," he wheezed, gesturing behind him even as he began desperately kicking dirt over the flames.

"Who?" asked Wirr, swiftly moving to help. The light of the fire began to dim.

"Shen."

"Fates." Wirr's heart pounded; Administration would have been much easier to deal with. The Travel Stones didn't emit much energy, but if an alert enough Gifted got close, it was possible they would detect it.

He whirled on Dras as the light faded further. "You are not to make a sound or do anything to give us away. You are to do exactly as any of us tell you."

Dras's lip curled and his eyes smoldered, but he didn't call out.

The fire finally hissed out, the clearing plunging into near darkness. The air felt immediately colder, the crisp bite of the unusually chilly late spring night returning; only the moonlight filtering through the boughs of the surrounding trees provided any illumination. Muffled shouts penetrated the dense surrounding brush as Wirr held his breath, trying to determine the direction from which they were coming.

"Smoke!" he heard one of the voices exclaim. "This way!"

Wirr grabbed Dras's arm, cautiously moving away from the sound and toward where the portal was hidden, settling down on his stomach about twenty feet away from the clearing where the brush was thickest. The moisture beading on the grass seeped through his tunic, and thin, thorny boughs from the bushes prodded at the still-sensitive scar beneath his ribs, but he ignored the sensations. The others were lying beside him moments later, flat to the ground, well concealed by the undergrowth. Laiman's labored gasps quickly slowed to a soft pant as he recovered his breath.

The clumsy crashing of someone fighting their way through the low branches grew closer, and soon bobbing spheres of Essence showed through the trees.

Wirr schooled himself to stillness, watching intently as Laiman's red-cloaked pursuers—two men and two women—stumbled into the clearing, their breath misting in front of them in the sharp Essence-light. One of them, a portly blond man, spied the disturbed earth and hurried over to it, hovering his hand just above where the fire had burned a minute earlier. Wirr's heart dropped.

"Someone was here. It's still warm."

There was silence as the members of the patrol gazed around, and Wirr felt his breath catch as their eyes swept over where he and the others were lying. But the shadows were deep and the foliage thick, and the patrol gave no sign that they saw anything untoward.

"We need to send the signal," said one of the women, her voice taut with worry. "It's too close to the wall. If he was meeting with Administration…"

"Agreed," said the blond man, and the others indicated their assent. The woman who had spoken raised an arm.

"Stop."

Wirr murmured the word, his focus on the woman. This was dangerous; if there were any members of the patrol he couldn't see—someone bringing up the rear, or who had cut off in a different direction to search—then the potential for exposure was high. He couldn't bind people who he couldn't see and hadn't met.

The woman frowned, her arm still raised. Nothing happened.

"What are you waiting for?" asked one of the men, puzzled.

Wirr expanded his focus to include all four Gifted. "You will not signal Tol Shen tonight." He thought furiously, trying to cover all the variables. "You will forget that you found a campfire. You will doubt any evidence you saw or heard during the chase, and conclude that the man you were following turned back and fled along the road, away from the Tol. You will feel convinced that there is no reason to concern the Council with any of this, and will also convince anyone else of the same if need be." He said it all in a whisper, eyes never leaving the group. "Now return to your patrol."

There was a frozen moment, and then the woman's arm lowered. She rubbed her eyes, as if waking from sleep.

"Fates. What a waste of effort," muttered one of the men.

"Jumping at shadows," another agreed. "Come on."

As one, the four left the clearing and began making their way back to the road.

Wirr released the breath he'd been holding, closing his eyes and going over what he had bound the Gifted to before nodding to himself. It wasn't perfect, but should be good enough.

He opened his eyes again, levering himself into a crouch and brushing loose twigs and grass from his clothing. He turned to the others.

Driscin and Dras were staring at him, wide-eyed; even in the deep shadows, Wirr could see that the blood had drained from Driscin's face. The Shen Gifted rose from his hiding spot, his gaze never leaving Wirr.

"Fates," he murmured, finally finding his voice. "It's really that easy? A few words and you can...tell them what to think? What to remember? How to *feel*?" There was a nervous edge to his tone that bordered on panic.

"Easy, Driscin," said Taeris, walking over and helping the man to his feet. He gripped him by the shoulder, a sympathetic gesture. "You knew this. It's just hard to see it in full flight, the first time."

"You mean terrifying?" asked Driscin, with an awkward chuckle that was clearly an effort to avoid offending Wirr.

"I mean terrifying." Taeris held Driscin's gaze. "Which is why Torin wanted to wait for Laiman. It's why he's so serious about not using this ability whenever he feels like it. He could just take our loyalty, Driscin, but he hasn't." He glanced over at Wirr. "Trust isn't just a word here—and if we have to give our trust to anyone, we should be glad it's him. Believe me."

"You are a fool if you believe that," muttered Dras, who had scrambled to his feet. "He is dangerous."

"Be quiet, Dras," said Driscin tiredly in a dismissive, almost automatic response. He exhaled, acknowledging Taeris's words. "You're right. Sorry," he added as an aside to Wirr. "It just... took me by surprise."

"No apology necessary," Wirr assured him as they started heading back to the clearing. As far as reactions from the Gifted or Administrators went, this was among the most mild he'd seen.

"Quick thinking, by the way," added Laiman to Wirr, giving him an approving clap on the back. "There could well have been more than the four of them; I only heard the shouts behind me just after I left the road. I thought I'd taken appropriate measures, but they must have been following me for a while, keeping their distance until I did something suspicious." He squinted through the trees in the direction in which the patrol had disappeared. "I don't believe they'll be back, but we should probably make do without a fire now."

Wirr screwed up his face—the chill of the night was made even worse by his now-damp clothes—but nodded an agreement along with the others. Better discomfort, severe though it was going to be, than being caught.

Soon enough they had settled down, cloaks pulled tight against the sharp air. Wirr took a deep breath, then turned to the former Representative, whose expression suggested he knew exactly what was coming.

"Now, Dras," said Wirr quietly. "It's finally time for you to talk."

Chapter 2

Dras shifted, the fear that had hovered at the edge of his features since his arrival finally creeping into his eyes.

"You are making a mistake, Prince Torin," he said quickly. "Whatever he's told you about what will happen from here, you cannot trust Taeris. The Assembly won't be able to ignore—"

"You may talk to *answer questions*," Wirr corrected himself in a growl. He shook his head. "I have given you and Tol Shen plenty of opportunities to come forward of your own free will. I have tried every diplomatic channel for a year, Dras. So now you are here to provide information. You will do that, and you will do so fully and truthfully, ensuring that you do not omit or gloss over anything that you think I may be even vaguely interested in knowing. Do you understand?"

"I understand," said Dras, the words sounding as though they were torn from his lips.

"Good." Wirr leaned forward, staring across at the moonlight-framed man, who had folded in on himself and looked considerably shorter as a result. "First question. Were you responsible, or do you know who was responsible, for my uncle's illness and behavior when the Blind attacked Ilin Illan?"

Dras's lip curled, and Wirr could see him trying to stop the answer from escaping.

"Yes. I was responsible. My proximity to King Andras allowed me to use Vessels called Cyrrings, but we only had three of them." He flexed his fingers nervously. "It was meant to be Control, with no sign of illness. We thought not having the full set of five might result in weaker, less perfect Control—which it did—but we didn't anticipate the side effects."

Wirr felt a chill at the reluctantly delivered words, and he heard Taeris exhale sharply beside him. They had long suspected Dras, enough to believe that his involvement in King Andras's illness had been a major factor behind—possibly even the catalyst for— Tol Shen's decision to withdraw from the capital. It made sense; the drastic measure had not only allowed Shen to publicly take the moral high ground against Wirr, but also led to the continued safety of one of their most politically damaging secrets. It was why Wirr was here, why he had decided that taking this risk was justified.

Still, having it all confirmed was as sickening as it was a relief.

"We?" Wirr pressed.

"The Shen Council. Elder Dain authorized it, but I believe many in the Shen Council knew of the plan."

Wirr felt his jaw tighten. "Many, or all?"

"Not all. Some, like Driscin over there, would have caused trouble. They were omitted."

Wirr glanced across at the others, gauging their reactions. Taeris and Laiman looked furious, but unsurprised. Across from them, Driscin's expression was impassive, but Wirr noticed that his fists were clenched so hard that the knuckles had turned white. Driscin had agreed to help Wirr because he'd wanted to know the truth, but he had to have been hoping that the Shen Council—the people with whom he had worked his entire life—were not outright traitors.

Before Wirr could speak again, Laiman leaned forward, eyes bright in the cold moonlight. "Do you have the missing pages from the Journal?"

Dras just looked at him stonily.

Wirr sighed. "You will answer the others' questions as completely and honestly as if they were my own."

Dras scowled. "Yes," he breathed, a puff of silvery steam drifting from his mouth. "We have the pages. They're how we knew that the Blind would be repelled with the Gifted's help. We wanted to make sure that our contribution was properly appreciated, and that the king and the Assembly could claim no credit for what we did."

"Where are the pages?"

"How did Shen get them?"

"What else is in them?"

"How did you know you could trust them?"

Taeris and Laiman spoke over the top of each other in their eagerness; before Dras could open his mouth, Wirr waved them back to silence. "Let's allow him to answer." To the side, Driscin continued to watch, his shadowed expression growing grimmer with each passing second. He'd known that there was an old vision of the Blind attacking Ilin Illan—the entire Shen Council had, in fact—but he'd believed it to be a copy, transcribed from memory and not necessarily reliable. He had also assured Wirr, via Laiman, that there was no possibility Tol Shen had the famously missing section of the Augurs' Journal.

Dras's face was set into a permanent glare now. "The pages are locked away in Tol Shen. In our vault. Do you remember Diriana Traleth?"

"The Scribe. From before the war," said Laiman.

"Yes." Dras licked his lips. "A few months before it all began, she became involved with Lyrus Dain. Romantically. He was... told things."

Wirr just frowned, but the reaction of the other three men was far more incredulous.

"The *Scribe* fed him information? That's preposterous," sputtered Taeris, louder than he should have, looking as if he'd just been insulted.

"Would never have happened," Driscin agreed vehemently. "That was a sacred position. The Augurs Read everyone they chose for it; if someone had even hinted that they *could* betray the visions, then they would never have been allowed the job." Across from him, Laiman nodded along emphatically.

"You are fools if you think the system was perfect," sneered Dras. "I'm sure that when Diriana started, her intent was not to do anything untoward. But you all remember how quickly things changed." His glower deepened, clearly still trying to prevent himself from talking. "Besides. As far as passing along the information went, she had *permission*."

Both Laiman and Taeris shifted, and Wirr found his stomach suddenly unsettled at their expressions. Driscin had seen the same thing; his eyes became sharp, appraising as he watched.

"Permission?" asked Taeris, dread threaded through his voice.

Dras hesitated again, but Wirr's binding pulled him onward. "One of the Augurs knew about the rebellion before it happened."

"Who?" asked Laiman heavily.

"Jakarris." Dras's eyebrows rose as he saw the two men's expressions. "You don't look surprised."

"Tell us *exactly* what Jakarris did." Taeris's voice was hard.

Dras shifted, looking irritated at not getting a response, and even more so at being unable to pursue the matter. "He knew about Diriana's relationship with Lyrus. The Augurs were already having trouble with their visions by that point, so of course Diriana knew better than anyone that there was a real problem. Jakarris came to her and told her that there was going to be a rebellion, and that nothing anyone did could stop it. He said he knew which of the visions she'd been receiving were trustworthy."

Laiman sucked air through his front teeth. "So you knew that he was a traitor."

Dras's eyes darted nervously, as if he were still looking for a way to escape. "Yes. At least, we speculated that he must have been in on it, somehow. There's no other way to explain why one Augur, over all the others, would know which visions were true and which were not."

Wirr gazed at the former Representative, his distaste mirrored in Taeris and Laiman's expressions. It fit—fit with what he knew, fit with what his father had written about Jakarris. Still, the three of them had learned the depths of that betrayal only a year ago. Dras had carried the knowledge of it for more than twenty.

Driscin's face had drained of blood, but he somehow looked even more dazed as he read the others' expressions and realized that he had been the only one not to know.

"Why...why would he tell Diriana the truth, then? Or get Lyrus involved in the first place?" the Shen Gifted eventually whispered, his voice trembling. He did nothing to conceal his shock, and Wirr couldn't blame him. The Augurs' failure, their fall, had been the great mystery of his generation. To discover that it had come about because of treachery within their own ranks would have been a confusing, painful revelation for any Gifted, let alone a former sig'nari.

"Jakarris wanted something from the Tol's vault, and he wanted it kept secret," explained Dras to Driscin, the words tumbling out of him. "But back then it was Tarav leading Tol Shen—and you remember what he was like. Not a man to break protocol. He would have died before going into that vault without permission from the other Augurs, too."

Driscin stared at Dras wide-eyed, but in the end reluctantly acknowledged the statement. Wirr watched intently, frowning. Davian had told him about the vault at Tol Shen—about how it had been designed to prevent even Augurs from unauthorized access.

"Jakarris already knew that Tol Shen would survive the war," continued Dras, "so he equipped Lyrus. Made sure that he would be the one credited with its defense."

"Which led to us choosing him to lead the Council when Tarav died." Driscin's eyes were hard. "Was Tarav's death really an accident?"

"No."

Driscin's jaw clenched. "And you were party to it? *That's* why you were chosen to be Representative?" he asked, voice suddenly dangerously taut.

"Yes."

There was a shocked second of stillness and then Driscin abruptly surged at Dras with a snarl of rage, Dras falling over backward in fearful surprise as he tried to scramble away. Taeris and Laiman both moved swiftly to restrain Driscin, but not before the former sig'nari had managed to land a savage kick to Dras's face. A cry of pain shattered the still night.

"Enough!" Wirr snapped out the word, though he kept his voice low, not wanting the sound to penetrate too far through the surrounding brush.

The three Gifted immediately stopped, reluctantly resuming their seats, Driscin's glare still murderous and Dras moving dazedly as blood leaked from an evidently broken nose. Laiman stood motionless, blinking in surprise before shooting Wirr a cautious nod and copying them.

Wirr waited until the furious breathing of the men had calmed, then shook his head angrily. "We have already established that he is a disgusting excuse for a man," he said, addressing Driscin more than the other two, "and that he has much to answer for." He peered at Dras's face. "You will need to heal him before you return."

Driscin's lip curled. "I'll do it on the way back."

"Fair enough. Just see that you do."

Driscin clenched and unclenched his hands, plainly still bringing his emotions back under control. "I apologize. I just...I didn't expect that. Tarav was a good man. A great leader. One of the last sig'nari. And my friend." He turned to Dras, eyes flat and cold. "What did Jakarris want from the vault?"

"An amulet." Dras's voice was nasal now; he had tilted his head back, pinching his nose with one hand while trying to gently stanch the leaking fluid with the corner of his cloak. "Lyrus agreed to go through with the plan, but once the other Augurs died—and knowing what he knew from Diriana—he realized that there was a chance for Shen to lead all of Andarra, without any Augur influence whatsoever. He guessed that Jakarris couldn't have Seen his betrayal, given that Jakarris had chosen him in the first place. So rather than handing over the amulet, Lyrus ambushed and killed him."

There was silence.

"The Vessel Davian took from the vault," Wirr said suddenly to the other three, looking in particular at Driscin.

Driscin nodded slowly. "It could be. There is more than one amulet down there, though." Despite the words, his voice held a note of concern.

Dras froze, still holding his nose, looking as though he had just put the pieces together. "The Vessel that can stop an Augur from using their powers? It's the same one," he said. "I heard it was stolen before I got back, when that Augur who caused all the problems last year was killed, but..." He trailed off.

"Fates," Taeris cursed. "That cannot be a coincidence."

"Do you know who did the killing? Who took it?" asked Laiman quietly, as Wirr felt a sudden surge of disquiet. He wanted to hear what the two men from Tol Shen had to say, but he already knew the answer.

Dras and Driscin both shook their heads. "We assumed that it was one of our people. Rohin had certainly done enough to motivate them," admitted Driscin.

"The Council had been considering how he might have been useful, but...nobody wept any tears over his death. There was no real investigation," agreed Dras.

There was only the whispering of the frigid night breeze for a few seconds.

"Jakarris killed Rohin and took it," Wirr said, feeling sick. The other men all stared at him, evidently hearing the certainty in his tone. "Erran told me. I'd almost forgotten—it didn't seem important at the time, given that we were fleeing for our lives. But he mentioned that Jakarris had the amulet when he and Asha met with him, just before Asha restored the Boundary."

"What in fates are you talking about? Jakarris is dead," snapped Dras irritably. "Your Augur friend was mistaken."

Driscin studied Wirr intently. "Davian would have known Jakarris as a man called Scyner?"

Wirr's chest ached a little at the reminder of his missing friend, but he dipped his head.

Driscin's shoulders slumped. "Fates. Rohin claimed that a prewar Augur sent him to the Tol," he said. "A Shadow. Davian said it had to have been Scyner. I didn't recognize the name or description, but..."

Dras gaped at Driscin, and the other three considered the words in horror.

"So he set it up. The whole thing," said Laiman eventually. "If Lyrus really did try to betray Jakarris, then this sequence of events—Tol Shen being taken over by Rohin, Lyrus's death, the amulet being free of the vault—cannot be coincidence."

"Twenty years is a long time to wait for revenge," observed Taeris.

"Not if he knew it would happen, and get him the amulet, too."

"True. Depending on why it is so important in the first

place…" Taeris rubbed his chin, gazing at Dras. "What do you know of the Vessel? Its origin, its purpose?"

"Only that it was capable of disabling an Augur." Dras sneered at Taeris's penetrating look. "That is all."

Taeris's lip curled and he opened his mouth to respond, but Laiman laid a hand on the Athian Representative's arm. "A mystery for another day, my friend. Our time here is running short. Let us get the answers we can, and worry about the rest later." When Taeris gave a curt nod of assent, Laiman turned to Dras. "How many people had knowledge of this?"

"Only a few—I am the last left alive, as far as I know. The rest of the Council members who were involved knew to trust Lyrus's judgment on the visions, and most of them realized that he must have figured out a way to tell which ones were reliable. But none of them were aware that he'd made the deal with Jakarris, or that he had known the war was coming before it began."

"What about the Scribe?" asked Wirr.

"She is dead," confirmed Taeris grimly, before Dras could reply. "The night of the rebellion. I saw her body."

"Lyrus probably saw that coming, too," muttered Driscin bitterly.

"Focus, gentlemen," murmured Laiman. "We have minutes, not hours." He glanced up through the trees toward where they all knew the Essence-lit walls of the Tol lay, then back to Dras. "Why tear out the pages? Why not take the entire book, or copy them?"

"According to Lyrus, there wasn't time. He was there in the palace that night. He knew that if the Journal was missing, the rebellion would hunt to the ends of the earth for it; even with the Augurs' failure to see what was coming, it was still a prize for Vardin Shal and his men. Pages missing would be suspicious, but in the chaos—and with the Augurs and Diriana dead—Lyrus guessed that there would be no reason for them to devote an inordinate amount of resources to figuring out why. He was right, too."

"Makes sense," admitted Taeris reluctantly.

The questioning continued for a while after that, somewhat haphazardly due to the need for haste; as soon as something occurred to Taeris, Laiman, or occasionally Driscin, they would immediately set about trying to pry details from Dras's unwilling lips. Sometimes the focus was on events during the war, sometimes it was information about things currently happening within Tol Shen's Council.

Wirr, for his part, mostly listened with mute unease. The others knew Tol Shen better than he, and he had to trust them to ask the right questions.

Gradually, a clear picture began to form. Twenty years ago the Shen Gifted, under the new leadership of Lyrus Dain, had waited out the rebellion behind their walls and begun planning to take control of the new generation of Augurs. Then, using information from the visions Jakarris had told him were reliable, Elder Dain had started forging political alliances with an unusual series of Houses—many of them insignificant at the time, distant from the capital, the benefits of the relationships unapparent until years later.

Eventually, knowing the Blind's invasion would be defeated, Lyrus had instructed Dras to Control the king when it finally came—ensuring that the Gifted would get the lion's share of the credit for the victory. And then, even after the Augur Amnesty was passed, Lyrus had felt no need to send the Augurs north: thanks again to the visions, he had been confident that the Boundary would be made strong again regardless.

Every move had been cold, calculated, often accumulating power at great cost to others—but never with any obvious correlation, never with any way to lay blame. Wirr would have admired the brilliance and daring of it all, if it hadn't disgusted him to his core.

It wasn't until their time was almost over, though, Driscin casting constant nervous glances in the direction of the Tol, that the worst of the revelations came.

"Something still doesn't feel quite right." It was Laiman speaking up, looking thoughtful. "Lyrus focused heavily on his relationships with the southern Houses. That makes sense to an extent; the north was hit hard by the Blind's invasion, which placed a lot more importance on the south's resources and massively increased their influence." He frowned. "That should have been exacerbated by the presence of the Banes—but instead, Shen encouraged those southern Houses to *withdraw* from the Assembly. If it's control of Andarra that they want, the smarter move would have been to leverage the north's need, not slap those who live there in the face."

He turned and looked questioningly at Dras; when the other man just stared impudently back, Laiman rolled his eyes. "Dras. Why, and how, did you convince the southern Houses to withdraw along with Shen? What advantage did you all see in it?"

Dras's breathing became short, and a vein on his neck started to bulge. Wirr leaned forward, suddenly intent. If Dras had been reluctant before, he was all but bursting from the effort of remaining silent now.

"Ilin Illan will be destroyed," he finally growled, lips drawn back in a snarl of frustration. "Possibly soon."

There was utter, disbelieving silence as Wirr and the others stared at Dras. The moonlight temporarily faded as a cloud passed overhead.

"*What?*" Taeris and Driscin both spoke at the same time, and Wirr's heartbeat was suddenly loud in his own ears. The moon emerged again, coating everything in stark silvers and blacks. Next to Wirr, Laiman was leaning slightly away from Dras, as if the man's words were poison.

"The last set of visions in the Journal show Ilin Illan in ruins, abandoned. Irreparable without years of work. Structures melted to the ground, the Builders' creations destroyed." Dras kept his gaze on the ground as he spoke. "Other correlating visions show that the south survives. One in particular suggests that it all happens close to the Festival of Ravens, which is why we got the Houses to leave before the festival last year. We don't know the exact year it will happen, but as Prythe is Andarra's second-largest city, and easily its most important in the south, we made the assumption—and the Council continues to believe—that the capital will shift to there, at least temporarily, after it does."

Another heavy, shocked silence greeted the words.

"And if Ilin Illan falls, the north is presumably either lost or suffers greatly." It was Laiman, the first of them to recover enough to speak; even so, his voice had an uncharacteristic quaver to it. "Withdrawing from the Assembly leaves the southern Houses with no obligation to provide manpower, supplies, other resources—if they're not part of the government, then they are simply wealthy families with vast holdings. King Andras would have no legal way to compel them to contribute to a defense. And be in no position to enforce such demands, even if he tried."

"Yes." Dras's confirmation held no emotion. "This way, we get to form a government with allies who still have much to offer. The surviving part of the country will stay strong."

The words ignited a dark fury in Wirr. "And everyone in the north is...what? Unimportant?"

"To an extent," conceded Dras.

Wirr gaped at him, not knowing how to respond. This year's festival was only two weeks away.

Though Laiman, Taeris, and Driscin immediately began firing related questions, Dras knew little more than he'd already said: Ilin Illan would be completely scorched, leveled by fire, but there was no indication of how or why it would happen.

After a few minutes, Driscin shifted, eyes glinting as he glanced up at the position of the moon and then in the direction of Tol Shen.

"We are out of time. In fact, we should already have started heading back. Someone will be checking on him very soon."

Wirr gave a short nod. He wanted nothing more than to keep Dras here, or better yet to force him to return to Ilin Illan and admit to all he had done. But Tol Shen would just drown out the truth with claims of a forced, false confession. For now, the information they had gained would have to be enough.

He stretched cramped, cold muscles as he rose from his seat, the others following his example. The surrounding forest was blessedly silent except for the occasional rustle of leaves in the breeze.

"How did Tol Shen find out about my ability to bind people?" Wirr asked Dras suddenly. It was by far the least of their concerns, right now, but it had been vexing him. This would be his last chance to find out for a while.

"Rethgar told us," said Dras. "It's why we tried to have you assassinated during your dinner at the Tel'Rath estate."

Everyone froze, and Wirr heard Driscin muttering a disbelieving curse under his breath.

"*You* were behind that?" Wirr asked, though his tone was more weary than angry now. Any other time the information would have shocked him; on the heels of learning about the destruction of Ilin Illan, it seemed like little more than a footnote.

Then he cocked his head to the side, registering the timing. "Wait—you knew about my ability before I did? How?"

"Rethgar told us," repeated Dras.

The name meant nothing to Wirr, but Laiman and Taeris both wore utterly stunned, horrified expressions. "Rethgar Tel'An?" clarified Laiman, his voice hollow.

"Yes."

"Sire, we really need to go," said Driscin, apologetic urgency in his voice. "You need to bind Dras now."

"Just wait." Wirr glared at Dras. "Who is this Rethgar? How did *he* find out, then?"

"He was one of the sig'nari, and a Council member for Tol Athian," interjected Driscin quickly before Dras could respond, tightness increasingly threaded through his tone. "Taeris can probably tell you more about who he was; I'd assumed he'd died in the war. I have no idea how he's been communicating with anyone in Shen—I've been kept in the dark about far too many things, apparently." He sounded nauseous. "I'll find out what I can from Dras on the way back, but we truly have to go. *Now.*"

"He passed on information mostly through Lyrus," added Dras. "I haven't heard from him since Lyrus's death. I don't know how he knew about you. Lyrus knew even before the Blind attacked, but he didn't want to take action until you'd changed the Tenets."

Wirr groaned in frustration. There were so many more answers he wanted from Dras, and simply not enough time to get them all from him.

"How in fates did you convince former Administrators to—"

"*Sire.*"

Wirr gritted his teeth, but he knew the mounting panic in Driscin's voice wasn't without reason. The portal back to Daren Tel would be running out of Essence soon, too. "Dras, you will return with Driscin and do everything you can to avoid being discovered. You'll tell him everything you know about Rethgar on the way back. Once you're in your bed, you will fall asleep and completely forget everything that has happened this evening, believing yourself to have slept the entire night through."

Driscin gave a sharp, relieved nod. "I'll send word when I can."

He grabbed Dras roughly by the arm and dragged him away into the darkness.

As the sounds of Driscin and Dras making their way through the undergrowth faded beneath the breeze, Wirr exhaled, turning to his other companions. The two men were still silent, but it took only a glance to know that something was badly amiss.

"You know who this Rethgar is?" he asked.

Taeris opened his mouth as if to reply, then shut it again and glanced at Laiman, who nodded slowly.

"We do. We killed him more than twenty years ago. An accident," the king's adviser explained softly.

"He was our first attempt at a sha'teth."

Chapter 3

Davian strolled the quiet streets of Caladel, his step light, enjoying the crisp warmth of the early-morning sun as it competed with a fresh breeze sweeping in off the harbor.

Mistress Alita had woken him before dawn to fetch supplies from town, but he found himself not minding today. The walk here along the cliff top, with the sun barely peeking over the horizon, had been especially peaceful as he'd watched Caladel's fleet of fishing boats far below slide out into the Vashian Ocean for their day's work. Even now, in the town itself, the rhythmic lapping of waves was still audible over the idle chatter of merchants setting up in the next street. The harborside village felt sleepy rather than its usual, bustling self. He liked it.

He paused, getting his bearings, then ducked down an alley and into a side street. If he was quick enough in completing his chores today, there might even be time to swim before returning to the school.

Footsteps echoed abruptly behind him, and before he thought to turn, a meaty hand was roughly grasping his arm.

Davian flinched, instinctively trying to shrug off the iron grip. He twisted to see a large man with blond hair and weather-beaten skin looming over him, expression sour; two more men stood off to the side, their eyes cold as they watched.

"What are you doing?" asked Davian indignantly, trying again to squirm out of the big man's grasp. Had these men mistaken him for someone else? The street was empty behind them, he realized to his sudden concern.

"He's just a child, Tanner," said the one with a strong jaw and muscular physique, looking bored. They were all fishermen, from the looks of them, though why they weren't out with their boats already, Davian couldn't imagine. "Not worth it."

Tanner—the big man—ignored his companion and stared at Davian, lip curled.

"You working for the bleeders, boy?" Tanner asked, his breathing oddly heavy. Davian's nose wrinkled at the sharp tang of alcohol. Mistress Alita was always muttering about men who drank early, and this was definitely early.

"Gifted," corrected Davian automatically. He'd used that other word in Mistress Alita's presence, once. It was possible that he was physically incapable of saying it anymore.

The polite term was the wrong thing to say here, though, clearly. Tanner's eyes flashed and he spun, not relinquishing his grip on Davian's arm, dragging him wordlessly toward a nearby building. A tavern, from the sign. Silent at this hour, but clearly open.

Davian struggled in vain, shoulder aching where his arm had been yanked, protesting vigorously. The two other men trailed after them into the dingy building, looking uneasy.

The tavern smelled of sweat and stale wine. Only two people were inside: an older man sweeping—probably the owner—and another, younger man in a blue cloak, halfway through what looked like breakfast. Davian felt Tanner's grip on his arm tighten.

"What is this?" The Administrator had stopped eating and stood, studying the scene with a frown as the sweeper halted his work and disappeared silently into the kitchen. The door locked behind him with a firm click.

"He works for the bleeders," Tanner said roughly, a slight slur to his words. "You going to make trouble?"

Davian locked eyes with the Administrator, silently pleading for him to help. The man wavered, then walked over. He reached down and pushed back Davian's left sleeve, revealing clear skin.

"No Mark. Not my place," said the blue-cloaked man. Davian thought he saw something approaching shame in his eyes.

The Administrator gave a slight nod to Tanner and the other two men, then headed for the door.

Davian was watching him go, mouth agape, when the punch took him in his stomach.

Air exploded from his lungs and he went to the floor, wheezing from the blow. A vicious kick followed that clipped him on the chin, snapping his head back, sending his vision spinning and ears ringing. There was laughter, then shouting, then more blows followed by a confusion of angry voices as he curled up into a ball, his world red and hazy.

Then, miraculously, it all stopped.

Davian rasped and moaned; there was someone else in the room now, furiously protesting what was happening, though he couldn't lift his head to see who. His arm dangled uselessly at his side, and something—multiple things—in his chest felt broken.

As he lay there, though, some of the pain began to just...dissipate. He was doing something. Something natural, something he'd done his entire life but never deliberately. Like a child recognizing for the first time that they could control their breathing, purposefully drawing in deep lungfuls of air.

His head cleared a little.

"This has gone far enough," the new voice was snarling. "Let him go."

Davian forced his gaze up to see a handsome, middle-aged man clad in red at the door, bodily restrained by Tanner's two companions. He looked a mixture of furious and terrified.

Tanner gestured, not noticing that Davian had recovered enough to observe. "Too late for that, bleeder," he said, words slurred, a wild glee in his eyes. "You shouldn't have started this. When you came to me, did you know that my father was murdered by your people? He did nothing wrong, but the fates-cursed Augurs said he'd killed someone. They muddied his name and then they hanged him. He cried at the end, you know? Begged for mercy? But they didn't give it to him. I even believed that they were telling the truth about him." His eyes were red rimmed and he jutted out his jaw, teeth bared. "And then three years later, we found out that they were all frauds. Just making it all up. They

were criminals, and all of you who were helping them are just...
evil. This thing you can do makes you that way. It needs to stop."

The Gifted man had paled under the onslaught of drunken
words, desperation in his eyes now.

"He's just a boy," he said, more to the two men holding him
than to Tanner. "Do what you need to with me, but let him go."

There was silence, and the burly, bearded man on the left hesi-
tated, looking like he was about to agree.

Then the one on the right started, staring at Davian.

"Tanner," he murmured. "His arm."

Everyone turned to look at Davian and the red-cloaked man
gasped, suddenly renewing his struggling.

It took Davian a second, woozy as he was, to realize why.

Tanner had drawn a knife from somewhere on his person.
Short but with a wicked edge, the kind used to gut fish. It didn't
look as if it had been cleaned since its last use.

A surge of panic went through Davian as he comprehended the
threat, but his shout was cut off by Tanner's massive hand across
his mouth.

Then the knife was large in his vision, blotting out the rest of
the world.

The sharp steel started biting into his cheek, slow and deep, trac-
ing a burning line down his face. He bucked, trying to tear himself
away, but he may as well have been trying to shrug off a building.
Fear and panic and helpless rage all coalesced in his chest, a feral
tangle of wild emotions that balled up inside him, tight and hot.

Everything...dimmed. There was something else there. Some-
thing dark and powerful and violent.

Something that could help.

He reached out.

The cutting stopped, and Tanner's suffocating grip on him
loosened.

Davian wrenched himself free and stumbled away before trip-
ping gracelessly, taking great, heaving breaths as he collapsed on
the dirty wooden floor, vision blurred by tears and blood. When
hands failed to grasp at him again he summoned the courage to
lever himself up and twist back toward his assailants, teeth bared

in defiance.

Tanner hadn't moved to follow him. Instead his eyes were wide, staring at the bloodstained knife in his hand.

"Tanner?" The bearded man, still holding the Gifted back, looked increasingly anxious. "What are you doing?"

Slowly, Tanner raised the knife to his own cheek. His hands trembled as they began slicing an unsteady line down his skin. The cut was deep; blood spilled silently from the wound, gushing onto the collar of his shirt.

Everyone else watched in frozen, wide-eyed disbelief.

"Please," Tanner whimpered, confusion in his eyes.

Then he began to scream, even as he continued to cut.

Davian scrambled madly backward with a cry, unable to look away from the horrific sight. Behind Tanner, the other three men—including the Gifted—had started to move, too.

One drew a blade from his belt; the other two fetched knives from the settings at nearby tables.

And then they started to cut themselves too, their panicked, pained cries creating a nightmarish chorus with Tanner's.

"Stop!" Davian screamed, putting his bloodied hands over his ears to blot out their shrieks. "Just stop!"

An abrupt quiet, almost as shocking as the screams.

All four men crumpled to the ground, blades clattering from their hands. Davian stayed scrunched up where he'd collapsed beneath a table, breath coming in short, sharp gasps. His three attackers weren't moving but the Gifted was stirring, dragging himself over to where Davian lay cowering. Blood streamed freely down his face, dark red and glistening. He reached out gently, but Davian couldn't help but flinch away.

The Gifted swallowed as he forced his hand to Davian's chest.

"I never wanted this. Not this," he whispered as a trickle of healing Essence began to flow into Davian, tears of shame in his eyes. "I'm so, so sorry."

Everything faded.

Davian woke to find the featureless darkstone roof of his cell staring back at him.

He gazed at it, steadying his breathing. For so many years, that one day in Caladel had been nothing but a blur; his mind had shied away from touching on it, even his dreams of it nothing more than a hazy mélange of events.

Since Rethgar's visit, he had relived it in excruciating detail... five times, now? He knew what was happening, too—that it was more than a simple memory. His ability to See had started taking him back to that moment in his life, again and again. Just as had happened to Malshash with his wedding day.

He rubbed his face and then hauled himself up into a sitting position, swiveling to perch on the side of his small cot.

He had killed those men, instinctively Controlled them and then drained too much of their Essence—he'd been certain of that since the first time he'd relived it. There was still a lingering horror at the thought: not guilt, necessarily, but certainly regret.

More to the point, though, it meant that Taeris had willingly taken the blame for what Davian had done.

Wirr had told him that he needed to give Taeris another chance, the last time they had spoken. Had he known, somehow?

And were Taeris's scars—his ongoing cutting of his own face— a result of what Davian had done that day? Some remnant of the Control he'd used?

Davian shook his head with a heavy sigh, levering himself to his feet. Tanner's form had been the one he had accidentally taken on when he'd shape-shifted in Deilannis, too. He had thought long and hard about that—suspected he knew what it meant, now. It would certainly explain why Malshash had seemed so horrified at the time.

There was little point in dwelling on it now, though.

It was just another problem for after he got out of here.

He began his daily routine. Walking the perimeter of his near-empty, twenty-foot-wide cell to loosen his muscles, then dashing from wall to wall for a few minutes, then a series of strengthening exercises he knew from his memories of Aelric's training. Those drills had been hard, the first few months. Now he barely felt a mild burn in his muscles after he finished.

Food came next. As it did at the same time every day, the small section in the darkstone wall slid away around dawn, a steel bowl and fresh bucket pushed smoothly through the slot on a rotating shelf before the opening immediately ground shut again. He didn't bother trying to thread kan through that brief gap anymore. It had taken six months for him to gain enough control here to attempt that—only to discover that the meals were delivered through some sort of interconnecting chamber, and that there was a secondary darkstone barrier between him and his guards anyway.

That had been...disappointing, to say the least.

He ate—the food in Tel'Tarthen Prison was surprisingly palatable, albeit bland—until the familiar angular symbol etched into the bottom of the dish became fully visible. Thirteen curling slashes, each joined to another, forming the vague impression of a stylized man.

He stared at the image bleakly, then carefully tapped the Vessel, draining it of the Essence it contained. Just enough to comfortably get him through another day. A deliberate choice by Gassandrid, undoubtedly.

He left the bowl on the rotating shelf, then swapped the bucket that served as his privy. The shelf would rotate back at some point during the morning.

He spent the next three hours practicing with kan. Though darkstone—the Essence-absorbing, kan-blocking black bedrock of Ilshan Gathdel Teth—had interfered with most things he'd tried, there were still several techniques he could attempt to perfect. Besides, the difficulty of merely grasping the power here in Talan Gol had forced him to improve. There was no way for him to measure how far he'd come, but he was undoubtedly stronger than he had ever been before.

That hadn't mattered, so far, but still. He was determined to be ready when the opportunity to get out of here finally presented itself.

He was halfway through testing a new variant of his Disruption shield when he caught the slight scratching of a key sliding into a lock.

He froze, for a split second unwilling to trust his ears. Excluding Rethgar's intrusions, he had been visited exactly three times since his capture. Three times in a year.

Then he swiveled smoothly, tensed, readying his attack.

The door began to swing open.

Davian stepped outside of time, arrowing multiple whisper-thin threads of kan toward the new crack in his darkstone cage, extending his senses along with them. Some of those threads would drain Essence, others would attempt Control, others would merely stun. All he needed was to get one through. *One.*

As they reached the door, they were met with . . . a torrent.

Hundreds of strands of dark energy flooded into the cell, meeting Davian's and overwhelming them before slithering on unimpeded. Davian watched in horror as they coalesced; a moment later thick, oily black chains burst into existence, snaking around him before he could react. He gasped as the links snapped tight, lifting him from the floor and slamming him bodily against the wall opposite the cell's entrance.

When his head had cleared enough for him to look up again, a muscular, blond-haired figure stood in the doorway, the end of the black chain attached to a glowing steel bracer on his arm. The man studied him with glazed, lifeless eyes.

"A pleasure to see you again, Davian," said Gassandrid.

Despite its wanness, Ilshan Gathdel Teth's dusk still managed to sting Davian's eyes as he stepped out of Tel'Tarthen Prison for the first time in a year.

He winced, squinting against the glare, trying instinctively to bring his hands up to shade his eyes. They were firmly bound, though, rough rope chafing against his wrists.

He reached for kan and immediately ground his teeth against the pain that shot through his mind, barely avoiding dropping to his knees again. The same as when those kan-blocking black chains had still been wrapped around him, back in his cell.

Beside him, Gassandrid—the man who had given his life to be part of Gassandrid, anyway—gave him a gentle nudge forward.

"It is temporary," he assured Davian.

Davian didn't respond, still unsettled by the man's glassy eyes and slightly off, stiff way of moving. He was a corpse—animated by Essence and distantly Controlled by Gassandrid, who by his own admission managed thirteen such proxies at any one time.

They allowed him to split his mind across multiple bodies, duplicate important knowledge. Be in several places at once.

These bodies weren't like Davian's, though. They didn't require food or sleep, and lasted for only a few months before Gassandrid had to find new ones. All were supposedly volunteers from within the city, as if that somehow made it better. Gassandrid had explained the necessity of it all in calm, unapologetic detail to Davian, the first time they had met.

"Where are you taking me?" asked Davian as Gassandrid began guiding him down the street, tension tightening his words. "And why now?"

Gassandrid eyed him. "Did you think our patience with you would be unending? After all we have shown you—after explaining the situation so clearly, treating you with respect, giving you plenty of opportunity to dwell upon the things you've learned—you still choose to fight for the other side."

"You've treated me with respect?" repeated Davian bitterly. "Are we pretending Rethgar's visits didn't happen now?"

Gassandrid's mouth twisted in displeasure. "As I have said before: that was a mistake."

"A mistake that tortured me for two straight days and nearly killed me." Davian's stomach twisted at the memory. "I'd go as far as to call that a *large* mistake."

Gassandrid grunted. "Your point is made, Davian. It does not change anything. So now, given your refusal to change and a lack of better options, you will be ... put to better use."

Davian just shook his head, falling silent as he processed the ominous words. Gassandrid was right about one thing: the Venerate—specifically Gassandrid and Diara—*had* explained their position to him. In those first days after freeing Caeden, Davian had barely slept as he'd braced himself for reprisals, picturing the sort of agonizing torture to which he'd seen his friend subjected.

Instead, when the two Venerate had finally visited him in his cell, everything had been surprisingly ... civil.

He could tell from the icy hatred in her eyes that Diara would have liked nothing more than to do to him all the things he'd been imagining. And yet she had simply tried to Read him—

unsuccessfully, thanks to Malshash's training—while Gassandrid went about detailing their perspective on things. Telling him how Shammaeloth's grand plan was currently enslaving the world, about their efforts to help El escape and Caeden's desire to prevent that from happening. Making special mention, of course, of Caeden's goal being to kill each and every person able to access kan.

Davian hadn't believed a word of it, that first time.

"He is not coming, you know," said Gassandrid suddenly, interrupting Davian's thoughts. "Not until he needs you."

Davian clenched his jaw, keeping his eyes forward. Ilshan Gathdel Teth was as black and brooding as he remembered it, the darkstone buildings all jagged and angular, as if every element of the architecture was meant to evoke some sort of weapon. The people, normal enough though they seemed, scrambled out of the way with wide-eyed reverence when they spotted Gassandrid.

"I don't know what you're talking about," Davian said eventually.

"Yes you do." Gassandrid looked across at him. "I can see you still anticipating it. Still waiting for something to happen, even after what we showed you. But he has abandoned you, just as he abandoned us. He has no care for people, Davian. To him, only his goals matter."

Davian scowled, the accusation striking home.

A year. He'd been carefully tracking the passage of time, and he was confident it had been that long. A year, and no sign of Caeden. No contact. No evidence at all that his friend was working to get him out, as he had promised in those desperate moments before his bizarre, nightmarish escape.

Even now, even after everything Davian had learned, it was hard to believe that what he'd done had actually set Caeden free. He certainly hadn't believed it when Caeden's head had rolled to a stop at his feet, lifeless eyes staring accusingly at him.

After Gassandrid and Diara's second visit to his cell, though, he'd known it to be true.

That had been about two months after their first conversation, but there had been no talking this time: instead he had felt images pouring into his mind almost as soon as the two Venerate entered the room. With his shields focused on stopping information from leaving his mind rather than entering it, there had been little he could do to prevent the onslaught of memories. Visions of Caeden as Tal'kamar, as Aarkein Devaed. Memories of the lengths he had gone to and the atrocities he had perpetrated in pursuit of his goals. Of the *millions* he had sentenced to death because of what he believed—often to the horror of even the other Venerate.

And then, after what felt like uninterrupted hours of forced experience, a final memory—not originating from Gassandrid or Diara, this time, but from Caeden himself. Something Caeden had shared with the others in an attempt to uncover the identity of the man he had killed, rattled as he had been by the stranger's words, and desperate as he was to prove him a liar.

That memory, above all, Davian had done everything he could to forget.

It was no easy thing, to watch your own death.

He shuddered, forcing down the sense of helplessness that always accompanied those images. It had, unsurprisingly, badly shaken him. For weeks after, he had sat in that lonely cell and just...wondered.

Not about which side he was on—the Venerate had tried to destroy Andarra and kill everyone he loved, so there was no debating that. But he *had* started to doubt his choices. Freeing his friend. Supporting him. Believing in him as he had.

If Caeden got his memories back, started reverting to who he had once been...

He sucked in a breath. Ultimately, he'd come to the conclusion that he had a simple choice: have faith in the man he had come to know, or condemn him for a past that Caeden himself had tried to reject. And if Davian chose the latter, all the things he had said to Caeden—the advice he'd given, the assurances of friendship he'd made—had been nothing more than words.

Which was why he was able to meet Gassandrid's gaze with confidence, this time.

"That's not the Caeden I know," he replied quietly. "If he's not coming, then he's not coming. But it isn't because he doesn't want to."

Gassandrid watched him, then dipped his head.

"I cannot help but admire your faith in Tal'kamar, even if I think it is misplaced," he said sincerely. "Perhaps it is part of why you were able to sway him, when so many before you could not."

There was no talk for a while after that; people began to flow around them as their downward-sloping street merged with a main road, which in turn ended in a massive marketplace to the east. Several more passersby stuttered to a stop and gawked as they recognized Gassandrid's proxy, his passage leaving a trail of hushed, excited murmurs. Davian's presence, despite his bonds and the Runner's mark clearly cut into his neck, was by comparison barely acknowledged.

He gazed around as they walked, a little intimidated by the crowds after having been isolated for so long. The sun had fully slipped below the horizon now, and torches were being lit at regular intervals along the streets, which—like everything else in the city—were carved from darkstone. The sharp black lines of the buildings stood out starkly against the fading light in the west.

Despite its alien appearance, everything else here truly seemed...normal. Merchants hawked wares in the distance. People chattered and laughed and shouted and bustled from place to place, going about their business at the end of the day. Children trailed after parents. The sounds of singing filtered out of a nearby tavern. The rhythm of the song felt strange, not quite right—but otherwise, this could have been any city in Andarra.

As they walked, Gassandrid abruptly dug into a pocket, pulling out something small and holding it up for Davian to see.

"I have to ask—my curiosity has been piqued for some time. How, exactly, did you obtain something so valuable?"

Davian stared at the silver ring, nonplussed.

His mind raced. The familiar three intertwining strands were unmistakable: it was the Vessel Asha had given him, the one Malshash had used to draw him through time in Deilannis. The one he had been wearing when he'd been captured a year earlier.

But Gassandrid's question felt...off. The Vessel was useful, but hardly remarkable. The ring itself was finely made, but far from singular in its craftsmanship.

Why would Gassandrid, of all people, describe it as *valuable*?

He held his tongue; the silence drew out and Gassandrid gave a snort of disgust, pocketing the Vessel again and marching onward.

They finally made their way into a large square. Davian recognized it immediately: the enormous sphere that dominated its center, blue Essence pulsing through cracks that spiderwebbed across it, was a landmark he had noted when he and Fessi had first been brought here.

The thought gave him a flicker of sadness, an echo of the grief he'd felt a year ago. Fessi was dead, now. Her death had been confirmed by Gassandrid, and the man had shared his memory of examining her torn body as proof. She'd fled into a section of the city called Seclusion, apparently—an area dangerous even for the Venerate, if Gassandrid was to be believed.

That news had shaken Davian, left him feeling empty and alone in a way nothing else had during his imprisonment. Not only had Fessi been his friend, but the thought of her out there—escaping, maybe even getting help—had been one of the few bright lights of those early days.

In the time since, Davian had guessed that she must have run because she'd recognized something from one of her visions. Likely the one of her own death, given the timing and how scared she had been.

He'd never know for sure, though.

He frowned as he and Gassandrid approached a large darkstone archway at the side of the square, beyond which lay stairs that vanished down into the bowels of the city. A trickle of people were entering, talking excitedly among themselves; Gassandrid nodded for Davian to proceed, and they joined the downward flow.

Voices echoed in the tunnel as the sounds of the square began to fade behind them. The people up ahead were talking enthusiastically about someone called Metaniel; though his expression gave away little, Davian thought he saw a flicker of irritation in Gassandrid's eyes at the repeated mentions of the name.

They continued their descent for several minutes until the comparative quiet of the passageway was gradually covered over by a low rumble, the muttering sounds of a crowd barely audible. After another minute that had grown to a dull roar, crescendoing and dampening and then crescendoing again as thousands of voices thundered. Davian's heart began to pound with the pulsating noise as he finally saw the way ahead smooth out and open up.

He stepped off the last stair, stomach lurching at the sight before him.

They had emerged onto a pathway high above a massive, bowl-shaped cavern, the entire space clearly carved from the surrounding darkstone. Row upon row of staggered seating had been hewn into its sides, interspersed with carefully cut stairways. The seating ran all the way to the bottom, which leveled out to form a rectangular arena, though that too was floored by darkstone—this surface worn smooth, but with its immediate walls ugly and jagged, viciously sharp protrusions everywhere. Those spikes would prevent anyone in the arena itself from climbing out, and from the wine-colored, viscous liquid dripping from some of them, Davian suspected that they had been tested quite recently.

The benches were three-quarters filled with people—a massive crowd—though most weren't sitting. Animal-like screams and wild-eyed jeers came from every direction at the arena far below, which currently held a half dozen occupants. Even from this height Davian could see the tension in those fighters' shoulders, the sweat glistening on their faces as they circled and slashed wearily with their weapons.

Scattered across the arena were several more people. Each of them was prone and still.

Bile rose in Davian's throat as he understood what he was seeing; he stuttered to a halt, his attention more on the crowd than the combatants. There was something feral in their expressions, a fierce, lusting glee that exploded every time someone down in the center drew blood.

"Why...why are we here?" he asked Gassandrid, voice barely more than a whisper.

Gassandrid didn't answer, moving to the side and unlocking a thick iron gate, quickly ushering Davian through, and locking it again before anyone passing had a chance to notice. They walked along an elevated pathway; many of those in the highest seats spotted their passage, cheering and taunting them in equal measure, though their distraction from the bloodshed below was brief.

Davian put one foot after another in a daze. He had heard of such things: contests of blood, men and women fighting to the death for the entertainment of others. Supposedly a staple in Nesk, the Isles of Calandra, and other far-off, barbaric realms. Certainly nothing he'd ever expected to see in person.

They came to another set of stairs and started down again, away from the seething cauldron, the frenzied, crashing noise of the crowd soon muted by thick darkstone walls.

"You expect me to fight," said Davian, voice unsteady.

Gassandrid pulled him to a stop as they reached the bottom of the stairs and came to a heavy-looking iron door. He looked Davian in the eye.

"I expect you to win," he said softly.

He rapped on the door.

Before Davian could respond, a heavy lock clicked and the door swung open, revealing a pretty young woman with short-cropped brown hair, fine features, and pale skin waiting warily on the other side. She examined Davian coolly, one hand on the hilt of her blade. Aside from the absence of a helmet, she was clad entirely in the black, light-drinking armor of Telesthaesia.

Her entire demeanor changed and she dropped to one knee when she spotted Gassandrid's proxy.

"Lord Gassandrid," she said reverently, head bowed. "My name is Isaire. In the Protector's name, welcome."

Gassandrid bent down and pulled the woman gently to her feet. "There is no need to kneel, Isaire. Not to me." He gave Davian, whose head ached as he tried to process what was happening, a small push forward. "I have today's challenger for you."

Isaire's expression clouded with sudden confusion. "Lord Alaris's chosen fighter—"

"Will not be required today." Gassandrid's voice was firm. "This man is to be announced as Ethemiel. Keep a close watch on him and if anything seems out of place, do not hesitate to bring him back to me. Even at the cost of delaying the proceedings."

Isaire still looked surprised, but obviously knew not to argue. She bowed low.

The proxy gave a nod of satisfaction and disappeared back up the stairwell.

"Lord Gassandrid is confident," observed Isaire, casually drawing her blade and slicing through Davian's bonds before poking at him to move through the doorway. "Ethemiel. Destroyer of false idols. He must have great faith in your abilities, to publicly name you so."

Davian barely heard the words, thoughts racing as he allowed himself to be moved along. Though Isaire acted casually, Davian could see that every movement was balanced, every glance alert. She looked comfortable in Telesthaesia, too.

He reached out for kan, stumbling as pain ricocheted through his head. Not as crippling as before, but he still couldn't touch the power. Even with Gassandrid gone, there was no way to escape just yet.

"I have seen Metaniel fight," continued Isaire, despite Davian's obvious lack of interest in the conversation. She looked him over with an assessing, dubious glance. "Lord Gassandrid...clearly knows something that I do not."

Davian remained taciturn as the oppressively narrow passageway branched in five different directions; his guard ushered him into the leftmost one, and they were soon emerging into a large chamber, which was empty save for several racks of battered-looking weapons and armor lining the walls. Smoke from torches mingled with the acrid smell of sweat and blood.

"This Metaniel," said Davian finally, staring at the blades. "That's who I'm about to face?"

Isaire gave him a baffled look.

"You...haven't heard of him?" The woman seemed incredulous when Davian shook his head. "Where have you *been* for the past half a year?"

"Tel'Tarthen Prison."

Isaire started to smile, though the expression faded to something more thoughtful as she realized that he wasn't joking.

"Metaniel started fighting in the Arena six months ago. His skills have made him very popular, and he has a reputation— justified, so far—of being unbeatable. He has also been a... somewhat divisive figure." Isaire hesitated, as if debating how much to say. "Outside of the Arena, he has spoken out against

the preparations for war. Challenged people not to blindly hate the south, criticized the Venerate and questioned their motives. He claims knowledge of their secrets, too—will tell anyone who listens of the atrocities he believes they commit against the people of this city. He has stirred up more dissent here than anyone in recent memory."

Davian's heart sank. So not only was he being forced to fight, but it was against an enemy of the Venerate.

"Why don't they just kill him?" he asked eventually, walking over to the rack of swords. These blades were dented, and he could see where blood had soaked into many of the hilts. Davian picked one up and hefted it with a grimace. It was unbalanced. Poorly made.

Isaire shrugged. "Martyrs are powerful things. If he does not die in the Arena, everyone will know why, and assume that what he says is true." She studied him. "As I said. If you are being pitted against him, then Lord Gassandrid evidently knows something I do not."

Davian tried another sword, Aelric's memories telling him that the craftsmanship was as lacking as that of the first. He'd already decided not to wear any of the armor on offer: even if the quality was significantly better than that of these blades, he wasn't accustomed to it, and it would only serve to slow him down. "Then he has made a mistake. If Metaniel is an opponent of the Venerate, I'll make sure that I don't kill him."

"Defeat in the Arena means death—regardless of whether the final blow comes during the fight or after it is over. And if you each refuse to fight, then you will simply both be executed." There was certainty in Isaire's voice. "If you truly do not wish to kill him, then you will need to sacrifice yourself."

Davian fell silent, thinking furiously. There had to be a way out of this.

"Why are you telling me all of this?" he asked suddenly. He stopped, examining his guard, the faintest flicker of hope igniting in his chest. "You...you don't *want* me to fight him. You believe in what Metaniel says, don't you?"

Isaire looked at him. "I am giving you information that is already common knowledge. Nothing more."

There was a familiar stabbing pain in Davian's head.

His pulse quickened. "I know you're lying. You could get me out of here," he pressed. The lingering effect of the black chains, or possibly Telesthaesia, must be affecting his ability similarly to a mental shield. "We are on the same side—you saw my bindings when I got here. I am no friend to the Venerate."

To his surprise Isaire just laughed, the sound musical and without malice. "I would never betray Lord Gassandrid." More pain. "Besides—even if you were right, it would not matter. Willing or not, you will be dead within the hour."

The latter statement was apparently not a lie, as far as Isaire was concerned.

Davian's lip curled, but he quickly reined in his frustration. "What if you're wrong? What if I end up killing the one man who could make a difference in this city?" He leaned forward, willing her to change her mind. "You want to know why Gassandrid brought me here to fight him? I am an Augur, Isaire. And I am *not* fated to die today," he finished firmly.

The slender woman's eyes widened, and for the first time she looked off balance as she stared at him. There was dead silence for a few seconds.

"That is…unexpected," she admitted, "but…in some ways that would make things harder still. The Venerate would hunt me to the ends of the earth if I set you free."

"You have to," pleaded Davian. "I can help. This may be the only chance I get. *Please.*"

Isaire looked at him, her expression still considering. Processing what he had told her.

Then she reluctantly shook her head.

"It is too much of a risk. I do want to help you, but…there are bigger things than even Metaniel's safety to worry about. I am sorry and I hope that this somehow works out for you, but I owe you nothing."

Davian opened his mouth to further his case but was interrupted by the sound of a horn, loud and harsh. His heart dropped as the far door opened, flooding the room with bright light. Banishing whatever chance he'd thought he had.

Isaire was already on her feet, her back straight and her face cold, every inch the elite guard. She nodded to the hulking, silhouetted figure in the entrance, then turned to Davian. "It's time. Go."

Davian rose slowly, the weight of what felt like a missed opportunity heavy on his shoulders. He couldn't blame her—he knew that. It didn't lessen the pain of having those few moments of desperate hope slip away again so quickly.

He hefted the poorly made blade he had chosen and trudged past Isaire, not looking in her direction.

"I *am* sorry," she whispered as he passed, her lips barely moving, despite the attention of the man in the doorway being back on the crowd.

Davian paused. Inclined his head in the barest of acknowledgments.

For now, it would have to be enough that there were allies here. To know that, just maybe, he wasn't completely alone in this nightmare.

He squared his shoulders, then walked out of the tunnel and into the thundering, drumming, pulsing roar of the Arena.

Chapter 4

Davian waited at the lowest level of the black stone amphitheater, body tensed against the bone-rattling sound that assaulted him from all sides, only dull metal bars now between him and the violence taking place beyond.

Both the gate and the passageway he was standing in were capped by thick darkstone, completely in shadow and out of sight of the crowd above. Davian could hear them well enough, though. Stamping feet drummed chaos above his head. A thousand voices screamed their delight or anger as events in the center unfolded, thundering waves of emotion followed by troughs of jeering, or support, or anything in between.

Every moment of it made Davian sick.

He glanced across at the hulking man who had fetched him from his conversation with Isaire and was now standing beside him, peering through the bars in fascination. Telesthaesia rippled black around his body, dark even in the shadows. All the guards here wore it, apparently.

"How long until it's over?"

The huge man turned; even the muscles in his thick neck stood out. He considered Davian with sharp, appraising green eyes. "A minute until you're out there. Two at most." He eyed Davian's attire disapprovingly. "And maybe thirty more seconds until you are dead. Pride will get you killed, Runner," he added gruffly, returning to his watching through the bars.

Davian didn't respond, turning back to the battle out in the center as he thought furiously of ways that he might still get out of this. The guard hadn't been wrong: the fight currently under-way was nearly over. One combatant was still defending but his movements were sluggish, desperate in their jerkiness; whether he had been wounded or was dizzy from a blow to the head, it barely mattered. His opponent had the advantage and knew it, raining down blow after blow in what was close to a frenzy, not with any particular skill but rather with sheer, heavy force.

A thin spray of glittering red suddenly colored the torch-lit air; a roar echoed around the arena as the wounded man crumpled. The other dropped to his knees and stabbed down with feverish intensity several times as the feral cheers of the crowd urged him on, before finally rocking back and lifting his bloodied blade, looking at the stone ceiling far above and screaming his relief to the enthusiastic onlookers.

"Protector take it," muttered the man to Davian's side, flicking the bars in front of him in irritation at what Davian assumed was a lost wager.

Davian watched silently as the victor was ushered away and the loser's corpse dragged unceremoniously from the arena. This vio-lence was awful, barbaric, but he had seen far worse over the past few years. Such things didn't shock him as they once would have.

That worried him, sometimes.

The crowd's fervor quieted to a low, dull roar, equal parts anticipation and restlessness. Davian closed his eyes, taking deep breaths and focusing on a series of mental techniques designed to block out emotional distractions. It was another routine inher-ited from Aelric, one of the memories the brilliant young swords-man had allowed Davian to Read from him before their defense against the Blind, what seemed like an age ago now.

He knew he was going to need everything he'd taken from Ael-ric. Diligent though he'd been in his exercises over the past year, doing them in a locked room and without an actual weapon was hardly a suitable replacement for proper training. Not to mention that if what Isaire had said was even vaguely accurate, then his opponent was both practiced and very, very good.

And as little as Davian wanted to fight, he had no intention of dying tonight.

He took another calming breath, then hesitantly reached for kan once again.

Fire scorched through his mind; he gritted his teeth, clawing desperately through the haze of red toward the dark energy that he knew lay just beyond. There was resistance, like being underwater and swimming for the surface.

And then, abruptly, a bursting of the pressure.

He was through.

Davian opened his eyes again, not releasing his grip on kan, relief mingling with a tingle running down his spine at the sudden tension in the air. How long had he been focusing? An aura of pent-up expectation filled the stadium; the crowd above had to be at least five thousand strong now, packed in so that they were almost spilling over the balconies above. Whether that was normal or if people were expecting something special tonight, he had no idea.

Suddenly, the way ahead was opening.

"Protector with you, Runner," muttered the guard as he prodded Davian through.

Davian half stumbled out onto the black, barren stone, the worn-smooth surface stretching away in front of him for at least two hundred feet. Iron clanged behind him as the barred gate slammed shut again, the sound barely audible over the exulting bellows of the crowd. Davian stood still for a moment, feeling the uneven weight of the steel in his hand, quickly trying to take in what else was happening around him.

It didn't take long to realize that this would not be a simple duel.

The gates to either side of him—perhaps thirty feet away to his left and right—had also opened, three fighters clad in Telesthaesia emerging from each and barely pausing before arrowing toward him. On the far side of the arena he could see more motion: a single figure directly opposite, and another half dozen opponents streaming in its direction, too.

Assuming that other figure was Metaniel, the fight was being kept even. That was something.

He took another deep, calming breath as the black-armored combatants—four men and two women—flew toward him, preternaturally fast. His heart pounded as he took the measure of the blurring dark forms.

Davian waited until the closest of his attackers was less than ten feet away, and stepped outside of time.

Even already holding it as he was, kan was difficult to wield here in Talan Gol, thin and oily and commanding a good deal of his concentration to use. Still, a year of constant practice had helped. The noise of the crowd was suddenly a little quieter, distorted, as if he were hearing it through a long and echoing tunnel. The people in the stands were still moving but at half their previous pace, mouths opening and shutting sluggishly, clenched fists seeming to wave almost lazily above their heads.

To either side of Davian, the men and women in Telesthaesia came more sharply into view. Not slower than him—that was too much to hope for. But close to the same speed now.

A spear flicked out like a forked tongue from the frontmost fighter's hand; Davian moved smoothly to the side, letting the wicked edge pass beneath his left armpit and then spinning, wrenching the weapon from the shocked man's hands. An undisciplined attack, despite the Telesthaesia. The man—another Runner, interestingly, judging from the symbol burned into his neck—must have thought to score a quick kill and gain the resulting glory all for himself.

Davian maintained his grip on the plain wooden haft and continued his twirling motion, snapping the spear around and slashing hard. Like all the fighters racing at him, the attacker wore no helmet. The sharp steel raked deep in a diagonal line down the stunned man's right cheek, then across his throat. He went down in a gurgling shower of blood.

Davian didn't pause to watch; he could wield a spear well enough, but it wasn't his preference. He braced and the weapon blurred as it left his hands, sprouting through the open mouth of the next attacker, who flipped backward at the force of the throw, dead before she hit the ground.

Four left. They stuttered to a brief, shocked halt but quickly recovered, spreading out, working together now. More respectful of him than the first man. One barked an instruction to the others, the exact words lost to Davian beneath the pulsating thrum of the crowd. His assailants began to separate farther, circling him, hunting for a blind spot.

Davian snatched some Essence from a nearby torch and flicked it at the fighter to his left, eliciting an appreciative gasp from the crowd as the red-bearded man flinched; Telesthaesia would block the energy, of course, but most people still shied away when a blinding bolt of it was fired at their face. Davian simultaneously dove to his left, just past the singing blade of another attacker, his elbow smashing a third in the nose with a wet crunch before he got in close and grappled for their weapon.

The sudden, searing pain in his side warned him that the fourth fighter had scored a hit.

Davian ignored the sensation and the subsequent temptation to panic, instead driving his elbow viciously back again, rewarded with a muted cry of pain as he wrested the contested sword free from the athletic-looking young man's grasp. He staggered back with the second blade now held in his left hand, still on guard, doing his best not to let on that there was a fiery numbness creeping up his side. The injury was a bad one, possibly life-threatening for anyone unable to heal themselves. Maybe still was. He forced Essence from his dangerously low artificial Reserve to the wound—with the nearby torch out and his opponents in Telesthaesia, there were no other sources at hand—but while the pain eased, it did not vanish.

He growled in frustration as the sliced-open cloth of his tunic slapped wetly against his skin, the heavily stained fabric no doubt displaying to everyone his weakness. The flow of blood had been stanched, but he hadn't been able to heal himself enough to regain full mobility.

Even taking into account the now-disarmed fighter, who was wiping blood from beneath his broken nose but otherwise looking alert again, Davian's task had become near impossible. He tensed, preparing to launch himself at the nearest of his opponents. He would have to trust the added advantage of the extra weapon, and fate. He couldn't afford to wait for an opening...

He faltered.

Beyond his assailants, toward the center of the arena, there was movement. His heart sank. There hadn't been enough time for

73

Metaniel to overcome the Telesthaesia-clad fighters on the other side, which meant that he must have instead succumbed quickly. Davian would soon be fighting even greater numbers.

He let his gaze slip past his attackers to focus on the lone black-clad figure flying toward them, and froze.

The thin, long-limbed fighter was wearing a Telesthaesia helmet to go along with the rest of his armor.

Davian's shock almost cost him; the woman to his right had seen his hesitation and lashed out with her sword. He jerked back, barely keeping his balance, the blade slicing perilously close to where his right arm had just been. The woman shouted in triumph as she saw the opening, darting forward.

Her head rolled from her shoulders in a spray of red as Metaniel's sword slashed from behind.

Davian scrambled to set his guard again but Metaniel was already moving on, past him, close enough to strike at had Davian been fast enough. There was a clash of steel; Davian spun, dazed, to find the man whose nose he had broken slumping to the ground with thick red dribbling from his gaping throat, while the next fighter's sword was already cartwheeling through the air.

Metaniel moved with grace and purpose, elegance, somehow looking unhurried despite the terrifyingly cold efficiency with which he put his blade to work. He slid to one side; the third fighter went down screaming, blinded as steel sliced cleanly across his eyes. The final of Davian's original foes attacked; Metaniel simply stepped underneath the blow and caught the man's arm as it descended, then thrust forward with clinical force, the tip of his viscera-coated blade abruptly protruding from the back of his opponent's skull. Metaniel withdrew the blade instantly, spinning back to the writhing man on the ground and going smoothly to one knee, silencing the fighter's agonized cries with a single, icily efficient blow.

Davian could only watch, barely able to believe what he was seeing.

Five seconds. That was how long this man had taken to kill four opponents in Telesthaesia.

He forced himself to snap back into action, putting distance between himself and Metaniel's tall, wiry frame, even as he registered the half dozen prone forms on the other side of the arena. It wasn't that Metaniel had somehow evaded his own attackers, then. He had simply dealt with them that quickly.

Davian gripped his dual blades firmly, mouth dry as the warrior in front of him stood again, smoothly withdrawing his sword from the dead man's skull. He faced Davian, and that symbol—the same symbol that had been carved into the side of Davian's neck a year ago—stared back like a giant, deformed eye.

The crowd had gone quiet; Davian could make out that much, even from inside the time bubble. Whether they were sharing in his shock at Metaniel's inhuman efficiency or simply anticipating what was about to happen, he had no idea. He couldn't afford to look, couldn't afford to take his eyes off the man in front of him.

Metaniel simply stared at Davian, motionless, almost casual in his stance—clearly confident, and with what felt like good reason. Davian shifted his weight onto the balls of his feet, muscles bunching as he prepared to launch himself forward. His injury was not going to improve any further. Waiting in this weakened state was the worst thing he could do, no matter how good his opponent.

Left hand by his waist, Metaniel flicked three fingers at the ground.

Davian blinked. Hesitated.

The motion had been small, almost imperceptible, so fast that Davian wondered whether he'd imagined it. Outside of his time bubble, there was no way he would have seen it at all.

Even so, it was enough to fire a memory—one he knew was not his own.

His heart pounded loud in his ears, confusion suddenly making kan even harder to hold on to. The gesture was one that Unguin, Aelric's mentor, had used. A message between swordsmen—though usually ones who were on the same side, working together to take on a common foe.

Wait.

Davian's breathing was heavy; though his actual exertion had been brief, his wound had taken too much out of him. He knew—logically—that he had to win here. Was *destined* to win, no matter the choice he made now.

But...in his condition, against this man...he simply could not see how that was possible.

He made his decision. Forced his muscles to ease, then cautiously took a step back, putting distance between himself and Metaniel. Davian's faceless opponent immediately drew a secondary, shorter sword from his belt; Davian tensed again, suddenly certain he had made a mistake.

Metaniel raised the blade to his own shoulder.

A thrill ran around the stadium as he carefully cut away the leather bindings of his Telesthaesia breastplate, then shrugged it off and threw it to the side. The crowd, like Davian, thought they knew what was happening—Metaniel was removing his armor as a statement, a challenge, a way of matching Davian's own lack.

It wasn't until a few seconds later that Davian saw what no one else possibly could.

Metaniel's hands were trembling.

The shaking became more pronounced as the warrior's shortsword came up again. This time, though, the crowd's murmurs turned to a hushed confusion almost as complete as Davian's. Both of Metaniel's hands were on the hilt but gripping it upside down, the blade pointing toward the ground.

For a moment, everything paused. Metaniel's head tilted up slightly, and Davian thought he gave the slightest of nods in his direction.

Then the blade snapped inward, the tip at Metaniel's chest.

Before anyone could react, the warrior was driving the steel hard and deep into his own flesh.

Davian lowered his bloodied dual blades until they hung limply at his sides, a symbol of his utter, disbelieving bewilderment as he watched Metaniel crumple to the ground. He let his time bubble drop, gaze drifting dazedly to the thousands of faces staring back at him from the crowd. Had someone intervened on his behalf? Controlled Metaniel, somehow? But no—that was impossible. Telesthaesia should have blocked any attempt to reach the man's mind with kan.

Confused, concerned shouts started raining down from the onlookers above. This wasn't what they had come here to see. There was motion around the edges of the arena as guards behind the various gates peered uncertainly through the bars, knowing they were meant to collect the victor once the fight was finished, but evidently perplexed—and probably alarmed—by what they had just witnessed.

Davian finally moved, gripping his two swords alertly again as he limped forward, face contorting at the pain in his side. His caution was unnecessary; Metaniel was dead, his chest still, even as dark blood continued to spill from his self-inflicted wound. Davian finally dropped his blades, kneeling next to the body and placing his hands on Metaniel's helmet.

The indignant buzz of the crowd swelled as they saw what he was about to do, though presumably more because they realized that it meant Metaniel was truly dead than because they didn't want Davian touching him. Perhaps fifty feet away, one of the gates to the arena was finally swinging open and a dozen men emerged, bearing a heavy chain over their shoulders. The metal of it was black, oily in the torchlight.

Davian recognized it immediately.

The first boos began to rain down as Davian hurriedly began wrestling Metaniel's helmet from his head, certain he would not get another chance once the guards reached him. The fastenings were tight and adrenaline made his hands shake as he worked feverishly, all too aware of the men now running toward him, yelling in taut voices for him to stop, to get away from the body and to lie on the ground so that they could secure him.

Just as hands began looping under his armpits to fling him to the ground, the black covering finally slid away to reveal Metaniel's face. A man not much older than Davian, brown haired and clean-shaven, hazel eyes staring sightlessly at the darkstone roof.

A stranger. Davian was quite certain he had never laid eyes on him before.

Then he was on his stomach, the wind knocked out of him and knees pressing hard into his back as the Telesthaesia-armored men began rapidly looping the black chain around him, pinning his arms to his sides. He didn't resist beyond trying to protect his aching side; whatever was going on, he was in no condition to put up more of a fight. He couldn't see much with his face pressed into the darkstone, but the booing around them had intensified to an ugly, heavy drone, and flecks of motion behind the men holding him down suggested that the crowd were now flinging things onto the arena in protest.

The chains around him seemed to tighten and slither together, pulsing with darkness as they did so. Davian winced at the renewed pain of his wound but made certain not to move otherwise, not wishing to show these men any signs of resistance. From their panicked sideways glances at him, it would clearly not take much to invite further violence.

As soon as his captors were satisfied that the bindings had taken hold, he was being hauled to his feet and half carried, half dragged toward the nearest gate. He was surrounded by Telesthaesia, still couldn't see a lot, but several of the men flinched as they neared the edge of the arena, and the sounds of ill-aimed projectiles striking rock were obvious even over the continued snarl of the crowd.

Then, finally, they were past the iron bars and hurrying down the shadowed passageway.

The petulant, impotent railing of Ilshan Gathdel Teth's citizens chased them into the darkness.

Chapter 5

Asha reclined on the couch in front of the tall, narrow arch of glass, soaking up the pleasant late-morning sun as she flipped the page.

She paused in her study, gazing out the roof-to-ceiling window next to her, one of the many that lined the wood-paneled walls of the massive library. Beyond, sunlight glittered off rippling streams, hues spinning through fountains as bursts of water rhythmically showered the air in a spectacular dance of motion. The gently sloping grounds were alive with such displays, interspersed with vibrant green manicured lawns and brilliant white stone pathways. In the distance, past the immediate grounds at the beginning of the valley, a lush forest swayed gently in what was no doubt a pleasantly warm breeze.

She stretched, turning back to the book.

Her breath caught.

There it was again. It had happened twice since she'd settled down here an hour ago: a flicker of dark movement in the corner of her eye, something flitting along the dappled tree line below.

She swiveled, eyes darting as she searched unsuccessfully for the source of her concern.

Was it just the motion of the fountains? A mild paranoia? She shifted restlessly and tried to resume her reading; after a few seconds, though, she sighed, snapping the book shut and pushing it to the side.

Even one moment out of place here was unusual. It *could* have been her imagination, but ignoring it would be foolish.

She checked her Reserve absently, though there was little need: the great ocean of Essence thrummed there as always, pulsing so bright that she had learned to ignore it out of necessity. She adjusted the summery yellow dress she was wearing and made her way out onto the nearest balcony, sweeping back her loose hair as the soft wind nudged it across her face. As always out here, the temperature was...perfect. The sun was warm, but the breeze took away its edge and kept the air invigoratingly fresh.

Asha started down the winding stairs, between and sometimes beneath the streams and fountains that created the constant joyful dance around her. Short tunnels made of crystal and glass wound through the water, casting a gentle, softly shifting deep blue on the white stone underfoot as the sun filtered through the clear pools.

About halfway down she tarried, turning to gaze back up at the palace. It was a beacon through the bursts of water, the crystal facade glittering and refracting light in every direction for miles, bright but not enough to be blinding, not enough that she had any desire to look away. It did that all day, and any night when there was even a sliver of moon.

It still felt strange to think of it as her home.

She tore herself from the dazzling sight and continued down the hill, breathing deeply as a light mist from one of the fountains wafted across her face, pleasantly refreshing. Before long she had reached the bottom, the edge of the grounds giving way to the dappled light of the forest ahead. With the tinkling of water now behind her, the warbling of birds tickled cheerfully at her ears, and the soft sigh of wind through the treetops was a comforting susurrus.

She wound her way along the path, alert for any hint of something unusual, not rushing—there was no need—but not wandering, either. After a few minutes, she reached the point where the trail began to close in and the trees grew more closely, threading together in order to block her path.

Asha lingered, then shrugged to herself: she'd come this far now. She edged her way through, forcing aside the unnaturally resistant, thickly leafed branches until she finally broke out onto the open plateau beyond.

She brushed herself off, strolling to the edge of the grassy cliff top and making herself comfortable, legs dangling over the sheer drop as she stared out contemplatively at the blue sky stretching to the horizon and the distant, inaccessible rolling plains below. It was a stunning vista. Perfect, just like everything else here.

She breathed deeply. Concentrated.

A section beyond the edge of the cliff... *rippled.*

And then she was looking at a barrier of writhing, pulsing shadow, the wall that formed the edge of the dok'en now impossibly juxtaposed against the clean light of noon.

She swallowed, steadying herself against the dizzying sight and studying the swirling black mass intently. This was the weakest point in the mental construct—the one she had needed to reinforce three times so far. It looked stable enough right now, though.

Asha chewed her lip, observing the pulsing barrier for a few more moments before looking away, letting the illusion of sun and sky reassert itself. Whatever was going on, this wasn't the problem.

She frowned at where the barrier had been, dissatisfied. Her knowledge of how the dok'en worked felt relatively complete— one of her first tasks here had been to read each of the comprehensive books in the library on the subject, after all—but something was off, and this time she couldn't put her finger on what it was.

That was a problem. Though she had a semblance of control over the stability of this place, it was Caeden's creation, not hers— at least she'd deduced it was, given the tiny pieces she'd gleaned from Elli. Yet Caeden himself seemed to have only the most tenuous of connections to it. If it collapsed—as it so nearly had several times, during those first, terrifying few weeks here—then at best she would be permanently cast into the constant agony of the Tributary.

And at worst, her mind would disintegrate along with the dok'en.

She shivered at the thought and began heading back to the palace, mentally cataloguing the books on the subject that were worth revisiting. She would have to ask Elli her opinion, too. All she had to do was—

The ground trembled, and Asha's heart went to her throat.

The midday sun suddenly waned, then flickered, Asha's surroundings disorienting as reality began to spin in and out of darkness. The air rippled all around her and sounds became warped, the delicate tinkling of the fountains up the hill morphing into something sullen and unsettling.

She braced herself, breathing heavily, trying to hold back tears. Not a collapse, but...still. There had been a Shift only a week ago. It was too soon. Too soon.

There was a roar, and she was ripped back to *there*.

She forced her eyes open, vision blurring through the tears; she blinked to clear them, unable to move. Searing pain sliced through her body everywhere, forcing her breaths to come in short, panicked gasps; despite her having been through this a dozen times before, it was worse than she remembered, worse than she could have anticipated.

It wasn't just the pain—it was the inability to do anything about it. To feel so helpless, so trapped, while the needle-thin blades cut her everywhere.

Outside the Tributary, through the pane in front of her face, she could see the pavilion outlined in pulsing blue Essence. It was starting to shift, pieces groaning into motion, whirring and rotating and realigning, snapping together with crackles of energy. She didn't know if it always did that or if it was just during the Shifts, but it was at least something to focus on. Some small distraction from the pain that tore her concentration apart every few seconds.

Beyond the moving parts outside she was occasionally able to glimpse the world beyond. The cliff side, the ocean, the Boundary itself. It was night, clouds masking most of the sky, but the pulsing Boundary lit everything for miles around. The strength of that glow gave her the slightest measure of comfort as she struggled against the agony.

It was still standing. What she was doing here was worthwhile.

Soon enough her muscles were screaming from the tension of trying to stay perfectly still; whenever she relaxed them the slight shift meant that every blade cut savagely, causing those same muscles to tense up again instinctively, which in turn forced the razor-sharp edges running through her back into flesh that had just barely healed. She knew that was how it worked—knew that this was happening to her day in and day out while she was in the dok'en. But inside, it was nothing more than an unpleasant thought.

She tried to focus on anything else—a technique from one of the books she had read recently, plans for what she wished to train in next—but nothing could take away from the constant, mind-breaking pain.

It went on for what felt like an eternity.

Asha woke.

She just lay there, barely breathing, still afraid to move. She was lying on her back atop her massive, impossibly soft four-poster bed, tucked carefully underneath the covers. The sun was setting through the enormous and intricately designed open window that formed the entirety of the western wall of the room. A silhouetted flock of birds glided in front of light clouds tinged pink and orange, and the Essence-lights beneath the fountains outside were beginning to pulse to life as the grounds leisurely melted into dusk. A warm breeze danced around the room and caressed her hair.

As if nothing had happened, just like always.

She closed her eyes, letting tears of both grief and relief fall silently for a minute, phantom pains still cutting into her body as she tried to stop herself from twitching uncontrollably. She almost managed to forget her real situation, sometimes, here in this perfect paradise. Almost managed to ignore the horrors of what she'd been through, and stop wondering—even if it was just for a few minutes—what might be going on out there in the real world. How her friends were faring, Davian in particular. What had changed. Who lived now, and who had died.

Whether anybody was left to remember her.

The Shifts brought it all back. She could handle the physical pain—even if it didn't feel like it at the time, she always knew it was going to end. But what it *meant*, the reminder, stuck with her for much longer and hurt far worse.

"Welcome back."

Asha opened her eyes again, wiping the moisture away and sitting up. Elli was standing in the doorway. Though her tone was light, even cheerful, her eyes were full of concern.

"It was too soon." Asha's voice was hoarse. "I should have had weeks."

The young woman—she was perhaps five years older than Asha herself—nodded, her waist-length, straight black hair swinging with the motion. "Something is wrong," she agreed.

Asha's breath caught at the words. "Do you know what?"

"My best guess is some sort of external disruption." Though she was undoubtedly perturbed, Elli's tone was as calm as ever. "Was the Shift any different from usual?"

"No," said Asha automatically.

Then she swallowed and held up a hand, forcing herself to think back properly.

"The beginning *was* odd," she conceded. "Usually when it happens, the Tributary machinery is already in motion. This time... this time it felt like it started as I woke up. *Because* I woke up."

"A disruption to the dok'en, then, rather than the Tributary itself. The Shift mechanism was reacting to your altered state, rather than causing it." Elli crossed her arms, giving her a mock-stern look. "What did you do?"

"Nothing. Nothing!" said Asha quickly, defensive despite herself. "I'd just checked whether the dok'en needed reinforcing, but I've done that plenty of times before. I thought I saw something down near the forest not long before that, but...I don't know what it was. If anything. Something just didn't feel right," she finished lamely. "You can't...do some sort of test, I suppose?"

Elli shook her head apologetically. "You know I cannot," she chided gently. "The changes I can make here are superficial; I am still governed by the laws of this place. Whereas the dok'en is drawing on your Essence, which is why you have enough access to its underlying structure to stabilize it." She shrugged. "I can play with the facade, but you're the only one here who has any level of access to the foundations."

Asha conceded the point tiredly. That was about all she was likely to get out of the woman.

She still, even after all her research, didn't completely grasp how Elli's existence was possible. A dok'en was a kind of Vessel, constructed from kan to mimic a place from its creator's memory—and then using a small, ongoing connection to that person's mind to keep the rules within consistent. Which was why Asha wasn't suddenly able to fly, or control kan, or will a building to change into something else: if it wouldn't be possible for her in the real world, then it wasn't possible here.

That all made sense to her. But Elli? Despite by her own admission being part of the dok'en, Elli acted almost like a real person. She clearly had memories of a life here with Tal'kamar—Caeden—as she had absently mentioned him more than once, and yet she refused to share them. She was incredibly knowledgeable in every area Asha had thought to ask her about, but she also learned, acted independently, reacted, remembered. She was caring, too, even witty. Asha *liked* her.

But the books all suggested that mimicking something as complex as a person within a dok'en simply wasn't feasible.

Still—despite feeling occasionally unsettled by that knowledge, Asha wasn't complaining. It was Elli who had saved her, those first few weeks after she had entered the Tributary. Asha had woken up here in this extraordinarily beautiful, peaceful place, confused and alone and terrified. Wondered, briefly, if she had somehow escaped her fate.

And then the edges of the dok'en had trembled, shadows rushing in on her. She'd been ripped from tranquility to burning misery. After a while reality would stutter, and she would be reclining in a soft bed in the palace. And then, seconds later, she would be in agony again. And on, and on, for longer than she could fathom, until she almost lost her grip on what was real. Constantly a heartbeat away from just letting go, giving in.

Asha wasn't sure how long had passed before she'd heard Elli's voice, instructing her on what to do. How to steady the walls of the dok'en, solidify and push them outward. It had been close to impossible, focusing in that state, and she had fallen agonizingly short so many times before finally gaining a foothold and stabilizing this place.

She was determined to never let things go back to that way again.

Elli held out her hand; Asha grasped it gratefully, allowing the other woman to haul her to her feet. She stumbled a little, but her legs quickly steadied. The physical effects of a Shift never bled through into the dok'en for long; besides, rest would only bring with it the chance to wallow.

She needed to be up, and out, and *doing* something.

"Do you have any suggestions for investigating?" she asked, stretching.

Elli frowned thoughtfully. "If the dok'en is stable—and I believe it is—then...I'm afraid not. And you've already read every book in the library that even touches on the subject. Twice." She gave Asha an apologetic look. "We will simply need to be on guard for anything unusual."

Asha made a face, but inclined her head. "Then I think perhaps it's time for some training," she said, forcing some cheer into her voice. "The exercise will do me good."

"Already?" Elli eyed her dubiously.

Asha glared at her. "Yes. Already. Let's go."

She strode past the other woman without waiting for a response, drawing a sliver of energy from her Reserve to make sure she didn't stumble again. Though she wasn't really accessing the power—everything here was in her head, including her use of Essence—she still did her best not to tap it to excess. If she ever got to use it outside the dok'en again, drawing too much would pull Essence away from the Shadows and Lyth connected to her, potentially to dangerous levels. Asha had been on the receiving end of that connection herself. She had long ago resolved to practice accordingly, and not to take her enormous pool of energy for granted.

Elli trailed after her as she made her way out to the open courtyard, which was bathed in the last rosy light of dusk. Like everything else here it was perfect, the white stone underfoot inlaid with polished obsidian, the designs elegant and flowing. Cushioned stone benches lined the long, slightly sunken space, and perfectly manicured firs bordered it at regular intervals, marking the shallow man-made stream that formed one edge. In its center three fountains spouted in time with one another, ejecting thin streams that seemed to hang in the air, sparkling in the dying light, before dropping gracefully back into their pools with barely a splash.

A gleaming weapon lay on one of the nearby benches: a proper blade today, Asha was pleased to see. Elli would sometimes, apparently on a whim, conjure something different for her to use—axes, spears, even flails—always touting the importance of understanding how each was wielded. Today, though, Asha just wanted to spar using something with which she actually felt comfortable.

She picked up the weapon as she passed, breathed deeply of the fresh air, then turned to Elli and carefully tapped her Reserve.

Golden light began to seep from her skin—not focused at one point as was normal, but rather appearing as hundreds of tiny, burning threads, all curling out at different points, interweaving and tightening to conform to the shape of her body. Asha's arms and legs began to shimmer as the power solidified, molding itself to her beneath her clothing as well as over exposed skin. She could feel the energy creeping up her neck and over her head, too, though it never reached a point on her face where it might obstruct her vision.

Within seconds the Essence armor had fully formed, pulsing around her and seeping into her skin, bright but no longer as distracting as it had once been. Asha flexed the fingers of her free hand, watching as the protective energy shifted smoothly with the motion.

It had taken her six months of daily practice to learn this, after reading of it in one of the books Elli had recommended—even with constant coaching from Elli herself. The armor's direct connection to Asha's flesh made it partially internal, allowing her body to act like a Vessel, largely protecting the Essence from decay. It would stop anything short of a direct attack with kan, and its open connection to her Reserve meant that if any Essence was expended, it would be instantly replaced.

It still used more energy than she would necessarily have liked, but if it came down to it—if she needed to fight—then this was an advantage she would happily use.

Elli was watching from the edge of the courtyard. She sighed theatrically. "That really is very unfair, you know."

Asha shrugged. "You're the one who keeps saying that defense is my biggest concern." It was true enough; Asha's raw strength gave her incredible destructive power, but it wouldn't stop an arrow or blade that she didn't see coming. "Besides. Being unfair is kind of the point."

Elli raised an eyebrow. "Is that so?"

A massive blow crashed across Asha's back, sending her flying forward. Her armor absorbed most of the damage but pain still wrenched through her torso as she rolled, digging her heels into the courtyard, stone scraping and cracking as she ground to a halt. She shook her head dazedly.

Where she had been standing, another version of Elli stood—clad in exactly the same armor as Asha's.

Asha scrambled to her feet and shot the first Elli a dirty look, letting Essence flow into her muscles, loosening them again.

"I suppose I asked for that," she muttered.

Then both versions of the woman—one shining bright, one not—dashed toward her.

Weapons appeared in her opponents' hands: dual short, curved blades of Essence for the original, and a long spear—steel, rather than one made of energy—for her copy. They were on her in a moment; Asha swayed back calmly as the spear cut the air inches from her eyes, then flicked her hands and unleashed a carefully directed, concentrated blast of Essence at the other, unprotected version of Elli.

The force of the explosion shattered the white stone underfoot, cracks rippling across the entire courtyard away from where the stream traveled. Asha's movements had given her away, though; Elli blocked almost disdainfully with an Essence shield of her own, perfectly formed. Despite the crackling torrent of power rushing around her, she remained untouched, though she at least skidded backward from the impact.

Asha spun back to face the Elli with the spear, but the armored woman had stopped, her eyes disapproving through the glowing visor.

"You're using your hands again," she said chidingly. "Remember—no gestures, no words. These are the signs of a mind poor in discipline. A mind that needs trickery as a crutch to perform its tasks."

Asha grunted, blade still up and keeping one eye on the other

Elli, who had dismissed her shield again and was circling into Asha's blind spot. "In a real fight, I'm going to do everything I can to win."

"If you need to do it in a real fight, there's a good chance you won't—"

Elli stopped midsentence, lurching to a complete halt.

Asha felt her brow crease, glancing bemusedly behind her. The unarmored version of Elli was motionless, too. Frozen.

"Fascinating," murmured an unfamiliar woman's voice from behind Asha's left ear.

Asha leaped and spun with a shout of surprise; a stranger had appeared next to her in the middle of the now-shattered courtyard, though Asha couldn't see how she'd made it there unnoticed. The short, athletic-looking woman wasn't paying her any attention, though. She was instead studying the two versions of Elli, arms crossed thoughtfully.

"A training partner built into the dok'en?" she mused. "Impressive. Tal'kamar went to some effort."

"Who are you?" snapped Asha, pointing her steel at the woman in what she hoped was a threatening manner, trying to get the shock in her voice under control. Other than Elli, this was the first person she had seen in…a year? "What did you do to her?"

The intruder continued her examination of Elli, then turned in unhurried fashion to look at Asha. Her eyes were deep brown, almost black.

"You are shorter than I expected," she said. Her gaze held Asha's, and somehow Asha knew what was coming before she spoke again.

"My name is Diara—I am here to represent the Venerate. It is nice to finally meet you, Ashalia," she finished quietly.

Chapter 6

Asha didn't hesitate.

She tapped her Reserve and gestured, sending a massive, slicing blade of energy scything toward Diara, for once not holding back. The solid razor of light smashed into the stone, the fountain, and one of the benches beyond, splitting it all with a thundering crack and an explosion of rubble, the hissing of water turning to steam audible as the din settled.

"That sparring construct was right," said Diara as she emerged from the dust, waving her hand in front of her face and then brushing some grit from her sleeve in a vaguely irritated fashion. "You need to learn not to use gestures. You're strong, but I've known blind men who could have dodged that."

Asha scowled, drawing deeper from her Reserve this time. She didn't need to worry about the Tributary here, or the Shadows. She could use more.

Much more.

She unleashed a wave of utter, burning destruction. Similar to the one she had used a year ago against the tek'ryl, but more controlled this time.

Everything in front of her...*melted.*

The water in the fountains evaporated in an instant, surrounding stone liquefying and sliding to the ground in a red, glowing mass where it didn't burst apart and fly away. The green grass vanished and at the bottom of the hill, trees that had been swaying gently in the wind burned angrily through the miasma of smoke and destruction.

In a single moment, the beauty of the palace gardens had been transformed into something terrible to behold.

Asha breathed heavily as she dropped her outstretched hands, dizzy, unaccustomed to drawing that much power at once. The air in front of her shimmered, the haze of heat distorting everything beyond.

Her heart sank as a line of glowing stone suddenly dulled and hardened within the chaos, and she spotted the figure emerging along the newly made path.

Diara walked through the boiling heat at an unhurried pace, clearly protecting herself with a bubble of kan. She stepped calmly out of the destruction and back onto the broken white stones of the courtyard.

"A blind man may have had trouble with that one," the Venerate conceded drily.

Asha glared and dashed at her, blade in hand: perhaps kan could protect Diara from Essence, but steel was another matter. She would never be a master with the weapon, but Asha's confidence with it had grown greatly over the past six months. The Essence coursing through her limbs made her stronger, too—and her reactions faster than any normal person could possibly hope to match.

Diara blurred, near-impossible to track even with Asha's enhanced senses. Asha adjusted but too slowly; a blow to her side sent her stumbling and then she was looking up from the ground to where Diara stood, the other woman holding the sword Asha had just dropped.

Diara sighed. "Now. Before you bring the Crystalline Palace to the ground as well, perhaps we can talk?"

"I know who you are." Asha scrambled to her feet warily, not dropping her armor or her guard. She refrained from another attack, though, at least for now. "I don't think we have much to talk about."

Her pulse raced; everything had changed, and so quickly that she could barely comprehend it. The Venerate had found her. She'd known that they would search—of course they would search—but to have one of them here, so soon...

"You would be surprised," said Diara with a cold smile, reading Asha's expression. "Let us start with the obvious: I am here to

give you a choice, not to kill you. Killing you would be easy, but…
of little gain. Your mind would likely be healed by that ridiculous
store of Essence—and even if it was not, your body would still be
linked to the Siphon and continue to supply the Tributary. I *will*
try it, if it comes to that," she admitted calmly, "but I would prefer to explore more…positive outcomes, for both of us."

Asha took a moment, processing the words. Diara either didn't
know where the Tributary was—entirely possible, as her access
to the dok'en could have been from anywhere if she had the right
tools—or couldn't get past its defenses. Information that the Venerate obviously didn't mind Asha knowing. A strange thing to
admit to so quickly.

"I won't leave the Tributary, and I will not tell you where it is."
Asha put iron into her voice. "There is no deal you can make that
would convince me to do either of those things."

"Which is why I am not going to ask you to," said Diara.

Asha opened her mouth but then shut it again, brow furrowing
as she searched Diara's expression for a clue to her intent. What
other bargain could the Venerate possibly wish to make with her?

"Then what…" Asha trailed off. "Why are you here?"

Diara held up a hand. "First, I would like to show you something while the opportunity presents itself. What is happening
where I am in the physical world."

Asha's vision suddenly went black, and then she was somewhere else.

A wave of nausea washed through her, followed by lurching
disorientation as she tried to grasp something to steady herself,
only to discover that she was no longer in control of her own body.
She was seated in a small, black stone room; the large window she
could see through overlooked a massive torch-lit stadium, which
appeared to be entirely underground. Voices howled from the
writhing crowd packed inside. Below, one man stood amid a sea
of motionless forms, the blades in his hands glistening red.

She gasped as she recognized him even from this distance,
though the body she was in made no sound.

His shoulders looked broader now, his dark hair was long, and
there was a new scar on his neck—a scar she had seen only once
before.

93

Davian looked dazed as the angry sounds of the crowd began to intensify. He stumbled toward one of the fallen men, dropping to his knees beside the body as gates in the arena opened and soldiers poured through, each in the black armor of the Blind. They dashed as one toward him—so fast it was startling, almost impossible to follow.

Davian ignored them, wrestling with the helmet of the fallen warrior, apparently trying to remove it. The crowd screamed now, jeered. Scraps of food and other, heavier objects began to rain down onto the arena as the chorus of disapproval swelled.

And then she was back in the dok'en.

She reeled as she tried to grasp what had just happened, doing her best to master the deep, aching sense of loss her glimpse of Davian had abruptly revived. Diara hadn't Read her—Asha had been practicing her mental defenses regularly over the past year, and they were still holding strong—but clearly she had just used kan on her in some way.

Asha's hands shook. The last time she had seen Davian—the moment she had sealed him behind the Boundary—still haunted her dreams more nights than she cared to admit. He had looked older when he'd traveled back in time to speak to her, so she'd known he'd had at least a couple of more years to live...but that hadn't stopped her from feeling sick at what she must have put him through, stranding him there.

It had been the right thing to do. She knew it. Elli had said the same thing several times early on, when she had found Asha thrashing in bed from the nightmares, then comforted her through the tears of grief and regret. It had helped Asha make peace with her decision, over the course of months. But it didn't make her hate it any less.

And now this. A glimpse of the horror he was living.

Asha did what she could to refocus, checking her surroundings and her Essence armor even as she trembled. She couldn't afford to be thrown off balance like this, not now.

"Is he all right?" she asked, relieved to find her voice steady. Diara had to know that there was a connection between her and Davian, else she wouldn't have bothered showing her what she just had.

"Remarkably, yes. He is." Diara shook her head, looking irritated, then absently waved away Asha's subsequent glower. "I am neither surprised nor upset at his survival. Just the manner of it."

"So why show me that?" Asha snapped.

"Because I wished to prove that Davian was still our prisoner. That this offer is being made in good faith." Diara's words were clipped, the woman evidently still considering whatever had just happened in the real world. "I am offering you the chance to have him released, Ashalia."

"In exchange for?"

Diara gestured behind her at the apocalyptic, burning wasteland that had once been the palace gardens.

"An assurance that something like this can never actually happen," she said quietly. "A binding, to take effect upon Davian's release, ensuring that this confluence of power within you is *only* used to fuel the ilshara. I have already accepted that no volunteer for a Tributary could be convinced to leave—but nor can I in good conscience leave a weapon like you in the hands of Tal'kamar."

"I'm not a weapon," said Asha angrily, as much to buy time to process what was being said as from any real outrage. The Venerate wanted to exchange Davian for...a guarantee that she wouldn't use Essence outside the Tributary?

Diara raised an eyebrow, casting a pointedly dubious glance behind her before continuing. "Then this should be an easy choice. Make no mistake, though, Ashalia: you *are* a weapon, and weapons are rarely left idle. Perhaps you were never going to be used as such, and this proves to be a poor deal for me. But as my bargaining chip is rather unique—specific to you, and with a limited time to trade—I will take what I can get for him."

Asha rubbed her face, her unease growing.

"'Limited time'?" she asked pensively.

Diara opened her mouth and then paused, for the first time looking surprised.

"You...don't know?" Her eyes were suddenly sorrowful. "Tal'kamar did not tell you? Ashalia, I...I am so sorry."

"Sorry for what?" Asha whispered.

Diara's expression was almost reluctant as the dok'en faded again.

This time, when the burning remnants of the palace gardens returned to Asha's view, the sight was blurred through tears.

She gasped a breath as she realized that she was back in front of Diara, scrubbing her eyes and doing her best to suppress the emotions that threatened to overwhelm her after what she had just witnessed. A memory, this time—she'd known that immediately, somehow—and yet every detail had been painfully clear.

Davian stumbling from a building. Not much older than when he had traveled back in time to talk to her. Scarred, tired looking.

Accusing her—accusing Tal'kamar, Caeden—of being on the wrong side of the fight. Of killing friends and loved ones. Caeden shouting at him to stop but Davian refusing to be silenced, plowing on.

The blade lashing out.

Davian's severed head on the glowing, red-and-gold-flecked stone of Deilannis, blood everywhere. Then on a pike.

"You...you cannot fool me," she said eventually, roughly, though she was barely able to force the words out, and her sharp, distressed breathing surely gave her away.

"Forging memories is not something of which I am capable." Diara's voice was gentle. "Davian will go to Deilannis. He will use the Jha'vett and travel back in time, planning to confront Tal'kamar—to make him doubt the things he did while using the name Aarkein Devaed. An ultimately successful move, I might add. But in doing so, Tal'kamar kills him. *Has already* killed him." She shook her head sadly. "It is...not something either of us wants. But it *has* already happened. That cannot be changed."

Asha's vision swam. "Aarkein Devaed?" she whispered. In the memory Davian had said...something...

Diara shook her head in horrified disbelief.

"Tal'kamar has thoroughly deceived you. I see that now," she said softly. "I have given you much to grapple with, Ashalia—a heavier burden than I ever expected to impart—and there is even more that you should know. But...news of your decision is being awaited in Ilshan Gathdel Teth, so I must ask. Will you accept this deal to free Davian?"

Asha squeezed her eyes shut, fighting against shock and confused grief. She couldn't help but see the image of Davian in

Deilannis again—seeing those eyes, which had always looked at her with such warmth, now sightless and cold. If she did not take this deal, she might not ever see him again. Even though that had always been a possibility, her heart broke at the thought.

Still.

Through that pain, she knew that Diara couldn't be trusted: even if she was telling the truth, there was no disputing that she was Andarra's enemy. Perhaps this was the best deal Diara thought she could get Asha to accept, and it was certainly a tempting one—*fates*, it was tempting—but there could easily be more to it. Some advantage to the Venerate that Asha couldn't see.

Swallowing, she shook her head.

"I need time to think," she said numbly, the statement true enough. She already knew, deep down, that she was not going to agree to Diara's offer...but there was no reason to tell the Venerate that. Not after the woman had just displayed how easily she could defeat Asha in a fight.

Diara said nothing for a moment; Asha thought she saw a flash of frustration in the Venerate's eyes, but it was so quick that she could well have been imagining it.

"Of course. Of course," said Diara eventually. "I cannot rightly ask a decision of you so quickly, given the magnitude of what you have just learned." She brushed a strand of dark hair from her face. "One week, Ashalia. That, I hope, will give you enough time to process all of this. I will return then for your answer."

Asha felt a dim thread of relief wind its way through her battling emotions. "And...if I decide to say no?"

"Then Davian will remain in our custody, I will kill you, and we will see whether that store of Essence can restore your mind as well as your body," said Diara matter-of-factly. "If it does not, then I get the same outcome. If it does, then...I am no worse off. But I hope it does not come to that."

Asha swallowed. The words hadn't been delivered with any malice—they were just a calm assessment of a likely sequence of events. Somehow that made them even more intimidating.

Diara studied her, then gave a short nod. "In a week, then. Think well, Ashalia, and do not let your loyalties be blind ones."

Without anything further, she blinked out of existence.

The next few minutes passed in a haze.

Asha let out a gasping breath as soon as she was certain she was alone, trembling and collapsing to her knees, hands shaking violently despite her best efforts. It had all happened so *fast*. The things she had just learned crashed around inside her head, a maelstrom of information that changed so much. She struggled to grasp it all, to properly comprehend what it meant.

She wasn't even sure that she *could* understand it all—not fully. Caeden was, or at least had been, Aarkein Devaed? The man everyone knew as the epitome of evil? Scyner had explained a little of the Venerate and their nature to her, that day before she had entered the Tributary. He had even admitted that Caeden had once been one of them, had changed sides.

But never once had he mentioned Devaed.

And as for the other information she had learned, about Davian...she couldn't quite bring herself to think about it yet, not with any sort of dispassion. The emotion that memory had left her with was too deep and too raw. Even the afterimages of it, flashing unbidden through her mind, left her nauseous and dizzy.

She wasn't sure how long she had been kneeling there when a tentative touch brushed her shoulder. She stirred, raising her head to find Elli looking at her concernedly.

"I...believe I may have missed something," the other woman said, glancing pensively toward the still-burning gardens.

Asha choked out a laugh, then rubbed her face, taking a few deep breaths. "One of the Venerate was here. Diara."

"Ah," said Elli. Asha had already explained what little she knew of the Venerate to her. "And you...defeated her?"

"Not exactly." Asha slowly climbed to her feet. "She left. Though not before showing me some things that..."

She swallowed, trailing off.

Still unsteady, she walked over to sit heavily on one of the unbroken benches, staring out numbly over the apocalyptic scene down the hill. Elli joined her.

As they watched, the molten stone started to rise and re-form, as Asha had known it ultimately would. The burning red gradually faded to black, then burst into bright greens as the grass was swiftly restored. Stone mended itself. Smoke cleared. Water began to flow once again with a pleasant, gentle burbling.

Within five minutes, it was as if the battle had never happened.

"What did she do to you?" Asha asked eventually, gazing past the now-pristine gardens toward the fully rejuvenated forest below. "You were just frozen in place for the entire thing. She thought you were a...training construct, or something."

Elli rubbed her forehead. "Some form of kan, I would assume. She would not be able to Control me as she could a person, but she could do enough to interfere with my...mental processes, I suppose you would say. It was probably fortunate that she thought I was less than I am. She could have done much worse." The woman gave her an apologetic look. "I know of the mental techniques to block Reading and Control, but I cannot implement them myself. It seems I would be of little benefit to you in a fight, and potentially a hindrance, should she return."

"Which she is going to do. In one week." Asha stared into the distance. "I was like a child against her, Elli. Even with all this power, even with everything I've learned and practiced. She just...*ignored* it." She sighed. "You cannot think of a way to stop her? Use your ability to manipulate this place, somehow?"

Elli shook her head ruefully, gesturing to the gardens. "The dok'en will always revert to its natural state. With enough warning, if I stay out of sight, I might be able to change things to your advantage here and there for a few minutes, but...it would be like everything else I can do here. Fading away too swiftly to be of any true use." She shrugged, the words practical rather than bitter. "She can manipulate kan, Ashalia—and that will work the same here as it does in the real world. No matter what we do, if she is not caught completely by surprise, then she cannot be beaten using only Essence."

Asha acknowledged the statement ruefully. "How did she even find a way in? I'm certain she doesn't have physical access to the Tributary, else our conversation would have gone very differently."

Elli frowned. "She must have found another key, then." She hesitated. "Unless she had direct access to the dok'en creator's mind, of course."

"Tal'kamar," said Asha absently. "Diara said it was Tal'kamar's dok'en." It was good to have that confirmed. "And I don't believe Diara has easy access to him. That is something that I rather suspect she would have brought up."

"Likely so," agreed Elli thoughtfully, a flicker of emotion crossing her face. Asha wondered why, and then realized how important that information probably was to the woman. Human or not, being certain of who was responsible for your existence had to mean something.

Asha decided not to mention what Diara had said about Caeden being Aarkein Devaed.

"So if we don't know how she's getting in, we can't figure out if there's a way to block it." Asha chewed her lip. "Could I...set up wards using Essence, for example, to let me know when she returns? Traps, even?"

Elli's eyebrows rose.

"I don't see why not," she said slowly. "You would have to renew them every few days—they will decay just as they would in the real world. But...she will surely be on her guard when she comes back. Even if she triggers them, I don't think you will be able to stop her that way."

"It would slow her down, though. Keep her busy and let me know that she was here," said Asha. "Which would give me enough time to weaken the dok'en while she was still in it."

"That..." Elli looked thrown at the suggestion. "You likely couldn't collapse it fast enough. She would know what was happening and leave again—as I suspect she did last time, when her initial entry must have caused that destabilization. It would take her only a few moments, and then you would be left to endure another Shift."

"But she would know I could do it—and she'd know how badly her mind could be damaged if it was still connected. It wouldn't be something she could ignore," said Asha. She saw Elli's expression and shrugged, despite her stomach churning at the very thought. "She will *kill* me when she comes back, Elli. The best outcome from that happening would be me going through a Shift again anyway. At least this way, it would force her to be more cautious. It would buy us time."

"Time for what, though?" asked Elli quietly. "You cannot keep triggering Shifts every time she breaks in. The ones you already have to go through take enough of a toll."

Asha paused, thinking.

"I know you can't mimic kan," she said, "but could you mimic its *effects*? Not Control or Reading or Seeing, but...stepping through time. Being unaffected by my Essence attacks. If we sparred, you could replicate that well enough, couldn't you? Make the illusion the same thing?"

Elli's brow furrowed. "I cannot. It touches too much on the underlying rules of this place." She considered. "As far as training goes, there *may* be a way I can help. But I doubt you'll enjoy it."

"I'll do whatever's necessary," said Asha as if that settled the matter, stretching and turning back to the courtyard. She wasn't going to think about Davian or even Caeden—not for now. She needed to focus.

"We have a lot of practicing to do."

Chapter 7

Pain, and cold.

Those were the only two things Caeden had known for what felt like a very long time, now. His breathing was labored and his thoughts crawled; he forced his eyes open to a red-and-white smear of light as he tried to make sense of where he was, what had happened.

He had been in Alkathronen. Fought Alaris.

Fallen.

He allowed a soft, wheezing moan to escape his lips as he registered his injuries and what they meant. He had misestimated. Any other man would be dead after the shattering impact of the three-thousand-foot fall, but—even with every bone broken, lungs collapsed and chest caved in, his body an utter ruin—he was, somehow, still here.

That was a problem.

He'd assumed that one of two things would happen: either his injuries would be so devastating that he would wake up in a new body, or—at worst—he would be able to adequately heal himself within a day or two. Unpleasant either way, but an acceptable trade-off for the chance to capture Alaris.

What he hadn't counted on was the awful, biting cold that sliced into him constantly as he lay exposed, splayed on a large rock that was mostly—but not entirely—protected from the driving snow by a jutting outcrop above. He'd landed here, apparently, no doubt bouncing off other protrusions until he'd finally stuck. If he had fallen into the deeper drifts at the bottom as expected, then the surrounding snow would have encased him, keeping him out of the freezing wind and preventing those few flakes that found their way onto him from melting and soaking him through.

Now, though, too much Essence was needed to simply keep his body warm. He *was* healing, but it was at such a slow rate as to be nearly imperceptible.

It could be weeks before he could move his limbs again, and he didn't have that sort of time.

He lay there, gazing blankly into the driving white, for... hours? Impossible to tell. He dozed at some point, somehow, through the pain.

When he woke, his marginally less blurry vision picked out a dark, person-shaped shadow against the white.

"Fates," muttered a voice through the howl of the wind, unfamiliar to him. "What a mess."

Caeden cracked open his mouth to speak, but no words came out, only a soft sigh. The stranger standing over him crouched, leaning in close. Coming more into focus, this time.

He didn't recognize the angular, black-scarred face above the scruffy beard. A Shadow. That reminded him of something, but he couldn't latch on to what.

Caeden's gaze traveled downward to the dangling chain that had slipped from beneath the middle-aged man's shirt. At its end was a distinctive golden eagle, its wings spread wide.

Warmth began to spread through his mind, a familiarity. That medallion. He *did* know that medallion.

He drifted again.

Caeden stared pensively ahead as they trudged the long, muddy, overgrown path to Ilshan Tereth Kal.

To his right, his companion glanced across at him. He was short but well muscled beneath the thick furs he was wearing, his brown eyes keen and sparkling with their usual barely contained mirth as they assessed Caeden's expression. "You really need to stop brooding, Tal. Keep worrying like this and you're going to start showing your age."

Caeden gave a chuckle, the sound nervous despite his best efforts. "Sorry, my friend. I'll be worried until all of this is done. Over for good, one way or another."

Alchesh grunted. "Well it's terribly unbecoming for an immortal. You're just making the whole 'live forever' thing seem rather dour and unappealing."

Caeden snorted, allowing himself a small smile at the friendly jibe, though it faded quickly.

There was just too much pain at the memories this journey brought back.

Silence ruled for a time as they leaned into the heavy rain and sharply biting wind, which whipped down off the snowy mountains and through the narrow pass.

"How long has it been since you made this climb?" Alchesh asked. Though his tone was conversational, there was an underlying mildness to it, a gentleness indicating that he knew the question was approaching sensitive ground.

For a long moment, Caeden considered not replying.

"A thousand years. Give or take," he said quietly. "And before that, another several hundred."

"Changed much?"

Caeden responded with an amused glare. "A little."

"Good. I'd hate to think you were bored, on top of worried and sad and generally depressed." Alchesh didn't look at him, but his tone remained soft. "A thousand years is a long time for most of us, you know. Far too long to hold on to any mistakes we may have made." Before Caeden could respond, the other man stretched. "So I saw you were talking with Sariette de la Teirs, just before we left."

Caeden blinked at the abrupt switch in conversation. "I was."

"She is very beautiful."

"I suppose."

"And witty. Terribly witty. Renowned for her wit."

Caeden frowned. "True enough."

"And extremely eligible."

Caeden sighed, glancing across at Alchesh. "Fortunate, then, seeing as you appear so enamored of her."

"I saw the two of you flirting. Don't tell me there's nothing

there. You must have at least thought *about it,"* Alchesh
wheedled.

Caeden *glowered at him.* "You know how I sometimes
complain that dealing with mortals can be like dealing with
children?"

*"Honesty and innocence. Purity of intention. All just part of
our charm," replied Alchesh cheerfully.*

Caeden *shook his head, though this time a genuine grin slid
onto his face. Alchesh was working hard to lighten his mood, and
he couldn't help but appreciate the effort. It wouldn't make coming back here pleasant, but it might at least make it easier.*

*He allowed himself to relax, for a while pushing back the dark
thoughts that had plagued him since they had arrived and allowing himself to participate in the more lively, cheerful conversation that Alchesh was trying to foster. They had been friends for
decades, and for all his effervescent-to-the-point-of-rudeness
demeanor, Alchesh was, beneath it all, a wise man. Wiser than
most, in fact.*

*It was an hour later that their shared laughter at a joke died
as they crested the final rise and the blackened, long-abandoned
ruins of Ilshan Tereth Kal peered back up at them from the valley.*

*Only two of the nine towers were distinguishable within the
remains, though even those poked feebly at the sky now, jagged tops cracked and crumbling where the crystal had shattered.
The surrounding forest had reclaimed much of the structure
over the past millennium, vines curling through gaping holes and
entire trees sprouting in the courtyard where he had once trained.
The walls were dark, the guardians' streaking, flowing blue
energy gone. Snuffed out forever.*

*"El's name. You didn't leave much to chance, did you," mur-
mured Alchesh, gazing down upon the ruins.*

*"It was..." Caeden stopped himself. "We thought it was nec-
essary. Not that that is an excuse."*

*"I know," said Alchesh, his quiet tone indicating the response
was to both statements. He gestured. "Shall we?"*

*They began picking their way down the treacherously steep
path into the valley. Once they reached the floor, the thick forest murmured and rustled with life around them, a stark con-*

trast to what poked through the tops of the trees ahead. Despite Alchesh's efforts, now that they were here, Caeden's feet dragged as the memories he had worked so hard to forget began to weigh him down.

They passed through the scorched entrance, where once he had knelt before the entirety of the Cluster and sworn never to reveal their secrets. The courtyard—where he had truly learned to use Essence, all those years ago—was achingly familiar, even with the layers of grime and overgrowth. They made their way down the stairs where—

"Agh!" Alchesh's strangled grunt of surprise interrupted Caeden's thoughts, making him flinch.

He spun, then gave a low chuckle as his gaze followed Alchesh's to the image etched in the crystal wall. Eleven feet tall, the sinuous red-scaled shape rose majestically, her gaze determined and wise. Cracks ran through the etching but still, as the sunlight caught it it seemed to shimmer, coming alive and moving, looking as much like the real thing as any picture could.

"What is it?" murmured Alchesh, looking mildly abashed.

"Sarrin. First of the Shalis," said Caeden, a touch of reverence in his tone.

"You knew her?"

"She was the one who let me in here." He pushed past Alchesh, unable to look at the Shalis's great leader any longer. "Both times."

He assumed that his friend would follow, but instead Alchesh continued to stare at the etching, fascinated as the sunlight played off it. "Is the picture as accurate as it looks?"

Caeden shuffled his feet. "It is like she is here with us again," he admitted softly, raising his gaze to meet Sarrin's soulful eyes once more.

Alchesh was silent for a few seconds. "They look...different, than how I had imagined. More...personable," he admitted. "How many of them were there?"

"One hundred and forty-four in the Cluster," said Caeden. He gazed around the courtyard. "All of them here when it happened."

Alchesh nodded, not really listening. "Amazing," he said, still staring at Sarrin. "She looks so...wise."

"She was." Caeden's jaw clenched. "The only mistake I believe she ever made was trusting me."

He tore his eyes from the image and moved on before Alchesh could respond.

They came to the sloping ramp leading into the lower level and began the long descent, made all the harder by the severity of the smooth floor's angle. Caeden found himself adjusting naturally; though it had been so long ago, he had been up and down here every day for months on end. Twice he had to reach out and steady Alchesh as the other man almost slipped, despite a hand firmly against the wall as they made their way downward.

"Not exactly practical," the usually light-footed man muttered, taking another stuttering step.

"It wasn't made for walking," replied Caeden absently. "Nothing in this place was."

Alchesh eyed the seamless white walls. "But it's Builder-made."

"It is."

"So...it was made specifically for the Shalis?" Alchesh's voice was thick with skepticism.

Caeden nodded. "Sarrin and Ordan never said so, but I believe they knew them."

"The Shalis knew the Builders," repeated Alchesh slowly.

"Sarrin and Ordan knew the Builders," Caeden corrected him.

The other man stumbled and almost fell again as his focus strayed from the descent. "You cannot be serious. I've never heard anything to suggest that."

"You hadn't heard of the Forge before I told you about it, either," observed Caeden. "What you know comes from our history books, and our history books come from us. The Venerate. They are...incomplete, at best. Filled only with what we want others to know."

Alchesh looked across at Caeden. "I try not to press you about this time in your life, Tal—you know that—but...why did you keep the whereabouts of the Forge from everyone? You stood against the Shalis with the others, so if there is a Vessel of such immense power hidden away down here, why not—"

"Because sometimes we know that the things we do are

wrong," interrupted Caeden quietly. "Even after so long away, even after hearing all of the reasoning, I hated betraying Sarrin and her kin. They saw something in me, taught me, and I repaid them with death. And this..." He sighed. "The Forge was a secret that, even after they let me in, I was not supposed to know. Ordan revealed it to me and when the Cluster found out, there was a vote on what to do with me. It was a tie, and Sarrin held the deciding vote." He licked his lips. "I was made to swear never to reveal its existence. Even as we burned this place down, I could not bring myself to break that vow."

Alchesh frowned. "But you told me," he observed. "If it was such a secret, why didn't they just bind you?"

"They would have found the very concept repugnant." They finally reached the bottom of the twisting ramp, Alchesh breathing out a sigh of relief. "The Shalis believed that kan was the source of all death and destruction in this world. The reason we feel pain, and loss, and hunger for the things that are not healthy for us. Power. Unlimited freedom."

"Cake," added Alchesh.

Caeden barked a soft laugh. "The point being, they refused to use it. They could have, but to them it was a power never meant to be touched."

"But the Forge..."

Caeden glanced across at him. "One of the reasons its knowledge was forbidden to outsiders." He shook his head. "I do not believe it was the Shalis's choice, being linked to it—no more than it was ours. But if people had known that their rebirth was tied to kan, after all they preached against it..." He shook his head. "They would not have understood. They would have jumped to conclusions and assumed the worst, just as they always do. Just as Gassandrid did."

A passageway stretched out before them, the ground uncomfortably curving upward at both sides so that the center was the only place that was truly flat. They walked for a while until dark holes—no more than three feet wide—began to appear at regular intervals, just a few at first but then more and more, until the wall itself seemed to be little more than a latticework separating the circular entrances.

"It's where they slept," said Caeden absently in response to Alchesh's wondering look. He trailed a hand along the stone. Warm and dry, just as he remembered it.

"Looks uncomfortable."

"It definitely was for a human."

Alchesh smirked. "You actually slept in one?"

"Not much choice in the matter. You live with the Cluster, you do what they tell you to do." Caeden allowed himself a small smile at the memory. "It wasn't so bad. You would be surprised at how much less intimidating they were after I had to listen to some of them snore for a few weeks."

Alchesh chuckled. "That, I can relate to."

Caeden shot him a mock glare, though once again conceding to himself how glad he was to have chosen his friend for this task. Alchesh had manned the first of the new Ironsails with him from the Shining Lands, had fought alongside him almost since he'd been old enough to wield Essence. Most of the men were terrified of Caeden, obeyed him without pause—without thought—but Alchesh, intensely loyal though he was, had never feared speaking up. Never feared questioning what they were doing or why they were doing it.

People like that were harder and harder to find, since Dareci.

They walked for a while longer. Though Ilshan Tereth Kal had held only the hundred and forty-four, the curving hallway was long; with each new gaping, empty hole they passed, the significance of what had been lost here became heavier and heavier, even Alchesh for once seemingly content to settle into contemplative silence.

"If we go through with this," the other man said after a while, "and the worst eventuates. We find…something. Evidence that this man you killed was truly from the future, and that everything we've been fighting for is a lie. Are you really going to let Andrael and the Darecians activate this ilshara you've built?"

Caeden grunted. "Depends on the strength of the proof, I suppose. Let us hope it's something that can convince the others— because if it isn't, I cannot think of anything else I can do to make them question El's divinity."

Alchesh shivered, looking uncomfortable at the mere thought.

"Andrael and Asar were obviously willing to. And you convinced Cyr—enough for him to volunteer for a Tributary, of all things. That has to mean there's hope for the rest of them, surely."

"Cyr agreed to it because he's endlessly curious. He's as much fascinated by the idea, the logic and the mechanics, as he is by the cause." He waved away Alchesh's expression. "I'm not suggesting that he's doing it purely as an experiment, or that he doesn't want to know the truth as much as the rest of us. In fact, his being on board might be one of the most convincing proofs I've had that this is worth doing. If he felt that El's story was indisputable, he would never have agreed to help power the ilshara." He rubbed his forehead. "I still despise the need, though. I worry for him in that thing."

Alchesh raised an eyebrow. "He will be in the dok'en. From what he told me, he's set aside all of his knowledge, arranged it so that he will be able to spend his days focusing on study and reflection. No need to feel bad, Tal. As far as he's concerned, he's in paradise for the next decade."

Caeden rolled his shoulders. "Except during the Shifts."

"He'll probably enjoy those, too, in his own sick way. He'll be fascinated by the entire process. And it's not as if he can't get out if he wants to." He shrugged. "Ten years sounds like a long time to me, but I know it's nothing to you. My equivalent of a month or two, perhaps."

Caeden acceded with a nod. "And I do think that will be long enough. If the ilshara can contain El for such an extended period, then that should surely be proof that investigation is needed into why." He gnawed his lip nervously at the thought. Ten years. Nothing, compared to how long they had worked toward this goal, and yet…was it still too much? The others hadn't even been able to countenance the thought of testing El, of seeing whether their understanding of Him was all it could be.

But no. There were too many questions now, after Deilannis. Too many uncertainties after the Jha'vett had exploded and the mysterious stranger had appeared. If the young man calling himself Davian had been telling the truth, then El's claim that they could break Shammaeloth's hold over time—change things, destroy fate itself by going back—was false.

The thought was close to inconceivable, even after he had at first ignored it, then denied it, and finally wrestled with it each day for the past seven years. He had done everything he could to raise the question with the others as their armies had pushed farther and farther south against the Darecian defenses, going so far as to show them the memory itself—not his part in the destruction of the Jha'vett or his saving of the High Darecians, of course, as the repercussions of that would have been severe—but he had shown them Davian.

It hadn't made a difference. Still they remained resistant to investigating, confident that the question he was asking had been answered long ago. They thought it was simply jitters, brought on by a combination of Andrael's betrayal and being so close to the end.

"Any word on Isiliar?" Alchesh's voice cut through his thoughts.

A fresh fist of guilt hit Caeden in the gut. "No," he said. "Already the others are wondering if she was killed somehow. Postulating that Andrael has created another weapon like Licanius. We are keeping watch over one another now, with Traces to ensure that no one else is lost. If I go to visit her—or Cyr, for that matter—it would risk too much."

"Won't they know you're here, then?"

"Probably. Certainly if Gassandrid notices where I am, he will ask." Caeden shrugged. "But he also believes that we are nearing the end of this journey. I will tell him that I am revisiting the past, reminding myself of sacrifices made. He knows destroying the Shalis was one of my great regrets. He will not question it—and even if he does and decides to come here himself, he will find exactly what he found a thousand years ago. Which is to say, nothing."

Alchesh frowned. "How can you be so sure?"

Caeden gave a grim smile as they turned the final corner. "You are about to find out."

The other man started as he spotted the figure of a Shalis, eyes closed, sleeping against what appeared to be a solid wall at the end of the hallway. Alchesh shuffled closer, studying it curiously. "Another etching? Amazing," he said in wonder. "It is truly like *they are here." He poked at the Shalis's chest, brow furrowing at what was clearly an unexpected sensation.*

One of the creature's eyes opened, rolling toward Alchesh and Caeden.

"Why does he think I am an etching, Tal'kamar?" the red-scaled snake asked in a hissing lisp.

Alchesh stood frozen for a long, shocked moment before screeching in a most undignified manner, flinching backward and letting fly an enormous bolt of Essence. The snakelike creature didn't move a muscle, but a shield of answering Essence sprang into place; blue power sizzled but the blast did not penetrate it.

Caeden smiled.

"It is good to see you again, Ordan," he said quietly.

Chapter 8

Caeden moaned.

Something was happening. Though his entire body was numbed from the cold, he managed to open his eyes enough to register that he was moving. Being hauled, in fact. Slung in undignified fashion across someone's back as they trudged up a series of steep steps through driving snow.

"A mountain," a voice was muttering to itself—the same one as from earlier, he thought. The Shadow with the medallion. "Of all places, falling down a fates-cursed *mountain*. Stupid, Tal'kamar. Just stupid. This is going to take forever."

Caeden let the irritated voice fade to a dull buzz as his attention wandered back to the memory that had come unbidden. There was something important there, something that had been hovering for a while now at the edge of his mind—even from before his injury. A puzzle that he needed to solve.

Alchesh's hands trembled as he leaned back against the far wall, his eyes glued to Ordan's imposing, red-scaled figure.

"You told me they were all dead," he said.

"They were." Caeden studied Ordan warily, relief and new tension layered within him all at once. "How are you, old friend?"

Ordan cocked his head to the side. "Are we friends again, Tal'kamar?" he hissed, a quietly dangerous note to his voice. "I have seen what remains above—seen what your fires wrought of Tereth Kal. I remember what you did."

"I know. But I was also the one who put you in the Forge." Caeden waved down Alchesh as he spotted the other man tensing at the Shalis's aggressive tone. "I never broke my vow, Ordan. Never revealed Aloia Elanai to the others." He dug into his satchel, then produced a leather bag that clinked as he held it out to Ordan. "One hundred and forty-two scales—one from each of the dead. The attack here was always about weakening Dareci, Ordan. I was never with Gassandrid in his war against your people."

Ordan considered the bag, not reaching for it.

"Who is missing?" he asked eventually, though Caeden felt from his tone that he already knew the answer.

"Esdin." Caeden said the name calmly, doing his best to hide the regret that came with it.

"Why?"

"A tale perhaps I can tell when we are a little more—"

"I would hear it now."

Caeden exhaled, shutting his eyes. He had forgotten Ordan's people's penchant for bluntness. Best to be done with this part, then, and quickly.

"Gassandrid captured her. When the Forge could not be found, and she would not reveal its location, Cyr was...given access to her." From the corner of his eye Caeden could see Alchesh shift uneasily, but thankfully the other man didn't feel the need to elaborate. "Cyr was able to detect her connection to the Forge, and engineer a way to use it with his own Vessel. The Furnace, he called it. It drew on her tie to the Forge, and produced...creatures in her likeness, I suppose. Creatures who will fight for us. Dar'gaithin."

Ordan said nothing for several seconds.

"'Dar'gaithin.' Copies," he finally translated, more emotion in his lisping voice than Caeden could ever remember hearing. "They would be soulless. Abominations."

"Fairly accurate," murmured Alchesh.

Caeden gave him a sharp look to indicate that he should keep silent, then turned back to Ordan. "Not soulless—that is the argument of the others. The dar'gaithin each have their own minds, their own personalities, their own sources. They are more than simply animated shells. But yes," he conceded heavily. "They are still a pale, subservient imitation. I tried to stop it, but you know how our war was going against the Darecians. The others were desperate. They said that a creature without a soul was no creature at all—that if we had created those same beings from steel rather than flesh, there would have been no objections. That I was imposing an illogical morality on the proposal, and that in fact making such creatures would save the lives of those with souls." He tried to keep the defensiveness from his tone, but knew he was failing.

Ordan hissed again. "And if they had been human shells, rather than Shalis?"

Caeden looked away. "That has happened, too," he said softly. "We call them Echoes. And others—others from the Ilinar, from the Doth. Even the Vaal—we made them bigger, made them blind with rage by making them need regular submersion to survive. None of them as intelligent as the dar'gaithin, and none with enough Essence to even survive the journey through a Gate, but all strong. All fighters. And all derived from Cyr's Furnace." He swallowed. "I am sorry, Ordan. The world has become much darker since you last knew it."

"And you along with it, apparently." Ordan's voice was heavy. "You speak of this in the past tense. What of Esdin now?"

Caeden hesitated.

"She is gone," he admitted.

Ordan released a breath, to Caeden's surprise seeming relieved by the statement. "She used her Sever? Cut her tie to the Forge?" He frowned. "If she had it with her, why would she not have done that straight away?"

Caeden nodded; the 'Sever' terminology was unfamiliar to him, but he thought he understood to what Ordan was referring. "Andrael and some of the others turned against us after… not long after the attack here. We think he was convinced by Esdin, at least in part." He refused to mention how he'd created and used the Essence-eating Columns to destroy Dareci, wiping away millions with the great weapon. He had enough shame to deal with without seeing Ordan's reaction to that news. "Esdin gave him her…Sever, you called it? The Vessel that would unlink *her, anyway. She thought it was more important that Andrael study it, than that she use it herself. So that he could kill the rest of us," he added drily. "When he had learned enough from it, he found her again, and…" Caeden gestured.*

Ordan's intelligent, serpentine eyes stared at Caeden intently. "For one of you to have deciphered even part of the Builders' handiwork would have taken several lifetimes." He spoke steadily, but Caeden marked the rising tension behind his words. "When I was reborn, I had little choice but to remain here, sleeping—I could not leave the Forge unguarded. I thought that whoever resurrected me would return fairly soon thereafter to explain why they had done so."

He let the question hang in the air.

"A millennium." Caeden said the words simply and honestly. It was not a blow that he knew how to soften, even if he'd thought his old mentor would appreciate it.

Ordan closed his eyes, though against the pain of that news or simply in thought, Caeden couldn't tell. "You return not for friendship, then, but because you require something of me. That is the only reason to come back after so long," he said as he finally reached out, taking the bag from Caeden's outstretched hand. "I would know more of Esdin's last days, of Dareci, and of everything else that has happened beyond these walls—but first, I would know why you are here. Because if I do not like the answer, then this may be a short reunion indeed."

His gaze slid briefly to Alchesh, who twitched nervously beneath it.

Caeden winced, but nodded. He accepted what Ordan was saying—knew he deserved it, and far worse besides.

"The reason? I have doubts," he said simply. "The Dareci are defeated, Ordan. Broken, fled from the Shining Lands. We commandeered Ironsails, followed to a distant continent and are even now on the cusp of victory, but…" He scowled, shaking his head. "Questions have been raised—questions which I cannot ignore, even if the others insist on doing so. I do not concede that El is anyone but who He says He is"—he held up a hand warningly, half expecting Ordan to launch into a lecture—"and yet. I met a man who claimed to have traveled from the future. A man

who told me that…that none of the things that have been done can be undone." The words still left a dry, foul taste in his mouth.

Ordan studied him. "Words which have been said before," he observed.

"He said that he was my friend, and then I killed him." Caeden stared vacantly at the ground, remembering. "And I cannot help but wonder. If it was true. If he came back to tell me that, and if traveling through time truly cannot alter events, whether…"

"Whether he knew?"

"Yes." Caeden felt his lip curl in frustration; as always he couldn't tell whether it was at the thought, or because he had not yet been able to dismiss it. Had he killed someone whom he would come to respect, to love? And had Davian come back, said those things and accepted death itself, because he'd known that his words would stick in Caeden's mind like needles? Prick at him day in and day out until he finally took action—did exactly what he was doing right now?

"Anything that makes you actually question this path of yours is a blessing, Tal'kamar," said Ordan, "but I fail to see why that brings you here."

"I searched for years for proof that this man lied—that he in fact existed in this time. But I found nothing." Caeden licked his lips. "As you well know, El took each of the Venerate's ability to See through time when we swore ourselves to Him—which for most of us was a blessing, anyway—but it was always a great act of trust, too. It's meant that for the longest time, the only visions of the future we have seen are the ones which He has given us."

He fell silent. It felt wrong, even just implying this. But he had to be certain, didn't he?

Ordan's gaze slid back to Alchesh, who had been mercifully silent. Though the Shalis's expression barely changed, Caeden saw that he understood now.

He turned back to Caeden. "You still do not believe you are wrong."

Caeden met his gaze. "No. But if I am, then I want to know."

Ordan studied him, then turned and placed a scaled hand against the wall. Nothing happened, and for the longest of moments, Caeden wondered whether anything would.

Then a blue light flickered.

Caeden squeezed his eyes shut against a sudden surge of emotion. There was still life here.

The blue energy—similar to that which had once shimmered and darted around the walls above—coalesced, bathing all three of them in an eerie glow.

"Stand still," Caeden cautioned Alchesh. "Let it mark you. It is the only way you will be allowed inside."

Alchesh did as he was instructed, looking wary and a touch startled as the energy flitted around him. "What is it doing?"

"Deciding whether you are a threat."

There was a humming sound, and suddenly the stone in front of them just...melted.

Alchesh gaped, for perhaps the first time since Caeden had known him looking lost for words.

The room curved gently outward away from them, vertically as well as horizontally, a large oval space that stretched out into the darkness. The crystal walls began to glitter as golden light spread through them, seeping away from the entrance and gradually revealing more of the chamber, the illumination at first seeming to cover the entire surface, but on closer inspection running along thousands of minutely etched, intricate designs. Representative of kan mechanisms, Caeden believed, though he had never been able to verify that. The crystal was not only an indestructible barrier, but it hid kan from his vision completely. In his thousands of years, it was something he had never seen replicated.

Aloia Elanai, the Shalis had called it. The Serpent's Head.

The Venerate—all of whom bar Caeden had seen this place only from the inside, and that merely in glimpses—knew it simply as the Chamber.

Ordan entered; Caeden gave Alchesh a small nudge forward and stepped after him onto the gently sloping crystal surface. The wall silently materialized behind them again, sealing them in, the golden glow close to blinding as it continued to crawl through the countless whisper-thin lines all around them. Some of those lines were ordered, uniform, systematic. Others curved and intertwined and swirled seemingly at random, more art than mechanism. Whether it showed precisely what went on behind the crystal barrier or not, Caeden had no idea.

Having seen the unshielded kan mechanisms in Deilannis, though, he could only begin to imagine how fine, how complex, the kan of this place might be.

"What in El's name?" whispered Alchesh.

Caeden followed his gaze to the far end of the room, perhaps two hundred feet away, which was now lit. Three holes in the crystal were visible: The largest was set in the floor, almost ten feet wide and filled with a clear liquid. It was flanked by two slightly smaller holes in the wall at about head height, hearth-like—but rather than flames, golden Essence burned within.

"That's the Forge itself." Caeden gestured to the upper two pulsing cavities. "Formally, those are known as the Forges of Rebirth. Eye of Soul, Eye of Mind."

Alchesh nodded, gaze fixed on the golden fires, looking as mesmerized as Caeden remembered being the first time Ordan had brought him here. "And the lower one?"

"The Waters of Renewal," said Ordan, not glancing back at them. Caeden heard the irritation in his tone, though Alchesh appeared not to. Before today, Caeden had been the only human to ever have been allowed inside Aloia Elanai.

Alchesh gazed at the two fires. "So this place...this is what you see, every time you...?"

"No. When I was first brought here in the flesh, I didn't recognize it at all. But after a few times, you might remember something—a glimpse. After a dozen deaths, maybe an image sticks in your head." Caeden grimaced. "Cyr killed himself deliberately near two hundred times over the course of a single year, just to see how much information he could glean about this place. It was before I met him, but I am certain he did it, because he shared the memory of what he eventually saw with all of us."

Ordan glanced at him. "This is how Gassandrid came to learn of it?"

"Yes. I never told them anything, denied knowledge of it, but..." He turned back to Alchesh. "The Shalis only ever came here to begin the resurrection of one of their number, and

121

their deaths were almost as uncommon as ours. The chances of a Venerate glimpsing someone in here would normally be infinitesimal."

"But if Cyr died more than every other day for a year..." Alchesh nodded slowly. *"Still unlikely, but much better odds."*

"Exactly."

Ordan continued to watch Alchesh, who still looked overawed at his surroundings. *"So Cyr actually witnessed one of us in here. That explains much."*

Caeden acknowledged the statement morosely. *"Gassandrid already blamed you for destroying Zvaelar; when he found out what Cyr had seen, the thought of you intruding upon the gift El had given us, too... well, it didn't sit well with him. The others were not so easily convinced, but once your people began actively supporting Dareci, it didn't take much for them to give more weight to his arguments than mine."*

"He is a zealot, Tal'kamar—misled about Zvaelar and so much more—and as I have told you before: your god is outright lying to you if he claims your immortality is a gift from him." Ordan's voice dripped with disdain. *"The Forge was made by the Builders. By men. I do not know how this creature you serve tied you to it—or how he did it without our knowledge—but there is no doubt that he did."*

Caeden held up a hand as Alchesh scowled. *"And as I have said before: El making use of the Forge does not preclude our link to it being a gift from Him,"* he said quietly. *"We are not here to start up old arguments, Ordan."*

"No. We are not." Ordan shook his head as if remembering what he was doing, then slithered over to a section of wall next to the Forge. He placed his hands carefully against two specific positions on the shining surface.

The golden light running through the crystal in that section suddenly faded, and then the crystal itself melted away, revealing row upon row of small shelves.

"What are you doing?" Caeden asked, a pensive note entering his voice. He had never seen this before. The shelves were lined with small objects—beautifully crafted ornaments, medallions, and pendants made of gold, each in its own distinct shape.

Ordan didn't answer. He carefully picked up one of the medallions, then with equal reverence drew a red scale from the bag Caeden had given him. It was a mottled red, glinting in the light of Essence.

"Uldan," he murmured.

Ordan touched the medallion to the scale, and there was a flash from the two Essence-fires to his side, each one burning brighter for just a moment.

The medallion crumbled, and the scale turned to dust in Ordan's hand.

Caeden and Alchesh looked at each other in confusion.

"What are you doing?" Caeden repeated as the Shalis took another medallion from the shelves on the wall and another scale from the bag. This one was a brighter shade of red, almost crimson.

"Onasis," he said softly. Another flash, and scale and medallion once again dissipated.

Caeden felt a chill. "Ordan," he said uneasily. "Those . . . those aren't Severs, are they?"

"They are," replied Ordan, his back still to Caeden, reaching for the next scale.

"Stop!" Caeden rushed forward and placed a restraining hand on the Shalis's arm; the next thing he knew he was lying on the floor on the other side of Aloia Elanai, blinking spots from his vision as Alchesh stood protectively over him, glaring at Ordan. The tall red serpent was ignoring them, continuing his work.

"Indral," murmured Ordan, and the Essence burned sharper for an instant yet again.

"Why?" Caeden shouted as he stumbled to his feet, confusion and horror mingling. "I risked *everything to retrieve those. I gave them to you to restore your people! El take it, Ordan—tell me why!"*

Ordan finally stopped. To Caeden's shock, the Shalis's arms were trembling.

He turned, and Caeden recoiled.

Ordan's expression, as always, had barely changed. But there was something now—something furious and terribly, terribly sad—that emanated from him like a physical force. From the 123 *corner of his eye, Caeden could see Alchesh taking a hesitant step back.*

"Because it has fallen to me to do so," said Ordan. His voice was calm but even so, that heavy grief remained in the air. "Because after this long, I cannot risk them coming back. I cannot risk them becoming koth."

"I don't understand," said Caeden, his voice almost a whisper. He didn't recognize the word.

Ordan paused, then hung his head.

"They have been in Markaathan, Tal'kamar." He finally looked across at Caeden, almost defiant now. "That is where we go when we die. The Darklands, you call it. And the Forge…the Forge pulls us back here again. Or more precisely, it forces our link to the Darklands to push us back here."

Caeden stared at him, trying to process the words. The Darklands. The fate that Andrael feared El was trying to unleash upon the world. He knew it was real—El Himself had said that it was where Nethgalla had originated, and Alaris had spoken of it as well.

It was a place of nothing but terror and pain, if what others had said was to be believed.

"I am sorry," he said roughly. "But surely that means severing their link now will just strand them there?"

"Perhaps. We do not know." Ordan looked to the side. "Our origins—how we came to be this way—are a mystery to us. Some of us believed that we were from the Darklands originally, and that our time spent here was nothing but a reprieve from that place. Some thought that using the Sever would mean nothingness, an end. Others—those who believe in Dreth—considered that it might be a chance to move on to somewhere else. Somewhere better." He shook his head, red-scaled body swaying slightly from side to side as he balanced on his thick tail. "It does not matter. All agreed that longer than a day there, and the risk of what may come back—something mad, something corrupt— was too great. That is why we never strayed far from Tereth Kal without Travel Stones. Without a way to swiftly return."

Caeden frowned. "But rebirth takes several months."

"Rebirth takes minutes, Tal'kamar," Ordan corrected. "The

body forms, and mind and soul are restored in an instant. The months are for the memories. We lie here, submersed, and it works away the worst of what we have experienced. Never all—but enough to function. Enough to control ourselves once again." He shook his head. "Longer than a day, and the Waters would never be enough. I cannot imagine what a thousand years would have wrought on their minds."

Caeden felt the blood drain from his face as Ordan elaborated. He sat on the ground abruptly, knees weak.

"I didn't know," he whispered.

"That is no excuse," replied Ordan.

He turned back to his task.

Caeden and Alchesh watched silently now as Ordan picked out each scale solemnly, recognizing it, naming its owner before reverently touching a Sever to it. Each one crumbled into nothing, dissipating like smoke.

Eventually, finally, only one medallion remained. A golden eagle, wings spread wide. Ordan picked it up, examining it; Caeden stiffened where he sat, heart suddenly in his throat.

Ordan put the Sever back on its shelf and slithered over to Caeden and Alchesh.

"You understand what Tal'kamar is asking of you?" he asked Alchesh abruptly.

Alchesh started, evidently not having expected to be addressed. "I believe so."

"And he told you that it may destroy you?"

Alchesh coughed, glancing across at Caeden with a raised eyebrow. "He may have...skimmed over that particular part. But I trust him."

"It is not about trust." Ordan's words were reproachful. "I can connect you to the Forge, but no one can tell you the consequences. You may become like Tal'kamar—bound to be reborn in a different body whenever you die. Or you could become like the Shalis, bound to the Darklands but able to be restored. You could become Shalis in truth, for all I know."

"Very funny," said Alchesh quickly, a nervous smile on his face. It faded as he watched Ordan. "That was meant to be funny. Right?"

"The last is unlikely," conceded Ordan cheerlessly. "But it is illustrative. I do not know the consequences. Nor does Tal'kamar, no matter what he has told you. It may be that you will become something entirely different—something new. Stronger. Weaker. Better. Worse. There is no way to tell before it is attempted."

There was silence; Alchesh glanced up, seeing Caeden watching him intently.

"I am going to need a few seconds," he said drily.

Caeden gave a small smile, hearing Alchesh's answer in his voice. The man was nothing if not brave.

Ordan sighed, then—clearly having heard the answer, too— guided Alchesh over to the wall. "Place your hand here," he instructed, indicating a flat, smoothly shining section of crystal to the left of the burning Essence.

Alchesh did so, looking calm. A hundred times more confident than Caeden felt. Cyr had theorized more on the Forge than on any other Vessel in existence—they all had—and connecting Alchesh to it should allow him unfettered use of kan.

But ultimately, that was all they had. Theories.

"You should be able to see kan now—in particular, the threads that tie Tal'kamar and me to this device," said Ordan. "They are hardened kan, unbreakable except by kan made before it—kan that was made alongside the device itself. When I activate the endpoint you will see the beginnings of other threads, ones which are loose. You must reach out and take one of these, drawing it into yourself. That will connect you to the Forge."

Alchesh's brow was furrowed, beads of sweat standing out on it now. "Sounds simple enough," he murmured through gritted teeth.

Ordan inclined his head, and flicked the Initiation endpoint.

Alchesh at first didn't react, then suddenly stiffened as the first wave of kan swept through him. He didn't scream, didn't make a sound, but his eyes went wide and Caeden could see his knuckles turning white as his hand pressed hard against the crystal.

Caeden tried to watch the flows of kan as they entered his friend, but they were too fast, too complex. Alchesh himself was still quiet but Caeden could see the veins on his neck beginning to stand out, his face turning red with strain now. He wished, again, that he understood more of how the Forge worked. Was it a tie to the soul, as the Shalis seemed to believe? Or did it conserve the mind, copy it at the moment of death and store it away in full, ready to be delivered to a new body?

Caeden and Andrael and Cyr had favored that last theory; it was the one closest to their understanding of kan, the one that allowed them to explain how it could work. But it equally unsettled them. They each agreed that the body was an integral part of identity—so when they died, did they truly come back the same person? Did their always having the same Essence signature somehow indicate some sort of physical consistency, despite external appearances? Or did they come back slightly different, with memories simply recorded from someone else?

"He is taking too long," said Ordan suddenly.

Caeden looked sharply at Alchesh. Several lines of kan were attached to him now, and yet more snaked toward him, affixing deep into his chest. Caeden frowned, moving around for a better view, and froze.

Alchesh's eyes were wide and black, as if they would burst from darkness.

The waves of kan continued to flow, and Caeden stepped forward, concerned now.

"He's taking as many strands as he can," Ordan abruptly hissed, shock in his voice. Before Caeden could move he darted forward and ripped Alchesh away from the wall, throwing him forcefully back to the floor. The hum that had been building to a crescendo finally died away.

Caeden skidded to his knees beside Alchesh, wincing at a gash on the man's brow where he had struck his head. He shook his friend by the shoulders, then carefully pried open his eyelids, examining his eyes worriedly. They had returned to clear brown, he was relieved to see, and Alchesh's chest rose and fell rhythmically.

"What happened?" asked Caeden dazedly, eyeing Ordan's looming figure with trepidation.

"He was greedy." Ordan watched Alchesh's motionless form warily. "He saw multiple connections and drew them all into himself."

Caeden's expression twisted. "Not greedy," he corrected. "Loyal. Desperately, stupidly loyal. I have been frantic to know the truth, and Alchesh knows it." He swallowed. "What will happen to him?"

Ordan contorted his serpentine body, hovering low to the ground above Alchesh, examining him.

"I do not know," he admitted, a tension to his words that concerned Caeden. "He has taken on thirteen connections, Tal'kamar. Thirteen. I did not realize that was even possible."

"And?"

"And he cannot be allowed to stay like this." He gazed at Alchesh, considering. "A connection to the Darklands like that... it is too strong. We cannot risk something coming through. Escaping."

Caeden stared at him, aghast. "I will not let you kill him."

Ordan snorted. "A solution that shows how little you have grown, Tal'kamar." He shook his head, clearly troubled. "We are beyond that now, anyway. If your friend dies, there is no telling what will happen to his connections. He may be reborn with them somewhere else, for all I know, in which case his death will merely inconvenience us. No—the only way to fix this is to use the last Sever on him, and quickly." He rose and moved to the row of near-empty shelves, picking up the final medallion.

"What?" Caeden shook his head in confusion. "Isn't that meant for you?"

"I will seek out Andrael instead."

Caeden swallowed. "His will kill you. It is not designed for anything else."

Ordan, to Caeden's surprise, smiled at that, albeit sadly. "There is no point in life for the sake of living, Tal'kamar. My people are gone, and this fight was one we already knew that we could never outlive. Death is a journey I am willing to take, now." He leaned in toward Alchesh, Sever outstretched.

"Wait!" Caeden held up his hand. "Just... wait." He thought furiously; he'd come too far and risked too much to have it end like this. "You said that you were willing to do this, to link Alchesh, because you thought it was important that I believe. So

just hold off, a little longer. A few weeks. Let him try and come to grips with this power and See into the future. If he shows even a hint of being dangerous, I will use the Sever on him myself. You have my word."

Ordan hesitated.

"No." He held up a hand as Caeden made to argue further. "Leave him here under my care. A month, Tal'kamar. Return in a month. By then he will either have Seen what you need or have grown too dangerous. Either way, he will be unlinked."

"Easier to give me the Sever, Ordan," said Caeden. "Gassandrid does not know you are alive, and he has my Trace. I can get away with coming here once, but twice..."

"You will find a way." Ordan's tone was firm.

Caeden scowled. "You do not trust me."

Ordan shook his head.

"I still remember the man who feared what he would become," he said softly. "If he had seen who you are now, Tal'kamar, he would have torn out his eyes from grief."

On the ground, Alchesh stirred.

Caeden gaped at Ordan, then hurried back to his friend, kneeling beside him. Alchesh felt the pressure on his arm and gasped, flailing, hands wandering like a blind man's. Caeden's heart sank as he saw the other man's eyes had turned entirely black once again.

"What can you see, Alchesh?" he asked urgently, fearing the worst.

Alchesh's breathing was heavy. Panicked.

"I see everything," he whispered.

Chapter 9

Davian grunted as he endured another violent shove from his guards, this time stumbling to his knees in the middle of the torch-lit, near-empty darkstone street.

He glanced down at his tender side, the slice in his shirt exposing it to the chill night air. The still-raw wound hadn't broken open again from the sudden motion, thankfully. There hadn't been an opportunity to heal himself further since the fight.

He gulped a lungful of air, and gingerly struggled back to his feet.

He had been abandoned, alone and wrapped in those kan-suppressing chains, for what felt like hours after they had dragged him out of the furious maelstrom of the Arena. The pain of his injury had dulled to a numb ache now, but the adrenaline of the fight had worn off long ago; by the time he had finally been fetched by this dozen-strong group of men in Telesthaesia, the onset of exhaustion had robbed him of his clarity of thought.

Which was a problem, because he was beginning to realize that wherever they were taking him right now, it wasn't back to his cell in Tel'Tarthen.

He did his best to keep his balance as he was pushed unceremoniously along once again, feeling a vague sense of amusement despite the situation. His entire escort was making sure to stay to his side or behind him as they pushed him forward, nervous caution in every inch of their postures. They had clearly either seen or heard what had happened in the Arena.

Still, as he risked a glance behind at his captors—catching a glimpse of a dozen tense, glaring faces above glimmering black

Telesthaesia before another almost-blow forced him onward—he suspected that there was more to their concern than just him. He could see it in the way they eyed the surrounding streets, this section of Ilshan Gathdel Teth distinctly abandoned save for Davian and his escort. Even their footsteps seemed eerily muted here.

After another minute they emerged into a long, narrow street that was bordered on one side by a massive spiked wall, their path turning sharply to follow alongside it. Davian stared at the structure, which stretched away in both directions for as far as he could see. It wasn't made of darkstone like the rest of the city: instead the wall appeared constructed entirely of plates of steel, clean and smooth, the lower section lighting up the street as its mirror-polish finish reflected the glow of regularly placed torches. In an odd way, it reminded him somewhat of Fedris Idri. It was as unusual a sight as Davian had yet seen here.

"What is this?" he murmured.

As expected, the only response he received was yet another sharp shove.

A pair of figures soon resolved up ahead; from their change of stance when they saw Davian's entourage, they had clearly been awaiting his arrival. The two men were standing in front of a large gate made from the same sleek steel as the wall.

Davian's stomach twisted as he drew closer, recognizing the younger of the two.

"That will be far enough," said the man Davian didn't know as they approached. He had distinguished gray hair and a kindly, grandfatherly face, though his green eyes were sharp. "Release him from those bonds."

One of Davian's captors took a half step forward, his voice full of protest. "Lord Gellen, he just—"

"Do not make me ask again, son," said the man—Gellen— quietly.

The guard swallowed, the scales of his Telesthaesia clicking against each other as he hurried to obey.

Davian fought to keep his face smooth as a soldier fumbled with his bonds. Once the rope finally slipped free he brought his hands up, stretching, flexing his fingers and rubbing out the sharp sensation as blood began to flow properly through them again.

Gellen glanced over Davian's shoulder. "Go."

Davian ignored the sound of the soldiers beating a rapid retreat, watching the man on the left. He was solidly built, perhaps ten years older than Davian, with reddish-blond hair. It was his skin that defined him, though: translucent white mixed with stark, raw red where sections of flesh had just...decayed. Sluiced off. Most noticeable was the palm-size patch on his cheek, though Davian knew that the man's tunic hid long strips missing from his arms, too.

"Rethgar," Davian said eventually, choosing to feign cheerfulness. It was the thing that would most annoy the man, from his experience. "A pleasure to see you again."

Rethgar returned his gaze coldly, not responding.

Gellen glanced between them. "So you have met?" His gaze focused on Davian. "You are...*brave*, to try and provoke the escherii." His emphasis indicated that 'brave' wasn't really the word he should have chosen.

Escherii. The term was familiar; Davian dredged his mind, arriving at the memory he'd taken from Ilseth Tenvar. The one in which Ilseth had received the Portal Box and discussed the attacks he had orchestrated on the Gifted schools around Andarra.

Of course. He still didn't know what it meant, but the context fit.

Davian forced his smile wider, though he could feel a tight ball of fury burning just beneath the surface.

For two straight days, this man had tortured him. It had been a vain attempt to break Davian's mental shield and Read Asha's location from him, not long into his imprisonment—perhaps a month after Caeden's escape?—but even with the intervening time since, Davian's memories of the experience hadn't come close to fading.

He still woke every other night drenched in sweat, thanks to what Rethgar had done.

The decaying man—the 'escherii'—was an Augur of some kind, as far as Davian had been able to tell. Rather than inflicting any bodily harm, he had instead used some sort of modified Control—manipulating elements of Davian's mind beyond his mental shield, apparently—to bring Davian back into the worst   133 moments of his life. The most painful, both emotionally and physically.

He had done it again, and again, and again.

And when that had not worked, Rethgar had chosen to show Davian a memory of his own.

Davian could still remember the feeling of anticipation as he gazed down on the Darecian-era castle, the calm waters of the Vashian Ocean just beyond. His excitement as he crept into the school. The barely restrained, savage glee as he flitted from room to room to room, murdering all who he came across. Elder Olin, Mistress Alita, Administrator Talean. Children and adults, male and female.

All except Asha. Her he had *wanted* to kill, so desperately. Had loomed over her bed, breathing heavily, watched her sleeping with his shadowy blade—just like the sha'teth's—poised inches from her throat. He had wanted to see her warm blood spilling everywhere. Coating the walls.

But Tal'kamar's binding was stronger, and he had left, sated but still disappointed.

Davian shuddered inwardly, though he kept his expression carefully smooth. It had taken two days before Gassandrid had apparently become aware of what was happening; one of his proxies had arrived, forcing Rethgar to leave and apologizing profusely for the man's actions. Rethgar had never appeared in Davian's cell again.

Which had been fortunate, as Davian didn't know how much longer he could have held out and kept his Lockbox sealed against the horror of that constant, merciless assault.

"I was told that he would be punished for what he did," said Davian to Gellen conversationally, ignoring Rethgar. "I see torturing your prisoners doesn't earn much of a penalty around here."

Gellen held up a hand as Rethgar's lip curled.

"Rethgar did the wrong thing, but he did it with the right motives. That didn't preclude him from discipline, nor did it preclude him from forgiveness. He is convinced of what is right, and that is more than I can say for you." Gellen's tone was calm, in
control.

He gave Rethgar a stern glance. "And you. He appears to know your temperament. Don't let him put you off balance. Lean harder on your other self, if need be. Where we are about to go, you need to be focused."

Rethgar just nodded, his eyes never leaving Davian. Clearly whoever Gellen was, he commanded respect.

Davian finally tore his gaze away from Rethgar. "And where *are* we going? Who are you, and why am I here?"

Gellen paused, hands clasped behind his back as he regarded Davian.

"My name is Gellen. I am the Voice of the Protector. I am the conduit through which El Himself makes His will known to the people of Ilshan Gathdel Teth." Gellen held Davian's gaze calmly. "As for the rest—we are about to enter a section of this city which is dangerous beyond measure. Normally it is off-limits to all, but Lord Gassandrid has asked me to bring you to him there, specifically."

"You...speak to El?" Davian repeated dubiously.

"He speaks to me," Gellen corrected as he turned to the massive steel doors, placing one hand on each. "And if He wills it, I can explain further at another time. For now, though, we must be moving. Quietly," he emphasized to Davian. "Believe me when I say that there would be no benefit to your causing a disturbance in here. You may not die, but there are worse things than death lurking within Seclusion."

Davian's breath caught. *Seclusion.* This was where Fessi had died, then, if Gassandrid was to be believed.

He took a half step back in surprise as lines of sharp blue suddenly appeared along the gate, the steel surrounding it beginning to shimmer with the bright, clean light of Essence. The gate slid open smoothly—disappearing inside the wall itself, it seemed—and Gellen walked through the opening, Rethgar shoving Davian to get him moving forward as well.

Davian glared around at the other man and then trailed after Gellen, passing beneath the square archway. His discomfort grew immediately; nothing had changed, visibly, but the air on this side of the wall felt...sullen. Darker and more ominous.

Like there were thousands of eyes in the shadows watching him hungrily.

Behind him, the gate slid shut again, closing off their exit with a heavy metallic clang that echoed away ominously into the darkness.

❦

The jagged, black architecture of Seclusion menaced them on all sides as they walked.

Davian did what he could to ignore the unnerving, oppressive atmosphere, focusing instead on trying to memorize their path through the streets. The buildings here had initially looked to have a similar style to the rest of Ilshan Gathdel Teth, but he'd soon noticed that they were less organized, didn't fit in with their surroundings as smoothly as in the rest of the city. Not many landmarks had presented themselves, either—though he did eventually spot three towers in the distance, each standing a little apart from the others, and each with its own distinctive shape. It wasn't much, but those might help him navigate if he had to run.

"Tell me about Isaire," said Gellen abruptly, breaking the grim hush of the past several minutes.

Davian took a second to realize that Gellen was speaking to him, then another to place the name.

"Who?" he asked, though he remembered now. The name of the guard who had seemed tempted to help him, before his fight in the Arena.

"The woman who was on duty tonight. She was with you before you killed Metaniel." Gellen continued to talk in little more than a whisper, but his voice carried disconcertingly along the dead streets.

Davian shrugged. "She seemed no different from the rest of your thugs in Telesthaesia."

Gellen didn't react, though Davian saw Rethgar twitch from the corner of his eye. "Simply a strange coincidence, then."

Davian knew he was being baited by the statement, but still. "Coincidence?"

"Do not play the fool," snapped Rethgar. "We found her dead in her house less than an hour ago. How in El's name did you do it?"

Davian shook his head in only half-feigned bemusement, though his heart sank at the news. Isaire had been the first person here who had seemed close to being an ally. "Nothing to do with me," he said honestly.

Gellen's face remained smooth, though Davian saw a flicker of frustration in his eyes as he glanced at Rethgar. He had probably wanted to probe further before revealing that information. Rethgar might be a powerful Augur, but subtlety and patience were clearly not among his strengths.

"A strange coincidence," Gellen repeated calmly. "And I suppose that you would describe Metaniel's death the same way?"

"Not at all. I definitely killed him," said Davian firmly. He'd been expecting this question for a while now. "Controlled him right through that Telesthaesia helmet of his."

Gellen's mouth twisted in irritation this time. "Be wary, Davian," he said. "Lord Gassandrid will wish to know as well, and he will not accept such dismissive answers as easily as I."

Silence fell again, the unconscious tension in both Rethgar's and Gellen's strides screaming for caution. The heavy stillness pushed in at them as they made their way down street after empty street, noticeably avoiding getting too close to the buildings on either side. Though neither man said anything to Davian, Rethgar in particular was clearly focused on the structures they passed, his eyes wide, twitching occasionally at what Davian could only assume was some imagined movement.

Nothing appeared, though. They finally arrived at one of the towers he had spotted earlier—the shortest of the three, he thought. Gellen unlocked a black iron gate, ushering them through and onto a downward-leading stairwell.

They descended for what felt like an age until finally, new light up ahead revealed a sight that Davian recognized.

The stairs leveled out into a narrow hallway, this one lit with clean lines of Essence rather than torches. The floor, walls, and ceiling were all made of plates of pure steel, reflecting the light almost like a mirror, polished and gleaming in stark contrast to the dirty black of darkstone that lay everywhere else in Ilshan Gathdel Teth. The corridor stretched away, Davian barely able to see where it branched off far ahead.

It was just like in his vision. He'd fought Gassandrid's proxies in a room of shifting steel plates that looked exactly like these.

"What is this place?" he asked.

Gellen glanced at him. "It is for Lord Gassandrid to decide whether you need to know," he replied firmly.

Davian rolled his eyes and turned back to examining his surroundings as they made their way along the empty corridors. This *was* the place from his vision—almost certainly—but it couldn't be the same time. There had been a dar'gaithin leading him then, not Gellen and Rethgar. The vision had started in a lower section, too—a much filthier, more dungeon-like area than this glimmering hallway.

Still, he doubted that there were many places like this in Ilshan Gathdel Teth. Something told him that in a city built on darkstone, hallways positively pulsing with energy were a rare thing indeed.

He shuffled along uncomfortably between his two captors for a while as they traversed the burnished passageways, several sharp turns finally leading them to a large room. Closed double doors loomed at the far end; Rethgar brought Davian roughly to a halt as Gellen continued forward and placed a hand against one of the doors.

There was nothing for a moment, and then the metal around his fingers seemed to ripple.

"Enter." The deep voice vibrated from every inch of steel in the room, making Davian jump. The doors swung open silently.

Davian marched forward before Gellen or Rethgar could try to make him, determined not to look intimidated.

The room was much as he remembered it. Shining, finely cut pieces of metal glimmered where they were sealed together with pulsing blue Essence; the configuration of the space was definitely different, but it was also without doubt the same area in which he had fought—or would fight—Gassandrid. Right now the floor was mostly flat, though a dais was raised at the far end, several people seated atop it.

A dozen, in fact, just as in his vision—though there were only a few faces he recognized, including the man who had fetched Davian from Tel'Tarthen earlier that evening.

Davian deliberately jerked to a stop well short of where he knew Gellen and Rethgar would want him, bracing himself.

When he felt Rethgar's hands shoving him hard in the back he feigned stumbling forward, dropping to his knees.

He needed to examine the floor, figure out how it worked and see if he could turn it to his advantage. If last time was any indication, long enough should have now passed since he'd been bound by the black chains.

Sure enough, he was able to force kan through his vision despite the fiery pain that accompanied the act, examining the steel plate beneath his palm.

He almost recoiled.

The kan was...complex. Not quite to the extent of the dizzying, mystifying design of the Boundary, but close enough that it immediately gave him that same overwhelmed feeling of dread and despair. How was he supposed to understand this? Endpoints were everywhere, and the steel itself seemed to shimmer strangely, even while his vision was extended through kan. That was odd, but there was no time to analyze it.

He got unhurriedly to his feet again. When his fight with Gassandrid did finally come, he knew he must figure out how to manipulate these Vessels—but there was no chance of that happening right now.

That didn't mean he couldn't draw Essence from them, though. Even as he straightened, he was already gaining just a trickle of energy from the plate underfoot.

He took a few unwilling steps forward, still allowing Essence to flow into him, and then looked up at the figures on the dais.

"What do you want?" he asked them tiredly.

"He has not revealed anything," interjected Gellen, his tone apologetic. It was also, Davian thought, laced with a hint of nervousness.

The figures above continued to study him. Then one in the middle—a long-haired young man, probably around Davian's age—spoke.

"You Controlled Metaniel," he said.

"You overcame Telesthaesia," said a young girl. Davian's stomach twisted as he remembered her from his vision.

"Or used some other trick," mused another young man standing to the right.

"A problem regardless," said a middle-aged woman with gray streaks in her hair.

"So now you will tell us how," concluded the long-haired man.

Davian gazed at the group, already feeling more clearheaded.

"You know how strange it is when you talk like that, right?" He carefully straightened the torn remnants of his clothing. He had been a prisoner for too long, knew that the Venerate didn't want him dead—couldn't kill him, in fact—and had no intention of acting daunted. "Can't you just choose one and make them do all the talking?"

There was a sharp intake of breath from behind him, and Davian thought the people up on the dais looked mildly taken aback.

"You are...not surprised by how my Vessels interact when together," an older gentleman murmured.

"You have already been told of this," said another.

"Or perhaps something else," mused a third.

"Still strange," said Davian cheerfully. "Very, very strange."

There was a grinding, crackling sound behind Davian; before he could turn there was steel slamming into his still-tender side, eliciting a grunt of pain and forcing him to his knees. He twisted to see exactly what had happened, but the floor was already settling back into its original position.

"Your lack of respect is meaningless," said the little girl calmly, a small smile on her lips. "Except for when it wastes time."

"I have been patient with you, but do not mistake that for weakness. Do not think your arrogance is not noted."

"A reckoning for every word, Davian. That is how you should live."

All twelve on the dais abruptly shifted their gazes to the men standing behind Davian, the synchronicity of the motion unsettling.

"Gellen, you may leave us."

"Your idea was sound, and yet the end result has obviously been...undesirable."

"Unforeseeably so, but I will nonetheless leave dealing with the repercussions to you."

Gellen quickly gave a deep, respectful bow. "Of course, Lord

Gassandrid." He seemed relieved; he shot Davian a final, considering look and then retreated from the room.

"And Rethgar." The Gassandrids' stares settled on the pallid, decaying man, who shuffled his feet and, for the first time since Davian had met him, looked humbled. "Find our guest a traveling companion to the Mines."

"A smart one—one who will stay with him, watch him at every turn."

"Explain to whomever you choose that if they do this, they alone of their peers will have the opportunity to return...intact."

"Ensure that they understand how this could be achieved. The importance of doing so, and why we know it is possible."

"Then prepare them as we would any other. Instill the usual commands."

"They may not be required tonight, but I am inclined to think that it will be soon, regardless."

Rethgar bowed as Gellen had, though worryingly, Davian thought he spotted a glimmer of vicious excitement in the Augur's eyes. "At once, Lord Gassandrid."

He retreated, the massive doors shutting silently after him. The dozen Gassandrid proxies on the dais contemplated Davian.

It was the little girl who spoke first.

"Herein lies the problem with fate," she said wearily, gaze fixed on Davian.

"I can toss a man into a deep pit with little fear, if fate dictates that he will survive—but the manner of his climbing out is always a risk," continued a blond-haired boy in his teens.

"Sometimes that risk is worthwhile. Today it was not."

"So tell us, and tell us true, Davian. How *did* you kill Metaniel?"

"I Controlled him," said Davian calmly.

"By which method?" asked a frail-looking man to the left who had not yet spoken.

Davian shrugged. "The usual one?"

"That should not be possible," observed the redheaded man.

"I'm very good," Davian assured him.

Another heavy blow to his legs, and this time Davian felt something give way in his knee. A shout of surprise and pain tore from him before he could bite it back.

"A reckoning for every word," murmured the middle-aged woman, sweeping a strand of gray hair back from her face.

"Discipline follows disrespect, Davian."

"I gave you fair warning, and hear me when I say that if you continue, the result will be the same."

"So enough of this false bravado, and speak with me plainly."

Davian stayed on the floor, his heart pounding. The effects of the black chain had finally worn off enough, and Essence was once again flowing into him smoothly. He hesitated, then sucked it in greedily from the steel plates beneath his hands, funneling it to both his knee and his still-tender side. The pain in both eased, and his mind immediately felt sharp once again.

He stood, the struggle to do so only half an act, though he didn't stop drawing thin lines of Essence from his surroundings. For the first time in over a year, he was going to be able to fill his Reserve.

He just had to make sure that Gassandrid didn't know it was happening.

"I didn't kill him," he said eventually. As much as he despised Gassandrid, what the Venerate had said was true enough. Withholding this information wasn't a battle worth fighting. "I didn't do anything. He committed suicide."

There was silence for a few long seconds. "Unlikely."

"I agree," said Davian bitterly. "And yet." He rubbed his forehead. "Why does it matter? You clearly wanted him dead, else you would not have dragged me into your fates-cursed Arena in the first place—and now he's dead. Surely you can see that if I was powerful enough to penetrate Telesthaesia, I wouldn't have waited to reveal it at such a pointless juncture."

A tall man on the right tapped a finger repeatedly against his other hand. Davian recognized the act—he had seen Gassandrid's other proxy do the same thing earlier that day. Clearly an absent-minded motion.

"You are angry that you were made to fight," he said.

Davian glared up at the group on the dais, continuing to siphon what he hoped was an unnoticeably small amount of Essence from his surroundings. "Of course I'm angry."

"You should not be." The middle-aged woman again. "It is the punishment reserved for all criminals here."

"You came into this city and you killed a man."

"My friend, as it happens."

"Your importance has shielded you from the wrath of the law until tonight, but do not mistake that for believing that you have been treated unjustly," one of the young men finished.

"So your punishment for my killing someone is to force me to kill more people," Davian said cynically. "Our definitions of justice are very different."

"You say 'force,'" said the gray-haired man on the left. "I am interested to hear you describing it thus."

Davian frowned. "What choice did I have? There were men trying to kill me, and besides—you knew that I was going to survive. So their deaths were guaranteed."

"What choice indeed?" murmured Gassandrid, the young girl speaking again.

"I used my foreknowledge and my position to manipulate events, coercing you into a particular action."

"I took away chance, and in doing so, I arguably took away your autonomy."

All twelve Gassandrids gazed at him. "Yet some would argue that the choice was very much still yours to make."

"So tell me, Davian. Is those fighters' blood on my hands, or yours?"

Davian looked away, gritting his teeth in frustration. "You're changing the subject," he growled, feeling absently at his side. It was healing, and his artificial Reserve was slowly, slowly filling up again. "You talk so much about right and wrong, about responsibility, and yet you have people out there dying for the entertainment of others. Criminals or not, how can you possibly defend that?"

Gassandrid leaned forward, his dozen faces darkening as one.

"If you think we are to blame, then perhaps you would like me to explain how when your *friend* sealed us behind the ilshara, it began sapping the very life from the earth."

"Perhaps you would like me to tell you of the moment we discovered that it affected even Gates, draining the source from all who traveled through them except for those with vast Reserves—and worse, corrupting even objects brought through. Making the food from outside rotten, inedible."

"Perhaps you would like me to recount the famine that followed. The starving families whom we had no way to help. The dying children. Everyone begging us for assistance, though they still thought of us as their enemy."

The tall woman in the center gestured angrily. "Or how when crime became rampant, and the prisons overflowed with desperate men and women whom we could barely feed, *the people* started organizing duels to the death for extra rations."

"One parent against another, more often than not. People who had done nothing wrong, dying for the chance to feed their families."

"How long would you have lasted, Davian?"

"How long could you have watched such suffering before it became too much for you to bear?"

"Would you have simply murdered those in your prisons, or citizens in the city, to reduce the need?"

"Would you have waited until enough people had starved, so that the few farms still providing crops could supply those who survived?"

"Or would you have tried, as we did, to arrive at a solution acceptable to all? A system of justice that still provided a chance at redemption, but reduced the population in the process?"

"Yes, the fights are seen as entertainment—because there is little else in this place for which to cheer, Davian."

"Because it distracts from hardship."

"Because it provides a shared experience for the people."

"Because it reminds those who watch not only of the consequences of breaking the law, but of the importance of their own work, their own sacrifices."

"You presume to make moral judgments on a society not your own, on people whose situation is vastly different from yours."

"You think the barbarity of it all pleases us, somehow."

"That we force these fights for our amusement."

"Yet this is what the people want."

144   "It is what the people—*your* people—demanded."

"So perhaps you think less of us than you should," Gassandrid concluded softly.

Davian listened mutely, the words making him uncomfortable despite his desire to just ignore them. Unless his ability didn't work with Gassandrid's proxies, the Venerate hadn't lied.

That didn't mean that the wild glee in the faces of the crowd, the bloodlust, the terror and sickening fear of the Arena were suddenly forgotten, though.

"I know these things are hard to accept." It was a young man with a muscular physique who spoke, his voice gentle. "Which is why we chose to give you adequate time to consider them."

"We have allowed you months to properly contemplate the things we revealed to you about Tal'kamar—his goals, his deeds, his person."

"You know of his atrocities."

"You know of his betrayals."

"And most importantly, you know that he now works to ensure none of it is *ever undone*."

"Even still, we do not ask you to betray him. To fight against him."

"You need answer only a single question."

"Answer it, and show your willingness to consider both sides of the argument. To be reasonable."

"Or do not, and accept that you will be sent to a place where you will be protected from Tal'kamar's desire to kill you. Protected, but not…comfortable."

Davian shook his head. "As I have said repeatedly—I don't know where Asha is, and would never tell you even if I did. Nor do I know anything about how she came to have so much power. If what you claim is even true," he added, trying to sound irritable.

"I am aware."

"Which is why that is not the question."

"All we wish to know, Davian, is anything you can tell us of the one known as the Shadraehin."

There was silence, Davian's mind racing as he did his best to look surprised by the question. He'd already known from his vision that the Venerate were searching for the Shadraehin—and he suspected, given what he'd learned from Asha the last time they had spoken, exactly why.

The Shadraehin was in fact Nethgalla, and also the one who had for a long time been gaining the benefits of the Siphon. Davian had no idea how much the Venerate knew, but they must at least have recognized that she'd had a role in orchestrating Asha's current situation in the Tributary—and, therefore, was likely aware of its physical location.

Finding her would probably be just as useful to them as getting to Asha herself. Maybe even more important, given that she was the one who had caused them so many of their recent problems.

"The 'Shadraehin,'" he said, pasting a puzzled look on his face and enunciating the word as if it were unfamiliar. "The leader of the Shadows in Ilin Illan? Why?"

"Our reasons are our own."

Davian shook his head. "I would tell you if I knew anything," he said, doing his best to sound bemused. "But I never had any interactions with him." He brightened. "Though—I did hear that he's an Augur. A prewar Augur. Does that help?"

Another silence, this one heavy.

"You should know that we have Read almost everyone in Ilin Illan over the past year, Davian," said the weak-looking man after a while.

"Many of your friends have admirable mental shields, but some do not."

"I find it hard to believe that they are more knowledgeable than you in this area."

Davian shook his head. "I have no idea what you mean," he said, though his heart sank. It made sense that the Venerate would have been making every effort to discover more information about Asha's location, but their having managed to worm their way inside so many people's heads in Ilin Illan was hardly encouraging.

The young girl sighed. "To begin with, we know the Shadraehin is a woman."

Davian once again did his best to look surprised, though he was painfully aware that acting had never been a strength of his.
146   "That's not what I heard."

The redheaded man frowned but before he could speak, several plates over to the left of the dais suddenly moved, steel sliding away smoothly with a crackle of blue energy.

The woman who walked through the new opening was short, her lean frame hugged by a deep-green dress. She paused as she took in Davian standing below, her dark-brown eyes hard.

Davian shivered inwardly, barely preventing himself from taking a half step back.

Diara.

He had met her only once, when she had accompanied Gassandrid to Tel'Tarthen. Like Gassandrid, she had never laid a finger on Davian...and yet every time she looked in his direction, he could feel her anger like a physical heat against his face. He was confident that both of the Venerate blamed him for turning Caeden against them, but Diara made no effort to hide her hatred.

He had always wondered whether she had somehow been responsible for Rethgar's access to him, too—or at least responsible for not stopping him. *One* of the Venerate had to have known it was happening.

"Already?" The Gassandrid proxy closest to Diara had turned; the gaze of the other eleven remained focused on Davian, though their expressions were blank and their eyes dead.

Diara moved closer to the man who had spoken, lowering her voice to an inaudible murmur. Gassandrid listened and then scowled, an eerily similar expression abruptly reflected on all dozen of his faces.

The redheaded proxy turned to Davian. "Don't move." He gestured and suddenly steel plates were moving again, snapping together, rapidly walling off both of the Venerate from Davian. Within moments, only one of Gassandrid's bodies—a young man with plain brown hair and a weedy physique—remained.

"Important conversation?" Davian asked casually.

The proxy didn't react, simply staring at him emptily, motionless. Gassandrid must be concentrating on the conversation with Diara, but presumably he could still see if Davian tried to escape.

Davian steeled himself and then pushed through kan, careful to keep the residual pain of the act from his face.

The proxy didn't move.

Davian kept his eyes on the man, but silently extended his senses toward the wall of steel. Gassandrid thought he was still incapacitated. The mechanism was complex, but it wasn't designed to block kan from getting through...

"...answer is no. She asked for more time, but her intent is clear," Diara was saying, irritation thick in her tone.

Davian breathed out. It was a trick he had learned a while ago; extending his senses this way didn't use a visible amount of kan. He should be able to listen to the Venerate without their realizing.

"Disappointing." He heard one of Gassandrid's proxies sigh. "You gave her a deadline?"

"One week, and she knows what will happen when I return. I was tempted to do it straight away and be done, but better to prove true to our word—just in case future negotiation with her is necessary. She is no threat as she is," Diara added absently.

"And if she contacts Tal'kamar?"

"I showed her who he is. What he did. Even if she had a way, I do not believe that she would, now."

"A risk nonetheless."

"Worth taking." Diara's voice lowered, her tone worried. "Alaris's Trace is still bright, so he's not dead, but...I cannot get a location from it. He won't have shape-shifted, and I doubt that it's because he's gone through the Chamber. He hasn't returned through the Gate you opened earlier, either, which makes two delays—he only has one opening left. It is not like him." A pause. "Perhaps it's time. This could be Tal'kamar making his move. With Alaris absent..."

Gassandrid said nothing, then exhaled.

"Agreed," he growled. "Rethgar is already preparing. Let him know."

After another second the crackling of energy indicated plates were moving again; Davian quickly released kan, keeping his expression smooth and forcing down the tiny spark of hope in his chest.

Perhaps Caeden was preparing to make good on his year-old promise?

The body that had been watching Davian finally shifted, relaxing as the other eleven came into view once again and regaining a semblance of normal posture. Davian mentally took note of the change. It appeared that, split though Gassandrid was, his proxies weren't completely independent when his full focus was elsewhere.

"It seems that we must make this brief." It was the young girl starting the conversation again; Davian wasn't sure whether she was somehow easier for Gassandrid to use, or whether he realized that using her to speak unsettled Davian the most.

"You will soon be fetched."

"Perhaps where you are going will provide you with the perspective I cannot."

"Know that I had no desire to do this, Davian—but as is often the case, it seems we are left with no choice." He gave a humorless smile at that last part.

Davian's heart skipped a beat. "And where exactly am I going?"

The dozen Gassandrids held Davian's gaze steadily.

"The deepest pit I know," said the little girl heavily.

Black chains erupted from the floor, snaking around Davian and tightening before he could react; steel suddenly began sliding and shifting, blue energy crackling as a new wall snapped together in front of Davian's eyes, hiding the dais from his sight and sealing Gassandrid away.

Within moments, he was alone.

❦

Davian waited silently in the pulsing steel room, deep in thought.

As always, Gassandrid had somehow managed to take the horrors he and his people were committing and make them sound... *legitimate*. He hated that. Gassandrid's arguments were so clinical, so reasoned out, that Davian could never quite see where the faults were—even though he knew that they had to be there.

He pondered for a bit longer and then shook his head irritably. There would be a time for thinking about these things further, but right now, he had to consider whether there was a way out. Wherever Gassandrid was intending to send him, it did not sound pleasant.

There was a sudden flash of blue followed by a grinding sound off to his left; he twisted to see one of the steel plates sliding away to reveal a lone, slim figure making her way hurriedly into the room.

"You," said Davian, staring in blank confusion as he recognized Isaire.

The woman whom Rethgar had claimed to be dead glanced around, raising a finger to her lips. She knelt, placing her hand against the floor; several thin lines of blue crackled outward from her touch, racing across surrounding plates and vanishing into the walls. After a couple of seconds she nodded, breathing out and standing again.

"We have a minute. Maybe two," she said quickly, her voice a whisper. "How did you kill Metaniel?"

Davian stared at her. "Get me out of here and I'll tell you."

Isaire shook her head. "If you have a way to overcome Telesthaesia—if you're really that strong or that smart—then you're worth the risk. But not otherwise." There was an edge of desperation to her voice, and she looked him in the eye. "If you're against the Venerate, you'll tell me the truth. I've risked a lot to come here."

Davian glared at her, heart pounding. The truth wasn't going to help him this time. "Then we're at an impasse."

Isaire glowered. "And this was a waste of my time." She spun and began heading back toward the opening in the wall.

"*Wait.*" Davian gritted his teeth. "They said you were dead."

Isaire stuttered to a stop.

"Already?" she cursed. She turned back to him. "Who told you? What did they say? *Exactly?*"

Davian hesitated. "Two men, called Gellen and Rethgar. They said that they found your body an hour or so ago."

"Fates. And this was such a suitable one," Isaire muttered. "Is Gellen still here?"

Davian shook his head, bemused. "Gassandrid sent him to deal with the fallout from the fight."

Isaire stared at him and then at the gap back out to the hallway, considering. Finally she sighed, evidently coming to some sort of decision.

She gestured, and suddenly Davian's mouth felt as though it were filled with sand.

He coughed furiously but no sound came out, though thankfully he could still breathe. He stared at Isaire, wide-eyed.

That hadn't been Essence she had just used.

"Sorry. This will take a few seconds, and I need you to be quiet," she said in exasperation. She eyed him severely. "Killing you would probably cause more trouble than it's worth. Probably. But if you breathe one word—one *word*—of what you're about to see...it will only hurt us both. I'm on your side. Don't forget that." She studied him, expression serious. "I don't know how you did what you did to Metaniel, but I hope for your sake that you're able to survive where I suspect you're going."

Before Davian could react, the woman's face began to writhe.

He restrained a gasp; he'd seen this before—had *done* this before—but when it was unexpected, it looked a hundred times worse. Skin warped and tore; bones cracked and grew. The woman's hair lengthened, turned blonde.

It was over within seconds. As Davian gaped, she gave him a small smile, then spun and walked swiftly away.

Davian tried to call out, but the gag of kan still stifled his words; he tried to take a step forward but the black chains clanked, yanking him back against the wall. In moments, the woman had vanished.

Nethgalla.

It had to have been Nethgalla. He was even fairly certain that the woman she had transformed into was the same one he had seen in his vision.

That meant that his fight against Gassandrid, his opportunity to escape, might not be too far away.

What was she doing here, though? She was *exactly* whom the Venerate were searching for; surely her presence was far too great a risk. Was she working with Caeden? She hadn't known who Davian was, which suggested not. Davian's mind spun.

The sensation of grit filling his mouth abruptly vanished, and he breathed deeply, quietly testing his voice to himself. Whatever Nethgalla had done to gag him had worn off.

He chewed his lip, considering the implications; at least five more minutes passed before a different section of wall slid aside and Rethgar's red-pocked, sallow form strode through—

accompanied by another. One that moved with an unsettling, sinuous motion.

Despite himself, Davian couldn't help but shuffle back as the dar'gaithin approached, its scales scratching menacingly against the shining steel floor.

The creature came to a halt in front of Davian. It stood at least nine feet tall, but it contorted itself, leaning down menacingly until its face was level with Davian's. It could have been the same one from his vision, or not—they all seemed to be virtually identical in appearance.

"Follow," it hissed.

It slithered away as the black chains holding Davian suddenly vanished.

Davian didn't move; even knowing that the creature in his vision had talked, he still found it unsettling to hear one of the Banes speak.

"You had best do as Theshesseth says," said Rethgar, jerking his head after the black-scaled creature. There was a vicious satisfaction in his eyes. "You don't want to get on his bad side, after all. You're about to be spending a lot of time with him."

Davian glanced back at the dar'gaithin. So that *was* the creature he would eventually kill. Good to know.

"What do you mean?" he asked as he started walking, keeping his pensiveness from his tone.

Rethgar's smirk widened. "You'll see."

He refused to respond to questions after that, clearly enjoying Davian's discomfort. They walked in silence, Davian calculating desperately as they reached a set of stairs and descended. He knew he couldn't escape; the aftereffect of the black chains was just as it had been before, and he was completely unable to touch kan. He could try to run—if he couldn't die, why not at least make the attempt?—but as if reading his thoughts, Rethgar shook his head warningly.

"Not worth it, Davian. Not down here," he murmured.

Davian gave their surroundings an uneasy glance. Rethgar's tone was solemn, and there *was* something off about this place, even if Davian couldn't put his finger on exactly what.

For now, at least, he would see where this was going.

After a few minutes, Davian frowned. The steel beneath his feet was beginning to vibrate, barely noticeably at first, but the quivering seemed to increase in intensity as they walked. Each step soon felt as though it were sending tiny shocks through his feet, and a low, uncomfortable buzzing began to press on his ears. The walls and ceiling around them were clearly affected, too; to Davian's eyes they gradually began to blur with constant, furious motion.

He wanted to ask what was happening but Rethgar didn't appear fazed, and Davian knew that he wouldn't get an answer out of the unsettling man, so he kept quiet.

It didn't take long after that for them to arrive at the room housing the portal.

The plates all around them were vibrating frantically now, a blur of steel, blue energy crackling and snapping furiously as if struggling to hold the individual pieces in place. The portal itself just hung in the center of it all, silent and menacing, a hole in the air that led to... nothing. Davian squinted, at first thinking that it must be dark on the other side, but there was nothing at all. Just... black.

Theshesseth glanced back at Rethgar and Davian, reptilian eyes glinting, then slithered through.

Davian swallowed as Rethgar pushed him closer. "Is it supposed to look like that?" he asked apprehensively.

"Not really," said Rethgar.

He shoved Davian firmly through the hole.

The thrum of the buzzing steel plates vanished; there was pain, something tearing at him—not just his body but his mind as well, pulling, clawing, grasping, raking at him from all directions. A flash of an unsettlingly familiar river of gray, though this time he was apart, somehow above it rather than within.

And then he was stumbling out the other side of the portal, and into madness.

Chapter 10

A dull-red crescent moon burned low in the cloudless sky, light seeping through the foliage overhead and barely illuminating Davian's surroundings as he burst through the other side of the portal.

He stumbled to a stop, gaping at the disquieting sight of the shadowy forest's black and crimson tints before spinning, trying to get his bearings. The hole through which he'd just been pushed was no longer there.

In its place stood a towering, twisting wall of gray void.

Davian's stunned gaze traveled slowly upward. The barrier stretched impossibly high, curving inward slightly so that it loomed over him; the farther up he looked the more translucent the gray became until finally it vanished, revealing the stark black of the night sky beyond. Stars shone up there, but the points of light didn't twinkle and glimmer as they should. Their light was cold. Dead.

Bewildered, he followed the line of gray to the right, and then the left.

There was no end to it that he could see.

That gray river raging through the wall looked all too familiar, though. And the journey here had been...not the *same* as when he had been caught in the rift in Deilannis, but similar. Too similar to be coincidence.

He pushed up his left sleeve. No Mark, the circle encapsulating the man, woman, and child vanished. Just clean skin once again.

The question, then, was no longer just where he had been sent.

It was when.

He recovered himself enough to force motion into his legs, stumbling to the nearest tree and pressing himself flat against the enormous trunk, doing his best to still his breathing as he finally remembered the dar'gaithin that had preceded him. Theshesseth would surely be looking for him.

There was nothing, though—no sign of the creature, or anything else living for that matter. Everything was still.

He waited for a few more seconds and then exhaled, staring around at his new surroundings dazedly. He was in some sort of forest—a very old one, judging from the enormity of the trees; the trunks were as wide as ten men standing shoulder to shoulder, and he couldn't even estimate how high some of them stretched. Moss covered many of the trunks, and vines hung everywhere, thin black silhouettes that added to the raw menace that exuded from every red-tinged shadow.

He quickly spotted where the gray wall curved around through the trees, far away to both his left and right—presumably unbroken, though the thick-leafed foliage hid much of it. It looked as though it was some sort of encircling barrier.

Which meant that at least for now, there was only one clear way forward.

He kept his back pressed against the rough, dry bark of the tree, gathering his thoughts. After a year of almost complete isolation and routine, the events of the past day had hit him hard, shaken him, even prepared as he had been for something to happen.

After a while his pulse slowed and his breathing steadied. Whatever this place was, he needed more information. If it was a prison, then where were the guards? Where was Theshesseth?

He started walking, the red light of the moon filtering through the branches above as he struck out in the only direction that wasn't obviously toward the wall. The air here was hot and dry, each breath feeling as if it took just a little more effort than it should. No moisture beaded on the foliage around him, the leaves papery dry to the touch and twigs cracking beneath his feet. There was an unnatural stillness, too—no chirping of birds or buzzing of insects. Just silence.

He reached for kan automatically, thinking to extend his senses out, spot any danger before he simply stumbled upon it. Based on his previous experiences, the effect of the black chains should almost have worn off now.

He stuttered to a stop.

There was no pain when he cleared his mind, no resistance when he searched for the shadowy power.

But there was also nothing there.

He closed his eyes, concentrating this time, brow furrowing. Even while unable to use it, he'd always been able to *sense* kan.

After a moment, his anxious tension loosened a fraction. It *was* there.

Just...*different*.

He frowned, examining the energy now, trying to determine what felt wrong about it. The process of grasping kan was always tricky, but this...this was as if it was further away, somehow. Distant.

He reached for it.

Nothing happened.

He tried again, more urgently this time, stretching. Again he failed. He knew immediately that this was different from when he'd first been learning under Malshash, or the added difficulty of handling kan within Talan Gol. It wasn't slippery, wasn't difficult to manage.

He simply couldn't reach it. Couldn't touch it at all.

He shivered, a surge of panic threatening to overwhelm him as he realized that he wasn't drawing Essence from his surroundings anymore. Even his most instinctual use of kan was gone.

Heart in his throat, he checked his Reserve.

Still almost full.

He released a shaky breath. That was...interesting. A relief, but still—even more confusing. If he really had just traveled through time, then any Essence within his body should have been ripped away.

For now, though, the reason it hadn't didn't matter. The Reserve was as large as he'd been able to make it, and he had taken a good amount of Essence during his conversation with Gassandrid. It should last him months, if he was careful.

And he wasn't going to die here. Reminding himself of that 157 eased his nerves somewhat, even if it couldn't completely dispel his reflexive anxiety at not being able to draw Essence. It was like swimming through a tunnel underwater—knowing that he would eventually surface made holding his breath bearable, but the need to breathe felt no less urgent.

Davian pressed on, more tentatively than before, experimenting cautiously as he went. He tapped his Reserve the way one of the Gifted would, breathing out in relief as a tiny ball of light appeared up ahead. He'd had very little practice using Essence without kan, though he knew the theory as well as anyone after his studies in Caladel. Manipulating Essence like this felt messy, wasteful. Compared to the efficiency of funneling it through kan, it was like requiring an entire river just to wash his hands.

Still—if he needed to defend or heal himself, he could, even if doing so would deplete his finite supply. He let the Essence-light dissipate—he could see well enough by the red moon's eerie illumination—and kept moving.

He had been making his way methodically through the tangle of vines dangling from thick, low-hanging branches for less than five minutes when he caught the flicker of movement up ahead. He slid carefully into the shadowed concealment of a nearby tree.

The red-rimmed silhouette of a serpentine head materialized beyond the foliage in his path a moment later and Davian held his breath, careful not to move. Another figure quickly appeared behind the dar'gaithin, the outline similar to a man's but too tall and thin, looming over even the Bane. Its movements seemed... off. Jerky. Like those of a marionette in the hands of an unskilled puppeteer.

A second humanoid figure appeared, slightly shorter than the first. Then a third. All were outlined against the sharp red light of the moon, features doused in black shadow.

The group didn't appear to notice or be looking for him; they moved along together, silent, heads occasionally swiveling to the sides but not with any particular purpose. Before long they were lost again behind the thick-trunked trees.

Davian vacillated, trying to decide if he should follow. The risks were obvious, but he had no idea where he was, or about the situation here. He had no food, no water, no shelter.

He glanced up at the towering gray wall curving around in the distance to either side. His choices of direction remained limited for now, anyway.

Best not to take any more risks than were necessary at this point.

He angled off away from where the dar'gaithin and its companions had disappeared, keeping an eye in that direction in case they doubled back for some reason. The forest pressed close as he walked; he kept his bearings by occasionally checking the walls to the right and left, ensuring that he wasn't straying closer to one or the other. After a few minutes he noticed that the trees were beginning to thin, and within one more he had reached the edge of the forest.

He stuttered to a halt at the tree line, staring blankly. He was at the top of a gentle rise, which overlooked the beginnings of what appeared to be a massive city.

One in ruins, though. Silent. Dead.

Davian frowned, brow creasing as he took in the mass of buildings, sandstone structures illuminated deep red or shadowed pitch-black in the disconcerting moonlight. This was unlike any city he had ever seen: there were no streets to speak of at all, and no apparent order to the mélange of stairs, tunnels, and snaking pathways that wound their way up to, around, and over the buildings. Worse, half of the structures he could see had collapsed, the facades of many buildings completely gone. Everywhere he looked there were deep shadows in narrow alleyways that seemed to simply end, while others branched out in confusing, haphazard directions, no apparent pattern to their layout.

He stayed there for another few minutes, watching carefully for any sign of movement. Clouds of dust occasionally appeared, tinged red in the light, but they appeared to be from the slight, dry breeze rather than having been stirred up by something else. Otherwise, everything was still.

Davian eventually stood, brushing off his clothes. He hadn't spotted anything to be concerned about, and there might be supplies that he could recover from the debris. A weapon, even.

He hurried down the slight incline and scrambled over the first pile of rubble, which he realized must have once been a low wall surrounding the city. His footsteps crunched on loose rock as he reached the outer area, the sound muted, swallowed by the heavy shadows.

Davian's disquiet intensified as he drew nearer to the close-set, looming structures. Charred spots were now visible on the sides of some, where walls had seemingly been blown apart.

Davian couldn't help but wonder if those marks had been made by Essence. Some sort of battle?

He peered into the inky shadows of the ruins as he passed, trying to spot anything that might be of use to him. There was nothing, though. It was as if these places had all been stripped, picked clean.

He chose to follow the perimeter for a few minutes rather than attempt to navigate the maze itself, moving cautiously, muscles tensed and ready to react to any sign of movement. There seemed to be no end to the buildings, and many of them were tall—almost towers. This city had to have housed tens of thousands of people. Maybe more.

So where had they all gone?

Finally he steeled himself and turned down one of the alleyways that led inward, away from what he felt was the comparative safety of the open air. The buildings that menaced him on either side looked to be as empty as the ones on the outer edge, though. The alley quickly narrowed to an impassable crack, so he took a nearby stairwell, following it up and then through several quick, sharp twists. The high buildings on all sides made the process confusing, and it was only the glow of the red moon that allowed Davian to keep his sense of direction. Oddly, though some time had passed, neither the crescent nor the dead stars around it seemed to have shifted across the sky at all.

He emerged onto a pathway, still elevated. The way ahead was wide—almost a street—but felt narrower thanks to a series of crumbling buildings that rose several stories high on either side, forming a sort of unnatural canyon.

He was so focused on looking inside each of those structures that for the first few seconds, he didn't even notice the bodies.

He froze as the first figure caught the corner of his eye, hanging limply as it was from the second story of a building he was

160

passing. He didn't move for a long moment, then forced his gaze upward.

A chill ran down his spine.

Illuminated starkly in the red moonlight was the lifeless form of a dar'gaithin, a black outline against the red-tinted wall. A single, thin spear of jagged rock protruded from its mouth and pinned it firmly to the stone behind.

Davian's heart began to pound as his gaze traveled to the next body, a little higher on the building.

And then the next. And the next.

He took a step back, breath shortening to nervous gasps as he finally grasped what he was seeing. Every building along this way had dar'gaithin corpses pinned to its facade, hanging motionless in the eerie light.

A hundred at least. Maybe more.

He forced himself to calm, assessing. The bodies were broken, many necks at odd angles, the serpentine figures mangled as if they had been smashed by some massive, unseen force. There was no particular arrangement to the bodies: they seemed to have been pinned to the buildings as a means of killing them, rather than as some sort of sick display.

Still.

He considered retreating, then shook his head firmly to himself and pressed forward, searching for a body hanging relatively close to the ground. The rough spears pinning the dar'gaithin were the closest things to weapons that he'd seen; if the stone spikes were good enough to kill the creatures, it was worth having one with him.

He soon spotted what he was looking for, the corpse's tail dangling almost within reach. He hurried over, swallowing his nerves as he slipped into the heavy darkness of the building's shadow.

A closer look at the creature made him flinch. It looked as if it had died in terrible pain, the thin stone fixing it to the wall having somehow speared beneath its scales and through its throat. The massive wound there suggested that the dar'gaithin had thrashed around long after the blow that had ultimately killed it.

Davian hesitated, then carefully tapped his Reserve, sending out a thin tendril of Essence and trying to wrap it around the sliver of stone. The black blood that slicked its surface seemed to act almost like the Banes' scales, though; without the fine control of kan to help, his thread simply slid off the spear without gaining purchase.

He scowled silently, then used more Essence to strengthen his arms and began dragging over a large piece of rubble to stand on. He was hesitant to use even these small amounts from his Reserve, but the opportunity to obtain a physical weapon was too good to pass up.

The heavy stone made a grinding sound that echoed painfully through the empty structures around him. Davian winced at the noise, pausing and lifting his head, scanning the wide pathway for any sign that he had been heard. There was nothing.

He moved to begin pulling again, and then froze.

A sound—definitely not from him. A wet, regular *crunching*.

Nearby, too.

Davian straightened, turning to face in the direction of the noise. Leaving his arms strengthened, he crept forward farther into the shadows of the hollowed-out building, sidling up to a window that looked down into the adjoining alleyway.

The dar'gaithin was easily visible in the red moonlight. It was bent double over something, its back to Davian and body blocking his view, grotesquely muscled arms tearing at whatever was on the ground.

Then it abruptly paused, its serpentine head flicking up and swiveling to stare around, revealing what it had been hunched over.

Davian bit back a gasp.

The mangled remains of what was clearly another dar'gaithin lay in a raw pile in the middle of the street, scales torn off and flesh shredded. Black blood surrounded it in a pool, as well as dripped from the hands and face of the dar'gaithin that was now moving, as if somehow sensing Davian's horror.

The dar'gaithin slithered off to the side, out of Davian's sight. Its motions were erratic, though. As if it was only sporadically remembering how to move.

Davian held his breath until he could no longer hear the sound of the dar'gaithin's scales against the stone of the street, shuddering to himself as he peered again at the mangled corpse. They *ate* one another? That felt wrong, even for Banes. But there was no denying what he'd just seen.

He made his way back over to the piece of rubble he'd been moving, hesitant to make more noise but painfully aware of his need for a weapon now. The stone rasped over the ground as he dragged it, but thankfully it was in place quickly. He tore a small bit of cloth from his shirt and then leaped atop his makeshift step, balancing precariously and reaching up to wipe the black blood from the revealed shaft. Once that was done, he strengthened himself with Essence. Braced to pull.

There was a dark blur from the corner of his eye, and then he was being smashed to the ground by a heavy, black, thrashing force, his ribs snapping with an audible crack.

He croaked a cry as the new dar'gaithin's bloodied maw opened and snapped at him several times in quick succession, only his Essence-enhanced arms saving him from having his face torn off by jagged teeth. He summoned more energy and desperately *pushed*, upward and away; the snakelike Bane flailed as it flew through the air, crashing hard into the wall opposite and then to the floor in a cloud of dust.

Davian gasped as he flooded Essence to his caved-in chest, the bones rapidly joining, his collapsed lungs expanding and filling with air once again. From the corner of his eye he could see by its rapidly growing shadow that the dar'gaithin had barely been dazed. He rolled and scrambled to his feet.

"Just wait," he said to the creature, holding out his hands to show that he had no weapon. "I know you can talk. We can—"

The slavering dar'gaithin leaped at him, jaws snapping together with maniacal fury as it tried to bite him yet again.

Davian dove to the side, eyes wide, panting as he tried to recover. There was something terribly wrong with this creature; even the way it looked at him was different from that of the other dar'gaithin Davian had come across. Less intelligent and more... crazed. It was hard to tell in the dim red light, but Davian thought that its eyes were bloodshot, too.

The creature came again; Davian moved more smoothly this time, allowing it to narrowly miss him and instead smash itself 163 into the wall with a thundering crash of broken stone. He quickly maneuvered himself out toward the open path, wishing desperately that he were able to step outside of time.

Even so, when the dar'gaithin attacked for a third time, Davian was ready.

He dashed to the side, bracing himself atop the stone he had placed earlier and *leaping*, his Essence-enhanced reflexes and strength allowing him to tear the stone spear free from the skewered dar'gaithin on the wall. He kept his momentum and spun in midair, hanging.

He hurled the spear as hard as he could.

He missed.

The unbalanced stone sheared off the scales of the dar'gaithin's cheek with a shower of sparks; the creature flinched away, shocked, as the weapon crashed to the ground behind it. Davian cursed but managed to land smoothly, crouching and sliding backward through the rubble as he came to a halt.

He tapped his Reserve again as the dar'gaithin slithered forward, lightning fast, recovered from Davian's failed attack. He fumbled with the unrefined power of Essence as the creature closed on him, then desperately snaked out a tendril. Wrapped it around the cleaned part of the spear and *pulled*.

The rough weapon spun wildly toward him, red in the moonlight where flecks of black blood didn't spray from it. Davian snatched it from the air, ignoring the burning in his hands as he touched the dark substance on it, putting all his weight behind it and thrusting hard just as the oncoming creature reached him.

The unwieldy weapon frustrated him again as it smashed slightly upward of where he was aiming, scraping across the dar'gaithin's eye and into its forehead, jagged stone tearing into his hands at the shivering impact. The dar'gaithin floundered back, stunned by the blow, its left eye a mess of black blood. It steadied, and for a heartbeat Davian thought it was simply going to rush at him again, injured or not.

Then, with another feral hiss, it slithered off into the surrounding ruins.

Davian just stood there panting, every nerve taut as he watched for the creature's return, hands shaking. He finally registered the pain in them; he held one up, stomach churning to see rotting flesh and suppurating ulcers forming where the globules of black blood had smeared across his skin. He gritted his teeth, reluctantly setting his spear within easy reach and then swiftly cleaning his hands with a torn strip of his shirt, relieved to see the unpleasant-looking damage rapidly fading as he forced more Essence to the injury. Within a minute, both hands were healed.

Once the process was complete, he checked his Reserve. Still fairly close to full—but noticeably emptier than it had been a half hour earlier.

As if to underscore his concern, there was a clattering from farther down the walkway.

Davian drew back into the shadows and then glanced around, spotting nearby stairs leading upward, still in good condition. If he wanted to get a good look at whatever else might have been drawn by the disturbance, he would be better served moving to higher ground.

He used another strip of cloth to collect and then clean the rest of his makeshift spear as he hurried quietly upward, traversing three winding flights before emerging onto an open, flat roof. He eyed the stone beneath his feet—it seemed solid enough, despite the missing wall below—and then lay on his stomach, worming forward until he was at the edge overlooking the elevated pathway.

All was still. No people, no dar'gaithin.

Davian frowned, staying motionless, scanning the area below but not spotting anything of note. And yet, he *had* heard a sound.

He let his vision drift; this was one of the taller buildings in the area, giving him his first good view of the city. As he'd suspected, it was enormous: the close-set buildings stretched away well into the distance, though even from here he could see that damage was prevalent everywhere. Half of the buildings were jagged outlines, their facades crumbled away; in other places he could see piles of rubble where entire structures had collapsed.

His brow furrowed as he focused on a point in the distance, perhaps a mile away. A sharp yellow light shone upward in a long line, splitting the entire city in half, reflecting off the tops of the buildings and tinting the slightly dusty air more strongly than the red moon. Davian peered along the line curiously, but there were too many things in the way. He couldn't see the source of the illumination.

Then he spotted the figure.

He squinted. It was sitting on a rooftop near the strange golden light, silhouetted against it. He wouldn't have seen it, or perhaps would have mistaken it for a statue, had he not caught it shifting positions. It was staring down into the light, Davian thought, though he was far enough away that it was hard to tell.

It was human, though. The more he watched, the more confident of that Davian became.

He fixed the direction in his mind and then scrambled back from the edge of the roof.

There was still no sign of danger when he reached the walkway again, thankfully; whatever he had heard before must have passed by. He didn't waste time, moving through tunnels, up and down stairs, and along paths and rooftops as quickly as caution would allow. He had no idea whether the person he'd seen would be friendly, but this place was too strange, too unsettling for him to keep enduring it without at least trying to make contact with someone.

He made good time, even if for the entire journey it felt as though there were hundreds of eyes peering at him from every red-tinged shadow. He moved at a slow, crouching run where he could, carefully skirting or climbing the sharpest rises when rubble meant that there was no other way forward. Once one of the darkest shadows underfoot proved to be a deep hole into which he very nearly stumbled, losing his spear to its depths during his desperate attempt to recover his balance. After that, he used a sliver of Essence wherever the red light from above was blocked.

The light he had spotted splitting the city seemed to grow in intensity as he drew near, coloring the air a sharp gold above the buildings up ahead. He glanced at it occasionally, bemused by what it could possibly be.

He rounded another corner; only a single line of structures separated him from where the light was originating now, intense illumination filtering through jagged holes in the nearby buildings. Davian hadn't spotted the figure again since setting out, but he was confident that he had managed to keep a relatively straight line toward where it had been.

He picked his way around the side of a building, then slowed to a shocked halt as he finally took in the source of the light.

Perhaps twenty feet away from where he stood, the ground ahead just... vanished.

Bright-yellow light poured upward from a massive rupture, a gaping wound in the stone that ran from left to right for as far as he could see. Davian couldn't begin to guess how deep it might go but it was certainly wide, encompassing where at least two rows of buildings would have been—fifty feet, perhaps more. Hundreds of structures on the other side had been sheared completely in half, and Davian could only assume that this side would look much the same. As he crept closer, a barely audible hum tugged at his ears, seemingly emanating from the depths.

He swallowed. There was no way of crossing the gap, as far as he could tell. Where the earth had been rent the stone itself was glowing, as if it had somehow been infused with pure energy.

Davian still didn't think it was the light of Essence, though. This was somehow dirtier than the illumination that would have provided: the yellow was hazy, smudged, as if saturated with greasy smoke.

He rubbed absently at his ears as he finally tore his gaze away from the sight, scanning the rooftops for any sign of the figure he'd seen perching there earlier.

There was nobody up above, but it didn't take long to spot whom he was looking for.

The man—it was a man, Davian could see now—had moved; he was seated at the very edge of this side of the chasm, the zigzagging lip angling him toward Davian. His legs cast strange shadows in the air as they dangled, the yellow light highlighting his narrow features. For a moment he looked almost familiar.

Davian frowned, studying the streaks glistening on the man's unshaven cheeks. Bloodshot eyes gazed blankly down into the light, though the glare must have been painful. Strands of black, unkempt curly hair hung limply around the stranger's face, which bore a vicious bruise just beneath the left eye.

Most likely a prisoner, then. Certainly not someone who looked as if he would pose a threat.

He hesitated, then stepped out of the shadows and politely cleared his throat.

The man gazing down into the light started violently, twisting without taking into account where he was and then scrabbling backward desperately as the motion almost sent him sliding over the edge. He ended with an ungainly half roll, half crawl away from the chasm, finishing a few feet away from Davian, who suddenly felt tempted to pretend he hadn't been watching.

"Sorry," he said, sheepish as he walked over and leaned down, extending his hand.

The man glared up at him. He was older than Davian—perhaps in his early thirties—and now that he was no longer staring into the golden light, his sharp ice-blue eyes were filled with a mixture of embarrassment and anger. He didn't take the proffered help.

"El take it," he muttered, shifting slightly back from Davian again before getting gingerly to his feet on his own. "There's not supposed to be anyone..." He trailed off, peering at Davian. "Why are you out here?" He spoke oddly—the language was Andarran, but the accent was hard to place, enunciated more carefully and precisely than Davian was accustomed to hearing.

Before Davian could answer, the man let out a groan and crumpled to his knees, face twisting. Davian took a couple of uncertain steps forward.

"What's wrong? Are you..."

He trailed off.

There was something on the man's arms. The sleeves of his tattered shirt were rolled up, and each arm looked as though it were encased in shadow—except that this shadow was glistening, liquid as it writhed from wrist to shoulder.

The man followed Davian's gaze, his anger dissipating into resignation.

"So. Now you know why *I* am out here," he said weakly, apparently assuming that Davian would recognize whatever was afflicting him. "But that does not explain your presence." He squinted. "I don't recognize you. Are you even from Isstharis's section? Who are you?"

Davian shook his head dazedly. "I'm Davian. I only just arrived."

The stranger stared in disbelief and then issued a short, bitter laugh.

"I know the name. You're the one they were looking for. You're supposed to be..." He trailed off, looking even more perplexed. "What do you mean, 'only just arrived'?"

Davian was saved from answering by the man's sudden, staggering weave to the side, followed quickly by his eyes rolling back into his head. The wiry man collapsed to the hard stone ground before Davian could jump forward to catch him.

Davian hurried closer to the stranger, concerned but fairly certain that he shouldn't risk touching the dark, shiny mass covering his arms. It wasn't the same as the dar'gaithin blood from earlier—in fact, in a lot of ways it looked worse. It seemed to... *crawl* along the skin as if alive, rippling, caressing it in a most unsettling manner.

He screwed up his face. Whatever it was, it was clearly hurting the man. Killing him, probably, judging by his waxy skin and labored breathing.

He knelt down and stretched out to touch the stranger's forehead, then snatched his hand away as the substance reacted to Davian's presence, pulling upward like inverted drops of tar toward him. It didn't surrender its grip on its current victim's flesh, though; after letting his thumping heart ease, Davian cautiously reached out again, keeping a wary eye on the unsettling, waving tendrils grasping in his direction.

He swallowed, then tapped his Reserve and began funneling Essence into the man.

At first nothing happened, the glistening mass somehow resisting the flow, forcing Davian's healing energy away from where it was attacking. Davian almost flinched back as he felt the depth of the injury to the man's flesh, tiny threads of darkness burrowing down into muscle and bone, sucking out life and leaving rot and decay in its place. It wasn't just on the stranger's arms, but beneath his shirt, too—across his chest, almost down to his stomach.

Davian gritted his teeth and pushed more Essence into the 169 man's body, flooding it with energy. Like a dam bursting, the black substance suddenly seemed to break, seeping away from the surface, its deep hooks dissolving as the damaged areas finally began to restore themselves. Color returned to the man's cheeks, and his breathing immediately eased to a more regular, relaxed rhythm.

Davian exhaled and sat back, relieved his efforts had made a difference but more than a little concerned about how much of his own Essence he had just expended. His Reserve was noticeably lower once again, and he had been here less than a single night.

He looked around, then picked up the still-unconscious man and half carried, half dragged him away from the chasm's edge, propping him up against a nearby wall. The stranger continued to breathe steadily, not stirring. It might be some time before he woke.

Davian did his best to ensure the man was comfortably situated, then ventured again over to where the yellow light was spilling upward. It wasn't as blinding as it had first appeared, and to his surprise he was able to see a fair distance into the depths without difficulty.

He stared downward for some time, studying the abyss.

The split in the earth ran as deep as he could see. Some of the light was emanating from the sides of the chasm; the broken stone surfaces were coated in golden luminescence, though that light was broken by dark holes—tunnels, judging from their regular size and shape, that had been sliced in two by whatever cataclysm had happened here.

Davian tested the anchoring of a nearby piece of stone and then used it to lean slightly, peering over the edge. The abyss stretched downward, ultimately disappearing into a haze of burning yellow. The constant, low, vibrating hum seemed to be coming from the depths, noticeably louder when his head was poked out over the edge.

He shivered, pulling back, rubbing spots from his eyes. What *was* this place?

The clattering of loose stone against stone caught his ear; he spun, peering in the direction from which it had come. Down the line of the chasm, somewhere behind a huge chunk of broken wall, the sound came again.

Davian didn't pause to think; he grabbed his unconscious companion under the armpits and dragged him as soundlessly as he could into the shelter of the nearest building. The entire facade was gone, but it still hid the both of them in deep shadow.

Moments passed, the skittering of stone getting louder, whoever was approaching not trying to remain silent. Footsteps crunched close by, and Davian held his breath, willing the unconscious man next to him to not make a sound.

A single figure strode into sight, silhouetted against the yellow light of the chasm and tinged in red from the competing moon. Like the figures Davian had seen earlier in the forest with the dar'gaithin, this one was too tall, limbs thin and stretched, movements jerky. It wore a simple pair of breeches but was otherwise naked, nothing on its torso or feet.

Then it turned, and Davian clamped his teeth together to keep from crying out.

The man's hair, brow, and nose were normal, but his mouth... his mouth was a gaping hole of needle-like fangs, lipless and permanently open, stretching down from beneath his nose almost to his chin. The red moonlight reflected off those razor-thin, elongated teeth, and they glistened with beaded moisture as if they were coated in congealing blood.

Davian's horrified gaze traveled up to where the creature's eyes should have been. There was... nothing. That part of its face was just skin.

The man's—creature's—head turned, pointing directly at Davian's hiding spot.

It paused. Cocked its head to the side slightly, as if puzzled.

Davian's heart pounded and he kept perfectly still, fearful that any motion—even something as slight as his pulling back farther—might somehow be detected, despite the creature's apparent lack of sight. The monster delayed a moment longer and then continued to sweep the area with its eyeless gaze, bulging muscle rippling along its bare arms and chest as it moved stiffly. It was strong, clearly, even if its movements did not appear particularly coordinated.

It gave a soft, rasping sound.

There was a strange blur in the air, and then the creature was just... gone. Vanished.

Davian crouched there, unmoving, for what felt like an age.

Finally, when his aching legs couldn't hold their position any longer, he stood again slowly, stretching out and peering pensively along the edge of the chasm. There was no movement, no sign of the creature.

He stared grimly at the glowing abyss, rubbing at his ears as that barely-there hum tugged at his senses again. It didn't seem wise to do anything else until he found out more about this place.

He settled back down into the shadows by the sleeping man to wait.

Chapter 11

The blood-red moon still hung in the same position, refusing to give any indication of time's passage, when the man beside Davian finally groaned.

Davian started, then positioned a hand near the stranger's mouth, ready to muffle any noise he might have been thinking of making. The creature Davian had seen had disappeared long ago now, but there was no telling what other horrors might be nearby.

The man's eyes snapped open, reflecting the yellow of the chasm's glow. He immediately tensed, staring up at Davian and then around at the building.

Then his jaw went slack and he levered himself up, raising a trembling arm up in front of his face.

"El," he whispered, flexing his hand in disbelief. "You...you did this?"

Davian nodded, relieved to see that the man didn't appear to be hostile. "I used Essence," he explained. He didn't think that mentioning he was an Augur was a good idea at this point.

The man didn't say anything for a long moment, looking dazedly at his arms.

"You're Darecian?" he said eventually. "I thought they killed all of you. Thank you," he added, before Davian could decide how to respond. He looked up at Davian, resolve suddenly in his eyes. He held out his hand. "I'm Raeleth."

"Davian," said Davian, grasping it firmly, something inside him unclenching at the friendly gesture.

"Davian? I know that name." Raeleth squinted. "I remember

now. You said...you said you had only *just arrived*?" His emphasis on the last part was unabashedly dubious.

"I came through the portal earlier tonight. I've only been here for this one evening," Davian confirmed, a touch defensively.

"That...doesn't make any sense." Raeleth rubbed his forehead, then held up a hand apologetically at Davian's mildly irritated expression. "I'm not calling you a liar. Not exactly. But... everyone else arrived at the same time—within *seconds* of one another." He fell silent, the last statement clearly a challenge.

Davian stared at him blankly. "I...don't know why I would have been different. I don't know anything about this place," he admitted, head spinning. "You said that there were others?"

"Thousands of us. Though not so many now," Raeleth conceded. "We got here almost three months ago, right when this delightful mess"—his gesture encompassed the chasm and the ruined city both—"was in the middle of happening." His skepticism faded to dazed disbelief again as he continued to examine his arm, as if not quite comprehending what he was seeing. "I recognize your name, you know. They've been looking for you."

"Who?"

"The snakes. One called Theshesseth, especially. He kept coming around and asking about you. Seemed convinced that you were still alive for weeks after they gave up on everyone else. I remember, because none of us could understand why they didn't just assume that you'd died along with all the others." Raeleth gazed out over the chasm, looking grim at the memory.

Davian nodded silently; he could only imagine what it must have been like here in the city when all of this destruction had taken place. His heart sank a little at the news that the dar'gaithin were in control, though.

"Do you know why he thought you were alive?" Raeleth continued. His tone was casual, but the way he eyed Davian showed that he was genuinely curious.

Davian hesitated. Theshesseth would have been told that Davian's fate wasn't to die here, but saying so would lead to questions that he had no desire to answer right now. "I have no idea what's—"

174   The ground started to tremble beneath Davian's feet.

He stumbled backward in drunken fashion as a low rumbling permeated the air, his eyes wide as he instinctively made to brace himself against the nearby wall. Raeleth was grabbing him by the arm and pulling hard in the opposite direction, though; Davian fell, and rubble smashed down onto the stone where he'd been standing a second earlier.

Crashes echoed across the vast expanse of the city, and Davian saw one structure collapse entirely in on itself across the chasm. Massive chunks of stone vanished into the abyss, trailing yellow-tinged streaks of dust behind them.

"Thanks," gasped Davian as the shaking eased to a stop.

Raeleth brushed himself off. "I suppose this is your first tremor, too? They're fairly common here. It's good practice not to let things fall on your head when they happen."

Davian glanced across, offering a weak smile. "I'll try to remember that." He got to his feet. "Seems like I could use as much advice as I can get. If you were willing to give it."

Raeleth said nothing for a few excruciatingly long seconds, the only sound the irritating low hum that pressed on the air.

Then he sighed, nodding.

"It would appear that El has brought us together. And with Him as my witness, you've earned the help. I haven't heard of anyone infected by Dark who has lived to see another dawn. Figuratively speaking," he amended softly.

"Dark?" repeated Davian. "That...black liquid?"

Raeleth raised an eyebrow. "You really *haven't* been here," he said, sounding vaguely surprised. "It's not the worst way to die around here, but it's close. If you see any, for the love of all that is good, do *not* let it touch you." He glanced up at the red moon without waiting for Davian's acknowledgment. "How long has it been?"

"An hour?" suggested Davian.

"Good—it's still before first bell, then. We need to move. We've been fortunate not to have any al'goriat find us out here."

Davian swallowed, scrambling after Raeleth as he began walking. "You're talking about those creatures with no eyes?" Al'goriat were, supposedly, the rarest and most dangerous of the Banes. According to legend, details about them were so scarce because so few who encountered them lived to tell the tale.

Raeleth cast a sideways glance at him. "You've seen one?"

"There was a group following around a dar'gaithin earlier. And one wandered past while you were unconscious," Davian admitted with a shiver. "That's why I dragged you into the building."

Raeleth blanched. "That close? And it didn't see you?" he asked disbelievingly.

"We were in the shadows, behind a wall," Davian assured him.

Raeleth snorted. "Doesn't matter," he said morosely. "I don't know how they see, but it's obviously not like you or me—darkness doesn't seem to affect them at all, and stone not much more." He shook his head dazedly. "El was watching over us, clearly. This far away from camp, they would have eaten us for sure." He glanced around nervously. "We should keep the talking to a minimum until we get somewhere safe. Their hearing is quite good."

Davian swallowed the several burning questions on the tip of his tongue, the memory of that gaping maw of needle-sharp teeth making him acknowledge the statement and follow as noiselessly as he could, mimicking Raeleth's sure footsteps as they started walking.

They kept to the edge of the chasm for a while, the journey proceeding tensely but without incident; eventually Raeleth gestured and they angled away from the yellow light, their progress slowing as they began picking their way through the darker, red-tinged ruins. Finally Raeleth held up a hand, bringing Davian to a halt.

"We're getting near the camp. The al'goriat shouldn't be a problem here," he said, voice still a whisper.

Davian released a breath in relief. "Camp?" He peered ahead, though he couldn't see anything notable. "Where? How many people?"

Raeleth jerked his head to a nearby building—almost a tower—inside which stood a mostly intact stairwell. "Better to show you."

Davian frowned but trailed after the other man, climbing carefully to the top of the structure and out onto the roof. The buildings here all had these rooftop accesses, it seemed.

Raeleth guided him over to the edge, then gestured.

Davian's eyes widened.

The flickering yellow-orange illumination of small fires spilled out of various structures for almost as far as he could see; occasionally a shadowy figure would cross by a window or doorway, briefly silhouetted before passing from sight once again. There appeared to be groups populating different areas of the city, one directly below and then the others segmented out, each batch of fires clearly separated by a combination of stagnant red moonlight and stark darkness.

"There must be hundreds of people here," Davian murmured, stunned.

"Closer to a thousand. It's late; a lot of the fires have already gone out." Raeleth shrugged at Davian's disbelieving look. "There used to be a lot more of us. Probably three times our current number when we first arrived."

Davian shook his head dazedly, still studying the scene. What looked like a large man-made lake sat a short distance beyond the lights; Davian licked his lips at the sight, suddenly reminded that it had been far too many hours since he'd had anything to drink. Essence sustained him, but that didn't mean his mouth and throat weren't dry.

"What would happen if someone else saw me?" he asked quietly, gaze focused on the rippling water. The dotted lights stood squarely in between.

Raeleth squinted at him.

"You're *going* to be seen," he said slowly. "Why do you think I brought you here, exactly?"

Davian frowned. "I..." He trailed off, horror seeping into his tone as he realized what Raeleth was saying. "You want me to join you down there? But...you're *prisoners*."

Raeleth snorted. "*We're* prisoners. Unless you have some way of getting out of here that I'm not aware of."

"But no one else knows about me yet," Davian protested.

"And they don't have to. Choose a different name. No one will guess who you really are," said Raeleth firmly. "I am sorry if I gave you false expectations when I said I'd help—but you have to understand how things work here. There's no food aside from the rations Isstharis gives out, and that lake is our only source of water. Those people you see down there aren't just here because they're afraid of what's out there. They're here because this is the *only* place where anyone can survive."

Davian's heart sank. "So...if I do join you down there. What happens if someone figures out who I am and turns me in to the dar'gaithin?"

"They won't," Raeleth assured him. "A few might realize you're not from this section, but there's always someone moving from area to area, looking for a new team to take them in. And the snakes circulated your description, but I guarantee that nobody will remember after this long. I certainly didn't until you said who you were." He shrugged. "As for the snakes themselves...they have trouble, sometimes, telling humans apart. You should be fine. Besides—there's only Isstharis in our section, and she always stays in the same place for metal delivery. More of them died than humans when we got here—the transition disoriented them more than us, for some reason. We took advantage where we could. You might go weeks without even seeing one now."

Davian scowled, though more to himself than to Raeleth this time. Every time the other man gave him answers, Davian found more questions arising.

"*One* dar'gaithin is guarding all these people?" he said, deciding to focus on one thing at a time.

"One here. Each other section south of the Breach has one, too," corrected Raeleth. "And it's the dar'gaithin, plus a couple of hundred hungry al'goriat."

Davian rubbed his forehead. "Oh. I thought you said there wouldn't be any of those to worry about here."

Raeleth gave Davian a rueful smile. "You misunderstood. They just don't *eat* us here. As long as we follow the rules," he amended bleakly. "They don't seem very intelligent, but they're certainly smart enough to obey the snakes."

Davian felt his shoulders slump. He had no way to know whether Raeleth was telling him the truth—kan remained frustratingly out of reach, which surely meant that his ability to see lies was also not working—but...it *felt* as if he was being honest.

Which made everything he was saying somehow much worse.

"Why are all the fires so spread out, even within the different sections?" he asked, gazing out at the scattered points of light. He could see inside a few of the buildings where the flames crackled; though there appeared to be room for plenty more, only a few dejected-looking figures were slumped in each, as far as he could tell. "Surely it would be better if everyone stayed together."

"It would be," agreed Raeleth, "but we're not allowed to gather in groups of more than four. That's one of the snakes' rules. One which I've seen the al'goriat enforce, too." His mouth twisted with distaste at the last.

Davian opened his mouth to ask more, but Raeleth shook his head firmly.

"I know you must have a thousand questions, but I need to get back. I can probably convince my team to let you join us—we're one short anyway, and they were desperate enough to take me in, a few weeks back—but only if they're not in the midst of wondering why I snuck away tonight. If they ever find out I was infected..." He grimaced at the thought. "I'll return as soon as I can."

"Ah." Davian shuffled his feet, feeling an abrupt sense of abandonment. "What am I supposed to do in the meantime?"

Raeleth shrugged, glancing down at the city.

"Go to the lake, get some water, then come back up here and wait. Don't worry if someone sees you tonight, but stay out of sight once you're back—especially after you hear first bell. Idle hands will get you noticed more quickly than anything else during work hours. I'll return after last bell tomorrow with food. And a plan," he added firmly.

Davian almost protested; the idea of just hiding, of leaving his fate entirely in this man's hands, was one with which he hardly felt comfortable. Particularly given his inability to see whether Raeleth was deceiving him.

The lack of that ability after so long taking it for granted—his lack of access to kan as a whole, in fact—made him feel naked. Terribly vulnerable, something only made worse by his ominous surroundings.

Eventually, though, he nodded. Partly it was the lack of a better choice. Partly it was events catching up to him; after a year in the silent calm of his cell, the shock of the past evening—had it been only one night?—was wearing on him.

And partly, too, there was just something about Raeleth, about the man's earnest demeanor, that Davian trusted.

Oblivious to Davian's thoughts, Raeleth clapped him on the shoulder, taking the nod as a sign of acceptance. "Good." He headed for the stairs, then threw a glance over his shoulder.

"Welcome to Zvaelar," he added wryly.

It was at least half a day later—though impossible to tell exactly how long, under the frozen glower of the red night sky—that Davian heard the crashing of stone below.

He rubbed his eyes; he'd been half dozing, huddled up against the low stone of the roof's edge, trying to rejuvenate himself without using more Essence. He was thirsty again, frustratingly; he'd made it to the lake and back without any problems before the juddering ring of a deep bell had echoed across the city, but he'd had nothing with which to carry any water back.

The sound of stone against stone came again from somewhere below, and Davian felt his muscles tighten. Everything had been deathly quiet since not long after that bell, when the camp had—briefly—come alive with activity, people marching along raised pathways and up and down twisting stairways with apparent purpose. There had been no chatter, though, just muttered whispers within groups, people moving in clumps of four or fewer. Just as Raeleth had said.

Everyone had disappeared farther into the red-tinged city, and ever since, there had been utter silence below. Davian hadn't been willing to risk venturing out again after Raeleth's warnings.

He shifted carefully, then peeked over the edge of the building, trying to see what had caused the disturbance. The crunching and scraping of loose stone came again, the rhythm uneven—and something else. A constant grinding, dragging sound. Directly below him now, on the lower floor of the same building atop which he currently perched.

Davian tensed. There was nowhere to hide if someone came up here.

There was abruptly motion below, something emerging from the hollowed-out shell of the building and into his vision.

Davian recoiled, barely managing to clap his hand over his mouth to stifle a cry.

Crimson light glinted off skin that was almost completely transparent, glass-like, revealing a mess of muscle and organ and fluid shifting unsettlingly just beneath the surface. The creature was dragging itself along with arms that ended abruptly in curved spines that sprouted outward, scraping weakly against the stone.

The limbs to which those claws were attached were emaciated, far too thin for the bulky body that would have been at least ten feet tall had the creature been standing. It made a wrenching motion, claws digging into rock, and hauled itself forward a few more feet. Davian's stomach lurched as its legs became visible. As thin as its arms, with glass-like skin that revealed shattered bone stabbing outward through torn muscle at multiple points.

The creature's chest rose and fell quickly, and it twisted to face the sky, now staring directly up at him. A ruined maw revealed needle-like teeth grinding and slicing into its own flesh, many of the fangs broken off and dark blood dribbling down its chin.

Its eyes, though, were wide. Intelligent.

Human.

Davian froze, heart thundering in his chest, resisting the urge to flinch back and possibly draw attention with the movement. Had it seen him? He realized what it was now. Or what it would resemble, anyway, if its body were whole.

An al'goriat.

But its eyes were not covered over in flesh. Brown and scared, they flickered as the creature stared upward, and Davian knew it had spotted him. It opened its mouth wide as if to speak, or scream.

A spear took it through the left eye, slamming into hard stone beneath and quivering there for a long, shocking second.

Davian just lay there, frozen, as a slithering sound came from somewhere below. Then the sinuous form of a dar'gaithin was by the dead creature's side, pulling out the spear with a short, sharp motion. The serpentine Bane contorted its body to lean in close to the deformed al'goriat's face, studying it.

It pulled away after a while, its sharp gaze raking the area; Davian didn't dare breathe, but the creature never looked upward.

Seemingly satisfied, the dar'gaithin proceeded to lean down and haul the deformed al'goriat onto its shoulder, the immense strength of its arms meaning it had little problem with the dead creature's weight.

Then it was slithering away, leaving only a dribble of black blood and the steadily dissipating sound of scales scraping against stone.

Finally, the camp was silent again.

Davian just stayed where he was, every muscle taut, trying to block out what he had just seen. Eventually he slid back and twisted into a seated position, steadying his shaky breathing.

He knew he wasn't going to die here, but right now, that was barely a comfort.

He didn't move again for a long time, peering over the edge only once the booming bell rang out again and he heard the sounds of people returning. The groups were once again moving together, everyone looking dusty and exhausted, clearly drained from whatever tasks they had been set.

It was another few hours before he heard the soft footfalls making their way up the stairs. He held his breath, then let it out again silently as a tired and grimy-looking Raeleth emerged onto the roof.

Raeleth gave Davian a weary smile, half of his face shadowed by the angle of the red moon. Then he walked over and thrust out a hand. It was filled with a dark, leafy plant of some kind, though Davian didn't recognize it.

"Food," he explained. "Not much, but—"

He cut off as Davian grabbed it, barely giving it a glance before biting in. Prisoner though he'd been for the last year, he had at least been properly fed, and it had been more than a day since he'd had anything to eat. His stomach had been gnawing at his insides for hours now.

He sputtered and almost spat out the vegetable—if that was what it was—before forcing himself to chew deliberately and swallow. Its tough outer surface had given way to a soft, soggy flesh that was extremely bitter.

"Sorry," said Raeleth apologetically. "These things taste better cooked, but it would have raised too many questions if I'd been seen preparing but not eating it."

Davian forced another bite, hunger trumping any misgivings he had about the flavor. "I'll survive," he assured Raeleth between chews. "Thank you." He swallowed, the bitter tang of the meal—small though it had been—burning his throat. "I have a lot of questions," he added.

Raeleth sat, gesturing for Davian to do the same, the motion barely visible in the darkness. "Then let's start there for now. I'll answer what I can."

"Where are we?"

"The dar'gaithin call it Zvaelar, and that's about the most any of us really know. Twenty miles, roughly, between the gray boundaries to the north and south—more than half of that is city. Perhaps ten miles between the east and west boundaries. No way over or around or under. Trust me, we've tried," Raeleth added drily.

Davian nodded thoughtfully. "*When* are we?"

Raeleth looked taken aback.

"Impossible to tell," he said. "Nobody I've met recognizes the city, and we seem to come from a range of eras. One member of my team was born almost a millennium after me, from what we can tell." He squinted at Davian. "How did you know?"

"Well it's not hard to see that time's not passing normally here," said Davian, gesturing to the stagnant red moon. "You said Theshesseth has been here for months, but he went through the portal only a few seconds before me. And you mentioned everyone else arriving at the same moment, too. It didn't seem like that much of a stretch." He tried to keep his tone casual. There were other reasons that he'd assumed time travel, of course—the raging gray void of the surrounding walls, for one thing—but he didn't see the need to reveal that information to Raeleth just yet.

Raeleth scratched his head. "You...are taking to the concept better than the rest of us did," he admitted, issuing a soft laugh and seeming to accept Davian's explanation. "Praise El for that. It wasn't a conversation I was looking forward to."

Davian smiled, though the expression quickly faded back to seriousness. "So there's no way back, that you know of?"

Raeleth vacillated.

"Not that I know of," he agreed slowly. "Though..."

183

Davian gave him an expectant look, and Raeleth made a face.

"Our teams scour the city for anything made of metal—mostly iron or steel—and in return for meeting quota, the snakes give us food," Raeleth explained. "That food comes from somewhere; there's too much of it for them to have some hidden store. And that metal is *going* somewhere, too. It has to be." There was a note of barely restrained desperation to the last, an acknowledgment that he had only guesses.

Davian contemplated. Hardly proof, but it was better than nothing. "Any idea where they take the metal, once you give it to them?"

"North," said Raeleth. "Across the Breach." He nodded toward where the city-splitting, illuminated chasm lay.

"There are ways over it?" asked Davian in surprise. The gap was massive where he'd seen it, and judging from the refracted yellow light in the sky, the abyss stretched the entire distance between the eastern and western boundaries of this place.

"Just the one. Impossible for us to cross, though. It's heavily guarded." Raeleth shook his head. "It's not an option worth exploring."

Davian frowned; there was a hesitation to Raeleth's voice that suggested there was something he wasn't saying, but this was hardly the time to press. He tucked away the information to investigate later.

"So everyone here is slave labor," he said. "That's where they all go, when that bell rings?"

"Essentially," admitted Raeleth.

Davian peered down at the mess of paths and buildings below, parts of which were now illuminated by firelight. Then he let his gaze wander further, to where the violent yellow of the Breach lit up nearby buildings, and beyond that to the darkened, empty-looking outline of the structures beyond.

If he wanted to find his way out of this place, it sounded like his path lay somewhere through there.

"So if I join your team," he said eventually, picking up the previous thread. "We'd just be searching the city for metal while we're awake?"

Raeleth chuckled humorlessly.

"If you want to put it like that," he said. "Of course, we've all been doing this for nearly three months, so it's getting harder and harder to find what we need. And you have to avoid stepping in pools of Dark. And getting trapped in collapsing buildings. And stray al'goriat, not to mention a dozen other things around here that could kill you." He shrugged at Davian's expression. "There's no point in me making it sound easier than it is. You're going to find this out soon enough anyway, and El as my witness, it's not like the alternative is any better."

Davian swallowed, the unpleasant aftertaste of the food Raeleth had given him still sharp against his tongue. "So what do we do now?"

"Right now? You sit there and you listen," said Raeleth firmly. "The others won't pay you much attention; the days are too long and too hard to bother with conversation, and all anyone wants to do once they get back is get enough sleep to be capable of doing it all again tomorrow. Plus, people die a lot around here. It's easier not getting to know them." He shrugged. "But they *will* notice if you're ignorant about how things should work."

Davian grimaced, but dipped his head in acquiescence.

He listened in silence for the next hour, gradually piecing together what life in Zvaelar was like for the prisoners. The cataclysm that had shattered this place and rent the city had, apparently, occurred just as everyone had arrived—whether as a consequence of their arrival or for some other reason, Raeleth didn't know. The other man described stumbling into a nightmare of raging fire and shattering ground and a strange red energy flecked with yellow coating everything in sight; people and dar'gaithin alike had fled, unable to tell between where was safe and where the ground was likely to swallow them whole.

Many of the thousands who had been sent through hadn't survived that first hour—but it was only after the earth had stopped shaking and the fires had died down that the real trials had begun.

Raeleth described scavenging in the city in a calm and concise manner, but it was impossible to mask the horror that leaked through as he did so. The terrors that lurked around every corner sounded like a nightmare made real, no matter how matter-of-fact he managed to be about it all.

Davian's heart sank as he listened. Part of him wanted nothing to do with any of this, but another part knew that he could help: his ability to wield Essence would give him an edge that, according to Raeleth, no one else here had. Assuming, of course, that he could find a way to replenish his Reserve.

Not to mention that if he was going to figure out how to get back—and there *had* to be a way—then he needed more information.

Finally Raeleth fell silent, and though he didn't look over at Davian, his anticipation was thick in the darkness.

"So?" he asked eventually. "Have I painted an enticing enough picture?"

"You make it sound delightful," Davian assured him drolly.

"But?"

Davian hesitated. "Why are you going to so much effort to help me? Why risk so much?" It was blunt, but what Raeleth had described was...grim. A life where expending this amount of energy to aid someone—even someone who had just saved one's life—brought plenty of risk and very little reward. He wanted to understand the other man's motivations.

Raeleth said nothing for a long moment.

"I thought El was ready to take me home, last night. That's why I was out there. The dar'gaithin take the corpses of anyone infected with Dark, and I...I didn't want them to have mine," he said, his voice soft. "I was sitting on the edge of the Breach and I could feel the stuff eating at me, and even in this place, even with all that pain..." His voice cracked a little. "I didn't want to go. I closed my eyes. I begged El for more time." He sucked in a breath. "And then you were there."

Davian blinked. "You're helping me because you think...*El* sent me?"

"I'm helping you because I was reminded that as unknowable as El's plan might be, there always is one. Even when we don't like where it takes us." Raeleth sighed. "A truth that is most important to accept when it's hardest, unfortunately. I was losing myself to this place, but you turning up made me remember that...well." He gave Davian a lopsided smile. "Leaving you out here to die may just not be the right thing to do."

186

Davian snorted soft amusement at the last part, but nodded. Coincidence or something else, it didn't really matter: Raeleth was clearly confident in what he was saying.

He didn't want to give himself up like this, but what choice did he have?

"Good enough," he said heavily, getting to his feet and gesturing to the stairwell.

"Lead the way."

Chapter 12

Wirr sprinted through the trees, dodging low-hanging branches and leaping over fallen logs even as he tried desperately to calculate where each of his squads should currently be.

A little ahead there was a flicker of movement as Erran appeared, the young man glancing back at Wirr and giving a cheerful salute before vanishing again. It had been to let him know that he was still there more than anything else; the Augur wasn't allowed to help him here, much to Wirr's chagrin. He would have given anything for the ability to move that quickly.

"Amadia," he gasped as he skidded to a halt, ignoring the slight pulling pain from his scarred stomach, finally reaching the edge of the cliff overlooking the forest below. Enemy reds were visible at various points through the gaps in the trees, as were the whites of his own troops. Heavily outnumbered, as always. "Tell Siara that your squad needs to move a half mile to the south. Right now." He spotted a trio of figures sliding through the trees, closer to his position. "Tell her Calder's scouts are there, too, but that they will be past by the time you get there. You should have..." He calculated quickly. "Ten minutes to set up an ambush on the lower road. He won't know you're there until it's too late."

He put his hands on his knees, catching his breath as he examined the tableau, nodding to himself as the flashes of white to the north started toward him at a good pace. He gave more orders as he spotted the courses of other squads through the thick foliage, though most were only minor adjustments. His people were very close to where he had envisaged them.

"You're winning."

Wirr flinched, turning to see Erran to his left now, the young Augur peering with keen interest at the events unfolding below.

"We're not losing." Wirr's gaze traveled to the slopes beyond Erran, and he spotted a couple of Calder's men making their way up. "Make sure you're not seen. If you get me caught, I'm going to look even worse than usual." The scouts were searching specifically for him, he knew, albeit more as a precaution than from any real belief that he would actually be here. Calder was a proponent of generals staying well out of the range of battle, and that attitude pervaded his ranks. To them, Wirr's being present so close to the conflict would be foolhardy.

"I'm being careful." Erran reluctantly sank lower as he said the words, though, making sure plenty of foliage sat between him and the enemy soldiers. "Just thought you might want to take a break and let me know what happened in Prythe," he added, sounding somewhat disgruntled.

Wirr glanced away from the scene, forcing a grin to hide his discomfort at the reminder of what he and Taeris had learned. "Working with the Council's been boring these past few days, I take it?"

"You have *no* idea." Erran grinned back, though.

Wirr looked again toward Calder's scouts. They were still a distance away, but they clearly knew this area gave a good view of the battlefield. "I don't suppose you want to make us invisible, seeing as you're here?"

Erran snorted. "I said I wanted to talk, not help you cheat." Shouts came from below, followed by the sounds of a clash— wooden weapons rather than steel, but still loud enough to cause a flock of birds to rise from their resting place. The scouts heard it, too, sprinting back in the direction from which they'd come. Erran peered down at the battle unfolding. "Not that you need it, apparently. You *are* getting better at this." He sounded mildly surprised.

"Thanks," said Wirr drily. He settled back against a thick trunk. He needed to stay vigilant, but it seemed that his gamble had paid off. He glanced across at Erran. "Do we have to do this right now? We could just use your ability to communicate privately later." It was going to be a heavy conversation, one that he didn't particularly want to have while distracted.

Erran grunted. "I saw Taeris this morning," he admitted. "He didn't say much—he was on his way to meet with the Council—but…I got the impression that things did not go entirely well." He shrugged. "I'd prefer to hear the bad news now than have to wait for it."

Wirr sighed, but nodded. He spent a grim few minutes sporadically relating the things he had learned on his sojourn south, occasionally pausing to issue orders or assess how a clash was going.

"Fates," murmured Erran after Wirr had finished. He raked a hand through his hair, the fighting below completely forgotten. "*Fates*. The entire city—and Shen think it happens close to the festival? So…any time from now?" A cracking note of panic entered his voice at that, though he quickly brought it under control. "That scum Rohin claimed that he'd Seen us getting annihilated, too…he was so unhinged, we thought he must have been talking about the Banes that got through a year ago. But now… *fates*. I can't comprehend it. *I* can't comprehend it, and I at least know what's still out there somewhere. How are we supposed to convince everyone else?"

Wirr watched as flashes of white darted through the trees toward another clash. The men he had diverted would arrive at the skirmish just in time. "Our options are limited," he conceded, recognizing the dread in Erran's tone all too well. He'd had the whole day before to think about this on the road back from Daren Tel, to argue over the options with Taeris, and there were no easy solutions. Both agreed that preparing the city for an evacuation would be the right course, but they couldn't simply go around announcing what they'd learned. Everyone would rightly demand proof, and if they admitted where the information had come from, then the source would inevitably be discounted as unreliable. Not to mention overshadowed by the equally inevitable uproar over Wirr's actions.

"What about if Ishelle and I both See something?" suggested Erran.

"You mean 'See' something?" said Wirr wryly. "Already considered it. You haven't had a confirmed vision since the two of you   191 were officially recognized, and that was... what? Almost a year ago?" He shot Erran an apologetic look. "Even if you could fool Celise into announcing it—and you know her loyalty is to Administration more than to her position as Scribe, so there will be no convincing her to just go along with it—the Assembly doesn't have enough confidence in you to simply believe something that big. You would need to have established a record of being consistently right before throwing that at them."

Erran raised an eyebrow in vague surprise, and Wirr shrugged back, shifting his position so that he could observe the progress of a battle farther to the north. "If I've learned one thing over the past year, it's that the law is important, but hardly the same thing as what's right," he said grimly. "This is about saving lives. If I thought that you two cheating the system was the best option, I'd take the risk. I still might have been tempted, if Ishelle was more reliable," he added absently.

"She's reliable." Erran's voice was sharp; he immediately waved a hand apologetically. "I know what she was like the last time you saw her, but... she's fine, as long as she stays within the walls of the Tol."

Neither man talked for a few seconds, and then Wirr scrambled to his feet. "I need a better view," he said, quickly checking that the general's scouts hadn't returned.

He jogged along the edge of the cliff, keeping just inside the tree line to avoid the off chance of being spotted from below, until he found a suitable position. Erran trailed after him, not bothering to step outside of time, keeping pace easily enough. The Augur was there ostensibly as an observer, making certain that Wirr did nothing to abuse the 'official' Oathstone he currently held. Normally he would be accompanied by both a Gifted and an Administrator while in possession of it, but today's exercise called for a level of independence that Wirr had, with great reluctance, been granted.

They were soon settled down again, Wirr making more adjustments. He gave the commands confidently now, not pausing too long or second-guessing himself as he once had. Assessing the state of the fight was important, but swift, decisive orders were equally so.

Eventually, though, he fell silent, just watching.

"So how are we going to deal with it?" asked Erran softly, continuing their conversation from earlier.

Wirr didn't take his eyes from the field. "We've been through all the options, believe me. Fates, we even discussed using a combination of my Oathstone and Control to force enough people in power to do something. But the moment we do that, rather than just telling the truth, we're no better than Tol Shen—no matter our motivations." He shook his head. "Which leads us to the obvious option."

Erran frowned, then his eyes widened and he shook his head. "No. *No.* Out of the question. You tell the truth about how you found out, and you're handing the country to Tol Shen regardless of whether the attack happens this year." Erran's tone was firm, almost commanding. "You would be arrested—don't have any doubt about that; if you weren't, the entire committee would come off as a complete sham—and your family would lose all the political capital you've worked so hard for over the past year. There would be calls for your uncle to abdicate and let another of the Great Houses take the throne. This awfully loose alliance of Administration and Gifted would fall apart. The army's only advantage against the Blind, and Desriel, and fates knows whatever else is coming would be gone. The south would be—"

"You don't have to convince me. I get it." Wirr couldn't keep the bitterness from his tone. He'd reluctantly come to the same conclusion, albeit only after a long argument on the journey back. "Taeris said the same thing. It's not just me who pays in that scenario, it's the country."

"Precisely." Erran sounded bleakly confident in his affirmation. "Tol Shen might see as far as the old Augurs' visions allowed them to, but they still—*still*—don't understand or even really believe in the threat from the north. They think they see an opportunity to rule; they won't be able to resist tearing down anything in their path to that. They will consolidate themselves in the south, maybe even figure out a way to hold off Nesk and Desriel. But they won't be able to stop what's coming."

"Will we?" asked Wirr quietly.

"We're going to try. That's better than the alternative."

Wirr sighed, agreeing. These were discussions he had already had, though part of him constantly wanted to revisit them, to try and find some angle he had missed.

"One thing I would ask you to do—not that it's anywhere near as effective as I'd like, given how little time we have—is to start some rumors," he said. "You spent years monitoring the city for information; you know how news flows around here better than anyone. Maybe even use some light Control on the more influential people, to make sure they're convinced..."

Erran looked thoughtful. "It's probably a better plan than you think," he admitted. "The right people start talking about this, and most of the city will know within days. Rumors might be enough to get at least some to leave straight away, and I guarantee the rest will be packed and ready for an evacuation. Nobody's going to take chances after the Blind."

Wirr exhaled. That was good to hear. "I *am* going to run this by Uncle," he added, holding up a hand as Erran made to protest again. "Fates, Erran, I know. It will make him complicit if he doesn't turn me in. But there are no good options, and he is the *king*. If nothing else, he needs to know the danger to his people. For the following years, if not this one."

Erran grimaced, but eventually indicated his agreement. "He can better move things in the background so that the city's prepared for an evacuation—similar to what we did when we learned of the Blind. And he always was willing to listen to you." His tone held a nostalgic twang, gone again immediately but noticeable nonetheless. Erran looked at Wirr sheepishly. "Sorry."

Wirr glanced at the Augur but said nothing, a strange mix of discomfort and affection washing over him as he saw the oddly familiar expression on Erran's face, this one no doubt unbeknownst to the other man.

They hadn't spoken of Erran's relationship to Wirr's father at first—there had been the constant dangers of the road back to Ilin Illan, and then the chaos of their arrival to deal with. But Erran had all but admitted it back at the Boundary, when Geladra had accused him. And the time Wirr had spent with him on the road had only confirmed it.

Erran had been the one Controlling his father.

He'd wrestled with that knowledge for many long nights. Part of him had been angry with Erran—part of him was *still* angry, deep down.

Part of him knew that the Augur had saved his life a hundred times over, too.

Wirr turned his attention back to the forest below. It had been Erran who had come to him, in the end, one cold night a few months after their return, when things had finally started to settle down. He'd been quiet at first, moving through the words as though he'd rehearsed them over and over, explaining in careful terms why he had taken the actions he had.

Then he'd broken down in tears, as if the weight of everything he'd done, everything he'd been through, was finally hitting him.

They'd talked for hours that night, and many nights thereafter, ultimately reaching an uneasy agreement that had gradually become a genuine, if still sometimes equally uneasy, friendship. The more Wirr looked, the more he saw of the father he'd known in Erran—and not just in the young man's outward mannerisms but in his process, in the way he thought about things and saw the world.

It was a bittersweet relationship, one in which Wirr constantly found himself catching glimpses of his father—and then second-guessing whether it had ever been his father in the first place. Erran had assured him that Elocien had loved him, even as he'd admitted that the man's hatred of the Gifted sometimes overwhelmed everything else. And when Wirr had told him about Elocien's journal from twenty years ago, Erran had confirmed much of the information it held—the missing memories, and the abrupt, irrational hatred of the Gifted that followed.

Neither Elocien nor Erran had ever considered that one of the Augurs might have altered Elocien's mind to make him feel that way—there was no logical reason for him to think it would have happened, after all—but as soon as the possibility had been raised, Erran had started nodding. And once the young Augur had really thought about it, he'd conceded that he could recognize the signs, too.

"I think you're done."

Wirr started, shaken from his thoughts by Erran's voice. The

Augur was right; the sounds of battle below had faded, and from the confident stride of his white-clothed troops as they emerged onto the open, grassy plains that stretched out toward Fedris Idri, they had done well.

"I think you're right." He stood, stretching, then unhooked the Oathstone from around his neck and handed it to Erran. "All yours."

They made their way down the slope carefully, not bothering to conceal their presence now. A few of the white-clad soldiers spotted Wirr and threw him friendly, cheerful salutes. His squads were made up of mainly younger soldiers, and though plenty of them had grumbled against him at the beginning, their mounting victories were starting to thaw the ice.

The red-clad soldiers, on the other hand, either ignored him or cast black looks in his direction. They had been defeated before, but this was the first time Wirr's success had been so resounding.

Wirr shaded his eyes against the near-midday sun as they walked, finally spotting two men standing a little apart, arms crossed and engaged in a quiet but clearly intense debate.

"Don't have to guess what they're arguing about," murmured Erran. He gave Wirr a deep nod, a respectful gesture that meant a lot in front of the soldiers. "Highness. I'll speak with you later."

Wirr smiled slightly at him in dismissal, then squared his shoulders, marching over to where the older men were talking animatedly.

"General Vis. General Calder," said Wirr politely as he approached.

"Sire." General Vis—a lean man in his sixties, with steel in his hair and a soldier's hardness to his weathered face—gave him a deferential nod, casting a glance behind Wirr up to the area from which he had just come. "Congratulations are in order."

"Let's not go that far." General Calder's face, as far as Wirr had ever been able to tell, was permanently set in a scowl. He was younger than Vis by a decade, and clearly still kept up his training, muscles bulging beneath his neatly pressed uniform.

"His forces—significantly smaller though they were—defeated ours," said General Vis calmly. "He made good, dare I say even clever tactical decisions. Something I would not have thought possible six months ago," he added, with a small smile in Wirr's direction to show he meant no insult.

Wirr smiled back, conceding the last point without protest. Though he had studied some light military strategy before leaving for Caladel, it wasn't an area any of his teachers at the school had been able to cover. It was fair to say that his training with the army had gone...poorly, in the beginning.

Calder snorted. "Good decisions? He took an enormous risk, exposing himself like that," he said irritably.

"It paid off," observed Wirr, managing to keep his own irritation from his tone. Calder's reaction was far from a surprise; the man hated Wirr almost as much as the Administrators and Gifted did. Accustomed to it though he was, the attitude still grated.

"And if it hadn't, Sire?" The red-bearded general glared at Wirr. "If my men had captured you? They could have forced you to tell your whole army to surrender. Or at the least, walk themselves into a trap of our own making."

"Come now, General," said Vis, before Wirr could respond. "There are protocols upon protocols for such an event. Prince Torin could attempt to get rid of the Oathstone to avoid any of that, or simply issue an order containing the right passphrase to alert his men to his capture. He gambled—sometimes gambling is needed on the battlefield. Let us simply be pleased at his progress."

Calder growled under his breath. "We will still need to review your decisions later, Sire," he said to Wirr, waiting until Wirr indicated his acceptance before striding off to see to his troops.

"Thanks," said Wirr once the general was out of earshot.

Vis waved away Wirr's gratitude absently. "He's right, you know," he said quietly. "Contingencies are all well and good, but you didn't have any protection whatsoever. If you had been taken..."

"I know." Wirr was all too aware of the risks, of how dangerous he could be to Andarra's security if he was captured with an Oathstone and somehow turned. It was why his itinerary was kept such a tightly guarded secret, why the Oathstones were locked away in Tol Athian, and why, when one was released for any purpose, he was required to have the somewhat excessive protection of an Augur present.

The sha'teth attack had only served to reinforce that he was a target. It had been only a week after his return when the remaining two of the creatures had appeared, mere moments after he had used Essence. That he had been in the middle of Tol Athian—with most of the Council members in attendance, not to mention Erran and Ishelle—was likely the only reason he was not now either dead or a prisoner of the Venerate.

Even so, many Gifted had died, and Erran and Ishelle had both suffered injuries in the attack, too. It had been a sudden, violent maelstrom of blood and death, all within the space of a single minute. Wirr still had nightmares about it. Even with the sha'teth now imprisoned, he had heavily restricted himself from touching Essence ever since.

Vis clapped him on the back. "Still. You did well, Sire."

Wirr shook his head, the thrill of victory fading as he considered the practicality of his actions further. "Better than previously, anyway. I think I have a long way to go."

The general chuckled. "You put yourself at risk today because you needed information—information you should be able to get from others, if you have enough resources at your disposal. This isn't about turning you into some kind of military savant, Sire. This is about using these small-scale skirmishes to make sure that you understand the fundamentals. Supply lines, rules of engagement, how fast a group can move based on their size and armor and experience. It is about making sure that you can assess the likely outcome of a clash based on your troops, the enemy, the terrain—and assess it fast enough to maneuver accordingly, if we are not around to assist." He gave Wirr an encouraging nod. "You have a head for it now. General Calder is a sore loser, but that's what makes him right for the job—and it's why, for all his grumbling, he'll continue to support you in the Assembly. As will I."

Wirr breathed out, grateful for the reassurance. It hadn't taken the military long to recognize the potential of his ability; the advantages it provided was one of the main reasons he hadn't simply been pushed from most political circles. For all the discomfort his presence now caused, he was considered a vital weapon against Andarra's foes. A necessary evil.

It wasn't the most pleasant way to be regarded, but he supposed it was better than being ignored.

They began walking back toward the gathered troops, Wirr lost in thought.

"Why are we really here, General?" he asked eventually. When Vis looked askance at him, he continued, "I agree that these exercises are important, but I only got back to the city late last night. Organizing one at such short notice suggests...some urgency."

The general hesitated.

"We have had some more reports over the past week, Sire." His gray eyes met Wirr's. "I did think that speaking of them face-to-face might be more prudent than shuffling it in with all your other paperwork."

Wirr glowered despite himself; what Vis really meant was that he didn't want it to be so easy for Wirr to ignore again. Vis was the military authority with whom Wirr got along best; it had no doubt fallen to him to have this conversation. "Desriel?"

Vis nodded dourly. "Every sign points to the Gil'shar moving, massing their troops." He took a breath. "And though the reports are less certain, there's movement in Nesk, too, I'm afraid."

Wirr sighed, feeling as if he were being pulled in several directions at once. Desriel and Nesk were undoubtedly a concern, but they would both be coming from the south: from what Dras had said, it seemed unlikely that they would be responsible for the razing of Ilin Illan. "And you want me to recall everyone still in the north."

Vis scratched his chin. "As many as we can without leaving it completely undefended," he admitted. "Sire, I won't pretend to know what you went through up there, and fates know those creatures are horrific. But we have had our people scouring the countryside for *months*. It's possible they haven't killed them all, but if there are stragglers, we can always send men back." His eyes searched Wirr's, and Wirr could see the concern in them.

Wirr rubbed his forehead. Vis was a good man, a good general. He could hardly be blamed for not putting all his faith in what Wirr, Karaliene, Erran, and Ishelle had reported; he had to balance the security of the country—from a threat with which he was familiar—against their word. While the stakes had been lower, he and everyone else had been content to mollify Wirr and send men to roam the north, searching for the creatures that Wirr knew had broken through the Boundary a year ago.

Two months past, though, the reports had started coming in from Desriel—particularly concerning signs of an increased presence across the border from Talmiel, which was the only viable crossing between the two countries. That was several weeks' march from the north, and Andarra's army was currently scattered, a large number of units devoted to combing the countryside in search of the missing Banes. It would take time to inform them all of the change in plans, let alone gather them back into one place.

The southern Houses posed another problem. They had agreed to place their forces and resources at the king's command under certain circumstances, and Wirr had no doubt that this would be one of them. As much as it stung, the army would be stronger and better supplied if they went south and took care of more immediate threats. Even General Vis and his counterparts, who usually liked to eschew politics, knew how important such a step would be to bridging the current divide in Andarra.

Another ploy of Tol Shen's, no doubt. Abandoning the doomed north to strengthen the south.

Wirr gritted his teeth. "How reliable are the reports?"

"Quite." The general drew in a breath. "Sire, ever since the Blind invaded, the Gil'shar have been stronger than we are—even with the help of the Gifted—and they know it. If they did attack and broke through at Talmiel, it would be a foothold which they would not easily be made to give up."

Wirr chewed his lip. "What about Deilannis?"

Vis shook his head. "Even if it weren't as dangerous as you've previously said, their religion won't allow it." He crossed his arms. "As for the rumblings from Nesk—we both know that they've never been shy about their claim on the south, and we won't have much warning if they do try something. I'm sorry, Sire, but...I think there is consensus now. The troops need to be brought back."

Wirr grimaced. He couldn't blame Vis—couldn't blame anyone, really—but the thought still left him with a sick feeling in the pit of his stomach. The Banes that had breached the Boundary had gone *somewhere*, and knowing what he now did about Ilin Illan, he couldn't help but wonder if the missing creatures were going to be at least partly responsible for what had been Seen. "I'm surprised you haven't asked my uncle," he said eventually.

"We went to King Andras with this three days ago," Vis said candidly. "He insisted that we get your agreement before proceeding."

Wirr gave Kevran a mental nod of gratitude. His uncle had been one of the few to steadfastly support his claims, backing Wirr and Karaliene against the advice of almost everyone else. It hadn't worked—Karaliene, furiously frustrated at the Assembly's inability to see the danger, had volunteered to oversee the relief efforts in the north as a means of quietly conducting a search herself—but even so, Wirr couldn't begin to say how much that faith had meant to him.

He squeezed his eyes closed, letting the crisp morning air burn his lungs. He'd been considering this for a while anyway, though it made the decision no easier.

"All right."

He opened his eyes to find Vis looking at him with an expression of incredulity and cautiously optimistic relief. "Really?"

"Yes." Wirr's heart was heavy in his chest, but he knew there was no choice. He didn't believe the rest of the dar'gaithin and ele-tai had been eliminated, but Vis was right—there simply wasn't anywhere else to look. They needed to address the most pressing threats first.

"But I want the units stationed at Beredren and Tar Anan to remain, and regular reports from every other area coming in weekly," he continued. "If anything happens, I want as much warning as we can get. And...I want word spread that everyone in those regions should be ready to evacuate south. Quickly, if need be."

Vis frowned slightly at the last part, but didn't comment on it. "Done." His shoulders relaxed in evident relief. "It is the smart decision, Sire."

"I know." Wirr looked out over the sunlit plains. "I just hope it's the right one."

They talked for a little longer, and then Wirr spoke briefly to some of his troops—congratulating them, making sure any minor injuries they had sustained were healed, and generally seeing to their morale—before wandering back over to where Erran was waiting alongside their already-saddled horses.

"Where to now for you?" asked Erran as they mounted.

"My uncle first. Then mostly catching up on paperwork and meetings for a few days, I suspect." Wirr turned his face toward the sun, which was nearly at its zenith now. This was probably the last chance he'd get to be outdoors today. "And at some point, as soon as Taeris can make arrangements, Tol Athian," he added reluctantly, giving his steed's flank a nudge with his heel and rubbing the scar across his abdomen absently.

"He thinks it's time we had another chat with the sha'teth."

Chapter 13

Asha used Essence to dive, letting the armored tail of the dar'gaithin sail through the space where her head had just been as she funneled more energy into her legs, skidding across the courtyard.

She screwed up her face in frustration, ripping up a section of stone and slamming it into the Bane's chest, using the incredible force of the blow to fling the black-scaled creature high into the air. Even as she did so another three appeared to the side, and in the corner of her eye she could see the dozen or so tek'ryl still scuttling toward her from the trees. A shadow flickered over her face, and she knew there were eletai somewhere above, too.

She split her focus, sending a maze of hot, thin beams of blazing red into the air; there was screeching from above, and bodies began falling around her. She had moved on before the first one hit, tearing more stone and flinging it at the oncoming Banes.

"Are you sure this is necessary?" she shouted as she dodged to the side, barely avoiding several black spears as they skewered the ground where she had been standing.

The only answer she received was more motion at the tree line below, two new creatures appearing. They were different from any of the others, though just as horrifying to look at: humanoid figures with no eyes and gaping mouths filled with rows of long, thin teeth that glistened red. A new kind of Bane? They were more than a hundred feet away; besides, the eletai remaining above were closing in fast. She ignored them.

A moment later, a shadow loomed over her and pain burned through her arm.

She let out a yell, panicked to find another of the creatures she had spotted with its mouth firmly clamped to her shoulder, teeth somehow penetrating the Essence armor to reach her flesh. She funneled Essence to the point and let it burst outward, into the creature's head.

There was no resistance; it exploded in a shower of viscera, but Asha's relief was short-lived as a second of the creatures raked its claws down her back, again cutting through her armor. She screamed this time, twisting and unleashing a concentrated beam of Essence that sliced through the monster's torso.

She gasped, dancing to the side as she healed and her armor rapidly restored itself. Where had they come from? There was no sign of the two she had seen over in the trees, and yet they had been far too far away to have reached her so quickly.

She rapidly finished off the few remaining Banes, pain temporarily forgotten. She thought she understood why Elli had chosen this method to train her, now. Each attacker had strengths mirroring a kan user's ability: dar'gaithin couldn't be hurt using Essence, eletai attacks could cut through an Essence shield, and the tek'ryl were able to drain the Essence from those they stung. The last, Asha hadn't even realized when she had fought them in the real world, but there had been too many here to completely avoid being hit. The sapping effect had never come close to emptying her Reserve, but they were nonetheless enemies she couldn't ignore.

"Not entirely bad."

Asha turned, still panting, raising an eyebrow at Elli as the other woman strode into view through the smoke. "Not bad?" she repeated, a touch piqued, as she let her Essence armor dissipate.

"You *barely* beat them. With all the power of the Lyth at your disposal." Elli's tone indicated that she was less than impressed. "They're only Banes—yes, they mimic some Augur abilities, but aside from the dar'gaithin they're still not much more than animals. Don't think that a victory here means that you could take on one of the Venerate."

Asha acknowledged the statement, rubbing her shoulder. "What were those things, at the end?"

"Al'goriat. You will never face one, but..." Elli shrugged. "They are able to manipulate time."

"They actually hurt me," said Asha, her tone vaguely irritated.

The wound was gone now—her Essence healed her remarkably quickly, at least in this place. But her memory of the injury remained uncomfortably fresh.

"We learn from mistakes, not perfection." Elli eyed the torn cloth on her arm and shoulder. "Be glad that we're in the dok'en. In real life, that would have left a scar that no amount of Essence could fully heal."

Asha said nothing to that, continuing to rub absently at where the wound had been.

"So they account for the Venerate's time manipulation abilities," she said eventually. "What about Control?"

"You've kept the dok'en stable for an entire year—there's nothing wrong with your mental discipline. And Diara has already had the opportunity to try something, anyway. Be alert with your shielding, but I don't think you need to be overly concerned, compared to the defenses you've already built up."

Asha nodded. What Elli was saying rang true; though Asha's curiosity had led her to read up on the Augurs previously, she had spent much of the past few days learning as much about their abilities as she could. The library here was surprisingly full of information in that regard.

"For the most part, I think I can adjust to these attacks as I go," she said, mind already back on what she'd just faced, "but the time manipulation ability is...tricky. How do I counter it?"

"In a fight, the only counter to someone who can move faster than you is to be smarter than them. Anticipate. And to some extent, be lucky." Elli shook her head apologetically at Asha's grimace. "There is simply no easy way to nullify their advantage. All you can do is look for predictability and overconfidence. Or better yet, get in a good first strike that ends the battle before it starts."

Asha sighed again, accepting Elli's assessment.

"I would like to practice some more. Just against the al'goriat, for now."

Elli frowned. "You're sure you wish to push on?" she asked, clearly observing Asha's tiredness.

Asha waved away her concern. "Start me off with one. And a blade."

Elli made a face but nodded, stepping back.

A sword materialized on the ground, which Asha stooped to pick up.

A moment later one of the monsters appeared, standing not more than fifty feet away.

Asha let Essence flood through her, every muscle tensed, watching the disgusting, eyeless creature closely. Essence didn't just increase her strength: it stimulated every sense, made everything clearer and brighter and sharper. If she could just focus—

The al'goriat spotted her, and vanished.

Asha swung, hard and fast.

She hit fresh air, overbalancing as pain seared down her left side; the creature had swiped there with a razor-sharp claw, scoring a deep hit and drawing blood. Asha let out an involuntary cry and twisted, but the creature was already gone again; another pain scraped down her back and she groaned, stumbling and dropping the sword.

She rolled desperately, the pain of the motion agonizing, only to find that the al'goriat had been frozen in place by Elli.

She snatched up the sword again and scrambled to her feet, breathing easier as her injuries healed. "I'd like to try again."

Elli's mouth twisted, but she agreed, the al'goriat vanishing and materializing back where it had started.

Asha's pulse raced as she dropped into a ready stance, eyes locked on the creature. Watching its breathing, its movements, the way its muscles tensed when—

Needle-like teeth slicing into her left arm.

She resisted the searing pain and unleashed a burst of Essence, connecting with the creature's shoulder, though it was far too late. The monster ripped itself free, taking a chunk of flesh with it in a shower of crimson blood. Asha gasped and went to her knees, head swimming as Essence flooded to the wound. When she steadied herself, the creature had vanished once again.

"This is a fight you cannot win, Ashalia," said Elli to the side. Asha twisted to see the woman staring concernedly at her. "The ability to manipulate time simply has no counter. You would be better served looking for other options."

Asha waited, letting her breathing calm, then rose to her feet.

"Again."

There had been something, that time. A flicker to her left in the breath before the al'goriat had struck, something she would have dismissed at any other time as being her imagination.

"Ashalia—"

"*Again*," repeated Asha. She had read enough about this ability to know that what she wanted to do wasn't impossible. The sheer volume of Essence coursing through her meant that both her reactions and the speed of her strikes were far faster than any normal person—or, realistically, even any Gifted—could achieve. And there *was* a moment, a heartbeat, between the al'goriat disappearing and its landing a blow.

Stepping outside the flow of time meant that the creature had more time to react than anyone could hope to match, but it didn't make them immune to being hit. No different, presumably, from an Augur. An Augur might have kan prepared to absorb an Essence attack, too, but if Asha could wait until the last second, against an overconfident opponent...

She set her feet. The al'goriat was probably going to get in a lot more hits before she had any chance of success.

Still—pain, she could deal with.

She motioned for Elli to begin again.

Asha breathed deeply of the sweet air as she moved through the forest, enjoying the way the vibrant pink-purple light of dawn colored the surrounding foliage.

She paused briefly to examine a couple of the wards she had set along this path, giving a small, satisfied nod when she saw that they needed no strengthening today. This was her morning and evening ritual now, since Diara had shown herself: performing this check, occasionally reinforcing or tweaking the wards, but mostly just reassuring herself that they were still in place.

There were still three days until the Venerate's deadline, but Asha had no confidence that Diara would keep her word.

She eyed a particularly dangerous ward as she passed, considering. She had spent an entire day setting these up in a solid perimeter around the Crystalline Palace, where Diara should be entering the dok'en. They were threaded throughout the woods and—she thought—very difficult to avoid setting off. Kan could dismantle them, of course, but Asha had gone to great lengths to hide any traces of visible Essence. They were hardly the most sophisticated of traps, but with the power at Asha's disposal, it hopefully wouldn't matter. At best, they might hurt Diara. At worst, they should give Asha some measure of warning when the Venerate returned.

She rolled her shoulder absently as she walked, though there was nothing physically wrong with it. Still, the memory of teeth sinking into it—again, and again, and *again*—made her twitch uncomfortably.

Her training against the al'goriat the day before had not gone as well as she had hoped, though she knew it was foolish to want better results after only a few hours. She was, now that she'd experienced failure time after excruciating time, beginning to see patterns she thought she could use. The way the creature's muscles tensed usually indicated in which direction it was going. That meant she then knew roughly where to look for the slight, barely distinguishable blur against the horizon, sometimes backed up by suddenly indented dirt or spots of crushed grass along the creature's path.

It all gave her the briefest of warnings for the likely direction of the assault upon her, and thus a rough approximation of where was best to attack. The trick, currently, was training herself—her mind and her muscles—to respond in that single moment. To see and react without needing to think in between. To make adapting to the time manipulation a reflex.

She thought that, perhaps, she might be getting better. A little closer.

She still hadn't stopped the al'goriat a single time, though.

She sighed. Even if she did manage to win against one of the unsettling creatures, she knew that Diara would be an entirely more difficult opponent. Not because she was better at manipulating time—according to Elli, al'goriat were more adept at that than most of the Venerate—but because she was simply smarter than one of the Banes. If Asha didn't strike a maiming blow on the first attempt, it was doubtful she would get a second.

Her thoughts drifted as she meandered through the next copse of trees, absently adjusting one of her wards as she did so to better conceal its presence. What Diara had shown her of Davian's current situation was weighing on her almost as much as his impending death; she kept replaying the scene in her mind—brief though it had been—and wondering what they had been making him do for the past year. Hoping that he was still all right, praying desperately that the decision she had made not to cooperate wouldn't bring him to any harm.

Still, she did have that message from him, from what seemed like a lifetime ago. He was in Ilshan Gathdel Teth, but they couldn't kill him. They *couldn't kill him*. Until now, she had always assumed that it was an exaggeration, and that Davian had only said it to reassure her.

She understood now why it was true.

Asha was abruptly shaken from her introspection by a flash of yellow beyond the Crystalline Palace, refracted and distorted through the glittering lens, but too familiar to mistake.

Essence.

A distant, thundering roar reached her ears.

She stood paralyzed for a moment. Then she began sprinting for the palace, heart suddenly pounding loud in her ears, all thoughts of Davian forgotten.

One of her traps had been triggered.

Diara had returned early.

Chapter 14

Caeden woke.

For a few seconds he just lay there, confused, a deep ache in every part of his body. Something had happened. He'd been injured. Badly.

With an effort, he forced his eyes open.

Alkathronen was around him once again, warm and bright; he was lying by a heatstone, which was staving off the chill and had helped dry his snow-sodden clothes. He frowned around in bemusement as memory started to return. He'd fought Alaris. Fooled him into that leap, the only way he could think to get his friend through a Gate. Physically forcing him would have been impossible, given the other man's strength.

But Caeden had crashed to the rocks below. How had he gotten back here?

His heart lurched, and he tried to sit up. Had Alaris *not* gone through the Gate? Had he somehow, already, figured out a way back from the Wells? It was an irrational thought, but panic began welling up inside him nonetheless.

His effort to sit up failed, and he winced instead, lying back and taking a steadying breath. He was sore, weak—but a quick check of his limbs revealed that he was without serious injury. The eternity he'd spent splayed on that rocky outcropping began to come back to him, and he knew he'd shattered bones and crushed organs in the landing. There was no way he could have had enough Essence left to heal so quickly; that would have taken focus, time. And there had been that figure...

"So you are Tal'kamar."

Caeden flinched at the unfamiliar voice. He turned his head to see a man standing off to the side. He was perhaps forty, wiry and with a narrow face that seemed to emphasize the black veins that streaked prominently across it and beneath his beard.

"Who are you?" Caeden rasped, discovering his throat was as rough and sore as the rest of him.

The man studied him. "I am Scyner," he said, saying the name as if it should mean something.

"Who?"

Scyner glared, clearly irritated, though the expression faded almost immediately. "I am an Augur," he said calmly, "and the one who saved you."

"You didn't save me. I would have recovered eventually." Caeden remembered the agonizing haze of his injuries. "But thank you," he added begrudgingly. "You healed me?"

Scyner nodded. "I wasn't sure there was anything left *to* heal, to begin with," he admitted with a visible shudder. "I have never seen a still-living body so badly injured. I am by no means a squeamish man but...El's name, it was unpleasant."

"Imagine how it felt."

Scyner allowed himself a small smile at that. "Quite."

Caeden stared around at Alkathronen. "How did you get to me, and then get me back up here?" There was no easy path down from Alkathronen, of that he was certain. "Are you able to make Gates?"

Scyner produced two stones from his pocket, displaying them to Caeden. "Not exactly." he conceded.

"Where did you get those?" Caeden asked, trying to stop his muscles from tensing with suspicion.

Then he squinted. They were similar in size and color to the Travel Stones he and Taeris had used to transport themselves inside Tol Athian, what seemed like an age ago. But these were different. For one, each had a symbol inscribed upon it.

A circle surrounding a man, woman, and child.

"Nethgalla," said Caeden dourly, answering his own question. "Of course."

Scyner sniffed, his lack of denial confirmation enough. "I

tossed one down, then used the other to open a portal. I had to go outside the city, though—it didn't seem to work from in here. The one I threw down landed *much* farther away from you than I would have liked," he added with a vaguely accusatory glare. "It was quite a walk. I barely got us both back through before the portal shut."

Caeden tried unsuccessfully to shift to a more comfortable position. That was a useful Vessel to have. He would need to confiscate it from Scyner before he left.

"How did you find me in the first place?" His aches were easing as he continued to drain Essence from the city around him; he propped himself up on one elbow, focusing. "I assume that you were not just passing through Alkathronen by happenstance."

The corners of Scyner's mouth quirked upward. "No. I was looking for you. I've been looking for you for a while, actually, but this was the first time you were somewhere I've actually known how to get to."

Caeden's eyes narrowed. "But how did you know I was *here*?" he clarified.

"A Trace." Scyner showed no embarrassment at the statement. "Elliavia gave it to me, and told me to seek you out."

There was silence for a few seconds.

"And how, exactly, did Nethgalla get my Trace?" Caeden asked wearily. "She didn't have one before for this body, when she was searching for me. And she didn't have the opportunity to take one at the Wells. Or at Deilannis." He held Scyner's gaze. "You can call her by her true name now, too. Elliavia was my wife's name, and I will not have it used to refer to that monster."

Scyner's expression darkened.

"*Elliavia* didn't say how she got the Trace," he said, defiant. "It is the name she prefers, and you are in no position to be giving orders, Tal'kamar."

Caeden gave a tired sigh.

He stepped outside of time.

He was still weak, but his mind was clear enough to manipulate kan; everything around him slowed almost to a stop as he levered himself to his feet and limped over to stand in front of Scyner, waiting patiently.

To Caeden's perception it took the Augur a good ten seconds to react, his eyes inching wider as he realized that Caeden was gone, and then his movements abruptly became close to matching Caeden's speed again.

Caeden drew more Essence from the surrounding lines.

Scyner hadn't even thought to raise a Disruption shield, so Caeden simply infused his arm with the energy—he was demonstrating a point, not aiming to injure the man. He casually blocked a panicked strike from Scyner and then lashed out, grasping the Augur by his shirt and walking forward, slamming the man upward against the nearby wall so that his feet dangled off the ground.

He restrained a grimace as snow that had built up on the rooftop shook free at the impact. Scyner's face went white.

He *might* have done that a little harder than was strictly necessary.

"Careful, Tal'kamar," Scyner gasped weakly. "Someone else is in the city."

Caeden frowned. What he'd just done shouldn't have attracted any attention, but he was glad that Scyner had mentioned it before he had decided to use Essence externally.

"Thank you for saving me," he said calmly, his face only inches from Scyner's. He casually blocked another feeble attempt from Scyner to attack him with kan. "But do not imagine for a second that it means you are stronger than me. The time for games or to debate who is in charge here is well past. So you can follow my instructions and answer my questions, or leave." He released his hold on Scyner's shirt. "Your decision."

Scyner stumbled as he slid back down the wall, the veneer of control he'd exuded up to that point vanished. He'd thought he was capable of competing, Caeden realized with vaguely pitying amusement—thought that, perhaps given Caeden's weakened state, he would be able to hold his own in a fight.

He knew the truth, now, at least.

Scyner finally regained his footing, though he stared awkwardly to the side, face flushed.

"Who is here?" Caeden continued calmly. "How many of them
are there?"

"I don't know. I felt them using Essence…" Scyner waved his hand toward the center of the city. "Somewhere that way."

Caeden chewed his lip. "Activate my Trace," he said, suddenly uneasy. It was almost certainly long enough since he'd used Essence—neither strengthening nor healing himself should have given him away, as the energy remained in his body rather than his using it as a focal point—but he wanted to be sure.

Scyner obediently drew a small, polished marble sphere from his pocket, staring at it. He shook his head. "Nothing."

"Good. We should be safe enough here, then. It's a big city." Caeden released a breath he hadn't realized he was holding. "Now. Why were you sent to find me?"

"Nethgalla wanted to give you a message." Scyner's tone held only faint traces of resentment at having to use the name. "She has gone to Ilshan Gathdel Teth to find Licanius—to get it back for you. She will send word when…"

He trailed off as he watched Caeden rubbing his face and nodding wearily. "You *knew*?"

"Yes," said Caeden in vague apology. "Please, continue."

"How did you know?" demanded Scyner.

"Davian told me." Caeden waved away Scyner's expression. "It's a story for which I doubt we have the time."

He walked stiffly over to a low wall and sat heavily, drawing more Essence from the city as he did so.

"Sit down, Scyner," he said reluctantly, gesturing to the space beside him.

"Tell me everything you know."

Caeden largely let Scyner do the talking for the next hour, only occasionally prodding for more information as he caught up on events from the past year.

Much of the news from Ilin Illan he already knew. The massive political divisions. The Assembly's struggle to exert their power. Scyner's frustration when he spoke of Wirr in particular was clear, though given the lengths to which he and Nethgalla had gone to put the prince in his current position—and Wirr's subsequent refusal to use it to force Andarra completely under his command—the Augur's vexation was hardly surprising. Caeden was at least glad that Scyner's observations backed up his own impression that the young man had been handling himself well, even thriving, despite the circumstances.

He was relieved to hear that Karaliene was well, too. He'd already learned during one of his cautious sojourns from Mor Aruil that the princess was overseeing relief efforts in the north—it had been easy enough to find out, as the Assembly had taken to making her reports from there public. Trying, no doubt, to stoke sentiment against the constant political unrest that plagued the city.

That suited Caeden just fine; Scyner had heard the most recent report, and Karaliene apparently remained in good health. She was as safe as she could be, so long as Caeden didn't draw any more attention to her. He still worried for her, wished he could risk seeing her again—but for now, it was all he needed to know.

There were other things, however, about which Caeden had been entirely unaware. This was the first he had heard of Desriel's apparent preparations for war; that was almost certainly at the Venerate's prompting, though he had no idea why they had chosen this moment to urge the Gil'shar to action. And while the additional rumor of a potential Neskian assault was unlikely to be connected—the Venerate had never bothered to foster much influence that far south—it was still a concern. Andarra's military simply couldn't stretch that thin.

And then, eventually, there was the other piece of news. The one Scyner mentioned almost offhandedly and seemed about to move on from when Caeden held up a hand, bringing the conversation to a halt.

"What do you mean, the sha'teth were *captured*?" he asked.

Scyner hesitated. "It was months ago—though I only heard of it recently," he admitted. "My source is reliable, but the Tol are obviously very tight-lipped about it all. I haven't had the chance to verify whether it's true."

"It would be a strange rumor to start if there wasn't something to it," Caeden allowed grimly, "but it also doesn't make any sense. I broke Tol Athian's control over the creatures myself; there's no reason for them to have allowed themselves to be captured."

Scyner raised an eyebrow. "There are two Augurs there, now. It may not have been that simple."

Caeden's frown deepened. If the sha'teth truly were imprisoned, it changed everything. He had assumed, from the moment he'd escaped a year ago, that the Venerate would have assigned the sha'teth to tracking him down. Even with the Watcher dead and their base of operations beneath Tol Athian gone, they were still a serious threat. Every time he had been forced to use Essence over the past year, he had all but fled the scene immediately afterward as a precaution.

"Do you know what the sha'teth are?" he asked Scyner.

The Augur shrugged. "Creatures from the Darklands. Like Echoes, but with close to full control."

"Like Nethgalla," said Caeden quietly. "But...worse. Nethgalla, and even the Echoes, are denizens of the Darklands—they escaped from there, but they were not *born* there. The sha'teth are more like...*leaders* in the Darklands. There from the beginning. They are older than any of us, any of the Venerate—and when a sha'teth is made, they are *chosen* to cross into the waiting body."

Scyner cocked his head to the side. "How do you know this?"

Caeden's heart twisted as he forced himself to consider the question. The memory brought on by seeing Ordan's Sever had been one of those that his mind had shied away from, but not because of what he'd seen.

It was what had come after that he'd wanted to forget.

His return to Ilshan Tereth Kal, he and Alchesh together convincing Ordan to let them leave with the Sever in order for Caeden to help the struggling Darecians raise the ilshara. Ordan's locking of the Forge, ensuring that it could never again be used, but dooming himself in the process.

Alchesh's years-long battle with the being from the Darklands as it began seeping through his connections—learning from it, at first, seeing more and more of the future, every time closer to the edge but every time promising that he had it under control. Promising that he could find out more about Davian, constantly convincing Caeden to wait just a bit longer.

And then Caeden's blindness to the sha'teth finally wresting control. Alchesh's rapid descent into madness as the creature began giving him glimpses into the Darklands, until finally Caeden, realizing the truth too late, tried to use the Sever.

The way it had taken such pleasure in killing Caeden's friend while Caeden was forced to watch.

It had taken Caeden years to fully grasp why the sha'teth had destroyed the body it had managed to take, sending itself back to the Darklands in the process. Years until the group of young men and women in Andarra had started showing signs of being able to use kan, and Caeden had finally understood that Alchesh's connections to the Forge had been released upon his death. Each one breaking off, attaching to a new individual.

Making it even harder to close the Rift.

"I just do," he finally said coldly. "The point is that the sha'teth should never have been captured by the Andarrans, even with Augurs on their side. They are simply too smart and too careful."

Scyner's brow furrowed. "You sound afraid of them."

"I am." Caeden held Scyner's gaze. "These creatures have *knowledge*, Scyner—far beyond anything in this world. Whatever dangers their abilities pose, they pale in comparison to that. When I released them from the Gifted, I added stipulations of my own: specifically, that they were not to share knowledge beyond what was already known in the world. But that was years ago. The other Venerate have had plenty of time to realize my deception and try to undo it. And the weapons that those creatures know how to make could wipe us all out in a heartbeat." He gestured to the medallion around Scyner's neck. "Speaking of Vessels. How did you come to be in possession of that particular one?"

Scyner started, his hand moving to his neck on instinct and clasping the medallion protectively.

"This?" He gave an uncertain laugh. "It was a gift. From Elli...from Nethgalla."

"You know what it does?"

"I do." Scyner forced his hand away from the amulet again. "It is for the end. When all the others are dead."

Caeden nodded slowly. "It breaks your tie to the Forge," he said, his stomach churning as flashes of memory returned. "You will no longer be able to use kan, but...you will not need to die in order for us to close the rift."

"Exactly." Scyner shuffled his feet, looking suddenly nervous.

Caeden was silent, immediately feeling a surge of pity for the man as a few pieces fell into place. Scyner was working for Nethgalla because she had told him that he could be saved. Even if he had convinced himself that it was for other reasons, there was no doubting his core motivation now.

But Nethgalla intended to give Caeden the Sever; it was so obvious that Caeden almost wanted to laugh. She had only ever inserted herself into this conflict—violently manipulated the political and social landscape of an entire country, ruining the lives of thousands upon thousands of Andarrans—because while she wanted the rift closed just as badly as Caeden did, she was also desperate to stop him from killing himself. Because she knew his plan, and she was determined to force her alternative upon him.

She wouldn't care about the cost, either. She never had. That *thing* had come through from the Darklands into his wife's body, taken Elliavia's memory of him—her love for him—and twisted it into something dark and fixated. And in all the years since that had happened, her pursuit, her belief that eventually he would end up with her, had never fallen anything short of obsession.

That should have been obvious to Scyner, too, by now. But whether his blindness was born of desperation, or whether Nethgalla had truly persuaded him, it didn't matter. She would discard him as soon as he was no longer useful. That was simply her nature.

Caeden considered the amulet. If he took it from Scyner, then perhaps Davian could use it... but then, he would die soon after, unable to draw Essence from his surroundings. Not to mention that Caeden was fated to take his life anyway. There *were* others fighting for Andarra who could use this, though—who were almost certainly more deserving than this man, if he had been working for Nethgalla.

Still. If Caeden took it, he would be necessitating Scyner's death. He didn't like the man much from what he had seen thus far, but he wasn't sure he was quite at that point.

"Why haven't you used it yet?" he asked eventually.

Scyner shrugged, still looking tense. "There's no reason to until everyone else is dead. This way, I can still be of use." His eyes searched Caeden's. "You have remembered much, then."

"Almost everything." Caeden left it at that.

His memories *had* mostly returned, and yet...since he'd remembered killing Davian, the vivid ones—the ones he relived, rather than simply recalled—had been rare. In fact, the memory he'd just seen of Alchesh had been one of only three over the past year. Instead, everything leaked back in a slow haze, now. Sometimes he would simply have facts at his fingertips that he hadn't realized had returned until his mind needed to conjure them.

He knew why, too. His mind was shying away from the trauma, or potential trauma, of experiencing those things all over again. Of exposing him to the kind of man he had once been.

He still wasn't sure if that was a good thing.

A distant boom shattered the silence.

Both men froze, then darted behind a low wall, looking toward the source of the noise. The sound had come from deep in the city, somewhere within the great haze of darkness caused by Isiliar's broken Tributary. The noise echoed away into nothing, but there were no physical signs of anything untoward.

"What was that?" whispered Scyner.

Caeden shook his head, eyes still fixed on the darkness. "Not sure."

It couldn't be coincidence that someone was here: so far as he knew, nobody except Nethgalla had come to Alkathronen in the two millennia of Isiliar's imprisonment. The city was a marvel, to be sure, but at the end of the day it was just...a city. There were no hidden treasures to be found, no unique wonders from which to learn.

He frowned to himself. When Scyner had first mentioned the presence of others, Caeden had assumed that it was someone reacting to his fight with Alaris—that his Trace had activated and one of the Venerate had come to look for clues to his whereabouts. Not ideal, but not especially dangerous so long as he and Scyner did nothing to attract their attention.

This, though...this was something else. Whatever was going on, it didn't feel like a search.

"Are we safe here?" Scyner's tone was uncertain.

"As I said. It's a big city." Caeden kept his own concern from his voice. Even if whoever it was did wander in their direction, the Essence flowing through Alkathronen should mask their presence from all but the most wary of passersby. But if it did not—if, somehow, they were discovered by one of the Venerate—Caeden was in no condition for a serious fight. Or flight, for that matter. "But we shouldn't linger."

Scyner indicated his agreement. "So...you'll help Nethgalla?" he asked, sounding cautiously optimistic. "She only went to Ilshan Gathdel Teth for you, you know," he added, seeing the hesitation in Caeden's stance.

"She went there for her own purposes," Caeden corrected him firmly. "Nethgalla is as afraid of Shammaeloth reaching the rift as you or I, but not because she fears the end of the world. It is because she doesn't want to live in the Darklands again. She simply doesn't want her time in this place—this paradise, by comparison—to come to an end."

"It doesn't *matter* why she is doing it," Scyner pressed, somewhat nervously now. "Your goals are clearly aligned. She wants to help you retrieve Licanius, and that is your sole purpose right now." He eyed Caeden's tattered, bedraggled state. "Surely you need every ally you can get."

Caeden studied Scyner.

"The old saying is wrong, you know," he said eventually. "A common enemy does not a friendship make. You can only ever be as good as the people you are willing to fight beside. And even ignoring her past, I am only in need of her help because she altered my plan for her own ends—she killed Asar, destroyed countless lives in Andarra to introduce her binding Vessel and make use of the Siphon, and then thrust the responsibility of maintaining the ilshara upon the shoulders of an innocent girl." He held the man's gaze steadily. "So...no. Alliances made from convenience only ever weaken a cause. I won't refuse Licanius if she places it in my hand, but I am not going to join with her."

Scyner paled; he gaped at Caeden, for the first time looking completely lost.

Caeden gave him a tight smile, only partly sympathetic. "You thought that I would be more pliable. More uncertain. You thought I would have enormous holes in my memory—that I wouldn't entirely understand everything that's happening, or who was a friend and who an enemy. Whether I was doing what I'd planned to do, or whether I was making a mess of things." Caeden watched the Augur calmly. "I am clear now, Scyner—clearer than I have been in a very long time. I despise my past but I have to learn from it, not wallow in its misery. My confusion, my desperation, is not something that you or Nethgalla or *anyone* can take advantage of anymore."

Scyner sat heavily. "She said that you would save her," he muttered.

"I still might. I'm just not going to pretend that's my goal." Caeden leaned forward, lending his tone some urgency. "You want to help her? Make my job easier. I'm not going to work with her but the faster I get to Ilshan Gathdel Teth, the more likely she is to survive."

Scyner looked up again. "How?"

"Two things." Caeden drew in a breath. "The first is easy enough. Go to Ilin Illan, and talk to the sha'teth. Try to determine their purpose there. They delight in using Darecian, but they know and can use the common tongue if pressed." He held Scyner's gaze. "When you have extracted all that you can, kill them. I don't know why those fools in Tol Athian are keeping them alive, but make certain they are dead before you leave."

"Why me?"

"Because they might be bait for me," said Caeden simply. "The Venerate haven't attacked Ilin Illan directly yet—partly because they do not see Andarra as much of a threat, but I think also because they believe I'll eventually try to contact my friends there. Add to that the sha'teth's capture, and ... it is hard for me to stay away." He spoke honestly; if Scyner were not here, he wasn't sure that he could stop himself from trying to sneak into the Andarran capital. "I cannot ignore them, Scyner. And the others know it."

"So you're sending me into a trap."

"Which shouldn't matter, seeing as you're not the one for whom it's set," observed Caeden. He shrugged. "I didn't say that it would be safe. But at the very least it will save me time. It might even be the difference between me making it to Talan Gol or not."

Scyner's face twisted, but he nodded reluctantly. "Perhaps it will be an opportunity to finally convince Prince Torin to actually use the power he's been given," he observed through gritted teeth. "We always knew it was possible that he might abuse it, but this...*indecisiveness* was not something we ever anticipated."

"It's not indecisiveness. It's him being principled, and El knows that you and Nethgalla should both be grateful for it," said Caeden sharply. He'd often thought that, ever since he'd remembered that the Mark was in fact Nethgalla's symbol—the one he and the rest of the Venerate had bound her to use, all those years ago.

"Tell me," he continued. "I see the purpose in a lot of what she has done, regardless of how I feel about it. Killing the Augurs to stop the Boundary from weakening, then using the Siphon to quietly accumulate enough power to restore it, all makes sense—and she knew that Is and I were the only two Venerate still alive who knew about the Siphon, so she was fairly safe in doing so." He shook his head slowly. "But then the Tenets exposed her. They make sense, practically—it was the only way she could bring the law for creating Shadows into effect—but that symbol appearing on everyone's wrists immediately meant that we knew who was responsible. She had to go into hiding for fifteen years because of that. So why risk it?"

Scyner gave him a reproving look. "I thought that would be obvious, Tal'kamar," he said gently. "She knew that the Venerate had been suspicious of you for some time, even back then. It was so that no blame could be placed on you."

Caeden closed his eyes at that. It *did* make sense, from Nethgalla's twisted point of view. The Venerate knew of their past, would never have believed that Caeden and she were working together.

"And choosing Torin's father?" he pressed, eager to clarify some of the questions that had been lingering this past year. "I assume that there was some sort of an implied right of acceptance necessary for the mass binding to work?" Bindings always required some form of agreement between initiator and bound, but what constituted agreement was sometimes...murky. With the Northwarden given such far-reaching, officially recognized authority over the Gifted, Caeden's best guess was that Nethgalla's Vessel had taken advantage of that fact—allowing him to somehow accept *on behalf* of the Gifted.

"There was," Scyner admitted. "And still is, as far as I know. If Torin was stripped of his position, or even stopped believing that he had a right to it, then his ability may well not work anymore."

"But you foresaw that he would be Gifted? That he would get this ability?"

"Of course."

Caeden scowled. "She certainly took a risk with him, then. He could have turned out to be a monster."

"A monster might be what Andarra needs, right now," said Scyner darkly.

Caeden snorted, then considered.

"That's why you became a Shadow," he said suddenly, another piece falling into place.

Scyner shook his head. "No. It was earlier than that." The uneasy way he shifted showed Caeden that he had guessed right, though.

"But you knew what was coming with the Tenets—not that you would have wanted to restrict yourself to them originally anyway," allowed Caeden. "You knew that if you wanted to use Essence, you would be bound; if you were bound, you would ultimately be at the mercy of Wirr's decisions. But you're an Augur—you get your Essence externally anyway. For you, being a Shadow is simply a shield from the Tenets. And a shield from Torin's influence."

Scyner looked displeased. "Something like that." He squinted at Caeden. "As we're on the topic. I've always been curious as to why the Venerate were not affected. When we discovered the binding had extended to countries other than Andarra, Nethgalla had hoped it would affect Gassandrid and the others, too."

Tal shook his head.

"The Gifted in the Cyrarium were affected," he said quietly. "But not us. Bindings require access to the mind, so our unique connection to the Forge would have interfered, the same way it does when someone tries to Read or Control us. The only bindings that have ever worked on us are those we've been willing to accept."

Scyner looked dissatisfied, but waved his hand in reluctant acceptance. There was a short, thoughtful silence.

"So. You mentioned that there were two things you required?" the Augur said eventually.

Caeden grimaced.

"I need a memory of yours," he admitted, a little sheepishly. "I need to know where Asha's Tributary is."

"You don't know?" Scyner gave him a puzzled look. "Didn't you *create* it?"

Caeden coughed. "I did. And I know enough that I could get within a few days' walk of it. But I don't have much time, and my memories...well. Try and picture somewhere you went for only an hour or two, say, thirty years ago—in enough detail that you could reliably call it 'familiar,' which is what is needed to form a Gate. Even if it was somewhere important, somewhere you wanted to remember. That's what it's like to recall a place where you spent a couple of weeks two millennia ago."

Scyner held up his hands. "All right. No need to get defensive," he said, sounding dangerously close to amused. "You can have the memory. Nothing else, though."

"Agreed."

Scyner stood. "Why do you need to go there, anyway?"

"It's complicated." Caeden kept his stare level, and Scyner looked away, nodding.

Caeden inwardly breathed a sigh of relief. He would have explained his reasons if he'd had to, but he didn't think Scyner would have liked them much.

Scyner eventually indicated his readiness, and Caeden stepped forward, placing two fingers against the Augur's forehead. Physical contact wasn't necessary for this, but it did make it much easier.

The memory transfer took mere moments, Caeden reliving the events just as Scyner had. Even that small glimpse into the man's mind reassured Caeden that his decision not to trust Nethgalla, and by extension Scyner, had been the right one. He had felt... nothing, as Asha had allowed herself to be consumed by that terrible device. He'd known what it would do to her, and there had been not even a sliver of pity, or remorse, or wondering if there was somehow a better way. Scyner was focused, driven, and completely untouched by the plight of those he had no care for.

Just the kind of man Nethgalla would choose.

Scyner shivered as Caeden lifted his hand again, then stepped back, looking questioningly at him.

"That is enough," Caeden confirmed. The island to the east, cloaked in so many kan wards that not even he could have found it again without help. He could make a Gate straight there now.

All that was left was to see whether he could save Ashalia.

"You know how to return to Ilin Illan from here?" he asked Scyner.

"The Builders' portal," said Scyner. "Then back up through the Sanctuary and into Tol Athian. It's not too far."

"Good." Caeden stretched. "Before you go, I'll be needing those Travel Stones." He held out his hand expectantly.

Scyner glared, moving slightly away. "Why? Can't you just make a Gate to wherever you need to go, like Ell... like Nethgalla?"

"Gates take time. These are a tool that I can almost certainly use." He already had an idea of how he might be able to make use of them, in fact. "But even if they were not, this isn't a discussion."

Scyner's expression didn't change, and for a moment Caeden thought that he might try to refuse. Then the black-veined man reluctantly dipped into his pocket, pulling the two parts of the Vessel out and pressing them into Caeden's outstretched hand, his anger evident in the motion.

Caeden pocketed the stones, casting another wary glance toward the center of Alkathronen. "Time to get out of here."

"I have questions of my own," Scyner immediately protested, clearly displeased at the dismissal.

"And I will help you with those when we next meet, if there is time," said Caeden firmly. "There's not a high chance of our being discovered here—but should it happen, the danger would be immense. And I'm about to be out in a howling blizzard, using all of my concentration on making a Gate for the next couple of hours."

"I will hold you to that," Scyner growled. He made to start toward Alkathronen's entrance, then paused. "At least answer me one thing."

Caeden sighed. "What?"

"Licanius—can it truly not be destroyed?"

Caeden cocked his head to the side. "Gassandrid tried it, once. He cast it into the Molten Sea—a massive lake of lava, far to the north," he clarified for Scyner. "Andrael retrieved it within a day. So…no. It cannot be destroyed, and it cannot be hidden. Only protected." He shrugged. "If the Lyth had not been such a threat, I believe the others would have happily left it in their possession forever."

"They were a threat?"

"They were capable of opening a portal to anywhere—except through the ilshara—and they had Licanius," said Caeden impatiently. "Andrael's deal let them use it, too, as long as it was outside of Res Kartha. Not long after the ilshara went up, they took Gassandrid by surprise when he tried to leave Talan Gol. Almost killed him. Being away from the lava pits ended up costing the would-be assassin her life, but it sent a message—showed us just how big a risk leaving the north, even briefly, was going to be." He gestured. "And that is your question, plus another. Now go."

Scyner glared, but slipped away without another word.

Caeden waited a few minutes and then moved as well, gazing down the long street toward the ominous darkness of the city's center. No more sounds had emanated from that direction. He wasn't sure whether that was good or bad.

He hurried out to the city's entrance, marching through the long canyon of portals and then wrapping himself as warmly as possible before braving the softly falling snow beyond. It would take longer to make a Gate out here—a few hours, probably—but it was too risky to do it too close to Alkathronen. The kan construct itself wouldn't be detected, but the Essence it used when he activated it could well be.

Another distant, booming echo from the city made him flinch as he trudged upward, somehow audible even through the dampening field of snow that surrounded him. He resisted the urge to turn back, to go and find out what was going on. Even if it was something he'd want to stop, he was far too weak for a confrontation right now. He needed to stick to the plan.

It was time to talk to Asha.

Chapter 15

Caeden stepped through the Gate and onto the plateau.

He pulled in a lungful of fresh sea air, shaking the snow from himself and then shedding his heavy coat, immediately struck by the change in climate. Even though it was late night here, with the moon almost at its zenith, the atmosphere was oven-like in comparison to Alkathronen. He draped the damp coat on a nearby rock and gazed around.

The pavilion on the far side of the open space glowed a faint blue; it would have been a beacon for miles around, had the entire island on which this mountain sat not been perfectly veiled by a complex screen of kan. He'd been involved in the construction of that veil, not long after the Jha'vett had exploded in Deilannis. Before the island had even existed, in fact.

It had been a great work to raise the land from the ocean once the veil was in place, but the Venerate had mapped Andarra long before invading, and he and Andrael had needed somewhere entirely unknown. Its position, so close to the Boundary itself, had been risky—the Cyrarium it connected to was hidden hundreds of miles away in the Menaath Mountains, after all—but keeping it physically close had made for easier access. Especially when the other Venerate had started paying so much more attention to his movements after Deilannis.

He shook his head, the information somehow both familiar and new as he accessed it. *Cyrarium.* A massive store of Essence fed by multiple sources, used to power Vessels that needed to last through hundreds of years of constant use. Named in typically mock-arrogant fashion by Cyr, who had first come up with the idea. And the name had stuck, even after they'd discovered that the Builders had figured out how to construct something almost identical millennia earlier.

Cyr was in the south, now. In Nesk, inside another Tributary, hidden deep in the ice and snow where the Venerate would never think to look for him. Just as with Meldier's Tributary, the distance to the Cyrarium meant that a significant amount of the Essence he provided was lost along the way, but the effectiveness of his concealment more than made up for it.

Caeden would have to kill him, too, once he had Licanius back.

He sighed. Beyond the plateau's edges, he could see the gently rolling waves stretching out, highlighted by the strong, healthy light of the ilshara. It calmed him, seeing the barrier that way. There was something eminently comforting about the solid wall of light. He knew that this was how he and Andrael had designed it, the way it was meant to be.

It also, very briefly, made him reconsider what he was about to do. This wasn't like the other Tributaries. It was directly connected to the Cyrarium, and thus was also able to draw from the Cyrarium to power its defenses if need be. Even if the Venerate did manage to figure out where it was—a difficult task, despite their knowing what they were looking for now—they could throw armies against it without getting inside.

So long as he didn't inadvertently let them in, anyway.

He stared over the expanse and then closed his eyes, feeling the soft breeze against his face and the gentle silence of the night. These quiet moments were too rare, and went unappreciated too often. How long had it been since he had just stopped and breathed? The past year had been a blur of pressing forward, of learning and planning and obsessing over all the different things he could try, going through every potential strategy and how likely it was to succeed or fail. In all that time, it hadn't felt like he had once just ... paused.

But there were good reasons for that.

He squared his shoulders and walked over to the pavilion, gazing at the sealed entrance pensively.

A sliver of blue Essence-light tinged the edges of the stone entrance, which was sealed shut. He focused, examining the intricate web of kan that sat layered over the top, following the lines from endpoint to endpoint, studying their functions. He had been involved in the construction of the defenses, but it had largely been Andrael's job. That had been a deliberate choice. Harder to find a way around such security measures when the maker was dead.

He walked closer, though he hesitated as the strangely curved structure glowed red in warning at the motion. Pushing carefully past the loose outer mesh of hardened kan, he extended his senses and examined the series of endpoints clustered in a circular pattern over the door itself. Impossible to spot if you didn't know where to look, and difficult to see them all even if you did.

He gnawed his lip as he studied them. There were more than a hundred, all told. They looked identical to one another, the kan lines to which they were attached vanishing into a complex web beyond, impossible to follow.

It was familiar, though. Sparked another memory.

Caeden carefully funneled Essence into one endpoint, then another, and then another. There was no significance or pattern to which ones needed to be activated and which ones did not; he had not wanted to risk one of the other Venerate somehow guessing the combination. Points on the ring began to glow red, then yellow as more endpoints were activated, and finally changed to a deep-blue hue. It was odd, the things he remembered sometimes. He hadn't been able to bring to mind a mental image of this place, yet he remembered this sequence well enough.

He activated the final endpoint, and the stone door slid away with a rasping groan.

Caeden exhaled and entered, the interior lighting up as he took his first step inside.

He examined the mass of steel and glass and black stone in front of him with a mixture of horror and fascination. It had been a surprise to him, that first time they had tested it, when he'd realized that it had shaped itself into a jagged wolf's head. A funny thing, really. He'd tried so hard to avoid placing his signature on the Tributaries themselves, done everything he could to avoid fulfilling the oath he'd Bound himself to centuries earlier.

And then it had been completed, and it had slid into place, and *that* had stared back at him.

Andrael had laughed and laughed, though Caeden had been less than amused at the time.

He stared at it now, stomach churning. This was it. This was the device within which he'd intended to seal himself, the one in which he'd decided to spend his last days while he waited for Asar to kill the remaining Venerate, the Augurs, and then finally him.

He shivered. Even now, even with his memories all but intact and his understanding of the situation firm, he still found that hard to comprehend.

He peered through the small window and winced as he saw Asha. She could have been merely sleeping, were it not for the hundreds of needles piercing her. Caeden instinctively pushed through kan, checking her source. All was well, though. While Essence drained away at a steady rate, sucked downward through the kan mechanism and drawn off to the Cyrarium, there was more than enough remaining for Asha to survive.

She *was* asleep, though—which meant she was in the dok'en. That was a relief.

He swallowed as his thoughts drifted, briefly and unwillingly, to Isiliar.

He pushed the dark memory aside, turning and reactivating the outer Tributary defenses, nodding in satisfaction as the shell ground back into place. There was little reason to believe he would be disturbed, and having the pavilion open would not increase the chance of discovery—but there was no reason not to take the precaution.

He pulled in a breath, then walked around to the side of the Tributary, searching for the shelf upon which he knew the iron ring would rest. Rings were the best Vessels for most things: portable, wearable, distinctive when they needed to be. Their size disallowed using them for more complex purposes—even before he'd lost his memories, he'd been dumbfounded that Garadis and the Lyth had somehow managed to fit the entire machinery of a flexible Gate into a small bronze cube—but for something simple like entry into an existing dok'en, rings were perfect.

The small band of iron was there, just where it should be. He stared at it, considering. What would he find in there? Would

Asha have recovered from the trauma of the Shifts enough to have even stabilized a small section of the dok'en? That it could still be in a state of flux had occurred to him—such a scenario shouldn't stop him from entering, but it could make things more difficult. He needed to be prepared to act quickly either way; it was unlikely that Ashalia would have been able to steady the illusion much beyond a small space. At least while he was in there, he would be able to teach her. Show her how to expand the dok'en to its fullest potential and live more comfortably.

He took a deep breath, and slipped the ring on his finger. The Tributary and the inside of the pavilion immediately vanished; sunlit trees and grass snapped into view all around him, and—

Fire.

Caeden gave a panicked yell, instinctively enhancing his legs with Essence and leaping to the side as searing flame screamed down from some unseen source above; he landed and rolled, his clothes alight from the sheer heat. Pain flooded through him from scorched skin; he quickly forced his mind to calm and directed Essence to the injury.

Before the cracked skin had even smoothed there was a warning flash from the corner of his eye; he dove again, propelled forward by a massive blast of pure energy where he'd just been standing. He stepped outside of time and moved, watching almost dazedly as impossibly thick beams of Essence seared through the air, slicing dangerously close to his head despite his increased speed.

What was this? Where was all this Essence coming from? He hastily erected an ilshara and scanned the now-blazing forest for the source of the attacks, but there was nothing—no one, and no Vessels that he could see, either. Just...Essence, coiled and waiting to be unleashed.

How was that possible?

Another streak of white-hot energy crashed against his newly formed shield, and to his astonishment it actually *shivered.*

He scowled, shaking his head and closing his eyes. This was supposed to be *his* dok'en.

He focused.

When he opened his eyes again, the raging storm of power outside his ilshara had vanished, and the forest was calm once again.

Caeden glared down at his burned leg, which was not crippled but still ached terribly. This was a preconstructed space, deliberately cordoned off in his mind; he could reset it, but there were still limits to what he could do with his own body. He funneled Essence to the wound, breathing out as the pain seeped away and flesh knitted together once again.

His drumming heart finally slowing, he took the time to assess. The forest around him was calm, peaceful; the sun was yellow white in the east where it had just risen. Dappled light penetrated the foliage overhead, and a warm breeze caressed him, belying the violence of only a minute earlier.

He frowned as he recognized where he was. This was the edge of the dok'en, quite some distance from the palace itself.

The *very* edge of to where he had created it to extend.

He inhaled, still confused, and started walking.

Vague memory told him the correct path to take; soon enough he could see the sparkling of a water garden flashing through the trees. His brow furrowed as more memories flickered. He knew this place—of course he did—but on his seeing it, the familiarity became deeper, something in his bones. The fountains he could see weren't just fountains; they were masterworks of Essence and engineering both, the Water Garden of Om.

He took the final step to the base of the hill, and something changed in the air. Before he could move, impossibly thick strands of Essence wrapped themselves tightly around him, immobilizing him. He almost lashed out to cut them with kan, then held off when the young woman appeared from behind a fountain in front of him.

"Ashalia," he said, relief thick in his voice. "It's me. I am glad to see you."

"Tal'kamar," said Asha, and her voice as much as the name itself told Caeden that this was not going to be a warm welcome. "How do I know that this is really you?"

"Last I saw you, we were in Deilannis. You stabbed Nethgalla with Whisper, which transferred her Reserve to you—along with the Reserves of everyone connected to the Siphon. We left the city, and I made a Gate for you to return to Ilin Illan."

234   Asha didn't react. "And what did you tell me, just before I left?"

Caeden licked his lips, thinking back.

"That it was a risk, you going back there."

Asha waved her hand, and the thick, vine-like Essence unwrapped itself from Caeden's legs. Caeden watched it go with fascination. He could have dispelled the Essence, but there was simply so much of it that it wouldn't have been easy.

"So. Care to explain why I was nearly killed entering my own dok'en?" he asked, keeping his tone light.

"Wards. Against intruders."

"Wards without containing Vessels, though," Caeden observed slowly. "You would need to be replenishing them every couple of days. Everywhere. And those are complex. You would need..."

He trailed off as he watched Asha's face, then looked around again, reassessing the perfectly formed dok'en.

"Well," he said, sitting against the edge of a nearby fountain. "This is a pleasant surprise."

"I wish I could say the same." There was a cold light in Asha's eyes. In control though she appeared to be, this was not the Ashalia whom Caeden had met a little over a year earlier in Deilannis. She seemed more confident now, but much older than her seventeen years, too. Wearier. Harder.

And very clearly not pleased to see him.

"Why are you here?" she asked bluntly.

"I need your help."

"You need..." Asha trailed off with a humorless laugh. "Of course you do." She looked him in the eye. "The thing is, Tal'kamar, I'm not sure that I want anything to do with you."

Caeden flinched.

"Tal'kamar," he repeated, shaking his head. "That's not my name now."

Asha's lip curled. "How about Aarkein Devaed?"

Caeden swallowed. It wasn't a guess—she knew. He could tell from her stance, from the dead, icy certainty in her eyes.

Asha's voice built, emotion flooding her words. "I saw what you did, too. I know you killed..." She choked off, then took a steadying breath, her gaze full of resolve. "I know that you killed Davian. Or will kill him. So do not imagine that we are friends. I will listen to what you have to say—mostly because *I* 235 need *your* help. Diara has already been here, and she is intending to return soon." She paused to let that sink in, then continued, "But if you think that I'm going to help you simply because you ask, then you are sorely mistaken. Now—I am going to repair the damage you just did in removing my wards, before someone who wants both of us dead gets back in. I'll find you in the palace when I'm ready."

Caeden gaped at her, a flood of shame filling his gut. He wanted so badly to tell her that she was wrong. That hurting Davian was the last thing he wanted to do.

"Fair enough," he all but whispered.

Asha threw a hate-filled glare in his direction, then turned and walked stiffly away.

There was nothing but the burbling of fountains, and then, suddenly, movement to his right. Still reeling, he turned.

His breath caught in his throat.

"I've missed you, Tal," said Elliavia.

Chapter 16

Asha watched Caeden and Elli from the library window, their heads bent low as they spoke to one another.

Caeden suddenly leaned back and laughed at something Elli had said, a genuine sound. Asha sighed, putting down the book she'd unsuccessfully been trying to distract herself with, steeling herself. She had returned from repairing the wards—and strengthening them a touch, given Caeden's ability to survive them—to find the two in deep conversation. She'd felt an irritating spark of jealousy, though it only stood to reason that Elli would like the man. Still.

Caeden had seen Asha enter the palace but hadn't come to find her, hadn't approached her or tried to encroach upon her space in the hours since his arrival. At first, she'd thought it was because he wanted to spend time with Elli.

The occasional sidelong glances he cast toward the palace, though, said otherwise. The longer he went without pursuing her, the more she realized that he was giving her time. Giving her space to come to the right decision.

It irked her, but mostly because she knew that he was trying to do the right thing. She still hated him for what he'd done—what he *would* do—to Davian, still stewed over it, even setting aside the knowledge of who he truly was. Every time she saw his face, she felt a seething anger at his presence, a desire to go and physically attack him. As if that could somehow stop what had already happened.

He'd done it before he'd come to know Davian, before he'd 237 switched sides, before any of this. On some level, Asha understood that. Logically, now, he was on her side. He wanted to work with her toward their common goal.

Her helping him might somehow result in Davian going back, might speed the death of the one she loved.

Not helping him could do exactly the same.

She stood, exiting the library and reluctantly navigating her way to the front of the palace. Caeden looked up when he heard footsteps.

"Ashalia," he said when he saw her, scrambling to his feet and moving to meet her, out of Elli's earshot. He looked... awkward. Nervous.

Asha watched him, then glanced at Elli before looking back at him, her tone cold despite the decision she had reached. "Who is she?"

"My wife." Caeden's face twisted. "The memory of her, anyway."

"Oh." Asha paused, thrown. She shuffled her feet uncomfortably. "I like her."

"Me too," murmured Caeden. He turned and shot a smile at Elli, but there was a depth of grief to the expression that, just for a moment, made Asha's heart swell with sympathy.

Then Caeden swallowed and straightened, as if remembering the situation. "You and I need to talk." He glanced over at Elli again, raising his voice so that she could hear. "I'll... find you a little later?" There was a conflicted reluctance behind his words.

Elli agreed amiably, as Asha had known she would. "Of course." She moved gracefully to her feet, giving the two of them a cheerful smile before walking off.

Caeden watched her go. "I am still not sure if I am torturing myself, having her here. Whether her presence is just a reminder of what I've lost." He shook his head wistfully. "I see glimpses, sometimes, but..."

"She's not real," finished Asha quietly.

Caeden nodded heavily. "And the heart always knows."

Even so, his gaze lingered on the spot where Elli had just been.

"Tell me about Diara," Caeden said eventually.

Asha relayed what had happened as succinctly as she could.

There wasn't really that much to tell; when she was finished Caeden just gestured wearily to the seat that Elli had vacated. Asha took it, though she couldn't help but sit on the edge, wary of the man across from her. Caeden evidently spotted her tension because he gave her a tight, rueful smile.

"I cannot imagine what you must think of me," he admitted. "El knows even I despise my past, hate the things I've done. But I cannot change what has happened. I can never make things right, never balance the ledger in my favor. I can only try to do what I can to..." He gestured. "I can only do what I can, for as long as I can."

Asha watched him. The words seemed real, the contrition—the shame at what he'd done—seemed absolutely genuine.

And yet this was the man who had murdered Davian.

"How can I possibly trust you?" she asked softly.

Caeden considered the question. "Do you know what has to happen, if we are to defeat this enemy?" he asked. "Do you understand what we're fighting—*why* we're fighting?"

Asha frowned. "I suppose..." She shook her head. "I suppose in my head, it was always...*you*."

Caeden barked a humorless laugh. "Yes. Well. I think it's time we corrected that."

He spent the next hour summarizing the situation. How he had once believed that the force now contained within the Boundary was El Himself. How he had fought alongside the other Venerate—at first for causes that seemed good and just, but increasingly focused on ends rather than means, until he'd finally accepted the task of destroying Dareci in order to force the creation of Deilannis.

The creation of the device that had subsequently torn wide the rift between here and the Darklands, giving Shammaeloth a chance to escape time and bring the horror of the Darklands to this world.

Asha nodded along as he spoke, following the conversation without difficulty. Many of the books she'd read over the past year had actually touched on these subjects. Some had been drily analytical, others densely religious. There were differing arguments on the nature of the rift, and on the consequences of its being opened. But the impression she had gained was largely the same as what Caeden was now telling her.

Finally, though, Caeden faltered, looking hesitant.

"So the only way to close the rift is to eliminate anything of our world that can draw directly upon kan. To erase the existence of any unnatural link between here and the Darklands," he concluded awkwardly. "That doesn't include things like the Banes—they rely on their connection to survive, but they do not draw kan from there. And it doesn't include the sha'teth or the Ath, either; the rift sealing would cut them off from kan, but they originated from the Darklands and so their ability to use its power is... harmless, in this context, I suppose you would say. Unlike the Augurs and the Venerate," he finished significantly.

He waited to let the last part sink in, watching uncomfortably as Asha processed the information.

"So you're saying that Davian *had* to die?" she asked, tone hardening as simmering fury suddenly ignited again in her chest. "You're trying to suggest you did what you did because you *had to?*"

"No. *No.* Not at all," said Caeden. "But... it will be true for others." His gaze pleaded with her to understand. "I do not want to, and I know that this is a hard truth to bear. One of the hardest. But I didn't wish to keep it from you, either. Truth can be a burden, but secrets are poison."

Asha's stomach lurched as she thought about Erran and Fessi. "Then I will not help you," she said coldly. "I cannot. They're my friends."

"Even if they make the choice themselves, once the situation is explained?" Caeden held her gaze. "I know this will be difficult to hear, but... I believe now that that's what Davian did. It in no way lessens my guilt or responsibility, but... if you have seen that memory, then you know that he sacrificed himself. He knew that we needed to shut the rift, and he knew that his words would change me—make me confront what I'd become." He paused, looking as if he was willing her to understand. "When he does go back, he *knows the outcome,* Ashalia. I see that every time I relive the moment in my mind, now. He came through the time stream, willing to die, in order to seal the rift and set me on the right path.

To save the man who kills him. He believes—or will believe—in what we are doing enough to give his life for it."

He watched her, genuine passion and sorrow in his eyes, and left the rest unsaid.

Asha turned her gaze to the ground, brow furrowing as she struggled to hold back a wash of emotions. She wanted to be angry at the implication. She *was* angry; Caeden was using Davian's death, turning it around to try and *make* his argument.

And as much as it ripped her apart, he was also right.

"So if I cannot trust you, I should trust him," she completed, unable to keep the bitterness from her voice.

"At least enough to hear me out." Caeden's tone was cautious, restrained; he clearly knew that he was treading a thin line here. "I am not asking that you help me to kill anyone, Ashalia. I am asking that you help me get the most important weapon in this war out of Ilshan Gathdel Teth—and rescue Davian from Talan Gol in the process. And, once he is free, help me fight to stop him from going back until the very last moment," he added, the words a promise. "He is my friend, too."

Asha couldn't bring herself to look at Caeden, but she heard the earnestness in his voice all the same. "How?"

"The first step would be to get you out of this Tributary."

Asha shook her head, despite the vain hope that flickered in her chest at the words. "You know as well as anyone that if I leave, the Boundary collapses." And Davian had said not to come for him. That he was being used as bait. That was part of why she hadn't risen to Diara's taunts in the first place; Davian had to have guessed that they would use him to get to her.

Caeden gazed at her steadily. "What if it didn't?" He leaned forward. "What if I told you that there was a way for you to come with me, to leave the Tributary, but still power the ilshara?"

Asha stared at him blankly, refusing to acknowledge the quickened beating of her heart. "Are you saying there *is* a way?"

Caeden hesitated.

"I believe so," he said slowly. "I have remembered a lot, this past year. Asar and Andrael and Cyr and I all had ideas about how this could be done—believe me when I say that none of us wanted to build these monstrosities, and we searched hard for an alternative. None of us had the technical knowledge to implement the theories, though." He exhaled. "I think I know who might, now. But there is no point in me pursuing it if you are not willing to help." He spoke matter-of-factly, with no rancor in his tone. It wasn't a threat. He was simply stating the practicalities of the situation as he saw them.

Asha closed her eyes. She wanted to say yes—yes to helping Davian, and most of all yes to getting out of the Tributary. It seemed too good to be true.

Davian's words still rang in her ears . . . but had he known that this was an option?

"I am listening," she said eventually.

Caeden gave her a tight smile, clearly relieved.

"The existence of the Siphon is proof that what we are considering is technically possible," he began. "It's what originally gave us the idea, to be honest. But the Siphon was created by a Venerate called Wereth, who died before all of this happened. And its workings are very, very complex—not to mention controversial. Wereth regretted even creating it, so he never told us the specifics of how it was made." He nodded at Asha's disappointed expression. "Exactly."

"So how . . ."

"Wereth was one of the first to break from the Venerate, and he *did* pass on much of his knowledge to the Darecians," explained Caeden, his voice soft. This was a memory for him, not just a history lesson. "He was one of the main reasons that their Vessels, their understanding of kan, were so advanced. We even think he provided them with the foundational theory and Vessels that allowed non-Augurs to manipulate kan."

Asha considered. "You think the solution might be in the Great Library?"

"No. It isn't." Caeden drew a breath. "But I do think that the surviving Darecians might be able to figure it out."

He quickly, dispassionately explained the origins of the Lyth to her, not shying away from his culpability. Despite the vaguely detached manner in which he related the events, Asha could still feel shame radiating from him as he described what had happened

in Deilannis during the hours leading up to Davian's death.

"So there's only one problem," he finished quietly, evidently having said all he wished to say.

"They are unlikely to help you." Asha shook her head, still trying to comprehend what she'd just been told. If there was anyone in the world who had a right to hate Caeden, it would be the Lyth.

"That is ... understating things." Caeden gave her a wry smile. "But they want Shammaeloth to succeed as little as we do. They may still be willing to bargain. It is worth the attempt, I believe."

"Do you even know where they are?"

Caeden rubbed his forehead. "I could make a Gate to where I left them in the Shining Lands, after I bound them with the Siphon. It's possible that they will detect it and find me," he conceded. "It is also possible that they will detect it and *hide* from me. Or that they have traveled far enough that they won't even be aware of my presence there. I doubt that Garadis will have liked the thought of my having easy access to what remains of his people."

"Aren't they all Shadows?" asked Asha, a little confused.

Caeden snorted. "They are Darecians. They didn't ask me to return them to their homeland simply for nostalgia—there had to be a reason why they agreed so easily to the deal which bound them. I wish I'd been more suspicious at the time," he admitted. "We never found the Vessels that allowed them to manipulate kan, so I don't doubt that some still remain. They will not be powerless for long."

"So what are you going to do?"

"I *was* going to simply try and approach them anyway. But now ... I'm hoping that you might be able to help. You are connected to them, after all." Caeden held her gaze. "The Siphon uses a light element of Control when tapping someone else's Reserve. A way of forcing the body to allow its energy to be taken. I think that you may be able to use that mental connection to send the Lyth a message."

Asha frowned. "Why would that be better?"

"To begin with? Garadis wouldn't view it as me making myself free to visit his new home," said Caeden drily. "It may save weeks of searching that we cannot afford. And he is far more likely to listen if contact is initiated by you." He gestured. "We lose nothing by trying, anyway."

Asha rubbed her forehead. "So how am I supposed to communicate with them, then?"

"I can help with that. To start with, I can show you what Garadis looks like—his precise Essence signature," said Caeden confidently. "It's not something one of the Lyth can really hide. It should help you find him amongst all the Reserves you're connected to, isolate him. We can go from there."

Asha nodded uncertainly, though part of her couldn't help but feel a thrill of unexpected excitement.

For the first time in a long time, she had the tiniest sliver of hope.

Asha ate silently, occasionally glancing across the table at Caeden, who was doing the same.

She had prepared the food herself tonight; Caeden had not asked for Elliavia's presence and despite the seething anger Asha still felt toward him, she couldn't bring herself to torment him by summoning her to the meal.

She stretched. She had spent the majority of the day memorizing Garadis's Essence signature, as well as reading up on the Lyth and being drilled by Caeden on how she might reach them. Even so, her first attempts at a message—or even at locating Garadis's Essence among all the other Reserves—had resulted in failure.

"So what exactly *is* this place, to you?" she asked, gesturing around. She was accustomed to having Elliavia to talk to, and the lack of conversation was becoming unnerving. "I know dok'ens are supposed to be representations of real places, and Diara recognized it. Elli calls it the Crystalline Palace, and she seems to know her way around, but she's never wanted to share anything about it."

"She didn't open up to you because, ultimately, she is still an extension of me." Caeden gazed out the window. "I am...protective of the things I love, I suppose. And these memories are by far my most precious."

There was a silence, and Asha began to wonder if Caeden was just going to leave it at that.

244   "This was the only place I ever felt at home," he continued

abruptly, shifting in his chair. "The Crystalline Palace is its correct name. There were actually two of them, but everyone knew that if you referred to just one, it was always this one." He glanced across at her finally. "I met her here."

"Elli?"

Caeden nodded. "I wasn't much, growing up. An orphan," he added with a small shrug. "But in my homeland, orphans were looked after with a care that I have never seen elsewhere. The ruling family—Elliavia's parents—took in any child who did not have a living relative. They trained them, fed them, nurtured them. An orphan's upbringing in my homeland was something of which people were genuinely jealous. It opened doors, made a success of many."

"Sounds nice," murmured Asha. Her own parents had been merchants, always focused on work and never kind to her; as soon as her Mark had appeared, they had dropped her at the school at Caladel and ridden away without even a backward glance. She'd learned not to spare them too much thought, over the years.

"It was." Caeden licked his lips. "This section of the palace, though—the library, the water garden out there—was Ell's private residence. I was an adventurous child; we could always hear the fountains from behind the wall, but—"

"The wall?" interjected Asha.

"I didn't include it in the dok'en," said Caeden quietly. He regathered his thoughts. "We heard the water, heard tales of it, but we were never able to see it. I wanted to, though. Fates, but I wanted to so badly. I couldn't even tell you why," he said with a soft laugh. "So one day, when I was fifteen, I snuck in. It was no mean feat—the guards were some of the best trained in the world—but a young boy's determination is a marvelous thing, sometimes."

"Did you get caught?"

Caeden raised an eyebrow. "Caught? Not exactly. I came upon Elliavia—she was fourteen—while she was bathing in the fountains. Not naked, understand, but in an...inappropriate enough state of dress that I lingered longer than was strictly necessary."

Asha hid a smile. "I see."

"I got out that day, but I'd figured out the way in," he continued. 245

"I could have told my friends about it. Part of me wanted to brag, in that idiotic way that teenaged boys do. But I didn't. I didn't, mostly because I knew that once the secret was out, someone would talk. And once those in charge found out, I would never be able to get back in. Never be able to see her again."

"You were that smitten?"

Caeden chuckled. "I was that lustful, at least." He shook his head. "But yes. There was something about her that I couldn't shake."

"So how did you actually meet her?"

Caeden looked caught between a laugh and an embarrassed smirk. "The third time I snuck in, she turned to the bushes where I was hiding and asked me if I was ever going to show my face. It turned out that she'd known I was there from the first. It was the most humiliating, terrifying, wonderful moment." His face glowed with the recollection.

"But Elliavia didn't turn me in—she just wanted to talk. She had no friends to speak of, no one that she especially trusted or liked. And her parents were...strict, in terms of who they let her spend time with."

Asha let Caeden talk now; she somehow doubted she could stop him even if she wanted to. He was lost in the memory.

"It was almost a year before High Councillor Deshrel realized that we'd been seeing each other," Caeden continued, a smile on his lips. "He caught us...there." He pointed out a window to a twirling fountain that was lit crimson in the dying light. "He was angry, of course, but ultimately he came to see that we were truly friends. In fact, at the time, that was all it was. I was infatuated, but Ell..." He sighed. "I wasn't sure of her reaction up until the moment I told her that I wanted to court her. And then even after the courting, even after all that time, it was hard to convince myself that she would say yes. There were so many others who were interested. Stronger men, more powerful men. But in the end, she said that didn't matter. She said it didn't matter because I was the *better* man."

He fell silent, and Asha saw his eyes were glistening.

They stayed like that for a while, not speaking, just gazing out at the beauty of the grounds. Eventually, though, Caeden stirred. Sucked in a breath. Forced a smile at Asha.

"Thank you," he said softly.

"For what?"

"For letting me relive that." His voice was quieter now, but stronger, too. There was something different about him. As if the storm that had been raging at his center had calmed, or at least quieted for a time. "It's been a long time since I've had a memory that good. That...pure."

Asha inclined her head, then hesitated. "You know she can join us for the meal, if you would like."

"No." Caeden smiled again, though there was pain in it. "She was here because I intended this to be the last place I ever was. She was here so that I could pretend, one last time." He swallowed. "Pretending is not a luxury that I can afford anymore."

There was silence, and then Caeden shifted.

"I have to leave soon," he announced.

Asha's heart skipped a beat. "Already?" she said uneasily. "What about Diara?"

"I will be back before she returns," Caeden said confidently. "But this deal she's offered you, along with some of the other things I've learned recently...it bothers me. I don't think I can waste any time before trying to find out what's going on." He smiled reassuringly at her. "I *will* be back."

Asha bit her lip worriedly, but nodded.

"Do you even need to return to the Tributary?" she asked suddenly. "If this is your dok'en, aren't you already connected to it?"

"This is a...more complicated version. A more detailed simulation. It's not just in my head—my unconscious mind is providing the handling of the rules, I suppose you'd say, but many of the specifics are actually stored within the Vessel itself." He saw her mildly confused look. "The library, for example. Those books you've been reading aren't full of information I necessarily know—some of it will be Andrael's, and other parts will have been contributed by Cyr. Probably many parts," Caeden admitted, somewhat drily. He shook his head, as if realizing he was digressing. "Regardless. The point being, my mind is providing the foundation, but not the building itself. Which means I need the key to access it just like everyone else."

Asha frowned. "Then how did Diara get in?"

"If I had to guess? She modified the keys from Isiliar's Tributary with some of the Essence that she took from me while I was their prisoner." Caeden scowled. "I was supposed to be the one in here, so in my original plan that wouldn't have been possible. It still must have been incredibly difficult—she had to have been working on it since the moment they found Isiliar—but..." He shrugged tiredly. "I miscalculated."

Asha let that pass without comment. "Where will you go for information?" she asked instead.

"I may have to go and talk to the sha'teth, though it's a risk," Caeden admitted. "Alaris would be my best source of information, but I have no way of forcing him to tell me."

Asha paused at that, and Caeden looked queryingly at her.

She wavered, still reluctant to trust him. Deep down, though, she knew that he was on her side.

She quickly explained about Knowing, Caeden's eyes widening as she described the blade.

"You're right," he said thoughtfully after she had finished. "Isiliar used it on me, and she discovered...everything. All my plans. It's why I had to put her in a Tributary in the first place." He grimaced. "That, and she knew how the Siphon worked. The plan was to use Knowing on her when I arrived, figure out how to use the Siphon, and then move on."

"So it should work on Alaris, too," said Asha.

"I believe it would—Andrael made those blades specifically with the Venerate in mind. I don't think it could kill him, but it should at least cut him." Caeden drew in a breath. "Thank you. I should go and get it as soon as we've made contact with the Lyth." He finished the last mouthful of his meal and wiped his mouth neatly with a napkin. "I think we're close, by the way."

Asha pushed back her plate, too.

"Then let's get to it," she said softly.

Chapter 17

Davian heaved at the torch-lit slab of broken stone, he and Raeleth giving a final half grunt, half shout of effort as together they lifted it and shoved it aside.

The thick stone crashed to the floor in a shower of grit, revealing splintered wood beneath where it had been. The remains of a desk. Wordlessly, Davian and Raeleth started pulling bits away, swiftly and efficiently looking for the precious metal they knew it would contain. Nails to hold everything together. Ornamentation of some description, too, if they were lucky. One such desk they'd found had filled almost a third of the sturdy pail they carried around, though that had been a spectacularly rare find.

He pried each piece he spotted free and tossed it into the bucket, the rattling sound a small but welcome reminder that they were one step closer to reaching quota. He allowed a small trickle of Essence to ease the ache in his muscles as he worked, though he was trying to use what was left in his Reserve as little as possible. This was harder work than he'd expected, the pace of it constant and tense and demanding, each day—they all thought of the time between bells as daytime, despite the unchanging red-and-black sky—a struggle to find enough metal for the four of them. He'd built up muscle during his stay in Tel'Tarthen, but he still didn't have the stamina for the hours of intense work that were required here.

He couldn't afford to show that. Not when he was supposed to have been here for more than three months already, rather than just a week.

He wiped sweat from his brow despite the chill of the air, glancing over at Ched and Ana, the other members of the team. They were working in the next room, focused on the process of tearing off an inner door to get at the hinges. Despite the hours they'd all spent together, the two were largely still strangers to Davian.

"Has he said anything, lately?" he panted to Raeleth in a low voice, eyeing Ched's hulking figure. The man had a ruddy complexion that was exacerbated by both torchlight and moon, stood a head taller than Davian, and was seemingly built entirely of muscle.

"No. By El's grace, I think he's let it go." Raeleth was breathing heavily but spoke quietly, too, not looking up from what he was doing. "He's more suspicious of the other teams than you, now."

Davian cast another discomfited glance over at Ched. His first week with the team had shown him just how little information he was going to get from them. Meaningful conversation during the day was impossible, beyond the necessities: every ounce of energy and focus was channeled toward making sure that no metal was missed, and, more importantly, toward avoiding the many dangers that lurked within the city. By the time evening came and they returned to camp, everyone seemed intent on eating quickly and sleeping as much as possible in order to prepare themselves for the next day.

Given that, Davian had decided to use some of his first evenings with the group to investigate the immediate area. He'd used precious Essence to banish the need for sleep, trying to familiarize himself with the layout of the city, hoping to stumble across some information about exactly where they were or what was going on here. He had always waited until the rest of the group were slumbering, of course—which happened rapidly after the evening meal was done—but three nights ago, something had disturbed Ched, and the large man had woken to realize that Davian was gone.

Ched had never been friendly, but things had been...tense, after that. Davian had stuck to his story that he had been out walking nearby because he couldn't sleep, but it was a thin excuse and everyone knew it.

Even so, Davian nodded, taking Raeleth at his word that no more questions had been asked. He had quickly grown to like the wiry, curly-haired man, even if their chances to talk freely had been limited to moments like this.

He kept working despite his entire body protesting, searching the jagged shadows for anything that glinted. They would need to start heading back soon.

They pushed on mutely for another ten minutes before the bell echoed across the city and a call from Ched—who was nominally in charge of the group—sounded out. Davian released an audible sigh, allowing his arms to drop, breathing hard. Raeleth followed suit, all but collapsing into a sitting position, snatching up his water skin and taking deep gulps. Sweat ran down the other man's face in rivulets, streaking through the grime that always accumulated as they worked in the thick dust of the ruins. Davian staggered a little as he searched for his own water, then took a long swig before allowing himself to slide down next to Raeleth.

There was dead silence for a minute as everyone focused on catching their breath.

"You all right?"

Davian turned to find Ana watching Raeleth, who was slumped against the wall, still breathing hard. The only woman in their crew of four, Ana was shorter than Davian, but her build was as solid as any warrior's he had seen. Surviving three months of this work would of necessity do that, he supposed.

Davian's gaze switched to Raeleth, and he saw why Ana was asking. The wiry man was dripping sweat and looked pale, even in the torchlight.

"Fine," snorted Raeleth, waving his hand dismissively and producing what was clearly meant to be a smile, though it came out as more of a grimace. "Slept badly last night, is all. Not a lot of energy today."

Ana accepted the explanation, though her green eyes remained thoughtful.

"You going to be able to haul?" Ched's expression was severe, though Davian had come to realize that the look was close to a permanent thing. He indicated the pail. "We need to get this to Isstharis before last bell. I'm not going to risk having this much uncredited overnight." His gaze flicked at the last to Davian, who just barely managed to keep his expression neutral.

251

Raeleth hesitated, and Davian saw the answer in his eyes. "I'll manage," he said eventually, his back straightening with resolve. Raeleth was their assigned hauler: the one both trusted and burdened with regularly running their pails of metal to the dar'gaithin and receiving their rations in return.

Davian frowned. Raeleth *did* look weaker than even today's exertion would account for.

The other man saw his expression, glaring at him briefly before struggling to his feet and stalking over to the pail, which was almost full—a good haul, two days' worth of rations at least. The reinforced buckets used by the scavenging teams were large, heavy and awkward when full; Raeleth took a deep breath and grasped the handle, pulling upward.

He didn't make it two steps before the pail dropped back to the ground with a rattling sound, tipping precariously before settling on its base again. Raeleth glanced at the others, red faced.

"Seems I'm more tired than I thought," he admitted sheepishly.

"We didn't take you in so that you could rest," rumbled Ched. The big man glared in exasperation, but it was clear to anyone with eyes that Raeleth was physically incapable of doing what was needed. "Very well. Shadat, you take it. Just make sure the snake knows who to credit."

Shadat was the name Davian had chosen to go by, given that his real name was widely known. His heart dropped, and he glanced at Raeleth, who was already shaking his head.

"You or Ana should go. Isstharis doesn't know him yet, and..." Raeleth gestured. "I thought it might be a bit soon," he finished meaningfully.

"All the more reason to send him. Last thing we need is the snake sniffing around because she thinks we're hiding something from her." Ched turned to Davian, and his green eyes were hard. "We're not hiding anything, are we, Shadat?"

Davian snorted, doing his best to cover over his nervousness. Raeleth was right; particularly given how suspicious the other two were of him, it was strange that he was now being entrusted with an entire day's worth of metal. If he had really wanted to try and steal something, this would likely be the perfect time.

"It's fine," he said, trying to pass off his concern as irritation. "I love the idea of finishing the day by carting a bucket full of metal up and down stairs for another half hour."

Ana chuckled, and Ched made a sound that might or might not have been an acknowledgment before turning away. The big, balding man with the thick black beard might have given up on asking around about Davian, as Raeleth had said, but he was still clearly intent on testing him.

As the other two moved to collect their tools, Davian edged closer to Raeleth.

"Is this going to be a problem?" he murmured. Raeleth had previously acknowledged that Davian might have to interact with Isstharis, but their limited time together had been focused on other things, both of them mistakenly assuming that this wouldn't happen so soon.

"Probably not," Raeleth replied softly, shuffling closer. "It's a simple exchange. Isstharis will have heard what you look like, but that doesn't mean she'll recognize you—the description of you they circulated was more for the humans than the snakes. They seem to have trouble recognizing people they've met before, let alone identifying them by specific features. Isstharis didn't even start to recognize me until two months in."

Davian grunted. "Well. No way to get out of it now, I suppose," he said, casting a glance back at the other two. There was no point in risking a scene over this. Life here was about survival, not loyalty—and he had no illusions that if Ched or Ana realized he was hiding something from the dar'gaithin, they would hesitate for even a second before looking to improve their circumstances. "Anything I need to know?"

Raeleth thought for a moment.

"It's the end of the day and early in the week, so you might run into Maresh." He winced at Davian's querying look. "Ah. Of course. You wouldn't have had the pleasure. Maresh and his team are..." He paused as if trying to think of a polite way to put it, then shrugged. "Well, they're the extortionists of our little corner of the city. They don't do any scavenging themselves, but instead wait around near Isstharis—often between second and last bell, when everyone's carting the last of what they've found—and demand a share of yours before you hand it over. Once they've

253

collected enough to get rations for a while, they turn it in and keep to themselves until they need more."

Davian felt his expression darken. "And everyone lets them get away with that?"

"They're bigger than everyone else—even Ched—and perfectly willing to employ violence." Raeleth said the words with a small shrug. "A few people resisted early on, and those ended up with broken bones. Which meant that they could barely work. Which meant that they ended up not meeting quota. Some of us tried to slip them food, but Isstharis takes note when a team doesn't deliver; in the end, they got carted away by the al'goriat. After that..." He sighed. "Not being able to gather in large groups means that we can't organize to take Maresh down. And Isstharis knows, but she doesn't care as long as she's getting her metal. I think she actually finds it useful. Someone to redirect everyone's anger away from her."

Davian scowled, and Raeleth placed a hand on his shoulder, expression serious. "I don't like it either, but I'm sure you've realized by now that we need to pick our battles here. Even if you thought you could beat them somehow, it's not worth the attention it would bring."

His hand slid from Davian's shoulder and he stumbled, steadying himself against the closest wall. Davian quickly forgot his anger as he examined Raeleth again.

"You really don't look great," he observed.

Raeleth glanced around. The other two had disappeared from view, already heading back to the hollowed-out building in which the four of them slept.

"I...I might need your help," he admitted.

He pulled up his shirt.

Davian recoiled at the sight of the glistening black mass, roughly the size of a man's hand, rippling over Raeleth's heart.

"Fates," he muttered. "Again? When?"

He had seen Dark around the city several times over the past week, though he hadn't thought Raeleth or anyone from their team had gotten close to it. It was deceptively hard to spot in the stark, dead shadows cast by the red moon; sometimes it would

form in a pool on the ground, but just as often it would drip silently from the roof, coagulating on the stone overhead and then gradually allowing gravity to suck it back down. Twice, Raeleth had held Davian back from walking directly beneath such a hazard. Davian was finding himself significantly more wary of his surroundings now.

"It's not new," said Raeleth, his tone vaguely apologetic. "I noticed it starting to form again a couple of days ago, but I... I don't know. I was hoping it was going to go away, I suppose. Wasn't going to mention it, but..." He gingerly lowered his shirt. "I might need to impose on you again after all."

Davian tried not to show his dismay. He hadn't explained his limited Reserve to Raeleth yet, nor the fact that he was an Augur: there had been no need thus far and though the other man seemed trustworthy, giving away too much information too quickly had seemed imprudent. It was a conversation that he was going to have to have sooner rather than later, it seemed.

Still, he couldn't leave Raeleth like this. He closed his eyes, funneling Essence carefully into the other man until the Dark retreated once again, shriveling like leaves in a fire. Gone to all outward appearances, but this time Davian thought he could still sense a faint, dark spot directly above Raeleth's heart. No matter how much Essence he poured in, that spot refused to disappear.

Trying to hide his concern, he opened his eyes again. This hadn't taken anywhere near as much Essence as last time—the infection was far less advanced, he assumed—but it had nonetheless used more than he could afford. He had four, maybe five more such expenditures before he would be unable to do this again.

If the Dark kept coming back every week, that gave Raeleth not much more than a month to live.

"Thank you," said Raeleth, standing a little straighter, oblivious to Davian's concern. He felt absently at his chest, then eyed the pail of bent, rusted metal pieces. "I could probably..."

"It's all right." Davian shook his head, albeit reluctantly. "Ched will definitely notice if you've not only suddenly recovered enough to haul, but volunteered to do the job for me. I was going to be seen eventually—better to stop the others getting suspicious and just get it out of the way early."

"As you say." Raeleth's relief was obvious. Davian had given him the Essence necessary to heal him, but nothing more. The man was still in dire need of some rest.

Davian bent down and hefted the pail, his expression contorting at its weight. He allowed another small trickle of Essence into the muscles of his right arm.

"I'll see you back at camp," he said grimly.

Davian kept his head down as he trudged along the elevated walkway with the heavy pail, trying not to flinch as an abrupt howl floated from the distant wall of gray smoke that raged on the horizon.

That happened a lot here, he'd discovered—once every day or two. Shrieks of pain echoing out over the dark, dead city. Agonized cries for help, sometimes. Raeleth said that some of the voices repeated, were familiar to him now.

That just made the pleas, when they came, all the more unsettling.

He strained forward as the sound echoed away, muscles in his right arm taut as he hauled the reinforced pail through the cold shadows, angling toward the lake. Isstharis kept her base of operations just south of the water, in one of the few buildings that were entirely intact. He'd seen it from a distance a couple of times, but never needed to approach before.

He passed plenty of people as he made his way up stairs and through short, winding tunnels in the main section of the southern camp, though there was little motion at this point in the day. Many were stretched out on the ground around unlit fires, either sleeping or too exhausted to move. Others simply sat on pieces of rubble, staring absently at nothing.

Most of the activity was provided by al'goriat, which lumbered everywhere between and through the buildings, the creatures often pausing and turning to examine prone figures before unhurriedly pacing on. Perhaps fifty of the Banes wandered the immediate area, from Davian's count, never in groups and never, seemingly, with any particular pattern or purpose. They just...patrolled. So long as the prisoners didn't threaten them, and didn't gather in too large a number, the al'goriat completely ignored them.

Until they didn't deliver their share of metal, of course. Davian shuddered at the memory of what Raeleth had told him about the consequences of not meeting quota too often.

"Who in fates are you?"

Davian flinched. He'd been lost in thought as he walked through the short tunnel, and hadn't heard anyone approach.

"My name is Shadat," he said as he turned, doing his best to speak politely. The tone of the initial question had been unduly aggressive, and he suspected he already knew who was asking it.

The hulking figure before him smiled forbiddingly as their eyes met.

The man who was presumably Maresh towered over Davian by almost a foot, his height matched by a muscle-bound bulk that was one of most naturally intimidating that Davian had ever seen. Just outside the tunnel stood two more men of almost equal stature, bathed in the red moonlight.

Maresh's eyes glittered as they slid toward the pail, taking note of its contents. "Who are you with, Shadat?"

Davian kept his breathing steady, calming himself. "Ched."

"Raeleth indisposed today?" Maresh waved lazily at the pail in Davian's hand, clearly not caring whether he received an answer. "About a third of that will do."

"A third?" Davian looked at him disbelievingly.

"No, you're right. I misspoke. A half." Maresh's gaze returned to settle on Davian calmly, and he tapped a thick wooden pole in his hand as the two men behind him shifted menacingly. "I don't know how things work in whichever section you came from, but here you will find that we have very little patience for those who waste our time."

Davian barely bit back a retort, remembering Raeleth's warning. Maresh continued to watch him as he gestured; one of the other men stepped forward, dropping an empty pail emphatically next to Davian's full one.

"Half," repeated the hulking man. "You fill. We'll choose which bucket to take with us."

Davian swallowed his anger and forced a nod, carefully taking chunks of metal from his pail and placing them in Maresh's. His fury burned hotter and hotter as he felt the three smug sets of eyes on him, but he focused on the work, reminding himself with each motion of what Raeleth had said. He had to pick his battles.

Soon enough he was done, having split the scraps as evenly as he could. Maresh picked up the pail closest to him, then tarried.

"You think we're traitors. Scum," he observed, studying Davian's expression.

"You think you aren't?" Davian replied, the words out of his mouth before he could stop them.

Maresh's eyes narrowed. "This is the world we live in now, Shadat. Nobody is getting out, nobody is going home. This"—he gestured around them—"is where we are all going to die. So if I have a way to *not* spend my days scrounging through ruins, in constant fear of buildings collapsing and Dark and wild Banes, then I am going to take it." He delivered his explanation calmly, as if it were the most logical thing in the world.

Davian stared at him, then forced a mocking laugh. He knew it was the wrong thing to do, but this was just...too hard to ignore.

"Fates," he chuckled bitterly. "What a wonderful justification for being a disgusting human being."

The blow caught him by surprise, despite his having known that he was inviting it. A backhand to the head, hard enough to snap him around and send him sprawling, his vision nothing but dizzying white light for several seconds. He choked out a groan, tensing for more, but nothing came.

When his vision cleared, Maresh was looming over him, expression dark.

"I normally don't like to injure people—it is of no benefit to anyone," he growled. "But do not make the mistake of thinking that I will not. It has been a while since an example was made. So I wouldn't try any harder to convince me that one is due." He nodded to one of the others, a light-skinned man with a completely bald pate and thick beard. "Ald, grab another few pieces. Payment for the unpleasantness."

Davian gasped another lungful of air as he tried to recover, silently berating himself but biting back any argument as Ald picked out several more chunks of metal from his pail. He was exhausted, frustrated, not a little concerned about his situation—and he'd allowed it all to shorten his temper. Large as these men were, he could probably take on all three with the help of Essence... but he knew no one else in the camp was Gifted. Which meant that revealing his ability here would inevitably attract the wrong kind of attention.

The smart thing to do was to accept this—infuriatingly *unjust* though it was—and be on his way.

He would need to apologize to Raeleth and the others later for losing more metal than he should have, too.

He didn't bother using Essence to clear his head, staying down until Maresh and his thugs wandered off, talking and laughing together as if nothing had happened. He wished again that he could just *touch* kan; he would have had little compunction in Controlling Maresh.

Fates, but he hated the sensation of being helpless. Even in his cell in Ilshan Gathdel Teth, he'd never felt quite like this. In fact, he couldn't remember feeling this bad since Caladel, practicing to pass his Trials.

He eventually picked himself up, dusting off his already-ripped clothing and peering bleakly into his pail. It was closer to a quarter full now, barely worth the grueling trek to deliver it.

He hefted the significantly lighter pail and squared his shoulders.

Now came the dangerous part.

He trudged forward again, and soon his pulse quickened as he spotted Isstharis—at least, Davian assumed that it was she—in the distance, the glistening black, serpentine body unmistakable as she slithered alongside the lake.

He made a beeline for the creature, doing his best not to shy away as a patrolling al'goriat wandered close to his position, its eyeless gaze roving, needle-like teeth dripping dark red. Davian kept walking, his neck itching as the al'goriat moved on behind him, though it was Isstharis herself who was commanding his attention now.

This was it. The creature had his description. The only question now was whether Raeleth was right in his assertion that the dar'gaithin had difficulty distinguishing between humans.

Isstharis looked up as Davian approached, noting the pail he was carrying.

"Bring it," she hissed peremptorily, sounding bored, as she slithered off toward the intact building.

Davian did as he was told, trailing after the dar'gaithin and into the deep shadows of the structure.

He squinted as his eyes adjusted to the meager red light filtering in through the windows, taking in a surprisingly ordered space. Three reinforced barrels filled with metal sat in one corner while several more sat in another, these with the gray-green tips of bitterroot sticking out of the tops. The rest of the space was spartan but clean, entirely empty aside from the dozen al'goriat lumbering aimlessly around the interior.

Each of them stopped as Davian and Isstharis entered, turning to watch silently.

Isstharis ignored them, reaching out with a muscular arm and taking the pail from him, hefting it as if it were nothing to her—which, Davian knew, it probably wasn't. The creatures were far stronger than any human.

"A small return." Isstharis's gaze went to Davian and lingered there, her expression turning almost quizzical. Davian did his best not to look nervous.

"Half rations," Isstharis said finally, turning to empty the pail into one of the barrels, then slithering over and dropping a few bitterroot stems into it.

Davian nodded, knowing not to argue, then dithered. "You know which team?"

Isstharis hissed impatiently. "Raeleth, yes?"

"Yes," said Davian, hiding his relief.

Isstharis stared at Davian, and he had the distinct impression that she was confused. The creature shook her serpentine head from side to side in evident irritation.

"Go," she hissed. "It will be credited."

Davian turned and resisted the urge to flee, instead collecting the pail and walking outside again as calmly as he could, heart pounding disconcertingly against his chest.

He flinched as a peal rang out loud behind him, then twisted to stare at the tower, one of the few structures still standing tall along the side of the lake. Crimson spilled off the swinging bell, though he couldn't see who, or what, was doing the ringing. The iron in there would probably have fed a team for weeks, but the dar'gaithin had clearly prioritized its function over whatever value the metal itself held for them.

His gaze switched absently to the stagnant spots of light surrounding the crimson crescent that hung, dead, in the sky. The same as always.

Almost absently, he focused and reached out for kan. He did it several times each day; he wasn't certain, but it felt as if he was getting closer and closer to touching it again. As if every mental stretch inched him nearer.

He released a pent-up breath after a moment, ignoring the brief flood of frustration. It was *there*, so close that it felt like his straining fingers were brushing against its surface.

But he still couldn't grasp it. Couldn't use it.

He sighed, then started the long trek to camp.

Chapter 18

Wirr sat in his office in the palace, flicking the sheet of paper in front of him absently.

It had only one line written on it, the handwriting familiar but beginning to fade after so long. Almost a year old, now.

Aelric taken to Nesk. Following.

Written hurriedly and sealed with the Shainwiere sigil, left with Administration to deliver. With so much chaos in the aftermath of the north-south split, it had taken two months—as far as he could determine—to reach him, and there was no telling if there had been other messages that hadn't made it at all.

He'd tried to find out more, of course. Dedicated resources he probably shouldn't have, though on that count he'd at least had the backing of his uncle and Karaliene, who both considered Aelric and Dezia all but family. But there had been nothing—not then, and not since.

He flicked the paper again, partly absently and partly in irritation at his helplessness. *Nesk.* Andarra and its southernmost neighbor had never, in their entire history, been on friendly terms, the Neskians persistent in their claims that the southernmost half of Andarra was theirs by ancestral right. The immense Mountains of Alai blocked most opportunities for major conflict; they were impassable in winter, and the crossing was extraordinarily dangerous during the rest of the year. Even so, regardless of who ruled in Nesk's capital city of Ishai—and that changed every few years without fail, sometimes several times before anyone in Andarra even heard about it—there was always a push to attempt another glorious retaking of 'Neskian' land.

Even if Dezia had made it past the border, what little Wirr knew of the country gave him scant comfort. The Neskians were a blood-thirsty people who traded in strange systems of honor, who out-lawed all religion and enslaved their prisoners. Neskian slave traders occasionally crossed into Andarra, disguised as merchants and taking back Andarran captives, who were highly valued for sport.

If Aelric had gone there, it wouldn't have been by choice.

He stared at Dezia's note for a long time before shaking his head. Dezia could look after herself—he knew that. Still, he missed her and worried about her; no amount of reasoning in the world could prevent that. He'd played her departure over and over again in his mind, wondering if he should have attempted to stop her. But every time he imagined it, he knew it wouldn't have done any good: Dezia was nothing if not independent and if she thought Aelric was in trouble, nothing would have prevented her from helping him. And for all Wirr wished he could have gone with her, he knew he'd done what was best.

Fates, but he hated duty.

"She can look after herself, you know."

Wirr started at the soft voice from the door, which had opened without his noticing. He turned, giving his younger sister a tired smile and motioning her inside.

"Del," he said affectionately. He glanced back at the paper in his hand, his smile slipping. Deldri knew about the message—she was one of the few people he'd felt comfortable confiding in. "I know," he added quietly.

"Which is why you're staring at that note and looking like you're going to burst into tears," retorted Deldri impudently as she shut the door behind her, slipping over to Wirr and giving him an impromptu hug around the shoulders before he could react.

"I am not," retorted Wirr in a growl, folding the paper care-fully and slotting it back into his desk drawer. "And knowing doesn't stop me from worrying," he added.

Deldri gave him a sympathetic smile, observing the stack of

pages at the corner of his desk that were covered in precise, elegantly flowing handwriting. "But it helps for Cousin Karaliene?"

"That's different. She...likes to keep us informed," Wirr understated with vague amusement, glancing at the letters. Those came with almost zealous regularity, and had done so ever since Kara had left six months ago. He hadn't really expected her to be so fastidious about staying in touch, but given her extended absence, both he and his uncle had appreciated not having to wonder whether she was all right.

He reached over, thumbing absently through his cousin's correspondence as he tried to remember when the next letter was due to arrive. A week, maybe? Publicly, the princess was still managing the official relief efforts in the north—distributing supplies where they were needed, and directing Assembly-sponsored work crews to help rebuild areas damaged by either the Blind or the Banes. Or both, in some cases. It was a worthy task, given how hard the Andarran people there had been hit over the past couple of years. Not to mention that her publicized, detailed monthly reports to the Assembly continued to generate some much-needed goodwill with the populace.

Privately, though, the princess was also looking for any clues as to where the Banes had gone. Those letters were sent in secret to Wirr every two weeks; he shared them with his uncle and Deldri, but no one else. Kara hadn't found anything yet—he could almost feel her frustration emanating from the page, sometimes—but it was nice to receive those more personable, familiar messages from her, too.

Deldri interrupted his distracted reverie as she threw herself into a chair opposite him, commanding his attention with an exaggerated sigh.

"So. I'm here because Administrator Tulean pulled me aside this morning. She didn't say anything *specifically* about you, but..."

Wirr rolled his eyes. "But she was trying to turn you against me." He scowled. "Sorry."

"Not your fault." Deldri still smiled but her eyes were tired, far beyond the sort of weariness a fourteen-year-old should know.

The scar across her forehead from Isiliar's attack had remained, an ugly reminder of when he'd nearly lost her. "At least they're being less obvious now. Nobody's *directly* accusing you of anything."

"I wish you'd tell me who was doing that."

"And I told you that I would, if I thought it would help. But if I do, you'll keep me away from them, and they'll figure out that I told you. And then the next time, when they try and actually *do* something, it won't involve me." Deldri smiled brightly at him. "Seems like if they're going to be treasonous, it would be good for us to know about it before the actual treason part."

Wirr snorted. "Have I mentioned that you're far too good at this?"

"Spending all that time around here with Mother was good for one thing, at least." The mixture of sadness and bitterness in Deldri's tone was undisguised.

Wirr winced. Deldri had been nothing but loyal to him over the past year, and yet events had conspired to put a gulf between them that had never been there before—one that Wirr was unsure could ever be fully bridged.

Despite Karaliene, Erran, and Ishelle's confirmation of what had happened at the Boundary, the narrative around the palace had remained much murkier: that Geladra, who was poised to remove Wirr from his position as Northwarden, had gone north to give her son one last chance to prove himself . . . and had mysteriously died in the process. While he, of course, had lived.

It was too easy a target for the more political elements of the city to ignore. Rumors that Wirr had somehow planned her death, or at least hoped for it, had sprung up almost immediately upon his return. Despite his fury at those who would whisper such accusations, they had never fully died down, and he had never been able to locate their source—if there even was just one.

Deldri maintained that she believed his version of events, and he believed that she did. Still—it was the sort of accusation that was hard to dismiss, hard to stop from worming its way into the back of your mind, no matter how much faith you had in someone.

"Thanks for letting me know," he said, shaking his head and

mentally adding Tulean to the list of Administrators he couldn't trust. Or, more accurately, removing her from the list of those he could. That list was much easier to maintain.

He leaned back, sighing. "How's everything else going? How are your studies?"

"Boring. Easy. Zala Tel'An and Paden Tel'Shan have the attention span of goats, and possibly the intelligence of them, so the tutors are constantly slowing down the rest of us so that they can catch up."

"I'll see about getting you some private lessons," said Wirr. He coughed. "And…it probably doesn't need to be said, but don't mention the goat thing outside of this room. Those are two Houses we kind of need right now."

Deldri snorted. "It's obvious enough that I probably don't need to point it out, anyway."

They shared a chuckle, and then Deldri stretched. "I saw Uncle this morning," she said conversationally. "He mentioned that he spoke with you after you got back from Daren Tel. He didn't say it in a particularly…*happy* way."

Wirr grunted. "No progress on our talks with the southern Houses, unfortunately," he said casually. He trusted Deldri—she knew about his private Oathstone, after all—but telling her what he'd done with it, what he'd learned, would only make her party to his illegal activities. Not to mention put even more on her young shoulders than she already had to bear. "And we didn't talk about it, but Erran says that there have been more reports coming in about Desriel massing their troops. And more rumors from Nesk, too," he added, glancing distractedly at the drawer that held Dezia's note. Just one more reason to worry about her.

Deldri shifted uncomfortably.

"About…him," she said awkwardly. "Augur Erran. He seems…awfully friendly, sometimes."

Wirr looked at her blankly, then suddenly guffawed.

Deldri glowered. "It's not *that* funny."

"No, it's not. It's just that he…" Wirr shook his head. "He was close to Father, and we both know how much Father loved you. I think Erran…sort of sees us through Father's eyes. He's the same way with me, sometimes." He hadn't been able to bring himself to explain what had happened with Elocien and Erran to anyone else; only he, Karaliene, and Erran himself knew the truth.

Deldri glared at him, and it occurred to Wirr that perhaps she had been flattered by the attention. Then she grinned.

"That makes sense," she said, looking vaguely relieved. "Whenever he's talked to me, Father *has* come up a lot. Perhaps he just misses him."

Wirr's smile faded. "We all do," he assured her. "And Mother."

Deldri nodded at that, but Wirr couldn't help but notice the tightening of her shoulders.

The moment passed and they chatted for a few minutes, the conversation casual and light, both of them enjoying the opportunity to talk unguardedly. Finally, though, Wirr stirred, glancing reluctantly at the Decay Clock in the corner.

"I have things I should do," he admitted, standing with an only half-exaggerated groan. "Taeris is waiting for me at the Tol."

Deldri stood, too, giving her brother a quick hug. "Dinner tomorrow night?"

"I'll be there," Wirr promised.

He smiled after his sister as she slipped out the door, marveling at how bright and cheerful she still managed to be, despite everything that had happened. He knew that it was partly put on; the past couple of years had taken their toll, without a doubt. Still, it always raised his spirits to see.

He informed Didos, the heavyset guard standing outside his door, that he required an escort—that wasn't optional these days, even for such a short trip—and started toward the front gate.

It was time to face the sha'teth once again.

Wirr walked the sun-drenched streets of Ilin Illan, doing his best not to glare at the clumps of people chatting and laughing and going about their daily business.

It ground at him, how everything here seemed so...*normal* again. Ilin Illan's white streets had been all but cleansed of signs of the Blind's attack, with the vast majority of the buildings—at least the ones in the wealthier areas—completely rebuilt.

Most who had fled the city had now returned, crowds throng-ing in the markets where vendors hawked their wares once again. Even the unease that had prevailed a year ago, when the attacks by the Blind and then Isiliar had been fresh, seemed to have sim-ply dissipated in the face of prolonged peace.

Worse still were the blue lanterns he spotted hanging outside some houses. Early, but a reminder of just how close this year's Festival of Ravens truly was.

The people who recognized him stared as he passed. That grated, too. He knew their whispers would be about politics, about how he had single-handedly caused the split with Tol Shen and the southern Houses—or sometimes, even more frivo-lously, about whom he might marry. So few of them were con-cerned about the terrors still stalking the land somewhere to the north. None, certainly, were concerned that his best friend was trapped beyond the Boundary, or that his other remaining child-hood friend was going through unimaginable suffering to ensure that their safe little existence here remained intact.

To them it was all in the past: the north had been close to lost, but that was over now. Most of the populace, from what he gath-ered, were still unclear on exactly how much of a threat there had even *been*. The general sense was that the time had come to focus on more immediate, more... *real* issues.

He exhaled heavily. If only they knew what was coming.

The massive iron gates of Tol Athian soon loomed up ahead, and Wirr slowed as he approached, quickly recognized by the half dozen red-cloaked guards on duty. The doors were opened, though not before Wirr and his accompanying guard underwent the same checks as everyone else; once he was on Athian ground, even being the Northwarden didn't exclude him from the rules.

He endured the checks with practiced patience, understanding their necessity even if they were also an irritation. Ever since Caeden and Taeris had used the Travel Stones to infiltrate Tol Athian, no unauthorized Vessels had been allowed in. It was a sensible precaution, particularly given the Tol's weakened state after the Blind's attack.

One of the Gifted guards had disappeared inside upon recognizing him; by the time he was cleared to enter, Elder Eilinar himself—the leader of Tol Athian's Council—was waiting just inside.

"Prince Torin," said the wiry older man, bowing slightly to show his respect.

"Nashrel." Circumstances had led to Wirr's becoming fairly familiar with the man over the past year. They were far from friends, but their relationship wasn't as bad as it could have been, all things considered. "Sorry to have dragged you away from whatever you were doing, but I'm just here to meet with Taeris today. He is expecting me."

"Of course. Before you do that, though, I thought we might have a quick word?" Nashrel hesitated, lowering his voice. "It is regarding Augur Devries."

Wirr glanced reluctantly down the cavernous Essence-lit main tunnel of the Tol, but motioned for Nashrel to lead on. He had been anticipating this conversation since the incident with Ishelle. There was no benefit to delaying it.

They set off through the spacious, always-bustling tunnels of Tol Athian, Wirr receiving more than one openly wary glance from red-cloaked men and women as they passed. As always, he felt the strange tension of being here. He was Gifted, and the Northwarden. He was bound by the Tol's laws rather than Andarra's, but equally—if he had an Oathstone—could take command of anyone here. Simply change those laws, if he wanted to.

And every single Gifted he passed knew it.

It wasn't long before Nashrel was pulling him aside into a room just off the main passageway. A Lockroom, Wirr noted with interest. Not unusual, necessarily, but clearly a deliberate choice.

The Elder waited for Wirr to take a seat and then settled opposite, hesitating as he gathered his thoughts.

"As you know, Augur Devries has been staying with us over the past year, thanks to her ... condition," he started, clearly choosing his words carefully. He knew that Wirr and Ishelle were on good terms, having made the journey back from the north together. "Her presence has been welcome, of course—a privilege—and the benefits of it to the Tol have been wonderful."

Wirr sighed. "But you don't want her here anymore," he finished flatly.

Nashrel shook his head, looking irritated. "I didn't say that. But lately, she…" He trailed off, chewing his lip, searching for the words.

Wirr waited patiently. He knew exactly what had happened, shivered a little inside as he remembered the gibbering wreck Ishelle had become when she'd attempted to accompany them to question Dras. They had set off on foot, intending to travel to Wirr's family estate before using the Travel Stones to get to Prythe, hopefully establishing to any spies that his leaving was nothing nefarious.

Ishelle hadn't lasted until noon.

Her connection to the eletai seemed to be blocked by Tol Athian's walls, but the moment she left the protection of the structure, her mind came under constant assault. Erran had done everything he could to minimize the problem before they left, but in the end, they had simply been forced to take her back.

"Is she causing problems?" asked Wirr directly.

"Yes." Nashrel gestured helplessly. "I don't wish to be rude but after rumors of her display the other day got out, Sire, things have been… tense. There is a growing concern that her behavior may soon become that erratic regularly, regardless of whether she is behind these walls. Even a few weeks ago, I would not have said anything of the sort. But whatever her condition is, it is worsening, and we simply have no way to combat it."

Wirr said nothing. The problem was, he knew that Nashrel was right: Ishelle *was* getting worse. Six months ago she had been able to last more than a week outside the Tol.

"What do you suggest?" asked Wirr.

"Nothing, for now." Nashrel's hazel eyes held his gaze. "That's why I wanted to make this chat an informal one. Augur Devries is a wonderful asset, and I happen to like her personally, too—most of us do. And we have not stopped trying to find more information on her condition. But we are looking after her at your request, and I needed to let you know that we may not be adequately equipped to do so for much longer."

"Thank you. I appreciate that." There wasn't much more that Wirr could say. The Gifted had no doubt made a genuine effort to help Ishelle: it was in their best interest, after all. "Give me some time—a few days, at least. I'll see if I can come up with a plan."

Nashrel looked relieved. "Now. I should let you press on to see the Representative. He told me you have some solemn business to attend to this morning."

Wirr covered his confusion with a nod, unsure to what the Elder was referring, but assuming that Taeris had given some excuse for their meeting. "Thank you, Elder Eilinar. I can find my way from here," he said politely.

It wasn't long before he was walking along the tunnel to Taeris's study. He paused at the door next to it, a combination of nostalgia and sadness washing over him as he gazed into the empty room. Asha's old study. He half expected to see her look up from her desk and wave him inside with that bright smile of hers.

There were only boxes, now; the Elders were using it for storage, apparently. Wirr had rebuffed Tol Athian's several requests to assign a new junior Representative to the palace—not directly, of course, but more ignored them by making sure that he had more important things to be dealing with. Taeris preferred to work alone, anyway. Someday soon, though, Wirr would have to allow the Council to make Asha's replacement official.

Fates, but he hoped that she was well.

Davian, too, wherever he was.

When he opened the door to Taeris's office, Wirr found Erran and Ishelle in the process of standing, apparently just finishing their conversation with the Representative.

"How did your meeting with Kevran go?" asked Erran immediately once the door was shut.

Wirr ignored Erran's familiarity, though he saw Taeris's eyebrows rise slightly. "Well enough. He...wasn't pleased with everything I'd done," he conceded, playing down his uncle's anger just a touch, "but there won't be consequences from him, at least. He appreciates the value of the information that we got."

"And the plan?" asked Taeris.

Wirr shrugged. "He agreed. He'll have people spread word of another suspected attack, make sure that there are extra ships on standby in the harbor, quietly prepare as many areas of the city as possible for a clean evacuation...that sort of thing. He eyed Erran. "He did say that he wanted to talk to you directly about it, though."

"Any idea why?" asked Erran, sounding more curious than worried.

"Just for clarity on what is being spread, I suspect." Wirr grimaced. "He wasn't feeling particularly inclined to share more than was necessary with me, to be honest."

Ishelle cleared her throat. She was a stunning young woman, but the dark circles beneath her eyes and a generally exhausted, unkempt appearance betrayed some of what she had been going through recently. "If that's the worst of his reaction, we should count ourselves fortunate."

"Agreed." Wirr coughed, glancing across at her.

"No," said Ishelle before he could ask. There was no irritation to her tone, though he wouldn't have blamed her. "There's been nothing from Davian or Fessi. No sense of them at all." She bit her lip. "Not even the other day, when..."

Wirr nodded quickly, accepting the statement without pressing, though it still hurt as the slight glimmer of hope that always sparked when he saw Ishelle faded once again. He couldn't bring himself to believe that his friend was dead—he'd made that mistake once before; he refused to do it again—but a year was a long time. And Ishelle had described the wastelands of Talan Gol in vivid detail.

Still—Davian was resourceful, and Erran constantly assured him that Fessi was as well.

And they were Augurs, of course. That didn't hurt their chances.

Ishelle stretched absently. "I really should get some rest, I think," she said abruptly, the shadows beneath her eyes seeming more pronounced than ever. "My head is..."

She trailed off, staring into nothing for a few uncomfortably long seconds before shaking herself, giving the others a wry smile. "Sorry."

"No need to apologize," Taeris assured her.

Erran lent Ishelle his arm as she swayed. "Nothing we need to know?" he asked Wirr, then sighed as Wirr shook his head. "Well. If the king wants to see me, then I suppose I should get over there." He made sure Ishelle was steady, then headed for the door alongside her.

"Erran?" Wirr shifted uncomfortably. "Just...remember who you're talking to, when you meet with him?"

Erran lingered, dipping his head in understanding before slipping out. Another effect of his having Controlled Elocien for so long was that Erran tended to think of the king as his brother, often more than he thought of him as his liege. It had resulted in some...interesting slips of propriety, early on.

Once Erran had shut the door, Wirr turned to Taeris. "Nashrel pulled me aside when I got here."

Taeris scowled. "Ishelle?" When Wirr nodded, he cursed under his breath. "The man's not a fool, but fates take him if he doesn't let the Council pressure him too far sometimes. I assume they want to get rid of her?"

"They're worried that she's going to snap," admitted Wirr. "Her little display when we brought her back didn't go unnoticed."

Taeris grunted. "That doesn't much surprise me."

Wirr indicated his agreement, shivering as he remembered the state Ishelle had been in when they had finally managed to drag her back into the Tol. Eyes red and wild, strange black lines striping her body, screaming nonsense, flecks of foam at her mouth.

Half a day, that had taken. Perhaps eight hours outside the protection of the Tol, and she had been reduced to little more than a feral animal. They had managed to get her back to her rooms without too many of the Gifted seeing—it had been late at night and they had done everything they could to avoid notice—but the damage had been done. Ishelle's deteriorating state had been the cause of much concern even before the event. Wirr had no doubt that word of what had happened had spread through the Tol like wildfire.

"There's nowhere else to take her, though," observed Wirr. "She needs this place."

"We'll sit down with her and Erran soon. Discuss our options," Taeris assured him. "Erran won't hesitate to put himself against the Council to help her—that may be enough. Or we might be able to convince the Assembly to amend the Amnesty again, make it so that if they are to be in charge of the Augurs, they must accept all of them—no matter their condition."

Wirr nodded. The Assembly had decreed that Tol Athian was now the sanctioned destination for Augurs, stripping Tol Shen of the right—for what that was worth, these days.

Taeris exhaled. "We have other things to worry about right now, anyway."

"Nashrel mentioned a...*solemn* purpose to what we were doing?"

"Ah." Taeris looked apologetic. "I told him that you would be paying your respects to Elder Olin today."

Wirr stared at him, nonplussed. "Elder Olin is buried here?"

"Entombed." Taeris shifted. "The tombs are normally off-limits to everyone but family. But given your position, and the role the Elder played in your protection and development in Caladel, Nashrel agreed that it would be appropriate."

"Oh." Wirr shook his head, somewhat dazedly. "Thank you. I would...actually like that." He'd never had the opportunity to say good-bye to anyone from Caladel—not properly. Elder Olin had not only taught him much of what he knew about being Gifted, but had been the one to keep his secret so faithfully over the years. It had cost the man his life.

He frowned slightly as he saw Taeris's expression, and opened his mouth to ask.

"I'll explain when we're down there," said Taeris firmly. "When it's secure."

Wirr resisted the urge to sigh. Taeris had told him about Tol Athian's Remembering not long after his return to Ilin Illan: a kind of ward, built into the stone of the Tol itself. Anything that was said within range of the Remembering could be recalled by one of the Council, if they knew the time and place of the conversation. Recalled *precisely*, as if they had been standing right there when it happened. It was one of the Council's most jealously guarded secrets, and something Taeris himself had been reluctant to reveal, even to Wirr.

"Then let's go," he said.

Wirr followed Taeris out of his office and downward, toward the center of the Tol, farther beneath Ilin Tora.

"Has Erran checked you this week?" asked Taeris absently as they walked.

"Of course." One of their first priorities upon Wirr's return to the capital last year—as the committee overseeing him drew up its charter—had been to do everything possible to protect him from Control by one of the Venerate, Scyner, or even another rogue Augur like Rohin. That included constant attention to his mental shield, and regular assessments by Erran.

"Good." Taeris waved away Wirr's look. "I'm not concerned. It's just nice to have the confirmation."

They walked for a while, Wirr letting Taeris take the lead. There seemed to be more Gifted than the last time Wirr had been here. That made sense, he supposed, with plenty of Gifted refugees from the northern schools having made their home in Tol Athian recently.

Soon enough Taeris was steering them down a deserted side tunnel; several twists and turns later they came to a heavy-looking oak door. The scarred man drew a key from his pocket, which slid into the lock and turned with a well-oiled click.

A set of stairs led them downward, much to Wirr's surprise. He knew that there was a lower section to the Tol—it was the only route to the Sanctuary, after all—but he had assumed that everything beyond the main floor had remained abandoned.

Then they reached *another* flight of stairs.

"Fates. How deep does this place go?" he wondered aloud as they began their next descent. The stairs had a different appearance from those leading from the level above, the steps thinner and longer, providing a more gradual descent. They were still made of pure white stone, though. Still very evidently created by the Builders.

"The Tol?" Taeris shrugged at him. "There are maps for the first five levels. Beyond that, nobody really knows. The paths are dangerous and the Essence lighting doesn't extend that far down; in fact, after a while, using Essence to light the way doesn't even seem to work. There have been a few efforts in my lifetime to map it—especially during the siege years—but whole groups of Gifted have disappeared down there. Most of it's been shut away for decades. Before that, it was entirely sealed off for centuries."

"*Five* levels?" Wirr began reassessing his understanding of the Tol's size.

"Of which we know," repeated Taeris. "They're not all as large as the upper level; they were mostly used for storage back in the days of the war." He gestured reassuringly. "The tomb is on this level."

Wirr nodded slightly, still a little dazed, as he followed Taeris along the corridor until they finally reached the end, passing through an open doorway.

The chamber beyond stood in sharp contrast to the dimly lit, spartan passages outside, the long room opening up into a vast, decorated, warmly illuminated area. The walls were lined with square stone doors, each only a few feet high and wide. Wirr couldn't see where they ended.

As he looked closer, he realized that each door had a name on it, written in Essence, which in turn gave the room its permanent, gentle glow. Fountains flowed at sporadic intervals along the wall, though from where they could possibly be drawing water— or where that water was going—Wirr had no idea.

"The bodies are all kept here?" Wirr had been vaguely aware that there was a tomb somewhere in Tol Athian, but it was rarely discussed. Only Council members and other honored Elders were afforded a burial here.

"When there are bodies to entomb, yes." Most of the doorways close to the entrance had names on them.

"Fates. Is that really Caravar Trelais?" asked Wirr, spotting a name. The man was a legend from the time of the Great War, more than a thousand years ago.

"Well. It's his body." Taeris scratched his chin, giving a shrug to Wirr's look. "He was important in his time, Sire, but there's a reason the Builders created this place. Everyone's equal here. There's no place of honor, no seniority, no rank. None of these graves can become a shrine." His gaze traveled the room. "I've always liked that. Great people should be remembered for their great deeds, but strangers visiting their graves strikes me as...odd." Taeris shut the tomb door behind them, then glanced around. "We can talk freely now. This place doesn't have any Remembering."

Wirr breathed out. "So. Why are we really here?"

Taeris gestured, somewhat sheepishly. "You *can* pay your respects to Elder Olin," he assured Wirr. "But Rethgar is entombed down here, too. Or is supposed to be," he added pensively. "It only occurred to me yesterday that I could check. This was the best way I could think to get us down here."

"Ah." Wirr felt the true purpose of the visit cheapened it somewhat, but he couldn't blame Taeris. The Representative had been fretting about Dras's revelations since the moment he'd heard them. "And if he's not there?"

"Then we have one more thing to question the sha'teth about."

Wirr nodded grimly.

"This is Elder Olin's tomb," said Taeris, arriving in front of a door with the Elder's name glowing gently on it. "Please pay your respects, Sire, then come and find me."

Wirr waited for Taeris to wander farther down the long room before turning toward the square marked with Elder Olin's name.

He touched the name, and flashes of images ran through his head. He saw the Elder laughing with his students, teaching classes, striding through the courtyard in Caladel with his robes streaming behind him as he went to discipline someone. There were more; moments more than anything else, but enough to bring back the memory of the man who had taught him and Davian and Asha for so many years. Who had shown them so much kindness as they'd grown from children to young adults.

Minutes passed, and when Wirr finally lowered his hand again, there was a genuine smile on his face, and a warmth—albeit still tinged with loss—in his chest. He took a second to collect himself, then walked over to where Taeris was standing.

"How does it do that?" he asked quietly.

Taeris shrugged. "Taps into your memories of the departed, somehow," he said. "Usually seems to find the good ones, if you have them. If you put your hand against the grave of someone you'd never met—say, old Caravar over there—nothing would happen. And if it was someone you'd barely known, you'd probably get a flash of their face but not much more." He smiled sadly. "But it is nice to remember the lost more clearly, sometimes."

"It is," agreed Wirr, swallowing a lump in his throat. It seemed like an age ago that he'd been at Caladel, but in reality it was only two years, and that after living there for three. That school had

been his home, and his bonds with the people there had been

as strong as any in his life before or since. It had been a simpler, much happier time in his life. Probably the happiest that he could remember.

Taeris gave him a sympathetic pat on the shoulder, then beckoned for Wirr to follow him to another door on the far wall.

"Rethgar Tel'An," Wirr read, then looked at Taeris, who tentatively reached out and touched the name, shuddering and closing his eyes.

"What did you see?" Wirr asked as Taeris's eyes opened again.

The Elder made a face. "My memories of Rethgar are..." He sighed. "I didn't know him well; my memories of him are mainly from the end. He was the first one. The first volunteer to be made into a sha'teth. We didn't really know what we were doing— Laiman did his best to make sure he understood the knowledge Jakarris had given him, but..." He shrugged. "His death was not a pleasant one. We very nearly gave up then and there."

There was silence; Taeris glanced to the side, seeing the expression on Wirr's face and interpreting it correctly.

"And we should have," he agreed heavily, as if suddenly recognizing the nonchalance of his previous tone. "But I'll say it again, Sire—the days before the war were a different time. Chaotic, close to lawless. You have to remember that the Augurs were all but in hiding, and the Gifted...more and more of them were using their power to take advantage of regular people." He cast another glance at Wirr, this one containing a familiar, unconscious hint of pleading for understanding. For forgiveness. "They thought that it was acceptable, too—that they had a *right* to do it—fates, when we imprisoned our own for their crimes, mobs of Gifted started forming to protest! The Councils were losing control, where they were even trying to keep it in the first place. Things were getting bloody, and we needed a weapon to scare our own people back into submission before we had a civil war on our hands. We needed a *threat*, and..."

He trailed off, as if suddenly recognizing how defensive he was sounding.

"None of which is an excuse," he eventually finished softly.

"I know." Wirr said the words gently, in response to both Taeris's explanation and his last statement. He'd heard much of it before, from both Taeris and Laiman. Both men were clearly haunted by the decisions they'd made back then, even as they desperately tried to contextualize them.

He turned his attention back to the door in front of them, choosing to focus on the task at hand. "So now we just...see if Rethgar's inside?" he asked, a touch queasily. Though they *were* just bones, vessels emptied of everything that made them important, it still felt disrespectful at best. "How do we do that?"

"I'm not sure. I haven't exactly been in this position before," Taeris admitted, sounding relieved that the conversation had moved on. "And it didn't seem like something that I could ask about." He closed his eyes, frowning in concentration as he examined the tomb.

"I think it's a Vessel," he concluded. "Just a latch. A touch of Essence here, and..."

The stone shivered, as if reluctant, and then sluggishly ground aside.

Wirr and Taeris peered inside as the warm Essence-light of the room revealed the interior of the tomb.

"There are two bodies in there," observed Wirr, bemused. The corpses were perfectly preserved, their faces unmarked, though the bodies themselves were badly damaged. "Is either of them Rethgar?"

He glanced across at Taeris, and froze. The scarred man's hands were shaking as he physically leaned away from the corpses, his face white.

"No. Neither of them is Rethgar," Taeris said hoarsely.

Wirr swallowed. "Who are they, then?"

Taeris didn't respond for a long moment, gazing at the faces as if transfixed.

"They're us," he eventually said.

"They're Thell and I."

Chapter 19

Wirr hurried to keep pace with Taeris, the older man's ground-eating strides a good indication of just how rattled he truly was.

"How did Rethgar make their faces look like yours?" It hadn't been immediately obvious to Wirr—he hadn't known Taeris before the scars that now covered his features—but he had been able to see it once Taeris had explained. Could see the likeness, even if the man lying in the tomb was a good twenty years younger.

The other man's face—Thell's, apparently—Wirr didn't recognize at all, but that was unsurprising. When Thell had changed his identity to Laiman Kardai, even his physical form had been remade by Jakarris.

"I don't know. Shape-shifting of some kind, I suppose," said Taeris, not slowing. "If Rethgar actually has a sha'teth's powers—even some of them—but isn't as restricted in what he can do..." He shook his head uneasily. "Whatever the case, the message is clear enough."

"But those bodies are from twenty years ago," pointed out Wirr. "If it was revenge he wanted, and he's that powerful, surely you would know about it by now?"

Taeris grunted. "One of the many questions we're going to ask our friends in black," he muttered. He glanced around at the walls, wincing. "And that's enough said until we get there."

Wirr stared blankly for a second and then screwed up his face. They'd both been rattled enough that they'd forgotten about the Tol's Remembering.

They walked for a minute more in tense silence. The sha'teth were being kept in the depths as well, though on a higher level; the emptiness of the Tol here, combined with their unsettling discovery in the tomb, made Wirr feel almost as on edge as Taeris looked.

Finally they came to a doorway, and Taeris stopped in front of it with heavy certainty.

"Here?" Wirr shifted, bracing himself. He hadn't seen the sha'teth since the attack almost a year ago.

Taeris nodded, opening the door and gesturing Wirr through. "This section of the Tol is...special. It is where they were created," he explained, slipping through and shutting it behind him. "The Conduit runs past here, but it's different from the Sanctuary—it's shielded, completely safe for us. Those same mechanisms interfere with the sha'teth's ability to touch kan. They're weakened here, barely able to stand."

Wirr raised an eyebrow. "That seems a very specific thing to know."

Taeris glanced around, the slight relaxing of his shoulders indicating a release of tension. "Laiman knew that it would have that effect on them. It was part of the knowledge Jakarris gave him." He rubbed his forehead. "We're outside the range of the Remembering again, by the way."

"I gathered." Wirr gazed around uncertainly. They were in a small, circular antechamber of some kind, smooth white walls curving around to meet at another doorway twenty feet away. "Aren't there any guards?"

"Too risky. Only the Council know that the sha'teth are still alive, and only a few specific members know where they're being kept." Taeris waved away Wirr's concerned expression. "No need to worry. We have someone checking down here three times a day, and the Tol has a whole raft of defenses for this section. It's probably going to take me a half hour just to get us through them."

He strode toward the far door, and then faltered.

"What is it?" Wirr asked.

In answer, Taeris touched the door lightly.

It swung silently open.

"And what of you, Sekariel?" A voice echoed from the

other room, quiet but clear. "Is your answer the same as your brother's?"

Taeris froze, gripping Wirr's arm warningly and holding a finger to his lips. He leaned over, putting his mouth close to Wirr's ear.

"There is not supposed to be anyone here," he breathed, the older man's every muscle tense as a rasping answer to the question they had heard—this one inaudible—came from the other room.

Wirr indicated his understanding; the two men positioned themselves at either side of the now-open door.

"That is disappointing," lamented the unfamiliar voice as they peered through the entrance and into the lit room.

The chamber within was not the uniform white of everywhere else in the Tol, but rather little more than a cavern; the walls were a matte black, rough-hewn, the facade sharp with jagged, vaguely misshapen edges. As if whoever had built the place had left it unfinished.

Wirr's stomach churned as he took in the scene within. At the far end of the chamber the two sha'teth hung, manacled to the wall, their hoods pushed back to reveal deathly white, wrinkled skin and horribly deformed features. Thin trickles of black—what Wirr assumed was blood—dripped from the mouth of one, though whether it was from some recent injury or not, he had no idea.

Neither creature struggled as the man standing in front of them watched, arms crossed, looking relaxed—albeit annoyed. He was tall, slim, with an unsettlingly confident bearing given what he was facing.

The man turned to face the entrance as Wirr and Taeris both jerked back to avoid being seen. "Please. Join me," the stranger said in vague amusement. "I have been meaning to speak with you again anyway, Prince Torin."

Wirr swallowed, mind racing, but silently motioned for Taeris to wait before walking out into the light of the second room as confidently as he could. When he'd turned, Wirr had spotted something else about the stranger.

The man was a Shadow.

"What are you doing here?" Wirr asked sharply. "Do the Council know you're talking to these things?"

"Bah." The man gestured irritably. "No time for that. I'd have to spend weeks just proving to that dolt Eilinar who I am. No thank you." His eyes narrowed as he looked at Wirr. "You, on the other hand, seem to have recognized me?"

"Scyner." Once he had seen the black markings on the man's face, it hadn't been hard to extrapolate. "The real you, this time. Not someone you're Controlling."

Scyner chuckled. "Well done." His gaze shifted over Wirr's shoulder. "And...Taeris Sarr," he added, quietly this time. "It has been a while, my old friend."

"Jakarris." Taeris walked forward slowly, staring at Scyner as if looking at a ghost. "It really is you, isn't it." His voice held a mélange of emotions, from wonder to sadness to fury.

"It is." Scyner gave the older man a tight smile.

"Fates." Taeris's expression hardened. "*Fates*, Jakarris. We trusted you."

Scyner gazed at Taeris, looking sorrowful. He clearly knew exactly what Taeris was referring to.

"I know," he said eventually.

A rasping laugh interrupted him before he could say more.

"*Atarin tel'teth*. What a delightful reunion," the sha'teth on the right sneered, its voice like stones being ground together. "Two of the men who made our passage to this world possible."

Scyner rolled his eyes, not bothering to turn and face the creature. "These monsters shouldn't be here," he said bluntly, addressing Taeris more than Wirr. "How were they captured?"

"First tell us what you're doing here," responded Wirr pointedly.

Scyner gave an exasperated sigh. "Investigating." He jerked his head toward the sha'teth. "Perhaps we can exchange notes later?"

Wirr considered, then grudgingly indicated his assent. The Augur clearly didn't want to say too much in front of the creatures, which made sense.

"They attacked me. That's how we caught them," he said eventually. He lifted his shirt slightly, revealing the pink, half-healed line across his stomach. "About a week after I got back to the city, after Asha..." He trailed off, glancing at the sha'teth warily. It probably wasn't the best idea to give them information they didn't have, even if it seemed unimportant.

Scyner seemed to understand what he was talking about anyway. "But *how*?" he pressed.

"The entire Council was there," explained Taeris. "As was I. More than half of us died in the fight."

Scyner glanced behind at the manacled creatures, then gestured to the opposite side of the room; Wirr and Taeris nodded their agreement and the three of them moved out of earshot before Taeris began explaining the sequence of events. How the sha'teth had burst into the chamber and arrowed for Wirr, giving him almost no time to react or defend himself. How Essence walls had lit the room and a hail of energy had rained down on the creatures, one of which had still managed to battle through a dozen Gifted to stab Wirr in the stomach with its dark, pulsing dagger.

Wirr couldn't fill in the gaps after that; he had woken to the worried ministrations of the Gifted, who despite their best efforts were unable to fully heal the wound. But he had heard the story several times now. How the entire Council had stood against them. How they had activated the protections of Tol Athian's Council room itself, the Builders' internal defenses springing to life for the first time in known memory.

The sha'teth had been restrained down here, and while there had been much debate about simply killing them—both Wirr and Taeris had advocated it—the Council had ultimately seen them as a valuable resource. Both for information and, Wirr suspected, because they vaguely hoped they might one day be turned back under their control.

Scyner listened with narrowed eyes, assessing, saying nothing until Taeris was finished. Then he glanced back over at the sha'teth, who had remained silent throughout, hanging from the wall and watching the three men with dead eyes.

"Is it not as we told you, Shalician?" called the one on the left, noting Scyner's look.

Scyner showed no reaction to the creature, though he looked pointedly at Taeris and Wirr. "It is."

Taeris scowled. "You doubt something about the account?"

"No." Scyner kept his voice low. "My concern is that they were captured at all."

"They killed a dozen of the most powerful Gifted in Andarra," pointed out Wirr. "And made it into the middle of Tol Athian to do so."

"But doesn't that strike you as odd?" Scyner pressed. "These are not animals, Prince Torin. They are not Banes, clumsy weapons that the Venerate would try to just smash against their enemies. I have no doubt that you were a target, but..." He shook his head. "If you were truly their only target, why attack at the very center of Tol Athian—and while you were with the entire Council? Why not pick you off somewhere outside the protections of the Tol?" He stared at Taeris pointedly, plainly expecting the scarred man to answer.

"Of course we considered that," said Wirr irritably before Taeris could respond. "But that Council meeting was one of the first times my whereabouts were widely known since I got back here. It was only made public because it was assumed to be safe."

"Not to mention the statement the attack made. The effects we still feel from it," added Taeris. "Everyone in the Tol knows that this is not necessarily a safe haven now—even with the Sanctuary entrance guarded. The time and energy that have gone into strengthening the defenses here, when they could have been put toward more important things, have been significant."

Scyner considered.

"Perhaps you are right," he conceded reluctantly. "But Tal'kamar sent me here to get information from these creatures, and that is what I intend to do."

"You've seen Caeden?" asked Wirr immediately, brightening. He leaned forward excitedly. "How is he? *Where* is he?" He had not seen his friend since the Blind's attack on Ilin Illan nearly two years earlier, though he knew Asha had seen him since in Deilannis.

Scyner studied Wirr curiously.

"He is well enough. He is attempting to retrieve Licanius from the Venerate," the black-veined man said. "And to save your friend."

286 Wirr's heart leaped. "Davian's alive?"

"He is." Scyner seemed privately amused about something in the conversation. "I do not know much more than that," he added quickly, seeing the questions on the tip of Wirr's tongue. "He helped free Tal'kamar from Ilshan Gathdel Teth, and now is being held by the Venerate. That is all Tal'kamar told me before sending me here." Scyner paused. "And on that subject—why are *you* here? I assume that you didn't come all the way down here for casual conversation."

Wirr glanced across at Taeris, who hesitated.

"Do you...remember Rethgar?" Taeris asked.

Taeris quickly explained what they had learned from Dras, then moved swiftly through their subsequent findings. Scyner listened with a steadily deepening frown, which changed to an expression of outright concern as Taeris described Rethgar's tomb.

"El take it," he muttered. "An escherii? Tal'kamar needs to know."

"Escherii?" Wirr looked at the other two men blankly, but from Taeris's grimace, Wirr was the only one who didn't know the word.

"An unbound sha'teth. One with more agency, free to share its knowledge, to use its connection to the Darklands without limitations. There has only ever been one other, and the information on it is...slim, at best." Taeris licked his lips as Scyner nodded approvingly; this was evidently coming from the memories the Augur had stored within Taeris. "Their only limitation is the body they inhabit; the more power they use, the more it will break down, until ultimately it will just...disintegrate."

"That's not the worst of it," murmured Scyner bleakly. "Its creation will have taken one of the connections to the Forge." There was silence; Scyner looked up at them, glowering at their blank looks as if only just remembering whom he was talking to. "It's your missing Augur," he clarified impatiently. "And now we're going to have to find a way to kill it. Another delightful side effect of your misusing what I left to you, Thell, and Nihim." The last was directed squarely at Taeris.

The scarred man blanched for a second before his expression darkened. "No. *No. Your* betrayal is what led us to grasp at that particular straw," he said, ire raising his voice sharply. "Fates, at the time, we thought that maybe making the sha'teth was *why* you gave us that information!"

"I gave Thell *every* scrap of research I had on the Darklands—the sha'teth were one piece amongst thousands," said Scyner, matching Taeris's tone. "Just as I gave you everything I knew of the Boundary, and Nihim everything I'd learned of our enemy. I knew I wouldn't be able to risk showing myself again for years; it was all meant to inform, to ensure you had the most complete picture possible of what Andarra was facing. It was meant to help you and the Tols prepare, so that you could actually *help* when the time came." His expression hardened. "You were the three Gifted who I knew would survive the war; I assumed that together, you would be able to convince everyone of the danger. Instead, you created *these*"—he gestured back at the manacled sha'teth in disgust—"and got yourselves disgraced before the rebellion even started."

He locked eyes with Taeris, who glared back defiantly, their surroundings temporarily forgotten.

Then Scyner sighed, shaking his head.

"We don't have time for this—I need to ask some more pointed questions about Rethgar," he said grimly, looking around at the sha'teth. "You may stay, or leave. But do not interfere."

Wirr coughed, almost unwilling to remind the two men that he was there. "They have already been questioned. A lot."

"Not by me." Scyner looked like he was bracing himself for something unpleasant.

Taeris gave him a black look. "These are the Tol's prisoners. What happens to them while in our custody is our responsibility." The tension in his voice suggested that he was still working hard not to pursue the previous argument with Scyner.

"Then stay and observe. This will be painful for them, but it is not torture." Scyner peered at Taeris. "I am the only one who has the ability and knowledge to do this. Who can get *real* answers. And I am going to do it whether you try to stop me or not."

Taeris and Wirr exchanged a glance. Wirr's stomach churned, but he nodded.

"Do it," he muttered.

Scyner strode back over to the sha'teth. "Sekariel. Deonidius." He smiled cheerlessly at the creatures. "Time to talk."

The pale, scarred faces regarded the Augur with almost identical sneers.

"*Kelorin sa etemiel.* We have already answered your questions," said the one on the left—the one called Sekariel, Wirr thought.

"Yet if you have more, we are of course pleased to cooperate," rasped the other. It glanced across at Taeris. "Particularly for you, Taeris Sarr."

"I want to know about Rethgar," said Scyner, ignoring the words.

"The one Taeris Sarr killed?" asked Deonidius mockingly.

"The one he and Taranor sacrificed to keep secret their mistake?" the other crowed, its black-eyed, empty gaze fixed on Taeris. "Surely there is someone here better to ask?"

Scyner sighed.

"Here is the thing, Sekariel," he said. "You obviously believe that you have me at a disadvantage right now. You are thousands of years old, no doubt bound against revealing your purpose, and you think that I...I am just an Augur."

He smiled slightly, as if he knew something that the sha'teth did not.

"In those thousands of years, though," he continued, "did you ever hear of the Ath?"

Deonidius rasped a laugh, though it had lost some of its bite this time. "You are not her."

"No." Scyner closed his eyes, stretching out his hand toward the sha'teth. "But she *has* been teaching me."

Deonidius screamed.

Wirr and Taeris both leaped in alarm at the horrific, earsplitting sound, the unnatural screeches of pain ricocheting around the enclosed space, assaulting their senses. The other sha'teth—Sekariel—shouted something furiously in Darecian, obviously demanding that the Augur stop, but Scyner didn't react to any of it.

Wirr shuddered, hands over his ears, as he watched Deonidius. The sha'teth's back was arched, its mouth so wide its pallid face looked stretched almost to the breaking point as it shrieked, every muscle trembling and convulsing as it thrashed maniacally against its manacles. Wirr tensed as tiny clouds of dust burst from the wall where the metal was secured, concerned that the creature was about to somehow—impossibly—break free with sheer, demented strength.

"Stop." Wirr couldn't take it anymore; regardless of the creature's nature, it was impossible not to feel just how much pain it was in. "Scyner, just—"

He trailed off as Taeris gripped him firmly by the arm. Wirr turned to the scarred man, who shook his head silently.

Wirr pushed Taeris's hand away vexedly, but he didn't move any closer.

Scyner abruptly opened his eyes, staring directly at Deonidius, who was still thrashing as if being lashed again and again by invisible whips.

"Let him speak," Scyner said in a commanding voice.

Beside him, Wirr heard Taeris inhale sharply.

"You are a fool!" snarled Sekariel, and this time the note of panic in his voice was unmistakable. "You cannot—"

Scyner gestured tersely and Sekariel's eyes bulged as he cut off abruptly, apparently unable to say anything else.

"Elder Tolliver. I know he is still in there." Scyner said the words calmly, almost drowned out by the screams. "Deonidius, you will let him speak if you do not wish to be entirely cut off from Markaathan."

"You...waste...your energy," gasped the creature. "You will kill us, and then this will be for naught."

"And yet I do not believe you wish to die. If you did, you would never have allowed yourself to be taken by mere Gifted," replied Scyner calmly. "So I will continue, and we will see. If I am wrong, then I am wrong."

There was nothing for what seemed an eternity, before suddenly a final screech of defiance and anger. The sha'teth went limp against its restraints, its cries silenced. For a moment Wirr was certain it was dead.

Then, impossibly, its face started changing. The pallid facade gained a hint of color. The drooping skin pulled tighter.

The sha'teth raised its head, and the eyes it gazed at the three

men with were human.

"Jakarris." The weak voice that came out of the sha'teth's mouth was hoarse, but...*real*. Colored with emotion in a way the sha'teth's never were. "Traitor."

"Do you remember the last time I saw you, Tolliver?" Scyner asked briskly, ignoring the accusation.

A pause.

"The day...before the war. You sent me to...Tol Athian. Told me you needed me to...stay there for a couple of days." A broken laugh. "Turned out to be...longer."

Scyner nodded. There was sweat on his brow, and Wirr could tell that there was an unseen struggle taking place.

"We do not have long," the Augur said, voice strained with effort. "Why are you here?"

"Told...to come here. Get...caught."

Wirr's heart pounded, and Taeris shifted expectantly beside him. This is what they needed to know.

"Why?"

"Not...sure."

Scyner gritted his teeth. "We need to know, Tolliver. Quickly." To the left, Wirr could see the other sha'teth straining angrily against its restraints, but they all ignored it, hanging on Tolliver's every word.

"All...Deonidius knows," Tolliver gasped. "Not...trusted."

Scyner bared his teeth, looking as frustrated as Wirr felt. "Stay with me," he muttered, more to himself than the sha'teth.

"What do you know about Rethgar?" It was Taeris breaking the silence, stepping forward. Scyner scowled at the interruption but didn't say anything.

Tolliver's disfigured face turned deliberately to Taeris. "Sarr," he gasped. "Rethgar is the...one who sent us. He is...escherii. He...hates you. Wants you to see...all you have worked for...destroyed before he kills you." Another rasping, coughing laugh. "I...cannot blame him."

Taeris took a half step forward.

"Forgive me," he said, a tremor to his voice that Wirr hadn't heard before.

Those eyes, full of pain, gazed at Taeris.

"Never," came the whispered reply.

"Enough," snarled Scyner, beads forming on his forehead now, clearly struggling in whatever battle he was fighting. "What else can you tell us, Tolliver? We need to know their plans."

"We are ordered. Nothing... is explained. The Venerate do not... trust us because they do... not trust the one who turned us."

Scyner staggered and there was a *twisting* in the air; suddenly the sha'teth's face drained of color, the skin sagging and deforming once again. Scyner groaned as the sha'teth glared at him balefully.

"So," it said, and the grinding, unnatural rasp to its voice was back. "Did that help you, Shalician? Do you feel accomplished?"

Scyner steadied himself against the wall, pale from the effort of whatever he had done. "It was enough," he croaked. He just stood there, breathing for several seconds, and then looked at Wirr and Taeris.

"I'm going to try with Sekariel, now," he said quietly.

The next few minutes were painful to sit through as the other sha'teth endured the same agony as its brother, arching and spasming and shrieking. It was to no avail, though; Scyner finally sagged back, hands shaking, as the sha'teth's screams faded to moans.

"I need to rest," he admitted, head bowed, breath coming in short, sharp gasps. "A few hours, at least."

"You are weak," rasped Sekariel, though the pain in his grinding voice was still evident. The sha'teth leaned forward against its restraints menacingly, looking at Wirr now. "Perhaps I can tell you more. Perhaps you would like to know more about Rethgar's deeds? Did you know that he was the one assigned to hunt you down? He told us of that night at your school. How he ripped the Gifted apart, feasted on their terror. He delighted in what he did to your friends, boy. He *laughed* as he told us of it."

Wirr swallowed the furious surge of emotions that suddenly roiled in his chest. The friends he had lost that night were many.

"And yet he failed, and I'm alive," he replied coldly, pushing down the pain. "Whatever Devaed's plan is, my being here is clearly a problem for him."

The sha'teth looked at him, and then to Wirr's horror it burst out laughing—a rasping, hacking sound, but clearly one of amusement.

"You still do not know? He *still* has not explained?" The sha'teth's eyes gleamed. "Your friend is—"

It cut off with a gargle, and Wirr realized that Scyner had gagged it again.

Wirr glared at the Augur. "I want to hear what it has to say."

"It is only trying to cause divisions," Scyner said quickly.

"And I know that. But I still want to know what it thinks I don't," said Wirr firmly.

Scyner rubbed his forehead tiredly.

"Then let me be the one to tell you," he said heavily. "Aarkein Devaed is still alive—but he switched sides a long time ago. He is fighting against the Venerate, now."

Wirr barked a laugh, and Taeris gave Scyner a disbelieving look. "Aarkein Devaed is on *our side*," repeated Wirr incredulously.

Scyner's face was impassive.

"More than that—you've met him. Devaed was what the Darecians named him. His real name is Tal'kamar," he said quietly.

"You know him as Caeden."

Chapter 20

Caeden sat opposite Asha on the lip of a fountain, occasionally glancing sideways at Ell.

She always smiled when he did; he was never sure whether that made him happy or not. The dok'en as a whole was as bittersweet a thing as he had experienced since he had wiped his memories. Had he really thought that having Ell here, reliving this part of his life, was the best way for him to live out his final days? It all seemed so...*sad*. The design of a man who had given up.

And yet he didn't want to leave, either. It brought him back to a time before all of this had started. He'd been young, of course—almost unimaginably young—but he'd been *free*.

He smiled back automatically, as always with a touch of hesitancy that he immediately regretted, and then was irritated at himself for regretting. Ell wasn't real, even if she wasn't as predictable as he would have expected a construct of his own mind to be. She only reluctantly answered to Ell, for one, insisting that she be called Elli instead.

He remembered that—something that had never quite stuck. He'd called her Ell for years in private; it had been the running joke of a child, then his affectionate name for her. But a week before their wedding, she'd brought it up. Told him that as much as she loved their shared history with the epithet, it might be time to start using something less...disrespectful.

He'd understood, of course. It was just a name, and they had both long since outgrown the rebellious humor of it. But even so, she'd still been firmly anchored in his mind as Ell when...

He sighed, shaking his head heavily.

He turned back to Asha, studying the young woman outlined by the soft blue glow of the water garden. Night had fallen hours ago, and the grounds were illuminated by the lights of the dancing fountains, though the air had kept its gentle warmth.

"Any luck?" he asked tentatively, not wishing to interrupt but feeling impatience encroaching upon his thoughts.

Asha opened her eyes, looking up at him ruefully. "It's harder than I expected," she admitted. "Can you show me again?"

Caeden nodded, fixing his image of Garadis in his mind and then *focusing*. His ability to manipulate the dok'en directly was frustratingly limited, but he'd finally remembered why: to make certain that he couldn't get out. Couldn't simply break it apart and leave the Tributary. He hadn't *thought* that he would break down and try, but it had felt wise to remove even the temptation.

He was still able to conjure illusions easily enough, though.

The dark was flung back as Garadis's imposing form burst into existence, forcing Caeden and his two companions to shield their eyes. It wasn't Caeden's most recent memory of the Lyth—the one in which he had been attached to the Siphon, dimmed from his former glory. This was Garadis as Caeden still thought of him: blue eyes burning almost as bright as the rest of him as he moved slightly, chest rising and falling, shifting from one leg to the other in a mildly impatient dance.

He did nothing else, though. It was just an illusion, a way of helping Asha to identify him.

"His Essence signature," said Asha, studying the image. "You're sure it's accurate?"

"Fairly sure." Caeden gave her an appraising look as the young woman examined the image intently. He'd known that she was strong, even skilled—his entry into the dok'en had more than proven that—but her being able to distinguish Essence signatures from one another was particularly impressive. There was a great deal of focus involved in being able to identify someone purely from the unique pulse and hue and strength of their Essence. A signature was something of a physical characteristic, too—it could change over time, age with the person. Still be recognizably them, but not necessarily appear just as it once had. "Hold on a moment."

He closed his eyes, using kan to sharpen the memory a little. He'd found that he could do that—not go back as he had with some of his other, older memories, but clarify the ones he had made since Eryth Mmorg. He wasn't sure if it was a skill he had always had, or whether this was something new. It was useful right now, though.

"There," he said, tweaking the image of Garadis—the *deeper* image of Garadis—and exhaling from the effort of concentration. "That's..." He shrugged. "It's close. It might not be perfect, but it should help."

"Thanks." Asha closed her eyes again.

Caeden watched her for a while in silence.

"She's tenacious."

Caeden smiled slightly at Ell's voice in his ear, the familiar light scent of her hair reaching his nostrils as he turned, her face only inches away. "Seems that way," he agreed softly. He hesitated. "How has her time been here?" It felt strange to ask questions of someone who was an extension of his own mind, but Ell was as carefully cordoned off as the rest of the dok'en. If she had learned new things in here, his mind wouldn't be able to access them.

"Lonely." Ell's smile faded and she looked sad. "I tried to keep her company as best I could, but..."

Caeden nodded his understanding. Ell knew what she was.

"You did what you could. That's all anyone could ask." Again, it felt strange to be comforting what was essentially himself, but the illusion was too strong to ignore. "How about her state of mind? Her determination? Her drive?" He'd only met Asha briefly at Deilannis, and though Davian had spoken extremely highly of her, Caeden really knew very little about her character.

Ell thought for a moment, then shook her head.

"She was a mess when she got here," she said quietly. "But she pulled herself together fast enough to stabilize the dok'en—without even knowing what she was doing. She's trained, and studied, and worked every single day. She takes the Shifts as well as anyone can be expected to. She's as good as you could possibly hope for, and better than you deserve." Ell smiled. "Which is all to say, I quite like her. So if you do anything more to hurt that girl—if you take *anything* more away from her than you already have—then you will have me to answer to."

Caeden held up his hands defensively, giving Ell a grin. "Understood." Ell's tone had been light, but her eyes told a different story. She knew that he was responsible for what Asha had gone through—perhaps not completely, but all of this was at least partly his doing. And Asha had deserved none of it.

He fell silent, lost in thought. He hoped that Davian could forgive him for dragging Ashalia back into the fight. His friend had explicitly warned her against going to Ilshan Gathdel Teth, but… he hadn't known the circumstances. Hadn't known that she might be able to leave the Tributary safely, or that it appeared the Venerate wanted to keep her in it.

He considered again telling Asha that he knew about that message—explaining about Zvaelar, comforting her with the knowledge of how much stronger Davian would emerge from that wretched place. Again, though, he dismissed the idea. The young woman certainly deserved to know, but there was too little time, and he needed her focused. That took precedence.

Caeden opened his mouth to say more when Asha made a small, surprised, and vaguely concerned sound, distracting him. He turned. She was looking at the image of Garadis, eyes wide.

Then he realized that the illusion had shifted.

Was now staring right at him.

"Tal'kamar," it growled, blue eyes flashing with fury, skin smoldering and burning hair curling around its forehead. "I told you that we were not finished with one another."

The blast of Essence was as powerful as it was unexpected, lifting Caeden off his feet and throwing him thirty feet back. He felt ribs crack as he tumbled, his mind going numb from the pain; this was his dok'en and he should be able to stop Garadis even without kan, but all of his focus was taken up by the Essence rushing to heal the massive trauma.

"Stop!" Asha's voice was distant, a mixture of fearful and angry. She knew as well as Caeden did what would happen if he died in here. "*Stop!*"

Garadis ignored her; Caeden wasn't even sure that he could

hear anyone or anything, so intent was he upon Caeden. The Lyth sprinted toward where Caeden had fallen, not giving him time to heal as he threw his hands forward and a twisted, molten blade of Essence the likes of which Caeden had never seen appeared in his hand. Caeden stretched for kan but the surprise attack had been effective, dazing him utterly; there was nothing he could do, no way he could react in time. His head flinched to the side as he braced for what would surely be a killing blow.

Nothing happened.

He sluggishly raised his head again, squinting. A figure stood in front of him, its brilliantly pulsing armor made of pure Essence.

"If you kill him, we all die!" Asha shouted at Garadis, holding back the blade with her Essence-gloved hands. "This is *his* dok'en! Stop!"

Essence flared and Garadis's eyes went wide as the young woman shoved the enormous blade to one side, stepping closer to him as she yelled. The words finally seemed to reach the Lyth; he stuttered, then slowly dropped his hands, though Caeden could tell he was ready to engage in the fight again at the slightest sign of provocation.

Caeden forced Essence to his body, feeling the bones snap back together; though in real life his physical form would be uninjured, the rules of the dok'en followed the rules of the real world—and that included how forces interacted with flesh. As far as his mind was concerned, his body here *was* real. And that was all that mattered.

He staggered to his feet, watching the Lyth warily.

"Good to see you again, Garadis," he gasped.

Garadis didn't say much for the first hour.

He demanded to know where he was, of course, and then how Caeden had had the temerity—after everything he had done to Garadis and his people—to forcibly draw him into a dok'en. The second question was somewhat difficult to answer, seeing as it wasn't something Caeden had specifically intended. Even now, he still had no idea exactly *how* Asha had managed to bring the Lyth here. He had theories—Asha's Essence underpinning the dok'en, combined with her connection to Garadis via the Siphon, must have allowed for it—but it was clearly a unique, unintended interaction between the two Vessels, and something that would probably require significant study before the actual cause could be determined.

Garadis had come close to attacking again when he'd realized that Ashalia was the one who held the power of the Siphon, and though Caeden felt confident that they could keep the Lyth in check now, he was glad they hadn't needed to try. He wasn't sure why Garadis was able to use Essence here, when the Siphon was physically blocking him in real life—but he very clearly could.

In the end, though, Caeden and Asha between them had managed to explain the situation. Garadis had calmed, even appeared to be listening. He seemed...*different* from when Caeden had left him and his people in the Shining Lands. Harder and yet less reserved, his fury and hatred no longer contained to his eyes.

Finally Caeden fell silent, the things he'd felt the need to explain now said.

"So once again you call on us," said Garadis heavily, just as the silence began to stretch. "You save us from imprisonment, only to bind our powers. And now you tell me that we are not safe. That after all your efforts, the rift may still be torn open and the Darklands unleashed upon us. Upon the entire world." He closed his eyes. "Every time our lives touch yours, Tal'kamar, we are left poorer. And every time, it seems that we have no choice. You are always the lesser of two evils. But never by much."

There was grief rather than anger in his tone, and Caeden felt a flush of shame. Garadis was right: he had always brought pain to the Lyth, even if he had managed to free them from Res Kartha.

Caeden didn't say anything in response. There wasn't anything he *could* say, really.

"Is it possible?" he asked eventually, quietly. "Your people were close with Wereth. You know all about the Siphon." He hesitated. "And I have to think that you have been researching it further, since you were all bound. So if anyone will know, it is you."

Garadis's glower was enough to tell Caeden he'd been right. It wasn't unexpected; the Lyth were nothing if not knowledgeable and so binding them with a Vessel was always a risk, even if they knew that they could not afford to break the connection while Asha powered the Boundary.

Caeden leaned forward, seeing Garadis's hesitation. "You are helping yourselves by helping us—beyond simply preventing the end of the world, of course," he said wryly.

"I do not see how that is the case," said Garadis. "We are best served by Ashalia remaining in the Tributary."

"Except that that is what it appears the Venerate *want*," emphasized Caeden.

"I am not going to help you on a guess." Garadis's tone was disdainful. "To think that I would help at all is ambitious, even for you, Tal'kamar."

"You need to grow up."

Both men stopped at Asha's words; Caeden blinked, and he could see the anger flaring in Garadis's eyes as the Lyth turned toward her. But she didn't look intimidated.

"You think that you're alone in hating him? Hating what he's done?" she spat, jerking her head toward Caeden without looking at him. "He murdered the man I love. I've *seen* it. It is a memory for Tal'kamar here, but for Davian? It is the future. He's not dead yet. But this man is going to kill him." There was grief and rage and fear in her voice all at once, and Caeden felt a chill of sadness. "He is the reason we are here. But he is also on our side, now. We have to work with him. It doesn't mean we have to forgive him."

Caeden stared at the ground. The words cut deep, all the more so for his knowing that they were completely deserved.

Garadis glared, but to Caeden's surprise there was also hesitation in his stance now.

"You think that is reason for hate?" the Lyth snarled. "He killed my *people*."

"He *hurt* your people. Not working with him is what will kill them." Asha glared at Garadis. "I think he's right, by the way. There's something that the Venerate are hiding from us."

Garadis stared at the ground, not answering for a long few seconds.

"What you wish to do is...likely possible," he finally said, albeit reluctantly. "The theory is sound, and the practice is in evidence." He gestured at Asha, but then shook his head as Asha 301 started to relax. "That is not the same as me agreeing to help. I need to consult with my people. I cannot do this alone, and I will..." He grimaced.

Caeden frowned. "What?"

"I need to see if they will be willing. I cannot command them anymore, Tal'kamar. I am no longer the leader of the Lyth." He said the words simply, without self-pity, but Caeden could see that there was hurt behind them.

Caeden inclined his head, the motion an acknowledgment of Garadis's pain. Saying anything would likely only make matters worse. "How long until you know?"

"A few hours." Garadis nodded to himself. "That will be enough."

Caeden turned to Asha. "Can you bring him in again?"

"I'm still not sure what I did, exactly, but..." The young woman shrugged. "I suppose so." She ran a hand through her hair. "The bigger question is, how do I send him back?"

"That should be easy enough." Caeden closed his eyes, feeling the different connections to the dok'en. He had restricted himself from being able to alter it too much, but hadn't been blind to the possibility of intruders, either. "I'll release the connection."

"Then do it," said Garadis. His gaze locked with Caeden's. "Three hours, Tal'kamar. I will return with your answer then."

Caeden broke the glowing line. When he opened his eyes again, Garadis was gone.

Asha and Caeden stared at the spot where the Lyth had been. Dusk had turned into night, and though the lights from the fountains still lit the area clearly, everything seemed just a little dimmer.

"I meant what I said, you know," Asha said suddenly into the silence. "All of it."

Caeden gave her a sad smile. "I know."

They headed back inside the Crystalline Palace, and settled down to wait.

Garadis, thankfully, showed no inclination to initiate further violence upon his return.

The Lyth seemed to orient himself quickly this time, looking composed as he took in their location in the library and then acknowledging Asha and Caeden. Something glimmered in his blue eyes as he looked at Caeden.

"Well?" asked Caeden, not bothering to dance around the issue.

"We believe that there is a way to do what you are looking to do," said Garadis.

Caeden exhaled in relief, and beside him he could hear Asha doing the same. "But?"

"But there are some...conditions."

Asha's expression darkened, but Caeden just nodded. He had expected as much. "What do you want?"

Garadis said nothing for a few moments, though he didn't look as if he was thinking about his answer. More like he was sizing Caeden up, trying to decide whether his terms would be accepted.

"The first is not so much a price, as it is a restriction. A practicality, given the speed at which you will need this developed." His gaze flicked between Asha and Caeden. "The solution at which we have arrived will allow Ashalia to keep control of her power, but by necessity we will need to mimic at least some of the kan machinery of the Siphon. Which means that we cannot attach it to the Tributary itself."

Caeden winced, Asha's face twisting as she realized at almost the same time what Garadis was saying.

"You need someone to take her place," said Caeden.

"Not an option," Asha said firmly. "I'm not going to subject someone else to this."

Garadis looked at her mildly. "The others are uncertain whether it could ever be done without a living conduit, and I am inclined to agree. And even if we found a way around the hard limitations involved, it could take months of research. Possibly years." His gaze was steady. "Copying these elements of the Siphon isn't just a shortcut, Ashalia. It is your only option."

"We'll take it," said Caeden. He held up a hand as Asha made to protest again. "We'll find someone willing, Ashalia. And if they choose to make the same sacrifice that you have for this past year, then it is not your place to naysay them." He wasn't sure where they would get a volunteer, but he'd find one.

Asha subsided. She still looked as if she wanted to argue, but she clearly also saw his point.

Caeden faced Garadis again. "You mentioned a price?"

"Yes. We want you to bind yourself, Tal'kamar," Garadis said without preamble. "We want you to commit yourself to your own death. Even if you find a way to do what you wish without it, you *must* agree to end your own life once the other Venerate are dead."

"What?" exclaimed Asha, taking a half step forward in anger. "That's a preposterous thing to—"

"Done." Caeden ignored Asha's look of horror.

"Caeden, you don't have to—"

"Of course I do." Caeden turned to Asha, his voice calm, though his heart still skipped an unsettled beat at the thought of what he was agreeing to. "It's necessary, Asha. Planned. I've been resolved to this longer than you have been alive. Binding myself to it...all it does is make it official."

Garadis watched intently as Asha fell silent, the young woman gazing at Caeden in shock. "Further. We want you to bind yourself to leaving the remaining Augurs unharmed."

Caeden's heart sank, and he hung his head this time, mind racing.

"Still, Garadis?" he asked, hearing the frustration in his own voice. He'd suspected this, too, but had held out hope that perhaps sanity would prevail.

"Always." Garadis spoke softly, but there was a fierceness to his voice. "We will never give up, Tal'kamar. Not until the last of my people are gone."

"You cannot stop Shammaeloth without sealing the rift."

"We do not believe that is true. We never have."

Caeden clenched his fists; he glanced to the side, seeing Asha's mildly confused expression.

She didn't know that while the Lyth wanted the Venerate dead, they also believed that those deaths would be enough to make the rift...manageable. Something they could fashion into a door, one that they could open and close at will. Their failure with the Jha'vett, their transformation and subsequent confinement to Res Kartha—none of it had lessened their drive.

Just like the Venerate, Garadis and his people still believed that they could go back and change things.

And Caeden knew all too well that no matter how much he argued, he couldn't sway them from that.

"I'd like to know the wording first, of course. Written down for review," he said heavily. He motioned to the desk in the corner. "There's paper and pen over there."

"Of course." Garadis's eyes gleamed. "I will need a moment."

The Lyth moved a small way away, and Asha turned to him.

"You *knew*," whispered Asha accusingly. "You knew that this would be what he asked."

"Not him. The Lyth. The *Darecians*," Caeden corrected her quietly. "But yes. Trapping them as I did with the Siphon, placing them in such an impossible position...it was always going to be this."

"You're giving up."

"I'm doing what I already told you must be done." Caeden allowed a hint of irritation into his tone, but was prevented from saying more by Garadis proffering a sheet of paper. Despite the Lyth's burning skin, the page remained unsinged.

Caeden scanned what had been written, then shook his head. "I'm going to stipulate that this is void if the Vessel doesn't work exactly as described."

"You think that we would betray our word?"

"I think that there is no need to allow for the possibility," said Caeden calmly.

Garadis wavered, then gave a sharp nod. "Done."

"Then let's get it over with." He stepped forward, refusing to flinch as Garadis raised a glowing hand and pressed two fingers against Caeden's forehead.

"Say it."

Caeden took a deep breath. This was necessary. It would make things more difficult, certainly, but it didn't change anything—not really.

The words were still hard to utter.

" 'I will do nothing to harm the remaining Augurs.' " He faltered, just for a moment, and then continued. " 'As soon as I am satisfied that the other Venerate are all dead, I will use Licanius   305 to end my own life. I bind myself to this agreement upon the condition that the Vessel provided will successfully link Ashalia's Reserve to a proxy, allowing her to leave the Tributary while still powering the ilshara. If it does not, or if the Vessel has any other mechanism added to it without my consent, then this binding will no longer apply.' "

"And the rest," said Garadis, not removing his hand.

Caeden scowled. " 'I will honor this binding in the spirit in which it was agreed upon, not to the letter in which it was said.' " He held Garadis's gaze as he said the last words.

Garadis released a long breath, and the tension that had been in his shoulders since he had appeared seemed to melt away.

"An ending, Tal'kamar," he murmured, shaking his head dazedly. "To think, now—after all this time. Finally."

"An ending," agreed Caeden quietly, trying to ignore the still-horrified look on Asha's face.

Garadis cocked his head to the side, studying him. "So. What of your plan for the others? Have you determined a way to deal with Alaris?"

"Alaris is imprisoned. Somewhere even safer than Res Kartha."

Garadis nodded thoughtfully. "Is the Traveler not a risk?"

"Nethgalla is with me on this. She will not release him."

"You are working with her?" Garadis couldn't disguise his surprise this time. "You truly have changed, Tal'kamar."

Caeden restrained a grimace, but didn't correct the Lyth. Giving Garadis and his people more information than necessary was always a bad idea.

"Do not worry about the others," said Caeden. "Just design this device. I'll take care of the rest."

"We will get to work immediately," said Garadis firmly. He glanced at Caeden, something sharp in his eyes, almost gleeful. "We will bring the Vessel to you when it is ready."

Caeden indicated his agreement even as he swallowed, the implications unsettling. So the Lyth were able to create the Vessel themselves. And to deliver it they would have to use a Gate, given that they didn't have access to their own Essence.

That meant that they could use kan again.

And had his Trace, too, apparently.

Worrying, but at least he knew now.

"Good. Then we are done, and it is time for you to release me from this place." Garadis's gaze turned to Asha, becoming stern. "We have every motivation to deliver the Vessel as quickly as we can, now. I do not expect to be summoned again."

Asha gazed back, and Caeden found himself struck again by the calm confidence in the young woman's demeanor. There was no way that she'd missed the unspoken threat, but she looked unfazed.

"Understood," she said.

Caeden gave Garadis a slight nod, then closed his eyes and located the Lyth's connection to the dok'en, severing it. When he opened them again, he and Asha were alone once more.

Asha gazed at the spot where Garadis had been, and Caeden felt certain that she was about to berate him for his choices. Eventually, though, she just rolled her shoulders.

"I suppose the plan is still the same?" she asked.

Caeden sighed.

"It's time for me to pay Alaris a visit," he agreed heavily.

Chapter 21

Most of the camp had already turned in by the time Davian made it back from his meeting with Isstharis, meager rations in hand.

He paused behind a still-standing wall just before the firelight would reveal his presence, listening with a frown to the sound of tense voices within. Everyone still had rations stockpiled from the previous day, so they should all have eaten dinner by now and be preparing to retire for the night—if not already be asleep.

And until that happened, he wouldn't be able to slip away again and keep examining the area as he'd intended.

"...things we need to consider, Ana. I know it can be hard to think about anything except surviving here, but that just makes this more important."

"Important to you, perhaps," growled Ana. Davian blinked, doubting for a moment that it was actually her. The woman was usually the quietest of the group, and he didn't think that he had ever heard her sound even irritated before. "Tell yourself what you must, but don't bother me with this nonsense."

"Just dismissing something as nonsense doesn't make it so." It was Raeleth's voice. "I am not asking you to agree with me, but just to talk. Just to consider—"

"She is right." It was Ched this time, a bit farther away, sounding annoyed and vaguely sleepy. "Perhaps El exists, Raeleth, but if he does then he is certainly not here. Why bring this up now? The sooner we sleep, the easier it will be to get through tomorrow. And you especially need the rest."

There was silence, and then Raeleth exhaled heavily.

"You're right—for now. But I will not give up on you. Either of you," he added firmly.

Neither Ana nor Ched responded; Davian waited a couple of minutes longer and then moved into view, giving Raeleth a small nod and walking around the dying fire to sit beside him, placing the near-empty pail of rations to the side. He was relieved to see the other two lying tucked in the corners of the room, steady breathing indicating that both of them were already slumbering. That wasn't unusual. After a full day of scavenging, no one had the energy to do much more than chew their food and collapse onto the softest, most sheltered piece of ground that they could find.

They would be angry, and probably suspicious, at how little he'd brought back—but at least he wouldn't have to deal with that until first bell tomorrow.

He stared into the fire for a while. The flames were for light more than heat; the air here in Zvaelar was always dry, hot, and heavy, as if it had no way to escape.

"Maresh?" asked Raeleth abruptly, finally looking at the bucket.

Davian nodded dourly, skewering his bitterroot on a makeshift spit and holding it over the fire to take away the worst of its edge before eating it. "He took three-quarters."

"Three-quarters," Raeleth repeated in a dismayed murmur. He glanced up at Davian. "Didn't manage to keep your temper, I take it?"

Davian gave a short, bitter laugh. "Almost, but…no."

Raeleth said nothing for a few seconds, then smiled slightly.

"He took the same from me, the first time," he admitted. "I called him a coward and a bully and…a collection of names much worse than that. And then the second time, he took the whole thing."

Davian raised an eyebrow. "I did get the impression that he didn't like you much. What did you do the second time?"

Raeleth coughed. "I may have…used the pail to relieve myself of the previous night's bitterroot, a few minutes before I suspected that he was going to ambush me. He was so busy joking with his team about how spineless I was that he didn't even notice, until he went to grab two big handfuls of metal to put in his own bucket."

Davian stared, then guffawed. Raeleth's face split into a grin and he followed suit, the two of them laughing quietly into the fire for several seconds.

"What did he do?" Davian asked between snickers.

Raeleth shrugged. "Straight after? Not sure, because the moment he pulled his hands back out, I ran as fast as I could." He shook his head ruefully, his smile fading. "He's smarter than he looks, though. He didn't bother trying to hurt me. Instead, he spread the word that any team I belonged to would have to give him a quarter-bucket extra, every time. So now I'm a living reminder of what happens when you get on his bad side."

Davian gazed at Raeleth, a few of the things he had been wondering about coming together. "So that's what Ched meant when he said that he took you in." Raeleth, Davian had quickly noticed, was always assigned the worst and hardest jobs on the team—and never complained. This, presumably, explained why.

Raeleth shrugged, then grinned absently at the fire. "I can tell you one thing, though. Maresh doesn't take anyone's metal with his own hands anymore. And every time he tells me to put it in his bucket, it makes my day just a little bit brighter."

They chuckled again, and Davian found the tension in his shoulders easing slightly. It felt good to laugh, even here, even briefly.

"How are you feeling?" asked Davian eventually, casting a cautious glance over toward Ana and Ched. Both were still sleeping soundly.

"Like my eyes are trying to drag themselves shut," admitted Raeleth. "But otherwise, much better. Thank you again," he added sincerely.

Davian inclined his head. "Glad to be in someone's good graces. I suspect you'll be the only one, come morning."

Raeleth grunted. "They'll grumble, but I wouldn't worry about those two," he said reassuringly. "They say they only let me join their team from desperation—but the truth is, someone else would have come along soon enough. I think they just enjoy the idea of Maresh still having to deal with me."

Davian chuckled. "Good to know." He shifted slightly. This was the first real conversation he'd been able to have with Raeleth since he'd arrived at camp. "So you had a different team, before Ched and Ana?"

"Three of them, actually," said Raeleth. "The first months here, before everyone figured out what they were doing...well. Let's just say that El was looking out for me." He stared into the fire. "You can't cure it, can you. It's going to keep coming back."

Davian was mystified for a moment, until he followed the abrupt change of topic.

He shook his head slowly.

"No," he admitted, looking Raeleth in the eye. "I don't think so, anyway. It retreats whenever I use Essence on it, but there's a spot that I can't seem to get rid of completely."

Raeleth took a couple of shaky breaths. "Well. Now I'm *really* glad that I didn't leave you alone out there to die," he said with a forced grin.

Davian winced.

"I...can't heal it past a few times more, either," he said quietly. "It's difficult to explain, but...I'm not like a normal Gifted. I'm running out of Essence, here, and I don't have a way of replenishing it yet." He chewed his lip. "Which means that I need to find out all I can about this place. Sooner rather than later."

Raeleth paled, but to Davian's surprise did not react with the outright dismay he'd expected.

"You want to find out where the metal's going," he said eventually. "You want to go north, across the Breach."

"I know you said that it was impossible, but there have to be answers there." Davian rubbed his forehead. "There are certainly none around here—I've been looking, during the evenings. There's just...more of what we see during the day. Buildings falling down, pools of Dark, al'goriat and the occasional crazy dar'gaithin. That's where I was when Ched woke up the other night," he added, a touch ashamedly.

"I assumed," admitted Raeleth. "I thought about telling you to stop, but you know the risks and I'm not your father, so..." He shrugged.

Davian took a breath. He hadn't been intending to bring this up for a while yet—a week hadn't been nearly enough time to build up any significant trust—but they were talking about it now. "I can figure out a way across myself, but it would be ten times easier if someone who knew—"

"You don't need to sell it. I'll help however I can," Raeleth said, holding up his hand to stop Davian. "El brought us together for a reason—maybe this is it. Plus it sounds like it's in my best interests," he observed wryly.

Davian exhaled. He'd been prepared to tackle this alone, and part of him didn't even want to risk bringing Raeleth into it—that he himself couldn't die didn't exclude those around him from harm by association—but still, it was a relief.

"Have you seen the bridge?" asked Raeleth, the way he asked clearly indicating that he knew just how difficult an obstacle it would be.

Davian nodded grimly. The bridge itself—if it could even be called that—had seemingly formed from the remains of a massive tower, which had fallen across the Breach and somehow not broken apart in the process. Instead, it had left a fairly wide and smooth, if incredibly precarious-looking, path across.

A tremor had hit during the night he'd spent observing it, as he'd been trying to figure out a way across. He'd crouched in the shadows and watched, wide-eyed, as the al'goriat that constantly swarmed its surface had started stumbling around drunkenly, a few flailing and falling off, disappearing soundlessly into the burning yellow chasm along with great chunks of stone that had shaken loose.

It had *not* looked safe.

"There's really no other way?" he asked, holding his breath slightly. The al'goriat made crossing there impossible, but when Raeleth had first mentioned the bridge, there had been...something. A hesitation that suggested there might be more to say, but he'd chosen not to.

Raeleth rubbed his face.

"I may know of one," he finally admitted. "But it won't exactly be easy. It involves something of a...jump."

Davian's heart skipped a beat. "Can you show me?"

Raeleth's gaze slid to the sleeping forms on the other side of the 313 fire, and he gave a long, wide yawn. "Tonight might be too soon," he admitted wearily.

Davian thought. They didn't *need* to do it tonight, but he'd been itching to take action. Plus, the work they did was dangerous: tomorrow Raeleth might be injured, or his Dark infection might return more quickly this time, sapping Davian's Reserve even further.

He reluctantly tapped his Reserve and held up a hand that now gave off a gentle light, palm out toward Raeleth. "I can fix that. May I?"

Raeleth nodded after a pause for consideration, and Davian clasped him on the shoulder, letting Essence drain into the other man. After a few seconds Raeleth's eyes stopped drooping and he sat up straight, breathing deeply.

"That is... remarkable," he said softly. "I don't feel like I need to sleep at all now."

"It's not a replacement for sleep, but it's close," explained Davian. "You should be able to nap later for only a couple of hours, and still feel as though you got a full night's rest."

Raeleth stood, stretching. "Good enough for me," he said, a slight spring to his step now. He glanced again at Ana and Ched to check that they were still slumbering before motioning into the darkness. "Well. If we're going to do this..."

Davian stood, too, feeling both more nervous and more purposeful than he had since he'd arrived.

They struck out northward, past and over and under buildings as they made their way through the messy maze of the city, picking their way adeptly around any rubble in their path. It was hard to move soundlessly, every skitter and crunch of stone feeling like it was giving away their position. Nothing stirred in the red-tinged darkness, though, and every campfire still burning that they passed revealed only people sleeping.

Raeleth led the way, pausing occasionally to get his bearings and leading them in a seemingly zigzagging pattern along smaller, narrower paths and tunnels than they would usually choose to travel. He saw Davian's concerned glance at one point and shook his head slightly.

"I know where we are," he assured Davian. "Some of us spent

the first week here hiding out in these areas until it was either surrender or starve—that's when I found where we're going. The al'goriat don't seem to bother patrolling as much around these ways, either."

Davian accepted the statement, allowing Raeleth to lead them off in yet another new direction. If the man knew a route that avoided the creatures, it seemed wise to let him take it.

As they moved, Davian reached out for kan again, the attempt almost an absent, nervous habit now. He was *so close*. Every time he stretched he could *feel* the dark power, as if it were flowing over the very tips of his fingers. Just a little further, and he would be able to grasp it. Use it to draw in Essence once more.

They came to an abrupt stop in the shell of a hollowed-out building, and Davian abandoned his efforts, watching curiously as Raeleth started dragging aside some smaller pieces of stone that had fallen on the floor. After a moment, Davian moved to help him.

"So why are we doing this?" he asked between breaths.

"Because of...that," Raeleth panted as he hauled aside the final chunk, indicating the space on the floor that had been cleared.

Davian squinted at the dusty surface, finally spotting the faint square outline in the grit. A trapdoor.

Raeleth fumbled around in his pockets, then produced a long, fat key. The silver glistened in the dull red light.

"Metal?" Davian gazed at the key in disbelief. "You've been hiding *metal*?" He'd only been here a week, but he knew how risky a proposition that was.

"I thought about adding it to the bucket almost every day," said Raeleth, dusting off a section of the trapdoor to reveal the keyhole. "But...this is where I hid, that first week. Giving it up felt too much like giving up." He gave Davian a grim smile. "Told you. All in El's plan."

Davian shook his head dazedly as Raeleth inserted the key, giving it a sharp twist. The lock clunked beneath the sturdy wood; Raeleth scrabbled around the edge of the trapdoor and proceeded to haul it open.

Davian and Raeleth both winced as a sharp creaking sound echoed among the buildings, and Davian held his breath. There was no response from the city, though.

Davian allowed himself to breathe again, then peered down. He could see the first few stairs vanishing quickly into the darkness, but nothing beyond that.

At Raeleth's nod, he reluctantly sent a sliver of Essence out ahead of him and started downward.

He paused a few steps in, waiting patiently as Raeleth carefully closed the trapdoor behind him, locking it again. That was probably smart; even if someone spotted the uncovered entrance, they wouldn't be able to open it. The wood had looked thick, too. No one scavenging for metal would risk wasting time trying to break it in.

"What is this place?" Davian asked as Raeleth pocketed the key and they began their descent, Davian's tiny ball of Essence their only illumination now. "I assume it's not just a cellar."

"There's a massive network of tunnels that run beneath the city, and this is the only way down that I've seen. I think they may have been mines, once." Raeleth gave a half shrug. "I've come across old equipment down here, anyway. A couple of ropes. Some pickaxes I ended up turning in for the metal."

"If they were mines, then surely there are other entrances," Davian pointed out uneasily. "Bigger and more obvious ones than this, too."

"There probably are. But I think those must be on the northern side." Raeleth gestured. "You'll see."

They reached the bottom of the stairs, and Davian realized that his Essence was no longer the only illumination. He let his light wink out as Raeleth hurried over to a corner of the small room, picking up a chunk of stone about the size of Davian's fist. It glowed a virulent yellow.

"Breachlight," he said, snagging the two long coils of rope that had lain alongside it and looping them over his shoulder. "Cut it off myself."

Davian frowned. A piece of the glowing chasm wall. "Is it dangerous?"

"Hasn't killed me yet," said Raeleth cheerfully. He saw Davian's expression and shrugged. "It was pitch-black down here, and you know how dangerous it can be even *with* light. I had to try something."

Davian snorted, but gestured for Raeleth to lead the way.

"So tell me more about your era," said Raeleth as they began walking. He spoke quietly, but from his relaxed tone obviously didn't think that there was much chance of their being discovered down here.

Davian gave him a surprised glance.

"I...had the impression that subject was off-limits," he said carefully. He'd made similar inquiries of the entire team when he'd first arrived. On that occasion, he'd been told by Ched in no uncertain terms to let the matter lie.

"Not off-limits, exactly." Raeleth shrugged awkwardly. "It was the only thing anyone talked about, for the first few weeks, but... well. We soon realized that there were two common threads to every conversation. One"—he held up a finger—"that the Venerate are still alive and in control, and two"—he held up another— "the further into the future things go, the worse things in Ilshan Gathdel Teth get. The harder it is for the resistance. The more of our people who become loyal to them, and despise the rest of our country." He shook his head heavily. "The longer the Venerate rule, the more they have managed to shape our city—our society—to suit their views. Most of us are in here because of our opposition to those views, one way or another. So hearing about our failure to make a difference can be a touch..."

"Depressing," finished Davian, understanding. "So why ask me?"

"Because we have time. And because you arrived three months after everyone else," Raeleth reminded him. "Part of me hopes that you might have something different to say."

He glanced across at Davian, and Davian felt an irrational twinge of guilt at the painfully hopeful gaze.

Still, he nodded slowly.

"What do you want to know?"

He spent the next twenty minutes answering questions as they navigated the narrow, rough-hewn tunnels. Davian was, much to Raeleth's excitement, from much further into the future than anyone he had met thus far; Ana and Ched were both from almost a millennium before Davian's time, apparently, and Raeleth was only a generation removed from the creation of the Boundary itself. By Davian's reckoning, the most 'recent' prisoner Raeleth had spoken to was from more than three hundred years ago.

Davian had a thousand questions of his own but he kept them to himself for now, instead telling Raeleth what he knew of recent history, of Ilshan Gathdel Teth, of the Venerate and the current state of the Boundary. He left out the important details, though, skirting around anything he thought the Venerate could take advantage of in his own time. That wasn't from any mistrust of Raeleth, but simply for the sake of prudence.

The tunnels often branched off in different directions, but Raeleth walked confidently, never hesitating at any of the forks, holding the yellow Breachlight aloft but clearly distracted as he listened to what Davian was saying.

Which was why Davian had to rush forward and haul him back after they turned a sharp corner.

"What are you..." Raeleth scrambled to his feet indignantly but trailed off as he saw where he had been about to step. "Oh. Oh no."

The tunnel ahead, at first glance, looked no different from the others that they had been trudging down, but as Davian stared at it, it seemed to...glisten. The more he watched, the more he could see the walls, floor, and roof all shifting slightly, rippling and crawling with the wet, shadowy black of Dark.

"That...wasn't here, last time," said Raeleth. "Thank you."

"El's plan?" Davian asked, unable to resist.

Raeleth just gave him a wry smile. "There will be another way. We're close."

They backtracked, silent now as Raeleth guided them through a new set of passageways. The other man didn't move with quite as much confidence as previously, but he still seemed unfazed by the detour.

"You know your way around," observed Davian. He rubbed at his ears absently, a vague, low humming beginning to press down on them.

Raeleth gave a modest shrug. "I have a good memory." He lowered the glowing stone in his hand and gestured ahead. "See?"

Davian blinked as he saw what Raeleth had already noticed: there was light farther down the passageway.

The two men increased their pace as it became easier to see, but Davian stuttered to a stop as he rounded the next corner, forced to shield his eyes against the abrupt blaze of yellow light. He stood there for several seconds, squinting, letting his eyes adjust—as much as they could—to the glare that surrounded them.

"Fates," he murmured as his vision finally cleared.

He and Raeleth had emerged onto a narrow ledge, which had plainly once been another tunnel—one that had run parallel to where the massive split in the earth now lay. A single wall of the passageway had been shorn away, leaving a brief run of about thirty feet where it was possible to walk.

He steadied himself against the nearby wall, daring to lean slightly and peer upward.

"*Fates*," he muttered again.

"We're about a hundred feet down," confirmed Raeleth, his starkly lit expression vaguely pleased at Davian's reaction. "The bridge is...over there." He waved his hand upward and to the left. "But even if someone was watching, I don't think that they could see this deep. There's just too much light."

Davian licked his lips, frowning around at the burning yellow that coated the walls. "So...*how* do we get across from here, exactly?"

Raeleth silently pointed down and to the right from their position. Davian followed the gesture, not understanding.

Then he spotted it.

"That?" His heart sank as he examined the ledge that Raeleth was indicating. Perhaps ten feet down, it *did* jut out farther than everything else on the other side.

But it was still...fifteen feet away? More?

"I told you we'd need to jump." Raeleth coughed. "Or...I suppose I was thinking that *you* could jump. With the rope. And then I would sort of...climb."

Davian glared at him, then turned back and reassessed the gap. He could make it, with Essence lending his legs some extra strength.

Assuming that he didn't slip, of course.

"All right," he said reluctantly, unable to keep the growl from his voice. He glanced at the rope that Raeleth was uncoiling from around his shoulder, scowling. "You could have mentioned it was a *big* jump, though."

Raeleth grinned. "Didn't want you to worry about it until you had to."

Davian grunted, carefully looping the rope around his waist and knotting it firmly as Raeleth secured the other end to a sturdy-looking piece of stone jutting from the wall. Davian tested it several times with a hard tug before nodding grimly.

He stared at the opposite ledge. It seemed an *awfully* long way away.

"No point in wasting time, I suppose," he said with a tight smile.

He pulled in a breath, backing up against the wall to give himself as much of a run-up as possible.

Then he infused his legs with Essence. Sprinted.

Jumped.

Chapter 22

Davian reached the top of the stairs, scanning for any hint of movement on the flat rooftop before beckoning for Raeleth to follow.

The two of them crept forward onto the smooth sandstone surface, crouching low to avoid being obvious in the diffuse red moonlight. It had been almost two hours since he had leaped across the Breach, securing the rope to the northern wall and watching with his heart in his throat as Raeleth had shimmied—somewhat clumsily—across, bringing with him the spare coil in case something happened to the first. The other man had made it without issue, though, and no sounds had come from above to suggest they had been seen.

Since then, they had spent the entire time finding their way back to the surface through stairwells and passageways similar to those on the southern side—many more of these, though, coated in thick, rippling layers of grasping Dark. Davian was dreading the return trip; each step down there had been fraught, every motion burdened with the fear of a single lapse in concentration. They had even been forced to jump through a narrow section of corridor at one point, every surface for five feet entirely covered in glistening shadow. The oily black liquid had stretched greedily toward them from all sides when they'd leaped, perilously close to making contact.

But they had made it. Now all that remained was to watch the northern side of the bridge and wait for Isstharis to show herself.

"How long do you think until they move it?" murmured

Davian, settling down and eyeing the al'goriat swarming the bridge below.

"Not for a while, I think." Raeleth rubbed his hands together nervously. "The time I saw them taking the barrels across the bridge, it was later than this by a few hours."

Davian accepted the statement—that lined up with what he'd seen, the night that he'd watched from the other side—and neither man talked for a minute as they observed the meandering Banes below.

"So were you a priest, or something? In your time?" he asked conversationally, keeping his voice low. While he didn't want to make an excess of noise, there didn't appear to be any al'goriat nearby. There was no danger in talking while they waited.

Raeleth glanced across at him. "What? No. I was a craftsman—mostly employed to make jewelry for wealthy women, to be honest," he said, giving a small chuckle at Davian's guess. "What did you do?"

"Me? I was training, learning to use Essence, until a couple of years ago. After that..." Davian shrugged. "Fighting against the Venerate, I suppose. Trying to stop the Boundary from collapsing."

"It is hard to believe that the ilshara is still standing, after all that time," Raeleth murmured.

"Hard to believe that you knew people who saw it go up." Davian shook his head. "So what *did* you do, anyway? To be sent here, I mean. This hardly seems like the place they would send a simple craftsman."

Raeleth didn't answer for a few seconds, evidently ordering his thoughts.

"My parents' generation were children when the Venerate came," he finally said slowly. "The story goes that when the ilshara was raised, the Venerate went out of their way to make peace with those left in the north, when they could easily have wiped them out. They gathered the people together and told them that the rule of law would remain. They explained why they had invaded and what they believed about El, and insisted that others were free to believe otherwise—just so long as they accepted one another. They said that the Andarrans had been trapped just as much as they, and that until that wall of Essence could be over-come, we would all need to . . . get along."

He shook his head dourly. "My grandparents hated them—a lot of people in their generation were killed in the war. There were protests, violent uprisings, a lot of unrest to begin with. But then the crops started dying, and the Venerate said it was because of the ilshara. They started working to create arable land around Ilshan Gathdel Teth, using their power to help the people. They did that for *years*. Legend has it that Cyr spent a month with-out sleep to create the Vessel that protects the city's crops from decaying."

"They spread stories," said Davian.

"Not at all. They did all those things," said Raeleth firmly. "And people started to realize that their best chance of survival was to work *with* them. Protesters gradually became unpopu-lar, opposed by their fellow Andarrans. By the time my genera-tion became adults, the Venerate were well on their way to being accepted. Many people my age even saw them as a cause to get behind, to advocate. They became the symbol of a united society, and those who dissented from that view were considered destruc-tive by nature." He shrugged. "Which meant that when the Ven-erate continued to scoff at believers in the, shall we say, 'original' El, people started to listen. To follow suit."

He peered out over the edge of the building as he spoke, eyes fixed on the bridge below. "That doesn't sound so bad, right? Something you could just ignore?" When Davian nodded slightly, he grunted. "The belittling was in private at first, but it wasn't long before it became public. Often. It became a . . . rite of passage. Something people did to feel and look like they belonged. Many of us privately still believed in the old ways but in our silence, we were becoming fewer. Socially outcast, sneered at, told that we believed against proof and obvious moral right. So I started to speak out against the Venerate and what they were telling us to believe." He spread his hands. "And here I am."

"So they sent you here for having a difference of opinion, after explicitly saying that it was allowed?" asked Davian disbelievingly.

Raeleth gave a cheerless chuckle. "I was told that I should not lose my life because I disagreed, but that my beliefs—and my desire to voice them—were...*socially destructive*. That it was fine for me to have them, but detrimental for *everyone* if I tried to convince others of them. They said that it was contrary to objective truth, and therefore misleading. So I was given the opportunity to think the right way, or be sent here." He smiled wryly. "I still remember when they told me, completely unironically, that they were doing it to display the truth of El to people. To show me that if I desired His plan to be fulfilled, then I would have to accept that this was part of it."

He fell silent, and Davian didn't say anything for a while, turning his words over.

"So you did?" he asked. "Accept it, I mean."

Raeleth gave a soft chuckle. "Not straight away, no. Not truly until I met you, in fact. Until a week ago, I had been wondering what I had done to deserve being sent here. What mistake I had made to be punished this way by El." Raeleth gave him a lopsided smile. "Which you reminded me are ridiculous questions to ask."

Davian frowned. "How so?"

Raeleth shrugged slightly. "Because that's not how it works. Faithful people suffer and evil people prosper all the time, Davian—you must know that is true. Besides, if our actions are driven only by reward or punishment—eternal or otherwise—then they are motivated by greed and selfishness, not faith or love. That is where so many people go wrong, even those who say they believe in El. They obey because they think it will make their *lives* better, rather than *themselves*. And that is very much the wrong reason."

Davian considered for a while as he gazed down onto the bridge. The light of the Breach rose all around it, casting the al'goriat walking its surface in an unsettling, dirty yellow.

"So you know what the Venerate believe," he said eventually. "But you seem...you seem certain that they're wrong."

Raeleth shot Davian a vaguely surprised glance. "Are you not?"

Davian grimaced. "I don't agree with what they've done, of course. Of *course*. But so much of what they say makes sense. They're not wrong when they say that our side has acted just as badly as theirs." The words sickened him, but saying them out loud helped him accept an important truth.

He had doubted, this past year. Had wondered.

Raeleth paused, eyes still fixed below, rubbing his chin as he thought.

"What you just said—like so many of their arguments—is a distraction."

Davian felt his brow furrow. "How so?"

"Because it is like...like listening to a piece of music and judging the composer by how skillfully the musician is playing it. The question that needs answering isn't ever 'who acts better.' It is easy to seize upon the worst of groups—but every group is a collection of individuals, and every individual is flawed. Some are contrary, some are outright liars when they say that they believe in something. So every action has to be assessed *against* what someone claims they believe, not simply seen as a result of it." He shrugged. "Does that make sense? You should never judge the sides of an argument simply by who is doing the arguing."

Davian nodded slowly. "So what *is* the question that needs answering, then?"

"The one that got me sent here? The one which the Venerate don't want asked?" Raeleth leaned forward. "Simply put—do you believe that mankind should have no authority higher than itself?"

"Surely...surely that's not what the Venerate are suggesting."

"It is—and they would tell you the same. It is *exactly* what their version of El is offering. A world where all possibilities are promised is, by necessity, a world in which God cannot take part. Cannot choose to affect the world in any way. If He exerts His will even a fraction, He is by definition changing how things could have been. He is removing possible outcomes." Raeleth held Davian's gaze, calm certainty in his eyes. "They are trying to convince everyone that our creator wished to create a world in which He could not take part. Could not help, guide, or save. In which He was *functionally irrelevant*."

Davian was quiet for a long few moments. He'd never thought of it in those terms, but...Raeleth was right. That *was* the world the Venerate wanted.

"So their El really is nothing like the one I was taught about as a child," Davian said eventually. Somehow he had always pictured the god the Venerate spoke about as being the same as the one he had grown up with, but simply…trapped. His role in the stories reversed with Shammaeloth's.

"If we are talking about the same one? Then yes, he is very different," said Raeleth quietly. "The El I believe in is not just the creator of this world, but inextricably tied to it—if He were to withdraw from it, it would cease to be as we know it. It would become a place where all the things we value, all things that have beauty and life and meaning, are simply not possible. His absence wouldn't mean a lack of authority—it would mean complete and utter desolation."

Davian rubbed his forehead. That *was* what the Old Religion still taught. "And he doesn't just reveal himself, clear up the confusion, because…?"

Raeleth shrugged. "Because we're meant to realize that this is important, and figure it out for ourselves. 'No decision without doubt,'" he added, clearly quoting something. "El could convince the world in a heartbeat—but if He did, it would no longer be our choice to follow Him. Instead, He *enables* us to choose Him."

Davian sniffed. "And how did the Venerate respond to you saying all of this?"

"Well—I'm here," said Raeleth with a rueful smile. He shrugged. "They defended their position. They said that those were lies created by Shammaeloth, and that El created the world for us to live free, to make our own decisions—that giving us our independence would, in fact, be his greatest act of love. That we were meant to make our own mistakes, hopefully recognize and potentially right them—and yes, potentially fail, too. But that it would be our path, either way. Our own choices that led to whatever outcome came." Raeleth shook his head. "But it never sounded right to me. What kind of god would create us and then leave us with no guiding hand, no plan, to the mercies of chance alone? Is a lack of discipline caring? Is absence somehow love? Should a father take his newborn and cast it out into the wild, helpless and alone, all because he does not want to unduly influence its life?" Raeleth's eyes were hard. "So no—I *do not believe the Venerate*. The very idea of their El sickens me to my stomach.

And even if what they say is somehow true, I would never follow a god that would abandon us to ourselves."

Raeleth fell silent, then gave a rueful shake of his head. "Sorry. I know I can go on, when it comes to this—and it's a lot to think on—but this place...you never know how long you have." His fingers brushed absently at his chest, where Davian knew the lingering Dark still lay. "That realization hit me hard, this past week. I do not know what you believe, Davian, but the thought of someone else being taken in by their arguments, when I could have done something about it with the time I have left, is something I cannot let pass anymore."

Davian nodded slowly. "Thank you," he said, meaning it. Raeleth had spoken passionately, but...*logically*, too. That helped. It hadn't completely eliminated his doubts—he suspected that he needed to think long and hard on what had just been said—but it was enough to ease his mind for now.

He was about to say more, when he realized that there was movement on the far side of the Breach.

He stiffened, gripping Raeleth silently by the arm and indicating the motion. Isstharis was slithering toward them along the bridge, trailed by three al'goriat, the latter all carrying barrels as easily as if they had been empty.

The dar'gaithin and her unsettling retinue made their way across the shadowed bridge, the al'goriat not paying them any attention as they passed by. Once on the nearer side of the Breach, Isstharis continued to move purposefully northward, quickly vanishing among the maze of red-tinted buildings.

Davian exchanged a glance with Raeleth, and the two men crept as fast as they dared in the same direction.

Davian and Raeleth half sneaked, half jogged after Isstharis, keeping low behind broken walls and piles of rubble to avoid being spotted by an errant glance.

They had already discussed at some length how best to follow the dar'gaithin. The twisting, circuitous layout of Zvaelar made simple shadowing almost impossible, but by keeping to the higher ways, they were able to catch occasional glimpses of Isstharis and

327

her followers. Enough to determine their quarry's general direction, and to make sure they didn't get too close or too far behind.

It was ten minutes into their pursuit that they rounded a corner and came face-to-face with the al'goriat.

Davian skidded to a stop, Raeleth crashing hard into his back. Davian barely noticed, his entire attention focused on the creature ahead. It was facing them, blocking the path, not twenty feet from where they stood.

It cocked its head to the side, needle-like teeth glistening red in a lipless mouth. The smooth skin where its eyes should have been seemed to examine them.

Davian heard Raeleth's intake of breath from behind him. There was nowhere to go, no way they could run from this.

From desperate, horrified instinct, he reached for kan.

The al'goriat's mouth somehow widened, and it took a lumbering step toward them. More curious than aggressive. They seemed to operate on a predatory instinct, though; this felt as if the thing was playing with them. Waiting for them to react.

There was a moment when his effort to reach kan was just like every other time; he stretched for the dark energy, strained and scrabbled at the power that was right there if he could just reach a *little further.*

And then he was pushing through it.

He froze, almost losing his grip again in shock before focusing. He'd managed to grasp kan but the connection was...tenuous. Barely there. He couldn't do much, and he couldn't do it for long.

But now that Davian was finally holding kan, he realized that the same power was emanating from the Bane.

He had only a heartbeat to process what he was seeing. Thousands of dark threads waving like living things, like a cloud of snakes, from the creature's body. They wormed their way outward and everywhere for what appeared to be hundreds of feet, touching buildings, ground, rubble.

Davian and Raeleth.

Davian fumbled with the little kan he was able to use and threw up a hardened shield, cutting off the tendrils attached to himself and Raeleth. It was thin, weak. Barely anything. But it was the best he could do.

The al'goriat stopped.

A soft gargling sound erupted from its throat—the first time Davian had heard one of the creatures make such a noise. Davian gripped Raeleth by the shoulder and gradually, cautiously pulled him back.

The tendrils waved around them, flapped at his shield and slid off. The al'goriat continued to make the strange noise, but hadn't moved. It seemed to be still staring at the spot where Davian and Raeleth had been when it had first spotted them.

Davian carefully took two steps to the side, pulling Raeleth with him.

The al'goriat didn't track the motion.

Sight. That was what those kan threads were for. That *had* to be it.

The al'goriat abruptly vanished, then reappeared immediately in the space where Davian and Raeleth had been standing a few seconds earlier. With its unnaturally long legs, it was perhaps one or two strides away from being able to touch them.

Its head waved around wildly, as if in confusion. It vanished again.

This time, it didn't reappear.

Davian exhaled, every limb trembling; beside him he could see Raeleth still frozen to the spot, clearly unwilling to move for fear that the creature was still nearby.

"What...what just happened?" the other man whispered, voice shaking.

Davian swallowed. "We need to catch up to Isstharis. I'll explain later," he murmured. "For now, I think we're safe."

"*Safe?*" repeated Raeleth, the word coming out close to a hiss. He evidently heard the near panic in his own voice because he held up a hand apologetically, nodding, though Davian could see that he was still shaken. "You're right. Go."

They hurried forward, Davian suddenly feeling more confident than he had since he had arrived. He'd done it. He was *using kan again*. He still doubted that he could do much more than he was currently—in fact, he didn't think that he'd be able to maintain even this flimsy shield for long; the focus needed was far more than it should have been. The only reason he forced himself to maintain it now was that he feared that if he let go, he wouldn't be able to get it back again.

But it was progress. He would be able to fill his Reserve once more. He would be able to keep healing Raeleth, maybe even try eliminating the Dark in him entirely if he could find an Essence source big enough.

It was two minutes before Raeleth grabbed Davian's arm, pointing silently to the north. Davian followed the gesture, spotting the outline of an al'goriat hauling a barrel through the moonlight just before it disappeared over a rise.

They hurried in that direction, approaching the spot where the al'goriat had been. Davian frowned. The buildings immediately in front of them were little more than piles of rubble; clearly the destruction had hit hard here, even harder than in the other parts of the city. But beyond them...beyond them he couldn't see anything. No other buildings, no raised pathways or tunnels. Just open air.

A cliff.

He crept forward alongside Raeleth, doing his best not to send loose stones skittering. Raeleth climbed carefully around one of the piles of rubble and then lay on his stomach, motioning for Davian to do the same. The two of them wormed forward until their heads peeked over the edge of the drop.

Davian swallowed as the dingy, red-tinged scene below came into view.

A deep, circular dip in the ground stretched away before them. Perhaps a mile wide, it had bowl-like sides that curved upward, smooth and looking virtually unclimbable except for three separate points Davian could see, each of which was guarded by two dar'gaithin. Structures architecturally similar to the ones up top dotted its base, which appeared relatively flat. The indentation had to have been made before the city's destruction, rather than being due to it, then.

It was the center, though, that drew Davian's eye. A massive expanse of flat ground—a few hundred feet in diameter, at least—was bare of buildings or even rubble except for a few small structures in the middle, which were in turn clustered tightly around a square tower. The edifice was tall, almost the same height as the crater's edge. It glimmered in the dull light, glinted and shone.

Metal. The entire thing was made of metal.

He swallowed, hearing an almost desirous sigh from Raeleth as the other man spotted the same thing. After a moment he tore his eyes from the sight, gaze flicking away and down.

Surrounding the area containing the tower and its ancillary structures—flooding the open, otherwise cleared space—at least a hundred al'goriat roamed.

Raeleth tentatively shifted closer to Davian. "So. This is where they take it," he said softly, motioning to the west. Davian twisted slightly, spotting Isstharis and her al'goriat as they carted the barrels of metal down one of the pathways. "Now what?"

Davian swallowed. "I'm not sure," he admitted. Getting here was as far ahead as he'd thought.

"That's a forge," said Raeleth suddenly, gesturing to one of the other buildings in the center, off to the right of the tower. Thin black smoke rose from a chimney jutting from its roof. "They must melt it all down. El alone knows why, though."

They observed for a while, Davian's muscles beginning to stiffen from the awkwardly held position. He was just about to consider getting a better view when suddenly a flurry of activity from one of the pathways into the crater drew his eye.

Three dar'gaithin were descending, a single man shepherded among them, shoved forcefully every few steps despite not giving any apparent sign of resistance. Davian didn't recognize him, but he walked calmly, head forward, looking neither to the right nor the left as other dar'gaithin nearby stopped what they were doing and stared at him.

The dar'gaithin escorted him calmly along the basin floor and out into the sea of roaming al'goriat; the tall, eyeless creatures turned as soon as the prisoner stepped out onto the cleared space, some of them blinking in an instant from the far side of the glimmering tower to where the intrusion was occurring.

The man ignored the creatures, walking on unfazed between the dar'gaithin, who were apparently there to prevent him from being eaten. They crossed the wide-open space within thirty seconds, vanishing into the metal tower.

Davian turned to Raeleth, and his heart skipped a beat. Raeleth had gone white, his hands trembling, looking unable to tear his eyes from the scene. When Davian placed a gentle hand on Raeleth's shoulder, the other man flinched.

"What is it?" Davian asked nervously.

Raeleth swallowed, then began inching backward. "We have to go," he whispered. "Now." There was a shortness of breath to his words, a genuine panic.

Davian frowned but followed him. "Why? What did you see?" He glanced over his shoulder, back at where the man had been. "Did you recognize him?"

Raeleth nodded slowly, clearly still aghast, eyes full of fear. He leaned in close and kept his voice almost inaudibly low, as if the words themselves might bring down some sort of harm.

"Have you ever heard the name Aarkein Devaed?" he whispered.

Chapter 23

The Wells were eerily silent as Caeden stepped through the newly opened Gate and swiftly slashed behind himself with kan, cutting through the machinery of the portal.

He allowed himself to breathe again as it winked out of existence. He had built the Gate to open in a section of the Wells where Alaris had no reason to be, but he also knew his friend would be desperate. Caeden still half expected Alaris to appear in front of him at any moment, vainly attempting to rush to the portal before it closed. The Venerate would certainly have detected its opening, particularly as there was precious little else to demand his attention down here.

But there was nothing. The shimmering, coalescing veins of color trickled all around Caeden, but there was no sound, no other sign of movement.

He closed his eyes, envisaging the layout of the Wells. He'd spent a lot of time down here—not just the month with Asar trying to restore his memory, but much of the past year as well. It was as secure a base as he could hope to find, and though Nethgalla was able to access it, he didn't fear her as he once had. She was manipulative and terribly dangerous to those he loved, but not to him. Never to him.

He started walking. Though the network of tunnels was vast—the amount of Essence the Darecians had drawn from the earth had been simply staggering—there were only a few places that were actually designed for occupation. During his own time down here he had naturally gravitated to Asar's quarters: a comfortable bed, close to the vast stores of stockpiled food and water, and plenty of reading and writing material. There wasn't a great deal else to do, aside from sitting and thinking—which had occupied plenty of Caeden's time as well, to be fair.

His footsteps echoed as he walked; despite the familiar surroundings he found himself tense, ready to leap at every shadow. Alaris would not have taken kindly to being tricked. In fact, as far as Caeden knew, the man had *never* suffered a defeat quite like this one. Though the Alaris he knew was always calm, always rational and looking for a peaceable solution, Caeden also knew that much of that attitude came from the knowledge that he was all but impossible to beat. It wasn't a veneer, exactly—he *was* a good man, of that Caeden had no doubt.

But he'd seen the flashes of anger to which his friend was prone, too.

Still, no surprise attack came, and the longer the silence stretched, the more nervous Caeden became. He had expected desperation, resistance at the least. Was Alaris even still here? There was no way he could have escaped, surely. Nethgalla was off in Talan Gol, according to Scyner, so she could not have stumbled in here and let him go by accident—though that was the kind of mistake she would never have made anyway. And Gassandrid had never been here, had access to no one who had, and had no way of divining that Alaris was being kept here in the first place.

There was still the concern—sitting in the back of his mind, ever since his conversation with Scyner—that Nethgalla had been captured, and that Gassandrid had forced her to show him her memory of the Wells. But while that was possible, he felt it was highly unlikely. Nethgalla was nothing if not good at hiding.

Finally he came to the door to Asar's room. It was ajar; Caeden nudged it open.

The room both looked and felt as if a hurricane of fire had torn through it.

The books that had once lined the walls—Asar's carefully accumulated works from a thousand years, detailing the collected truth about Shammaeloth—were ash. Gone. Hot pressure blasted his face from where the walls had absorbed the heat. Charred scraps of paper littered the floor everywhere, along with the occasional splintered piece of bookshelf, which appeared to have been ripped apart.

Caeden leaned against the door post, stunned. It wasn't as if he had expected Alaris to be converted by reading—though the sheer volume of observations about Shammaeloth were compelling, they said nothing that had not already been said—but he hadn't expected *this*.

"I hope you like the new decor."

Caeden flinched at the voice, twisting to see what he hadn't noticed amid the devastation. Alaris, sitting in the sole remaining chair in the corner, almost hidden in shadow.

He looked...beyond weary.

"You did this?" It was a rhetorical question; he'd known before seeing Alaris there, but he still had to ask. "Why?"

Alaris smiled tiredly. "Something to do."

Caeden shook his head. "You think this will make a difference?"

"We do what we can. This was what was left to me," said Alaris, a touch bitterly. "If you prevail, if you make this world a prison, I do not want to leave anything that claims it is not. I cannot stand the thought that not only will all people be prisoners—but that they might accept it as *right*."

Caeden glared. "You don't think that this is part of the problem, Alaris?" he asked. "We were always so...dogmatic. Early on we actually *thought*—we discussed, we listened. We fought amongst ourselves and disagreed. We allowed for dissenting opinions. But after a while, we did exactly what we used to mock everyone else for doing. We settled. We no longer questioned." He licked his lips. "And it made us lose respect for what others thought—especially those who did not live as long as us, had not seen the things we had seen. We bought into the lie that we were smarter than all of them. *Better* than all of them. And so we did things like this." He gestured. "We tried to destroy *ideas*, Alaris! Shouldn't the arrogance of that concept make you cringe?"

Alaris was silent for a moment.

"When something is self-evident. When something is *inescapably true*. Then yes. I believe it is right to crush the concepts that oppose it from existence. Because they are not ideas, Tal'kamar.   335

They are lies." His lip curled. "It is calling it *idea* or *belief* that is the problem. It is seductive. It can fool even the smartest of people." He gave Caeden a pointed look.

Caeden shook his head. "That does not gel with what you taught me," he said grimly. "That was not what you would have said when—"

"That man died a long time ago, Tal. Idealism is one thing, but this is about the fate of the world."

Caeden studied the scene. The lingering heat indicated that this had just happened; Alaris had decided to do this as soon as he had detected Caeden entering the Wells, not before.

Alaris's gaze slid to the sheathed blade hanging at Caeden's side. "So. I did not think you would retrieve it as quickly as you did," he said heavily. There was a note of something in his voice—not fear, exactly, but definite unease. "I may be outmatched, Tal, but know this—I *will* fight. And I wonder. When it comes time, when you have to do it—will you? Can you? After all we've been through, can you truly strike the killing blow without hesitation?"

Caeden said nothing, though inwardly he understood. Of course. Alaris thought the blade at his side was Licanius—why else risk coming here? And Alaris was preparing for a fight that he knew he could not possibly win, given how much stronger Caeden would be with Licanius. He was doing everything he could to sow seeds of doubt, give himself the faintest hint of an advantage.

Caeden gazed at Alaris sadly.

"Will you talk with me? One last time?" He hadn't expected this, but... part of him needed to try.

"I told you at Alkathronen. The time for talking has passed," said Alaris. He straightened, looking Caeden in the eye. "Tell me one thing, though, Tal'kamar—because I am curious. Are you going to keep your promise to him?"

"To who?"

"The boy." Alaris's lip curled, as if he were unable to bring himself to say the name. "The one who saved you. The one you promised to save in return." Alaris held his gaze. "We Read that much from him, early on—it was all he could think about for a while. I even thought you might have meant it, those first few months."

"Circumstances changed."

"But not your heart, apparently," rejoined Alaris harshly.

Caeden scowled. There was no benefit to giving Alaris the reason, but...Caeden needed him to know.

"You want to know why I didn't try and rescue him?" he asked. "Because he didn't need it. Because the only thing I needed to do was ensure that he was sent to Zvaelar." He held Alaris's gaze coldly.

Alaris stared back, puzzled at first, then eyes slowly widening.

"El take it," he muttered bitterly, hanging his head.

"I cannot tell you how disappointed I was to hear that he was tortured, though," Caeden continued quietly. "You had to have known that the escherii would not hold back. That evil is on you, Alaris."

"I don't understand why you *care*." Alaris's voice was suddenly vicious again, full of pent-up frustration. "He is just a boy, Tal! Of all the lives to cross our paths—of all the people—why him? What makes him so special?"

Caeden shifted. "If I didn't know any better, Alaris, I would say that you are jealous."

Alaris looked at him incredulously.

"Of *course* I am jealous," he said, laughing in bitter disbelief. "We all are! The man who was more convincing to you in a few minutes than we were able to be in thousands of years. The man whose friendship you have valued over those whom you have spent hundreds of lifetimes alongside. The ghost against which we could never compete, the perfect ideal of self-sacrifice and truth. And as a result, the man who might have single-handedly enslaved the world." His face hardened. "That has always been your curse, Tal. You enshrine those whom you have lost, whom you have killed. You raise them above the living; their voices drown out all others who try to reason with you. *They* are your gods."

Caeden was silent.

"Perhaps you are right," he said softly. "But it goes both ways. Elliavia drove me for so long—you know that as well as anyone—and that was entirely to Shammaeloth's benefit." He sighed. "Davian's sacrifice has driven me as well, true—but far from blindly. You want to know why he moved me? He gave me the gift of doubt. He made me examine myself. He made me *question*."

He drew Knowing, trying to ignore the sick feeling that holding the blade imparted.

"And that is the only way we can ever find answers, Alaris."

Alaris's eyes went wide as he saw the blade, but Caeden already knew that this was the easy part. Alaris had no weapon of his own, and they were relatively equally matched—perhaps not across a long fight like the one at Alkathronen, but here in these close quarters, for the time Caeden needed? It was more than enough.

Alaris leaped to his feet, snatched up his chair with Essence and flung it, but Caeden was already moving, smoothly sidestepping the attack and letting time flow around him. He lunged forward, Alaris barely avoiding the blade as it slid by his shoulder; the Venerate backed away, wide-eyed, time bending around him, too, now.

"You came here for *information*?" gasped Alaris. He was suddenly alert, more alive than he had seemed at any point during their conversation. He thought he had a chance, now; if Caeden had no way to kill him, then he had to instead get out while leaving Alaris behind. A much more difficult task.

Caeden blurred forward, the blade slashing again and again and again, increasingly close to Alaris until finally an attack caught him—just a cut across the forearm, but it was enough. Caeden could feel the knowledge seeping into him.

He searched through it, focusing internally, seeking out what he was after. The flow of information was unpleasant, as if it were coated in filth, but Caeden gritted his teeth and allowed it in. Some of it was vague, more feeling than fact—the cut had been small and Knowing would focus on taking what Caeden wanted to know, rather than everything it could—but it was enough.

He backed away, eyes going wide.

"El take it," he said, feeling the blood drain from his face. His heart started to pound and he gazed at Alaris in shock; when he spoke he couldn't keep the ache from his voice. "*Why?*"

Alaris's face twisted, and Caeden saw a flicker of the guilt that was hiding behind the facade.

A guilt he knew all too well.

"Because you forced us," panted Alaris eventually, nursing his arm, though he sounded unconvinced even as he said it. "Because *you* led us here, Tal."

"Shammaeloth has led you here. Just as he led me," replied Caeden. If ever he had wondered since he had woken in the forest with no memories, if ever he had doubted that he was on the right side...those doubts were gone now. He heard the red-hot anger in his voice, but he didn't care, was barely able to think straight from the fury bubbling within him. "You say we were friends? How could you keep this from me? From *me*?"

"Because we all knew how you would react. Like *this*." Alaris nodded to Caeden's fists, which were clenched so tightly around the hilt of Knowing that his knuckles had turned bright white. "Davian may have been the feather that caused the roof to collapse, but we all know the true cause. Dareci was not your fault—it was Shammaeloth's. The *real* Shammaeloth, the one who has imprisoned us all. But you were never able to fully accept that its burden was not yours to bear. It was too great a thing, too great a shame. And our reactions...they did not help," Alaris conceded bleakly. "But when the ilshara was raised, when the plan was suggested, we all agreed. We needed the contingency."

Caeden took a step back, dazed, horrified. "I thought that you'd kept me away from the Desrielites because...because you were suspicious," he admitted faintly.

"Oh, there was that too," Alaris assured him drily. "In retrospect, I am still unsure how you convinced us that Andrael had fooled you into helping him with the ilshara. Hindsight sees perfectly and all that, I suppose."

"I just assumed you were using them as a backup. A secondary army of zealots, should the need arise. I *understood* that." It had seemed logical enough at the time, and had especially seemed like something that would appeal to Gassandrid. "But giving them *Columns*? Giving them the ability to wipe out..." He trailed off, not knowing what else to say.

There was silence for a few seconds.

"And now you have given them the order," Caeden finally finished. "You were intending to lead them in the fight yourself? After everything you saw the Columns do—to Dareci, to me—you still volunteered to be the one to use them?" He swallowed, everything coming together in his head. "Isiliar's Tributary. That's why it was so easy for you to meet with me. You wanted to run the test from Alkathronen one more time. You had to be certain that you had the exact location of the Cyrarium," he said, voice tinged with horror.

It shouldn't have been possible, but Diara had seemingly found a flaw in the Tributary's design, devised a way to trace the flow of Essence to its destination. The Venerate already knew where the Cyrarium was; Alaris had been scheduled to return to Alkathronen simply to make sure that there had been no errors in their calculations. Once he had finished there, he had been meant to return briefly to Ilshan Gathdel Teth—and then go straight to Desriel to lead the assault.

One that would have been delayed by his absence, but only fleetingly.

Alaris's gaze was hard. "I tried, you know. I did everything I could to stop this from happening. Even after the Boundary was strengthened again, I argued for finding that last Tributary, for convincing the girl inside of it to leave." He shook his head. "Ultimately the lives lost in this war, the aftermath of the Columns draining the Cyrarium—none of it matters. We will each have our opportunities for redemption once El reaches Deilannis. Even you, Tal, though you don't deserve it. All that is done will be undone."

Caeden closed his eyes. The ilshara itself could have withstood an attack like this; it was a vast, complex construction, hundreds of interconnected parts distributed over thousands of miles that would reinforce and repair each other. Not even the Columns, staggeringly destructive though they were, could strike every section of it at once.

The store of Essence that powered it, though... that was a different story. Like the Tributaries, part of the Cyrarium's strength had been the fact that it was hidden. It had been built to be nigh impregnable nonetheless, but against the annihilating strength of the Columns, its defenses would simply have no chance.

If the Columns were arrayed in the right place, the Cyrarium would be ripped apart just as surely as anything else.

Caeden opened his eyes again, a few points of confusion finally becoming clear. This was why Diara had offered the deal to Asha, why the Venerate had switched their focus to finding Nethgalla.

The Ath had caused countless problems for them over the years, and they no doubt wanted to be certain that she would not be able to interfere again so close to the end. She was, perhaps, the last remaining unknown for them.

But Caeden knew she had already done all she could. If the Cyrarium was destroyed, Asha's power would simply have nowhere to go. The Boundary would fall, the forces beyond would sweep through Andarra's remaining defenses—probably few, after what Desriel was about to do—and then...

And then the Darklands. An end to all that was good.

"Well. That makes things easy," said Caeden quietly, pain still coloring each word. There was nothing else to do here. If his old friend was willing to go through with this—had kept this hidden from him, all this time—then there would be no swaying him.

Caeden stepped outside of time, and ran.

Alaris was quickly after him, but a second or two of hesitation had cost him; Caeden was already away down the tunnels, colorful lines streaking past as he drew the white stone from his pocket, Nethgalla's symbol engraved on its surface. He fed Essence into it, not stopping, then glanced over his shoulder as a bolt of energy streaked past him. Alaris was within sight, but he was too far back.

Caeden could see the desperation on his friend's face and, despite everything, couldn't help but feel a twinge of guilt.

The portal opened in front of him, and the moment he dove through—the stone still in his hand—it winked out again behind him, cutting short Alaris's frantic, frustrated shout.

He rolled as he let go of time, skidding along the white sand of the beach. It was just past noon, and the sun beat down with a pleasant intensity. Waves lapped gently on the shore, with the constant crashing of larger ones audible on the reef a little farther out.

He lay there, panting. This island had once been a Darecian outpost, tiny and strategically unimportant though it was. It had been a very long time indeed before the Venerate had uncovered its true value: a massive source of Essence, deep within the earth. The Darecians had used the Wells to draw that Essence to the surface, giving them fuel for everything from their Ironsails to their Light Cannons.

Caeden glanced around. There were enough trees that he couldn't see the other side of the island, but it was a near thing, only a thousand feet separating the farthest points. The entire place was little more than a gentle hump in the ocean. The remains of a Darecian fortress sat crumbling at its center, abandoned for millennia and yet still largely intact. They'd never achieved the Builders' level of skill in engineering—no one had— but their structures had certainly stood the test of time.

He groaned, staggering to his feet and picking up the black counterpart to the white Travel Stone, taking a minute to charge them again. It was a precaution he'd remembered learning to take every time they were used; the same Essence signature was needed in each stone for them to work, meaning that if they got separated prematurely, they became useless. He'd found that out the hard way, many centuries ago. That had been a long month of walking.

When he was done he slipped the stones back in his pocket, stretching and contemplating the crystal-blue ocean. He could Gate back to where he needed to go, now.

His face grew grim as he considered where that was.

Ilin Illan. He would simply have to hope that he was not further delayed once there. And if he was...then Asha would just have to handle Diara by herself. He felt a stab of guilt at risking her like this when he had promised to return, but more than anything right now, Wirr needed to be warned of what was coming. The Darecians would not be attacking from Talmiel, as the Andarrans would expect. And the Gil'shar had Banes. All of the dar'gaithin and eletai that had breached the ilshara a year ago.

If Wirr and the Assembly were not forewarned, they would be wiped out—and the Boundary along with them.

He did his best to ignore the growing apprehension worming its way into his gut, and settled down to work on the Gate.

Chapter 24

Asha winced and brushed a light sheen of sweat from her forehead, allowing Elli to help her to her feet.

She funneled Essence to the torn muscle in her leg, the searing pain—which once would have had her curled up in a ball on the ground in tears—now something she knew to simply grit her teeth against until it was healed. She kept her breathing even as she tried not to focus on the uncomfortable sensation of flesh knitting together, gazing instead at the dead al'goriat lying a few feet away, its eyeless face smashed in, slivers of teeth broken where she had punched it repeatedly.

"You can do better than that," observed Elli as Asha released her grip on the woman's shoulder, able to stand on her own two feet again. "You are distracted."

Asha walked over to the nearest fountain, cupping her hand and drinking from the crisp, clear water, then splashing more on her face.

"Hard not to be," she muttered eventually, stomach twisted into knots as she cast a worried eye toward the forest.

It had been a week since Diara's threat. Over two days since Caeden's promise to return in time to help Asha with the inevitable confrontation. Had something happened to him? Had he ever been intending to return? As little as she trusted him, she saw no real advantage to him in lying to her: he wanted the Boundary stable just as much as she did. But he had spoken of his task in terms of hours, a day at most, confident that he would be back in time. Which surely meant that something *had* to have delayed him.

"He isn't someone to make promises lightly," Elli assured her, evidently having no difficulty discerning her thoughts. "If he can make it, he will."

Asha squinted at her. "You're sure you don't know what's going on?" Elli was supposed to be at least partly constructed from Caeden's mind. On some level, she had a direct connection to him.

The woman shrugged and shook her head.

"I am part of the dok'en far more than part of him," she said, again as if reading Asha's thoughts. "He designed this place—me—to be an illusion. That illusion would too easily have been broken if I had been able to simply know what he was thinking."

Asha acceded the point without argument, turning her face toward the clear sun and drinking in its warmth. "Do I have any chance against Diara, if he isn't here?"

"Your training gives you a chance, but your paths to victory are still . . . significantly fewer, without him. Your window of opportunity will be small." Elli's voice was calm. "Diara will initially assume that her ability to manipulate time is more than enough to deal with you—as it was last time—and attack at close quarters. That gives you one, possibly two opportunities to land a hit that will end the fight." She shrugged. "Once she realizes that you're a threat, she will switch tactics. Keep her distance. The amount of Essence you have at your disposal means that it will be harder for her to simply cut through your defenses with kan, and it is still possible that she will make a mistake. But the likelihood is that she would win, if it came to that."

Asha snorted. "I am filled with confidence."

"Some people need to be told what they want to hear to make them perform better, but others need the truth. You are the latter," said Elli confidently.

"I'll take that as a compliment, I suppose." Asha glanced at the sun, the butterflies in her stomach only intensifying. She still desperately hoped that Caeden would appear at the last moment, but deep down she knew—had known since she'd woken this morning to an empty palace—that he wasn't coming. There was no way that he would leave his arrival until this close to the deadline.

344   As if in response to her thoughts, a boom shivered the Crystal-

line Palace behind her and a fiery bloom of energy exploded from the treetops below, followed by several smaller bursts in quick succession. Asha pulled in a few steadying breaths, forcing herself to calm and reigniting her Essence armor as Elli placed a reassuring hand on her shoulder.

Diara had returned.

✺

It was ten minutes later that the Venerate finally strode into view.

Asha's heart sank at the sight, though at least Diara's clothing was tattered and scorched, an indication—along with her dark expression—that she had not dealt with the wards as easily as had Caeden. That was good; far better if she was distracted, irritated as well as weakened.

Asha stood patiently at the top of the hill, watching tensely, allowing Essence to heighten her senses in case Diara simply decided to attack. Elli had long since made herself scarce, concerned that the Venerate would turn her ability to manipulate the dok'en against Asha. A concern that Asha shared, if she was being honest.

The dark-haired woman glared up at Asha, coming to a slow stop by one of the fountains, perhaps fifty feet away.

"So you have made the foolish choice," she called, a statement rather than a question. "Yet I understand. You are young. You are reckless. I will still give you this last chance to change your mind."

Asha kept her breathing steady, despite every nerve being taut. "No."

Diara sighed, looking almost bored. "You could save the man you love, and continue protecting your country. What more could you ask for? Why won't you accept this offer?"

"Because I don't trust you," Asha replied simply. "Perhaps you're telling the truth, perhaps you're not. But I know who you are, and I know the things you've done."

Diara's expression darkened further. "I see," she said. "Then it seems that we have nothing more to say to one another."

She vanished.

Asha breathed in the cool, sharp air; she had been watching, 345 waiting for this moment. She had seen the way Diara's muscles had tensed. Saw, in a fraction of a second, the terrifyingly fast footsteps as they bent blades of grass. Spotted the hazy blur against the horizon off to her left.

Her instincts—honed over the past week of constant punishment for failure—kicked in. Her body was already flooded to bursting with Essence, allowing her to move with a grace and speed impossible for any other human.

She flickered forward, *toward* the blur. Drew the steel that was hanging at her side and thrust hard, as fast as she had ever done before.

Asha's arm shivered as the blade struck home.

She gasped, feeling almost as stunned as Diara looked as the Venerate appeared abruptly at the end of her blade, scarlet blood already beginning to seep from the deep wound. Asha snarled and thrust again, forcing herself closer, pushing it deeper as the other woman batted feebly at the steel, clearly in shock. The sword had caught Diara in the stomach—not a killing blow, but a serious one.

Asha reached out. There was no time for hesitation or sportsmanship here. She needed to incinerate the Venerate, and the only way to do that without being blocked was through physical contact.

Diara recovered.

It happened so fast that Asha didn't comprehend it for a second. One moment her hand was almost to Diara's forehead; the next the woman was lurching away, ripping herself off the blade by sheer force of will, screaming in fury and pain as bright droplets of crimson sprayed the air. Asha took a half step after her and unleashed a molten torrent of energy at the Venerate, but it dissipated against an invisible wall almost a foot from Diara's face.

Diara vanished again; Asha tensed but the telltale signs this time said that the woman was retreating, moving back almost to where she had started. Asha directed another scything beam of energy at the point at which she anticipated Diara was going to stop, but even as she did so she could feel her stomach twisting into a knot of fear.

346   "El take it," snarled Diara, stumbling as she appeared, hands

covered in blood as she clutched at where the sword had struck home. She was standing slightly to the left of where Asha had aimed her Essence; to Asha's horror her opponent straightened, the stomach wound already almost fully healed. The Venerate's eyes blazed as they focused on Asha.

"You will pay for that," she promised.

Asha took a deep breath, and attacked with everything she had.

The world became a whirlwind of fire and chaos, Asha running and leaping, constantly moving and surrounding herself in swathes of deadly fire, which not only forced Diara to focus on protecting herself, but better revealed exactly where the other woman was as she scythed through it with her kan shield. Several times more Diara attempted to attack, only for Asha to anticipate correctly—or correctly enough—and either dodge or, in some cases, actually try a counterstrike. None were anywhere near as successful as her first effort, though, and Diara's relatively cautious attacks came closer and closer to landing, a few even scoring hits and causing Asha to stagger, barely recovering in time to deflect the next.

The palace grounds were in cinders, with shattered or melted stone and ground scorched clear of foliage all that remained. Still Diara worried at her, blinking in and out of sight every few seconds. Sometimes it would be to attack; other times it would simply be to force Asha to react, to focus on where she might be. Diara started sending out curling swathes of kan as distractions, creating disturbances in the swirling, fiery Essence that looked similar to the ones made by her Disruption shield, more than once forcing Asha to hesitate longer than she could afford.

In the midst of it all—in a surreal, out-of-body way—Asha found herself surprised. She was resisting one of the Venerate. One of the most powerful people to ever have lived, and Asha was holding her own.

It couldn't last, though, of course.

Asha lashed out in rhythm at what she could have sworn was Diara launching another attack, only to discover that she was thrusting at empty air. She turned too late, reacted too slowly to the sudden shadow at her shoulder. The dark dagger plunged into her back, forcing its way through the Essence armor, kan rapidly

347

infecting her body and sealing away all that power beyond her grasp. She lashed out with what Essence she had left, but it wasn't enough.

She went to her knees, pain shooting through her spine as her eyes rolled toward her attacker.

Diara was a ghastly sight, even though she was already healing. She was naked, every inch of her flesh—including her face—burned away, scorched, black and red. Her bared teeth were too visible through missing lips that were gradually filling out again, blistered skin easing and then covered over.

Diara had fooled her, Asha realized vaguely. She almost laughed. She had been tracking movements through the fiery Essence first, and then verifying them by looking for imprints on the ground and the telltale blur of motion. Diara had realized that. Had faked moving with a kan shield again, but this time allowed herself to be burned nearly to death in order to conceal her true whereabouts.

Asha wished that she could take comfort in moral victories right now.

"I'll tell Davian you'll be waiting for him," hissed the monstrosity that was the Venerate as her outer layer of skin began to reform, the last of the Essence-fire dying around her as she extinguished it with kan.

She stabbed again, ferocious, eyes wild. Asha barely felt the steel slip into her chest.

Her breathing grew sharp, panicked. Her vision became hazy.

She focused, using every remaining scrap of her concentration. She could still see the connected Reserves, inaccessible though they now were.

She'd considered this, though she knew it was ill-advised. Incredibly risky. Stupid, even.

Except that there were no other options, now.

She forced her eyes open again to find Diara—her face restored—peering down at her, expression coldly triumphant.

"You put up quite a fight, but there's nothing left for you to do now, girl," she said in smug satisfaction. "You were never going to be able to beat me."

Asha tried to respond, but her breath caught; blood was filling her lungs. She coughed instead, swallowing her words.

Diara smiled. "Slow down. Try again," she said, relaxed now that her victory was assured. Her Disruption shield seemed to have dropped, too.

Asha leaned forward so that her mouth was close to Diara's ear.

"I said, 'I know,'" she rasped weakly.

The thin sliver of Essence was snaking into Diara's ear before the Venerate knew what was happening.

Diara didn't even register it at first; she had been entirely focused on Asha, not anticipating anything from behind. Then something plainly warned her—a moment of sensation, a feeling—and her eyes went wide.

She screamed.

She fell back, agonized shrieks only growing in intensity as the kan barrier separating Asha from Essence vanished. Asha gasped as energy flooded to her wounds; she scrambled backward away from the Venerate and the glowing figure now standing behind her.

Garadis stared grimly down, another thread of Essence sliding out from his hand and lodging itself in Diara's other ear. Her entire head began to glow.

"You drew me here, and risked my life in the process," he said to Asha, ignoring the shrieks. "Had she caught even a hint of my presence, I would be dead."

"Didn't have much choice," choked Asha, still recovering, her gaze fixed in horror on the writhing woman. "What are you doing to her?"

"Hurting her mind. Making her unfocused, unable to manipulate kan." Garadis's words were calm but something in his eyes was feral, more so than Asha had ever seen before. He walked around in front of the Venerate, so that she could see who it was that was hurting her. "She is reaping her own harvest, Ashalia. Do not feel pity for her."

A blade of Essence lashed out, and suddenly Diara's arm was dropping to the ground and rolling away, cleanly severed. There was no blood.

Diara's screams somehow increased in pitch and intensity again.

"Stop." Asha stumbled weakly to her feet. "Surely you can just knock her out."

"And where would the justice be in that?" asked Garadis, his tone controlled. There was something underneath it, though. A hardness that made Asha shiver. "There is no point in hesitating here, Ashalia."

"*Stop.*" Asha said the word with more authority this time, stepping forward and raising her hands threateningly. "Caeden said that if she dies in here, Gassandrid will be able to tell. He will just kill her in reality and let her come back in a different body. This would be for nothing."

Garadis ignored her.

Asha let white energy ignite around both her hands. Already her Essence was nearly finished its restoration of her body. "I will stop you by force if I have to," she said harshly, still slightly out of breath.

There was nothing for a few seconds, and then finally Garadis scowled. He gestured sharply and Diara's screams cut short, the naked woman slumping to the ground. She was, Asha was relieved to see, unconscious but alive.

"Where is Tal'kamar?" asked Garadis, breathing heavily.

"I don't know," admitted Asha, head still spinning. "He was supposed to be here."

Garadis snorted. "Unsurprising."

"What did you do to her?" Asha chewed her lip as she stared at the Venerate's limp form, still unsure whether it was entirely safe to approach. "How did you stop her without using kan?"

"Essence is a powerful tool when applied with finesse," said Garadis absently. "She will not be able to use kan. Or Essence. Or probably be able to walk, for that matter. The ward in her mind disrupts almost everything. It will decay in due course, but that will take weeks. Regular bindings will be enough to restrain her for now."

He slung Diara over his shoulder and stomped off, clearly angry, though whether at Asha or himself, she couldn't tell.

Then he paused, glancing back at her.

"Your timing was good," he added. "The Vessel is almost complete, and will be delivered soon." He gazed at her grimly. "Once Tal'kamar returns from wherever he is, you can finally get out of this place."

He turned and continued, leaving Asha gaping after him.

Asha and Garadis sat opposite each other, the table between them, Diara lying on a couch in the corner.

Despite the woman's bonds, Asha couldn't help but cast constant glances in her direction. Garadis, on the other hand, seemed wholly unconcerned about her presence now.

"So you really can get me out of here. And keep the Boundary up," said Asha finally, no longer able to take the silence. There had been no conversation as she had followed Garadis back to the palace, her head spinning, still recovering from the fight and trying to keep her wits about her as the intense thrill and panic of battle wore off. "As long as we find a ... replacement." Even saying it out loud left a bad taste in her mouth. "You're still sure there's no other way?"

"I am. There is not," said Garadis. There was neither satisfaction nor regret in the words. Just simple, calm certainty.

Asha grimaced. "How would it work?"

"You would share a Reserve with whomever you were linked to," said Garadis. "We have built in a fail-safe—you will be able to break the connection with them at any time—though that would ultimately bring down the ilshara, of course. Not to mention kill whoever was in the Tributary."

Asha blanched. She still couldn't imagine how she was going to bring herself to subject someone else to that torture.

And yet Caeden had done it to his friends. She gave an unconscious shiver at the thought and, not for the first time, prayed that Davian truly understood the man he had chosen to support.

When she refocused on Garadis, he was staring to the left, down at Diara's sleeping form. Asha flinched at the look in his eyes. She had seen it a couple of times, now, when the Lyth had thought she wasn't paying attention. Something savage.

Garadis caught her glance and glowered, looking away.

"You hate her," said Asha quietly.

Garadis issued a barking laugh of surprise, short and loud. "You could say that." He shook his head, but didn't look at Diara again. "Has Tal'kamar explained to you about Licanius? About his history with the Lyth?"

"A little. He said it was why he needed to erase his memories—so that he could get it back—and that it was the only thing that could kill the Venerate. But that's all I know," she admitted.

Garadis grunted. "Not long after the ilshara was raised, Andrael—the man who originally made Licanius, and who was once a member of the Venerate—came to us with an offer. He had finally managed to take back the blade from Gassandrid, Tal'kamar, and the others, and would give us stewardship of her as a deterrent to the other Venerate from leaving Talan Gol." He shook his head at the memory. "We were at war with them, so that was a gift too good to pass up."

He drew in a breath. "However, Andrael also made a number of...unusual stipulations surrounding the blade's release. The other Venerate had to come for it without the intention of taking it. We could use it against them if they left the safety of the ilshara, but they were to be allowed safe passage within Res Kartha and, once they found their way there, also allowed to return to Talan Gol."

He paused. "And—our own stipulation—once Licanius was taken, whoever took it had to release us from Res Kartha within a year and a day, or its ownership would revert to us in full. After which, we would be able to use it however we pleased, whenever we pleased. It would have let us use kan again, with enough precision that doing so would not have killed us. It would have freed us, let us travel inside the ilshara to destroy the Venerate once and for all. Given us more than enough control to rebuild the Jha'vett, too. It would have changed everything," he finished softly.

Asha swallowed. "Why would Andrael do all of that?"

"I can only assume because he knew the future. Others of my people have suggested that he also saw Shammaeloth's corruption in each of the Venerate, and knew that the only way to ensure whoever controlled Licanius was truly free of his influence was to have their memories erased." Garadis shrugged tiredly. "He obviously had his motives, but...there are some deals you simply do not turn down."

Asha nodded slowly. "So how does this relate to Diara?"

"Perhaps five hundred years ago, the Venerate finally figured out ways to reach Res Kartha through our defenses. Started trying to get to Licanius. Though all the Lyth were bound to protect it, I was the Guardian, the one truly responsible for it and so the one who spoke to each of them. They tried so many methods—direct attacks, deception, bribery—but none of them ever worked. Res Kartha was a prison, but it was a prison that gave us near-unlimited power. Not even all the Venerate combined could face us down there, and they knew it." He held her gaze. "And, of course, they were terrified of Licanius falling into our hands unrestricted. They feared one of their number relenting, taking the bargain, and then being unable to fulfil it. They knew exactly what we would do with it, given the chance."

His face twisted, blue eyes hard. "Diara was amongst the first to decide to test the limits of the binding. She came into Res Kartha and kidnapped a dozen of my people. My friends." He swallowed. "Those she captured, she tried to take back through the ilshara. It was an experiment, you see. She had been told it would kill them, but she wanted to see if we were telling the truth."

Asha swallowed. "That's horrible."

"That is far from the worst of it." Garadis's voice was taut with restrained fury. "My people—my *dying* people—have been at war with the Venerate for millennia, and of all of them, Diara is the worst." Garadis all but spat the name. "Not responsible for the most deaths, perhaps—but certainly the ones we all remember. She was the one who tortured, who taunted, who was more than willing to use our friends and loved ones in the most horrific ways to try and get control of that cursed blade. Ask any of the Lyth which of the Venerate they would kill first, and none would have a moment's hesitation. Even Tal'kamar, who has caused us so much pain, is not considered in the same breath."

Garadis's tone was thick with spite and disgusted, almost visceral hatred. If he were left alone with Diara, Asha suddenly had no doubt that he would happily torture and ultimately kill her—regardless of the consequences.

353

She swallowed. These grudges were so deep, built across life-times, centuries. It was hard to imagine what Garadis must be feeling. Hard even to comprehend, sometimes.

"So why are you making things so difficult for Caeden—Tal'kamar—then?" she asked. "Don't you have the same enemies? The same goals?"

"The same enemies," agreed Garadis. "But Tal'kamar wants to seal the rift. He wants to eliminate any chance of the past—a past in which he *destroyed* us—being changed." He waved his hand as he saw her about to protest. "Oh, I know that he does not believe it is possible. But there is a difference between belief and knowing. And my people have not survived as we have by resigning ourselves to fate."

"You're saying...you want to keep the rift open?" Asha mulled over the concept. The binding that Garadis had forced Caeden into meant that Caeden couldn't kill any of the Augurs—not that that meant anything for Davian—and she had a hard time thinking of it as a problem. But Caeden had explained to her the terrifying consequences of Shammaeloth getting to the rift, too.

"With the Venerate dead, there will be no one capable of releasing Shammaeloth from the ilshara. And even if they did, knowing his weakness to Essence, we believe we can protect the rift from him." Garadis's tone was confident. "If we are given time and opportunity, there truly is a chance that we can undo all of this, Ashalia."

Asha said nothing to that—there was not much she could say, really. It sounded like desperation to her, given everything she'd been told. But she wasn't about to provoke Garadis by admitting as much.

Garadis watched her, then sighed. "I feel that I must also fore-warn you: should Tal'kamar succeed—should he close the rift—then you will become a target." He said the words simply, a vague apology in them. "If the opportunity to go back is denied us, then we will be forced to come for you. Because with the rift gone, we will be able to survive without the Siphon's protection—and as far as we have been able to tell, the only way to break its connection is through your death." He held Asha's gaze. "I am sorry.

That is just the way it is."

The threat—delivered as a statement of fact, nothing more—sent a chill through her.

"But if the rift is closed, wouldn't the Siphon cease to function anyway?" she asked eventually, pleased to hear the words come out calm and steady.

Garadis gave her a surprised look.

"Of course not. Kan as a power will be eliminated from this world, and will no longer be able to be drawn from the Darklands—the creatures which rely on it will die, and no one will have the ability to manipulate it anymore. But that which is already in this world will remain," he assured her. "We are sealing off the quarry, but destroying the stone we have already mined from it would be another matter entirely. Kan is the underlying machinery of this world, as certain and unavoidable as death itself. It will never truly disappear."

There was silence as Asha processed the words. The revelation had little impact on her—it was a concern that seemed for a very distant future right now—but it was still interesting to know.

"Well. If it comes to that, Garadis, then I will be ready for you," she said, holding the burning man's gaze.

Garadis studied her, then gave a short, approving nod.

"What will you do now?" asked Asha, moving on from the uncomfortable topic. A sliver of guilt needled at her. "I can't release you from the dok'en."

Garadis shrugged. "I will abide until Tal'kamar returns," he said. "The palace is large enough for the two of us. And you will need me to restore the mental block on Diara, should Tal'kamar not show himself for a while." He eyed the walls. "Of course, I do hope that he comes back before the next Shift. Because while I do not know the consequences, I imagine that it could get...unpleasant for all concerned."

Asha found herself ruefully agreeing. The Shift *might* disconnect Garadis and Diara safely...but the abrupt shutting down of the dok'en could also very well destroy their minds. "And if he doesn't return by then?"

"He will." Garadis's blue eyes were certain. "You are far too important, and Diara far too great a prize, for him to stay away for long."

The conversation met a natural if somewhat abrupt end after that, Garadis clearly disinterested in small talk. Soon enough the Lyth bade her a polite good evening and retired, leaving Asha alone in the room with the bound, still-unconscious Venerate.

She stared out the window at the Essence-lit fountains for a while, only starting from her reverie at a hand on her shoulder.

"Elli!" she said, blinking. The woman had kept out of sight since the fight.

"Are you all right?" Elli glanced across at the bound Venerate. "I thought it best to remain hidden while Garadis was here, but I see things went...well."

"As well as they could," agreed Asha. She rubbed her face tiredly as she stared at Diara's sleeping form. "Garadis says that the Lyth have come up with a way for me to leave."

"And this troubles you?"

Asha shook her head. "No. Yes. I don't know," she admitted heavily. "Of course I want to leave. But asking someone else to be in here for the Shifts is...I am not certain that I can do it."

Elli was silent for a moment.

"Sometimes not wanting to share the burden is a form of selfishness, too," she said quietly. "You are strong, Asha, but so are others. *You* are the only one who has the sort of power that Tal needs. You need to trust that you are not the only one who can do this part."

Asha flushed. "That's not the problem."

"Isn't it?" Elli gave her a chiding look. "I know you well enough to know that you will offer, not force. There are many out there who would give their lives for this cause just as willingly as you, but whose abilities are far, far less. Why not give them the chance to help, too?"

Asha stared at the ground. The words hit home, harder than she cared to admit.

"Perhaps you're right," she conceded eventually, softly.

They talked for a while longer, Asha occasionally still worrying over what Elli had said. In the end, though, tiredness overcame her concerns; she found her way to bed, sighing as she sank onto the luxuriously soft mattress and closed her eyes.

There was little more she could achieve until Caeden returned.

All she could do now was wait.

Chapter 25

A scream—familiar; Davian must have heard the same one a half dozen times before—emanated from the gray wall of smoke in the distance, echoing over rooftops and through the winding pathways of Zvaelar.

He barely twitched at the sound now, though it still made some part of him inwardly clench. He, Raeleth, Ana, and Ched walked in silence through shadowed tunnels and up scarlet stairwells, Ched's flickering torch leading the way, their footsteps marked by the crunching of loose stones. The distant, muted sounds of other teams leaving in various directions were still audible, as were the occasional sounds of patrolling al'goriat, but otherwise only the elongated shriek of pain from the distance broke the eerie hush.

Davian cast a glance across at Raeleth, but the other man was staring thoughtfully at the ground and didn't notice the look. Davian wasn't sure if it was a deliberate avoidance. Raeleth had asked for time to think, after they had made the treacherous return trip from the northern side of the Breach. Davian didn't want to press him further than he already had.

He silently berated himself again for not being more tactful, that night. Raeleth had been shaken to his core after seeing the man he knew as Aarkein Devaed; Davian should have known to approach the matter much more carefully. Instead, in a poor, spur-of-the-moment decision, he had tried to allay Raeleth's concerns. Tried whispering that the man down there might not be the monster Raeleth thought he knew. That in Davian's time, Devaed had become Caeden. Changed. Switched sides.

All it had done was make Raeleth look pained. Betrayed.

As if *Davian*, suddenly, were the enemy.

The other man hadn't said anything further, but he had clearly been too shaken for them to remain, despite Davian's reassurances. And Davian couldn't simply ask Raeleth to go back alone. Not while he was in such a state, not to mention that he had risked so much to help in the first place.

Besides—Davian didn't actually know whether the man they had seen was going to be of any assistance to him. The fact that Devaed—or Tal'kamar, or whatever he was currently calling himself—was here certainly *suggested* he wasn't currently aligned with the other Venerate, but it was no guarantee that he would be amenable to helping Davian.

Or even know who Davian was, yet.

So they had returned, navigating the Dark-filled mines and shimmying back across the rope to the southern side. Davian had kept his mouth firmly shut on the trip back, afraid that anything he said would simply make matters worse.

That had been a week ago, now. He had tried talking to Raeleth a couple of times since, but on each occasion Raeleth had stopped him short. Said that he was still thinking, and asked for more time.

Davian sighed to himself as they turned down a now-familiar alleyway. There was still a good fifteen minutes of walking before they got to their destination. They had been working the same section of the city for several days now, scouring each ruined building for any hint of metal. It had clearly been picked over before, but Ched thought it had been during the early days, when it had been much easier to make quota. That would mean that there was nothing obvious left, but still plenty to find beneath the rubble.

Soon enough they reached where they'd left off the previous day, moving to their positions wordlessly. The heavy clunking and grinding of stone on stone quickly filled the air, along with the labored breathing of all four of them as they struggled with their work.

Davian hauled aside a large chunk of stone, relieved to find that he needed extra Essence in his arms less and less now. His physique had changed a lot over the past month, the thinner diet and hard labor having burned away every ounce of fat from his body. His shoulders had broadened and his arms thickened, too—partly due to the exercise and partly due to his using Essence to recover from it, which appeared to have bolstered his muscles' growth even further.

He paused, fumbling with kan, relaxing only when he managed to grasp it. He had been practicing in every spare moment since his and Raeleth's encounter with the al'goriat, but neither the amount of kan he could access, nor his ability with the power, had seemed to improve. He could create a thin shield and, more importantly, could draw a little Essence into his Reserve now.

But that was all. He had to fiercely concentrate to do either of those things, and his instinctual drawing of Essence from his surroundings still didn't work. Not that there were many sources, anyway, here among the stone and darkness. He couldn't draw from the rest of his team—they needed the energy just as much as he did. So he'd been restricted to a thin trickle from the fire in the evening, thus far. Enough to keep him alive, but not much more.

He stretched, glancing toward Raeleth. The other man was already drenched in sweat, using a long piece of wood to try and lever aside a fallen slab too large to lift. Even at this early stage of the day, the other man was struggling.

"How are you?" asked Davian quietly, noting that Ana and Ched were out of earshot.

Raeleth stuttered midheave, the stone shifting a few inches but not budging. He changed his grip absently, breathing hard, not looking at Davian.

"The Dark is back again. It returned toward the end of yesterday," he admitted. "I was going to tell you tonight."

Davian stared at him worriedly. "It's been back that long already? You should have said something." He hesitated. "This... makes it more important than ever that I go back. He could help."

"Which is why I did not want to say anything," Raeleth growled. "If you are bent on approaching him, you *cannot* go to him desperate."

Davian shook his head. "If he's the man I am hoping he is, then it won't matter," he said firmly. He glanced toward the building into which Ana and Ched had disappeared, then stepped over to Raeleth, placing a hand on his arm. The Essence did its work quickly, and soon the Dark had retreated once again.

Raeleth breathed deeply, the color returning to his cheeks. He rubbed his forehead, looking vaguely ashamed, as they both resumed their work.

"I am sorry I've not been...communicative."

Davian nodded slowly. "I know what he did. I've *seen* some of what he did."

Raeleth gave a short, bitter laugh.

"Have you now?" he said softly. "My grandparents told stories of him, you know—secret stories, ones that I was warned never to repeat, but ones that I equally knew were true. How their parents before them had been raised on Ironsails, knowing nothing but the ocean and begging port to port for food, always running, never sure how far behind Aarkein Devaed would be. Fleeing in terror because he had destroyed my people's homeland and killed *millions* of them."

Davian swallowed, lowering the stone he was holding.

"I am sorry, Raeleth." He closed his eyes. In a perfect world, he would let the matter lie for a while, give Raeleth's emotions the chance to calm.

"I'm not asking you to trust him. Nor forgive him," he continued reluctantly. "I'm asking you to do what you can to let go of your hatred of him, and trust me."

Raeleth flinched. "It's not *hatred*," he said quickly, defensively. "It's just..."

He trailed off, and his shoulders slumped.

"El alone knows...I am trying to work through what you told me, Davian. Truly I am. Trying to at least accept it in my head, as a beginning..."

He turned back to the stone and gave the wooden lever a vicious heave, rolling the slab aside.

Davian said nothing to that. He couldn't blame Raeleth, no matter how frustrating it was. It had been hard enough for Davian to accept Caeden's true identity—taken months for him to truly reconcile himself to the fact, and that for someone he already knew quite well. Whom he *liked*. The fact that Raeleth was able to even *discuss* what Davian wanted to do was a minor miracle.

Still.

"I am going to try and see him, with or without your help. After last bell tonight."

Raeleth didn't say anything, sweeping aside some smaller stones with his foot as he examined the area he had just uncovered.

Davian opened his mouth to say more, but was interrupted.

"Raeleth! Shadat!" It was Ana, sounding unusually enthusiastic. Excited, even.

Raeleth and Davian exchanged a glance, then hurried over to where the other two had been working.

Ched and Ana were standing at the entrance to a near-intact building, peering inside. Ched glanced around at the sound of the other two approaching, beckoning them over.

"Think we may have found something," the big man said with a gesture, sounding pleased.

Davian joined them at the doorway.

The building itself stood several stories high, but the metal scattered around the vast first floor alone was enough to make Davian's eyes go wide. Pickaxes and hammers and shovels glinted dully against the red light streaming in from the sole window to the east, some of the tools hanging on the walls from hooks— again, metal—and the rest scattered across benches and the floor. Once a workshop of some kind, clearly.

"Fates," murmured Davian wonderingly, hearing an equally astonished intake of breath from Raeleth behind him. This room alone could keep the four of them fed for weeks. "How is this still here?" He took a step forward.

Ched grabbed him by the shirt, yanking him back before he could step inside.

"Look with your eyes," he growled, pointing upward.

Davian's heart sank as he understood.

The ceiling wasn't just shadowed: black and oily, the entire thing crawled with a slight, rippling motion, indiscernible unless you were watching for it. The Dark wasn't a barrier to their collecting the contents of the room, but it would naturally stretch toward anything living.

And if it dripped onto one of them, then that would be that.

"We have to risk it," said Ana grimly.

Raeleth glanced at Davian, then stepped forward.

"Let me do it." He was directing the words at Ched, but Ana was clearly included in the request. "I owe you for taking me in when—"

"No."

It was Ana who growled the word and though Ched hesitated, he eventually agreed. "It would take too long for just one person," he said gruffly. "And we need you to haul, anyway."

Raeleth opened his mouth to protest, but Davian put a hand on his shoulder. Raeleth was already infected, which was no doubt part of the reason he was volunteering—but that didn't make him immune to getting worse. His infection was from a single drop; from the stories the others told, even a small puddle of Dark could kill in seconds. And there were several pools' worth crawling on the surface of the roof inside.

Raeleth sighed, then nodded his acceptance.

They got to work, moving cautiously through the building, agreeing that they should start with the smaller items first. There was too much to take to Isstharis all at once: the resulting rations—even if they were awarded them—would be too difficult to hide away, and be too tempting a target for other groups. They would end up having to leave someone behind at camp just to guard their stash.

So they would try for two pails today—an enormous haul by any standard, anyway—and systematically move the rest of the metal away from the Dark. Ready to collect over a period of time. No other teams were combing this particular area, so they should be able to make this find last for weeks.

After an hour, Davian paused. Ana and Ched had been responsible for carrying some of the metal away to be stashed, but now Davian could hear faint voices.

He cocked his head to the side. There was Ana's distinct, feminine voice and then...

He and Raeleth both froze at the same time as they heard the hissing lisp in the reply, if not the exact words. It didn't sound like Isstharis, either.

"Go," said Raeleth calmly. He indicated the three-quarters-full pail on the ground. "Take that with you."

Davian pumped Essence into his arm and snatched up the bucket, moving as quickly and noiselessly as he could in the opposite direction to the discussion. He had barely made it through the far door and out of sight when the harsh sound of scale against stone ground against his ears, too close for him to risk more movement. He winced, gently putting the pail on the ground.

"Stop what you are doing." The hissing voice was loud; the dar'gaithin couldn't have been more than ten feet away from Davian. He closed his eyes, steadying his breathing. "Name?"

"Raeleth. How can I help you...?"

"Theshesseth."

Davian's pulse quickened.

"Where is Shadat?" It was Ched's voice, thick with suspicion.

"We've already filled a pail, and we can likely fill another before the end of the day. So he's hauling it to Isstharis now," replied Raeleth casually. "If you want to speak to him, he only left a few minutes ago. You might be able to catch up with him," he added, presumably to Theshesseth.

"Irrelevant." Theshesseth sounded irritated, but not especially concerned. "You have heard of the fugitive Davian?"

Davian's stomach lurched.

"I remember. From months ago. I assumed that he was either caught or dead by now, though," Raeleth added blithely.

"He may be." Theshesseth sounded displeased at the thought. "However, we had word of someone matching his description working this section."

Raeleth grunted. "You're talking about me? I already went through this. Months ago," he repeated, tone vaguely bored.

Silence again, and Davian held his breath.

"You look similar enough, I suppose," Theshesseth hissed irritably. "The man who sent me here will be beaten for wasting my time. Still. I have reason to believe that he may yet be alive, and the reward stands. Whoever is responsible for his capture will be set free, sent back to their own time. Remember that."

Davian's breath caught. Raeleth had never mentioned *that*.

There was a scraping sound as Theshesseth slithered away. Nobody spoke until it had faded.

"Shadat is hauling today?" Ched finally asked, doubt thick in his tone.

"I asked him to," said Raeleth.

"He does fit the description, you know," Ana observed.

Raeleth chuckled. "So do I, and about twenty other people I've seen this week. Besides, even if Shadat *was* some kind of mastermind who had managed to hide from the snakes this long...would either of you really turn him in? On the chance that those creatures would actually honor their word? Because I don't think I would."

Ched snorted. "Then you're a better man than me, Raeleth. And I hope El comforts you with that knowledge while you're scavenging rusty nails and I'm back in Ilshan Gathdel Teth with my wife and daughter."

There was a grunt from Ana, which sounded very much like she was agreeing with Ched.

Davian's heart sank. He'd known, deep down, that he couldn't trust either of them—but part of him had still faintly hoped that they might protect him, if it came down to it.

There was the sound of footsteps retreating, and soon enough he heard Raeleth resuming his work. After a full minute had passed, Davian steeled himself and hefted the pail, making certain to keep silent and to the shadows until he was well clear of the area. He should be on his way, make sure that Raeleth's claim that he was hauling could be verified—either by Ched or by Theshesseth himself.

He had only been walking for a few minutes when the tremor hit.

A deep rumbling split the air, punctuated by occasional ear-splitting cracks; Davian almost lost his footing as the ground beneath his feet shook violently. Several of the buildings around him shed chunks of sandstone wall, and a few lost the last of their support, crashing to the ground in an explosion of dust tinted red in the light. Davian staggered away from the closest one, wide-eyed as he searched for any hint of something about to collapse on him. This was far worse than any of the tremors he'd experienced since arriving—and many of the others had had aftershocks.

As the shuddering earth began to settle, a thrill of fear suddenly ran through him. The others.

He dropped the pail where he was, infused his legs with Essence, and began sprinting back the way he had come.

The choking dust was so thick that Davian couldn't even see the facade of the building anymore.

He skidded to a halt and then forced his way forward to where he knew the entrance lay, raising a hand to his face against the clouds still billowing out of the structure. Inside was lighter than it had been before, but completely obscured nonetheless, the grit in the air as thick as any fog.

"Raeleth?" he shouted desperately as he approached, slowing. "Ched? Ana?"

"Shadat!" It was Ana's voice, more muffled than it should have been and laced with relief. The latter was reason enough for concern; usually the strongest expression of emotion the woman showed was a grunt of either approval or disapproval. "Watch your step!"

Davian heeded the warning, drawing Essence and using it to clear away the dust in front of him, immediately spotting the glistening black patina on sections of the floor. He balked as he sent the Essence farther, carving a path of visibility inside.

There were puddles of Dark *everywhere*.

He tapped his Reserve further and forced back the dirty red fog, eyes widening as he took in the full extent of the destruction.

Then he spotted the body among the rubble.

Ched had never stood a chance; the massive section of roof had fallen hard across his back and the base of his skull, crushing both. The massive man's eyes stared blankly toward the entrance, and for an unsettling moment, Davian imagined that he could still see the desperation in them. He had been less than ten feet from safety.

Davian swallowed, scanning the wreckage of the long hall. Head-height piles of stone blocked his view of several areas, collapsed there from the vanished upper stories. Red moonlight streamed in from gaps in the roof, though to Davian's discomfort, he noted that not all of the roof was gone. If there were aftershocks—and there had already been one during his mad sprint back here—then that remaining stone could very easily come down, too.

"Where are you?" he yelled, stepping carefully inside. Where he had cleared the dust he could see Dark oozing from the floor and walls, pulling inexorably toward him as he passed.

"Here!"

Davian grimaced; he was in the midst of the cloud and the voice seemed to be coming from all around him. He drew even more Essence, sweeping aside as much as he could.

A black pit revealed itself up ahead.

Davian hurried carefully toward the twenty-foot-wide hole in the floor, which entirely divided the long room. On the other side of the crevasse, Ana was lying flat on her stomach, peering over the edge worriedly. Her eyes glinted with fear as she looked up at Davian's approach.

"Careful," she warned, voice shaking. "There was some kind of shaft underneath the floor, and the roof caving in made it collapse. I'm not sure how stable the edge is." She glanced at the Essence-light he was casting, but said nothing.

Davian nodded, each footstep cautious as he approached; when he got within a few feet he moved carefully to his knees, crawling forward to peer over.

About twenty feet below Ana was Raeleth.

The wiry man was on a narrow ledge, pressed up hard against the wall; another heavy tremor could cause his precarious perch to vanish entirely. His face was deathly white even in the warm glow of Essence, though his fearful stare was directed upward rather than at the yawning pit below him.

Davian frowned, for a moment not understanding. Raeleth wasn't the most physically gifted of people, but it was only twenty feet, and there looked to be plenty of handholds between him and Ana. Why...

Then he spotted it. The slash of wet darkness flashing by between him and Raeleth, perilously close to the other man.

Davian cursed, glancing up at the roof above the pit. A large crack ran across it, through which the Dark appeared to be escaping, dripping with a slow but steady rhythm. He forced some lightness into his tone as he considered. "You could have waited for some rope, Raeleth."

"I know, I know." Raeleth's reply was bravely cheerful, but the tremor in his tone gave him away. "I just *really* wanted to get a good look at some Dark up close." Davian could see more of the substance trickling down the sides of the pit now, almost indistinguishable from shadow, seeping from several large cracks.

"Maybe next time," Davian called out, flinching as a soft rumble echoed through the city outside and the ground trembled. A tiny aftershock. He stared up at the roof, trying to make out the source of the Dark. He could try lifting Raeleth out using Essence, but that was far from a guaranteed solution. Though Davian had been able to drive the infection from Raeleth's body, he knew from experimenting that Dark in its pure form cut through Essence as effectively as kan; if Davian tried supporting Raeleth with the energy, he had no way of ensuring that the other man wouldn't get hit by stray drops—or that the Essence bond wouldn't be destroyed, plunging him into the apparently bottomless depths of the pit.

The ground shivered beneath Davian's feet again and he shifted back slightly, glancing up to where Ana was steadying herself too. Their eyes met.

"Go," he mouthed to her desperately. There was no way she could help. The entrance that had been behind her was completely covered with rubble now, but she might be able to climb up some of the debris and find a way out through the roof.

Ana hesitated, then her eyes hardened and she shook her head stubbornly. Davian watched in dismay as another tremor sent Raeleth teetering dangerously; he looked around, spotting several large chunks of stone.

He breathed out, then reached for his Reserve.

The shadows were thrown back by the sudden burst of light, and he heard Ana's intake of breath even from across the pit. Davian ignored it, snatching up the largest of the stones he could see and wrapping them with Essence, sending them smashing upward and then wedging them into the gap from which the Dark appeared to be dripping. He waited for a few seconds, holding his breath, then carefully pasted a thin layer of Essence underneath. Just enough to hold the stones in place for a minute.

The Essence stayed bright, and the stones stayed in place.

"It won't hold for long!" he shouted.

Raeleth was already moving, scrambling up toward Ana, movements scrabbling and desperate.

Ana was so intent on watching Raeleth as he neared that she didn't notice the cracking in the ceiling above her.

There was a frozen moment as shadows coalesced and then oozed down, quivering and stretching. Davian screamed a warning, but Ana's reaction was far too slow.

The Dark poured over her greedily. Covered her head.

Smothered any last sounds she might have made.

Davian's heart wrenched. He tore his gaze back to Raeleth, who had stopped climbing and was frozen in horror.

The Dark that had just taken Ana was now rushing toward him.

Davian tapped his Reserve and sent a long, thick tendril of Essence toward Raeleth, wrapping it around the other man's body and pulling him upward and toward him in one violent, jerking motion. The slim man came flying across the pit, arms flailing, even as the temporary plug in the roof finally broke and the sealing stones plummeted behind him, a steady stream of pent-up Dark quickly following.

Raeleth hit Davian hard and the two men collapsed in a tangle of arms and legs, the breath temporarily knocked from Davian. He stumbled to his feet, gasping and hauling up a stunned-looking Raeleth with him.

"Nothing we could do," he said wretchedly, following Raeleth's gaze across to the glistening black mound that had been Ana, which was already mostly obscured by the combination of falling debris and shadow. "Come on."

He funneled a small amount of Essence into his muscles, all too aware of how low his Reserve was getting, even with his ability to tap other sources now. This morning, he'd comfortably had weeks' worth left in it.

Now it was closer to days'.

Heart heavy, he lent a limping Raeleth his shoulder, and they
started the long journey back to camp.

Chapter 26

Davian sat on the smooth chunk of rubble, gazing into the fire and focusing with all his will on draining it of Essence.

Time passed; after too long he looked away again, breathing heavily, having managed to trickle only the tiniest bit of extra energy into his Reserve. The surrounding buildings were silent, despite its being only just past last bell. Raeleth slept in the corner, huddled under his cloak. Davian had healed the man's injuries as much as he'd dared. No broken bones, thankfully, but a badly sprained ankle had needed attention. His stiffness and bruises would remain for a while, though.

He screwed up his face and chewed absently on some bitter-root, glancing at the half-full pail of metal sitting beside Raeleth. He had another one tucked behind him, and yet another pile of iron and steel scraps were stashed back at the collapsed building. The remainder of what he'd been able to retrieve. Enough to supplement whatever else Davian managed to scrounge while Raeleth recovered, and then some.

It was no consolation for losing Ana and Ched.

He sighed heavily. He would wait until Raeleth was well enough to find another team—no one would take him in his current state—and then Davian would leave to talk to Caeden. Aarkein Devaed. Whoever he was right now.

He closed his eyes and concentrated again, gritting his teeth as he put all his focus into this one task. Reached out, grasped once again for the elusive dark power.

It was there. Right *there*. He could touch it.

He slowly, carefully manipulated it. Drew in more Essence from the fire.

He wiped sweat from his brow and steadied his shaking limbs, noting that the fire was little more than embers now. There was no way that he could keep focusing like that—not regularly, certainly not in anything except ideal conditions. He needed weeks more to practice, maybe months, before he could easily perform these once-simple tasks.

"You look tired, Shadat."

Davian flinched, turning.

Maresh's hulking form stood silhouetted against the light from the fire in the building opposite, flanked by two of his men.

Davian scrambled to his feet, trying not to glance around at the bucket behind him. All three of the intruders were carrying clubs fashioned from wood, hefty-looking weapons that would be sure to do serious damage upon contact.

Maresh's gaze swept through the building, coming to a stop on the spot where Davian knew the pail was sitting.

"Seems like you have some extra there, Shadat," he observed coldly.

Davian squeezed his eyes shut, barely able to believe that this was happening.

"Two of our team were killed today," he said. "Raeleth is recovering from almost being killed. And you want to do *this*?"

"It's a shame that Raeleth wasn't one of the two," said Maresh calmly. "But even if he had been, the tremor has meant that collection is down. We need a little extra, and it appears that you have a little extra. So that's fortuitous."

Davian clenched his fists silently. He hadn't known Ched or Ana particularly well, and neither had exactly been friendly— but their deaths still stung. It had been a sharp reminder that no matter his abilities, this place was too dangerous for him to save everyone.

That pain had been festering, a frustration he had pushed aside, but now . . .

"No," he said softly.

"No?" Maresh chuckled. "I don't think you understand the

way this works, Shadat. We are not negotiating." His voice was ugly and low.

Davian tapped his Reserve. So little left, but more than enough for this. He couldn't give away the fact that he could use Essence, but that wouldn't be an issue. These men were strong but they were also thugs, far from trained fighters. He had Aelric's memories and a year of running through exercises in his prison cell.

"We are not," agreed Davian. He smiled grimly, a flood of energy unrelated to Essence rushing through him. He was sick to his stomach of being beaten down, of being a captive, of *hiding*. "So here is my offer, Maresh. If you think that you can take this metal by force, then you are welcome to try. Otherwise, leave me alone." He deliberately turned his back on the man and sat down again next to the pail.

There was utter, shocked stillness, and he didn't need the sliver of kan he was using to monitor Maresh's position to know what would happen next.

Maresh charged.

Davian waited until the very last moment and then flooded his right arm with energizing Essence, snatching up the pail and moving smoothly to his feet as he pivoted, swinging the enormously heavy bucket with all his pent-up anger. The metal-filled container blurred as he spun until it came to a sudden, crunching, jarring halt, connecting cleanly just below Maresh's right shoulder.

Maresh fell, his screams echoing across the silent camp, clutching his arm and rolling in pain, the limb jutting at entirely the wrong angle. Blood was already seeping outward across the big man's shirt, the snapped bone protruding through his flesh.

Davian calmly bent down and used his left hand to pick up Maresh's club, which had rolled to his feet. He still held the pail in his right.

He stared coldly at the other two men, then turned and sat down again.

There was nothing but Maresh's furious, pained curses for several seconds, and Davian almost dared to hope that his men wouldn't be foolish enough to try anything more. But then

Maresh coughed out a vulgarity-laden order, and the two men were sprinting at him.

He carefully put down the pail.

He hadn't wanted this, but if he was left with no choice, he had no compunction about teaching these men a lesson.

He once again tracked their movements using kan, keeping his back to them until the last moment. It wasn't for showmanship so much as to emphasize to them just how futile their attack really was. Just how insignificant he regarded the threat. He didn't want to merely injure these men so that they could no longer pursue their attempts at extortion.

He needed them to realize that taking him on in the future was an utterly hopeless cause.

The first came in with a hard, cowardly punch at the base of his skull; Davian leaned aside smoothly, Aelric's training and his own heightened senses giving him much finer control over his timing and movements than he had ever had before. He reached up and caught the arm as it breezed by him, twisting viciously and then jerking it hard across him, bracing his own shoulder against it.

There was resistance, followed by a sharp snap and a scream. Davian released the now-dangling limb and finally stood, turning to face the third attacker, who had faltered at his companion's lack of success. Ulf, if Davian remembered the name correctly.

"If we keep going, there will be only one person on your team left capable of scavenging, wherever they are right now," said Davian, barely audible over the other two men's agonized moans. "Working with two—perhaps with these two hauling between them—you might be able to make quota like everyone else. Work with one, and you're all eventually starving. Probably taken away by the al'goriat." He eyed Maresh. "And no one's going to take you in. Trust me."

The dark-haired man wavered; Maresh snarled at him to attack, but Davian could see from Ulf's expression that his message had gotten through.

"No more taking from other teams. If I hear it's happening, I'll come back and finish the job." Davian held Ulf's gaze; better to address him, dismiss Maresh entirely. "Nod if you understand."

There was a long moment of silence.

Ulf nodded.

Davian deliberately turned his back on the three men again, and sat down tiredly. Remarkably, he noted, Raeleth had slept through the entire incident. That was good. The man needed sleep more than anything else right now.

He ignored the gasping, pained curses of Maresh as they gradually faded into the distance, until finally everything was hushed once again.

It was hours later when a hand on his shoulder was shaking Davian awake.

He sat up with a start, alert immediately, making Raeleth—who had been leaning over him—flinch back in mild alarm.

"What's wrong?" asked the other man, looking concerned at his reaction.

Davian's drumming heart eased and he let his shoulders relax. He had stayed awake for as long as he could the night before, worried that Maresh or one of his people would come back to exact vengeance while he was asleep. He had drifted off at some point, but thankfully it appeared that his efforts at intimidation had worked.

"Nothing," he assured Raeleth, rubbing his eyes tiredly. He glanced around, noting the lack of movement in the camp. "This is early."

"Sorry. I woke up and I just..." Raeleth shook his head. "I've been thinking about Ana and Ched. I realized that we never remembered them. Never sat down and really acknowledged their deaths."

Davian blinked blearily. "And you want to do that now?"

"If not now, then when? I almost didn't wake you because we both need sleep. Because it felt...*frivolous*," Raeleth finished, his expression indicating how distasteful he found the concept.

Davian vacillated, still rubbing sleep from his eyes.

"I don't want to sound callous, but are you sure it's not?" he asked. "It won't bring them back." He hated saying the words, but Zvaelar demanded practicality.

Raeleth stared at him seriously. "It's not for them."

Davian grimaced, but levered himself up.

"It wasn't your fault, you know," he said.

"I know. That's not why I want to do this," Raeleth said softly. "I just...can't stop thinking about how little I actually knew them after more than a month of this. About how, in this place, it feels like so much effort to talk. To learn about someone, and especially to discuss with them what is important. Even when you know how easily things could change, it feels like something you can always put off until tomorrow." He exhaled. "I know they found me an irritation because I talked to them so much about El...but the truth is, now they're gone, I don't think I talked to them about Him anywhere near enough."

Davian gazed at him sympathetically. "It wouldn't have saved them."

"It wouldn't have stopped them from dying," Raeleth corrected him quietly. "El alone knows the other." He waved a hand at Davian's expression. "Don't get me wrong—this isn't from guilt. It's not to make myself feel better. It's to make sure I don't forget."

Davian sighed, but nodded. He was tired, but this was clearly important to Raeleth—and part of him acknowledged that the man had a point. They couldn't let trying to survive here strip them of everything that made that survival mean something.

They spent the next fifteen minutes sitting by the newly stoked fire, remembering their experiences with Ana and Ched. Neither had known the pair well, but they each had stories to share. Davian even found himself smiling at some of Raeleth's anecdotes—something he had too rarely done since arriving in Zvaelar.

After, they sat silently for a while, waiting for first bell to be rung.

"You never said the reward was freedom," Davian said suddenly. "For turning me in, I mean."

Raeleth gave him a surprised glance, then shrugged. "It didn't seem relevant."

"Still. A lot of people would have taken the risk."

Neither man spoke for a few seconds.

"So when are you going to talk to him?" Raeleth asked, his

gaze focused on the steadily lightening eastern sky. From the way he had said "him," it was clear about whom he was talking.

Davian glanced at the other man cautiously.

"Today," he said. "It cannot wait any longer." His Reserve was almost empty after his fight against Maresh. "You could come with me," he added, though without much hope.

Raeleth chuckled. "Despite everything, if I were in a better state I might actually take you up on the offer," he conceded. "As I am right now, though, I'll slow you down. Probably get us both killed." He shook his head firmly. "We have enough metal stowed away for weeks—and by the time that runs out, if you haven't figured out how to get more Essence, I'm dead anyway. So I'll stay." He hesitated. "I do have one request of you, though."

"Which is?"

"That your association with him does not compromise what you think is right." Raeleth held Davian's gaze steadily. "Even if you think it will mean escape, or saving lives, or..." He gestured. "Given what he has done—even if he *has* changed—I fear what he will ask of you. Evil men rarely convince others to their side by asking them to perform dark deeds for no good reason. They will always start with the lightest shade of gray. They so often use what seems like a good cause."

"You don't think it's possible that a little gray is what's needed, sometimes?" asked Davian.

Raeleth snorted.

"No," he said severely. "Gray is the color of cowardice and ignorance and sheer laziness, Davian—never let anyone tell you otherwise. If something is not clearly right or wrong then it bears actually *figuring out* which one it is, not dismissal into some nebulous third category. If you have a basis for your morality, a foundation for it, then there will always be an answer—and if you do not, then trying to decide whether *anything* is right or wrong is an exercise in futility and irrelevance."

Davian held up his hands in mock surrender at the intensity in Raeleth's voice.

"I'll keep that in mind," he promised. He glanced at the pail of metal in the corner. "By the way—you shouldn't have to worry about Maresh, now. Or anyone else trying to take advantage in the meantime."

He briefly explained what had happened the previous night. Raeleth listened with a frown, to Davian's surprise taking no obvious delight in Maresh's defeat.

"Good to know," was all he said.

They talked a while longer, for once not needing to force themselves up and about with the other teams. Davian ignored the wondering, vaguely concerned stares that they received from a few that passed. Word had spread fast about Maresh, apparently.

Eventually, though, Davian stood. There was no reason to wait until after last bell to sneak away, now.

"I think it's time," he said, a touch pensively. He forced a grin. "I'll see you soon."

Raeleth smiled slightly. "Of course," he said quietly. He dug around in his pocket and produced the silver key, pressing it into Davian's hand. "El with you, Davian. Be careful out there."

Davian gave him an acknowledging nod, then sucked in a lungful of dry air and headed out toward the Breach.

The moon hung sullenly on the horizon behind him as Davian reached the edge of the crater, silently shrugging his right shoulder and letting the spare coil of rope from the Breach slide down into his hands.

His relief at the uneventfulness of the journey was short-lived as he peered over the rubble-strewn rise at the scene below, contemplating what came next. The crater was secure mostly because it had only three obvious exits—all of them still guarded by alert-looking dar'gaithin. Its walls, though—thirty feet high as they were—would be easy enough to climb down using his rope.

Though Davian would be briefly silhouetted against the red moon at the lip of the crater, it also meant that the wall he was about to descend was deep in shadow. He paused, glancing again toward the center of the space below, where the al'goriat roamed. The flat, open expanse separating the ring of outer buildings from the ones near the shining metal tower was a wash of black, from this distance a single rippling mass of kan as the creatures' "vision" intersected and overlapped. At least the thin kan shield he was managing to maintain should hide him from that. Should allow him to reach the oasis of buildings around the tower that, from everything he'd seen, the defending Banes avoided entering.

Should.

There didn't seem to be any emphasis on guarding against intruders—logical, really, given that the al'goriat would surely be expected to take care of anyone foolish enough to enter that patrolled inner ring.

Davian held his breath, wishing once again that he had enough control of kan to direct Essence into a full invisibility shield, and then scrambled over the rise. Within seconds he was grabbing the rope and lowering himself down, disappearing into the deep shadows. He hung there, holding his breath, ears straining.

Nothing. If anyone had noticed him, they hadn't raised the alarm.

Exhaling, he continued, occasionally allowing a tiny trickle of Essence into his arms to ensure that he had the energy to keep the descent slow and smooth. The coarse rope burned against his hands but he kept moving at a steady pace; within a minute he was gently touching the ground, eyes darting along the narrow path ahead between two buildings. No movement, only the distant crunching of feet on loose stone.

He released the rope, leaving it there; it was at risk of discovery, but was also the only way out if he didn't want to raise the alarm. This section of the crater was pitch-black thanks to the angle of the moon, but the dull red reflection off the opposite side allowed him enough light to navigate.

He slipped between buildings, resisting the urge to peer inside. Strange smells emanated from more than one, a stench that, the first time it caught his nose, came close to making him retch. The structures were largely made of stone, though clearly shored up in places with wood—whether the damage was from the recent tremors or had been there already, Davian didn't know. Either way, it was even more obvious now that nothing around him had been constructed within the last few months. There was an *age* to everything here, a sense that these structures had been around for a long, long time before their current occupants. Before the rest of the city, in fact.

He reached the corner of a building, peering around it into the expanse of red-illuminated space beyond.

Creeping fear tightened his chest.

Al'goriat roamed everywhere here; there were perhaps a dozen within a hundred feet of Davian, and perhaps another twenty or thirty just beyond that. The creatures shambled, appearing to walk aimlessly from place to place and rarely even keeping to a straight line, although they did manage to avoid jostling each other. None of them seemed inclined to stray from the open area between the buildings and the metal tower, though, keeping firmly within the unsettling ocean of kan threads they were creating. Liquid dripped from their needle-like teeth, and their eyeless gazes seemed to encompass everything.

Davian shuddered, flinching back. In camp, even from his view above, this plan had made sense. Al'goriat *clearly* "saw" by using kan; therefore, he was able to make himself invisible to them. All he had to do was maintain his shield and walk right by them.

But now—seeing the impossibly muscular ten-foot forms dragging themselves ominously across the ground, panting softly, slavering mouths agape—the logic of it all suddenly mattered a whole lot less. Even *knowing* that he wasn't going to die here didn't help.

The two-hundred-foot stretch of open ground between him and the tower was, simply put, terrifying.

He stood there, back pressed against cold stone, for a full minute as he reconsidered. The tower into which he'd seen Devaed being led was in the absolute center of the crater, completely encircled by al'goriat-filled open space. There was no better way in. No other way in at all, in fact.

Davian peered around the corner again. The dark form of a dar'gaithin was slithering among the structures up ahead, but it wasn't looking in his direction and soon disappeared from view.

He took a deep breath, then stepped out from the shadows and into the crimson light of the moon.

He flinched slightly as the eerie illumination hit him, feeling more exposed than he could ever remember. If a single one of the al'goriat did manage to detect him, he wouldn't be able to escape, let alone fight them off.

The dozen or so creatures close by initially didn't seem to react to his presence, and for a moment Davian started to relax.

Then the nearest one stopped its wandering. Turned its head.

Stared directly at him.

Then three more al'goriat did the same.

Davian felt the blood drain from his face as he checked his kan shield. Still up, though sweat already beaded on his forehead from maintaining it.

He watched the creatures, heart pounding and breath held. They didn't move.

Then, as if at some unspoken signal, they turned and resumed their patrols.

Davian barely avoided exhaling loudly in relief, stilling his shaking hands and forcing himself to calm. They had sensed something, clearly, but it wasn't enough to raise an alarm. He should try and avoid getting too close to any of them—something he had already intended to do anyway—but nothing had really changed.

He took one step forward. Then another.

The al'goriat continued to move, not reacting.

Davian braced himself, then began deliberately making his way across the vast, open space, resisting the urge to break into a sprint despite the risk of being seen by any dar'gaithin passing nearby. That tower had to be a prison of some kind; if Devaed was being kept there, it made sense that it was for the most important prisoners. The most dangerous. Which meant that if he made too much noise here, alerted the al'goriat that something was wrong, the creatures wouldn't hesitate to tear him apart.

The journey seemed to last an eternity, though Davian knew that it had to have taken only a few minutes at most. At last he was stepping into shadow once again, past the edge of the circuit the al'goriat seemed intent on patrolling. The skin on the back of his neck crawled as he finally turned his focus away from the Banes and onto the structure up ahead.

Now that he was up close, Davian could see just how much metal had gone into its construction. His chest tightened.

The steel on it could keep a scavenging team fed for *years*.

He shook his head, stealing quietly toward the door he had seen Devaed being led through, then pressing back sharply as it abruptly opened and three people emerged. Two men and a woman, looking weary, albeit healthy enough. Their attire was dusty and worn, but didn't have the ragged tears and frayed edges that marked those who worked on the scavenging teams.

Davian frowned as he watched. There didn't appear to be a lock on the door, nor were the people themselves bound in any way. The al'goriat nearby didn't react to their presence, either, though they were no more than fifty feet away.

The group made their way to a squat, square building not far from where they had appeared, entering as gloomily silent as they had emerged.

Davian watched from the shadows for a few seconds, then moved on to the glimmering tower, keeping one eye on the building into which the people had just disappeared. They might well be prisoners, but he was wary of revealing himself to anyone at this stage.

He held his breath, then pushed open the door and slipped inside.

The interior was much like the outside, with gleaming steel plates lining the walls, though reflected torchlight made it seem positively bright by comparison. Similar to the Venerate's underground complex in Ilshan Gathdel Teth, where the portal to Zvaelar had been housed. Was that significant? He quickly checked the metal and, sure enough, thin lines of kan ran through most of the plates—though just as back in his own time, it was far too complex for him to grasp its purpose.

A set of narrow stairs wound its way up around the outer edge of the tower, while there was a doorway to the center straight ahead that was ajar. Bright, pulsing light spilled through the slight opening, casting shadows in the hallway where he stood.

Davian took a breath, listening to the silence before creeping forward, hesitantly placing his hand against the door and inching it open farther.

He peered through, squinting against the blinding light.

The floor of the room beyond was *glowing*.

It took a few seconds for his eyes to adjust; once they did, he could see that one edge of the floor—which was steel, just like everything else—had several rough-spun mats lying along it. Resting on each one was a figure, their features initially hard to make out, but clearly human.

Essence poured off those figures and into the polished metal below.

Davian stared. The steel plates on the ground pulsed a constant, clean white, not serving any purpose that he could see except storing Essence—more Essence than Davian had seen in what felt like forever. He licked his lips, looking at the floor longingly for a second. With even a modicum more control of kan, he would be able to refill his Reserve in its entirety here.

He cracked the door a little more, and his breath caught.

The portal was in the corner of the room, opposite to where the figures lay. The familiar gray, twisting void thrashed along its surface. It seemed more…violent than usual, menacing, as if the time stream were trying to break free and seep into the tower itself.

He watched, transfixed, for almost a full minute, not willing to step inside. None of the half dozen people in the room looked like the man whom he and Raeleth had seen. That made sense, he supposed; Devaed would be a special prisoner and surely wouldn't be kept with any others.

He sighed, then pulled the door closed again and started nervously up the stairs.

The tension in his body built with each passing step; the stairway was walled with steel and without his ability to easily manipulate kan, there would be no way to hide from anyone if he encountered them here. And while he could always go back down, if he was trapped between someone ascending and someone descending, there would be no escaping.

He climbed for what felt like ages, though it couldn't have been more than a minute. The tower gave an occasional crackle as energy seemed to dart through it, making Davian flinch, but there was no sign or sound of any movement up ahead.

He emerged onto the next level of the tower: a narrow hallway with a high ceiling, finishing at a closed door twenty feet away. The only other way forward was the continuation of the staircase.

Davian deliberated, then crept toward the door. There were no guards, but the steel made it look more than sturdy; smooth and rust-free, it glimmered in the dim light cast by the lit torches that lined the walls. Davian hesitated as he reached it, then braced himself and placed his hand against the metal, pushing gently.

It swung open silently.

Davian flinched back, pressing up against the cold wall and peering inside. A sole man occupied the room, his back to Davian. He was seated at a desk, a candle illuminating his work space. His head was bowed, and the scratching of quill upon paper filled the room.

The sound came to a slow stop.

"If you have come to kill me, you have wasted your time," said the man tiredly, not turning.

Davian said nothing. Was it the same prisoner he'd seen? The hair color and build looked right, but it was hard to say with the stranger's back turned.

He stepped inside. "I'm—"

Then something heavy struck him hard across the stomach and he was lurching sideways into the wall, the breath knocked out of him.

He braced himself against the metal plates and tried to rise, to recover and get into a position to defend himself, but froze immediately as something sharp and cold pressed at his throat.

"—not here to kill you," he wheezed, directing the comment more to the diminutive olive-skinned woman at the other end of the half-length stone spear than to the man at the desk.

No one spoke for a second. The woman holding the weapon—the thin shaft stone as well, he noted, not just the point—was lean, perhaps a few years older than himself, brown eyes flashing beneath a mop of curly brown hair. She seemed entirely at ease with both the spear and the situation, plainly confident in her ability to stop Davian from retaliating.

Still, something changed in her expression as she examined his face; she seemed almost taken aback as the pressure on his throat decreased slightly. Her grip on the spear shifted, and Davian resisted the temptation to flood his body with Essence and fight.

"I'm looking for information. I just want to talk," said Davian, as calmly as he could now that he was able to breathe properly again, eyes finally tearing away from the woman and traveling to the man at the desk.

The stranger cocked his head to the side. "Wait, Niha. I know that voice."

He finally turned.

It *was* the man he and Raeleth had seen. Davian almost sagged with relief, forgetting for a moment that he still had something sharp pressed against his neck.

The man pushed back his chair as he stood abruptly, eyes wide. He was tall, with dark hair and a smile that split his features as recognition flooded his face.

"Davian?" He stepped forward, looking stunned. "*Davian?*" He waved his hand toward the woman excitedly. "Niha, it's all right! Please let him go."

The young woman—Niha—was still looking at him with a strange expression; she eventually lowered the spear, twirling it in a vaguely ostentatious display before calmly hanging it on her belt.

Davian shook his head bemusedly and focused back on the man, who had paused a few steps away and was examining him dazedly. "You're Aarkein Devaed."

The man blanched. "Tal. Just... Tal, please," he said with a wave of his hand.

"So you know me." This version of Tal'kamar—Davian was fine with calling him that, as it was hard to think of him as Caeden—was from some time after he had beheaded Davian in Deilannis, then.

"Yes!" Tal's expression suddenly cleared. "Oh. Of course. You knew me in other forms. And by a different name," he conceded to himself wryly. "I called myself Malshash." He peered at Davian expectantly.

Davian just looked at him in bafflement, mind freezing. "What?"

Tal grinned and to the side, Davian saw Niha smirk at his obviously shocked expression.

Davian's mind raced. "So...*you* were the one who taught me..." He shook his head as he tried to order the sequence of events, stunned, a few things that had been puzzling him over the past couple of years finally coming together. "You tied me to the Portal Box so that I would bring it to you." He'd always wondered about Malshash's involvement in everything. Now, so many of the things he'd said and done made so much more sense.

Davian rubbed his bruised shoulder absently and then shot a glare at Niha, which only seemed to increase her amusement. He gnawed his lip as he thought back to those few weeks in Deilannis, when Malshash had taught him how to use kan.

"My ring," he said suddenly, eyes going wide. "Fates. You said I dropped it, but..."

He swallowed, trailing off.

Tal's smile faded. He nodded slowly as he examined Davian's expression.

"Ah. So you know that, now, too," he said. There was genuine remorse in his eyes.

"You were trying to save me." Davian had figured out that much about Malshash already over the past year; after being shown his own death, he knew it had to have been the reason Malshash had tried to prevent him from going back. But now that he understood it had actually been Tal—Caeden—that made even more sense.

It helped, too. Caeden hadn't just been trying to undo his wife's death. He'd been trying to undo Davian's as well.

"Unsuccessfully, of course," Tal conceded heavily. "But that is a conversation for another time. How are you here? *Why* are you here? Did the dar'gaithin finally figure out where you've been hiding?" He rubbed his face. "Were you with the scavengers all this time, or have you found another source of food out in the wild? The dar'gaithin were looking *everywhere* for you. I thought you must have already escaped."

"I've been with a scavenging team, but I only got here a few weeks ago," Davian admitted.

Niha snorted, and Tal shook his head firmly. "Impossible."

"Apparently not," said Davian, somewhat defensively. "Because I got here three months after everyone else." He scowled at Tal's disbelieving expression. "I assume that my experience in Deilannis must have altered my path here, somehow. Though I don't understand how all of this works. If what Malshash—*you*—told me back then is true, then everyone else here should have died the moment they entered the rift," he observed.

"We survived it because it wasn't the rift. Not like what you went through when we last met, anyway," said Tal, studying Davian with a frown. "This is Zvaelar."

He said the name as if it should be significant to Davian, but Davian had only ever heard it used by Raeleth and the others. He shrugged, indicating he was lost.

Tal searched for the words before shaking his head. "There will be time for a proper explanation later. But right now—are you truly telling me that the dar'gaithin don't know that you're here?" When Davian nodded, Tal exhaled. "Well. We have some time, then." He cast a critical eye out the window at the red-soaked landscape, al'goriat below moving on their unpredictable patrols. "You're safe enough in here for now."

"How did you get past the al'goriat?" Niha asked abruptly, her eyes narrowed. "They should have torn you apart." Her tone was vaguely accusatory.

"They can't see him. No source," realized Tal before Davian could respond, giving a low chuckle. "Well. *There's* an advantage."

"What does my not having a source have to do with anything?"

Tal's smile faded. "You don't know? Then how..." He trailed off, brow furrowing as something else occurred to him. "And how in El's name are you surviving here without kan?"

Davian's heart dropped. He'd been assuming that Zvaelar was somehow the cause of his difficulties with kan, rather than its being something wrong within himself—but part of him had still hoped that Tal would be able to use it.

"I made a Reserve of Essence for myself before I came here. It was close to full when I arrived, and it's been enough. Until now," he said heavily. "So you can't manipulate it either? I can't do much more than create a shield—that's how I got past the al'goriat—and even that feels like I'm lifting a building with my mind."

He glanced up again to see both Tal and Niha looking at him strangely.

"You...you think you touched it? Used it?" Tal asked, sounding nonplussed. "Davian, the al'goriat identify their prey through looking for a source. *That's* how you got past them."

"No—I definitely used a shield," Davian said slowly. "Kan is just...different, here, somehow. Much harder to reach and use. It takes every ounce of my focus to do anything with it."

"You're sure?" There was a low, restrained confusion to Tal's tone.

"Yes." Davian felt his brow furrow. "Why?"

"Because it's impossible." Tal shook his head. "No one can use kan here, Davian. No one can *sense* kan here."

"The al'goriat can," pointed out Davian.

"Because they are *made* here," said Tal firmly. "Their creation in this...broken time stream allows them to access kan. But *we cannot*."

Davian closed his eyes. Focused. Fumbled for kan for a few long seconds, gritting his teeth as he stretched, scrabbled, trying not to let it slip through his fingers.

He shuddered as he finally caught it. Manipulating it here was like trying to carry a boulder.

With a groan, he snuffed out the candle on Tal's desk.

He gasped, opening his eyes to see Tal and Niha staring at him in utter shock.

"How..." Tal's voice was shaking; he was looking at the still-smoking candle dazedly. "Davian, that shouldn't be possible."

"Well it is. Not that it helps us much," observed Davian bleakly. "That is the very best I can do, and I've been trying for weeks." He glanced across at Niha, still not feeling comfortable. The woman bared her teeth at him in what might or might not have been a smile.

Tal's expression turned thoughtful. "And you truly created your own Reserve?"

"Yes. That was before I was here, though."

"How long since you did that?"

Davian considered. "A little over a year."

Tal shook his head in disbelief. "And Talan Gol did not corrupt the Vessel?"

"Not that I noticed."

"You would have noticed," Tal assured him drily. He rubbed his chin, his eyes bright with an excitement that Davian couldn't quite understand. "That's strange, but... do you know what this means?"

Davian shook his head mutely, and Tal chuckled quietly at his bemused expression.

"It means we are saved," said Tal. He smiled, the expression full of hope.

"It means you're going to save us all."

Chapter 27

Wirr pored over the papers on Taeris's desk, so deep in thought that he didn't register Erran's presence until the Augur was almost next to him.

"Sire!" The young Augur leaned down and said the word loudly, a mixture of amusement and irritation in his voice as Wirr jumped, finally shaking his head and offering Erran a half-irritated, half-apologetic grin.

"Lost in thought," he admitted. He glanced around, noting that they were alone and that Erran had thought to close the door behind him. He gestured to the seat opposite. "What did my uncle want?"

Erran threw himself onto the chair. "Exactly what you thought. Getting the details straight. Making sure the rumors would be...entertaining enough, I suppose. If you want people to spread something, it can't just be true, or even important. It has to be *salacious*." He shrugged at Wirr's reproachful expression. "It's just the way it is. You need a villain," he continued. "People need someone to be outraged at. Say that everyone's going to die, and they'll be uneasy. But say that everyone's going to die and that someone's to blame?" He spread his hands, posture indicating his confidence in the theoretical rumor's success.

"Oh." Wirr rubbed his chin, nodding as he considered. No different from schoolyard rumors in Caladel, really. "I suppose you could say it was me, but—" He cut off as Erran laughed, a genuinely amused sound. "What?"

"Fates, Torin. You don't always have to be a martyr, you know.

I was thinking of Tol Shen?" He raised an eyebrow. "You know—the ones who actually knew and actually left? They're not hated, but the way they uprooted hasn't sat well with the people here. Most agree that they should have stayed and worked out their differences, rather than all but divide the country."

"Oh. Yes. Of course," Wirr coughed, relieved. He was getting too accustomed to being a scapegoat, apparently. "That sounds much better."

Erran chuckled again. "Good—because half the city's already heard it, by now." He leaned back, stretching. "How did your reunion go?"

Wirr made a face.

"You're...not going to like it," he admitted.

Wirr held his breath as Erran pushed ahead of him and stormed into the Lockroom, his glare poisonous as it focused on Scyner.

Scyner looked up, gazing back mildly at the other Augur. "Hello again, Erran."

Erran's every muscle was tense, as if he was close to violence. He could well be, Wirr had to concede, given the conversation they'd just had. Wirr hurriedly shut the door behind him and put a restraining hand on the young man's shoulder. Erran shrugged it off angrily, but the message seemed to get through.

"What are you doing here?" he spat.

Scyner looked reprovingly at Wirr, who shook his head slightly in response. "I explained everything before we came," he said with a pointed look in Erran's direction.

Erran's lip curled, and he deliberately ignored both Wirr and the black-scarred man, turning instead to Taeris and Ishelle, who were the only other people in the room. "Don't tell me you two are being as stupid as Torin and actually trusting him."

"That's 'as stupid as *Prince* Torin' to you, Erran," said Wirr severely, his voice cutting through the surprised silence before anyone else could react. He understood Erran's anger, but that didn't mean that he could let it go unchecked. "I know you're upset but if you cannot remember that much, then you can leave."

Erran glowered, then closed his eyes.

"I apologize, Sire." His teeth ground audibly. "But this man is a murderer. He is working for the Ath. He put Asha in that machine. He is responsible for starting the fates-cursed *rebellion* twenty years ago." He pulled in a frustrated breath. "That we cannot believe a word he says is an understatement, and you know it."

"We're not trusting him," said Ishelle promptly. The young woman looked exhausted, but Wirr was relieved to see that she seemed to be entirely under control today. "I Read him."

Scyner spread his hands in Erran's direction. "You can Read me too, if it will ease your mind."

Erran's eyes narrowed, then he shrugged. "All right." He walked forward swiftly, as if daring Scyner to change his mind.

Scyner didn't react as Erran reached out and—slightly more forcefully than was strictly necessary—touched two fingers to his forehead. Wirr watched Erran closely, but it wasn't long before Erran gave a reluctant grimace and dropped his hand.

"Well?" asked Scyner, his gaze steadily on Erran as the younger Augur's eyes opened.

Erran didn't reply for a long moment, thinking.

"Ishelle's right. He is telling the truth about Tal'kamar—about who he is and what he said. And he wants to find out more about the attack on the city," he said, sounding as though the words were being dragged from him. "That's his focus right now. I can't speak for his intentions beyond that, though."

"That's all we care about right now," observed Taeris, studying both Erran and Scyner from the corner. The Representative had been quieter since Scyner had appeared—not cowed, exactly, but certainly less inclined to speak up. Wirr thought that was likely due to his not trusting Scyner, more than any sense of intimidation, though the latter undoubtedly still played some small part in his newfound demeanor. "And he thinks there might be a way to get us some information."

"How?" asked Wirr and Erran simultaneously, though Wirr's tone was hopeful and Erran's laced with doubt.

"Me." Ishelle spoke calmly, though Wirr could see the weary concern in her eyes easily enough. "Taeris says that the sha'teth— the *host* of the sha'teth," she quickly corrected herself at a look 391 from both Taeris and Scyner, hands held up defensively in a flicker of her former self, "claimed that the Banes are involved. We all know that they're out there somewhere, and…well. I *do* have a connection to them."

Erran's eyes widened, and even Wirr recoiled. "You cannot be serious," said Erran immediately.

"Scyner thinks that he can dampen the effect the eletai have on her. Filter it, long enough for Ishelle to focus on the voices. Try and communicate with them," said Taeris.

"He thinks?" Wirr looked at Scyner dubiously.

"Yes." Scyner returned the look evenly. "I am sorry, Prince Torin, but this situation is hardly…regular. If you are looking for guarantees, look elsewhere. This *is* a risk."

"And our best chance," interjected Ishelle, irritation thick in her voice. "*And* also my decision. Even if the rest of you seem to think that I'm incapable of making those anymore."

Taeris and Erran both looked vaguely embarrassed at that last jab. Wirr understood their hesitation, though, feeling some of it himself. It *was* Ishelle's choice, naturally—but Ishelle had also hardly been herself lately. There was some question over whether her ability to make decisions was impaired, which was why they had already been gradually, quietly shifting some of her more vital responsibilities onto Erran's shoulders.

"You'd be putting a lot of faith in him," Erran said to her eventually. "He wants answers, but he hardly has your best interests at heart."

Ishelle snorted. "Thank you for that insight, Erran." She shook her head, and Wirr could see the determination in her eyes. "I have made my decision." She hesitated. "But I would very much like it if you were there to help. To make sure nothing goes wrong." She said the last softly, a genuine entreaty in her voice.

Nobody spoke as Erran stared, jaw jutting as if he was thinking of another argument to attack with. Finally, though, he gave a short nod.

"I'll be watching," he said, the words as much to Scyner as to Ishelle.

They quickly agreed to use the Observatory for the experiment, a rarely frequented upper section of Tol Athian that opened out high above on the slopes of Ilin Tora. There were no external entries to or exits from the rooftop courtyard; it had been created with the same smooth, high walls that characterized Fedris Idri, hiding even the city below from view.

But it was private, beyond the protective wards of the Tol—and only a short few steps if they needed to get Ishelle back behind the defenses. For their current purposes, that was all they needed. Ishelle was technically free to come and go from the Tol; though the Council would undoubtedly have liked to be informed of her plan, she was technically under no obligation to do so.

They left as a group, taking the little-used staircase upward. It was a long climb—a full fifteen minutes, by Wirr's estimate—and he found himself drawing a little on Essence toward the end. He suspected that some of the others were doing the same. Certainly everyone seemed content to keep conversation to a minimum, focusing instead on conserving their breath.

Finally they passed through the upper door and into the open air, and Wirr squinted against the sudden glare from above, dulled though it was with the sun behind clouds.

The Observatory was a strange area, one that Wirr had visited only a few times before. It was bowl-like, as if a large section had been scooped from the side of Ilin Tora, giving its occupants a clear view of the sky in all directions. He knew that there were plenty of theories about what it had originally been: everything from an actual observatory to mark and analyze the stars, to some sort of private retreat, a repose away from the distractions of daily life.

Wirr could see its potentially having been the latter. The sides of the Observatory were sheer, smooth rock that still somehow managed to exude an alien beauty, marred only by razor-thin edges at the top. Those were as sharp as they looked, Wirr had been told—an extra defensive measure, presumably, for anything somehow able to climb this high. Though there were no obvious Essence mechanisms, he had been assured that when the Tol's defenses were triggered, this area was as well guarded as any of the entrances down below.

The remains of a tower sat in the center of the Observatory. During the war, the Council had built it to see over the edge and down into the city below—both to mark the movements of the Loyalists, and as a means of potentially raining down destruction upon anyone who got too close. Its dismantling had been one very minor stipulation of the Treaty.

Ishelle took a deep, shaky breath as she paused in the doorway. They had taken her up here a few times, early on, after it had become clear that the walls of the Tol were somehow protecting her. It was by far the best place to test her limits. They had no idea what would happen to Ishelle if she was completely overcome by her connection to the eletai. What the consequences might be.

That was a terrifying thought not just for Ishelle, but for the entire city.

Erran laid a hand on Ishelle's arm as she visibly wavered. "We won't let it go too far."

Ishelle shot him a small smile, then stepped out over the threshold and into the open air.

Wirr found himself holding his breath as he watched, though he knew the reaction wouldn't be instantaneous. Ishelle wandered over to the middle of the fifty-foot-wide area, standing near the wreckage of the tower.

She suddenly groaned and sat heavily on a beam, head in her hands.

"Are you all right?" Erran hurried over to her.

Ishelle was motionless for a second.

Then she snarled and twisted quickly, leaping to her feet and sending Erran and Taeris stumbling backward in panic at the sudden motion. Wirr leaped forward and tapped Essence immediately, readying himself to try to subdue her.

Then his heart slowed to something resembling an acceptable pace as Ishelle started laughing.

"Fates. That's not funny," grumbled Taeris, shooting an angry look at the young woman, who simply stuck out her tongue at him impudently.

"If you'd been able to see the looks on your faces, you'd think differently," Ishelle retorted cheerfully, still chuckling. "Fates, Taeris. It's been less than a minute. How far gone do you think I am?"

Taeris growled something under his breath, and even Erran

gave her a disapproving look. Scyner didn't seem to have any opinion on the joke, merely seating himself opposite Ishelle.

"Has it started?" he asked her directly.

Ishelle frowned. "What did I just say?"

"I heard you," said Scyner patiently, "but your eyes say something different."

Erran pushed past Taeris to stare into Ishelle's eyes. He gave a gentle nod as Wirr saw what the Augurs had: Ishelle's eyes were cloudy, the clear blue and white hazing slightly toward gray.

"It's started," Erran confirmed quietly. "Do you feel anything?"

Scyner coughed politely before Ishelle could reply.

"I'm going to start studying the connection," he said, only half asking permission. Ishelle indicated her acceptance.

"The usual. Just that pressure in the back of my head," she replied to Erran. "But...yes. It's there." She spoke with some discomfort, and Wirr could hardly blame her. A few weeks ago, it had been almost an hour before she had reached this stage.

"You can watch, but silence would be best," said Scyner calmly, cracking open an eye to indicate he was directing the comment mostly at Erran.

Erran scowled, but at a look from Ishelle, relented.

Wirr observed for a while, but everything happening was related to kan: there was simply nothing for him to see. He wandered a short distance away, gazing at the gardens that grew around the edges of the Observatory.

"Have you given any thought as to how much to tell the Council, Sire?"

Wirr started, not having realized that Taeris had joined him. They were slightly apart from the others, isolated enough that their conversation was private.

"You mean about Caeden?" Wirr shook his head. "Not yet. But..." He shrugged awkwardly. "My initial reaction is that it's not a good idea to say anything."

Scyner had spent almost a half hour trying to convince them of Caeden's past as Aarkein Devaed. It was only after the Augur's willingness to let Ishelle Read him, and her confirmation of the information, that Wirr had even been able to consider the news.

He still didn't know what to make of it. He was confident that the man he'd come to know was on their side—Caeden's actions had said enough, as far as Wirr was concerned—but knowing what he was capable of...

"I agree." Taeris kept his voice low. "No good would come of it. Half of them would say we were making things up again, and the other half would want to lock Caeden away until it was all sorted out and verified. There certainly wouldn't be enough of them willing to simply accept the information and adjust appropriately." He sighed. "As strange as it sounds, I don't think it's information that they need to have, either. They don't trust Caeden as it is. Making that worse would be a mistake."

Wirr nodded thoughtfully. "So if this works"—he cast a quick glance across at Ishelle, who was still quiet and motionless—"and we actually figure out where in fates the Banes are, then we go to the Council and the Assembly with our proof."

"What about the sha'teth?" asked Taeris uneasily.

"I...still agree with Scyner," Wirr said reluctantly. "From what that sha'teth's host—Elder Tolliver—said, they have a part to play in whatever the Venerate are planning. We need to get rid of them."

"You mean kill them."

"I mean kill them." It was hard for Wirr to say the words; there were clearly still people, or the remnants of them, locked away somewhere beneath the sha'teth's control. But it also seemed clear that there was no saving them.

"The Council will never agree."

"The Council will not be involved." Wirr made the statement firmly. "This is a time for decisions, Taeris, not committees."

Taeris snorted. "It wasn't so long ago that you would have said the opposite. That our taking these matters into our own hands was very much against the law."

Wirr gave him a wry grin. "I've had a year of politics to shake me out of that bad habit." He quickly sobered at Taeris's vaguely reproving look. "I still think we should try to uphold the law, but I also understand now that what's right isn't always what's legal. And that the opposite can be true, too."

"Law is about order, not right and wrong," Taeris agreed. "And the latter should always trump the former." He gave a soft laugh. "You've come a long way since we met."

Wirr chuckled, too. "I don't know whether—"

"Ishelle?"

The sudden concern in Erran's raised voice cut through the conversation. Wirr and Taeris turned at once, hurrying over to the others.

Wirr blanched as he saw Ishelle, spotting the signs that were becoming familiar to him now. Ishelle's hands were trembling—not violently yet, and the rest of her body remained under her control so far, but enough to be obvious at a glance.

"I thought you said that you could dampen the effects," said Erran anxiously.

"You need to focus, Ishelle," said Scyner steadily, ignoring Erran. "This connection is like a...noose around your mind. Every time you pull away, it tightens, digs in harder and makes things worse. It's hurting you because you're resisting it so much."

"I'm scared," whispered Ishelle, her eyes wide and blank as she stared into nothing. "I don't want to let them in."

"I'll protect you." Scyner's voice was gentle. "But I can't until you get out of the way."

Ishelle gave a tremulous nod, the usually brash young woman as obviously frightened as Wirr had ever seen her.

She gave a sudden, soft sigh, her shoulders slumping and head bowing.

When she looked up, her eyes were completely black.

"They're here," she said faintly, terror still in her voice. "They want to know about me. They are trying to burrow in. They're trying to get in further." The words were barely more than a whimper.

"Ask them about the sha'teth. About the attack," said Scyner, the urgency in his tone rising. "Ask them where they are and what is being planned. What they're seeing. *Anything.*"

A tear rolled down Ishelle's cheek, and her body was shaking now, though she hadn't started the mad ramblings that had previously accompanied that stage. A good sign, Wirr thought. Erran moved behind her, grasping her gently by the shoulders to stop her from falling over.

Everyone watched mutely, holding their breath.

"I...I'm trying," said Ishelle shakily. "They won't answer.

They keep asking—" She gasped, face contorted in pain; Wirr and Erran both stepped forward but she recovered quickly, sitting straight again. "They're asking to be let in. For me to... *join* them." The last was said in a horrified whisper.

Scyner shook his head. "Keep going," he said firmly. "We have to know."

Wirr moved closer, his disquiet growing. "Scyner. We need the information, but not at the expense of her health," he said firmly.

"She can handle it." Scyner glanced at him. "Trust me, Prince Torin."

Wirr hesitated. "Ishelle, if you want to stop—"

"I'm all right." Ishelle's voice told a different story, but Wirr accepted the statement, exchanging nervous glances with Erran and Taeris before reluctantly indicating that Scyner should continue.

A few minutes passed breathlessly, only Scyner's occasional promptings breaking the silence. Eventually the older Augur shifted.

"Ishelle," he said quietly, "you may not be able to get your answers just by asking."

"What do you mean?" Ishelle asked, still trembling in Erran's grasp.

"You need to use the connection yourself. *Read* them."

"Are you sure—" began Erran, but he reluctantly subsided at Scyner's glare.

The uneasy hush fell again for what seemed like an eternity.

"I see something," Ishelle suddenly gasped. Everyone leaned forward unconsciously as she spoke. "They're in a forest. Some sort of... temple. There are huge statues lining the entrance, each with a symbol. Men and women. Nine of them. The other ele-tai are everywhere here." A shudder ran through her. She spoke urgently but also absently, as if in a trance. "Dar'gaithin too. Hundreds of them. And people—but the Banes aren't attacking them. They're carrying things out of the temple."

"What are they carrying?" asked Scyner. "Do you recognize where this is?"

Ishelle didn't respond, but beside Wirr, Taeris shifted.

398   "Desriel," said the scarred man. When the others looked at him

questioningly, he gave a firm nod. "That's their sacred vault—I haven't seen it myself, but I've heard of it. Those statues are their gods, and they're supposed to be the only ones who can open it."

"And their gods are the Venerate," murmured Wirr, swallowing.

"They've seen me," Ishelle whispered suddenly, as if trying to make sure that the eletai couldn't hear her. "They know I'm here."

"What else do you see?" pressed Scyner, before anyone else could speak.

"No. No. I have to get out." There was panic in Ishelle's tone. "Let me out."

"Tell us what you see," said Scyner firmly.

"They know I'm here. They're going to tell the others." Ishelle's voice was getting louder as it became more urgent. "They know we know, now. They were waiting for something, but they're going to launch the attack now. Oh fates. It's our fault. They're going to hit Ilin Illan, use the eletai to try to cripple us before we can react. And they're coming for us now. They're coming."

Wirr felt the blood drain from his face, and he heard a sharp intake of breath from Taeris.

"That's enough, Scyner," said Taeris, and Erran began pulling Ishelle toward the door.

"*Stop.*" Scyner's voice cracked like a whip. "Ishelle, it's too late to take it back now, and we need more information. What about the sha'teth?"

"They're coming, they're coming." Ishelle's voice was breaking now, and she was shaking violently, Erran having to adjust his grip to hold on to her. Suddenly she gasped and her eyes, still completely black, went wide. She gripped Erran's arm so tightly that the young man grunted in pain. "They know the sha'teth are here. We're not safe. Nowhere here is safe. We need to leave. Fates oh fates they're coming WE NEED TO LEAVE!"

Ishelle screamed as she writhed and broke free of Erran's grip, black lines creeping along her body. Erran reached for her but somehow she twisted and *threw* him, sending him sailing through the air to land in a heap ten feet away.

"Grab her!" shouted Wirr, strengthening himself with Essence and seeing Taeris do the same. Scyner helped, too; they wrestled with Ishelle as she resisted like a wild animal, clawing and shrieking and thrashing with every inch of her body.

"We need to get her inside," growled Taeris as a flailing limb caught him across the chest.

"We need to tie her up and keep questioning her." Scyner yelled the response above Ishelle's frenzied screams. "She was getting answers. I just need—"

"No." Wirr glared across at Scyner, doing his best to restrain Ishelle while still being gentle. "She goes back inside. *Now.*"

Scyner's lip curled, but after a second he looked away with a brief, frustrated dip of the head. More black lines were spreading across Ishelle's face and limbs, almost like a Shadow's except these were far thicker and straighter, somehow more disturbing. Whatever they were seemed to be giving her near-inhuman strength, because it took all three of them—four, once Erran had recovered enough to help—to drag her twenty feet to the door and finally through it.

Ishelle gave a final gasp as she crossed the threshold, then went limp.

Their exhausted, shocked panting was the only sound to break the silence as they looked at her with a mixture of trepidation and concern. She was unconscious, the black lines on her skin not fading yet, her breaths coming in what looked like dangerously short and uneven bursts.

Erran was the first to move.

He punched Scyner in the face.

"You said you would *protect* her," he snarled as the older Augur staggered back, the attack clearly having taken him by surprise. "Are you actually *capable* of not doing fates-cursed awful things?"

Wirr placed a restraining hand on Erran's shoulder as Scyner steadied himself, shaking his head dazedly.

"I chose to prioritize everyone else. You heard what she said." He looked around at the other three. There was no defensiveness to his tone, only cold certainty. "We should have tried to get more. Now we know that Desriel has Banes and that they are going to

send the eletai to attack us here."

"Have already sent," corrected Taeris bleakly.

"Have already sent," agreed Scyner. "And she said that they know the sha'teth are here, too. It *sounded* like there was a purpose to that." There was clear frustration in his tone.

"We'll tell the Council," said Wirr, "and advise that they kill them immediately. But right now, we need to alert the city that there are eletai on the way." Saying the words suddenly made the horror of the situation more real, and a queasy wave of fear washed through him, though he quickly forced back the sensation. He turned to look at Ishelle. "Erran, do you think that you can take her somewhere to recover? And then inform the Council of what's happened. Tell them that they need to deal with the sha'teth before...whatever's coming."

"I'll do it," said Scyner. "The Council will take too long."

"No. I need you with me," said Wirr. He deliberated, then motioned to Taeris. "You too."

He gazed at the two men grimly. "We need to convince the Assembly to evacuate Ilin Illan."

Chapter 28

Davian sat on the sole chair in Tal's room, eyes close to drooping shut despite the seriousness of his situation.

First bell, fainter but still audible here, had rung out a while ago, but he was still no wiser than when he had arrived. He'd had ten minutes of excited discussion with Tal—mostly answering questions, to his vague irritation—and then Tal and Niha had needed to leave. A scheduled requirement of their time, was all he'd been able to gather; Tal had been suitably apologetic, but had told him in no uncertain terms to stay put. Tal, apparently, trusted the others imprisoned here in the crater about as much as he did the dar'gaithin.

Davian had been promised answers upon their return, but that had been hours ago. He'd watched out the window for a while—not that there was a great deal to see—and then done his best to rest. His Reserve remained dangerously low, and he couldn't afford to keep draining it just to stay alert.

The door abruptly opened and he leaped to his feet, his heart skipping a beat.

He sank back into the chair as Tal and Niha walked through. The two of them looked exhausted, Tal in particular seeming a hollow shell of the man who had greeted him just a few hours earlier. Dark bags sat under his eyes, and every movement was slow, strained, clearly taking effort.

He gave Davian a cheerless smile, trudging over to the bed and collapsing onto it. Niha—who also looked tired—shut and locked the door behind her, then took up position by it, giving

Davian a cool glance as she did so. Their movements had the feel of an established routine.

"What happened?" asked Davian tentatively.

"Nothing." It was Tal, staring at the ceiling from his prone position on the bed. "Which is always good."

Davian glared at him. "I don't know what that means."

"Sorry." Tal groaned, levering himself up into a sitting position again and waving away Niha's look of concern. The woman threw an accusatory glare at Davian, who shrank a little beneath it. "You're probably wondering what in El's name is going on."

"You could say that," admitted Davian drily. "Where were you?"

"Down below. Lending Essence to the cause." Tal rubbed his face tiredly, seeing Davian's expression. "Right. Where to begin." He glanced over at Niha, pleading for help.

"This tower is a Vessel. If it doesn't get enough Essence, everything in Zvaelar collapses," said Niha, sounding bored. "And then we all die."

"Everything collapses?" Davian repeated pensively.

Tal sighed, giving Niha a wry look.

"What do you know about this place?" he asked Davian.

"Not a lot," Davian admitted. "The scavenging teams figured out pretty quickly that we traveled through time to get here. Other than that..." He shrugged.

"So nothing, then," muttered Niha.

Tal closed his eyes; when he opened them again he seemed stronger, sitting straighter.

"This city—Zvaelar—was the capital of a desert nation, on a continent far to the north. Around...three and a half thousand years ago now, give or take, by both our reckoning." He hesitated, as if loath to reveal what he was about to. "It was where Gassandrid was born."

Davian raised an eyebrow. "I take it the city wasn't like this, back then."

"From the way he tells it, it was pleasant enough. As good as any other place where large groups of people congregate. He certainly has a nostalgia for it." Tal sounded sad. "When he was twelve, Gassandrid took part in a trial—a sort of test to pass into manhood—in which he had to go into the desert and kill a sand serpent. When he returned three days later, Zvaelar was gone. Collapsed in upon itself, withered to dust, everyone who had lived there dead. Including Gassandrid's parents and three sisters.

"Everyone who bore witness to the destruction said that it happened in an instant—that it had been a deliberate attack. There was only one group in the region who had the sort of power that could effect such a strike. A race called the Shalis."

Tal paused, sentiment in his voice as he continued. "The Shalis denied responsibility, but the survivors of the Zvael remained convinced of their guilt—particularly after a few years, when it was discovered that Gassandrid was able to wield kan. It was a power that the Shalis were known to abhor as a rare and dangerous weapon, and one that they immediately called upon him to abandon." He shook his head. "Gassandrid became convinced that the Shalis had destroyed Zvaelar to kill him, to stop him from coming into his power. He eventually led the war against them. And though it ultimately destroyed his people, he won many years later. With our help."

Tal shifted, the story unmistakably painful to tell. "Gassandrid's motivation to go back in time has always been this place. It's always been to save his family, his friends. His people. After the ilshara went up—after I broke the Jha'vett and Gassandrid realized that his goal might still be lifetimes away—he tried to replicate what the Darecians had done in Deilannis. Against our advice, he built on their work and made...a portal to the past, I suppose. To Zvaelar of old."

Davian glanced out the window at the ruined city. "That obviously didn't go as planned?"

Tal gave a low, humorless laugh. "No. Instead, Gassandrid created this mess. Closer than anyone has ever come to being able to go back, but still an unmitigated disaster." He shook his head sadly. "We're fairly certain now that he actually destroyed the city. That in his efforts to save Zvaelar, he was the one who caused its destruction."

Davian swallowed, trying to parse the information. "So we're...somewhere in those three days when Gassandrid left the city, as a child?"

"Inside the very moment when it was destroyed, in fact. He   405 did manage to open a portal back, obviously—one that could be safely traversed," Tal said quietly. "But in doing so, he miscalculated. He had a series of Vessels set up to dampen the effects of the portal in Ilshan Gathdel Teth, but he needed a duplicate set of those same Vessels here. So when it opened, it caused a cataclysm on this end. A massive distortion that ripped Zvaelar almost entirely from the time stream."

"Like when we let time flow around us?" asked Davian.

Tal screwed up his face. "Yes and no. We use the parallel of the river because what we do is much gentler by comparison: when we push against the flow of time, we resist it—but we're never in danger of separating ourselves from it. Never threaten to truly break away from it." He shook his head. "Whereas Zvaelar... Zvaelar was violent. Messy. A better analogy for what happened here would be that it was like a limb that was almost torn off. One that's now just hanging on to the body by a few pieces of sinew."

Davian felt a chill run through him. "Which means?"

Caeden glanced across at Niha, who shrugged. "It's too far out of step, essentially—you only have to look at the sky to know it. Nearly four months here, and probably only a few seconds back in Gassandrid's childhood. And El knows how long has passed in our own eras. Time is *broken* here. And the result is that the time stream isn't trying to drag Zvaelar back into alignment. It's trying to exorcise it."

Davian looked around at the steel tower. "So all of this is..."

"Everything we could do to slow that process down."

Davian walked over to one of the steel plates, touching it wonderingly. "But if you can't use kan, how did you make the Vessels?" They were clearly more than simple Essence conduits. "And why out of metal?"

Niha chuckled, a small smile playing on her lips as she watched Davian. "My rations for a week if you guess."

"It's complicated," Tal assured Davian, giving Niha a stern look.

"I have time," said Davian drily. "I need to..."

He trailed off.

There was a grinding sound coming from outside the door.

Tal gestured urgently to Davian, but it was already too late;

the door was swinging open and three dar'gaithin were slithering through.

Davian's heart sank as he took in the creatures. Each of them at least nine feet tall, they had to contort to fit through the doorway. Short, obscenely muscular arms hung from powerful serpentine frames as they came to an abrupt halt.

All three were staring at Davian.

"So he is here," hissed the first. "Did you think his rope would not be found?"

Davian winced. He'd forgotten about the rope he'd left dangling at the edge of the crater.

"Theshesseth was right," said the second, sounding amused. "You were hiding him all along, Devaed. This does not bode well for our deal."

Tal's gaze flicked from the Banes to Davian, then to Niha. He rubbed his face tiredly.

"I suppose it doesn't," he said heavily.

He gave a reluctant nod to Niha.

Niha flicked her hand out, the spear already off her belt, sizzling with Essence.

In one smooth motion, she pivoted and threw the spear, taking the nearest dar'gaithin through the mouth.

The remaining two creatures hissed in alarm as they spun to face the threat; Davian watched in openmouthed shock as Niha calmly gestured, the whip of Essence that had lashed out along with the spear flashing as the dead dar'gaithin began slumping to the floor. She ripped the weapon free in a shower of black blood and spun it, the sharp-edged stone moving in a deadly dance as it flew at the two dar'gaithin, snaking at one and then the other in rapid succession, targeting the soft spots of mouth and eyes.

Davian stepped forward but Tal put a restraining hand on his arm, shaking his head. "You'll only get in the way."

Davian accepted the statement reluctantly, gazing in wonder as the short spear blurred between the two creatures, sparks flying every time it connected. Finally the weapon struck home again and the second Bane crumpled, the edged stone through its eye.

The final dar'gaithin snarled and vanished out the door before Niha could wrest the spear free again.

Davian's heart leaped to his throat and he made to go after the creature, but again Tal restrained him. The other man gestured to the ground where the fight had taken place. "No need."

Heart still pounding, Davian stared in confusion as he spotted what Tal had indicated: several dar'gaithin scales scattered across the steel, clearly torn off during the fighting. He watched mutely as Niha calmly snapped the spear back into her hand, taking a cloth from her pocket and wiping it carefully. She tucked it at her side again once it was clean, then proceeded to stroll over to the window.

"There he goes," she said, sounding like she was commentating for them. "Athsissis always was a cowardly little creature. He's so excited that he hasn't even realized. He's going as fast as he can. He's reached the edge. The al'goriat have seen him. And...oh. *Oh.*" She watched for a moment longer, then made a face. "That did not end well for him."

Davian stared, head spinning, as Tal wandered over to the dead dar'gaithin, giving one of them an irritated prod with his toe. "El take it," he muttered. "We can't afford this."

Niha turned back from the window. The two both seemed more frustrated than anything else. "Three more down. That leaves...a dozen? We can't afford to lose any more," she agreed bleakly.

"You...didn't want them dead?" asked Davian in confusion.

Tal reached out and shut the door. "Not really." He rubbed his chin worriedly. "They are how we are getting food through the portal. They take the metal to Ilshan Gathdel Teth, and in exchange they get sent back with supplies."

"Except that the journey sends them insane, they come back at random positions along the edge of the dome around the city, and then Tal and I have to help the other dar'gaithin hunt them down and kill them just to get the food," said Niha. "So they are a limited resource."

Davian thought back to his first night in the city. "I saw one, I think," he said, shifting uncomfortably at the memory. "It was... *eating* one of its own."

"Southeast section of the city?" Niha nodded cheerfully at Davian's affirming gesture. "We're responsible for the decorations. The smell of their own dead seems to attract them, so even though they could come back anywhere around the perimeter, they always seem to end up there. It's made our job a lot easier."

Davian shuddered, as much at Niha's casual attitude toward the grisly scene he'd witnessed as anything else.

"What sends them insane?" he asked. "You said that the portal could be safely traversed, and the portal's just down below. Why haven't you just gone back the other way?"

Niha snorted. "Why didn't we think of that?" She looked at Tal. "Why haven't we just done that, Tal?"

"All right," said Tal with a small smile, shooting a vaguely warning glance at Niha. "Don't forget that you asked exactly the same question when we got here."

Niha glowered at him, but subsided.

"The portal protects passage to the past. To here," Tal explained to Davian. "The other way is essentially like the rift in Deilannis. *You* should be able to use it, but we certainly can't."

"Oh." Davian chewed his lip. "But the dar'gaithin..."

"The dar'gaithin survive because of their armor. Their scales provide a natural protection against being drained; it's a perfect shield, almost impossible to replicate. The Darecians nearly succeeded with the devices you know as Shackles, but even they couldn't get it right. As soon as Shackles start interacting with the Darklands, they become...overzealous. Start stripping away anything that might dampen Essence." Tal shrugged. "The dar'gaithin are ultimately not people, though—they're smarter than animals, but they don't have the mental capacity of a human. We think they sort of...drift, once they enter the time stream. Spend eons in there, an eternity of just flailing around, slowly going mad until eventually the time stream spits them back out where it thinks they're supposed to be." He rubbed his chin. "It's like...if we were stranded at sea but we could see gulls circling in the distance, we'd recognize that there might be land and swim toward it. The dar'gaithin don't have that level of ability to discern. They have to just swim blindly in any direction. If the possible directions included all of space and time," he finished drily.

Davian rubbed his head. Things were becoming clearer. Gradually.

"Speaking of dar'gaithin," said Niha from the corner, eyeing the two bodies on the floor. "I'll start cleaning these up if you two are going to talk forever." She wandered over to the corpses without waiting for a response, and Davian grimaced as she started using her spear to pry scales loose, revealing an oily dark-green skin underneath.

"All right," he said to Tal, turning away from the grisly sight. He assumed that there was a purpose to what the woman was doing, but he didn't want to know right now. "So they arrive back in their own time—insane from the journey—and then are sent back with supplies." He paused. "*Why*, exactly, do they agree to all of that?"

"They don't," Tal assured him. "They're Controlled—their minds get altered before they're sent here. By Gassandrid, unfortunately," he added, seeing Davian's briefly hopeful look. "He's the only one of us strong enough to do it. They still mostly think and act for themselves, but they have overarching commands that they can't ignore—they'd never have organized enough to be in charge here, otherwise." He shrugged. "And once they've gone mad back in Ilshan Gathdel Teth, there's not a lot of negotiation. Gassandrid can Control them just long enough to keep them calm while we load them with food, and then we send them back through."

Davian considered. "When they get back here, I assume they don't come back at the beginning again? When you all arrived?"

"No. They return immediately. The length of time they spend in the outside world doesn't seem to affect when they come back," admitted Tal. "It lines up with a study Cyr did on some of the creatures that had been here, early on. He said that they all had these almost indiscernible...markers. A kind of time decay that permeated their body—harmless enough, but more pronounced the longer that they had been in Zvaelar. An invisible clock on their time here."

Davian frowned. "So you think that the portal here adjusts when we arrive accordingly?" He shook his head. "That doesn't make sense for me. I haven't been here before."

"You've traveled through time before. Perhaps you have similar markers," observed Tal. He shrugged at Davian's look. "It's the best guess I have. And before you ask, no. I don't know how long passes in the real world compared to here, but time *is* passing. The dar'gaithin who returned to Ilshan Gathdel Teth with metal all did so weeks after entering the portal, not seconds."

Davian relented with a sigh. He glanced around at the sound of the door opening, making a face as he saw Niha dragging one of the dar'gaithin corpses—thoroughly descaled and smearing black blood everywhere—outside. He opened his mouth to ask, then shook his head and snapped it shut again, turning back to Tal.

"What is it about this metal?" he asked suddenly. It had been one of the questions burning in him since he'd joined Raeleth's scavenging team. "I think I understand the rest—up until the Venerate started throwing prisoners in here. What in all fates is so important about this particular metal that the Venerate are going to all this effort, sending people to their deaths just to get it?"

"It's not just metal. It might actually be the most important resource in Ilshan Gathdel Teth," said Tal. "It's why Gassandrid insists on everyone calling this place the Mines—it's his way of focusing on Zvaelar's new purpose, dissociating from the truth of what really happened. You know about the problem with Vessels in Talan Gol?"

Davian shook his head.

"They corrupt," explained Tal. "After a few months, the kan just starts to . . . corrode whatever it's touching. The others blame it on the portal here, or the ilshara, but we've been able to find nothing about either that should cause it. Personally, I think it's something to do with Shammaeloth's constant proximity—he was never in the one place for long before Talan Gol. But that's an unpopular opinion amongst the others, to say the least." He shrugged. "Regardless. Metal taken from here—so long as it's been reforged into something new since the portal opened—is different. It's . . . time-locked, I suppose is the best explanation. It holds that same time decay marker that I mentioned earlier. When we send that reforged metal from here back to the outside world, the Vessels we make with it are immune to the corruption."

Davian exhaled as he put the pieces together in his head. Everything was beginning to make sense now. "The metal plates in Ilshan Gathdel Teth."

"Exactly. They are the equivalent of these towers—suppressing the time corruption from the portal. Gassandrid made those Vessels from normal metal originally, but it was early on after the ilshara went up. Before we understood what would happen. Once they started to corrupt, we replaced them with the metal that came through. Almost all of the metal from here has gone toward that purpose," Tal added.

Davian rubbed his face. "I don't understand how you could have figured that out in the first place," he admitted.

"We got a nudge from here, actually." Tal gave a wry nod to his blank expression. "Following the flow of information between here and the outside world is...complicated, sometimes, to say the least. You have to remember that we're all from different eras; we converge here and so, depending on who we talk to, it's possible to hear news from a time much later than our own. And the dar'gaithin are no different. So when they go back to their own times, they can—in theory—take any information they've learned about the future with them."

"Except they go insane," observed Davian.

"Which isn't an insurmountable obstacle," countered Tal. "When Gassandrid first opened this portal, we sent several dar'gaithin through—we knew that they were most likely to survive the journey—along with a couple of volunteers. Actual volunteers," he added, at Davian's look. "Loyal people, good men and women. There was nothing for days, and we all assumed that it had been a failure. And then one of the dar'gaithin came back. It was mad, but it was carrying a steel plate inscribed with information. It told us what had happened. The cataclysm. The thousands of people from different eras, all arriving at the same point in time. The need for ongoing supplies."

He shrugged. "Diara noticed straight away that the metal was strange; we were already seeing the corruption of Vessels in Talan Gol, so it wasn't long before we experimented and discovered just how valuable that steel was. And of course, everyone saw the potential for getting information about the future. The description of the cataclysm was enough for Gassandrid to figure out what had gone wrong on the Zvaelar end, so we made the Vessels to build this tower, and sent them through the portal along with instructions."

Tal sighed. "After that, it seemed logical to keep sending through dar'gaithin every few years with some food, knowledge of the current era, requests for more information—and any prisoners who were particularly...difficult. Ones who we couldn't execute by law, but who could become martyrs if left locked up in Tel'Tarthen. The idea was that our people already there would manage messages and the reforging of the metal, the dar'gaithin would bring it all back, and the prisoners would do everything else."

"So there are people in charge here, somewhere? They're sending messages back?"

"No." Tal looked troubled. "I wrote the first and only message. I actually already had the Vessels for the tower—they'd arrived here at the same moment I did—but I knew that if I didn't send that information back, it meant that someone else would eventually decide to. And having anyone else communicating with the Venerate was dangerous, because they'd be able to relay anything they had learned about the Venerate's future—as well as the fact that I was here, which would have raised all sorts of questions. So I did it, and then I gathered all the volunteers we'd sent through over the years. Convinced them that I was here to oversee things, and..."

He gestured, sighing heavily. "Took care of them," he finished.

Davian didn't follow for a second, then swallowed as he understood. "I see." He shook his head dazedly. "Is that why the dar'gaithin turned on you?"

"No. They didn't know. I thought that Niha and I were the ones from furthest along the timeline," admitted Tal. "I came through alone, and she'd already killed the dar'gaithin sent through with her, so I assumed that none of the others would know that I'd switched sides. But there was one."

"Theshesseth," completed Davian, nodding.

Tal spread his hands. "And here we are. The dar'gaithin understand this tower's purpose enough to let us maintain it, and the other Gifted know that if they don't help supply it with Essence, we'll all die. But the dar'gaithin also know that I'm a traitor, and most of the other people in this tower were sent to Zvaelar specifically because they wanted to kill me in their respective eras."

"He is a *very* popular man," chimed in Niha as she joined them   413 again, wiping her hands on her clothes. Davian turned, gazing in vaguely disturbed admiration at the floor where the bodies had been. Completely clean, now. As if it had never happened.

"You need to rest," added Niha to Tal, this time without any hint of playfulness in her voice. She studied Davian assessingly. "You too, actually. I'm assuming that you don't always look this terrible."

Davian scowled at her, but Tal just chuckled. "She's right. You're going to need your energy."

Davian frowned. "For what?"

Tal smiled.

"To resume your training, of course," he said quietly.

The crimson light filtered through the sole window, glinting dully off the steel floor, illuminating Tal as he finally stirred.

Davian glanced up from his study at the desk, where he'd been scrutinizing the reams of notes that Tal had been making about Zvaelar for the past few months. Tal had offered them to him the previous night, and they had been well worth the read.

He'd slept only a little, his body accustomed to wrenching itself up at first bell. Even so, he felt better than he had in a long time. Before retiring, Tal had restored a portion of Davian's Reserve—it was nowhere near full, but neither was it close to running out anymore. That was enough, for now.

"Learn anything interesting?" asked Tal with a yawn, glancing at the sheets in Davian's hand.

"A few things," Davian admitted. He flicked around, then held up one entry in particular. "You say here that you think the al'goriat might be created from some combination of human bodies and Dark—but you don't know for sure?" That had seemed strange to Davian. Al'goriat were supposed to be Banes, and Banes were supposed to be the creations of the Venerate.

Tal stretched. "I actually thought that they were a myth until I got here. Something the Andarran resistance made up to make us sound even more evil. Rumors of them have been around for almost as long as the ilshara, but trust me—if we'd known how to make and command creatures who could manipulate time, the war with the Darecians would have been over before it started." He rubbed his face. "I don't think that they could do what they do, or even exist, away from Zvaelar though: they cannot seem to come within the radius of this tower's suppression, even though they are equally attracted to the well of Dark sitting underneath."

He shrugged. "The other Banes are all inextricably tied to the Darklands, to the rift—without that connection, they die—so the dar'gaithin, and now you, are proof that it is on some level accessible from here. But it's clearly still... barely so. The al'goriat seem more linked to the inherent corruption of this place. I think their abilities might actually stem from it—which may be why they're able to manipulate time, even within the time bubble Gassandrid created."

Davian nodded thoughtfully. He had wondered that about the al'goriat.

Tal watched his expression. "I made the assumption about the bodies because of the human likeness, and because we didn't see any for the first week or so here. It's all just speculation, though. I couldn't even tell you whether the dar'gaithin have been the ones making them, somehow, or whether they are happening as a result of something else. By accident, even. The only thing I'm sure of is that the al'goriat obey the dar'gaithin, so long as they can't see their source. And anything that they *can* see with a source... well. You've probably experienced that by now." He rubbed his eyes. "Any other burning questions before we get started?"

Davian hesitated, then put the sheaf of paper down.

"Why haven't you just killed yourself?" he asked quietly.

Tal stared at him, then nodded in vague approval at the question.

"Partly because I have no idea what would happen. I'm linked to a Vessel called the Forge—that's what brings me back when I die. But if I die now, when does it bring me back? In this time? In my own time? Still inside Zvaelar? I obviously do get out, but..." He shrugged. "Also partly because there was the possibility of talking to you. As soon as I found out about Theshesseth, I knew I had a chance to learn more about what was coming."

He glanced toward the door. "And partly because of Niha," he finished.

"Are you and she...?"

"No. *No.*" Tal chuckled. "I'm not sure that there's a man alive strong enough to keep up with her. But I do owe her."

Davian gave him a sideways look. "She seems a bit...intense."

"She is, but you can trust her with your life. Yesterday was just...well, she's accustomed to everyone here wanting to kill me." Tal grunted. "I rather think she likes you, actually. She doesn't usually give the people who come into my room uninvited the chance to explain themselves."

"She knows who you are, I assume?" asked Davian.

"Everyone here does. She's the only one willing to look past it. That alone should tell you something about her." Tal glanced out the window, noting the sun. "Has she stuck her head in yet?"

"Not since I woke up."

Tal gazed at the door for a second, then sighed, walking over and opening it a crack.

"You need rest," he said sternly. Davian could see Niha standing just outside, clearly guarding the entrance to Tal's room.

"And you need privacy. The idiots downstairs are going to notice if you start playing with Essence."

The two of them exchanged semi-jesting glares before Tal sniffed. "Fine. Give us an hour. Then *rest.*"

He shut the door again before Niha could respond.

"So," said Tal, turning back to Davian. "Let's talk about how you're going to save us. Now, and in your present."

Davian nodded, though somewhat uncertainly.

"I can barely touch kan. It takes virtually all my focus just to hang on to it," he reminded the other man warningly. "I'm not sure how much help I can really be."

"A problem that we can fix," Tal assured him. "If I drew a diagram for you, could you create some basic kan machinery? Nothing particularly delicate or complex—just a few pieces of kan here and there. You could stop to recover in between setting each line, if you needed to."

Davian frowned. "I think so. You want me to create a Vessel?" He thought for a moment. "It would have to be big. I don't think I could be exact enough if the lines were too small."

"That's fine. You remember what I did to you in Deilannis, to...encourage your learning?"

Davian snorted, half in irritation and half fondly. "Of course." He'd barely slept over those three weeks, devouring almost as much information as during his entire three years studying at Caladel.

"I can't do that to you here, but we can make a Vessel that provides the same effect—giving you massively increased focus. Once you have that, you should be able to handle kan more easily. You could then make a more effective version of the same Vessel, if you wanted. One that's smaller, lasts longer."

Davian's pulse quickened. "That might work." He looked up at Tal. "But then what?"

"Then we work on Vessels that can help us withstand the journey back. Help us all survive the time stream." Tal's eyes shone with anticipation. "That's a subject I've already been thinking about for *centuries*, Davian. I'll teach you as much as I can. Together, we can figure out a solution."

"Do you really think we can do what even the Darecians couldn't?" asked Davian, unable to keep the dubiousness from his tone. "You said it was impossible, back in Deilannis."

"We both know that I get out of here," observed Tal. "If not this way, then how?"

Davian thought, then conceded the point. If Tal was telling the truth and he'd come here more than a decade before Davian's birth, then he *must* escape—otherwise Davian would never have met Caeden.

"You really think I can learn what to do quickly enough?" he asked, a pit in his stomach. He was glad that there might be a way out for everyone—of course he was—but suddenly, the weight on his shoulders seemed very heavy indeed.

Tal smiled. "After Deilannis? Yes. I am confident."

Davian accepted the implied compliment with a cautious nod.

"It's going to take months, isn't it," he said quietly. "Even if we get this focus Vessel working straight away."

"Yes."

Davian shook his head, mind straying to the dar'gaithin that had interrupted them the previous day.

"How am I possibly going to stay safely hidden for that length of time?" he wondered. "Even if I end up able to use kan effectively, 417

I'm going to need to carry around that Vessel every moment of every day."

Tal clapped him on the shoulder, eyes burning. "That's the truly exciting part, Davian—the thing that's going to let you escape from Ilshan Gathdel Teth when you do get out of here, and that will let you take on *any* of the Venerate. You created a Reserve within yourself. From kan. Without side effects. Just think—what does that mean?"

Davian considered. "That I'm immune to the side effects of kan within the body, I suppose. So?"

Tal just watched him patiently, waiting.

Davian felt his eyes go wide as he understood.

"You...want me to build Vessels...using my own body?" he asked faintly.

Tal's grin widened.

"Think about it, Davian," he said excitedly. "Think about the *possibilities*."

Davian swallowed, mind racing. "And if I build a Vessel the wrong way?" He shuddered as he considered the ramifications. "I read about Vessel construction back in Deilannis, you know. The Darecians used to make sure the novices were isolated, because sometimes the things they made *exploded*."

"You had all your limbs when I killed you," observed Tal. He held up his hands at Davian's expression. "Just saying."

Davian found himself caught between a glare and a laugh, eventually relenting to the latter. "Hard to argue with that." He took a breath, still trying to grasp the possibilities. "Fates."

"So what *do* you know about creating Vessels?"

Davian shook his head ruefully. "Not much," he admitted. "Only what we skimmed in Deilannis, and then I think I learned a bit more when we were studying to fix the Boundary, but..." He shrugged helplessly. "There hasn't exactly been a lot of time to tinker."

"The basics aren't difficult," Tal assured him. "And a Vessel to increase your concentration isn't especially complicated. You're simply targeting certain points in the mind, stimulating them."

"Sounds safe," said Davian drily.

"You handled it just fine in Deilannis. And you'll have more opportunity to study this time around." Tal's gaze roved around the room, his expression turning thoughtful. "Hiding you in here will be tricky until we can create something to make you invisible, but the dar'gaithin provide us with enough food to go around. We'll have to figure out where you're going to sleep, too," he added absently.

Davian hesitated.

"There's someone back south of the Breach," he said suddenly, coming to a decision. Even discounting that the man needed him to survive, he couldn't just abandon Raeleth. "I'm going to bring him here too."

Tal's brow crinkled.

"No." He said the word gently but firmly. "I assume that this was the man you mentioned—the one who helped you when you arrived—and I am sorry that you cannot return the favor. But he would be dead weight here. If he has no Reserve, he cannot help supply the tower. And we get enough rations to stretch to one more, but not two."

Davian scowled. "Then he can share mine. The scavengers don't have long before they've picked the city clean, and from what you've said so far, I don't imagine that the dar'gaithin will have much use for them once that happens. I know I can't save all of them, but I *can* save him." He gestured out the window. "Raeleth was a craftsman, worked with metal. I'm sure he has experience operating a forge."

"His name is Raeleth?" Something about the way Tal asked indicated a shifting of his position, a sudden increase in interest.

"You know him?"

Tal shook his head. "Only by reputation. And that's if it's the same man," he said thoughtfully. "Would he even be willing? Most people here aren't exactly...admirers of mine. And if he's who I'm thinking of..."

"I'll convince him," said Davian firmly.

Tal vacillated, then gestured in defeat.

"No more favors after this," he said. "And for the love of El, do not get caught. I know you don't die but from what you've said, Gassandrid still has information that he wants from you—and he knows that you get out in the end, too. That means you're only   419 in here to buy him time, to keep you away from me in your present for as long as possible. He'll still want you getting out on his terms, though, so by now, Theshesseth probably intends to take you back as soon as he finds you."

"It's not a favor, because I wasn't asking," Davian said firmly. He smiled slightly. "But thank you, and yes, I'll be careful. I'll get rid of the rope this time, too."

Tal chuckled, then eyed the red-tinged shadows out the window. "Well. If you're going to do it..."

They headed for the door.

Niha was still outside; when she saw Davian she frowned, her gaze immediately sliding to Tal in askance.

"He's fetching a friend," said Tal, a touch wryly.

"Out of the question," Niha said immediately.

"Clearly not." Davian glared at her. The woman glared back until finally Davian just shook his head, breaking the gaze. "I'll see you both soon."

"Make sure we're the only ones," Tal emphasized. "If the dar'gaithin or any of the Gifted here spot you, it's going to make things difficult. And I'm not sure how many more bodies we can make disappear."

Davian shifted uncomfortably. From the way he said it, Tal wasn't specifically talking about the dar'gaithin.

They exited the tower, Tal going first to ensure that there was no one around to see. Davian lingered at the edge of the unpatrolled space, watching the wandering al'goriat ahead uneasily.

"The black substance. Dark, the scavengers call it," he said. "I've seen people infected. Is there a cure?"

Tal studied him intently. "None of which I know. Essence seems to push it back, but that's the best it can do."

Davian's heart sank. Still, he wasn't about to reveal Raeleth's affliction before he brought him here. Too easy for Tal to change his mind.

"What is it?" he asked eventually.

Tal considered.

"Time is damaged here. Irreparably," he said. "The substance you're talking about is a kind of...rot. Like a wound expelling infection to the surface, time is trying to reject what Gassandrid did—and that is the result." Tal held his gaze. "Don't go near it, Davian. It's well beyond our power to deal with."

Davian took a deep breath, and nodded.

"I'll see you soon," he said quietly.

He stepped out into the sea of al'goriat once again.

Chapter 29

Davian moved from room to room absently, his mind more on convincing Raeleth than on the task at hand.

"Shadat. *Shadat.*" The mildly irritated voice broke him from his reverie; he looked up to see Raeleth standing next to a desk, arms crossed. "I know you're trying to decide...whatever it is you're trying to decide, but *I* still need metal to avoid starving. So if you could please try not to ignore entire pieces of furniture held together with nails..."

Davian blinked, then shook his head ruefully. "Sorry." He backtracked to the desk and started pulling out drawers, breaking apart the wood to get to the nails.

The journey back south of the Breach had taken longer than Davian had anticipated last night; he had arrived just after first bell, only to discover that Raeleth had already left. Fortunately the man had been scouring the area close to their hidden stash of metal, and after only an hour of searching, Davian had managed to locate his friend again.

"Why are you even out here?" Davian asked as he worked. "You should be resting. We still have lots of metal left."

"But it won't last forever." Neither man spoke for a few moments, and then Raeleth sighed. "I don't suppose that you were daydreaming about something *not* to do with Aarkein Devaed?"

Davian grimaced, prying apart two thin boards. "He's trying to help. He didn't have to let me come back."

"He wants you to stay here and help him escape, when you could potentially just get out. Of course he's doing you favors." Raeleth's voice was scornful. "I doubt those favors will extend to me for long, though. And you still want me to come and work with him. In an al'goriat-surrounded prison."

"We've been through this," said Davian irritably. They had—too many times, over the past few hours. "Even if you're right—and I don't believe you are—there's simply no future here, Raeleth. You'll *die* if you don't come with me."

Raeleth snorted, but didn't respond. Davian watched him, his frustration only growing.

"You need to get past this," he said, keeping his voice calmer this time. "You talk to me about believing in El, about what it entails. About hating the acts of those who do evil, but not the people themselves." He met Raeleth's gaze. "Do you really believe that?"

Raeleth stared at him, wide-eyed, for a second.

Then he chuckled ruefully.

"Well," he said. "At least you've been listening."

He didn't say anything else, just returned to his work. Davian hesitated, then continued what he was doing as well. The silence was somehow more companionable this time.

Raeleth hadn't agreed to anything, but he was thinking, now—Davian could see that much. It was something.

The rest of the day passed in their regular rhythm; as soon as last bell rang out they finished up and headed back. Not long before they would have reached their own camp, they walked past a campfire crackling in the gutted remains of a building, and Davian realized with a start that Maresh was one of the men around it. The big man had his arm in a sling and was asleep, as were two others. The final member of their team stared morosely into the flames, expression haunted.

Davian grunted in satisfaction, despite a sliver of guilt worming its way into his gut. Raeleth had mentioned that word of Maresh's injury had spread quickly, and that the other teams were no longer handing over their shares. Some had even taken to threatening Maresh in return, forcing his team to pay back some of the metal they had taken. The rumor was, they hadn't been left with enough to get any rations for the past two days.

Combined with injuries that prevented any meaningful scavenging, it was doubtful they would survive for much longer.

Raeleth saw them, too. He paused, then got a determined expression in his eyes, turning and starting toward the fire.

"Raeleth," said Davian softly. "They've learned their lesson."

Raeleth ignored him, marching straight into the circle of light. The man on watch started as he realized that someone was there, his expression immediately darkening as he spotted Davian trailing after Raeleth.

"Come to gloat?" the man snarled. "Better be quick, else the al'goriat will have us all for a snack. And that's going to happen to us sooner rather than later now, anyway."

"You're short?" asked Raeleth.

The hulking man gestured to Maresh and the other injured man. "What do you think?" he asked bitterly. His eyes slid to the half-full bucket in Davian's hand, and for a second his eyes glittered with greed. The expression quickly passed as his gaze switched to Davian himself, though.

Raeleth studied the man silently, then turned to Davian, holding out his hand. "The pail."

Davian felt his brow crease, but he silently handed Raeleth the bucket containing their day's scavenge.

To his horror, Raeleth walked forward and held it out, offering it. "We have enough already."

The man stared at Raeleth with a mixture of shock and suspicion, as if barely able to believe that this wasn't some kind of trap. When Raeleth shook the pail at him impatiently, the metal inside rattling, the other man snatched it away and scrambled back as if fearful that Raeleth would change his mind.

Raeleth turned on his heel and strode off without another word.

Davian gaped at the man peering into the bucket, who was looking disbelieving at his good fortune, and then hurried after Raeleth.

"Why?" he asked furiously, still stunned. "We *worked* for that;

you could have stored it and used it another time. And they, of all people...they did *not* deserve the help."

"No?" Raeleth gave him a sharp look. "Then why did I deserve help, when you first met me? I could have been Maresh, and you wouldn't have known."

Davian gave him a nonplussed look. "That's different. I didn't know you. I like to assume the best, until I know otherwise."

"So it's not about being deserving or not deserving," said Raeleth quietly. "It's about whether you have a grudge."

Davian threw his hands into the air. "Fine. I'm holding the fact that Maresh is a terrible person against him. You're a better man than I am. Well done," he said tiredly.

Raeleth winced, clearly considering whether to let the comment pass, then sighed.

"Do you really think that's why I did it?"

Davian shook his head. "I don't *know* why you did it."

"Because hurting someone is not teaching them a lesson, Davian. As you pointed out earlier—we can hate what they do, but we should never hate *them*." He shifted. "And I'm not 'better' than you. That's not how it works. Believing in El, trying to follow His rules, doesn't make you in some way superior. If anything, it makes you more aware that *none* of us can claim to be truly good. That's why forgiveness is so important." He saw Davian's dubious expression and shook his head. "I'm not suggesting that enemies should suddenly be friends, but I *am* choosing to forgive. Because if I don't, I'm nothing more than empty words."

"But how can you possibly just forgive someone who's been so awful to so many..."

Davian trailed off.

"We're not talking about Maresh anymore, are we," he said with a small, rueful smile.

Raeleth exhaled, nodding. "I'll come with you."

"But you said—"

"I said that I don't trust Aarkein Devaed. But I trust you."

Davian felt a sudden weight lift off his shoulders. "Tonight?"

Raeleth glanced back the way they'd come.

"No point in delaying it," he said, the words sounding forced.

"If we hand in what we have in the stash, it probably gives us a week's head start before Isstharis decides to come looking for us."

Davian gave a tight smile in agreement.

"Tonight it is, then," he said quietly.

◦✲◦

Davian glanced across at Raeleth, feeling a flash of sympathy at the other man's expression as they looked into the sea of al'goriat between them and the square steel tower.

The red moon hung dead at their backs as they sat deep in the shadow of the crater. Their journey had been typically nerve-racking—navigating pools of Dark, making the perilous trip across the Breach and then slinking down into the crater itself, Davian making certain to remove their rope this time—but otherwise uneventful. Safe, as far as these things went.

"You...want to go through *there*," said Raeleth flatly.

"They see using strands of kan, and they'll only attack if they spot an Essence source. I'm already basically invisible to them, so I'll make a shield for you, and they won't even know that we're there." He patted the dark-haired man on the back, as much to cover his own doubt as to reassure his friend. "Don't worry. It's why that al'goriat left us alone, the first night we met—it must have thought that you were dying from the Dark infection, and it didn't see me."

Raeleth tapped a finger into his palm nervously. "You're forgetting the part where you say 'in theory.'"

"Well I feel like it's a *fairly* good guess." Davian smiled as Raeleth gave him a dirty look. "Trust me. We'll be fine."

Raeleth's expression remained dubious, but he gestured, indicating that he was ready.

Davian motioned Raeleth closer and then closed his eyes.

It took almost a minute of straining, and another of wrestling with the dark power, before Davian finally snared a proper hold on kan. Sweat slid down his skin as he carefully formed a messy but complete shield, completely encircling Raeleth. He would have liked to include himself within it, but he simply didn't have that kind of focus.

427

"Stay close," he said, opening his eyes and wiping his forehead. He eyed the sides of the shield nervously. "Really close."

Raeleth was watching him concernedly. "Are you all right?"

"Just move," said Davian through gritted teeth, noting that there were neither dar'gaithin nor prisoners in sight for the moment. "Slowly and quietly."

They inched forward, out of the shadowy cover of the buildings.

Too soon they were stepping into the vast, open expanse of dusty ground that separated the tower and its surrounding structures from everywhere else. Davian didn't have to look across at Raeleth to feel the sheer terror emanating off the man; if he was being honest with himself, he wasn't feeling much more comfortable. Banes grunted and snuffled all around them, their eyeless gazes sweeping back and forth as they shambled along, teeth bared and dripping in the garish red of the moon.

They were about halfway toward the center when one of the creatures stopped in front of them.

Davian's heart lurched as the al'goriat turned deliberately toward them. His focus wavered for just an instant; he desperately reached out, fumbling with kan and then snatching it back, keeping the shield up through sheer force of will. The al'goriat stared at them.

Then another, a little farther away, stuttered to a halt and turned, too.

The one closer to them growled.

Davian felt a small squeeze on his arm; he glanced to the side to see Raeleth watching him, eyebrow quirked questioningly. Though his demeanor suggested that he wasn't concerned, Davian could see the terror hiding just behind his eyes.

Davian forced out a breath and nodded slightly to Raeleth, starting out in a different direction, trying to skirt the al'goriat that had stopped.

More growls joined the first, a low, threatening chorus that deepened and got more aggressive by the moment. Davian felt his heart pounding.

"Keep moving," he whispered.

428   The first Bane to have stopped suddenly blinked into the space

where they had been only a few seconds earlier. It twisted around, snuffling as if testing the air.

Davian and Raeleth crept forward, moving as fast as Davian dared now. More and more al'goriat were being attracted to the scene; the ones that had seemingly detected their passing were growling more angrily now, vanishing and then appearing where Davian and Raeleth had just been, as if chasing their afterimage.

The journey to the tower seemed to take forever, Davian refusing to look back as snarls turned to a chorus, still relatively soft but spine-chillingly menacing. Step by painful step they moved forward.

Then finally, miraculously, they were stepping into the shadow of one of the tower's ancillary buildings, and safety.

Davian let the kan shield drop—through inability to maintain it more than choice—and turned, flinching back in horror.

Perhaps fifty al'goriat stared at him, gathered along the invisible border of their area, hissing and with teeth bared in rictuses.

"Is that normal?" asked Raeleth shakily.

Davian barked an almost hysterical laugh, opening his mouth to reply, only to shut it again with a snap as he saw two figures hurrying toward them.

"I believe the idea was to *not* attract attention," Niha called as she approached.

Raeleth's eyes hardened as he recognized Tal walking behind her, and the al'goriat—terrifying though they were—seemed all but forgotten as he glared at the newcomers.

Davian put a hand gently on the man's shoulder, feeling the rock-hard tension there. "This isn't the place."

Raeleth released a shaky breath, then nodded sharply.

Davian turned back to Niha as she arrived. She was studying Raeleth with open disapproval.

"*This* is who you wanted to save?" she said eventually to Davian.

Raeleth snorted before Davian could reply. "First impressions here aren't exactly spectacular, either," he told her, meeting her eyes calmly.

Niha said nothing, holding the gaze, then gave the slightest hint of a smile and just shook her head.

429

Tal jerked his head toward the tower. "We should get inside. If any dar'gaithin see the al'goriat acting like that, they're going to come and find out why."

Niha agreed, eyeing Raeleth again curiously before turning and joining Tal as he strode back the way he had come.

Davian exchanged a glance with Raeleth, and they trailed after the other two into the tower.

Davian sat with his back against the cool steel of the wall, tapping his fingers together in an absent, vaguely anxious motion as he watched Tal's closed door.

From the corner of his eye, he could see Niha studying him intently. He sighed, turning to face her.

"Yes?" he asked irritably.

Niha continued to gaze at him, openly and unperturbed.

"Your friend," she said. "You are concerned that Tal will do something to hurt him."

Davian shook his head. "No. That's already happened," he said. "I'm concerned that Raeleth may not be able to look past it." He grimaced. "I'm not sure that I could."

Niha, to Davian's surprise, nodded.

"Few who have been affected by his history can," she admitted frankly.

"So you weren't?" Davian asked. "From what I understand, this place is full of people just like Raeleth. Why are you so loyal to Tal?"

Niha said nothing for a few seconds; abruptly she held up her hand, a sliver of Essence springing to life at her fingertips. Davian watched admiringly as the hard sphere of Essence rolled smoothly between her fingers, pulsing and dancing. Her control was impressive.

"He saved me." Niha continued playing absently with Essence, another ball joining the first, spinning and intertwining and then separating again.

"From what?" asked Davian, realizing that Niha was going to leave it there.

"I was part of Diara's personal guard from the moment I could hold a weapon—right up until they discovered that I could use Essence. That was six years ago. The other Venerate discovered it, I mean. Do you know what that means, in Ilshan Gathdel Teth?"

Davian shook his head silently.

"A trip to the Cyrarium." She gestured vaguely at his blank expression. "It's why there are so few Gifted here—they need them back at home. It means prison, though they don't call it that. Death, eventually. They say that it is an honor to go into the machines, a noble sacrifice, but..." She shook her head, a haunted look in her eyes. "Tal'kamar sacrificed himself to get us out. I had two glorious years in the resistance before the other Venerate caught me again and threw me in here."

Davian frowned. "What do you mean, 'sacrificed himself'?"

"They knew it was him. They knew he was the one who'd let us go free. He was already in trouble for not leaving us in the machines for as long as he was supposed to, and they suspected his motives even before any of that—but as soon as he helped us to escape, they knew that he was truly against them." She rolled her shoulders. "He was still in Tel'Tarthen when they caught me."

Davian gazed at her. Something about the softness of her voice told him she was being genuine. "So there's actually opposition to the Venerate in Ilshan Gathdel Teth?" he asked, somewhat dubiously.

"A much stronger one after Tal released everyone like me to join them," Niha said with a proud smile.

Davian cocked his head to the side, trying to put together the pieces. "So he does that *after* he gets out of here," he said, calculating. Shuffling people around in timelines still hurt his head, but he was getting better at it. "You're...not from much before my time, then."

"Word of the rebellion against the Augurs was just reaching Ilshan Gathdel Teth when Tal got me out," clarified Niha.

Davian nodded slowly. Perhaps twenty years ago, for him. That fit.

"He didn't happen to mention how he got out of here?" he asked drily.

Niha shook her head. "I never actually met him. He set everything up so that the resistance could set us free. He could have spoken to me, I think, if he had tried. But it must have been too risky." There was a sliver of doubt in her tone at that, but the moment quickly passed.

Davian scratched his head, something suddenly occurring to him.

"So the Venerate only figured out he'd betrayed them *then*?" He rubbed his forehead in confusion. "But...I assumed that was why he was here."

"None of the Venerate have any idea he's here. He snuck in," confirmed Niha. "Once he knew from talking to you in Deilannis that he would get out again, he thought it was worth the risk."

"He knew I would be here?"

"That, you would have to ask him." She glanced at him appraisingly. "He certainly had no idea that he would be trying to turn you into the most powerful Augur to ever live, that much is certain. Even knowing what you will sacrifice, I think he is hesitant to give any man that much power." She waved her hand, suddenly looking irritated. "But we are straying far from the topic."

Davian raised an eyebrow. "You want to know more about Raeleth?"

"Yes. What is his background? Can he fight?"

Davian hesitated. "I...don't know. He was a jeweler," he finished awkwardly.

Niha looked displeased.

"He is a good man," said Davian firmly.

Niha sniffed. "I would prefer a useful man."

Davian glared at her. "If you don't think that there's a need for good people here, then maybe you need to take a better look around."

Niha rolled her eyes, though whether it was in amusement or derision, Davian wasn't sure.

"Why were you so intent on saving him?" she asked.

"Because if there's anyone worth saving in this place, it's him," Davian replied quietly. "Why do you want to know?"

"Because he is going to end up as my responsibility. I can already tell," said Niha, sounding irked at the prospect.

Davian was about to say more when the door opened, and
432   Davian tensed. From the corner of his eye he could see Niha brac-

ing herself, too. No matter what she said, she had been concerned that Raeleth might try to cause trouble.

Raeleth emerged first, and Davian was relieved to see that while the tension still remained in his shoulders, his demeanor was considerably calmer than it had been going in. Tal followed, looking thoughtful but not especially worried. That was a good sign, too.

Davian caught Raeleth's gaze with a pointedly inquiring look. Raeleth glanced over his shoulder and then stepped closer, keeping his voice low so that only Davian could hear.

"We've reached an understanding." He pulled in a breath. "I'm not at peace with any of this—not yet. But I'm closer to believing what you say about him than I was." He chewed his lip. "It's not easy."

Davian nodded. "I can only ask that you try."

"Niha." It was Tal. "Raeleth has metalworking expertise; I think we can slip him in with the others in the forge without raising any alarms. We'll just say that Athsissis brought him in for his expertise. Even if they realize the timing's suspicious once they notice Athsissis is gone, not even the dar'gaithin would imagine that Raeleth had managed to get past the al'goriat otherwise."

Niha eyed Raeleth. "Davian says you made jewelry." Her tone dripped with disdain.

"I'm not going to make you any, no matter how much you beg." Raeleth smiled cheerfully at her. "Now I believe you need to show me to my new accommodations?"

Niha stared with narrowed eyes, then snorted and shook her head, though a smile clearly played around her lips as she beckoned for Raeleth to follow her down the stairs. The other man dipped his head to Tal and Davian and then did so, looking pleased with himself.

Tal sidled over to Davian.

"You...saw that, right?" he whispered.

"I did," Davian whispered back. "I definitely did."

Tal and Davian shared a quick grin, then turned to watch until Raeleth and Niha's footsteps had echoed away.

"He reminds me of you," Tal said eventually, gaze still on the staircase.

"I'll take that as a compliment."

"You should." Tal turned to him. "He is an intelligent man who is unafraid of being mocked or even harmed for his beliefs. He not only has morals, but he understands *why* he has morals—which is why even though being here with me is testing him, he is able to remain civil. He is the sort of man who got thrown in here too easily and without us listening to him," he admitted.

Davian thought of Maresh. "I don't know whether he's right about everything, but...I admire him, admire his conviction. He's no hypocrite, of that much I'm certain."

Tal nodded thoughtfully. "As far as role models go, you could do far worse."

Davian glanced across at him. "So was he the man you were thinking of, when I mentioned his name?"

Tal rubbed his chin.

"Yes," he said slowly. "He says not, but he is also very open about not trusting me. He is from the right time, and the name was never that common. The chances of us having sent two Raeleths here from the same era are...slim."

Davian cocked his head to the side. "So who do you think he is, then?"

Tal rolled his shoulders. "The man who started the rebellion in Talan Gol."

"Raeleth?" Davian said skeptically before he could stop himself.

Tal raised an eyebrow. "Do not discount him. He is an eloquent man of clear ideas and strong conviction. The Raeleth who I am thinking of wrote a treatise against El—against Shammaeloth—just as we were finally bringing Ilshan Gathdel Teth into line. Some of what he put to paper has echoed across millennia." He sighed. "Either way, I will make certain that he is protected, Davian—to the utmost extent of what I can do here. You have my word." He frowned at Davian pointedly. "Even if he is infected by Dark."

Davian flushed. "He told you?"

Tal nodded.

"I wasn't certain you would have agreed to let him come if you'd known," Davian confessed.

Tal grunted. "It would have changed the conversation," he conceded, a touch irritably. "But he is here now. Your responsibility, though. I cannot ask the other Gifted to use Essence on him, when we need as much as we can spare for the tower itself."

"Understood. And thank you," said Davian, meaning it. He felt lighter and more hopeful than he had in days. "What now?"

"Now?" Tal stretched his arms out and cracked his knuckles, giving a sudden grin of anticipation. "Now, it's time to get to work." He clapped Davian on the shoulder.

"It's time to finally finish what we started in Deilannis."

Chapter 30

Wirr gritted his teeth as he watched the members of the Assembly process the news he'd just told them.

The Assembly chambers were located in the northern section of the palace, one side nestled against Ilin Tora. It was a large amphitheater, with seating enough for more than a hundred, and balconies farther up to allow for public viewing on certain formal occasions. This was not one of them, and the area above was vacant.

As were almost half the seats below, unfortunately. Calling a meeting of the Assembly at a day's notice was hardly uncommon, but it was summer and close to the Festival of Ravens; many lords tended to pretend that they never received summons around this time of year. Others, Wirr knew, had already left the city: he had given Erran permission to accelerate their plan by using Control on those who were most influential, spreading word of the danger and ensuring that a constant stream of worried-looking citizens had flowed out through Fedris Idri since morning.

Of course, the absence of the southern Houses—almost a third of the Assembly as a whole—didn't help the empty feel of the building, either.

"What other reports do you have, Sire?" asked Lord si'Bandin eventually, his reedy voice echoing off the smooth white stone. The building's acoustics were remarkable: no matter where the speaker was, anything louder than a whisper would always carry to everyone else present. "We do not doubt the danger and we are all aware of the rumors, but surely if there is an attack coming, then there should be a way to verify it."

Wirr caught a half-frustrated, half-sympathetic glance from Deldri off to the side; he'd let his sister know what was happening as soon as he had arrived at the palace, and she had insisted on attending this meeting. Her look was mirrored by his uncle, who had opened the meeting by pleading with the Assembly to listen to what Wirr had to say. Wirr didn't think he'd ever been so grateful to the king as at the moment.

Wirr shook his head. "It doesn't work like that. Not with these creatures," he said bleakly. "They are fast, Lord si'Bandin, and they can *fly*. Ishelle says that they are coming. We will get no further warning before they get here."

"Which you believe to be when?" asked Lord Tel'An.

"We're not sure. She says that they are—or were—in Desriel. Near some sort of sacred temple, but we're not sure where in the country it's located." His stomach churned as he thought about it. "We don't know how fast they are, either. It could be within the next few days."

"Surely the Desrielites wouldn't sacrifice such a powerful advantage, if they have it." It was General Calder this time. "If they are going to invade, why not just supplement their forces with such creatures?"

"Ishelle believes that they are moving to strike us now, here, as quickly as possible. They know that she saw what they were doing, and that seems to have accelerated their schedule. We're not sure why," he admitted calmly. He needed to convince these men of the danger, but they needed to have the facts, too.

"And why is this Augur not here, then?" asked Lord si'Rel.

"As I explained earlier—her connection to the eletai hurts her," said Wirr, keeping the frustration from his voice. "The Tol is the only place where that connection is broken."

"So it is not under her control." Si'Rel sounded dubious. "Quite aside from the fact that this has been kept from us—something which we will address later," he added ominously, "how do we know that she can even be trusted?"

"And why has she not made another attempt to find out more?" added Lord si'Garthen. "Surely if she is our only source of information, she should be doing her utmost to make sure that it is accurate? Asking us to evacuate the city on the word of one person, even an Augur, is a tall order. Why would we not simply ready our defenses?"

More voices joined the chorus of questions and doubt, though just as many argued that it was far safer to act and be wrong than to risk having the debate.

Wirr scowled. There was no time for this.

"There was a vision!" he shouted over the hubbub.

From the corner of his eye he saw his uncle grimace, but he didn't care: right now, all that mattered was convincing these men to get as many people out of Ilin Illan as possible. The rumors had worked well, and Erran had done a wonderful job, but there were still thousands left in the city.

"There was a vision," he repeated as the shouts died down, frowns turned toward him. "The rumors you may have heard are true. I cannot go into detail, but you must trust me—the city's destruction has been foreseen. This isn't like the Blind. I cannot tell you what the eletai will do once they get here, but they are not conquerors, they are not here to take what we have. They are here to end our lives—*nothing more*. And they will do just that unless we prepare. *Now*."

The entire room was still, and then suddenly Lord Tel'Rath stood.

"I am going. As are my family," he announced, eyes locked with Wirr's. "If Prince Torin says that the threat is so great, then we would be fools to ignore him."

"And flee Ilin Illan?" asked Lord si'Eridos incredulously. "On the word of a man who has apparently kept this information from us all?" His disbelief was echoed by a dozen other voices that quickly devolved back into angry shouts. Wirr heard the words 'coward' and 'traitor' repeated more than once in the jumble.

He looked around; some of the lords—presumably those who were taking his warning seriously—were already hurrying for the exits, murmuring urgent instructions to various messengers as they did so. Other lords were yelling after them, some of them jeering at the concerns of those leaving.

He turned to Administrator Ilen and Elder Kien, who repre-sented Administration's and the Tol's interests, respectively, to the committee members who oversaw Wirr's use of the Oathstone. For once, the two looked grimly united.

439

"I need to use the Oathstone to get everyone organized," he said to them urgently. "People should be safe behind the walls of Tol Athian."

The pair looked at him as if not comprehending what he was asking, and then Ilen gave a derisive snort.

"You want everyone—Administrators, regular citizens, nobility, *everyone*—to go to Tol Athian. Where the only law is that which the Gifted make?" He shook his head, expression resolved. "No, Prince Torin. *No*."

"Not that you have permission from the Council, anyway," added Elder Kien, her hazel eyes cold. "We do not have the supplies to house an entire city. It's not practical. There are too many..."

She trailed off.

Faint screams had penetrated the chamber, barely audible over the chatter of voices.

There was a moment of shock as everyone processed what the sound might mean, and then as one they were rushing for the windows, peering out at the city below. For a second Wirr thought a storm had rapidly approached; the sky was unnaturally dark, swirling with motion.

His heart plummeted as he made out the individual forms.

The eletai were everywhere. People ran like frenzied ants in the streets; Wirr could already see bodies scattered, motionless. Essence and arrows filled the air, downing many of the creatures, but for each one that fell, two seemed to take its place.

Wirr squeezed his eyes shut. Even accounting for the temple Ishelle had seen being right on the border, they'd expected to have at least another day.

They'd severely underestimated how fast the Banes could travel.

His head spun. He'd already forewarned General Oran to ready troops, to position Wirr's squads in various sections of the city in preparation—but that had been only a few hours ago.

They were too late.

"Tor!" It was Deldri rushing up to him, her face as pale as everyone else's in the room. She hurriedly dug something from her pocket and pressed it into his hand. "I took it from your room earlier," she added quietly. "Thought you might need it."

Wirr blinked down at the Oathstone in his hand.

He'd given Deldri the ability to access his safe months earlier. She'd already known about the existence of his Oathstone, and if anything happened to him, he'd wanted her to be able to retrieve it. It wouldn't have worked the same way for her—she wasn't Gifted—but still.

"Thank you," he whispered, giving her a brief, fierce hug. "We're about to go to Tol Athian. Stay close."

He hurried over to Scyner and Taeris, discreetly showing them what Deldri had given him. "I'm going to get everyone I can to Tol Athian."

Taeris nodded immediately, but Scyner hesitated.

"Get anyone nearby to rally at the palace gates," he said quickly. He subtly motioned to the room, particularly over at the king, who was busy giving orders of his own. "You, and he, and the rest of the Assembly need to survive."

"And you," muttered Wirr under his breath, but he caught a glimpse of Deldri out of the corner of his eye. He clasped the Oathstone in his pocket, facing the window again so as to conceal what he was doing.

The next few minutes consisted mainly of him standing with eyes closed, trying to block out the panicked sounds around him as Scyner and Taeris fended off the lords clamoring to speak with him, picturing faces and names in turn and directing them to their various duties. It was tricky, draining, even with all the training he had undergone over the past year. There was no time to consult with General Oran—if the man even still lived—or anyone else; he had to remember everyone's positioning and responsibilities throughout the city on his own, and tailor the instructions he gave accordingly. Assuming that they were all actually in place, of course.

Finally, he was done. He took a deep breath, getting an approving nod from Taeris and a dubious one from Scyner. His gaze slid past them, to where his uncle and Deldri were watching silently.

Kevran beckoned. "Coming?"

Wirr joined him, and without another word they both started ushering the others toward the exit.

The first few minutes of hurrying through the palace passed

almost uneventfully, but when they reached the upper western hallway—the one with tall, wide windows that overlooked Ilin Illan—they stopped. A crowd of people had gathered at the glass, watching the disastrous scenes below with a mixture of fascination and fear. Several Administrators were gradually pulling people away, but the majority were just staring, transfixed.

"Fools," snarled Kevran. He opened his mouth to bellow something.

Then suddenly there were yells of terror, a few screams, and a stampede of people fleeing from their viewing spots.

The windows shattered, and eletai burst violently into the hallway.

Wirr flicked up an Essence shield against the shards of flying glass at the same moment as Taeris; Deldri, Kevran, and the others around them were unharmed, but farther down the hall he saw people stumbling and clutching various body parts as jagged shards knifed into their skin. Nobody had time to do more than cry out, though; the creatures barely paused despite the damage done to them by their entrance, black blades whipping out, slicing everywhere. Wirr flung one man to the side to save him from a cut that would have beheaded him, only to see a young woman scream as the creature in front of her skewered her through the stomach, its sludge-covered spear releasing from its body and remaining inside its writhing victim.

Taeris and Wirr immediately began slicing at the eletai with Essence, trying to both minimize the damage the creatures were doing and allow those in their path to scramble away. But there were too many of them and nowhere to run; there had to be at least thirty of the creatures in the hallway now, ripping and tearing everywhere in a dark, buzzing frenzy of death and blood.

Wirr was about to push the others back into the chamber— though he had no idea how much safer that would be—when Scyner stepped forward, hands outstretched.

A wall of white flame exploded from his fingertips.

There was a high-pitched screeching sound as the flames seared along the length of the hallway in an instant, incinerating everything they touched. The heat was almost too much, even from behind Scyner; Wirr raised his hand in front of his face instinctively, flinching back from the blaze. The eletai's shrieking was by far the loudest, but it was the terrified screams of those still alive—brief though they were—that froze Wirr to the spot.

The flames died as quickly as they had appeared, leaving only an acrid smell in their wake. Pools of melted glass glinted wetly on the marble floor, and the walls and roof appeared untouched, but everything else—the bodies, the eletai, even the furniture that had been in the hallway—had vanished.

"You killed them," gasped Wirr.

"They were already dead. And you know what an eletai wound does," said Scyner coldly. "We need to go."

"Tor."

Wirr spun at the sound of Deldri's voice, small and terrified and in pain.

She was on one knee, Kevran's face as he crouched next to her white and haunted. For a second Wirr thought that they were just examining one of the eletai spears that had jammed into the ground close to her.

Then he saw her almost lose her balance, pain ripping across her face as the spear quivered.

"It's in my foot," she said, tears trickling down her cheeks.

Scyner made to move forward, but Taeris was there first. He knelt down, putting his hand on Deldri's forehead.

She stared at him, confused, and then slumped forward, one side caught by the Representative, the other by Kevran.

"Fates, Taeris. What did you—"

"She's asleep," said Taeris grimly.

Scyner looked at Wirr. "I'm sorry, Sire, but—"

There was a brief, blindingly bright flash of Essence, and the smell of burning flesh filled the hallway.

When Wirr looked again, Taeris was lowering his hand and scooping Deldri up. The spear—and her severed foot, cut off above the ankle—remained on the floor.

"It was seconds. It won't have had time to spread," said Taeris, glaring defiantly at Scyner as if daring him to disagree.

Wirr stared at the stump at the bottom of Deldri's leg, heart aching for his sister. Blistered, the wound cauterized closed by the intense heat of the Essence Taeris had used. But no Gifted would be able to heal that.

Wirr's horrified gaze switched to the others. His uncle was looking at Taeris bleakly, but eventually gave a slight, acknowledging nod.

"Lead on," he said shortly. "Before more of them arrive."

They hurried through the palace, Taeris carrying a thankfully still-unconscious Deldri, pausing only to help anyone confused about where to go. Other areas of the building had suffered attacks too; whenever they encountered bodies, Scyner incinerated them, along with any eletai in their path.

A crowd had already gathered in front of the palace gates when they arrived; Wirr was relieved to see that as instructed, the Gifted were providing a patchy but relatively effective defense, using Essence to heft soldiers' shields high above and creating a constantly shifting physical barrier against any attacks from the sky. The eletai—at least for now—appeared to be ignoring the people below it, focusing instead on more obvious, vulnerable targets elsewhere.

Administrators were there as well, looking terrified but wielding weapons and forming a defensive perimeter around the Gifted, in case any of the eletai that occasionally tested the barrier managed to break through. That had been part of Wirr's instructions, too.

A few stragglers still sprinted desperately toward the shield when they spotted it, but Wirr could already tell that the group was as big as it was likely to get; the surrounding streets had gone quiet, and from his vantage point he could see little movement among the buildings in the rest of the city. Smashed doors and windows were visible everywhere, and he felt a pang of despair for those who must have seen what was happening and tried to hide inside. There were so many families here, so many civilians. Even after the Blind, even after the rumors and warnings he had tried to spread, nobody could have woken that morning and anticipated this nightmare.

They reached the group of perhaps two hundred people, Essence pulsing and flashing everywhere, the metal shields floating above reflecting some of the glow. Each Gifted looked to be in charge of two or three shields—or in some cases, just large slabs of stone—adjusting their position each time they spotted an eletai coming close.

It was holding for now, but once the eletai attacked in numbers, it wouldn't be nearly enough.

They needed to get to Tol Athian.

"We have to start moving," said Taeris, echoing Wirr's thoughts.

Wirr nodded, hurrying over to the nearest Gifted, rubbing at his ears. There was a strange, distant hum from somewhere in the city, a sound unsettlingly like the Boundary. "Start everyone moving toward Tol Athian."

There was a commotion among the Gifted, and a man with bags under his eyes and a haunted look shook his head. Wirr recognized him: one of the men who had agreed to take his orders, named Saric.

"Sire. My family are still out there," Saric said miserably. "I was on my way to find them when I just…felt compelled to come here instead." His jaw clenched. "But I'm not leaving here without them. They might still be coming."

"Or they might already be at Tol Athian," said Wirr tightly, his heart breaking.

"Let me go and look for them," pleaded the man. "I just need to check the house."

Wirr hesitated. Saric was one of the stronger Gifted, which was why he had been chosen in the first place. Even as he spoke he was controlling four separate shields up above. And Wirr could tell that several other Gifted and Administrators nearby were listening intently to the conversation, similarly anxious looks on their faces.

None of it made Wirr feel any better about what he had to say.

"We cannot afford to lose anyone here," he said softly, hating himself for the words. "I'm sorry." He didn't add that if the man's family had been in their house when the attack came, then they were already dead. He raised his voice so that all those nearby could hear. "Everyone. We're going to start moving toward Tol Athian as quickly as we can." Swallowing, he touched the Oathstone in his pocket. "You too, Saric."

There were tears in the man's eyes as he moved to comply.

Scyner had been watching; he paused, then headed over to Saric. "Your family. Where were they?"

"Middle District," said the Gifted distractedly as the group began methodically moving along the street, ensuring that everyone was still relatively covered by the shifting shields above. "Near the Great Market."

"There is nobody near there," said Scyner immediately. "Nobody in the Middle District at all, in fact. If your family are still alive, they will be at Tol Athian."

Saric stared for a moment, then turned back to his task, concern mixing with renewed resolve. Immediately, the shields he controlled above steadied a little, and one flicked to the side, catching an eletai spear as it arrowed down from on high.

Wirr and Scyner dropped back, and Wirr cast a curious glance at the Augur. "You can really tell that from this distance?"

Scyner didn't take his eyes from the road. "Of course not. But it is very likely true, and it was what he needed to hear." He glanced at Wirr, then sighed as he caught Wirr's expression. "If his family are not at Tol Athian, then they are dead. And if they are not waiting for him when we get there, at least he will be able to comfort himself that he did not abandon them when he could have saved them. What I said was a kindness, Torin."

Wirr wasn't sure he agreed, but he simply gave a sharp nod and moved on. There wasn't time to argue.

The streets had gone eerily quiet, and most of the group moved without speaking now, too, fearful eyes fixed warily upon the skies. The bodies of both people and eletai littered the way ahead, though Scyner quickly cremated anything in their path as they moved along. Wirr understood the purpose of his actions, but it made him no less nauseous. He couldn't help but be reminded of the outpost, the day the Boundary had almost collapsed. The day his mother had died.

"Thank fates Kara's not here right now," muttered Kevran. He was off to Wirr's left, still watching Taeris carry Deldri in front of him, both of them surrounded by the grim-looking royal guard.

Wirr silently indicated a morose agreement, his thoughts flashing to Dezia. For the first time in a long time, he was relieved that she wasn't anywhere near him. Nesk was far from a safe place, but it couldn't possibly be worse than this.

Their progress was slow but steady as the group finally managed to find a rhythm to its movement, though every minute or so someone was still snatched by an eletai spear that found a gap, and a few times the eletai actually broke through the perimeter, tearing and slashing for several seconds before one or another of the Gifted managed to burn them.

Finally they came within sight of Tol Athian, and Wirr realized what the low, powerful thrumming had been.

The street in front of the Tol Athian gate was ablaze with burning white light in the dusk. The rock into which the gate was set was pulsing a warning, ominous red; occasionally slashes of light flashed out where eletai got too close, cleaving through them and sending bodies spinning to the ground below.

Kevran shivered as he saw it. "I remember the last time it looked like that," he murmured, mostly to himself.

Wirr stared in dismay as they steadily approached and he spotted the thick layer of Essence blocking off the entrance, the Tol's gate sealed shut behind it. Though the defenses were active, a massive crowd of people—presumably those who had been gathering from other areas in the city—appeared to be stuck outside; several Gifted defended them valiantly, along with another figure he immediately recognized as Erran.

They reached the group, and he forced his way over to the Augur.

"Erran!" He flinched as a blast of kan-modified Essence seared over his shoulder, taking down an eletai in midflight. "Why in fates are the gates shut?"

Erran turned, relief in his expression as he saw Wirr, though it quickly turned to cold anger when he spotted Scyner hurrying along right behind him. "The Council won't open them. They say it's too dangerous, that no one will survive if they let everyone in."

Wirr felt his expression harden.

"We can fix that," he said grimly.

He clasped the Oathstone in his pocket.

"Elder Eilinar. Elder Haemish. Elder Kasperan," he muttered, focusing on the three most senior Gifted in the Tol. "Open the

Resolute Door and let everyone inside immediately. Tell anyone who argues that you have a responsibility to save lives, and do not allow them to stop you."

He let his grip on the stone go again, feeling the wash of power that told him his instructions were taking hold. He nodded to Taeris—who was still carrying Deldri; the scarred man had to have been using Essence to strengthen himself—and Erran before rushing over to the front ranks of the Gifted and assisting in the desperate defense of the crowd.

The next few minutes passed in a haze of screams and panic and blood as the eletai—they had to number in the hundreds, now—began to converge on the Tol, apparently having swept the remainder of the city clean. More and more of the creatures filled the sky, replacing any the defenders' bursts of fire managed to take down. Wirr realized with horror that many of the creatures were probably new eletai, created from the very citizens he had been trying to protect.

The Gifted's defenses were waning, and Wirr's own Reserve running dangerously low, when the Essence barrier winked out and the Resolute Door finally began to open.

The crowd gave a panicked surge, only Wirr's shouted orders and the discipline of his soldiers preventing an outright stampede. Wirr clasped his Oathstone, ordering Taeris to get Deldri inside— he couldn't see them anymore—and then fought his way across the defensive edge of the crowd, circling around until he finally spotted Elder Haemish, who had emerged from the Tol and was screaming angrily at people even as he allowed them past. Wirr was vaguely aware of Scyner by his side as he shouldered his way over to the Elder.

"Prince Torin," spat Haemish as soon as he saw Wirr. "I assume that you are responsible for this disaster?"

"You mean saving people's lives?" retorted Wirr. "Yes. Absolutely."

"We cannot take them all," protested the Elder angrily. "We do not have the resources to house them, let alone feed them."

"We're not intending for this to be a long siege, Haemish. But even if we were—we're not leaving these people out here to die!"

"You will be risking all of us, to save a few." The Elder stared back defiantly.

"He is right, Torin," said Scyner, speaking up for the first time. Wirr glanced across at him in surprise, and the Augur shook his head. "It is vital that the Gifted survive this—they will be needed in the fight to come. But everyone else..." He grimaced. "I don't wish to see them dead, but they contribute nothing."

Wirr felt his lip curl, restraining his fury. "No. *No*." He turned to the Elder, ignoring Scyner's black look. "You will keep the gate open until the very last second. You will let in *everyone* who needs refuge. And you will figure out a way to make it work."

The Elder gaped at him, mouth opening and closing as if he desperately wanted to continue the argument, but the flood of people surging forward into the long main tunnel of Tol Athian continued unabated.

Wirr turned away from Haemish dismissively, keeping a tired eye on the continuing fight. How many had survived this assault? A thousand? The population had never returned to the level it had been at prior to the Blind's attack; many in the lower Districts had been waiting until their homes were rebuilt, or had simply chosen to move away, the memories of lost loved ones too painful. And many more had left thanks to the rumors Erran had been spreading.

But it had still been the capital of Andarra, a bustling metropolis. And now only the smallest portion of those living here were going to survive.

Wirr watched with a heavy heart. Had he made a mistake in not revealing what he had learned from Dras earlier? It wouldn't have saved the city, but might it have sparked an earlier evacuation? It was impossible to say. He knew, deep down, that the route they had taken was probably the right one—had provided the highest probability of success. In fact, there was a good chance that if he had come forward earlier, his words would have been dismissed, and everyone now safe in the Tol would instead have died in this attack.

Still.

Wirr breathed a sigh of relief as the number of waiting survivors began to thin; though there had been some urgency at the beginning, those who had been left until last—mostly soldiers and Gifted—were relatively orderly in their retreat.

"Sire." It was one of his uncle's men, ushering him onward. "Time to get you inside."

Wirr shook his head. "I need to be out here, where I can see what's happening. If there are any—"

"No discussion. King's orders. He'll oversee the rest."

Wirr hesitated briefly, then nodded for the man to lead on.

He hurried by the people still waiting to get in, a gap forced open by the soldiers, feeling vaguely guilty as he was moved past them. The main tunnel was crowded, chaotic. It was impossible to make out anyone with whom he needed to speak.

He had been forcing his way along for only a couple of minutes, searching for Taeris or anyone else to coordinate with, when the crashing sound came at the entrance.

Wirr froze as screams started echoing down the tunnel.

"What was that?" he asked, trying to turn around and see. The flow of people had rapidly increased, though; suddenly a crush was pushing him back, farther from the fighting. He spotted Elder Eilinar off to the side, his expression one of pure horror.

There were more screams, flashes. An echoing bang.

Wirr felt a chill as he realized he could no longer see the sky outside.

The Resolute Door was shut.

"Open the gate!" yelled Wirr in frustration, running over and grabbing Eilinar by the shoulder, shaking him angrily. "There are people still out there! Fates, the *king* is still out there!" He realized it as he said it, heard the rising panic in his voice but didn't care.

"It's the Tol's defenses, not us," said the Elder helplessly, voice hollow. "We have no control over it."

The doors were thick but did not completely block the noise from outside; Wirr's stomach roiled as the area closest to the gate quickly became vacant, and desperate cries sounded faintly from beyond, crescendoing quickly to screams of terror.

Followed by an eerie, unsettling silence.

Wirr stared emptily at the steel doors, which remained closed despite the best efforts of the Gifted to reopen them.

His shoulders slumped, and he turned back to Nashrel.

"Get the Council together," he said to the Elder, doing everything he could to keep his voice steady and commanding. "Let them know that they will be negotiating with me, now." He turned away from the doors, his chest heavy with shock and heartbreak.

"We have much to discuss."

Chapter 31

Shouts of alarm continued to echo through Tol Athian as Wirr entered the Council's chambers, steeling himself for what was to come.

Most of the Athian Council were already there; whether the missing few were busy helping sort through the chaos of the Tol or dead, Wirr had no idea. The Elders sat huddled together on the balcony above while Wirr, Scyner, and Erran were forced to stand below in the center, like supplicants. Or prisoners waiting to be judged.

"Prince Torin." Elder Eilinar, Tol Athian's leader, wore a dark expression as he glared down at them. "You have my sincere condolences for your uncle's death, and for the other lives lost today. I apologize, but this situation is urgent. May I dispense with formalities and get straight to the point?"

"That would be for the best," replied Wirr calmly, though the mention of his uncle pushed him dangerously close to breaking for a moment. He was doing his best to mimic how he thought the king would have acted here, but grief and shock still warred within him, mixing with a near-fretful concern over those whose fate he didn't yet know. Deldri, in particular. Though the chamber doors were shut now, he imagined he could still feel the panic of those rushing around outside. The fear of everyone now huddled in the main passageway, waiting, wondering whether they were safe.

Wondering whether the Gifted were even going to let them stay.

Nashrel stared down at them. His hair had turned rapidly gray in the last year, dark strands hardly visible anymore. "Our first order of business is for you to relinquish your Oathstone. You are in violation of every safeguard we put in place. Your possession of it is clearly illegal, even if you were not currently on our sovereign—"

"No."

Wirr's voice cut through Nashrel's, loud and firm, echoing around the chamber.

He let the shocked hush speak for itself before continuing.

"Perhaps I should not have kept its existence a secret. But that is a discussion for another time. Right now, it's the only reason so many of Ilin Illan's people are safe. My having it saved lives that you would have thrown away from fear and panic. And to be honest? I suspect that my possession of it is the reason those lives are not being pushed back out to the mercy of the eletai as we speak."

"We would never do that," Nashrel spluttered indignantly.

"How would it be different from not giving them access to the Tol in the first place?"

Nashrel glowered, but said nothing.

Wirr paused, making sure he had his roiling emotions firmly in check before continuing. "Be warned: an attack on me, any attempt to take the Oathstone from me, will be considered an attack on Andarra now. In that event, I will use the Oathstone *however* I see fit."

Several faces went distinctly pale up above.

"That...that will not be necessary," said Nashrel hurriedly, his aggressive stance curtailed somewhat. His gaze slid to the two Augurs, as if hoping to see some form of support from them, but Erran and Scyner both stared back in stony silence. Wirr had instructed them not to speak—he needed the Council to be clear as to whom they were negotiating with—but their presence was undoubtedly helping reinforce that he was not to be trifled with.

Or assaulted, for that matter.

Nashrel glanced around at his colleagues, then sighed, making a calming motion. "I apologize, Sire. This is a...difficult situation. Perhaps we acted rashly in the heat of the moment." Wirr

couldn't tell if the apology was genuine or motivated by his threat, but Nashrel certainly appeared contrite. "You *are* on Tol Athian ground, though. By rights, Sire, even *you* are bound to uphold our law. Our decisions."

Wirr didn't flinch; he'd been expecting this.

"Ilin Illan is gone, Nashrel. I want to work with you—we *need* to work together—but the fact is, I don't trust you after what you just tried to do. The city is *lost*. So fates take your laws. Negotiate with me to fairly accommodate my people, or we will take over the Tol for ourselves. It's your decision."

There was an appalled silence, as if everyone in the Council chamber had taken a sharp breath and held it.

Nashrel's eyes bulged from repressed anger, but he eventually glanced around at the other Council members, speaking to them softly. There was a short argument—none of which reached Wirr's ears—and then Nashrel turned back.

He nodded curtly.

"We will not forget this," he said bluntly. "But very well. Let us talk."

❧

The next hour passed in tense discussion, broken only by regular updates on the state of the attack on the Tol's gates.

Every time the door opened, all conversation would cease, silence falling as the messenger shared their information. It seemed that the Tol's defenses were holding, despite the eletai's having now taken to throwing themselves at the gate. As soon as the door closed again the discussions would continue: Wirr wanting food and shelter for everyone, the Council equally insisting that the Tol was simply not capable of sustaining the refugees for any length of time. Various solutions were floated and rejected: everything from a lottery for who could stay, to a time limit on any non-Gifted being allowed within the Tol.

It didn't help matters that tensions remained high and the question of authority was still very much in dispute, despite Wirr's initial threat. To the Council, Wirr was impinging upon their territory—barging into the home they had created and demanding that he and his people be sheltered and fed, at the expense of their own. They took every suggestion that required risk to the Gifted as offensive, and every idea that might inconvenience them as something to be treated with disdain. Even his concerns regarding the sha'teth—which the previous day they had seemed to take seriously—were now met with bristling, Nashrel himself insisting that Ishelle's words had been too vague to warrant simply killing them, and that the creatures remained powerless where they were being held.

They were still arguing that point when the door opened once again, and this time the messenger looked deathly pale.

"Elder Eilinar," he said worriedly, ignoring Wirr. "We think there's been a breach."

All incidental conversation in the room stopped, and Wirr found himself holding his breath. "You think?" asked the Elder.

"The defenses picked up a surge of energy in the cells. Similar to the last time a portal was opened into the Tol," explained the messenger, looking faintly embarrassed. "When we sent people to check, there was some damage to one of the cells, but whoever it was was gone."

"Fates." Nashrel rubbed his forehead, then gestured to Wirr. "We should find out what's happening with this before we go any further."

Wirr indicated his agreement. "We'll come, too," he said firmly.

Nashrel looked displeased but evidently didn't feel that he had time to argue, instead jerking his head in an indication that Wirr should follow.

They hurried after the messenger along the corridors and out into the main thoroughfare. Wirr tarried as he took in the scene.

The massive main tunnel had been transformed in the past hour, Essence-light revealing small groups of people huddled everywhere against the walls and lying on the floor, a much thinner path than usual winding its way down the middle. Exhausted-looking Gifted still moved among the wounded, much to Wirr's relief. For all the Council's anger, they were not outright refusing aid to those who needed it.

People seemed calmer, though there were still unmistakably distraught individuals searching through the crowds, staring desperately at every face as they looked for lost loved ones. Wirr's heart twisted as he watched, thinking of Saric. There would be others like him who had been pressed into action by Wirr's commands, forcing them to leave their families behind.

Crashes echoed down the tunnel, each followed by a crackling sound that Wirr knew had to be a massive release of energy outside. The eletai were still attacking, still throwing themselves against the bastion of the Resolute Door. Each crunching clang was met with flinching from many in the tunnel, a thousand fearful intakes of breath whispering every time.

He scanned the crowd, his eyes landing on Taeris making his way toward them. The Representative must have been waiting for him to emerge.

Wirr waved Scyner and Erran on with Elder Eilinar. "I know the way. I'll catch up."

Erran gave him a slight nod, and they hurried off.

"Sire," said Taeris as he arrived, the relief in his voice undisguised. "I am glad to see you safe." From the inflection in his tone and his icy glance toward Eilinar's retreating form, he clearly wasn't referring to the dangers from outside the Tol.

Wirr gave him a tight smile. "It's going as well as can be expected," he said quietly. "Deldri?"

"Being cared for. By people I trust," added Taeris.

Wirr swallowed, clasping Taeris on the shoulder. "Thank you." He exhaled, one fear of many allayed for now, and glanced out across the sea of refugees. There was a lump in his throat as he formed the question that had to be asked. "How many?"

Taeris's face twisted.

"Easier to tell you who survived than who didn't," he admitted. "Less than half of the Assembly. A couple of hundred Administrators. Perhaps a thousand civilians, if we're lucky."

Wirr acknowledged the assessment, a little shakily. Not as bad as it could have been, but far from good.

"The army?"

"Five hundred soldiers, by my estimate. Another hundred Gifted who have been training with them." He hesitated. "A few captains, but in terms of leadership...General Vis and General Calder were both still outside with your uncle when the gate closed."

Wirr closed his eyes, rubbing his temples to try and ease the steady ache behind his eyes.

"So what's going to happen to them?" asked Taeris, his gaze encompassing the miserable-looking refugees. "I assume that the Council are...unimpressed with our presence. They wouldn't allow me into the meeting," he added bitterly.

Wirr snorted. "They know whose side you'd be on, I suppose." He shook his head. "They're stopping short of calling it an invasion. For now. But they claim that the Tol isn't outfitted to supply all of these people."

"They're...right." Taeris held up a hand as Wirr glared at him. "It doesn't justify anything they've done. But from a purely practical point of view..." He sighed, glancing toward where Nashrel, Erran, and Scyner had just disappeared. "So. What's going on?"

"The Gifted think that there was a breach in the cells. That someone—or something—got inside the Tol," said Wirr grimly. "We could use your help."

Wirr thought he saw a flicker of hesitation on Taeris's scarred face.

"I have one other thing I need to do first, Sire, if that's all right," he said thoughtfully. "But I'll join you shortly."

Wirr nodded his approval, and they parted ways.

He jogged after the others, catching up to them after only a minute as they made their way down a deserted side passage and toward the Tol's cells. Wirr knew their location but had never had reason to visit them himself. The area looked no different from the rest of the Tol in most respects, though once they passed the jailer—a concerned-looking man who was protesting to another Elder that he'd seen nothing since starting his shift—the surroundings changed dramatically. The cells were little more than hewn caves with bars for doors, barely high enough to accommodate a man standing or wide enough to allow someone to sleep. Clearly not made by the Builders.

They arrived in front of one of the cells, and Wirr grimaced.

The bars here were badly damaged, melted away.

"I thought these cells were supposed to stop people from using Essence?"

"They are," replied Nashrel uneasily, moving to the iron and holding his hand over the metal. "Still warm," he added.

Wirr looked around at the surrounding cells. Only one was occupied, the shadowed figure lying on the bed at the back.

"You." Wirr strode across to stand at the entrance to the cell. "Surely you saw something?"

There was no response, nor any movement from the prisoner within. Wirr peered through the bars, trying to make out whether the man was genuinely asleep. He could see only a single hand dangling down into the light, its forefinger missing.

Nashrel came to stand beside Wirr. "You won't get any answers from him. That's Ilseth Tenvar."

Wirr started as the name registered, a flash of surprised fury running through him. Tenvar had been the one to fool Davian back at the school, who had been complicit in the killings there and at other schools around Andarra. Davian had questioned him, had broken into the man's mental Lockbox and in doing so had accidentally caused him to enter a catatonic state.

Tenvar had been working for . . . well. They had always assumed that he had been working for Aarkein Devaed.

"He's still alive?" he muttered.

"His condition is unique," observed Nashrel. "He sleeps, eats, and will relieve himself when guided to do so. The healers bolster him with Essence every few days. We are uncertain as to whether the man himself remains in there—even the Vessels we have for restoring minds haven't worked on him—but we are not in the business of executing prisoners simply because they cannot communicate." His expression darkened. "Augur Erran has been asked several times to come and assess his condition, but thus far, hasn't found the time."

Erran, overhearing the comment, let out a snort. "There have been one or two other things to do," he observed mildly as he continued his inspection of the melted bars behind them.

Wirr scowled to himself, unhappy to find the traitorous Elder here. "I thought he would be in a more secure location."

"These cells are more than enough. And it is easier to manage his condition from here," said Nashrel. "I sincerely doubt that he will see any rescue attempt."

Wirr shook his head, gazing at the silhouette of the man before turning away. The sight only caused old pain and anger to stir inside him—emotions he didn't need or want to deal with right now. Ilseth had been an evil man, but his fate was as bad a one   459 as Wirr could have wished upon anyone. There was no point in dwelling upon his presence.

They inspected the area for a few minutes longer, but there were no obvious clues as to what had happened, and even Scyner couldn't detect anything out of the ordinary. It was clear that either a Vessel or kan had to have been involved to portal some-one into the cell—and then the same to destroy the bars from the inside—but it was impossible to deduce anything more.

Eventually Erran and Scyner glanced at each other, and Erran shook his head.

"I don't know," the Augur admitted. "It looks like something one of us could have done, but…" He shrugged helplessly.

"Scouring the Tol will be impossible. Particularly with so many unfamiliar faces already here," Nashrel added darkly. He looked up at movement in the doorway, his frown only deepening as he saw who it was. "Taeris."

"Nashrel." Taeris nodded politely to the leader of the Tol, ignoring the other man's tone, and walked over to Wirr. "Find anything?"

"Someone definitely got in here, but…" Wirr shook his head and trailed off.

Nashrel watched them. "We should reconvene in an hour," he said to Wirr. "You would no doubt like to see to your people." He eyed Taeris. "We need to talk soon, too."

"Of course," said Taeris smoothly. He turned to Wirr and the two Augurs. "Perhaps we can discuss courses of action in my office."

Wirr kept his expression neutral as he agreed. Taeris's office here was a Lockroom. What he had to say must be important.

They made their way along the passageway—all but empty, with the Gifted concentrated in the main tunnel, helping the survivors—until they finally reached Taeris's office. The four of them entered, Wirr watching as Taeris shut the door behind them.

"What's this about?" he asked impatiently as soon as it was closed. "We need to be out there helping."

There was movement from the corner, a shimmering, and sud-denly a figure appeared. Wirr's heart went to his throat and he tapped Essence, ready to attack; beside him, he could see Erran and Scyner reacting with similar alarm.

The figure stepped forward into the lamplight.

"Hello, Wirr," said Caeden, giving him a tired smile.

Wirr sat at the edge of his seat, processing what Caeden had just told him, unable to keep his gaze from repeatedly returning to the man—confirmed by his own admission now—who had once been known as Aarkein Devaed.

His emotions as he looked as his friend were still mixed, almost an hour after their reunion. The knowledge of what Caeden remembered doing warred with what Wirr knew of the man personally, and he couldn't help but wonder how much that remembering had changed him. Caeden *was* different, that much was clear. He was confident, driven, focused—and also harder.

But as they'd spoken, familiarity had begun to win out. Turns of phrase, even jests, fell back into the sort of easy rhythm that came only with being friends. Caeden's first question, after learning of the attack in the city, had been about Karaliene. And his first piece of news had been to assure Wirr that Davian was not only still alive, but stronger than ever—taking the time to explain their imprisonment together in Zvaelar, albeit in the briefest possible terms. That said a lot, too.

It *was* Caeden, without a doubt. Whoever else he had been, Wirr *did* know him.

Caeden watched Wirr, and his gaze suggested that he understood the complexity of Wirr's emotions. "It's a lot to take in," he observed.

Wirr chuckled drily. "Yes."

What Caeden had told him explained much, as well as confirming everything Ishelle had said, even if that wasn't really necessary now. Most concerning, of course, had been his revelation of Desriel's ultimate goal. Not to conquer Andarra, as everyone thought—but to instead carry out the Venerate's plan.

To bring down the Boundary, once and for all.

Caeden flashed a brief smile in response, but his expression soon turned serious. "How many fighting bodies do you have left?"

"Five hundred soldiers. Perhaps two hundred Administrators, and four hundred Gifted, though we won't be able to bring all of the last two groups along. We'll be lucky to get many of them, actually," Wirr amended unhappily.

"We're not exactly popular with the Council or Administration right now," added Taeris, who had largely been silent as he'd listened to the conversation. He'd guessed that the breach had been Caeden, apparently—had remembered that Caeden was familiar with Tol Athian's cells, enough so for him to use a Gate—and had headed back to his office, giving Caeden an opportunity to make contact away from prying eyes. Caeden had located him not long after.

"You may have to leave them with no choice," said Caeden, looking meaningfully at Wirr. "We need to put everything we have into protecting the Cyrarium. Any politics here will be irrelevant if we fail in that."

Wirr shifted, then agreed morosely. It would cause a rift from which he doubted he or any of the royal family could recover, but...there was simply too much at stake.

"And you're *sure* they will be coming from the north?" asked Taeris, a little uncertainly. "Talmiel is the only crossing, and—"

"You are thinking about the Gil'shar that you know," Caeden cut him off, not unkindly but firmly. "Gassandrid and the other Venerate set themselves up in Desriel the way they did for a purpose, Taeris. Do you know about their sacred vault?" When Taeris indicated he did, Caeden continued, "The Venerate filled it with Vessels—Vessels that don't require Gifted to be used," he added significantly. "This fight will not just be against Traps. They will be wielding *Essence* against you." He let the significance of that sink in. "I do not know how they are intending to cross, but there are any number of Vessels that could allow them to do so. Just think of your Travel Stones."

Taeris nodded reluctantly. "If they do have Travel Stones, how will we possibly—"

"Bad example." Caeden held up a hand apologetically. "Vessels that can create portals are very rare—and even if they were not, the Gil'shar couldn't transport the Columns that way. The Columns are...they'll disrupt any kan mechanisms they interact with. One of them would probably collapse a portal the moment they tried to pass it through. It's the same reason that I know they won't risk taking them through Deilannis." He rubbed his face, thinking. "No—however they're intending to come, it will involve marching. You can count on that much."

Wirr hesitated. "You're certain that what you Read from Alaris is correct?"

"I am." Caeden said the words calmly, though Wirr could tell they made his friend sick. "The Cyrarium is in the Menaath Mountains, and Alaris was intending to take the shortest possible route there. If you send your men to Talmiel—as they are expecting you to do—then we will lose."

"The Menaath Mountains are a long journey from here," observed Scyner.

"I'll make a Gate."

"Not if you don't want to be delayed. At best." It was Taeris this time, looking gloomy. "The Tol's mechanisms will detect it as soon as you start trying to make a portal, and the Council are on edge like never before. *And* they don't particularly trust you. There will be things that they're willing to allow, but opening a portal past their defenses won't be one of them."

Nobody said anything, and then Wirr brightened.

"What about the Sanctuary?" He addressed the question mostly to Scyner.

"I was able to protect the Shadows' children from the draining effect of the Conduit, but I could not do so for many more." Scyner paused, looking thoughtful. "But. I may be able to get a large group past it, into the catacombs, if we open the Gate there."

Caeden nodded. "Then that's what we'll do. Wirr, if you tell the Council that you're leaving via the Sanctuary, then they won't try and stop you. They'll probably throw in some Gifted just to get all those soldiers out of the Tol." He smiled humorlessly at that. "Don't tell them about me or the Gate, of course. Ilseth was the only agent of the Venerate that I knew of two years ago, but that doesn't mean that others haven't been turned in the meantime." He turned back to Scyner. "Now. Tell me about the sha'teth."

Scyner related their experience with the creatures, Caeden listening intently as one detail or another was supplied by Wirr and Taeris.

"You're right. We need to kill them," he said. "And then I need to speak with this other Augur. Ishelle." He shook his head. "I have never heard of anyone having direct communication with the Hive, but there may be a way to use it against the Venerate."

"I can show you the way to the sha'teth," Taeris offered.

Caeden shook his head. "I already know my way around those levels." There was a touch of shame to the words, though Wirr didn't know why. "You need to get people together and go. Now."

"Only those who can fight," amended Scyner quickly. "I know it will not be pleasant for those left behind, but civilians will slow us down."

"I'll see to it," Wirr said heavily. The people wouldn't be well-treated here, but once the majority of the soldiers and Administrators left, there would at least be less reason to accuse them of draining supplies.

"Good." Caeden stood. "As soon as everyone is gathered, I'll meet you down there and Gate you north."

Wirr hesitated, catching the meaning. "You're not coming with us?"

Caeden's expression was hard to read as he paused.

"If I am being honest, Wirr, the force that you will be bringing to this fight is simply not enough," he said eventually. "This is exactly why the Venerate made Asha their offer. If they destroy the Cyrarium, her being in the Tributary is pointless. We need her out here," he concluded. "We need her strength—both to retrieve Licanius, and to defend against the Gil'shar."

Wirr swallowed. "Assuming that she is all right." Caeden had told them about Diara.

"And that this Vessel you've been given actually works," added Taeris, with what Wirr considered to be reasonable concern in his voice. Caeden hadn't gone into detail about the Lyth, except to explain that they were 'helping.' They had delivered him the Vessel that would set Asha free not long before he had opened the Gate to the Tol, apparently.

"She is, and it will." Caeden gave them a confident nod.

"But I thought you said that someone would need to take her place in the Tributary," protested Scyner.

Caeden waved away the comment. "Let me worry about that." He headed for the door.

"Wait." Scyner leaped to his feet, holding out his hand. "It will help if you can reach us quickly, once you're done."

Caeden vacillated, then dug into a pocket and proffered a smooth black stone. Wirr squinted. It appeared to have the symbol of the Tenets carved into it. Scyner took it with obvious relief, tucking it away.

Caeden made to go again and then lingered at the door, glancing back at Wirr.

"For what it's worth—I am sorry," he said. "For the man I was. For dragging you and Dav and Asha into this. For all of it."

Wirr met his gaze squarely.

"I know," he said quietly.

Caeden inclined his head slightly in acknowledgment.

Then he was gone.

❦

Wirr lingered next to Scyner by the raised entrance to the Sanctuary, their shadows cast in sharp relief against the stone, watching pensively as hundreds of men and women filed past and congregated far below at the entrance to the catacombs.

He shielded his gaze from the massive pillar of Essence that pulsed blindingly in the center of the space. The Conduit, Scyner called it. The means by which energy flowed from Tol Athian's Cyrarium to power everything within the Tol. Which included, of course, its defenses.

Scyner glanced across at Wirr. "It is not normally this bright," he admitted softly. Even he sounded vaguely awed. "The amount of Essence that must be being pulled through..."

He trailed off, shaking his head at the thought. Wirr couldn't blame him. The Conduit burned like the sun itself, impossible to look at, intimidating everyone in the vast cavern by its mere presence.

"How is your shielding?" Wirr asked, somewhat nervously. It was for good reason that this was the first time he'd been down here.

"No issues." Scyner was clearly focused on what he was doing, though his voice was calm. "I wouldn't want to protect this many people for days on end, but getting everyone through should be fine."

Wirr nodded absently, noting the unhappy expressions of some of the Gifted, his mind straying to his most recent negotiation with the Council. It had all gone smoothly until he'd announced that he needed some of the Gifted to go, too; after that it had been…confrontational, to say the least. He hadn't needed to use his Oathstone, but it had come awfully close; Nashrel had vehemently argued that the Tol needed their own people to stay behind, to maintain the defenses and to look after the civilians. And for a long time, the Council as a whole had fiercely rejected the idea of those who did go being under Wirr's command.

In the end, though—whether through his negotiation skills or the ever-looming threat of his Oathstone—Wirr had won the argument. The only concession he'd made was that none of the Council were forced to come. That was a loss, to be sure, as they were among the most powerful Gifted in the Tol.

But given that Wirr now had three hundred Gifted under his command, he didn't mind so much.

He gnawed his lip, mind straying to Deldri. He'd visited his sister, of course; she was thankfully showing no sign of being affected by the eletai spear, but she still hadn't woken up. She would—the Gifted healers assured him that she was healthy, all things considered—but not for a while. Hours yet, possibly, given the severity of her injury.

He sighed to himself. The makeshift hospital had been filled with casualties far worse off than Del. He hoped that when she woke, she would be able to focus on how fortunate she was to have survived, rather than on her loss.

He shook his head slightly, resuming his observation of the proceedings. They continued for almost a half hour as people made their way along the cavern floor, into the catacombs and through the Gate that Caeden had opened for them earlier. The Gifted would no doubt question where that Gate had come from, but by the time they got their answers, they would be safely north and unable to tattle to the Council. And though Caeden had disappeared as soon as the Gate was finished, Scyner or Erran would destroy it from the other side once everyone was through. There would be no immediate way back here for anyone.

Finally the last of the group was trickling through the Sanctuary's entrance and down to where the Shadows had lived for so long. Wirr kept one eye on Scyner, who had begun to look less comfortable over the past few minutes, small beads of sweat forming on his brow.

"Ready?" he asked as the flow of people from the Tol stopped.

Scyner gave a tight nod and they moved down the stairs, Wirr ushering everyone toward the relative safety of the catacombs, where the effects of the Conduit would not reach. It was slow, but finally the crowd in the Sanctuary itself began to thin. Wirr eyed Scyner, giving him an encouraging smile.

The hum of the Conduit wavered, changing in intensity for the first time since they had arrived.

Both men frowned as one, shielding their eyes and squinting in the direction of the blinding light. The hum seemed…higher pitched, now. But less steady, too.

"Is that normal?" asked Wirr nervously.

"No. No, it—"

The light flickered.

It was so quick, just an instant, that Wirr wasn't sure he believed it had happened to begin with. As if he'd blinked and not realized. It was only Scyner's rapidly paling face that told him otherwise.

Some of the few remaining people—soldiers and Administrators, mostly—tarried, turning, clearly having noticed the change as well. Scyner scowled at them.

"Get moving. Now," he snarled, his voice like the crack of a whip. Nobody argued.

"What is it?" asked Wirr apprehensively as another flicker— this one longer, noticeably so—dropped the entire cavern into utter darkness for a full second before Essence pulsed back to life in the Conduit. It was dimmer this time, Wirr realized, sickening dread stealing over him. "Is the Cyrarium running out?"

"No." Scyner swallowed. "This...this is something else."

The hum suddenly wavered again, intensifying sharply, pressing against Wirr until it became almost a physical force. He covered his ears, face contorting, until just as abruptly the sound vanished.

A reverberating thrum sounded around the cavern.

This wasn't like the constant hum of the Conduit. This was a wave, and as it struck the Conduit, the light flickered out again.

Two seconds, this time.

Scyner staggered backward, eyes wide as he stared around him, though what exactly he was looking at, Wirr had no idea. "Scyner, what's happening?"

"We need to get out of here," replied Scyner grimly.

"Why?"

"We just do." Scyner gripped Wirr by the arm. "I'll explain soon but, Sire, we need to go. *Now*."

The light in the cavern blinked out.

Wirr stared blankly into the darkness, too shocked to react, until suddenly a small ball of Essence appeared in Scyner's hand.

"I don't understand how, but the Tol..." He shook his head dazedly. "It's been cut off from the Cyrarium. It is no longer getting any Essence."

Wirr felt the blood drain from his face and had to steady himself against the stone wall. "But the defenses..."

"Are already down."

Wirr's heart lurched. Deldri. Ishelle. Caeden was still there, but...

"You cannot make a difference up there. You can down here," Scyner said sternly, gripping Wirr's arm, clearly reading his expression. "Time to be responsible, Prince Torin." He held Wirr's gaze.

Wirr closed his eyes.

"Nashrel. Find Caeden. He will either be with the sha'teth, or with Ishelle," he said softly into the darkness, his hand closed around the Oathstone. "Get him to help you defend, or evacuate, or whatever else can be done."

Scyner watched, giving a sharp nod once Wirr was finished. "It's all you can do for them now."

Wirr stared out into the gloom, toward the silent, lifeless cylinder.

Then he turned and reluctantly followed the black-scarred Augur into the darkness of the catacombs.

Chapter 32

Caeden hurried through the Tol, moving almost absently through the network of tunnels.

His conversation with Wirr, all things considered, had gone remarkably well—as well as he'd dared hope, in fact. He had half expected his friend to demand that he turn himself in to the Council or the Assembly once he'd learned of Caeden's past. It had still been a hard truth to learn—Caeden could tell that much—but Wirr had grown, even from the man he had known a year ago.

He wondered again whether he should have told him everything.

It had made sense to avoid mentioning certain things, though. Such as that he needed to make certain that all the Augurs died in order to close the rift in Deilannis. Or that he had killed Davian. Part of him had wanted to admit it all, but the other part of him— the more practical part—knew that doing so was to no one's benefit right now. At best, it would have put Wirr in the position of feeling as though he had to choose between working with Caeden and the lives of his friends.

He dismissed the needling sense of guilt from his mind, focusing on where he was going. Third level. He knew the way, had been to deeper places than this in the Tol before.

A distant, strange whining sound touched his ears as he descended. Likely something to do with the defenses; the farther down he went into the bowels of the Tol, the closer he got to the mechanisms that protected it.

He touched his pocket as he walked, absently checking once again that the near-circular bands of metal were still safely tucked away there. Dual torcs, crudely made on first inspection, though the fine webs of kan layered between the metal were anything but. Caeden hadn't had anywhere near enough time to evaluate them, but the binding he'd felt take hold as soon as they had been handed over to him was security enough. They would work.

Their delivery had been both surprising and brief, taking place on the beach above the Wells not long after Caeden's encounter with Alaris. Caeden had felt the Gate materialize behind him, and for a desperate, clear moment, he'd been certain that one of the other Venerate had somehow found him.

Instead, the Siphon-bound form of one of the Lyth had stepped through. The exchange had been one sided and succinct: the dully burning man had thrust the torcs into Caeden's hands, told him how they worked, and brusquely reminded Caeden of the terms of his agreement with Garadis before striding away again. Caeden had been left staring dazedly after him as the Gate vanished from view again, barely a minute after it had first opened.

He still wasn't sure whether Garadis's absence and the stranger's haste had been from concern that Caeden would try something—an attack, some form of betrayal—or simply an indication of just how much every single one of the Lyth despised him.

He was still reflecting on the encounter when he came within sight of the chamber Wirr had described to him. He stuttered to a surprised halt.

A young woman was slumped at the entrance, head in her hands, fists clenched in apparent frustration. A long, unsheathed blade—far too large for her—lay on the ground next to her.

Caeden approached cautiously but saw quickly enough that she was not going to be a threat. She looked... tired. Disoriented.

"Who are you?" he asked, crouching beside her.

The young woman looked up, registering his presence for the first time. She flinched away from his outstretched hand.

"You," she whispered, looking haunted. "Have you come to kill me?"

Caeden looked at her, baffled. He had never seen this young woman before, as far as he remembered. "No."

The girl remained visibly uncomfortable, her eyes searching

472

the empty space behind Caeden, as if hoping to find someone else accompanying him. "Oh." She didn't sound convinced.

"My name is Caeden. I'm here to help."

"Ishelle." Ishelle shook her head violently, as if suddenly remembering something. "Fates. Oh, fates." She scrambled to her feet. "Can you get in there? I can't touch kan right now. Too… dizzy."

Caeden frowned. Ishelle was the other Augur Wirr had mentioned—the one affected by the eletai. "I can," he said slowly, suddenly suspicious. He cocked his head to the side. "Why?" He had to raise his voice a little; the strange whining sound was louder here, pressing against his ears.

"You need to get in there and stop them. The sha'teth. They're supposed to do…something…" She trailed off and clenched her hands so tightly that her knuckles turned white. "The attack. They've been waiting for it. But I couldn't see exactly…"

Caeden's heart dropped, and for the first time he focused on the whining all around them. *Really* focused on it.

"Do you know what that sound is?" he asked as he began rapidly working on unlocking the defenses on the door, one eye on Ishelle.

"No. It's getting louder, though."

"Why are you here by yourself?"

"I tried to warn the fates-cursed Elders, but they were too busy with other things," Ishelle said bitterly. "They know I've been having…trouble. Mentally. They didn't believe me."

The defensive wards came down, and Caeden hesitated.

"Stay here," he said abruptly.

"I'm going to come with—"

"I don't trust you." Caeden said the words coldly and calmly. Ishelle might be trying to help, but if she was being influenced by the eletai, then she might equally be here to trigger whatever attack was being planned. "If you end up in the same room as the sha'teth without my permission, I will kill you."

Ishelle bared her teeth angrily, but she didn't move. "Fine. Fates, fine. Just stop them."

Caeden gave a brief nod, moving into the chamber beyond without further discussion. He wasn't able to kill Ishelle now that

Asha's Vessel had been delivered to him—his deal with the Lyth made him incapable of trying—but she didn't need to know that.

He shivered as he entered, immediately recognizing the two sha'teth shackled to the wall.

"Tal'kamar," rasped Sekariel, its deformed face leering at Caeden as recognition sprang into its eyes, too. It shifted awkwardly, manacles clinking against the stone wall. "What an honor."

"It has been so long since we saw you here in Tol Athian," chuckled Deonidius in agreement. The differences between the sha'teth were slight, remnants from their original hosts—height and eyes, mostly, with vague hints of the face's original shape visible beneath the drooping, puffed-up white skin. Still, Caeden knew them. He had been forced to spend time with them extensively when he had unshackled them from the Gifted.

He looked around, confused. The whining sound was louder in here, but he couldn't pinpoint the source.

"You had us guide you through this section last time, too, did you not?" continued Sekariel. "Did you ever find the lowest level of this accursed place, Tal'kamar? Did you find the Mirrors? Or was it all simply so that you could convince that traitorous fool Ilseth to pass along the Portal Box?" He shook his head in mock pity. "Often, I think of that. You could have ordered him to point Rethgar elsewhere, to call off the attack on Caladel. And yet you instructed him to proceed."

"The deaths of all those children, Tal'kamar. On your head. Their blood on your hands."

Caeden let them talk, reaching through kan to examine the room.

"Nothing to say, Tal'kamar?" mocked Sekariel, the sha'teth's voice grinding against the air. It cocked its head to the side, face splitting in a grisly smile. "Or have you realized? Because even if you have, it is far too late."

Caeden barely heard, his heart suddenly pounding as he understood what was going on.

A massive cloud of kan surrounded the two sha'teth, strands of the dark energy twisting and intertwining faster and faster as the whining sound pressed louder on his ears.

Caeden forced his vision past the cloud, trying to examine the source of the kan. The sha'teth weren't triggering it, weren't controlling it at all—impossible for them anyway, given where they were. But it was coming from them. From their bodies.

His stomach lurched. It was draining him, targeting his Reserve but not the Essence in the rest of his body—as smoothly and rapidly as he'd ever seen any kan device destroy energy. It must have started happening the instant he'd walked into the room, and he hadn't even *felt* it.

The cloud suddenly tensed, hardening and contracting.

Then it exploded outward.

Wriggling, soft tendrils of kan flew through the air, randomly until they abruptly all changed direction, as if sucked by a giant funnel. In moments they were arrowing at—and then snaking into—the lines of Essence that lit the room.

Caeden cried out, moving desperately to grasp kan himself as clots of darkness began pulsing along those lines—away from him, vanishing beyond the walls.

To where the heart of the Tol's machinery lay.

It was already too late; he turned back to the sha'teth just in time for a massive blast of energy—from another Vessel hidden within their bodies, he thought dimly—to crash through the room, throwing him bodily against the far wall, almost knocking him out. He groaned as he tried to recover from the unexpected impact.

He looked up through a haze of blood to see a hole forming in the air.

A Gate.

He hauled himself to his feet, swaying unsteadily. His Reserve was so low. He needed to heal, but it would leave him completely drained, unable to stop what the sha'teth were doing.

A blade hewed into Deonidius, and the Gate winked out.

The smile on Sekariel's face faltered as Ishelle's furious, desperate scream reached Caeden's ears and the young woman drew back and swung again, Essence blazing from her arms as she gripped her broadsword with both hands. Sekariel opened his mouth to shriek as the blade cut through the sha'teth's stomach, severing its spine and cleaving it completely in two, its torso remaining hanging in grisly fashion from the manacles even as its lower half slid to the floor in a geyser of black blood.

The furious kan cloud vanished, too, and the only sound was Caeden and Ishelle's shocked panting.

"Please don't kill me," gasped Ishelle, the black-soaked blade dropping from her trembling fingers.

Caeden stared at her, wide-eyed. Those body-sundering strikes had to have taken an enormous amount of strength, but the kan cloud should have drained her of any extra Essence. How had she managed it?

He shook his head dazedly. It didn't matter—she'd needed to. Kan couldn't have halted those Vessels, once they had been activated. Dismantling them had been the only way to stop them.

Caeden levered himself up, letting Essence flow into his aching muscles. With the kan cloud gone, his Reserve would refill now, but he was still weak. "Vessels. They were Vessels. Made to attack the Tol's defenses," he said softly, horror flowing through his veins as he assessed what had just happened. "No way to do that except from the inside. Close to the machinery itself, to the flow of Essence from the Cyrarium." The Venerate must have been concerned about Andarra's ability to stop the Desrielites— or perhaps they had planted the sha'teth here early on as a fail-safe, and had simply decided that now was a good time to make use of them. They'd known that the Tol was one of the few secure buildings in Andarra, one that even they would have enormous trouble breaching if necessary.

"Did we stop it?" asked Ishelle.

"No." Caeden's mind raced as shock and fear warred for control. "You shut the Gate before they got anyone else inside, but the damage to the Tol is done. We have...I don't know. Minutes. Maybe a half hour." He gritted his teeth. "I should have seen this coming. I've seen it before. Aelrith had Gate mechanisms built into his body. Davian would be able to do it, too." He rubbed his face. "These ones must have had a trigger that the Venerate could activate from elsewhere."

He tried to stand, but his body hadn't fully recovered from the impact against the wall and he stumbled, falling back to his knees.

"We need to get Erran and the others, then," said Ishelle, not moving to assist him, her expression still cautious.

"They're gone—or going, anyway. Through a Gate," said Caeden. "And even if they could come back, I hope that they are smart enough not to. This is all to stop Wirr, Erran, and everyone with them from doing exactly what they are doing. The Venerate only care about ensuring the success of Desriel's attack. This is a distraction." He paused, feeling the Travel Stone Scyner had given him in his pocket. It would let some of them escape, but the portal would shut too soon once the Essence in the Vessel ran out. Not enough time to get everyone through. "There's no time to build another Gate to get everyone out of here, either. It's just us now. At least there's no way they could have anticipated that I would be here when this happened. I can make a difference," he finished, hoping rather than confident that it was true.

Ishelle seemed distracted, frowning into the distance before acknowledging Caeden's statement. "Then we should get to the entrance."

Caeden staggered to his feet, successfully this time. He nodded tightly and started toward the door.

Ishelle took one step to follow him, and collapsed.

Caeden dashed over to her, confused. He hadn't seen her take any injuries.

Ishelle looked up at Caeden, pain in her expression, and he recoiled. The whites of her eyes had darkened. Turned a murky, disturbing gray.

"Go," said Ishelle. "They need you up there."

Caeden closed his eyes in frustration, understanding. Her connection to the eletai.

He made to go for the door.

His feet wouldn't move.

He pressed against the imaginary barrier briefly before turning back, dropping to his knees beside Ishelle. "Not without helping you first."

"You have to—"

"I'm bound not to do anything that would harm an Augur." He said the words through gritted teeth. "And you are dying, now that the defenses are down. We both know it, so shut up and let me save you."

Ishelle wavered, then used him to haul herself determinedly back to her feet and staggered toward the door, gesturing weakly for him to follow. "Then you can help me on the way back," she said hazily.

Caeden shook his head and pressed her gently down into a seated position again. "It's a good thought," he admitted, "but this is delicate work. It will go quicker if you're holding still and I'm not trying to walk at the same time."

"You'd think after a few thousand years or so, you'd be able to multitask," grumbled Ishelle, but she slumped back to the floor without further argument. She was silent for a long moment, then shivered.

"I can already feel them," she whispered. She sounded terrified, as if the act of speaking might draw the attention of the eletai in her head. "They haven't noticed me yet. But the barrier that was keeping them out is gone."

"Let me know if anything changes," said Caeden calmly. He glanced back at the door. "I will do everything I can for you, understand?"

Ishelle nodded, eyes wide. Caeden could see a tear trickling down her cheek, though she quickly brushed it away.

"They talk about you. All the time." Her voice was little more than a whisper.

Caeden leaned forward, looking at her queryingly. Ishelle ignored him, her eyes roving, as if suddenly unable to focus on him.

"They say you are a monster," she said eventually. "They showed me things. The things you've done. The things you've said." She refocused on him. "They say you aim to kill all of us. All of the Augurs."

Caeden hesitated.

"Yes," he said. "To stop the evil that lies beyond the Boundary, we have to close the rift. To close the rift, every person able to draw kan through it must die. Myself included." He held up a hand. "But I've also been bound *not* to kill any Augurs. Right now, I just want to help you."

"Do you think that's even possible?" She squinted at him hazily. "No lies, please. I'm not in the mood."

Caeden said nothing for a second.

"Extended connection to the Hive has always killed," he finally admitted. "Some people hold on for years of exposure, others only days—I don't know whether it's down to mental strength, the severity of the infection, or something else entirely. But inevitably, they just...fade. Our belief was that their minds joined the Hive, somehow, without their physical bodies changing." He gave her an apologetic look. "Of all the Banes, the eletai are the ones we've always comprehended the least. When I left Talan Gol, the Venerate still had people studying them, observing them, trying to understand them more."

"Why?"

Caeden shrugged. "To better control them. They do our bidding, for the most part, and do not attack if we tell them not to. But they are far less reliable than the other Banes. The most independent of them, I think. The strongest willed." The information came to him almost as he spoke, dredged from some back corner of his mind, as so much had been recently.

"Scyner already tried to help me," said Ishelle, a touch uneasily. "It...did not go well."

Caeden grimaced. "From what I heard, he used you to get information about the attack. Whether he actually tried to help you is another question entirely." He held her gaze. "Even if he did make a genuine attempt to weaken the connection, I don't believe that he has the knowledge or ability to do so. I might."

Ishelle exhaled heavily. "You are asking for a lot of trust, for a man who wants me dead."

A flicker in the lines of Essence above caught Caeden's eye. "Strange times," he agreed bleakly. "If you can give it, then I can start right now, but I will need to Read you."

Ishelle wavered, then indicated her agreement. "I've been keeping everything personal in a Lockbox, anyway."

"Good. One of the prevailing theories is that absorption into the Hive is dependent on personal memories, as those seem to survive the integration process best. Your Lockbox may well be helping."

479

"I'll try to keep that in mind," said Ishelle with a weak grin.

Caeden gave a gentle snort of amusement and then walked forward, at Ishelle's nod placing two fingers against her forehead.

He pushed through kan, into Ishelle's mind.

"El," he whispered, recoiling immediately, barely holding the connection. He'd seen inside plenty of people's minds—people with mental illnesses, people with little but darkness inside them. But this...

There were just *waves* of voices, thoughts crashing in a dizzying maelstrom around him, images and memories swirling in crazed, unpredictable ways everywhere he looked. It was as if he were in the midst of a hurricane, and only the eye of the storm—in this case, Ishelle's Lockbox—stood still, protected by what looked like a Disruption shield. Everything else was ablaze with dizzying color and light and motion, making him nauseous.

He kept to the edge of her mind, small and quiet, doing his best to avoid notice. Making adjustments here and there, adding tiny pieces of hardened kan to deflect or mute signals, slowly but surely dampening the effect that the connection would be having on Ishelle. It was a slow process, though—too slow. The time it would take to fully seal her off was time that he didn't have.

He could see it now: the link, thin and odd looking though it was, connecting Ishelle's mind to the eletai Hive. Letting these *things* in uninhibited. No wonder Scyner hadn't been able to spot it. He could restrict it easily enough now that he knew what to look for, he thought, maybe even sever it if there was a way to get around that hard kan layer...

He froze, lifting his vision back to Ishelle's mind.

Everything had stopped. The maelstrom had frozen in place, and yet it was...intense.

Watching him.

He acted on instinct, jamming hardened kan around the breach just as everything began screaming toward him. It all happened in moments; suddenly it was as though his mind were being hit by a falling mountain, less pushed and more smashed backward, painfully forced away from the connection. He groaned, dizzy, as the chamber gradually came back into focus.

"Are...you all right?" murmured Ishelle, seeing his expression.

Caeden assessed and then nodded, exhaling. "That was…" He gazed at the young woman, trying not to show his concern. How did she manage it? Her mind was all but wreckage, and yet she stared back, determined. Scared, but fighting. "They realized that I was there. Broke the connection between us. I restricted the flow between you and the Hive, but…" He held up a hand. "May I try again?"

Ishelle dipped her head, and Caeden placed two fingers against her forehead again, closing his eyes.

Nothing happened.

It was as if a wall of hardened kan sat in his path now. Complete, impenetrable.

Ishelle's mind, somehow, was completely sealed off.

He shook his head, dazed. "I can't get back in."

"They are wary now," said Ishelle, sounding absent. "I think… I think they've only just realized that others could access my mind, too. They considered it a breach into the Hive itself, and they've… shored it up."

Caeden nodded slowly. They'd never been able to Read eletai; the creatures' natural construction seemed to block any kan connection to their minds. This was a little different, but just as effective.

"How do you feel?" he asked pensively.

"Better." Ishelle, to his relief, sounded sharper. More aware. "Can we go now?"

"Let's," said Caeden, relieved not to feel any compulsion to do otherwise. He had helped Ishelle as well as he could, for now.

The young woman scrambled to her feet and they began moving. Ishelle walked to the side and a step behind; he knew without looking that she was still staring at him, every muscle tense.

"Tell me about the Hive," she said abruptly, tentatively.

Caeden glanced at the young woman as they moved swiftly through the Tol's deserted corridors. "It's what we call their… collective consciousness, I suppose," he explained gently. He chewed his lip. "I've been told about the attack that you survived. That's rare, but I have heard of it happening before. The mental connection occurs, but the physical changes are prevented." He rubbed his chin. "Not with an Augur, though. That is… interesting."

"Interesting?" repeated Ishelle, arching an eyebrow at him.

Caeden flushed slightly. "Sorry." For just a moment, he had forgotten that she was a person. Had been looking at her from an almost academic standpoint.

Was that something the old him would have done? He gritted his teeth. He had to be wary of attitude changes like this, to be aware of when he started thinking about people without thinking *of* them. It had happened a few times over this past year as his memories had returned, and every time he realized what he was doing, it made him deeply uncomfortable.

He clung to that feeling.

"I suppose that there are worse things to be," sighed Ishelle, finally relaxing slightly, thankfully appearing to take no offense. She had deep, dark circles beneath her eyes, but she seemed calm. That was good.

She held out a hand as they walked. "Let's start again. Ishelle."

Caeden clasped it warmly. "Caeden. It is good to meet you, Ishelle."

Another fading flicker ran along the lines of Essence illuminating the hallway, and Ishelle chuckled drily. "If not under the best circumstances. I am...sorry, for that introduction. I should know not to trust what they show me."

"Don't be. I don't believe that the Hive is especially manipulative," said Caeden grimly. There was no point in trying to hide anything anymore. "I have done many, many things in my past of which I am deeply ashamed. But I am here to help now."

There was silence for a while.

"Was it true, what the sha'teth said? That you let Davian's school get attacked?" Ishelle asked quietly.

Caeden winced. That day had been at the forefront of his mind as he'd made his way here. His meeting with Ilseth was hard to forget, even alongside his true purpose at the Tol that day.

It had seemed so logical, at the time. He'd already known that the school at Caladel would be destroyed—Davian himself had told him, in Deilannis all those years ago—and he'd also known, of course, that Davian and Wirr would both escape. Even if he had called off the attack entirely, it would have happened at some point regardless—but more importantly, would have let the Venerate know that there was something important to him there. Allowing the attack to go ahead had by far been the most sensible option.

Would he make the same decision again, though? He wasn't so sure.

"Yes," he said, not attempting to mask the sorrow in his tone.

Ishelle watched him, then just nodded. She'd probably been shown worse by the eletai, anyway, Caeden realized morosely.

"And...have you really been to the lowest level?" she eventually pressed, curiosity threaded through her voice now.

Caeden considered not answering.

"I have," he said after a few more steps. "Twenty-four levels beneath this one. The journey there is..." He trailed off, shaking his head. "I do not recommend it."

"Noted," said Ishelle. "And did you find the 'Mirrors'?"

Caeden gave her a mild glare to indicate what he thought of the flow of questions, but Ishelle just stared brazenly back. He sighed.

"I did." He paused hopefully, but Ishelle's expression indicated that she was going to keep pressing. "The Shalis—a people I once knew—called them the Mirrors of Truth. My friend once told me that they were the Builders' greatest creation. And also what destroyed them." He walked without talking for a few seconds, mind wandering. He hadn't discussed this, hadn't even thought about this, in a long time.

"They're Vessels," he finally continued. "A grand white hallway of hundreds of the things, lining it. You have to look into each one before moving on, but at the end, you are allowed to remember only one of them. One truth that they show you, personal to you. Your life. And once through, you can never go back. Ever," he finished softly.

He still remembered the cathedral-like archways flooded with what looked exactly like sunlight, though there was no way it could have been, that far underground. The enormous mirrors flanking him for what felt like miles and years. He remembered passing them but whenever he focused, all he could see in them was his own reflection.

In all but the second-to-last one.

"Still. That sounds like it might be useful," observed Ishelle.

"I thought the same. I thought that I could finally...be sure. That there of all places, I would be able to find the certainty I had been looking for." He laughed hollowly. "And I did, in a round-about way. Just not in the manner I was hoping."

Ishelle hesitated.

"So what truth did they reveal to you?" she asked, quietly this time. "What did you choose to remember?"

Caeden glanced across at her, smiling sadly as voices began filtering down to them from up ahead.

"Perhaps another time," he said gently.

They finally reached the main tunnel, throngs of concerned Gifted milling everywhere between clusters of sapped-looking refugees. They hadn't been among the crowd for more than a couple of minutes when someone recognized them.

"You!"

Caeden tensed as a figure raced toward them, waving frantically. He recognized him after a moment, though he didn't relax. Elder Eilinar, head of Tol Athian.

"The Tol is no longer getting Essence," said the Elder abruptly as he came to a stop in front of Caeden. His tone indicated that while he wasn't necessarily pleased to see Caeden, he would be more than willing to accept his help.

"I know," said Caeden.

The Elder gestured, the crowd parting more readily for him than it had for Caeden and Ishelle. They jogged toward the entrance as fast as they could.

"She should stay back," said Elder Eilinar suddenly, nodding to Ishelle.

Caeden shook his head. "We may need her. I've restricted her connection to the eletai."

"But not severed?" Nashrel shook his head. "We cannot take the chance."

Caeden was about to argue further when the Essence lines on the wall flickered again. Violently, this time.

"We still have time," murmured Nashrel, the pleading prayer in his tone evident.

As if to mock his words, the tunnel plunged into blackness.

484   Sharp fear cut through the air as voices started chattering all at

once. Caeden quickly supplied a ball of light, which illuminated faces twisted in sudden terror.

"What do we do?" Nashrel and Ishelle were both looking at Caeden now. In the tunnel behind them, the voices of the refugees were getting increasingly loud and frantic.

A booming, resounding clang echoed from the entrance, making everyone flinch. Another followed, and then another, and then another.

"The Resolute Door," murmured Nashrel, his eyes wide.

The entrance was already lit again by Essence, this time generated by a group of perhaps twenty Gifted, who were watching with panicked expressions as the thick iron in front of them was slowly, impossibly bent inward a little more with each blow. They flinched at every thundering strike from outside.

Caeden drew a deep breath. "Go," he said, addressing Ishelle as well as Nashrel. "Take everyone you can and get to the Sanctuary. The Cyrariel—the Conduit—won't drain you now." He hesitated. "Stay in there. Don't try the catacombs unless you have no choice." Ishelle would be able to find her way, but if she succumbed to the eletai halfway through...

Nashrel opened his mouth to protest, but something in Caeden's expression must have convinced him, because he snapped it shut again. He hurried over to the group by the door, giving them swift instructions.

Ishelle looked at him. "Are you sure? I thought..."

"I have an idea, but anyone else here will just get in the way." Caeden didn't have time to be tactful. "And if I fail, I don't want everyone else dying because I made a mistake." He vacillated, then dug into his pocket and pressed the white Travel Stone into her hand. "This will take you to Erran and the others. If what I'm about to try doesn't work, get as many people through as you can before the Essence in it runs out—and even if it does work, they could still use your help against Desriel. I doubt any more Gifted will be willing to go, but there's not much point in your staying here now."

Ishelle frowned as she accepted the Vessel. She looked as if she wanted to ask questions, but instead just touched him encouragingly on the shoulder before hurrying away back down the tunnel after the rest of the retreating Gifted.

Eventually Caeden stood alone in the fifty-foot-high main tunnel of Tol Athian, lit only by the small globe of Essence in front of him, the crashes of the door being bashed down echoing away behind him into the darkness. He'd been here before, against the Blind. He could do this.

He didn't have Licanius this time, but he had something better. His memories.

He extended his senses, using kan to crack open the dormant line that would normally have lit the tunnel and seeking back along it, probing deeper and deeper into Tol Athian's machinery. Down the Cyrariel, deep into its bowels.

He hit the Cyrarium.

He almost lost focus at the size of the thing; even remembering the size of the Cyrarium they'd built to power the ilshara, this one seemed especially large. It wasn't full—Caeden wondered if it would even be possible to fill such a Vessel—but there was still almost more Essence here than he could comprehend.

Just like the one he'd made in the Menaath Mountains, the Cyrarium was all but impregnable—which was why Gassandrid had targeted the machinery drawing Essence up into the Tol. Usually that would have been impregnable, too, but the attack had come from deep within, behind almost all the protections. It was the smallest gap in the defenses, one added by design so that corrections and alterations could potentially be made to the Tol. Gassandrid had exploited it perfectly.

He wiped a bead of sweat from his brow. He couldn't simply tap the Essence with kan, here. A Cyrarium was always built with specific purposes in mind, and it allowed Essence to be withdrawn from it only in a certain way. Even for Caeden, with thousands of years of experience behind him, it was difficult.

He sucked the Essence along the line, breathing out as it finally reached the tunnel and he saw the golden light creeping along, gradually illuminating the depths of Tol Athian once again.

Another boom sounded behind him, followed by a screeching of torn metal.

The light finally reached him, and he carefully sliced through the retaining kan, letting the raw Essence spill out and be drawn into him.

Another boom, this one ominously followed by a cracking sound. Screeches and shrieks and the low, buzzing thrum of the eletai were audible now through the cracks in the door.

He gritted his teeth. Drew more Essence, as much as he could and then kept drawing, carefully connecting the line he had created to his own Reserve. It was loose, temporary, with decay already affecting the energy. But he thought it would be enough.

The door was halfway off its hinges now, and a black, dripping spear poked through, straining against the iron. Then another.

Caeden assessed the door. One more hit and it was about to collapse anyway.

He threw Essence at it.

The Resolute Door ripped off its last hinges and exploded outward, two twenty-foot-high walls of metal careening away faster than the eye could follow, smashing into the eletai gathered beyond in a shrieking shower of viscera and flying limbs. The monsters not hit by the doors hovered as if in shock; there was an odd second of everything being perfectly motionless, Caeden alone in the entrance to the mountainside against the roiling black cloud that confronted him.

Then the cloud descended, and Caeden unleashed the Essence that he'd been drawing from the Cyrarium.

He twisted it with kan as it left him, forcing it hotter and hotter until the flames were a pale, ethereal blue and he could see the stone on either side of the entrance beginning to turn red and melt away. Grimly he stalked forward, placing himself in the very entrance, and began to expand the range of his blaze.

Eletai were hurling themselves against him; just as with Tol Athian's entrance, they knew that their bodies would absorb the Essence, gradually drain it, make it more and more difficult for Caeden to use. But he wasn't going to let it go.

Slowly the creatures began to thin out, and Caeden pushed even farther. Red-white fire scorched the air for fifty feet in a semicircle away from the Tol's entrance. Then a hundred. Then two hundred.

Finally the last of the furious shrieks were gone, the sound of buzzing had vanished. Only silence remained.

Caeden trembled at the effort of sustaining what he was doing, but he still didn't let the power go. There would be no one left alive in the city, but the eletai had wreaked havoc among its citizens. If he didn't do this—and do it now—then they would have thousands more of the creatures to contend with by this time tomorrow.

Swallowing, he drew more from the Cyrarium. More. Pooled it outside himself when his body could take no more.

Unleashed it.

Ilin Illan exploded.

Waves of rippling, rolling fire raced along its streets, consuming everything in its path. First the Upper District vanished beneath the burning blue and white, then the Middle, and finally the Lower District and the docks. Buildings caught fire and collapsed; those carved of the pure white stone began to glow an unsettling red and then reluctantly melted into the ground.

Finally, gasping and dizzy, Caeden released the flow of Essence.

He stood there, panting for several seconds, lit by fire.

Then he turned back to the entrance to the Tol, still trembling. His work here was done. There was no point in staying, navigating the petty politics of the Council, having to explain himself at every turn.

It was time to see if Asha was still alive.

But there was someone he needed to fetch, first.

Chapter 33

Asha watched Diara's sleeping form from the other side of the room, arms crossed pensively.

The beauty visible out the bedroom window was lost on her this morning. It had been almost an entire day since Garadis had rendered Diara helpless, now. The Venerate's inability to access Essence or kan at all was typified by her misshapen form under the covers, the stump of her severed arm sealed but not healing any faster than a normal person's injury would.

She had stirred briefly only a few times since their battle, as far as Asha had been able to tell. She was securely bound; uncomfortably so, but Asha didn't particularly care at this point. She had kept watch as often as she could, Garadis briefly taking over when she needed to sleep.

Asha had acceded that that was necessary, even if she still didn't trust the Lyth around Diara. Her options were few. Elli had offered to stand guard, but Asha didn't want to take the chance if she could avoid it. She liked Elli, but ultimately, the woman was part of the dok'en. She couldn't help but feel a mild concern that Diara would be able to turn her, to Control her somehow.

She stared out the window for a while, so lost in thought that she almost didn't register when the form on the bed shifted.

When she did, Asha flinched and went to her feet with alacrity, heart pounding as Diara gave a soft groan. The woman stirred further, then—realizing that she was restrained—thrashed against her bonds before quickly calming again, struggling into a position in which she could raise her head and look around. She spotted Asha, blinking.

Her eyes cleared as she remembered. There was a long silence.

"So," Diara said, bitterness in her tone. "Here we are." She tried to shift again, pain flashing across her face. She waggled her stump of a shoulder at Asha. "I assume that you think this was justified?"

"No," Asha responded evenly. "But don't expect sympathy, either. You came in here and tried to kill me."

"Because you are serving the side of evil." Diara slumped back. Suddenly she looked tired, scared, and alone, nothing like the demonic force who had invaded the dok'en. Her voice was reedy. "Do you think I *wanted* to kill you, Ashalia? Or anyone? No matter what you have been told, I am not a monster. I was just doing what had to be done." She swallowed, her injury clearly painful. "So what now? Why am I still alive? Do you think that you can get information from me before you kill me? Or do you mistakenly believe that you can keep me here like this indefinitely?" She grimaced. "Garadis will not abide that, I promise you."

Asha said nothing, still wondering at the wisdom of engaging Diara any further. She'd thought about it a lot over the past day, though, and it didn't seem particularly risky, so long as she didn't let anything Diara said get to her.

On the other hand, the chances of one of the Venerate letting slip important information seemed slim at best. It might well be better to simply ignore her, leave her bound in this bed and wait for Caeden to return.

Diara's eyes suddenly narrowed.

"It's Tal'kamar, isn't it," she said quietly. "You have been communicating with him." She paled as Asha continued to say nothing, the silence evidently confirmation enough. "Ashalia, you must listen to me. He is not your friend. He is filling your head with one-sided arguments and half truths, twisting your perspective so that you believe that *he* is on the side of right. But if you just listen, really *listen*, to what I have to say—"

Asha shook her head. "You're trying to unleash the Darklands."

"With all respect to Tal, he is wrong about that. His is a theory based on speculation alone, mysticism and vague warnings from books whose origins are unknown—all while denying the word of the one who *made* this entire world. I am not talking of some distant authority figure looking down from on high, Ashalia," Diara continued earnestly, "but an actual being. Someone with power beyond anything we could imagine. The only one capable of fighting this prison."

"You mean Shammaeloth."

"I mean El." Diara's voice was filled with quiet confidence. "Tal'kamar has far too great an opinion of himself, and far too poor a one of us. Do you think that we would not *know* if we were dealing with Shammaeloth? Do you think that we could deceive ourselves about such an important thing, the central tenet of our lives, for thousands of years?" She shook her head. "I understand that you tell yourself what you must, Ashalia. That your drive is to survive above all else. But that does not make you right."

"So instead I should just listen to you and give up. Just…die," said Asha with a snort.

Diara sighed. "This version of you would end, Ashalia—but this version of you isn't *you*. All beings are made up of a series of choices; if those choices are not our own, then who are we? Why fight to keep a version of yourself that is nothing more than a character in a play, reciting lines written by someone else?" She shook her head. "Even if I am wrong. If we are working for Shammaeloth and El is truly in charge. Think back on the mistakes you've made, Ashalia. Think back on the worst decision you have ever made. Now—imagine that I revealed to you that I had manipulated you into it. Not Controlled you, but Read you so thoroughly that I knew exactly how you would react to things, and then tailored *everything* to lead you into that choice—which, if I had that much power, is the *equivalent* of Controlling you." Diara locked eyes with Asha. "What would you do to get away from that? To try and free yourself, and others, from such terrible tyranny?"

Asha remained silent; Diara was just trying to get inside her head. The woman knew that she had no other way out of her present situation.

She pulled in a breath. She'd never been good at this sort of debate. Give her time to think it through, privately—perhaps put down her rebuttals on paper—and she could do so quite cogently.

But in conversation, her mind simply didn't work that way. Not to mention that the Venerate no doubt had centuries of experience debating this exact issue.

Still—Diara seemed happy to talk, and there was a chance, however slim, that the woman would let something slip.

Asha settled back, trying to look relaxed.

"Tell me about the Venerate, then," she said. "If you truly believe that you've been working with El, I would be interested to hear about your history. The things you have done."

Diara paused, cocking her head to the side before giving a small, acknowledging smile. "Very well."

Diara began to speak—about small things, mostly, from her past. She talked of the terrible things she had done, how they haunted her but she lived with them in the knowledge that they were for a greater good. She talked of the good the Venerate had done, too. How they had saved people. Saved *nations.*

It was both the confession and the desperate grasping of a woman who knew her end was rapidly approaching, Asha realized after a while.

Asha didn't need to talk much herself. Diara seemed content to wander in her stories, jumping from tales of history that Asha knew to accounts of things that had happened thousands of years ago. Despite her wariness, Asha found it all fascinating; though Diara deftly steered clear of revealing strategic information, she otherwise seemed perfectly happy just to talk. Often her stories would revolve around El, or inevitability—her perspective on which, Asha had no doubt the Venerate was trying to push. To her mild discomfort, she found it hard not to listen.

It was hours later that the ground beneath Asha's feet shuddered slightly, and she tensed, suddenly afraid that another Shift was about to start. But the tremor quickly subsided, and she breathed a sigh of relief.

She glanced at Diara, who had cut off midsentence, clearly having felt it too. The look of fear in the other woman's eyes was unmistakable.

"He will tell you that I am a liar," said Diara quickly. "He will claim that I use truth to mask my lies, that I am manipulating you. That you must ignore everything I say." She held Asha's gaze.

"And I would say the same about him. Make your own decisions as best you can, Ashalia. That is all I wish for you."

Asha frowned, not acknowledging the comment. Diara plainly knew what the tremor meant just as well as Asha did.

Caeden had returned.

◈

"I know, I know. I'm late," said Caeden as he walked up the palace stairs, warm air ruffling his red hair as he gave Asha a wry nod.

Asha glared at him, torn between relief and anger, the tension of the past few days finally releasing into a vaguely happy irritation. "That's the best you can do?"

"I'm glad you're still alive?" Caeden held up both hands in half-amused defensiveness as Asha's glare deepened. "Sorry. I am sorry. Truly," he said, sincerity in his tone this time. He rubbed the back of his neck as he came to stand in front of Asha, looking embarrassed. "Believe it or not, there was a good reason."

"I assumed," said Asha drily.

Caeden gave a chuckle. "I just spoke to Garadis. He gave me the very briefest of explanations before demanding that I set him free of the dok'en again." A note of admiration crept into his tone. "That was smart, bringing him back like that. Quick thinking. But I'd be interested to hear—"

"Diara's secure. You first," interrupted Asha.

Caeden hesitated, then gave a rueful, apologetic nod.

It took only a few minutes for him to clinically run through what had happened since he'd left—his discovery of the Venerate's plan, his return to Ilin Illan, the attack and the destruction of the Tol's defenses.

Asha listened mutely as he recounted the scouring of the city in fire. She had spent an entire year there, knew the city as well as anywhere. Even after the Blind, the thought of the entire place being gone was just...incomprehensible.

"That's...a fairly good reason to be late," she said eventually, motioning for Caeden to follow her inside. "You're sure that Wirr and the others got away?"

"As sure as I can be. I'm hoping we can join up with him again once we're both out of here."

Asha balked. "But Davian—"

"I know when he gets out," said Caeden suddenly, not looking at her. "We have time."

Asha looked at him in bewilderment. "What?"

"Davian." Caeden shifted. "He'll escape from his prison in about a week. There's little point in going to Talan Gol before that, because we won't be able to get to him where he is right now."

Asha stared at him, anger swirling in her chest. "How do you know?" She shook her head disbelievingly. "And why are you just telling me this now?"

Caeden exhaled heavily.

"I'm sorry. I didn't want to mention it, in case the Lyth took too long to get us the Vessel. It would only have distracted you," he said quietly. "The prison he is in is a place called Zvaelar. Everyone who goes there is sent to the past. I was there with him, for a time, many years ago. It's complicated," he assured her, seeing her expression. "I'll tell you more about it if we have time. The point being, he is all right. He and Licanius will just have to wait a little longer."

Asha felt her brow furrow, but Caeden spoke again before she could say anything, seeing the struggle on her face.

"Even if you choose not to believe me," he said softly, "we cannot save him at the expense of the world, Ashalia. If the Boundary falls then Shammaeloth will drive the Banes in front of him, carving a path of death and destruction to Deilannis in…a day, without anyone or anything to oppose him. Maybe two. Wirr is very capable, but he has only a small force, and the Gil'shar are equipped in ways that they never have been before. He can delay them, but he has no chance of beating them alone."

Asha swallowed bitter disappointment and frustration, accepting the statement.

"So now we need to find someone to replace me in the Tributary," she said bleakly.

Caeden rolled his shoulders. "I have someone here, ready to go."

Asha stuttered midstep, not sure she had heard correctly.

"Who?"

"Ilseth Tenvar."

"Tenvar?" Asha repeated, confusion her primary emotion. "Isn't he...*dead*?" She knew that Davian had badly damaged the traitorous Elder's mind when he had Read him, not long before the Blind had attacked—but she had been given the impression by the Council, when she had thought to inquire months after, that he had not survived that encounter.

"By all the important measures, yes." Caeden made a face. "I know it sounds...ghoulish, but he is in many ways the best choice. When Davian broke into his Lockbox, he completely destroyed Tenvar's mind. The man eats and breathes, but there is nothing in his head anymore that is truly *him*. He is, to all intents and purposes, a shell. But that still suffices for what we want to do."

Asha recoiled. "So we're essentially using his corpse."

"Would you prefer that we get someone to suffer through the Shifts instead?" asked Caeden pointedly.

"But what if he...wakes up? Remembers who he is?" protested Asha. "What if he figures out how to exit the dok'en, release himself from the Tributary? The Boundary would fail *and* he'd have access to my Reserve."

She shivered at the thought. It had taken some getting accustomed to, but she did think of it as *hers* now—not some amalgamation of other people's Essence. It operated as easily and smoothly as if it were all her own, too.

The thought of sharing that with someone like Ilseth made her skin crawl.

"I've Read him, Ashalia—no part of his mind has survived. There is *no chance* of him recovering. It's perfectly safe." He sighed as he saw her still-uncertain expression. "It's not pleasant, but none of this is. The Tol was likely going to be evacuated; he would have had to be left behind anyway—which was a death sentence, as no one would have been there to care for him."

Asha scowled at him. "Don't try to frame this as a kindness," she said irritably. "I see your point, and I'll do it. But let's not pretend it's noble, at least."

Caeden held up his hands in surrender. "Very well." He watched Asha as they walked. "Now. Your turn."

Asha explained how Diara had been captured and suppressed. Caeden listened silently until she was done.

"I'm impressed," he conceded. "Especially that you managed to stop Garadis from killing her. That…that gives us a chance."

Asha glanced at him. "To do what, exactly?"

"To leave her in here when we go," said Caeden, though he looked unhappy at the thought. "I'll disconnect the dok'en from the Tributary, maintain its integrity myself. She won't die until I let it collapse. That should give us…more than a week, before the earliest that Garadis said she might break free? Almost two?"

"Won't someone notice that she's still in here, though? Wherever she actually is?"

"I doubt it. Diara isn't really the trusting type. Gassandrid would know what she's about, but she would have set up private rooms to do this. She wouldn't be able to stand the thought of someone, even Gassandrid, being in the same place as her while she was so helpless." Caeden scratched his chin. "It's possible that she set up a fail-safe—some instruction to kill her, should she not come out within a certain amount of time—but I doubt that, too. After killing you, I'm sure she was intending to poke around in here for a while, see if she couldn't find some new piece of information about me." He shrugged. "A week or two in isolation isn't unusual for any of the Venerate. We've spent enough time around each other that we don't really feel the need to keep each other's company constantly," he added sardonically.

Asha coughed. "What happens if they do realize, though?"

"They kill her," said Caeden simply. "She will come back somewhere else, and our job gets much harder. But for now, everything will look normal. If we can act fast enough, we can get to Ilshan Gathdel Teth, get Licanius back, find her while she's defenseless, and kill her before Gassandrid even suspects something is wrong."

Asha blanched, and Caeden frowned at her. "It's awful," he agreed seriously, "but this is the reality of our situation. Don't forget that she came in here expressly to kill you, Asha. She chose this path."

Asha paused at that, and Caeden sighed as he spotted her

hesitation.

"You spoke to her, didn't you."

"What was I supposed to do?"

"Keep her locked up, and not go near her until I returned." Caeden held up his hand as she made to protest. "I know. You didn't know whether I even would return, let alone when. You're not to blame." He held her gaze. "But Ashalia? Whatever she said, whatever she told you, you *must* ignore it. She was always the one good at talking, and she is very, *very* smart. She probably told you a hundred truths for every one lie, but those lies..." He shook his head. "Forget whatever she said, and steel yourself for what must be done," he concluded.

Caeden pushed open the door before she could respond, and they entered.

Diara looked up, the last sparks of hope leaving her eyes as she saw Caeden. The two Venerate watched each other for a few seconds, silent.

"I am sorry about your arm," said Caeden quietly, nodding toward Diara's stump.

Diara gave a dry, sad chuckle. "If you're really sorry, you could always heal it."

Asha said nothing, though she did keep an eye on Caeden to make sure he wasn't thinking of trying. Garadis had told her that using any Essence on Diara could disrupt the ward in her mind, either killing her or setting her free.

She didn't need to worry, though; Caeden smiled tiredly back, apparently taking it as a jest rather than a serious request. "It's been a while, Dee," he said, walking over and perching on the side of her bed, giving a friendly touch to her good shoulder in greeting.

Diara smiled up at him. "Too long."

Asha watched, stunned at the exchange, even if each word was burdened with underlying tension. It wasn't just acting. The two seemed to have a genuine affection for each other.

Tal glanced over at Asha, who understood the signal, stepping a short distance away to give them some privacy.

Tal bent, lowering his voice so that only Diara could hear. It mostly seemed to be Caeden talking over the next couple of minutes, only occasionally stopping so that Diara could reply. They both laughed once, sadness in the sound, Diara's chuckle a little choked.

Asha watched curiously, trying to decide what to make of it. Some paranoid part of her saw two old friends talking and couldn't help but wonder, briefly, if Diara was somehow going to sway Caeden—to turn him against Asha. She knew, rationally, that it wasn't going to happen, and yet she felt like an outsider right now. A stranger intruding on an intimate moment.

At last Caeden bent low, giving Diara a long, gentle kiss on the forehead before whispering a final something. Asha saw his eyes glisten as he turned away. Diara watched him. She had changed, somehow, during the conversation. Gained a measure of—if not peace, then at least acceptance.

Caeden motioned to Asha, indicating that she should follow him out of the room. She did so silently, giving Diara a last glance, though the Venerate was facing away from them now, gazing out the window. She didn't say anything. Adding a farewell after Caeden's would have felt wrong, somehow.

They walked down the palace hallway after Caeden shut the door, neither speaking for a few moments.

"That went...differently than I expected," admitted Asha softly as they walked.

Caeden glanced at her in surprise. "I've known that woman for thousands of years," he said, the emotion in his voice telling her that he was still recovering from the encounter.

"But you're trying to kill one another. She said—"

"She said what she thought would get her out of this situation," said Caeden firmly, cutting her off. "Imagine if Davian and Wirr believed the Venerate's arguments, became convinced and joined their attack on this world. You would be angry with them, yes— argue with them, do everything that you could to bring them back, maybe even fight them if you had to—but would you stop loving them?" His voice was soft. "I am frustrated by them, Asha- lia. Angry with them and hurt by them. And they by me. None of that erases centuries of friendship. It does not change the fact that they are my family, constants in my life in a way that no one could ever replicate." To Asha's surprise, a couple of tears began the slow journey down his cheeks, though Caeden didn't seem to notice. "I will kill them, Ashalia, because this world will end if I do not. But never imagine that it means I do not love them."

Asha swallowed, not saying anything more for a while.

They walked until they reached the sumptuous main hallway.

Elli was waiting for them.

Caeden, so confident up until now, faltered as he saw the woman. He knew as well as Asha that Elli wasn't real, that her vanishing when he destroyed the dok'en in due course wouldn't be the same as her dying.

That didn't mean the look he gave her wasn't filled with pain.

Asha walked ahead and tarried by Elli, placing a hand on the other woman's arm as she made to pass.

"Thank you," she said quietly. "You helped me keep my sanity in this place."

Elli smiled back, giving a small nod.

Asha walked on and exited the palace for the joyously spraying fountains, leaving Caeden and Elli to say their farewells in private. That was one conversation to which she didn't feel she needed to be privy.

It was only a minute later that Caeden rejoined her, his expression somber.

"Ready?" he asked, gazing out over the stunning vista. He didn't turn to look back at the palace.

"Ready."

Caeden gave her a tight smile. "See you soon."

He vanished.

Asha continued to stand there, warm air ruffling her loose hair. It was almost noon, and the sun shone bright in a cloudless azure sky, sending dazzling color through the mists of the fountains as they danced. Everything was bright, warm, and vibrant—and so peaceful, too. She knew that this was Caeden's idealized image of this place, knew that nowhere could ever be this calming. This perfect.

It was an illusion, but it was one she would miss.

Time passed; Asha did her best to relax but as the sun began to tinge the wispy clouds a light pink, she knew what was coming.

Finally, everything shuddered.

Darkness and fire tore at her body, and though she was braced for it, she screamed.

The agony was a familiar one, but that didn't make it any less unbearable; every muscle twitched and begged to jerk away from the razor-sharp needles, but there was nowhere to go and movement only made things worse.

And then suddenly, miraculously, there was a grinding sound. Outside the window a light slowly grew in her vision, stinging her eyes and forcing them shut. The first natural light that she'd seen in months.

There was a final, burning pain as the needles began to retract.

The capsule door melted away in front of her, and Caeden's visage appeared above hers.

"Welcome back, Ashalia," he said with a grim smile.

Chapter 34

Davian sat at Tal's desk, flipping through large sheets of paper as he looked for the sketch that should match the one he had just outlined from memory.

He did his best to ignore Tal hovering curiously over his shoulder, finding the drawing that he was searching for and comparing the two. Plans for a Vessel to manipulate time: a narrow Time endpoint, two separate Initiation endpoints, and a strange, complex mesh of hard and malleable kan in the middle where the power would twist to force the flow of time around the activator.

He sat back, breathing out in relief. They were almost identical.

"The length of your connector here is too short," said Tal, leaning forward and pointing to the plans Davian had written up. His finger traced along to a different line. "And you've looped this section back on itself."

Davian shook his head. "I did those deliberately—it should be more efficient this way," he said, a touch nervously. "We need every inch we can get in these Vessels. Unless there's something I've misunderstood?"

Tal was silent, studying the two designs, then grunted in begrudging agreement.

"Good. You're understanding rather than just memorizing. That's...very good," he said. "You've come a long way. Far from finished, but a long way."

Davian grinned. "You're not pleased I improved on your design?"

Tal snorted. "If space was not an issue, the original would be   501 better. Safer. Require less finesse in the actual construction," he said firmly, though a slight smile played around his lips as he did so. "So 'improved' is a strong word. But you did modify it so that it's more appropriate for what we will need, I suppose."

"Then...I have some ideas for modifying some of the *other* designs so that they're more appropriate for what we'll need, too."

Tal raised an eyebrow, then grinned. "Just try to make your other sketches smaller," he said, indicating the outline on the desk. "We're almost out of paper and ink."

Davian nodded his agreement. Tal had apparently been able to convince the dar'gaithin to let him have this stash of writing paraphernalia, gathered from the ruins of the city, early on—ostensibly, to help him design the tower. It hadn't been confiscated after the tower was completed, but it wasn't as if the Banes were going to provide them with any more, either.

The two men were silent, and then the metal beneath their feet trembled.

Davian grimaced as Tal reached for a chair to steady himself. The tremors had been coming more and more often lately, not to mention increasing in intensity. This was the third one since Davian had woken, and it wasn't even noon.

Zvaelar didn't have long, and both he and Tal knew it.

Tal waited until the shaking had passed, then pulled up the chair he'd grabbed and sat on it. "How are you feeling about all of this?" he asked, somewhat pensively.

"Good." Davian let his gaze stray over the plans one more time. He *was* feeling good. After four months of grueling, unrelenting study, every line—its angle, its thickness, the way it connected to the next—stood out to him now as something that he grasped, completely understood. Everything fit together logically, the pieces affecting each other in foreseeable, reliable ways. He knew that there was still so much more for him to learn—his memories of the dizzying complexity of the Boundary told him that, if nothing else—but the mystique that had always surrounded Vessels had finally faded away.

He hesitated, then pulled out the plan stowed to the side, the one he and Tal had been working on together for almost the entire four months.

His brief burst of optimism faded as he studied the design again, even though it was already burned into his brain from countless hours of trying to improve upon it.

"You still don't think you can do it?" asked Tal, seeing his expression.

Davian sighed heavily, shaking his head.

"The more I understand, the more I think it just can't be done. Something that completely, seamlessly protects against the Dark-lands?" He gave a soft, bitter laugh. "Fates. *Every* Vessel has inherent flaws. I need to make, what—fourteen of them to save everyone here? I could make a hundred *thousand* of these, and *perhaps* one might be perfect enough to resist being broken by the journey." He eyed Tal worriedly. "Especially at a size that I can smuggle back. You saw what happened to the last one."

"I remember," Tal assured him.

Davian paused as he relived their most recent experiment, shaking his head to himself. He'd sneaked out of the tower, searching the immediate area until he'd located a large stone—a boulder, really, the size of a small child—and then spent the next week laboriously using it as the base for a large-scale version of the Vessel that they'd spent so long designing. A difficult task, even at that size, but Davian had finally been satisfied that every line was as perfect as it could possibly be.

Then they'd infused it with Essence to simulate a source and, during one of Caeden and Niha's shifts in the tower, hauled it to the portal. They had touched it—just *touched* it—to the gray void.

The kan structure had trembled, bent, and then crumbled. In seconds the Essence within had vanished, the boulder itself turned to dust.

That failure still stung. The fact was, Davian just didn't know if he could do any better. Even if he did get the chance to try and create these Vessels once he returned to Ilshan Gathdel Teth, he simply didn't see how he could be *that* precise.

"I guess I'll just have to get a better handle on kan," he muttered, mostly to himself. On instinct he reached for the dark power, grasping it with only a moderate effort now.

He toyed with it, trying to refine his interactions but still unable 503 to manipulate the energy with any sort of truly delicate touch. The skin on his right wrist pulsed in reaction to his concentration, and he wondered again if he had advanced far enough to deconstruct and improve further upon that Vessel. It was his smallest version yet of the very large, very basic stone Vessel that he had made at the beginning—the one that had given him infinitely more focus, allowing him to manipulate kan with any finesse at all. That had taken him a month of sweat and practice and pure frustration to build.

After it had been constructed, though, things had gone much more smoothly.

"Don't push it," said Tal, noting Davian's wrist lighting up. "I know that thing gives you headaches."

Davian conceded the point reluctantly and deactivated the Vessel, letting kan slip through his fingers once again. It was unhealthy to increase his focus too much or for too long: the effect of the Vessel was more intense than what Tal had done to him in Deilannis, and while his mind was incredibly sharp when he used it to its full potential, doing so also often left him weary for hours after.

Tal watched him, then glanced out the window. "Probably time to visit Raeleth." He pushed up his sleeve, studying the three bands concealed there. They were ornately made, each a delicate pattern of swirls and slashes. "That man takes far too much pride in his work," he added absently.

Davian gave a small smile at that as he stared at the bands. One for invisibility, one for more efficient manipulation of Essence, one for strength. Davian had those Vessels, too—though his were built into his own body. Each one had been created first within stone, then made into a wearable, thoroughly tested Vessel before he had dared set it into his own flesh. But so far, at least, their presence hadn't caused any ill effects.

In addition to those, he'd constructed a Vessel within himself that he could use a simple physical motion to activate, one that allowed him to draw Essence from his surroundings. It wasn't perfect—it wouldn't discriminate between a plant and a person, for example, and it still required him being able to move to initiate the process—but it was reassuring to have. If he was ever stopped from manipulating kan again, at least he had another way to stay alive.

"You coming?" asked Tal as he stood, stretching and glancing out the window as last bell echoed through the crater.

Davian followed his gaze. "Ah. That time already." He frowned. "But wait. Then why would you need to visit...oh."

Tal grinned. "Exactly."

Davian grinned back; he sent a sliver of Essence to the Initiation endpoint of his invisibility Vessel, and then trailed after Tal out of the room and down the stairs.

Davian barely glanced at the group of Gifted lying on the mats by the portal as they passed, no longer concerned that they might somehow detect his presence. There were eleven other prisoners aside from Tal, Niha, and Raeleth, all Gifted who now took shifts to supply Essence to the tower. A few had previously worked the forge, but since Raeleth had arrived, it was Niha who largely provided the Essence needed for that process.

The group mostly ignored Tal and Niha, these days, and Raeleth by extension. Though clearly acrimony remained, it seemed that they had finally acknowledged how important Tal's contributions were to keeping Zvaelar from complete collapse.

Either that or, as Tal himself had pointed out, they had simply accepted that they wouldn't be able to kill him. Either way, the two groups kept well out of one another's way. Davian still didn't even know the names of some of the Gifted.

The walk from the tower to the forge was a short one, Davian trying to ignore the moat of al'goriat milling only twenty feet away. The number of creatures patrolling the tower's perimeter had grown significantly over the past four months.

The steady ringing of hammer against metal was audible soon enough, smoke emerging from one of the bloomeries Raeleth had had set up since his arrival. Raeleth, it had turned out, was by far a more experienced metalworker than any of the Gifted here. He'd taken to his new role easily.

He still made himself scarce on the odd occasion a dar'gaithin came to check on things, but he'd been seen by the creatures a few times in the distance and never been questioned. The Banes knew that the metal needed working; as long as it got done, they didn't seem to care overly much who was doing it.

Davian and Tal rounded the closest wall, and Davian deactivated his invisibility Vessel. Raeleth was hard at work, shirtless as he alternately worked the forge and then the metal. Niha stood over to the side, sweat on her brow too, assisting with long-handled tools.

Raeleth wiped at his grimy forehead and grinned as Tal and Davian came into view. "Gentlemen," he said with a cheerful nod.

Davian nodded back, glad as always to see Raeleth in such a fine mood. He enjoyed this work, even if Davian knew he still felt guilty about leaving the scavenging crews behind.

"Anything new for us?" asked Tal, after quickly checking that none of the other Gifted were around. They had been careful in their acquisition of metal destined for Ilshan Gathdel Teth. If anyone found out that they were taking it—*especially* if they found out that it was for Tal—then there was a good chance they would inform one of the dar'gaithin.

Raeleth shook his head. "The amount of scrap coming in is getting low," he admitted. "I'm not sure we can get away with filching much more."

Davian observed the exchange curiously. There was still a vague underlying tension to all Raeleth and Tal's interactions, even if it was barely there anymore, not visible unless you were looking for it. Davian wasn't sure if Raeleth considered Tal a friend—he didn't think that would ever happen, really—but he had seemed to at least accept that Tal was trying to do the right thing.

Tal reluctantly accepted the statement. "Let us know if you think you can get more." He turned to Niha. "Thought we might find you here," he added, giving a deliberately knowing smirk across at the woman, who had until now been standing silently to the side.

Niha flushed slightly at his look, glaring at him as if daring him to say more.

Davian restrained a grin.

Raeleth and Niha had seemed a...strange pairing, at first. The quiet but intense man's demeanor, combined with Niha's blunt, ruthless streak, had felt destined to end in disaster.

But, somehow, it was working. Davian had seen Niha and Raeleth together more often than he could count, often with heads bowed close, deep in discussion. Sometimes—to both Davian's and Tal's shock—they had even caught Niha laughing at something Raeleth had said, though she'd always replaced her mirth with a glower when she'd noticed them watching.

Still, actually mentioning the clearly blossoming relationship between the two was something no one was willing to do. Not with Niha within earshot, at least.

"You go ahead. I'll be there in a few minutes," said Niha eventually, wiping her hands and shooting Raeleth a smile—something she only ever seemed to do for him. Tal watched in open amusement, then turned to Raeleth.

"Tomorrow?" he asked.

Raeleth nodded immediately. "Of course." He looked questioningly at Davian. "You're welcome to come too, you know."

Davian shook his head, waving his hand apologetically. "Study." Tal had been scheduling more and more time to talk with Raeleth about religion—arguing El, fate, morality. They were interesting conversations, but...heavy. Requiring the sort of concentration that Davian needed to reserve for studying kan, at the moment. "Another time."

Raeleth dipped his head again, letting the matter drop. Davian always appreciated that. Raeleth would never give up on trying to teach him, but he was never going to pressure Davian into being taught, either.

Davian and Tal started back, and Davian cast a curious glance across at his friend.

"You and Raeleth seem to be getting along," he observed.

"He has never been anything but civil," agreed Tal, "and he is...intent on educating me in areas where he believes I am lacking. About which he may be right," he conceded. "But it remains a task, for him. A project, rather than a friendship." He shrugged. "He cannot be blamed for that. And it has been...instructive."

Davian cocked his head to the side. "I thought you'd read

his writings. The ones that established the resistance in Ilshan Gathdel Teth." After the first month of gradually building trust, Raeleth had finally admitted to what Tal had suspected from the beginning—that he had, in fact, been responsible for the treatise that the resistance in Ilshan Gathdel Teth apparently still referenced. Raeleth himself, though, had never been aware of its popularity, despite Tal's admitting that its growing recognition had been the reason Raeleth was thrown into Zvaelar in the first place.

Tal gave a rueful nod. "I did. Many years ago."

Davian shook his head. "They obviously didn't sway you then, so what's changed?"

"Me, I suppose." Tal shrugged at Davian's look. "Sometimes it's not the message. It's the timing."

They headed back to their room in the tower, but after perhaps ten minutes of casual conversation, Tal cast a vaguely irritated look at the door.

"Niha's taking too long."

Davian smirked. "Are you going to be the one to point that out to her?"

Tal chuckled but shook his head. "We're going to be late for our shift," he said, glancing out the window at the red-painted landscape. "Interested in some more exercise?"

Davian stretched. "I won't say no." He could theoretically go outside whenever he wanted, so long as he had the invisibility Vessel activated, but the slight added risk always made it hard to justify.

They made their way back toward the forge, the tension of raised voices reaching Davian's ears at the same time as Tal's.

"Trouble," murmured Tal, moving quickly and noiselessly toward the sound, clearly assuming that Davian would follow. The two of them stole toward the wall of the forge, angry words beginning to resolve themselves.

"You are mistaken," Niha was saying, her voice a mixture of desperation and cold fury. "Raeleth was brought here by Athsissis. How in El's name else would he have come to be here?"

"Athsissis would have informed me," hissed a voice, one that sent a chill down Davian's spine. The dar'gaithin tended to sound very similar to one another, but he recognized this one. "Instead, I believed this man was dead."

"Then why don't you ask him why he didn't tell you?" came Raeleth's voice, trying to sound casual but with an unmistakable underlying tension.

"Athsissis has been missing for months," replied Isstharis. Davian was certain it was the dar'gaithin from the scavengers' section now. "And I am running out of experienced workers. He is coming with me."

"Just let him go, Niha." The new voice—a male's—dripped with self-satisfaction. Davian didn't recognize it, but he saw Tal's scowl as his friend obviously did.

Davian peered around the corner, certain he wouldn't be seen thanks to his invisibility Vessel.

Raeleth stood by a still-hot forge, a long pair of tongs in his hand, looking a mixture of shocked and resigned. Niha stood between him and Isstharis, whose tail flicked back and forth in clear irritation. To the side a short, middle-aged man with watery eyes watched. Davian recognized him as one of the Gifted prisoners, though he didn't know his name.

Niha's gaze flicked to the stranger. "I know you did this, Ayron. I will deal with you soon enough," she said softly, ice in every word. "But for now"—she turned back to Isstharis—"no. You cannot have him. I will not allow it."

Tal moved, pushing past Davian—clumsily, as he'd had no way of knowing exactly where Davian was—and striding out into the open.

"What is the problem, Isstharis?"

The dar'gaithin faltered when it saw who had arrived, though its aggressive demeanor quickly reasserted itself. "There is not a problem, Tal'kamar. I am simply taking this man back to assist in scavenging."

"Out of the question." Tal's voice was calm. "He is too valuable here. Your removing him would slow production significantly."

No one spoke as Isstharis evidently considered.

"As will not having any metal to forge," hissed the creature eventually, shaking its head. "This is not a negotiation, Tal'kamar. Step aside. Both of you." She stared at Tal. "You know the consequences of trying to kill me. There are far more lives at stake than this one. So just let me—"

Niha's spear was flicking out from her side, glowing.

It took Isstharis through the mouth before Davian even realized what was happening.

He watched, wide-eyed in shock as the dar'gaithin flew backward through the air, propelled by the flying projectile until the Bane struck the side of the forge with a resounding crash, the quivering spear jutting from the back of its head and pinning it firmly to the brick.

"Niha!" It was Tal, staring at the woman in horror.

"You *idiot*," hissed Ayron. "We can't afford to kill them!"

Niha ignored him. "You said we get out of here. I figured it was time to trust you," she said softly to Tal.

"Um," said Raeleth nervously from behind them, still holding the tongs. He pointed with them.

Davian looked in the direction he was indicating, heart lurching.

The al'goriat were gathering, teeth bared, growling and slavering at the very edge of where they were allowed to go.

"Davian," Tal murmured. "I don't *think* that they can come any closer, but still. I don't suppose you would like to step in right around now?"

Davian nodded, even though Tal wouldn't be able to see. He activated his focus Vessel and then grasped kan, quickly but carefully extending a kan shield around the other four, hiding them—and Isstharis's corpse—from the al'goriats' view. It was a simple enough use of kan, though such a large shield was something he hadn't had to create in a while.

From the corner of his eye, he saw Ayron turn as if to flee.

"Don't move." Tal's voice cracked out like a whip.

Ayron wavered, and Davian could see the deep fear in his eyes, but some part of the man recognized that none of the others were moving, either. He closed his eyes and stayed still.

The al'goriat continued to snarl and watch but the sounds were confused now; more of the creatures blinked over from elsewhere to join the initial group, only to blink away again moments later, seeing nothing of interest. The Banes growled and sniffed, and a few shrieked angrily, but none broke the invisible barrier that separated them from the tower's surroundings.

Finally, they quietened. Began blinking away and resuming their lumbering, random patrols. Davian watched for a few more seconds, then carefully lowered the kan shield again.

Nothing happened.

"What in fates?" murmured Ayron, staring with a mixture of utter relief and complete bafflement at the creatures. He turned his gaze to Tal, apparently singling him out as responsible. "How did you do that, Devaed?"

Tal ignored him, walking over to Niha and Raeleth. "We'll need to get rid of the body," he said, jerking his head toward Isstharis.

"Devaed!" Ayron strode toward him, angrily now. "Do you know something the rest of us don't about these creatures? I demand—"

He cut off with a gurgle as Niha's spear ripped free of Isstharis's corpse and blurred at the Gifted, the black-blooded tip coming to a stop inches from his throat and hovering there menacingly.

"You." Niha's eyes held murder as she walked toward Ayron. "You brought Isstharis here. You've been looking for a way to get back at me, and so you thought you could do *this*?" Her voice shook with rage.

Ayron blanched. "I didn't—"

Niha's spear blurred, curving in an arc and smashing down hard on Ayron's arm. The man screamed as something cracked; he fell to the ground and the spear flipped again, hovering above his heart.

Niha raised her hand.

"*Niha.*"

Raeleth's voice cut through the shocked silence. The woman stopped with her spear still held high, then turned.

"He tried to have you taken away. Out of petty spite."

"Then he is to be pitied," said Raeleth quietly. "Not killed."

Niha's lips pressed into a thin line. She turned back to Ayron, studying the man.

She gestured again.

The spear snapped back into her hand.

Ayron breathed out as the woman stalked away, but his relief was short-lived as Tal took her place, looming over the Gifted.

"The relationship that you tried to exploit is what just saved you. From me, as well as her," he said softly. "But rest assured that if you say anything about this—if you try *anything* like this again—nothing will be able to dissuade me from ending you. Understood?"

Davian felt a chill as he watched. The words were delivered with a heavy menace that he wouldn't have thought possible from Tal. A promise of violence that lay just beneath the surface.

Ayron nodded, wide-eyed, but Tal was already striding away.

Davian swallowed, then hurried after him silently.

Chapter 35

First bell had just rung when Davian slipped around the corner of the forge, as always a little tense despite knowing that no one could see him.

It was the morning after the incident with Isstharis, and from everything he'd seen so far, there had been no serious consequences from the Bane's death. Still, he'd woken to find Tal sleeping and Niha gone, and had felt in need of some conversation rather than a leap straight back into his studies. Raeleth, thankfully, was always a willing ear.

To his surprise, voices floated out to him as he approached.

"What about Jordyn? Like the hero of the Five Reeds—bravest man to have ever lived," said Raeleth.

"Never heard of him. Next!" Davian gave a small start as he realized it was Niha's voice. It was almost unrecognizably light and cheerful. Playful.

Raeleth grunted. "Rian?"

"I knew a Rian, and...no."

Raeleth sighed, audibly and dramatically. "What would *you* suggest?"

"What about Sandin?"

Raeleth immediately snorted in mock derision. "Is that even a name? Terrible. Just terrible."

"It's my father's name. And his father's."

There was a moment's pause, and then laughter from both Raeleth and Niha.

"Very well," said Raeleth eventually. "What name are *you* going to use when you get out?"

Davian's amused smile faded; he quietly withdrew, leaving the two to their conversation. He was happy for them, but...they were putting so much *faith* in him. In his ability to get them out of here.

It was hard not to let his failures, and the feeling that he wasn't going to be able to overcome them, weigh on him.

He walked the perimeter of the tower for a while, stretching his legs, before finally returning to the forge. Niha had left; only Raeleth was there now, already hard at work.

Davian glanced around, then let his invisibility shield drop. Raeleth caught the motion and paused what he was doing, smiling merrily at Davian. The man was no longer surprised by Davian's sudden appearances.

"Davian! Just who I was hoping to see, actually."

Davian raised an eyebrow. There was a sort of nervous energy to Raeleth this morning. "Just wanted to see how you were after yesterday."

Raeleth inhaled. "Not the most pleasant of encounters," he admitted, his gaze wandering to where Isstharis had been skewered. Nothing was left except the hole where the Essence-strengthened spear had jammed in. "I'm fine. But it was...a good reminder, I suppose."

"A reminder?"

"That only El knows what's going to happen to us. That we don't have forever here." Raeleth spoke solemnly. "These past few months have been...surprisingly joyful, Davian. Something I never expected to find in this place. But that cannot last."

Davian nodded, wondering whether Raeleth's conversation with Niha had helped spark these thoughts in the other man. "True." He frowned, trying to see where Raeleth was going with this as the other man licked his lips, looking nervous. "Is...something wrong? Is your Dark infection getting worse again?"

Raeleth chuckled uneasily. "No, no. Nothing's wrong. Between you and Niha, the infection is under control," he assured him quickly. He rubbed his chin. "I just...ah. I *do* have another item for you to make into a Vessel."

Davian scratched his head. "All right," he said slowly.

Raeleth shuffled his feet. "The thing is…it's special. To me. I mean…I know it needs to be a Vessel, because we need everything to be a Vessel, but…"

He trailed off, then shook his head irritably at his own rambling and held out his hand, revealing what had been tucked in it.

Davian felt a chill as he saw the silver gleaming in Raeleth's palm. The ring was beautifully made, three lines intertwining with each other. It glinted red as it caught the moonlight.

"*You* made this?" Davian asked quietly, taking the ring and gazing at it in mild disbelief. It was exactly as he remembered. The last time he'd seen it, Gassandrid had—understandably, now—been asking him why he'd had a Vessel that was so valuable. "You *made* this?"

"Well it didn't just appear," Raeleth said, a little bemusedly. "I melted down the metal from my key."

Davian nodded, still stunned. Raeleth had been holding on to that key since his first week in Zvaelar. Since they had come north of the Breach, it had become…not quite a talisman, but close to it. Keeping it from the dar'gaithin had been Raeleth's small, continuing act of defiance.

"I know this ring," he said. "From my time."

Raeleth stared and then, to Davian's surprise, smiled.

"Excellent. That's excellent," he murmured. He held up a hand as Davian opened his mouth to elaborate. "No. I don't want to know the circumstances. It might…change what I want to do. The important thing is that it makes it out of this awful place." He motioned to the piece of jewelry. "Can you turn it into something useful?"

"Yes," Davian assured him dazedly. "I'll do it right now."

Raeleth looked strangely relieved. "Thank you." He hesitated. "And Davian? Please…don't mention it to Niha."

"Why not?" asked Davian absently, still looking at the ring.

"Because it's for her," said Raeleth hesitantly.

Davian nodded, then stopped as he registered what Raeleth was saying. He looked up at the other man, who was watching him with a mixture of nervousness and awkwardness.

"Oh. *Oh!*" A slow grin spread across his face. "Really?"

Raeleth shrugged, unable to help grinning back. "I love her. She loves me." He gave Davian a mock-stern look. "And no, before you ask. It has nothing to do with her saving my life yesterday. I've had this ready for days."

Davian chuckled, inclining his head. Four months didn't sound like long, but here—living in such close quarters, spending almost every waking second together—it was an eternity. The bonds he had forged with Tal, Niha, and Raeleth in this terrible place were stronger than anyone could possibly understand.

"Well for what it's worth, I hope she says yes," he said jovially, clapping Raeleth on the back. "Even if I do think that it makes you the bravest man alive."

Raeleth smiled at that. "Well it's either that, or be the stupidest one if I didn't try," he observed. "Finding her here has been like…finding a jewel in amongst the dirt. An emerald, dropped into the cup of a beggar."

Davian chuckled. "Raeleth the wordsmith, at work once again."

Raeleth made a face at him. "That joke was old after the first week, you know."

"I just enjoy seeing you react to it," Davian responded lightly.

They talked amicably for a while longer, but as always, Davian felt the pressing weight of responsibility before too long. He soon bade Raeleth farewell and activated his invisibility Vessel again, strolling back to the shining steel tower.

He sat at Tal's desk and drew the ring out of his pocket, gazing at it, barely daring to believe it was the same one. There was no mistaking it, though. He had worn that ring for months; the lines were an exact match to the one that Asha had handed him so long ago. The one Tal had destroyed in Deilannis to send him back to his own time.

He eventually closed his eyes, feeling the vague warmth in his right wrist as he activated his focus Vessel again, grasping kan. They still hadn't been able to determine why Davian was able to access the power here. Even with his own focus Vessel, Tal claimed that he was completely unable to even sense the dark energy.

Time passed as he worked. Last bell rang to signal the onset of night, but Davian barely noticed. He set fine lines, destroyed and then set them again, carefully intertwining and meshing kan structures on top of one another. He hadn't created a Vessel like this before, but these types weren't especially difficult to set in metal: the kan didn't do much more than convert Essence into a different form of energy—in this case, a concentrated blast of wind. The size of the Vessel made it a painstaking process, requiring multiple restarts, but Davian didn't mind. He enjoyed the creation, the act of actually putting his knowledge into effect, far more than studying. And if Tal found out and complained, then he could always argue that it was good practice.

Another two tremors forced him to pause as he worked. Worry continued to build in the back of his mind over that, but he ignored the feeling for now. He already knew that Zvaelar was getting closer to complete collapse, and that he needed to come up with a solution to help everyone withstand the journey through the rift before that happened. Dwelling on it wasn't going to help.

By the time he finished adding the tiny Initiation endpoint to the ring, the final peal of first bell had faded away.

Davian examined the end result with undisguised satisfaction. Though little else had changed since Davian had arrived here, *he* certainly felt different. His progress in his studies, his ability to use kan—even at a basic level—and the addition of the Vessels to his body had all served to change the terrifying nature of this place into something...manageable.

Reluctantly, he let the flow of Essence to his focus Vessel wane, gritting his teeth as pain shot through his head. He knew it wasn't healthy to use the Vessel too much—Tal had once told him that Cyr had used one for an entire year, and had had headaches for the rest of his life as a result. He wasn't going to do anything so extreme as that, though.

For now, all he needed was some sleep.

Tal had returned when Davian woke.

The morning was still relatively young, he was glad to discover; one of the benefits of using the focus Vessel was that he didn't need as much sleep as he would have otherwise. He yawned, letting his invisibility shield drop and acknowledging Tal as he stood, stretching.

"All's well?" he asked.

Tal snorted. "As well as it can be. The tower takes more Essence every day to keep back the corruption, now. And these tremors…" He shook his head, sounding as exhausted as he looked. "I think we may have less time than I've previously said."

Davian's heart sank. "How long?"

"Months." Tal made a cautioning movement as Davian sat up straighter, a thread of panic running through him. "I haven't mentioned this to any of the others yet, because I'm not sure. I just thought you should know, because…" He shrugged.

"Because whether everyone gets out depends on me," said Davian. He didn't put any self-pity into the statement, though the responsibility weighed heavily on him. It was simply fact.

"I wouldn't have suggested this until recently, but I think you should add the time Vessel to yourself," said Tal. He held up a hand, anticipating Davian's protest. "I know you can't test it in here, but you're past the need to create practice versions for everything, Dav. Besides—you could be going back at any point now. You may not have time to do it when you return to Ilshan Gathdel Teth, and you *are* going to need it if you want to escape."

Davian paused, but nodded reluctantly. Time manipulation didn't work in Zvaelar—at least, not for him. That made sense; the entire city was already inside an enormous time bubble, and everything Davian had read in Deilannis said that 'nested' time manipulation was impossible. Though given that, he and Tal had only theories as to why the al'goriat were able to do it.

"I think I had it in the fight against Gassandrid," Davian eventually admitted, rubbing his chin.

Tal grunted. "Have you had any more chance to make sense of that?"

Davian shook his head ruefully. He had explained his vision to Tal early on, and both had agreed that Theshesseth must be the one to take him back. But he'd had a chance to simply win that fight, escape of his own accord and make the Vessels necessary to bring back everyone else. So why had he allowed Gassandrid to win, gone out of his way to speak to Nethgalla? Tal had already explained that Nethgalla would have made herself a target by creating the Tenets Vessel—Davian's mind still reeled at that; she and Scyner must have lied to Wirr's father about its origins all those years ago—but Tal thought that that would be a compelling argument for avoiding her, not going to her for help.

"Never mind. I'm sure you'll have a good reason," said Tal quietly.

Davian gave a slight, grateful smile at the unfeigned confidence in Tal's tone. The two of them had slipped easily back into the same roles they'd had in Deilannis, but the extra time—and the complete honesty in the relationship, now—had helped forge an even stronger bond between them.

"Do you really think that the Venerate will be able to send me back in time to speak with Asha, without me leaving Talan Gol?" asked Davian. That was what Gassandrid had said was going to happen, in his vision. Asha had never mentioned anything to suggest that Davian had done so—but then, he was going to warn her not to. And he hadn't exactly mentioned his vision of his fight with Gassandrid to her, either.

He and Tal had agreed on the most important thing to tell her if it happened, anyway: not to be tempted to leave the Tributary, even briefly, to come for him. Davian didn't think she would, given the potential consequences—but Tal had said that if the Venerate knew of their relationship, they would almost certainly try to exploit it. At the very least, his message might give her some measure of comfort that she was making the right decision.

Tal gave him a grim nod.

"If this escherii you mentioned is there, then I imagine so— he'll be powerful, no matter what I do to bind him when the time comes. And Gassandrid obviously has the mechanical knowledge to do it, given where and when we are. It will only work because Asha's so significant to you, but combine that with your ability to survive the time stream, and...yes. I'd say it should be easy enough."

Davian nodded slowly. That made sense—Zvaelar was continents away from Andarra, as well as in the past. "How do you think they'll do it?"

Tal eyed him, hearing the curiosity in his tone.

"You're thinking that you might be able to do it by yourself. Skip Ilshan Gathdel Teth entirely when you go back." When Davian shrugged an admission, Tal shook his head. "Once you're in the rift, it *might* be possible," he conceded, an abundance of caution in his tone. "It's true that we use the rift to travel through space with Gates—but there's a reason why only Gassandrid, Nethgalla, and I are able to make them. They're complicated. As in, study-for-centuries complicated—and even then you need an instinct for it," he emphasized. "Traveling through time is difficult enough on the mind. To do both, and with any degree of accuracy..." He shook his head. "There are good reasons why I haven't suggested trying."

Davian reluctantly conceded the point, absently putting his hands in his pockets.

"Speaking of good reasons," he said suddenly with a small grin, feeling the cool metal against his fingers, "Raeleth wasn't *entirely* truthful about not having material for a new Vessel yesterday." He produced the silver ring from his pocket and tossed it to Tal, quickly explaining as Tal's shocked expression gradually morphed into a genuine smile.

When Davian finished, he nodded delightedly. "That's excellent news, Davian. For those two to find some measure of happiness here is wonderful. And who knows? Maybe we won't get death threats every time we tease her about him, now."

Davian snorted. "I wouldn't count on that."

"You're probably right." Tal shook his head, chuckling. "Brave man."

"That's what I said." Davian hefted the ring cheerfully. "And more importantly, it means that Niha very likely gets back."

Tal's smile widened at the thought. "True." The expression slipped a little. "Maybe I do need to tell them that we have months rather than years, then. If their relationship is that serious..."

"They'll want to know," agreed Davian, sobering at the thought. Even if they did all get out, they would be returning to their own times. And Raeleth and Niha had been born millennia apart.

Tal examined the ring. "You made it into the wind Vessel?"

"I thought that made sense. A weapon for Niha, and I already knew that it would work."

Tal grunted approvingly, turning the metal over in his fingers. "Another extrapolation? I didn't think we'd covered anything quite so...aggressive, yet."

"Something like that." Davian shrugged. "It's hardly complicated compared to the time manipulation machinery."

"Still." Tal returned the ring to Davian. "I think that while you're working on that time Vessel, we'll start covering the next phase of your training."

Davian looked at him questioningly. "Next phase?"

"Offensive and defensive Vessels." Tal smiled slightly, eyes glinting. "Defense first. We can create Vessels to block Reading and Control. To prevent Essence from being drained from you. To establish a Disruption shield that requires no concentration. After that..." His smile widened. "Well. Imagine any of the Vessels you've ever seen in action. If you can learn the mechanisms..."

Davian swallowed, pulse quickening. He'd considered the possibilities before, of course, but his focus Vessel had largely kept his mind on the tasks at hand.

"What about those black chains? The ones which prevent us from using kan?" he asked suddenly. "Is there any way to stop those?"

Tal thought for a moment. "Perhaps. Those were Cyr's creation, but..." He shrugged. "We can certainly try."

Davian nodded. "When do we start?"

Tal gestured to the desk.

"We may as well start right now," he said cheerfully.

"Let's figure out how to turn you into a weapon."

Chapter 36

Wirr studied the map between him and Administrator Ithar dourly, lantern fighting the fading twilight outside, trying to ignore the doubt radiating like a physical wave from the older man.

"We must be missing something," Wirr said firmly. His eyes traced the line of the Devliss. "There must be *somewhere* the scouts can't see."

His stomach clenched as he caught the look in Ithar's eyes. It had been just over a day since they had emerged from the Gate that Caeden had made into this heavily forested valley, surrounded on three sides by the Menaath Mountains and on the other by the massive gorge yawning down to the white torrent that was the Devliss. The valley was on their maps—it formed part of the border with Desriel, after all—but was close to inaccessible by normal means.

"Perhaps you would like them to check underwater, Sire?" The frustration in Ithar's tone was unmistakable. "Even with these forests to hide in, the vantages we've found on the mountainsides provide a perfect view of the valley; any scout up there can see for miles. An army would have been spotted—even on *Desriel's* side of the river. There is *no one here*."

Wirr chewed his lip, not for the first time considering whether it was possible that Caeden had made a mistake. He certainly didn't think that they had been betrayed—there were far more effective ways to abuse their trust than simply sending them to the wrong spot—but if Desriel was about to cross the border here, or was even intending to in the near future, then there would surely be signs.

Was it possible that they had made their way through before the Andarrans' arrival, and were already into the mountain passes? He didn't think that was the case, either, and nor did Ithar. Armies of any significant size couldn't hide all traces of their passage.

Scyner, who had been sitting unobtrusively to the side next to Taeris, shifted. "If Tal'kamar says that there will be an attack, then there will be an attack," he said calmly.

"We cannot just leave. Caeden would not have sent us here for no reason," agreed Taeris.

Ithar ignored both the Augur and the Gifted. "You evidently trust this Tal'kamar. Caeden. Whatever his name is," he said, modifying his tone slightly, "and I do not doubt that the man believed the information that he gave you. But information—particularly information from only one source—can be *wrong*, Sire."

Wirr said nothing for a long moment. The concern in his most senior surviving Administrator's voice was not for no reason: though Ithar had had the foresight to bring as many supplies from the Tol as he could demand, those wouldn't last long. He was a former captain in the army, had even worked with General Oran years before. He understood the practicalities of their situation as well as anyone.

"How long can we stay here?" Wirr finally asked.

Ithar sighed. "Most of the soldiers are accustomed to foraging for themselves. Some of the Gifted and Administrators can, too. And I know that the Gifted can sacrifice a little of their Reserves to reduce the amount they need to eat. But even given that... a week? Perhaps ten days?"

"Then that's what we do. Find us a defensive position that assumes some sort of attack from across the gorge, and we'll make camp there tomorrow. If nothing has happened once we're established, and no more information has come to light, then we'll have to risk using the Travel Stones to open a portal to wherever Caeden is. See if we can find out more." Wirr glanced over at

Scyner, who gave the slightest nod in confirmation.

Ithar nodded reluctantly, too. "Sire." He stood, then paused.

"Sire, if I may say one more thing?" When Wirr gestured for him to proceed, he took a breath. "These men who have come with us...they've just lost most of the people they trust to lead them, and they are not stupid. They know there's not enough food to last. They've heard the reports about the Neskian invasion, the unrest down at Talmiel and the sightings of forces massing there. And they know that there should be no way that Desriel can attack where we are now. Plenty of them signed on to earn a wage more than protect their country, but...it still makes them uncomfortable when the one who's supposed to be in charge looks like he's giving illogical orders. *Especially* when he has no actual experience."

He shifted uncomfortably, rushing on before Wirr could respond. "A lot of them have families and homes in Ilin Illan. The Gifted and my people are on edge, too, given that you have *that*." He indicated the Oathstone hanging around Wirr's neck. "I don't mean to suggest that you're about to have full-blown infighting on your hands. But I've already heard people muttering. This group you have here...they don't like each other, and most of them don't like or trust you. A day will be fine, but much longer than that of sitting in one place would be...ambitious, is all I'm saying," he finished awkwardly.

"I understand," Wirr said simply. "Please do your best to keep everyone together. Thank you for your honesty."

Ithar ducked his head in a half-embarrassed, half-relieved way and left the tent to make his arrangements.

In the corner, Scyner shifted.

"Tal'kamar would not have made a mistake," he said quietly.

"I agree." Wirr met the Augur's gaze steadily. "But it hardly matters if we can't find the people we're meant to fight."

A gloomy silence followed the pronouncement. Caeden had given him the exact location of the Cyrarium, but it would take their scouts several days to get there and back to determine whether the Desrielites had somehow already reached it. And Caeden had been certain about Desriel's point of ingress, anyway, even if his Reading of Alaris hadn't provided every single detail.

Wirr stood, mind straying to the Tol once again. His stomach twisted; with the chaos of their arrival and the disconcerting discovery that there was no enemy to fight, the memory had settled uncomfortably into the back of his mind for the past few hours. Deldri was still there, and the defenses had almost certainly been destroyed by the eletai by now.

There was nothing he could do about it. Using the Travel Stone now would be premature; once used, the stones had to be charged with Essence by the same person to work again—which, practically, meant that they would be able to open the portal back to Caeden only once. So he just had to deal with what was in front of him, and hope that Caeden and Ishelle had figured something out in Ilin Illan.

"You don't think there's *any* chance he was wrong?" he asked eventually. "He got his information from another Venerate, after all. I don't believe that Caeden deceived us, but we have to at least consider the possibility that *he* was deceived. In that respect, Ithar's right." He shook his head. "We're talking about the fate of the entire country."

"We are talking about the fate of the world, Sire," said Scyner. "Make no mistake about that." He motioned to the chain around Wirr's neck. "If it comes down to it..."

"You know how much I respect your restraint with that power," Taeris added seriously, "but if the Gifted and Administrators stay in line, I'm sure that most of the soldiers will, too. If it comes to keeping this force together—"

"I know." Wirr didn't like the thought of compelling these people to do anything, but if it was a choice between that or letting the world be destroyed, he knew which way he would decide. "I'll do what's necessary. You have my word."

The scarred man opened his mouth to say something more.

A line of bright-white Essence appeared down the middle of the tent.

Wirr leaped back, as did Taeris; Scyner moved as well, digging furiously in his pocket for something. The line of white spun, expanded.

Created a hole in the air.

Taeris and Wirr both tapped Essence, tensed as Scyner finally drew his hand from his pocket, the white stone in his grasp shining brightly.

"It's all right," he said to the others quickly, though his expression remained wary until he saw the figure stepping through the hole in the air. The portal winked out behind the newcomer, and she held up her hands in amusement as she saw Taeris and Wirr poised to attack.

"I surrender," said Ishelle with a tired grin, tossing the matching black stone to a stunned-looking Scyner and walking over to a nearby seat.

There was a shocked hush for a full five seconds as Ishelle made herself comfortable.

"Ishelle. *What happened?*" Wirr asked, finally breaking the silence. His heart wrenched as fears that had been dormant for the past several hours came rushing back. "Why didn't anyone else come through with you? Are they—"

"They're fine," Ishelle assured him quickly. "Everyone's... homeless, but fine."

Wirr opened his mouth to ask what she meant but there was a commotion at the entrance to the tent, and suddenly Erran was pushing his way inside, ignoring the irritated protests of the guards posted outside.

"Ishelle?" Erran stared at her dazedly, looking unsure whether to be happy or concerned. He had been overseeing resource allocation and organizing leadership structures within the camp; his memories from his link to Elocien had come in handy, even if the knowledge that they were being used still made Wirr uncomfortable.

As, to some extent, did the Mark currently visible on Erran's left wrist. He had deliberately drawn enough Essence to bind himself to the Tenets as soon as they had arrived, insisting that Wirr's being able to communicate with him directly was too important for him not to. Wirr didn't disagree, necessarily, but still.

Erran's gaze went to the two stones in Scyner's hand. "I assume that's what I just felt? What are you doing here?"

Ishelle shrugged. "Thought you might want some company."

Erran made a face at her. "What happened at the Tol?" Erran hadn't seen the disruption to the Conduit—he'd already been through the Gate by that stage—but he knew about it from Wirr. "And why aren't you..." He gestured to his head.

"Caeden blocked the eletai. Hid me from them, somehow," said Ishelle. "He said that it won't last, but I can help here for a while, at least." Her voice was strong, but Wirr could see the fear in her eyes as she spoke.

"If there's even anything to help with," Wirr said grimly. He shrugged at Ishelle's querying expression. "There's been no sign of the Gil'shar or any Banes. They're either not here yet, or long gone."

"That...can't be true," Ishelle said slowly.

"It is," Erran assured her gloomily.

"No." Ishelle shook her head. "I mean, I can *feel* them." She closed her eyes, shuddering delicately before opening them again. "They're that way." She pointed west, in the direction of the gorge.

"They're not." Wirr felt his brow furrow. "We just got a report from our scouts, not more than twenty minutes ago. Unless they've made it closer in the half hour it took for the scouts to get back down here, there's nothing there."

Ishelle's frown deepened, and she sucked in a breath, closing her eyes again.

"They're near the river," she said softly. "Grounded. Keeping out of sight. They..." She shook her head. "They're...reorganizing their mind. Adapting, trying to cover lost information."

Wirr exchanged pensive glances with the other three. "What?"

"Their mind works as a single entity," said Ishelle, her eyes still closed. "When Caeden destroyed Ilin Illan, he killed more of the Hive than they've ever experienced before. They're disoriented, confused."

There was another silence, this one disbelieving. "*What?*" repeated Wirr.

Ishelle opened her eyes and took in their expressions. "Oh. Right."

She proceeded to tell them about Ilin Illan—about the Resolute Door falling and Caeden's scouring of the city.

"But they didn't breach the Tol?" asked Wirr, his voice shaking slightly.

Ishelle nodded at the unasked question. "As I said. No one inside was hurt."

Wirr released the breath he'd been holding, grateful for at least that much. Ilin Illan was gone, but he couldn't think about that now. "So the eletai are close," he said bleakly, turning his mind back to the most pressing danger. "Are they waiting for the Gil'shar?"

"No." Ishelle glanced westward once again.

"From what I can tell, they're already here too," she said quietly.

It only took a few minutes to find a scout capable of leading them to the best vantage point for the river, and soon enough they were away from the camp, pushing through snarls of branches and following their guide's path as the woman forged ahead confidently through the thick undergrowth.

After another half hour of hauling themselves up a narrow track and enduring a short climb, the scout gestured, looking vaguely irritated.

"See for yourselves," she said.

Wirr stared down at the glittering Devliss, heart sinking as he took in the rushing blue-white water at the bottom of the sheer gorge.

Ithar had been right: he could see for miles here, and there was...nothing.

"There." Ishelle pointed to a spot where the Devliss bent sharply. "There are eletai there. I can feel them."

Wirr squinted. "Beneath the trees on the far side?" The forest across the gorge was thick, and certainly had the potential to hide a large group, if they were being careful enough. It was the only spot in that area that provided any cover, though.

"No. Closer to the edge. Grounded, but definitely within sight of the water." She shivered, falling silent.

Taeris exchanged glances with Wirr. "A memory, perhaps?" he mused. "Could they already be past?"

"Ishelle?" Wirr watched the young woman cautiously. She claimed that Caeden had helped her resist the eletai, but even during the journey here he had noticed occasions when she had seemed distracted, staring vacantly and needing her name repeated several times to get her attention.

"No. I'm sure. What I'm seeing is right now," Ishelle insisted, urgency and frustration in her tone. "I know what *we're* seeing right now, but...it's an illusion of some kind. It has to be."

Wirr was about to say more when there was a flash from down below.

He paused, turning. "What was that?"

Taeris, who had been facing away from the river, followed his gaze. "I didn't see..."

He trailed off.

"What?"

Taeris was motioning urgently for the group to get down; Wirr did so with alacrity, relieved to see the others copying him. After a moment he spotted what Taeris had seen through the trees: a detachment of three Gil'shar, working their way up the same hillside the Andarrans had traversed only a few minutes before. They hadn't spotted Wirr and his people yet, but were clearly aiming for the same vantage point to survey the area.

"Back," murmured Wirr, jerking his head to the tree line behind them. He turned to the scout who had led them here. "Circle around. Make sure there aren't any others nearby."

The woman darted away without question as the rest of them scurried fifty feet back toward the trees. "Administrator Ithar. Administrator Kestig. Elder Tanavar. Tell those who need to know that there are Gil'shar soldiers on this side of the Devliss," said Wirr quietly as they dashed into cover, holding his image of the men firmly in his mind. "Tell them that the enemy are scouting from the position overlooking the river." He knew that it was too late to communicate caution to the entire army. Cooking fires already flickered in among the trees where the Andarrans had made camp. They were distant, but easy enough to spot.

He exhaled, every muscle tense, as the Gil'shar soldiers crested the rise only moments later. There was a sudden, odd increase in pressure in the air, and Wirr realized that one of the three men must have been carrying a Trap.

"Where in fates did they come from?" muttered Taeris as they peered out cautiously.

"Told you," responded Ishelle in a whisper.

Taeris shifted, watching the men worriedly. "We're going to

have to deal with them," he said. "Maybe take at least one of them prisoner, if we can. We need to understand what's going on."

Wirr shook his head. "They have a Trap. I'm useless here." At least his ability to command people worked through a Trap; that was something they had experimented with early on.

He hesitated, remembering the assassination attempt that Scyner had foiled, what seemed like a lifetime ago now. "Could you Control them? Force them to turn on each other?" he whispered to Ishelle. "Then we could send one back and have them report no sighting of us."

Ishelle considered. "The Trap wouldn't stop me," she agreed. She rubbed her neck. "But kan might draw their attention. The eletai's," she clarified uneasily.

Wirr closed his eyes, wishing Erran had come with them, or even Scyner for that matter. "Are you still willing?" It was a risk, but if they simply killed the scouts—assuming that they even could—then the enemy soldiers would soon be missed. It would be almost as good as announcing their presence anyway.

"Can't be afraid of them forever, I suppose," said Ishelle, the cheerfulness in her voice clearly forced.

She visibly braced herself, then focused on the group of men at the cliff's edge, who had just started to point and mutter excitedly among themselves. They'd spotted something below, and Wirr doubted there was anything much of interest in the valley save the Andarran army.

The soldier closest to the rear suddenly stiffened.

His blade whipped around in a shining arc and another of the men managed only a shocked gurgle as he fell, blood gushing from the gash in his throat. The soldier's other companion spun in alarm, sword making it halfway out of its sheath before a foot in his side sent him flailing, crashing over the edge of the cliff.

Wirr winced. The drop was fifty feet onto rocks.

"Well done," he murmured.

"Fates." Ishelle didn't look pleased; if anything, she looked terrified. Beads of sweat stood out starkly on her forehead, evidence of the concentration she was using to keep control of the final soldier. "I'm Reading him. The Desrielites *are* here," she whispered. "And they're expecting a report. Follow me. Quickly."

Before any of them could react, she was running, the Gil'shar soldier jogging ahead of her.

Wirr let out a curse and dashed after her.

The chase was a slow one, Ishelle too focused to hear their whispered pleading for an explanation, and Wirr not daring to call out any louder for her to stop. The constant worried glances he exchanged with Taeris indicated that neither of them was entirely certain she was even fully in control of herself anymore.

They descended the hillside rapidly, heading at an oblique angle to their camp, toward the gorge and the abandoned Darecian castle that sat decaying near its edge. After a few minutes there was a flash and Wirr and Taeris both gasped, skidding to a stop beside Ishelle as a strange sensation washed over them.

Wirr's blood went cold as his vision cleared and he took in a scene suddenly alive with noise and motion.

"Fates. *Fates*," whispered Taeris, the horror in his voice reflecting Wirr's feelings perfectly.

They had passed through the edge of what seemed to be some sort of invisibility bubble—an enormous one, stretching the entire width of the Devliss. Where moments before there had been only water rushing by below, now three wide, shining bridges of Essence spanned the gorge.

The two outer bridges teemed with marching soldiers, a steady flow of them emerging from the forests on the far side.

Worse, interspersed with them came Banes—hundreds of them. More. Dar'gaithin slithered among the Gil'shar soldiers, who sometimes glanced at them with some discomfort but otherwise seemed content to accept their presence. The flow of bodies moved steadily toward the castle, and Wirr could tell from the movement within that plenty of soldiers were already inside.

Wirr hurried after Ishelle, their presence at the fringe of the massive bubble unnoticed as they took cover in some thick scrub.

"What is this?" he muttered dazedly.

Ishelle didn't respond, her focus clearly still on Controlling the soldier striding back into the camp.

"More to the point, why is no one using the middle bridge?" asked Taeris softly.

He got his answer almost immediately.

The dense, gloomy forest on the far side of the Devliss shook, and Wirr swallowed down a wave of fear as a crowd of thickly grouped men and women appeared from the trees.

They were carrying…something. A dark column of perfectly square stone, wet and sickly black, almost invisible against the shadows from which it was emerging. As Wirr watched, some of those doing the carrying dropped to the ground; others who were walking alongside moved swiftly to take their place, ignoring those who had fallen as they put all their strength into moving the pillar forward.

Wirr didn't have to ask to know what it was.

He closed his eyes. "Kestig. Tell everyone that the invasion is confirmed. Tell them that the Desrielites have some sort of Vessel that shields them from view, and that they are crossing on bridges made of Essence. Right by the old Darecian castle." He swallowed as he took in the consequences of that simple statement. The Gil'shar, using Vessels. Using *Essence*. Caeden had warned him, but still.

Even if the Desrielites didn't have any Gifted on their side, it changed everything.

"Seen enough?" It was Ishelle, the words spoken through gritted teeth. "He's already reported that they didn't spot anything. I can bring him back with us if we leave now, but I can't hold this connection forever."

Everyone nodded, and they retreated cautiously, the terrifying sight vanishing as they crossed the border of the dome. The skin on the back of Wirr's neck prickled as they hurried through the forest back toward their camp.

His mind raced as he ran. They needed to mount an assault on those bridges immediately, before the majority of the Gil'shar could cross. Before all the Columns did, certainly.

"Asha," he murmured suddenly, slightly out of breath. "If you're with Caeden, tell him that the Desrielites *are* attacking— and that they have the Columns." He swallowed. "Tell him that we need all the help we can get here."

Erran had mentioned a while ago that Asha's Mark had returned before she'd entered the Tributary—but Wirr still knew that even if all had gone to plan and she was out again, he wasn't achieving much more than confirming to Caeden what the other man already knew. For the moment, though, it was all he could think to do. With the dar'gaithin and eletai against them, not to mention whatever other Vessels Desriel had at their disposal, this was a more desperate situation than Wirr's worst nightmares could have conjured.

They would still fight—of course they would. They had no choice.

But he simply didn't see how they could win.

Chapter 37

Wirr watched Ishelle worriedly as she sat off to the side.

She had handed Control of the Gil'shar soldier over to Erran as soon as they'd arrived back at camp, but the strain of holding off the eletai had clearly taken its toll; she was drawn, her gaze vacant as she sat numbly on a fallen log. Did they dare take her into battle? Wirr wasn't sure how much use she could even be in her current condition—but more concerningly, none of them really knew what would happen if the eletai broke through Caeden's blocks and truly got to her. If the creatures were somehow able to turn her...

"We need a detachment here." Ithar was poring over one of their rough maps of the region; he stabbed a point to the side of the Darecian castle, one that would provide a good view of the Essence bridges. "A hundred Gifted should do it. They can take advantage of the height, target any Gil'shar trying to reinforce."

Wirr nodded slowly. Erran had Read the soldier they'd captured; the man hadn't known a lot, but he had at least been able to give them a logistical overview of what they were facing. Ten thousand men. At least two thousand Banes, mostly dar'gaithin, but still including hundreds of eletai that were apparently continuing to swell their numbers using Desrielite prisoners.

And, of course, Vessels from the Gil'shar's holy Vault. One of their 'gods'—Alar—had appeared to them, emerging from the sealed Vault itself after two thousand years and proclaiming that it was time. Though Alar himself was supposed to have returned to lead them, the Gil'shar had finally decided to act without him. 535

The captured soldier didn't know the army's specific destination, but based on everything that Caeden had explained to Wirr, their purpose was clear enough.

There *was* some good news, at least. The invasion had only just begun, and the majority of the dar'gaithin were still on Desriel's side of the gorge; Taeris suspected, from their captive's observations, that the way their scales absorbed Essence meant that the bridges wouldn't be able to handle too many of them crossing at once. And the Vessels that were creating those bridges were, apparently, pulling their energy directly from willing soldiers—entire squads were being rotated through and drained hourly to keep them up, and those men and women would probably need at least a full day to recover from the experience.

That was probably why the Gil'shar had chosen to expend even more energy powering the massive invisibility shield, despite what should have been an incredibly low likelihood of an opposing force being nearby. This stage of their invasion was Andarra's best—and perhaps only—opportunity to stop them.

Ithar continued to outline positioning. They mostly didn't need to worry about the eletai for now; those that had not attacked Ilin Illan were still recovering from the shock of the Hive's loss there, according to Ishelle. And it appeared that the Desrielites hadn't bothered to send out any more scouts yet. As long as the Andarrans continued to use the thick forest as cover, they should be able to avoid detection for a few more hours.

That was probably all they had, though.

Time passed, discussions quick and tense as Ithar, Wirr, and Erran planned their best course of action, with Taeris, Scyner, and Ishelle contributing whenever they had something to add. They had several key advantages, but at the end of the day they were badly outnumbered and every moment that they delayed, more Desrielites and dar'gaithin were crossing into Andarra. The Columns, given what they'd seen earlier, were likely already on the Andarran side, too. If they had been just a little earlier—even a day—they could have held their side of the gorge, had the Augurs deconstruct the Essence bridges, and probably stopped all of this before it had truly begun.

But there was no time to mourn what could have been. It would be a true battle now, and there was nothing anyone could do about it.

"Can we afford to wait until dark?" asked Wirr worriedly as the plan finally began to take shape. "If they're intent on building their defenses around those Columns..."

"It's only a couple of hours; we'd need that time to get ourselves in position anyway. The darkness will make it harder for them to react, and hopefully—considering that they don't know we're here—it means that we'll start the battle with many of them asleep. The Gil'shar are zealots, but they haven't fought an actual war in generations. We have to hope that their discipline isn't all it could be." Ithar rubbed his face tiredly. "We don't have much longer than that, though, either—our captured friend says that the rest of his scouting group is supposed to be relieved at nightfall. And while we could probably buy more time by Controlling the next group, I wouldn't want to bet on our staying hidden forever. A thousand is just too large a force for that, even with the terrain here in our favor."

No one spoke, and then Ithar leaned forward again, frowning at the map worriedly.

"How are we going to deal with this invisibility Vessel?" he asked quietly, looking uncomfortable at the mere concept. "It's going to make a coordinated assault almost impossible. Can we destroy it?"

Scyner hesitated. "If we can find it, then perhaps. Though judging from what it can do, it's going to be bigger and more complex than any I've ever seen," he admitted. "It seems to be adapting to what was there before the army arrived, too—grass, trees, the castle, *everything*—and only concealing anything that came afterward." He shook his head, his admiration evident even through his concern.

Erran leaned forward. "What about the bridges?" He rubbed his forehead. "Are you sure we can cut them?"

"They're contained by kan, but they are being created dynamically. There's no way for them to be shielded with hardened kan," said Scyner confidently. "If what the prisoner says is true, Alaris himself was supposed to lead this attack—and if he had, then he could have protected the bridges and made this almost impossible. 537

But Tal'kamar dealt with him before he got here. On that count, we've been very fortunate."

The discussions went on from there for what felt like too long, though Wirr knew that it was important to go over every detail they could manage before time ran out. There was no room for error, here. They were outnumbered ten to one, and failure meant disaster on a scale that he could still barely comprehend.

Finally, though, the small arguments were settled, positions for the men were determined, and the plan was set. Ithar, for all the man's flaws, was calm and methodical now that the danger was apparent, willing to listen and outlining his own thoughts in clear, concise terms. Wirr found himself genuinely glad that the Administrator was there.

Outside the tent, the sun was beginning to dip below the horizon. Wirr stood.

"Prepare your men," he said to the group, a tight knot of worry in his chest.

"We attack as soon as everyone is in place."

Wirr gazed down on the moonlit waters of the Devliss, heart pounding as he searched for any sign of the thousands of troops he knew were nearby.

The Desrielites had continued their crossing into the evening; Wirr's best scout had sneaked inside the shield again and had reported that the enemy numbered at least three thousand troops on this side of the river now, including dar'gaithin. And more still came, each one another body that would need to be bypassed to take control of the Columns.

Wirr had to remind himself to breathe as he watched the deceptively calm scene below. The scouting groups sent out by the Desrielites were due back soon. Wirr's people had intercepted all the ones who would have discovered them—as far as they could tell, anyway—but most of the enemy soldiers had been killed, and their absence would not go unnoticed. The Andarrans absolutely had to strike before that happened.

Erran and Scyner were down there somewhere. The two men should be inside the shield by now, hopefully having figured out a way to destroy at least one of the Columns—or even to just cast one into the gorge, where it would surely be impossible for the Gil'shar to retrieve it.

But regardless of their success in that, their primary task was to look for the Vessel creating the invisibility shield.

It was risky, but both men were skilled Augurs and should be able to take care of themselves, even in the midst of the enemy camp. They would have to Read soldiers to find out more about the Vessel's location; once they knew where it was, Erran was to bring it down, while Scyner was to position himself by the bridges.

If the shield didn't come down, Wirr was to attack regardless. The damage they would be able to do was significantly less, though. They would have to bombard the encampment blindly and charge the areas marked out by their scouts, hoping to get inside the shield before the Gil'shar got organized.

Far from a perfect plan, but the best they could do at such short notice.

The silence stretched as Wirr lay on his stomach, watching grimly. After a few minutes he glanced across at Ithar, who nodded.

"Taeris, signal if you're in place and ready," he murmured.

There was a moment of nothing, and then a glimmer of Essence from the east, halfway up the slope that overlooked the Darecian castle.

"Nora, signal if you're in place and ready." An answering glimmer.

Three more times he gave the command, and three more times he got the desired answer. Everything was set.

He took a deep breath. "Erran. Take down the shield."

He gazed down at the scene below.

Nothing happened.

Wirr's dismay began to grow as seconds stretched into minutes. What was happening down there?

Beside him Ithar stirred, glancing across at Wirr. He didn't speak, but his expression said enough.

Wirr shook his head. "We have to give them more time."

"The Desrielite scouts are overdue." Ithar said the words softly. "If they get suspicious, get organized before we attack, then we fail."

Wirr scowled, turning back to stare down below, willing something to happen.

As if on command, a flicker of light broke the darkness. Wirr's breath caught as the light faded, and for a moment nothing happened.

Then there was a ripple of energy, white and sharp against the black, a thread of motion as the dome peeled back in a wave, washing over the scene below and revealing the enemy camp.

Wirr swallowed.

Thousands of tents were pitched below. Campfires dotted the area everywhere he looked, some burning bright and surrounded by soldiers, others guttering out. The distant sound of laughter and even faint, foreign music reached his ears, though that was dying as calls of bemusement began echoing up to their position, people apparently recognizing that their shield had stopped working. Inside the castle itself, Wirr could see violent, sharp flashes of Essence illuminating the walls. A battle, with nearby men streaming up toward the structure to join in.

Beyond the encampment, the three Essence bridges shone, their light refracted by the torrential waters of the Devliss below. Men still flowed across them, interspersed with darker shapes that Wirr assumed had to be dar'gaithin.

His heart wrenched as he looked down. This was war, and he felt a righteous anger at these invaders, these men who wished to destroy them all.

But he also felt sadness for them. Sadness that so many of them had been fooled by the Venerate, had been manipulated into this moment by forces beyond their comprehension.

Wirr closed his eyes, picturing the recipients of his message as clearly as he could.

"Now," he whispered.

The darkness was ripped apart by Essence.

The Desrielite camp burst into chaos as death rained from above and the sides; fires broke out among the tents and screams echoed through the valley as men and women scrambled to find their weapons, units trying to form up and soldiers sprinting toward where they thought the attacks were originating.

Word had clearly spread to the bridges; Wirr watched as men

and women poured across them now, intent on supporting their countrymen. Feeling sick, he waited until the bridges were full. The Gifted had been instructed to use as much as they could in that first strike; it had been effective, but they wouldn't be able to keep it up.

"Give the signal now, Nora," he said heavily.

Immediately a powerful burst of Essence shot into the sky, casting everything below in a stark white light. A few seconds passed; Wirr could see many of those below slowing, staring upward, wondering whether this was some kind of new attack.

Then the burning Essence of the three bridges vanished.

A hollow chorus of desperate screams filled the air as men and dar'gaithin alike plunged toward the white-topped river, the water churning silver in the moonlight as they flailed, their armor pulling them swiftly under.

Hundreds of lives, just like that. Wirr tore his gaze away and back to the battle, doing his best not to think about it.

He issued more commands as the fight continued, pinpointing weaknesses, taking occasional advice from Ithar but generally reacting as he saw fit. The scene below was chaotic in the dark, but the quick signals he had arranged with his people helped him to keep track of everyone, maneuvering them into the best positions to ambush any Desrielites foolish enough to try and counterattack.

They were still outnumbered—there were probably two thousand Desrielites remaining on this side of the river, not to mention dar'gaithin—and now Wirr could see pockets of space in which Essence was simply dying as it entered. Traps were finally being activated.

His throat tightened, but he gritted his teeth and kept directing as the Gil'shar forces began to show the first signs of organization within their ranks.

The real fight was only just beginning.

"Taeris, focus on your right flank!" snarled Wirr, one eye on the battle below as he dodged the Gil'shar soldier's blade.

He flicked out with Essence, relieved to find that there were no Traps in effect nearby, catching the man in the chest and tossing him more than thirty feet away. The soldier crashed hard against 541 the trunk of a thick tree and lay still, his neck at an unnatural angle to his body.

Wirr kept his blade up, eyes darting to the nearby trees, looking for any other threats. None came. This wasn't the first attack on their position, but it was the first by a group that had taken the time to circle around, using the surrounding brush for cover.

It had worked, too.

Blood still seeped from Ithar's chest as he stared glassily up at the night sky, the man's motionless form lying only a few feet from where Wirr was standing. Wirr gave him a silent, sorrowful nod before forcing himself back to what was happening below. That was all the respect there was time to show, right now.

The fight below was going well—better than it had any right to be—but it was still something of a stalemate, with none of Wirr's detachments getting anywhere near the five Columns. The Desrielites had focused their defense around them, easily resisting any pushes by the Andarrans to get to them.

Not that it was entirely clear how they were going to destroy them anyway. Wirr had already observed that the long square pillars absorbed Essence. Traps had been activated in a wide perimeter around them, too, blocking even attempts to hurl other physical objects at them. Early on he had seen several Gil'shar soldiers dashing for the Columns, even a group that had managed to get one hoisted before being cut down by their fellow men. Erran, or Scyner, or both of them had clearly been doing all they could down there.

That had been a half hour ago, though. The lack of further attempts was ominous, to say the least.

And now, step-by-step, the Andarrans were being driven back. The element of surprise and the darkness had worked in their favor, but now the Desrielites were awake, organized, and had adapted to their losses.

Wirr and his people were losing.

Movement behind him made him spin, Essence glowing at his fingertips as he made ready to blast anyone sneaking up on him. He quickly let his hand drop as he saw Ishelle's face emerging from the darkness, turning back to the scene below, scanning desperately for any important changes he might have missed in the intervening seconds.

"Prince Torin." Ishelle sounded out of breath as she scrambled up beside him; he could almost hear the pause in her voice as she spotted Ithar's corpse. "Fates. Are you..."

"I'm fine." Wirr didn't take his eyes from the scene below. "I could use someone to watch my back, but you should be down there fighting. Why are you here?"

"I didn't know how else to get you a message." Ishelle's voice was full of dread. "The eletai are stirring."

Wirr turned to face her this time, concentration broken.

Her eyes had turned a dark, cloudy gray.

"Fates," he muttered, turning away again. "I'm sorry, Ishelle. How long do we have before they attack?"

"Not long." Ishelle's face was pale as she gazed down on the slaughter. This was probably the first time that she was fully aware of just how little progress they had made. "Is extra time even going to matter?"

"Probably not." The eletai joining the battle would mean annihilation for the Andarran forces. "Nora, move a hundred feet toward the river and put your soldiers out front. Tell your team that there's a detachment of Gil'shar trying to circle around in that direction, and that they likely have a Trap."

Ishelle watched him pensively. "When do we retreat?"

Wirr rubbed his eyes, which were red and dry from staring so intently at the scene below. How long had it been, now? Hours, certainly. The lightening sky in the east told him that dawn was approaching. What little advantage they had left—the Gil'shar's uncertainty surrounding their enemy's numbers—would soon disappear, too.

"Now," he said softly, despairingly. "If what you say is true, then it has to be now."

They'd done miraculously well—killed ten of the enemy for every one of their people who had fallen, he thought—but it still hadn't been enough. This had been their best chance. Now they would have to draw back, regroup, and try to figure out a way to fight along the path to the Cyrarium instead.

But the Desrielites would know that they were here. They would never again have the advantages they'd had tonight.

He began giving the orders, trying to implement all that he'd been taught, moving his forces methodically back so that they deliberately sagged away from the worst of the fighting, not exposing themselves to any hard counterattacks. As he'd expected, though, the Desrielites were content to let them withdraw. They knew as well as Wirr that they didn't need to overextend themselves, and were likely also cautious of some kind of secondary trap. From their perspective, this attack would have appeared highly coordinated. They were hardly to know that it had been put together in a matter of a couple of hours.

He watched for a few minutes, making occasional adjustments but pleased to see that their losses during the withdrawal were minimal. Two of his first-choice communication recipients had been killed, along with one of his secondaries, but he had managed to divert others into those groups quickly enough that everyone had remained synchronized throughout.

Beside him, Ishelle gasped.

He turned to her, about to ask what was wrong but instead following her horrified gaze.

Dawn was brightening the mountains behind them, but across the river, it illuminated a cloud of dark specks swirling upward, rising from the forest in Desriel.

Wirr stared numbly, knowing what it meant but almost too tired to properly take it in.

"How many?" he whispered. There had to be at least two hundred eletai in the swarm, maybe more.

"All of them. All the ones who are left." Ishelle's voice was hollow. "They don't want to, but they've been compelled."

She looked at him, meeting his gaze. For the first time since he had met her, she seemed... at peace. Completely clear, in control.

"Tell Davian he missed out," she said, the sadness in her eyes belying her lightness of tone. She hesitated. "And that I died a hero, of course. Don't forget that part."

"What are you talking about?" Wirr asked in bewilderment.

Ishelle closed her eyes, a tear leaking out of the left one. Her

brow furrowed in concentration.

She crumpled to the ground.

For a second Wirr stood frozen. Then he threw himself forward, skidding to his knees beside Ishelle's limp form, rolling her over onto her back. Sightless eyes gazed up at the steadily lightening sky, and her chest didn't move. He funneled Essence—what little he could still afford—into her, but there was nothing to fix.

It was as if she had simply...given up.

He ran his hands through his hair as he knelt there, bent over her body, gazing despairingly. What had just happened?

A thundering, rippling cheer suddenly went up from the soldiers below as the Desrielites spotted what Ishelle had a minute earlier, eletai blackening the skies now as they streaked across the river. Wirr tore himself from his position and hurried back to the edge of the cliff, staring down at his retreating forces, which were still being harried by dar'gaithin. Whether that was due to orders or bloodlust, Wirr had no idea.

Men and women in Gil'shar uniform held up weapons in triumph as the eletai passed overhead, flying low and fast.

Wirr's stomach twisted at the sight. The creatures were too fast. Even with the orderly retreat, he didn't see how the Andarrans could possibly survive this.

He held an image of his officers in his mind. "Everyone, keep to the trees and watch the skies. Do your best to stay under cover..."

He trailed off.

Panicked screams had started intermingling with the cheers below.

He squinted, looking urgently for the source of the sound, and quickly spotted it.

Eletai had broken off from the main pack and were swooping hard at targets on the far side of the Desrielite camp—dar'gaithin, Wirr realized with bemused shock. The snakelike creatures themselves seemed equally confused, slithering around agitatedly and lashing out at any of the eletai that came near them, though the eletai seemed intent on attacking from a distance, their glistening spear-like limbs ejecting viciously from their bodies. To Wirr's astonishment, those spears were penetrating the dar'gaithin's armor. Many of the serpentine creatures already lay still.

His gaze traveled to the main group of eletai, heartbeat quickening as he spotted the creatures diving at the dar'gaithin pursuing his people, too, screeches of anger and confusion echoing up to him. These attacks were at a greater cost to the eletai as they swooped low beneath the trees, many of them not rising again after they disappeared beneath the leafy canopy.

Chaos reigned below as the Desrielites reacted to what was happening, their attacks stuttering to a stop, retreating hurriedly into more defensible positions. They didn't seem to be under threat from the eletai—but, miraculously, nor did Wirr's people.

He swallowed the knot in his throat, casting another glance at Ishelle's body.

This *had* to have been her doing. Some final sacrifice that had allowed her to influence the creatures. He didn't know much about the eletai—none of them did, really—but it was the only explanation he could come up with.

He quickly reassessed the battlefield below. The Gil'shar weren't pressing anymore, intent on helping the dar'gaithin fight off the eletai now, though even with the humans joining the fray, the eletai seemed intent on killing only the other Banes.

The Columns still lay at the entrance to the castle, protected by a crowd of dar'gaithin and soldiers alike. The fighting was thickest there, a furious flurry of motion. Wirr had no way of telling who was winning.

He closed his eyes. His people were tired, hurt and depleted. The Gifted had expended the vast majority of their energy. It felt unfair to ask them to attack again...and yet, this might be their best remaining opportunity.

He opened his mouth to give the order.

Light blossomed from across the river.

Wirr's heart plummeted as three broad lines of solid Essence began creeping outward over the gorge, the bridges inexorably reforming, soldiers marching onto them before they were even complete. He stared desperately, willing them to be extinguished again. Where were Erran and Scyner? Keeping those bridges down had been one of their primary jobs; all they'd had to do was keep out of sight and disrupt any attempts to remake them.

"Everyone, draw back." There was no getting to the river's edge to meet the soldiers there, and even if they did, there would be *thousands* flooding across now.

He watched for a while in silence, exhaustion battling with his need to figure out what happened next. The struggle between eletai and dar'gaithin slowly resolved itself; a significant number of the dar'gaithin appeared to have died in the clash, though the vast majority of the eletai had as well. The ground through the trees below was littered with mangled black bodies.

Finally the last of the eletai—a dozen, perhaps?—limped into the air, movements sluggish and erratic. A hail of arrows and spears chased them, bringing a couple of more to the ground before the rest retreated—northward, Wirr noted with vague concern, rather than back to Desriel. There wouldn't be anyone for miles in that direction, but he still preferred that none of the creatures take refuge anywhere in Andarra.

The Desrielites showed no sign of trying to pursue the Andarrans, despite their reinforcements, once again content to simply surround the Columns. Wirr could sense their agitation even from this far away, but it was of little comfort to him.

He gave Ishelle's body one last, grateful glance, and hurried away to rejoin what remained of Andarra's forces.

Chapter 38

Asha drew in a deep lungful of fresh sea air, sitting on the edge of the cliff overlooking the pulsing Boundary, trying to adjust to her surroundings as Caeden worked at the Tributary behind her.

She was free. No more Shifts. No more feeling helpless whenever she remembered where she was, caught between wondering how things were going out here and trying not to think about it. It was a hard concept to grasp, even as she stared out over the sun-drenched island and beyond, across the gently undulating blue to the shining barrier that hid Talan Gol from view.

She absently touched her arm, feeling for wounds that had already disappeared. Would she heal as fast once Ilseth was connected to her? There was no way to measure exactly how much the Tributary had been taking from her Reserve, nor—as Caeden had warned her—how much Essence would be lost to decay in the transferal process. He was confident that she would still at least be a match for any Gifted, but to what degree she would be stronger was still to be seen.

She glanced behind her, stomach churning at the sight of Ilseth's pallid, slack-jawed expression as he lay slumped inside the open, coffin-like Tributary, his round glasses gone, eyes staring blankly into nothing. Only the regular rise and fall of his chest indicated that there was any life in him at all. Behind him, though the needles had retracted, she could still glimpse dark-red smears marring the inside of the capsule.

They had a few hours' grace, Caeden said, before Asha's absence triggered any disruption to the Boundary—he'd assured her that the Essence already stored in the Cyrarium would provide enough of a buffer to keep it up for at least that long. He'd gone on for a while about flow and efficiency and support machinery, too, but that was more to himself as he'd verbalized his calculations, and there was no point in distracting him by asking him to explain further.

Her gaze slid to Caeden, who was inside the pavilion, bright flashes of light illuminating the interior as he worked at separating the dok'en from the machinery. As she watched he gave a grunt of satisfaction, pulling away a flat disc the size of his palm, staring at it before pocketing it.

He turned, seeing her watching, and gave a tight smile. "Done." He squinted at her. "How are you feeling?"

"Still a little disoriented," admitted Asha.

"That's natural." Caeden moved down the steps, picking up a pair of torcs from the ground as he did so.

Asha eyed them uneasily. Caeden had already examined the Vessels that the Lyth had created, confirming that they appeared to be as promised—and noting that it wasn't in the Lyth's interests for them to be otherwise, anyway. A helpful reminder, if not enough to entirely dispel her concerns.

Caeden paused, then proffered one of the torcs. Asha took it, examining it with a frown. It was simply made, rough in places and constructed from solid iron. On each point, a small cube of metal had tiny inscriptions on it in a language she didn't recognize.

Asha turned the Vessel over in her hands. "Why torcs?"

Caeden rubbed his forehead. "The shape lends itself to a Vessel. Not much material necessary, but bigger than a bracelet or ring, and the space between allows for some complex kan with anchors on both sides. The Darecians were the first ones to figure that out, actually. They chose torcs, specifically, because they were a sign of status amongst their people. The old princes of Dareci used to wear them..." He trailed off.

Asha considered the information, vaguely surprised to find that she understood what Caeden was saying. She'd read enough about the nature of kan and its uses over the past year to follow the logic on at least a basic level, now.

"I suppose it's a design that makes sense for anything you need to wear," concluded Asha. She raised it to her arm. "So just like a Shackle?"

"No." Caeden shook his head. "This one goes around the neck." He smiled slightly at her expression. "Don't worry. It won't seal to you the way a Shackle would; Garadis didn't bother building in anything so complex as changing its physical structure. You just wear it."

Asha hesitated. "How will it feel?"

"I honestly don't know. But it shouldn't hurt," Caeden said gently.

Asha nodded, then, at an encouraging gesture from Caeden, carefully slipped the iron around her neck.

It was cold against her skin, and she flinched at the contact, but nothing happened as she fastened it. Caeden watched her silently, and Asha realized with some discomfort that he was making sure there was no obvious danger in simply wearing it.

Then he walked back over to Ilseth. "Ready?"

Asha steeled herself. "Ready."

Caeden pulled Ilseth's limp form forward slightly and slipped the other torc around the man's neck. Then he moved to the side, and pressed his hand against the steel edge of the Tributary.

The razor-thin needles ejected into Ilseth, pushing smoothly through his body and protruding, wicked hooks forming on their edges to hold the body in place. The grisly sight was quickly concealed from view as the opening melted closed, sealing Ilseth inside, accompanied by a low grinding as pieces of metal shifted and slid, gradually forming the massive image of the wolf's head.

For a brief second, nothing happened.

Then Essence deliberately, smoothly began to drain away from her, and the Tributary began to glow an eerie blue.

Her breath caught, and she forced herself to calm, closing her eyes and studying the flow. It had started as a trickle but already, within ten seconds, had strengthened to a steady stream.

And then within the next ten, an unsettling torrent.

The ocean of Essence within her began to dim. Shrink.

She opened her eyes again, looking over at Caeden. "There's a lot going out. My Reserve is getting smaller." She couldn't keep the concern from her tone.

"The Cyrarium is refilling. This is the equivalent of a Shift—it fills the buffer before easing off. It will take a few minutes to normalize," Caeden said confidently.

Asha glanced up at the pavilion; inside, the Tributary was making periodic grinding sounds as pieces shifted and recalibrated, the eerie blue light pulsing bright one moment, then completely vanishing the next. She bit her lip, but conceded to herself that she had to trust the redheaded man. "If you're sure." She took another steadying breath. "How long to make a Gate to Wirr?"

"Another couple of hours." Caeden was already at work. "I wouldn't want to leave before making sure that everything was operating as it should, anyway."

Asha acknowledged the statement, then walked back over to the edge of the cliff, peering down the path to the village below. It seemed like a lifetime ago that she'd leaped from here, dashing among the trees and flinging tek'ryl to their deaths wherever she could in defense of the Shadows. "Are they still down there?"

"I saw people walking around when I got here," Caeden reassured her.

Asha nodded absently, her gaze traveling to the massive open expanse between the village and the ocean. The villagers had plainly planted some crops in the fields she had razed, but mostly the ground remained bare, devoid of life.

"So the tek'ryl..."

"There haven't been any more." Caeden joined her at the edge. "I've checked in now and then to make sure. Of all the Banes, they are the ones with the least intelligence. They barely take instructions let alone think for themselves, but their senses are excellent. They were probably curious about this island for weeks, and so when you and Erran activated that bridge when you first came here, it must have been enough to draw them in numbers." He scratched his head. "The Venerate wouldn't know that, though. They might be aware that the creatures have disappeared, may even assume that they're dead—but they wouldn't know why, or where it happened. Too many Banes got through the Boundary and were killed; I doubt that it will have set off any alarms in Ilshan Gathdel Teth."

Asha continued to stare down at the buildings, considering. "I'd like to go down and talk to them. To the Shadows."

Caeden looked at her in surprise. "Why?"

"Because we have time while you make a Gate. And because they deserve to know what's going on. They're part of the reason that this has been possible, remember." She shrugged at his dubious expression. "They might also be willing to help—to come with us. They probably still have those Vessels from when they fought the Blind."

Caeden considered. "Don't tell them anything too specific about the Venerate. Or about me," he added, almost sheepishly. "They can know about the invasion, and that the Gil'shar are trying to bring the Boundary down. But sharing anything more will require...explanation."

Asha nodded brusquely. She understood Caeden's concerns.

Caeden made to turn back to his task, then hesitated. "And if you feel anything. *Anything* strange," he emphasized, "you get back up here and tell me straight away."

Asha nodded again, trying not to let the instruction make her anxious.

She left Caeden and headed down the steep path, blinking when she recognized the massive crater she'd left from her rapid descent last time. She was about halfway down when a shout from below indicated that she had been spotted; by the time she had reached the bottom a small, worried-looking crowd had gathered. Shana's familiar face—a little older than the last time Asha had seen her—was among those at the front.

"Ashalia?" Her eyes traveled back up the mountain, toward where the Tributary lay. "Is something wrong?" There was unmistakable tension in her tone.

"No," Asha replied quickly. She dithered. "Or...well, yes. But the Boundary is still secure."

A relieved murmur went up from the gathered crowd. Shana gave Asha a tight smile, though she seemed less convinced than the rest of them. "How?" She crossed her arms, a worried stance rather than a defensive one. "What's changed?"

Asha spent the next ten minutes explaining what she could of the situation. The need to stop the Gil'shar invasion. The fact that she was still supplying the Boundary, but doing it remotely now.

When she had finished, Shana looked thoughtful.

"We still have our Vessels. I can't speak for anyone else here," she said, "but I will go with you." She glanced around, raising her voice. "Spread the word. You only have...an hour?" She gave a questioning glance to Asha, who quickly concurred. "An hour to decide whether you want to help. But there is no shame if you stay."

"What about the Shadraehin?" someone called suddenly. "Is there any word from him?"

Asha barely managed to repress her scowl. Even after all this time, the Shadows still didn't know that Scyner had been little more than a puppet for Nethgalla—and worse, they still thought of him as someone to look up to. A hero.

She considered, as she had before, correcting that misconception...and once again she realized the futility of it. Its best outcome would be that the Shadows trusted Scyner less, but it could just as easily result in their losing faith in Asha instead. Scyner had been the one to help them, to give them food and shelter and hope, for *years* before she had even seen the inside of the Sanctuary. If she made these people choose between her and him, it was easy to imagine which way things would go.

"The Shadraehin is fighting too," she said, feeling vaguely dirty for using their misconceptions to encourage them. "He is already with Prince Torin at the defenses."

Another murmur went up, this one sounding more enthusiastic, a few people nodding to themselves.

"Go and let everyone else know. Discuss it with your families," Shana said loudly. "Everyone who wishes to fight, be back here in an hour."

Asha watched as people dispersed. "How many do you think will come?"

Shana shrugged, her expression not hopeful. "They want to help, but...we've had to work harder to get by, here, since the tek'ryl. Some of them have families, children who depend on them. I hope you will not blame them if they choose to stay."

"Of course not." She glanced at Shana. "You're sure you wish to join us?" Shana had a family, if Asha remembered correctly. A husband and child.

"I've had this discussion with Parth many times," Shana said quietly. "We always knew this day might come—not these exact circumstances, but we knew that we wouldn't be able to hide here forever. And I'm the...*leader* is the wrong word, but in the Shadraehin's absence, I seem to be left with most of the decisions. If I don't go, it's not a good precedent." She bit her lip. "Before Sed, I probably would never have considered it. But now...I don't see it as being any different from choosing the Sanctuary in the first place. I just couldn't forgive myself if I had the chance to make a difference for the world he'll grow up in, and I chose not to try."

Asha nodded. She could hear the reluctant determination in Shana's voice.

Once everyone had dispersed, Shana left to speak with Parth, leaving Asha to her own devices. She wandered for a while, out past the buildings and into the still-scorched fields, all the while nervously keeping one eye on the energy steadily draining away from her. It seemed that Caeden had been right about the initial rush: though the amount flowing from her remained unsettlingly high, it was no longer causing the pool of Essence she could draw upon to diminish. If anything, since the flow had eased, that pool had actually increased again.

After a half hour, she was confident that it was stable, and the result was...pleasing. She could certainly see that the amount of Essence she could now tap was diminished, but her Reserve was still vast beyond any other Gifted's wildest dreams.

She glanced up toward the top of the mountain, then back at the Boundary towering above the ocean. She would be joining Wirr soon. Going into battle. Her body had recovered rapidly from the abuse of the Tributary, but she hadn't actually *used* Essence since emerging—not for the past year, in fact.

Now that the flow was steady, it was probably wise to practice at least once before leaping into a fight.

She stopped in the middle of the barren field, closing her eyes, examining the interlocked pools of Essence within her. No different from when she had accessed them in the dok'en.

Carefully, she tapped Essence, keeping an eye on the amount vanishing into the ether. It didn't seem to falter, so she drew a little more, focusing and spinning the energy around her left hand, delicate strands twisting and meshing into a tight-fitting, golden glove.

She flexed her hand, a slow, excited smile spreading across her lips as the armor moved with her, just as strong and flexible as it had been in the dok'en. She'd known in theory that everything in the dok'en should work just as it did in real life, and yet some part of her had doubted. Worried that all the research she had done, her progress, all the work she had put in over the past year had been nothing more than an illusion.

Her smile growing, she tapped her Reserve again, this time without trying to limit herself.

Power sprang to life around her, the armor forming itself to her, settling into her skin with a familiar, thrilling warmth. An Essence blade appeared in her hands by instinct and she stretched, the feeling of pure life flowing across her body energizing. She spotted a small clump of trees on the horizon and aimed at it, breaking into a run.

To her delight, her speed was undiminished from what it had been in the dok'en, too.

She spent the next few minutes excitedly going through some of the simple training exercises Elli had shown her, keeping a close eye on her Reserve, testing each physical limit to see how it compared to what she expected. A few felt slightly different—she couldn't leap quite as high as she'd been able to in the dok'en, for example— but her reaction times, her speed and strength, all seemed intact.

And through it all, her Reserve remained completely steady.

After a few minutes she caught motion from the corner of her eye; she paused, then stopped with a flush as she realized that a small crowd had gathered at the edge of the village, the vast majority watching with awestruck expressions.

She went through a couple of more exercises, more out of stubbornness than anything else, before letting the Essence armor drop. She'd never particularly enjoyed being the center of attention, and after spending a year with only Elli for company, she found herself distinctly uncomfortable with an audience.

She jogged back toward the group, spotting Shana at the edge of the crowd, which had grown to a few dozen people now. She approached the woman with a half-embarrassed smile.

"That wasn't meant to be a spectacle," she said ruefully.

Shana grinned. "If you say so. And it worked," she added, softly enough that the others couldn't hear. "It's reminded them—all of us—of what happened when you came here. Fates, fifteen minutes ago, half of the people here were trying to convince me that I shouldn't be letting anyone go. Now they're convinced that they'll be safer with you."

Asha frowned. "Definitely not true," she assured Shana.

"I know," Shana said with a small chuckle. "But showing them the kind of strength that they will be fighting alongside—rather than focusing on all the dangers they'll be facing—has made a difference."

They stared out over the open expanse of scarred fields. A few patches of green poked up here and there, but even those were dotted with brown. It was clear that the crops were struggling.

"Are you getting enough food here?" Asha asked quietly.

"We're getting by," Shana said, the prevarication in her tone answer enough. "Next winter will be...interesting, though. Hard. We've tilled the soil, planted what we could from other areas of the island. But this section was our best-producing farmland. It will take a few years before it's back to the way it was." She gestured, preempting Asha's apology. "Not your fault."

"Yes it is," said Asha ruefully. She gazed at the plants struggling to grow in the blasted soil, crouching beside one and placing her hand against the earth.

She had learned the theory for this one idle afternoon in the dok'en—a book by a farming specialist, surprisingly interesting given its subject matter. It wasn't too different from healing someone.

Carefully she let Essence flow into the ground, into the roots of a struggling plant, letting it soak up the energy.

As she watched, green returned to its leaves, and thin new branches began shooting outward.

Asha hesitated, then closed her eyes and tapped more of her Reserve. More than she had to create her armor, more than she

557

had since she had emerged from the Tributary. She did so carefully, gently, but it still didn't seem to disrupt the flow to Ilseth.

She began pouring Essence into the ground.

Gasps came from behind her, followed by excited chattering. Asha let Essence drain away from her, flooding the fields with energy, infusing the dirt and coaxing seed and root to life. It was a simple use of Essence; even if she wasn't doing it as efficiently as someone with experience could have, the sheer breadth of the power she was able to access made that irrelevant.

The murmuring behind her grew until it crescendoed into joyful shouts.

When Asha finally opened her eyes, green fields spread away almost as far as she could see.

She turned, and the expression on Shana's face—and those behind her—brought a genuine smile to her face, for what felt like the first time in a long time.

Shana finally tore her gaze from the lush fields, smiling too as she gave a deep, thankful nod to Asha.

"That will help," she said approvingly.

"The least I could do." A warm feeling of accomplishment spread through her as she watched the excitement on the Shadows' faces. Since the moment she had been tied to the Siphon, everything she had done had been about fighting. About helping Andarra win.

This... this felt *right*, in a way none of that ever had.

She spoke for a while longer with Shana as more people gathered behind them, the murmuring continuing around astonished, delighted exclamations as newcomers spotted the sea of green spreading out toward the ocean.

Soon enough, though, their time was up. Asha watched as Shana knelt down by her young son, enveloping him in a long hug of farewell as Parth did the same with her. Elsewhere, shoulders shook with quiet sobs as families said their good-byes. Asha watched it all uneasily, heart wrenching as she realized that some of these people she'd just convinced to join her would likely not be coming home.

Once everyone was ready, they made their way up the long path to the top of the mountain. There were perhaps a hundred

Shadows with Vessels, all told: more than she'd expected, by a long way. Even Shana had worn a vaguely surprised look as she'd assessed the crowd.

Once they had gathered on the upper plateau outside the pavilion, Caeden—who had apparently just completed his task—ran an eye over them with an approving expression.

"They'll be useful," he conceded to Asha. He studied her. "I saw what you did below," he added quietly. "Well done."

Asha inclined her head slightly to the compliment.

Caeden turned, gesturing, and the Gate he had prepared blinked to life.

The Shadows stepped back as the blue light spun and widened, forming a circle through which a forest hazed into existence, visible only through the portal in the air. They would all have seen something similar when they had come here—Scyner had used Travel Stones to bring them from the Sanctuary, after all—but seeing it happen without the use of a Vessel still elicited hushed, awed murmurs.

Caeden gestured for the Shadows to start moving through. "It's safe," he assured Shana. "You'll come out more than a mile from where I sent Prince Torin, in an isolated part of the forest. There shouldn't be anyone around."

Shana nodded, barking some instructions of her own. The Shadows started cautiously through.

The process didn't take long, and soon enough it was only Caeden and Asha still standing on the plateau.

"Time to go," said Caeden.

Asha took one last glance around, her gaze lingering on the pavilion at the far end of the mountaintop. It still glowed a solid blue, outlined by the pulsing white illumination of the Boundary beyond.

She wasn't going to miss that view.

She took a deep breath, and stepped through the Gate.

Chapter 39

Davian woke to thundering crashes and the sensation of falling.

He flailed his arms wildly, failing to prevent his side from smashing into the steel floor of the tower, which continued to shake and boom with terrifying intensity, furniture in the room tipping and scattering and crashing everywhere. He lay in momentary shock before rolling to a crouch, activating his strength Vessel as he did so.

Energy flooded to his limbs, the Vessel improving and regulating the Essence flow to optimize his increased strength and agility. Another tremor. Eight months since he'd arrived in Zvaelar and while they were coming daily now, this one was worse than any he'd experienced by far. He braced himself against the still-trembling steel floor and looked up at the roof warily. Tal had assured him that these structures had been designed specifically to withstand the shaking—it was built into the Vessels—but for perhaps the first time, he briefly feared that the tower was about to collapse in upon itself.

He waited for the rumbling to fade and then got smoothly to his feet, directing Essence into the endpoint of his invisibility Vessel before hurrying out the door.

The screams reached his ears before he hit the stairs.

His heart stopped and he raced down the winding staircase as quickly as he dared, reaching the bottom and skidding to a halt outside the room that contained the portal.

Inside was blinding chaos.

Tal and Niha stood just inside the doorway, both of them

entirely focused on the room as brilliantly shining metal plates blurred, reconfiguring. Davian's stomach churned as he caught a brief glimpse of what they were trying to cover: a pool of Dark, seeping up through a gap in the ground and crawling over the steel, drinking in Essence wherever it touched. It had covered almost half the floor.

The screams had cut off, but Davian could see mounds beneath the writhing, wet black that looked human shaped. Right where the Gifted would have been lying as they took their shift. The portal still glimmered on the far wall, only ten feet from the crawling darkness now.

He let his invisibility drop. "What can I do?" He didn't know if any of the Gifted were still alive elsewhere, but this wasn't the time for caution.

"Get out." The strain in Tal's voice was evident.

Davian didn't argue; he didn't know enough about the workings of these Vessels to be of any practical assistance, and Tal wasn't the type to refuse help if he thought it would make a difference. He dashed out the door, then turned and took another few steps back, watching in awe.

Glimmering red steel flew from the roof and walls, the upper section of the tower gradually dismantling itself, plates rearranging at a dizzying rate as another tremor—this one less severe, but still noticeable—shook the ground beneath him. He felt a vague, dazed sense of loss as he spotted the desk in Tal's room topple and then disappear into where he knew the pool of Dark lay. He'd been working on several new plans, all of them stored in those drawers.

He could see Tal and Niha now, taking step after agonizingly slow step back, the tower's walls dissembling and reforming at dizzying speeds as they worked. It wasn't a tower anymore, really. More of a steel dome, less than half the height it had been previously.

Finally, the last piece of steel snapped into place with a crackling hiss, and Tal's shoulders slumped. Davian hurried over to lend a shoulder as he staggered. He looked as tired as Davian had ever seen him.

"It will hold." Tal gazed at the shining steel mound, looking
briefly at Niha—who had slumped to her knees, clearly spent—

before starting to pour Essence into it again, sweat on his brow. "For now."

"What happened?"

"The tremor caused a disruption. A split second where two plates weren't properly connected," said Tal distractedly, grimacing as he swayed beneath the force of another tremor, the rumbling of Zvaelar intensifying. "Dark broke through, dissolved some of the mechanism. It all happened so fast."

"We were just outside," added Niha, staggering to her feet again. "It was almost our shift. No one inside stood a chance," she finished, speaking louder to be heard over the noise.

Davian opened his mouth to say more, but stopped as he spotted Raeleth staggering toward them from the direction of the forge, which apparently still stood.

"Niha," he gasped urgently, slowing to a halt and putting his hands on his knees as he saw the remains of the tower. "What's happening?"

Niha quickly repeated what Tal had told Davian. Raeleth's face paled.

"How long?"

Tal shook his head. "A few hours before it collapses; it's taking more Essence than before and I can't provide enough for long. This is a patch, nothing more."

"And then?"

Tal flinched as another thundering crack echoed around the city. "This all ends. We need to—"

Pain.

Davian's mind went blank at the searing fire that slashed across his face, blinding him, the blow leaving him dizzy as he heard urgent shouts and then felt hands grabbing his arms and dragging him back. He struggled instinctively, feeling hot blood gushing down his cheek before suddenly there was Essence and the pain was easing, flesh knitting back together.

He activated the pain Vessel in the nape of his neck and gasped, fighting to sit up straight, wiping desperately at the sticky blood as his vision gradually returned. The injury was still tender to the touch, even with the Vessel's dampening effect active. It was going to be unpleasant when he turned that Vessel off again.

"What..."

"Al'goriat." Niha spoke; she and Raeleth were both kneeling beside him. "We were all so focused on the tower that we didn't think to watch them."

"The suppression of the time corruption isn't as strong now. They can get closer," added Tal from behind them, still working at providing Essence to the mound of steel.

Davian propped himself up on an elbow, gazing out at the sea of al'goriat, which were now only twenty feet from the newly made steel dome. Several of the creatures' bodies lay, motionless, significantly farther from where the rest were crowding forward.

Niha held up her hand, waggling the finger on which the silver ring sat. "About time I got to try it out," she said with a small smile. It faded quickly. "But I only have enough left for another blast or two. Helping fix that tower took most of my Reserve."

Davian nodded dazedly, still focused on the mass of agitated Banes. The number of the creatures patrolling here had continued to increase, particularly after the metal had stopped coming. Tal suspected—and Davian agreed, however heavyheartedly—that the new al'goriat were probably the last survivors from the scavenging groups, sacrificed once the dar'gaithin were satisfied that the city had been picked clean.

He groaned. "The steel we were going to use," he said to Niha. "It was inside."

Niha glanced over at Tal, who rolled up his sleeve, removing the three bands around his arm.

"You can remake these," he said, waggling them for Raeleth to take.

Niha leaned forward, wiping the blood from Davian's cheek. "That cut isn't healing properly," she said, moving as if to put more Essence into it.

Davian pushed her hand away gently. "You're going to need everything you can get in the next few hours," he said, scrambling to his feet and taking the metal bands from Raeleth. He kept his movements confident as he pushed the metal onto his arm, concealing it beneath his shirt, though his stomach churned and a feeling of dread slowly enveloped him as he considered what was coming.

He wasn't ready. After all this time, after months and months of study and practice, he *still* couldn't make Vessels perfect enough to withstand the Darklands. It just *wasn't possible.*

Tal glanced at them, then nodded to the distance. "Theshesseth."

Davian spotted the Bane's form slithering rapidly through the al'goriat. Theshesseth was one of only three remaining dar'gaithin in Zvaelar, the others having been executed after returning with food. Theshesseth was the only one who wasn't often in the crater, though. To their ongoing amusement, Tal thought it was probably because the creature was still scouring the city for Davian.

"Well. It's not as if we can delay this any longer, I suppose," Davian said in grim acknowledgment, using his sleeve to clean the rest of the blood from his face. "Probably best if you stay back and just let him take me through the portal. No point in making this more complicated than it needs to be." He eyed the metal dome. "Is there a way inside?"

"I'll open one when you need it," Tal assured him.

"Thanks. Time to go, then." Davian took a steadying breath. "Look after them," he added to Niha.

Niha chuckled, though to Davian's surprise there was a slight cracking of emotion in the sound.

"Don't forget to activate those Vessels of yours as soon as you get back. They'll probably deactivate going through the rift."

"I know."

"Keep an eye on that cut, too. It really doesn't look like it's going to heal properly."

"I will."

"And be careful with Nethgalla. From what Tal says, she's—"

"Come on, my love," said Raeleth, grabbing Niha's arm and pulling her away. "He's a grown man." He cast a glance back over Niha's head, giving Davian a wink that belied the concern in his eyes.

Tal made to follow, then glanced over his shoulder.

"If we're right then you'll come back to the same point in time that you leave here, but it could be anywhere along the perimeter," Tal reminded him. "Those al'goriat will be able to get closer as the dampening here weakens, and that Dark under the tower's only going to get worse, too, so...you know. Don't take too long."

Davian gave him a tight grin. "I'll do my best."

He walked away from the others and toward Theshesseth, who was almost at the inner edge of the al'goriat. The dar'gaithin spotted him, freezing in sheer disbelief before slithering forward at an alarming pace.

"On your knees," hissed Theshesseth over yet another crashing rumble as he got within earshot.

Davian knelt.

"So I guess you finally caught me," he said calmly.

Traveling back, the time stream was nothing like how it had been in Deilannis.

Maneuvering through the current back then had been like swimming in a river; this was like being swept over a waterfall. Tal had warned him that that might be the case: time was already working hard to correct itself here, was likely to violently latch on to anything out of place. Davian fought desperately to maintain his sense of balance as he kept watch for the telltale beacon of light that he knew he needed to move toward. Even with all his practice focusing over the past eight months, it was a strain to keep everything straight as he was tossed about.

He could still sense Theshesseth, too, somehow clinging to him through it all. The creature was using him as a guide, making sure he didn't get lost in time like all the other dar'gaithin before him. That made sense; Davian vaguely recalled Rethgar's being told to forewarn the creature about this part. It was no doubt why Theshesseth had been so obsessive in his search for Davian, knowing that the only way that he could return with his mind intact was by finding him.

Of course, Theshesseth didn't know what happened once they got back. The brief thought sent a shiver through Davian, almost making him lose his concentration. He'd lived for so long with the certain knowledge that there was something still to happen, something to come before he went back in time and died at Tal's

hand.

That event was about to be in the past.

The light in the distance was there abruptly, almost blinding in the gray. He willed himself forward, across the raging current toward it.

Then he was on the floor, cold steel at his back, sharp pain slashing at his cheek, eyes so tired he couldn't pry them open. Couldn't move. He thought he sensed movement somewhere nearby but it was a distant thought, hazy.

He reached out on instinct.

Suddenly Essence was flooding into him, restoring his energy; he drew more and more, feeling the power course through him, bringing life back into every limb. The fire along his cheek eased to a dull ache; a slight burning sensation on his left arm told him that the act of healing himself had restored his Mark, too. An irritation, but unavoidable.

He was still stiff, sore all over, but not so much that he needed to reactivate his pain Vessel. He finally pried his eyes open to see a serpentine face peering down at him.

"On your feet," hissed Theshesseth, spite and anger still in his tone, apparently not inclined to show any gratitude for having been brought back safely.

Davian breathed out, recovering, then sluggishly levered himself up, noting the heavy quivering of the air around him, the thrum pressing down on his ears. He was far too close to the distortion of the portal to try out his time manipulation Vessel just yet. Instead he cautiously activated his focus Vessel to steady himself, and then reached out for kan.

He almost stumbled.

Kan was there—*everywhere*—so easy to grasp that it was almost comical. He smiled despite himself as he manipulated the dark energy, effortlessly creating lines so fine that they would be invisible to even another Augur.

"Where have you been?" snarled the dar'gaithin, face inches from Davian's. The rage in Theshesseth's eyes was unmistakable. "Where did you hide?"

Davian took a breath, and gazed back calmly. "Around. It really wasn't that hard."

Theshesseth continued to glare. "You seem unconcerned, 567

given that you have just left your friends to die." He waited for a reaction and then when he didn't get one, made a disgusted sound and shoved Davian forward, forcing him to walk down the tunnel, away from the portal. "You would be wise to reconsider your disrespectful attitude. Lord Gassandrid will not stand for it, and he will undoubtedly be wondering at the delay in our return."

Davian shrugged off Theshesseth's scaled hand absently, still focused on his surroundings. "I'll have to just explain to him that I liked it there. Good people, interesting place. Great exercise. No point in leaving *too* quickly."

Theshesseth scowled, as much as that was possible with his reptilian visage. "You fear this less than you should," he snarled, the restrained anger in his voice evident. He seemed irritated that Davian wasn't intimidated by him. A strange thought, given that Davian knew he wasn't long from killing the creature.

"Funny. I was about to say the same to you," observed Davian distractedly, still studying the metal surrounding them. Metal from Zvaelar. Maybe some that he himself had collected.

"Why here, Theshesseth? Darkstone everywhere in this cursed city, but in these hallways, metal that never rusts. To what purpose?"

He knew exactly why; the words were spoken partially to feign ignorance, and partially to give him an excuse to gawp, to walk unhurriedly as he gazed around at the steel. He pressed through kan, hearing Theshesseth's voice but not really listening to the creature's response, instead examining the underlying structure of the plates that surrounded them.

He restrained a relieved smile. He remembered his initial trip down here, looking at the lines of kan threaded through the metal and being bemused by the overwhelming complexity of it all. But this...this was comprehensible now. Still a web of fine lines, but logically laid out, even simple in places. Had he ever thought that *this* was beyond his grasp?

Much of the kan was, unsurprisingly, related to time: a suppression mechanism, creating a barrier around the portal. A safety measure like the tower back in Zvaelar—the time corruption emanating from the portal was unstable, and this was to prevent it from spreading.

Other parts of the machinery allowed for minor physical manipulation of the steel, he quickly noticed. It appeared that there were alternate passageways down here, hidden but easily opened by activating the right sequence of endpoints. He couldn't determine where those led, but it was useful information. There would presumably be less traffic, far less chance of discovery if he took those during his intended flight back down here.

They walked in silence for a while, Davian still focusing on the mechanisms around him. Some of the plates were fitted together very specifically; the kan running through them made for a bigger, interconnected system. Gradually, he began to grasp just how much effort had been put into restricting the effects of Zvaelar from bleeding through. As much metal as there was down here, none of it had gone to waste.

Gassandrid's failed experiment had taken much to prevent it from becoming an unmitigated disaster.

Was there some way to use that? Probably not. The effects of a dying Zvaelar here would likely end up spreading too far if unleashed, killing everyone in Ilshan Gathdel Teth and maybe beyond. Enemies or not, he wasn't about to do that.

He contemplated. His biggest problem, of course, remained the Vessels that he needed to create. He resisted the urge to check the three bands of Zvaelar-forged metal sitting snugly around his left bicep. His ability to access and control kan here *was* significantly better, almost laughably so. And yet...the level of perfection required for all three Vessels was still out of reach.

He sighed, gazing at Theshesseth absently. If only he had a way to replicate those scales; they had apparently protected the dar'gaithin perfectly during the transition through time.

Then it struck him.

He absolutely could.

His heart skipped a beat, and his mind raced now as they walked. Would it work? Was it even possible? He knew it would be simple enough for Tal, assuming that he had the right Vessel. But Niha and Raeleth? Davian chewed his lip worriedly, his expectations of what was about to happen adjusting.

So *this* was why he'd chosen to fight Gassandrid. To let the Venerate win.

They climbed a set of winding stairs, the ground underfoot changing rapidly from grimy to spotless. Davian finally released kan and looked around. After so long in the dust and grit of Zvaelar, he couldn't help but admire the cleanliness.

"You really need to tell whoever cleans up here about those stairs. It's *much* nicer up here," he quipped cheerfully, attempting to mask his nervousness. It had been simple, before. He'd known he was going to meet Gassandrid, known that he would kill Theshesseth and speak to Nethgalla afterward. He had assumed that when he asked her to get him out, that was all he would need from her.

What he was considering now was *much* harder.

He thought furiously. Would Nethgalla really risk that much for him, simply on the strength of his having revealed where Caeden would be? Tal had been the one to first suggest passing that message to Asha, assuring him that it was the only way to put the Ath heavily enough in Davian's debt to secure her help. Finding Tal was, apparently, her obsession—the one thing she actually cared about, the only currency he thought she would recognize. And as Tal had also pointed out, simply telling her that the aim was to save him wouldn't work. In the present, he had already escaped Zvaelar regardless of whether she helped.

Davian had still been hesitant to risk Tal and Asar's plan, but as his friend had somewhat heavily noted: if Asha was in the Tributary, then it meant that something had already gone terribly wrong at the Wells, and Asar was likely dead. If that was going to happen anyway, then they might as well reap the benefits of being the ones to give Nethgalla the information.

Theshesseth glanced at him again as they approached the doors. The creature looked distinctly unsettled—unsurprising, all things considered. He still had no idea how Davian had hidden from him. He'd probably expected Davian to be broken after his time in Zvaelar, grateful to be out, and intimidated by having to meet with one of the Venerate again.

Theshesseth opened the door, and Davian walked calmly into the dazzling, cleanly lit room beyond.

It was just as he remembered it: comprised entirely of steel plates, with blue Essence pulsing in the tiny gaps, holding the structure together in its current configuration. Davian made certain to move leisurely, pushing through kan again and quickly examining the surrounding plates. Again he was surprised at the simplicity of the design, shocked that he hadn't been able to recognize the purpose of most of the endpoints before, even if a few did remain a mystery. As he already knew from his vision, the room could easily be reconfigured.

He forced himself to saunter, to show as much disrespect to Gassandrid as he could. Tal had often mentioned Gassandrid's vanity—but had also warned him that the man was as astute as anyone alive. He needed the Venerate angry, distracted. Unable to see that Davian had a plan, or of what he was now truly capable.

Gassandrid's dozen puppets rose as one as he entered. The sight—the knowledge of what they were—still caused Davian to shiver.

"Gassandrids," he said cheerfully, continuing to examine the metal plates carefully. He would need to activate them in quick succession after his time Vessel. He was confident in the Vessel's efficacy, but he couldn't be figuring out which endpoints did what once he started.

Gassandrid talked at him but Davian ignored the conversation for the most part, responding only when he had to and trying to keep his answers as light and infuriating as possible. He remembered the gist—idle threats combined with more pretense to being 'right.' Tal said that Gassandrid truly believed he was on the side that was doing the right thing, but these speeches...they felt forced. Davian thought Raeleth would describe Gassandrid as a man who was trying to convince *himself*, rather than Davian. The type who, by converting others, could feel better about their own actions.

Once Davian was comfortable that he knew what he had to do, he focused again on the blank faces in front of him, which were looking at him expectantly.

"Is there any order?" he asked, not really remembering what had just been said. Not that it mattered greatly.

"Order?" It was the child who spoke. Davian gazed at her, his insides twisting, though he made certain not to show it. Gassandrid had taken her life, because he simply didn't think it was worth anything. Davian's memory of this fight, the vision he'd had, was mostly a blur—but her, he always remembered.

"When you speak," explained Davian patiently, "I can't figure it out. Are you choosing people at random? I mean, what about this fellow over here? He's said nothing the entire—"

There was the slightest signal from one of the men, and Davian grunted as a great weight hit him across his shoulders. Despite his muscular bulk, the blow forced him to his knees.

"Impertinence, we can ignore. Waste our time again, though, and you will be punished."

Davian growled, remembering from his vision what they had been asking about now. Still looking for the Shadraehin, then, even after all this time. Tal had agreed that the Venerate must already know that she was really Nethgalla—and know that she had been instrumental in so much of what had been going on for the past twenty years, too. Tracing her through her identities was, apparently, the only reliable way to find her.

And—if she was caught—Tal had said that she would be brought before Shammaeloth. That because of her nature, she would be compelled to talk. To reveal everything she knew.

Which made her presence right here, in the heart of Talan Gol and under the noses of the Venerate, all the more concerning.

"I keep telling you. I don't *know* who she is. I never had any contact with this 'Shadraehin.' I can't tell you what she looks like, or sounds like, or smells like, or…" He forced himself back to his feet, pretending to struggle, though in reality the blow hadn't been anything his Zvaelar-hardened body couldn't take. "You see what I'm saying?"

"We know," said the old woman off to the left. "We also know that you know those who can tell."

"You're talking about Asha?" Davian made certain to sound amused, as if he didn't understand what they were really asking. "Isn't that the entire reason you want the Shadraehin, though? So that she can tell you where Asha is? I'm confused. So you want me to find Asha so that she can tell you what the Shadraehin looks like, so that you can find the Shadraehin in order to make her tell you where Asha is?" He sighed theatrically. "I think you're making that process needlessly complicated. Possibly some circular logic in there. You really need to—"

He was expecting the blow but this one still stung, leaving black spots dancing in his vision.

"You can go back." Gassandrid's puppets were unmoved by the violence, though he saw a glimmer of irritation reflected in all their eyes. "To a time when you know where she is. A time when she would not be so guarded."

Davian continued to feign ignorance. "Unless something's happened to the Boundary—ilshara, whatever you want to call it—I'm not entirely sure how you expect to get me to Deilannis."

"We can send you back from here."

"Here?" Davian forced a laugh. "When you split up that mind of yours, Gassandrid, I think you forgot part of it." It was strange, hearing himself say the same words with identical inflection to his vision: last time he hadn't been in control, but this time...this time everything just came out that way. He *felt* in control, but as soon as the words were uttered, he remembered saying them in just that manner.

He felt the Essence channel itself into the plate behind him, raising it as one of Gassandrid's puppets moved with kan-enhanced speed toward him, slamming him with surprising strength up against the wall. Davian thought he could probably have stopped him, but he remembered this part all too well. There was no point trying to change it. He didn't *want* to change it.

"It can be done. Little is impossible for the dead," whispered the man.

"I'm sure that's comforting to your puppet here," gasped Davian.

The man growled, releasing Davian and letting him slide back to his feet. "You will go back to Ashalia Chaedris. You will mark her; physical contact will echo across time, and the sha'teth will find her."

"Even saying that I believe that's possible. Which I don't," Davian added, wondering if he was pushing the idea of his ignorance too far, "there is nothing you can threaten me with. I know you cannot kill me."

"Cannot?" Though only one of them spoke, all of them sneered. "Your head will be on a pike soon enough. Do not mistake prudence for inability, traitor."

Davian blinked; he'd forgotten that jibe. Far more unsettling, this time.

Still, it didn't matter. It was time to act; Gassandrid was going to start pressing about his time in Zvaelar soon, and Davian didn't want to risk any of the Venerate trying to Read him. If they did, it would be only a matter of time before they discovered his inbuilt Vessels.

"Let's find out if that's true, then," he muttered.

He breathed deep, and activated the Vessel in his left arm for the first time.

Time stopped.

The abruptness and ease with which everything froze around him came as a shock, even expecting it as he had been. This had always been so *difficult* in Ilshan Gathdel Teth, and yet right now he wasn't even using kan himself.

He breathed out, then turned to the dar'gaithin beside him.

The most important part came first: killing Theshesseth.

Stomach churning a little, he ripped a scale from the dar'gaithin, using the wicked edge as a blade and plunging it into the creature's eye. Dark blood began to spurt as he turned, draining the Essence from the man to his left. Each of Gassandrid's proxies pulsed with the same Essence signature; Davian knew this room's endpoints were protected from just anyone tampering with it, but he had to assume that Gassandrid's Essence would be compatible with them.

He went to one knee and slammed his hand against the plate on which he was standing, guiding Gassandrid's Essence into the nearest Initiation endpoint. Blue lines streaked out from it.

Suddenly, Davian had control of the room.

He immediately shifted the metal plates beneath Gassandrid's proxies, throwing them off balance. He wasn't aiming to win this fight, but he did need to convince Gassandrid that he was trying to.

The floor beneath the eleven—the twelfth was just a pile of dust, now—dropped away, leveling out with the steel that he was standing on. Moments later, concern and shock registered on all of their faces as they began to fall.

Then something changed. Though time evidently still flowed

around him—the geyser of black blood continued to creep its way out of Theshesseth's face—the others in the room were suddenly moving faster. Still not as fast as Davian, but close.

Several landed, catlike, on their feet, but the rest were unbalanced enough to stumble and slip to the floor. Davian dove forward before they could recover, slashing left and right with the dar'gaithin scale. Bright-red blood appeared on each neck he cut, the scale razor sharp everywhere but the dripping black root where he held it. The acid burned his hand, but he ignored it.

A redheaded man—one of the ones who had landed on their feet—sprang at him from the left. Davian moved to the side and caught the assailant by his left arm, spinning and hurling him with all his strength. The arm that he was gripping snapped; the man flew gracelessly through the air, tangling with an older woman before colliding hard with a steel wall and sliding to the ground in a heap.

Davian snatched more Essence and slammed his palm into the ground again; the floor rippled once more, snapping upward beneath the feet of a man and a woman rushing toward him. The plates kept rising after the two had lost their balance, pressing them against the roof with incredible force.

There was an unpleasant squelching sound. When the steel floor lowered again, only bright-red viscera remained.

He turned to face his next opponent, only to hesitate.

The young girl stood in front of him after having finally regained her footing, eyes wide as she watched him.

The hesitation was all Gassandrid needed. Without warning the floor beneath Davian twisted; he tripped as chains emerged from the steel, rising up and wrapping around his torso. They burned; immediately Davian's sense of Essence was lost. He roared, partly in frustration, but it was mostly an act as he pretended to try and free himself.

Then he let himself calm and closed his eyes. Breathed.

Stopped the internal Essence flowing to his Vessel and let time wash over him again.

There was utter silence.

"Wonderful!" The redheaded man who had been thrown to the far side of the room stood, straightening his misshapen arm with a slight grimace. There was a flash of Essence and he flexed his fingers, the break healed. "Your progress is impressive. Better than I could have dreamed."

Davian kept his face smooth. Gassandrid must have been wondering whether he had been training in Zvaelar—probably why he hadn't used the kan-blocking chains as soon as Davian had walked in. He clearly had no idea that Davian had been using Vessels, though. "I'm glad you approve."

The child in front of him brushed her clothes, though there was no dust in here, no grime to speak of at all. "Tomorrow, Davian. Tomorrow you will go back and you will meet with Ashalia Chaedris." She placed a hand against one of the steel plates; it pulsed with blue light for a moment and then part of the wall slid aside, revealing another doorway.

"Aniria. Please escort our friend to his new accommodations and then clean this up," she said, satisfaction in her tone.

Nethgalla—Davian was certain it was Nethgalla; she still wore the same form as when he'd last seen her, though the scandalously scant clothing was certainly different—entered the room with head bowed. Her surrounds, clearly, were not unusual enough to throw her. "Of course, Lord Gassandrid."

She took Davian's bloodied hand, ignoring the dar'gaithin scale in the other, and calmly led him to the exit.

"That must have been quite a performance," she murmured once they were through, sweeping back a strand of long blonde hair. "But I have to admit, I am curious. Why the charade? Why allow them to send you back?"

Davian studied her. She must have been using her ability to listen in on at least some of the proceedings—perhaps even to watch. Had she somehow spotted that he was holding back when Gassandrid had not, or was she simply assuming something about his abilities after his performance against Metaniel?

"Because you said that you owed me nothing," Davian replied. "But I don't believe that is true anymore. My name—my real name—is Davian." He waited for Nethgalla's eyes to widen with surprised recognition, then nodded. "Now figure out a way to get me out of here, Nethgalla."

576   Nethgalla stared at him, clearly taken aback.

"Well," she murmured. "So that is how you knew he'd be in the Wells. I wondered when that debt would be due." She sighed. "And I will pay. But I cannot simply get you out of Talan Gol. The Venerate will know if I open a Gate—"

"I'm not talking about Talan Gol. Or even the city," said Davian bluntly. "I just need to get out of *here* for a few days after I talk to Asha tomorrow." He knew that last part would happen, now, else Nethgalla wouldn't have reacted the way she had. "Somewhere safe, but nearby. Somewhere they won't find me and put me back in Zvaelar. Not until you've finished helping me, anyway."

Nethgalla's eyebrows rose, though she looked more amused than shocked. "And what else, precisely, do you imagine I can do for you?"

"I need you to figure out how to make a Vessel that will allow someone—anyone—to shape-shift into a particular form."

Nethgalla stared at him blankly. "That's tricky, but I still don't understand why you need me."

Davian braced himself, then looked her in the eye.

"Because I want that form to be a dar'gaithin," he said grimly.

Chapter 40

Nethgalla came to a stop, staring at Davian blankly, completely silent.

"*What?*" she said eventually, though she kept her voice quiet enough not to penetrate too far down the steel-encased hallway. She glanced around before Davian could respond, looking caught between apprehension and confusion. Then she grabbed him by the arm, pulling him forward. "We cannot talk about this here. Come with me."

Davian resisted for a moment, a flash of nerves suddenly reminding him that he no longer knew what was coming next. Was no longer able to lean on the comfort of a vision that was yet to happen. He eventually relented, though, allowing Nethgalla to guide him on. She seemed at ease here, making turns with confidence, nodding to the occasional man or woman as they passed and receiving friendly enough acknowledgments in return.

Nethgalla slowed after a few minutes, glancing around and noting the lack of other people near them. They seemed to have been heading to a less-populated area of the complex, judging by the steadily dwindling traffic.

"When you get out, you'll need to find your way back here," Nethgalla murmured, gesturing almost imperceptibly to a hallway they were passing. Davian could see an end to the steel corridor as they walked by, a rough-hewn darkstone passage continuing on. "Take the second left; after a while you'll see a hole in the wall—you'll have to crawl, but you should fit. It leads to a small room, completely isolated. Safe. Wait there, and I'll find you."

She paused to check that he understood, then was nudging him past and forward once again.

"I'm surprised to see you still here in this form," said Davian as they walked, taking advantage of the empty hallway. "Eight months is a long time to be keeping up a lie so close to Gassandrid. Especially when he seems to be searching for you."

Nethgalla eyed him. "Eight months?" She shook her head. "It hasn't even been one."

Davian's stride faltered. Tal had warned him that time in the real world would be passing at a different pace—it was broken in Zvaelar, after all—but it still came as a shock.

He swallowed. It was good news, he supposed. He'd learned an enormous amount in Zvaelar: probably the equivalent of years of study, given his use of the focus Vessel as well. And yet he hadn't lost much time since he'd first been taken from Tel'Tarthen, what seemed like an eternity ago.

He was still grappling with the thought when they arrived at the cells.

Davian recognized them immediately for what they were; though they were made of steel like everything else, a quick examination showed that the mechanisms were blocked off by hardened kan, completely inaccessible once one was inside. Nethgalla nudged him through the door and then stepped inside herself, shutting it behind them. Immediately she straightened, her vaguely submissive pose vanished.

She crossed her arms, studying him.

"I hope you realize how dangerous this is for me," she said. She held up a hand as he made to talk. "And before you claim that you don't care, you should know that I'm trying to find a way to get them to move Licanius. Trying to help Tal get back the blade that *you* lost," she added pointedly.

Davian snorted; the jab was a little unfair, but at least he knew why Nethgalla was here now. "I wasn't intending to make things more difficult," he observed drily. "So you know where it is?"

Nethgalla grimaced, her confident facade slipping for once.

"It is with . . . *him*," she said. The way she said the last word, her voice dropping to an uncomfortable near whisper, made it clear to whom she was referring. "In his sanctuary beneath the city. That is all I have been able to discern, for now."

Davian filed away the information. "And Tal was the one who sent you?"

"Yes."

Davian restrained a glare at the sudden pain in his forehead, a sure indicator that the woman was lying and trying to keep it from him. He said nothing, though. If she didn't know about his ability, then there was no point in giving it away—certainly not to dispute something that he wasn't entirely sure mattered, anyway. She was looking for a way to get Licanius to Tal. That was good enough.

"Now," said Nethgalla, fixing him with a stare. "You want my help to do *what*, exactly? Because I'm quite certain that I didn't hear you correctly the first time."

Davian took a deep breath.

"I want to figure out if it's possible to shape-shift into a dar'gaithin," he said firmly. The plan *was* crazy—even he had to admit that—but it was all he could think to do. "And then if it is, I want to build three Vessels that will allow others to do it. I have Theshesseth's Imprint, now, but I don't have the knowledge. Shape-shifting, as far as I can tell, must take different types of endpoints—different kan structures. Ones I'm not yet familiar with."

Nethgalla's frown turned considering.

"You weren't idle while you were gone, were you," she murmured, giving him a reassessing look. "You're not just stronger. You've been *taught*."

Davian deliberated. Nethgalla was in love with Tal. Her knowing that this was all to assist him would probably help convince her.

He briefly explained about his time in Zvaelar, about why he had come back—and why he wanted to return. Nethgalla listened in silence as he went over the training he'd received thus far.

"I haven't been taught shape-shifting, though," he said. "It's clearly different. I don't know the kan structures that make it possible. I can *do* it, but it's on instinct. And it's not as if I can observe the lines as they activate on my own body."

Nethgalla studied him. "So you've shape-shifted before?"

"Yes."

"Good. That's a start." Nethgalla's expression was thoughtful now. "What else do you know about it?"

Davian hesitated.

"I know that you need to kill someone to take their Imprint," he said reluctantly. He'd suspected that for a long time, but his discussions with Tal in Zvaelar had confirmed it. "Other than that, though, not a lot. Even Tal didn't seem to really understand it properly. It's..." He trailed off, shrugging helplessly.

"It's the dirty secret of kan," finished Nethgalla. "No one understands it because they don't *want* to. It doesn't fit their conception of how kan should work, doesn't follow the same clean, logical rules. Everyone likes to believe that kan is pure mechanics. The very idea of there being an unknown to it makes them uneasy." She looked at him seriously. "It's also why I cannot be certain that this Vessel you wish to make is actually possible."

Davian's breath caught. "But you're going to help me try," he said, trying to reaffirm rather than question.

"I am. I am even inclined to believe it *might* work, given that I cannot think of any other way Tal could get out of Zvaelar. And if nothing else, it is an...intriguing project." Nethgalla leaned forward, tapping her lips, looking thoughtful as she gazed at Davian with piercing blue eyes.

"The source is the key," she said, her tone turning instructive. "When a kan user extinguishes a source, there's a moment of... connection to it. It's something..." She gestured, sighing. "I hesitate to call it spiritual, but that may very well be the best word for it. It is a bond that follows rules, but rules which are upheld in ways that we still do not fully comprehend. Through mechanisms which operate beyond our understanding."

Davian's heart sank somewhat at the description. "So this link to someone's source is what allows you to shape-shift into them?"

"Something like that. The connection is only for an instant, but it gives you a sort of...deep memory of the other source. A true understanding of it. What we call the Imprint." Nethgalla made a face, indicating that she was dissatisfied with how she was explaining what she knew of the process. "It's not a physical description of the person—that comes from your memory, and can be imperfect—it's more about…who that person *was*. Shape-shifting is a transformation down to the very core, and the Imprint is what allows for it. It's why I have been able to hide from the Venerate for so long, too. Shape-shifting affects Traces; changing into a new body doesn't affect your Essence signature but the Trace still takes a couple of days to adjust, to become useful in tracking again. And it cannot track someone who has shape-shifted at all, if the Imprint was taken after the Essence sample."

Davian nodded. That made sense; it lined up with what he'd read in Deilannis, as well as Tal's use of shape-shifting to hide from the other Venerate, back then. Though Tal had admitted since that it had also been part of his training to escape from Talan Gol, ensuring that he had practiced enough to swiftly and reliably shape-shift into a new, untraceable body before his memories vanished.

"So we need to figure out how to transfer this 'source memory' from me into a Vessel," he said slowly. "And then figure out the kan necessary to activate it."

Nethgalla considered. "Yes. It's more complicated than that, but…yes," she said eventually. "It is as strange a plan as I have ever heard, and yet…it may work."

Davian exhaled. He'd thought that he could convince the Ath to help—Tal's rescue had been a simple enough motivator—but it had been far from a guaranteed thing.

"And you think you can figure out the kan structures?"

Nethgalla nodded, more confident now. "I've never codified them before—not for a Vessel. But it *is* possible to shape-shift others, assuming that they are willing participants. I've even shown one of your Augurs how to do so, and he's done it successfully a few times. But before we begin, you need to understand the risks." Nethgalla looked at him seriously. "There are so many unknowns to a change such as this. So many unknowns about the process of shape-shifting itself, to be honest, even for me—and I, if I may be so bold, probably know more about it than anyone else alive."

Davian chewed his lip. He'd assumed that the Ath, of all people, would be complete in her expertise at this. "Such as?"

Nethgalla gestured. "Take our minds as an example. When we shape-shift, our physical bodies change, yet our minds *seem* to remain the same. But the mind is not some ethereal entity: it is part of that physical form, and it takes its cues from the body. If a man sustains a serious head injury, he may lose some of his ability to think—his mind sustains a physical damage. If you then shape-shifted into his form, what would happen?"

Davian frowned. "I don't know."

"And neither do I," Nethgalla admitted. "From my experience, it is likely that the mind—the actual, physical matter in your head—does *not* change, despite the skull shifting around it. I have never forgotten things or felt significantly more or less intelligent than previously, when I have Shifted." She paused. "And yet, I can also say that there are some bodies in which I am quite certain I thought *more clearly*, and some in which I was more influenced by emotion. Some bodies are a joy, others are depressing. There is definitely some level of symbiosis between the two, Davian." She leaned forward. "Now consider again what you wish to do. Consider that there is the possibility that someone doing this might lose things—like, for example, the knowledge of how to use the Vessel to change back. Or the desire to."

Davian paled, swallowing. He *had* thought about that briefly, but he had to concede that it had not been in great detail. Nethgalla was right. What would changing into a dar'gaithin *do* to someone? Would they experience a significant drop in intelligence? Would they be somehow bound to the orders of the Venerate, simply by possessing that body?

Nethgalla watched him, nodding slightly as she saw his expression. "So. Do you wish to proceed?"

Davian considered a little longer. "I'll take the risk," he said quietly.

Nethgalla inclined her head.

"Interesting times," she murmured, mostly to herself. "On to the Vessels themselves, then. You're going to want something that will survive the journey. Something that won't corrupt once it comes through..."

She trailed off as Davian rolled up his sleeve, loosening the three steel bands from around his bicep.

"And you want to make how many?" Nethgalla asked dubiously.

"Three."

"No." Nethgalla shook her head. "If you combined those, you would still be fortunate to squeeze in the required kan."

"We'll see," Davian said stubbornly.

Nethgalla sighed. "Regardless. I'm going to need to practice, and those are far too small for experimentation." She shrugged. "I'll find something, work on it over the next few days."

Davian shifted nervously. "Days?"

"This isn't a job that you want me to rush," said Nethgalla, a touch irritably. "You go back to speak with Ashalia tomorrow—that means that I have until at *least* tomorrow evening. If you escape and get to that room I told you about once you've spoken to her, that should buy you enough time." She scratched her head. "Rethgar will likely be in charge of sending you back, you know. I've heard that you two have a... history." She looked him in the eye. "His loss would hurt the Venerate."

"So I should just kill the escherii? That sounds easy," Davian said bitterly, despite the wave of anger that rose in him at the mere mention of Rethgar's name. Tal had explained to him what Rethgar truly was—a mixture of sha'teth and human, connected to the Forge. An Augur in all but name, working for the Venerate. For Shammaeloth.

Regardless of any of that, though—eight months away hadn't dulled Davian's memory of what the man had done.

Nethgalla studied him, then shrugged.

"You're certainly capable now, and if you know what he is, then you know it needs to be done anyway if we are to close the rift. I'll do my part. You do what you think is best, and we shall see how it goes." She took a breath, then put on the servile facade she had worn on the way to the cell.

"Fates with you tomorrow, Davian."

With that, she slipped outside and locked the cell door behind her with an audible click, leaving Davian alone once again. He stood there, considering what would come next.

Then he picked up the first of the metal bands again, studying the lines of kan carefully. Figuring out how to destroy them cleanly, leaving the steel ready for a fresh set of mechanisms.

He had some preparing to do.

Though it was impossible to tell in his windowless cell, it felt like morning when Rethgar came to fetch him.

The hateful man looked no different from Davian's memory of him. His expression was surly as he bound Davian with the black chains, their weight settling around his shoulders almost as soon as Rethgar came through the door.

That was good, for once, though he made certain not to show his relief. Davian had wanted an opportunity to test the Vessel he and Tal had come up with, to see whether their ideas for how to get around the chains' effects actually worked.

He cautiously reached out for kan. It was still there, but when he touched it, pain shot through his head, incinerating his ability to concentrate.

He trailed after Rethgar silently, then funneled Essence within his body—something the chains were unable to block. Activated his focus Vessel.

And then the one in the nape of his neck.

The latter was the more dangerous of the two by far: it absorbed pain. He hadn't made it to take away pain entirely—that, as Tal had explained firmly, was far too risky. Normally, the body warned the mind of pain for a reason. Shutting that down completely could be disastrous.

He clenched his fists nervously as the Vessel activated, then attempted to touch kan again.

A mild discomfort, this time. That was all.

Keeping an eye on Rethgar, Davian carefully took hold of kan. Manipulated a thin stream of it—too small for the escherii to notice.

It worked.

He breathed an internal sigh of relief. Tal had explained that these black chains were affecting his ability to use kan, rather than blocking his access to kan itself—it was by far the simpler of the two options. Not as elegant as the cells the Builders had constructed beneath Tol Shen, nor as bluntly effective as rooms made of darkstone.

Efficient enough, though. The chains' blocking of external Essence prevented the use of Vessels to circumvent the effect, too.

For anyone who didn't have the Vessels built into their own body, anyway.

Davian silently experimented for a few more seconds and then let kan drop away again, turning his attention instead to the chains themselves. They were coated with hardened kan, difficult to analyze as he walked along the corridor, but he could see a variety of mechanisms he recognized. He couldn't unshackle himself, but thought he could further dampen the Vessel's effects if he had to.

Davian was soon being pushed through a doorway and into an empty circular chamber, with the steel floor sloping downward slightly, creating a sort of bowl in the center of the room. Rethgar motioned to it.

"Stand in the center," he said firmly.

Davian glanced around, noting the absence of anyone else in the room. "Where are the Venerate?"

"Busy."

The chains suddenly yanked him forward, making him stumble. He carefully tamped down his anger, restraining himself from lashing out and revealing that he wasn't as restricted as Rethgar believed him to be.

"Now," said Rethgar, taking up a position at the edge of the room and staring down at Davian with his arms crossed. "The rules are simple. You cannot tell Ashalia, or even imply, what will happen—where she will end up or why we are contacting her. I will be able to hear what you say, Davian, and I will draw you back in a moment if I don't like what I hear. I will also be instructing you on what to say. Lord Gassandrid wishes to use this opportunity to pass legal judgment, and it is important that it is delivered precisely." He gazed at Davian steadily. "If it is not, it will go poorly for Ashalia. I promise you."

Davian felt his jaw clench, but he nodded.

Rethgar busied himself with something—Davian could see

lines of Essence and kan disappearing into a nearby plate—and Davian silently pushed through kan again himself, examining the metal beneath his feet. These plates clearly dealt with time, judging by the endpoints, but were...complex. Much more so than anything else he'd seen thus far.

"So you can send people back through time," he said to Rethgar, shaking his head with a frown. "Why not just go back yourself? Or send someone you trust?"

Rethgar snorted. "Many were sent before my time, and a few since I arrived. The living cannot survive the time stream, nor can Lord Gassandrid maintain his connection with his surrogates through it."

A low thrum filled the air, building in pitch, and Rethgar finally looked up. "You will need to make physical contact with her," he said calmly, a little louder to ensure he was heard. "Lord Gassandrid assumes that we are not able to find her currently because she is inside the Tributary. Let me assure you that if that is not the reason—if you resist—then what I did to you in Tel'Tarthen will be revisited a thousand times upon you before you go back to the Mines." His eyes gleamed with barely leashed anger.

Davian shook his head, silently reminding himself that he was going to kill this man. This *thing*.

"If the Tributary is blocking your ability to find her, then what is the point?" he asked suddenly.

"Reassurance." Rethgar's eyes narrowed, and he looked annoyed, as if he had given away something he hadn't meant to.

Davian watched the man. "I don't understand how I'm supposed to find her from here."

"Using Markaathan to travel through space is little different to doing so through time," said Rethgar, his lip curling in disdain. "It requires...emotion. A *desire* to be where you are going. Something—or in this case, someone—to whom you are truly connected. Who means much to you." He waved his arm. "I have already locked the time to which you will be traveling; it is the latest we can go that we are certain Tal'kamar did not have Licanius. All you need to do is find Ashalia."

Rethgar spoke idly as he worked, almost casually. He clearly had no concern that Davian might be able to break the blocking of his chains.

"Why does Tal having Licanius make a difference?" asked Davian, partly to keep the escherii distracted, but also from genuine curiosity.

Rethgar eyed him, as if suddenly realizing that he had been talking too much.

"Remember—focus on Ashalia, Davian," he said sternly. "And say only what I tell you."

Essence crackled and swirled around him, bright blue.

Half of the room faded to twisting void.

Davian barely had time to react before he was suddenly being thrown back by the black chains, thrust into the gray, Rethgar and the rest of the room vanishing. He hovered in space, disembodied, the feeling almost a familiar one now—and yet, this was different. He wasn't swimming a river, currents speeding toward a destination. This was more of a lake. Choppy, with waves that bobbed him around, perhaps, but...no discernible flow.

He took a moment to orient himself and then began looking around. Rethgar had said that this was no different from traveling through time.

A light—small but bright, pulsing against the shades of gray. Distant.

He willed himself toward it; the gray seemed to twist around him, as if he were lurching violently sideways, despite having no physical presence here.

And then he was somewhere else.

It was dark, though the faint outline nearby indicated a window with heavy, closed curtains. Davian collapsed against the wall, the chains around him clattering, head spinning as he tried to focus. This wasn't like the other times he'd traveled through time. He was here, and yet he could *feel* the part of him still back in Ilshan Gathdel Teth. The black chain was tethering him there more strongly, somehow. Some part of the kan mechanism he apparently hadn't understood.

He closed his eyes, breath coming in short, sharp gasps. His Essence had vanished once again in the transition, his Vessels ceasing to function. He panicked as he reached out for kan and was met only with terrible, blinding pain.

Desperately, limbs barely able to move, he slid his right hand under his shirt and touched his forefinger to his heart. Connected the two halves of the Vessel, activating it.

Essence began trickling into him.

He gasped, immediately funneling it to the pain Vessel in his neck, then dizzily grasping kan. He silently reached out, sensing a fire in a nearby room and a few other sources of energy. He drained each of them, using hardened kan to funnel the Essence past the decaying effect of the chains.

He breathed out, finally taking his hand from his chest again, feeling steady enough to disconnect the Essence-draining Vessel. He didn't need much—wouldn't be here for long—and his continuing to use it could be dangerous for anyone nearby.

Then he flinched back into the shadowy corner as the door to the room opened, light from the hallway outside spilling in.

He swallowed.

Asha looked…pensive. Younger than he had expected, too; though this should be only a couple of years ago, the image of her in his mind was always of someone his own age. His heart ached to see her again though, emotions that had been pushed aside for the past year and a half stirring quickly to the surface. The black marks on her face had never been able to conceal her smile, the way her eyes shone, all the quirks and expressions he had come to know so well.

Asha didn't notice him, didn't realize anyone else was in the room. She shut the door again and flopped down on her bed with a heavy sigh.

"Asha," said Davian, a little uncomfortably. He didn't want to scare her, but he knew that his time here was short. He could already feel the little Essence he had managed to gather draining away.

Asha leaped up as if shot, scrambling nervously for the lamp beside her bed and lighting it with a shaking hand. Davian made a face and then forced himself forward again, his chains clanking obnoxiously as he moved into the dim light.

"It's good to see you, Asha," Davian said with a tired grin, though his pulse was racing. He needed to deliver this message and then deal with Rethgar.

"Is this a dream? You...you're not real. They said you died. At Caladel." Her voice was trembling.

"They lied." Davian shuffled back as Asha made to get out of bed. "Please, don't come any closer. It's dangerous," he insisted.

Pain immediately shot through his head, so sharp that it was barely manageable despite the Vessel he was using to dull it.

No, Davian. That was a mistake, but there is still time to correct it. Now ask her about the Shadraehin.

"Why?" asked Asha, looking confused.

"I don't have time to explain. I'm...restricted in what I can say," Davian admitted heavily. As he spoke he focused again on the black chain, searching for the mechanism that was allowing Rethgar to see these events. Stop that—even for a few moments—and he could relay his true message and leave. "Who is the Shadraehin?" He knew that Asha didn't know at this point, so it was safe to ask.

"A man called Scyner. Why?"

She is lying.

"She's telling the truth. She doesn't know," Davian responded aloud. He gasped in discomfort as the black chains tightened around him in response. If he could feel that much through his pain-dampening Vessel, then the intended pain must have been near unbearable. "You have my word, Rethgar," he added with a snarl.

"Dav? What's going on?"

Very well. Repeat the following, and this only. "We know you have met with the Shadraehin. You helped her."

Davian did as he was told, still desperately examining the chains. There *had* to be a weakness that he could exploit.

"Her?" Asha looked confused. "Scyner is a man."

Davian took a deep, shaky breath. He thought he saw something.

Time to try it.

"Scyner is just the Shadraehin's lieutenant. A prewar, though. Don't trust him."

The chains flexed and pain ripped through him once again, a 591 sure indication that Rethgar had heard. *You have been warned, Davian. Repeat again.* "Ashalia Chaedris, for your part in assisting the Shadows, you have been found guilty. The sentence is death."

"Dav—" Asha had clearly seen that he was in pain, soft concern in her eyes.

"*Stay back.*" Davian put as much command as he could into the words, even as another wave of agony washed over him. Rethgar either didn't understand just how much this *should* be hurting, or had to be wondering how Davian was still withstanding it. Reluctantly, he repeated Rethgar's words. This was evidently the Venerate's attempt at justifying their trying to kill Asha—making it 'legal' in their eyes—and yet one that still avoided revealing to her anything about her future.

"*I'm* a Shadow, Dav," said Asha, and the pain in her voice was worse than anything Rethgar had done to him so far. She raised her lantern slightly, as if concerned that he somehow hadn't noticed the black marks streaked across her face.

Davian took another slow, shaking breath, then forced a smile.

"You won't always be, though," he assured her gently.

Pain again, this time almost too much, even with the dampening Vessel. Davian moaned. "She doesn't know anything. And this is the furthest we can go before Tal'kamar—"

Another wave of agony, but this time Davian saw it. The pulsing of the endpoint being activated, the stretching of kan along several different lines in unison.

He reached out and brutally squeezed the connection. Like closing a fist around a puppet's strings, making the puppet master's efforts futile.

The writhing black chains went gray. Froze.

The pain vanished.

Davian kept his eyes closed, his focus entirely on grasping the connection tightly enough that no matter how hard Rethgar tugged on the other end, it wouldn't affect him. While he did this, Rethgar was cut off. Completely blind.

"They can't hear us now, but I can't do this for long, either." He wished that he could see her face, just watch her as he talked to her. He missed her. Still—being in the same room, alone…it was enough, for now. "I know this must be confusing, but there's no time to explain so you are going to have to trust me. You'll be making a deal with the Shadraehin soon—the real one. When you do, I need you to tell her that Tal'kamar is taking Licanius to the Wells, and that the information is a gift from me. Can you do that?"

It felt...wrong, to give Nethgalla this information, valuable though he knew it was to the Ath. She was searching desperately for Tal while he was at his weakest, and it could well result in the death of Tal's friend Asar.

And yet, even if he was responsible, it had all already happened. It was a decision already made.

He listened as Asha repeated the message verbatim, then gave a satisfied nod.

"Good. Thank you, Ash. Now, this is equally important. When you find out that I'm at Ilshan Gathdel Teth, don't come after me. I'm fine. The Venerate can't kill me, but they will kill you—you are the one they want. I'm just the bait. Remember that." Gassandrid and Diara clearly knew about their relationship, would inevitably try to use his presence to draw her out. Asha was strong, and he didn't believe that she would allow that to happen, but telling her this would hopefully strengthen her resolve—and, maybe, relieve any feelings of guilt the Venerate tried to foist upon her.

He opened his eyes again, his grasp on the kan connection starting to slip as Rethgar's jerking on the other end became more and more frantic. Black began to bleed back into the chains, and he suddenly felt terribly, terribly tired.

With a start, he realized that the Essence he'd drawn earlier was all but gone.

"Don't tell anyone else that you saw me. Especially not me. They've Read...they've Read so many of us, now. There's no telling whose mind is safe, these days," he admitted, thinking back to what Gassandrid had told him. He shook his head, seeing her confusion. "I'm so sorry. You'll understand when the time comes."

His grip on kan finally slipped, and the chains flooded to black. He met Asha's gaze, for a split second able to just drink in the sight of her, fixing her face in his memory once again.

Then he was lurching backward into the steel-encased chamber, Asha vanishing into the gray of the void that still cut the room in half.

He groaned as he collapsed to the ground, limbs too heavy to lift, barely conscious even as he reactivated his pain Vessel once again.

It had worked, though. He had passed on the message.

To think, Asha had been living with that. Living with what must have seemed like cryptic statements since before the invasion of the Blind, unable to tell anyone. She had passed on his message to Nethgalla, too, though she had to have wondered about its purpose.

Not for the first time, he wondered how he had been so lucky as to have her in his life.

His ribs cracked as a heavy boot slammed into his chest.

"You fool," hissed Rethgar, drawing back his leg and delivering another deliberate, vicious kick as Davian tried weakly to roll away. The black chains clinked, restricting his feeble movement. "You utter *fool*. I warned you. I pleaded with you."

"Gassandrid will want me alive," gasped Davian hazily.

"He will get you alive. We already know that," said Rethgar disdainfully. "I can try to kill you all day long, and you will survive." He leaned in, breathing hard, his eyes black and cold. "But El knows I am going to enjoy the trying."

His next kick caught Davian full in the face, warm pain exploding across his cheek as it caved in, even with his suppressing Vessel still active. He tried to drag himself away and vomited, head spinning as more blows began to rain down on his back, his side, his legs. If he was hurting this much through the suppression, then his body was in bad shape. He needed Essence.

He desperately slipped his hand to his chest again, activating the Vessel that drew from his surroundings; Essence immediately began funneling from the steel plate touching his body, the readily available energy making the flow quick and steady.

And then, abruptly, it was cut off.

He summoned just enough strength to turn his head and see Rethgar, a manic rictus of a smile on his face, sliding the kan shield between him and Essence.

"I do not know how you are circumventing the chains," said the escherii, "but that is enough. No healing. No escaping the pain, Davian. If memories are not enough to break you, then perhaps we have been going about this all wrong. Perhaps all you need is some *physical encouragement.*"

The chains tightened painfully around his body; his bones creaked and muscles groaned until he finally could take it no more, screaming as the bone in his arm snapped, followed by his leg bending at an unnatural angle. Rethgar watched it all with a satisfied snarl, and Davian knew that he would not stop—not even if Davian offered to tell him everything.

He rolled onto his side. The gray void still hung there; Rethgar either was unable to shut it off or was too angry to have bothered yet. Davian closed his eyes, then forced every ounce of energy into his limbs and made for it. If he could just get away . . .

He was almost there when the chains forced him to a halt.

"No." Rethgar gave the chains a vicious tug, sending a blaze of pain coursing through Davian's body. "No, it's not that easy." More pain. "Do you know how Lord Gassandrid punished me, after Tel'Tarthen? Do you have any idea how *protected* you have been, this past year?" Another shiver of agony.

Davian resisted the urge to haul against the chains, to try and make it that last few feet into the time stream. He knew that it wouldn't work. The last vestiges of the Essence he'd managed to gather were draining away.

Desperately, he used it to activate his focus Vessel.

Kan immediately became easier to grasp; he pushed through and examined the chains again, trying to make sense of the complex mess of mechanisms. Distantly, he could sense his body failing.

There.

He snaked out a line of kan, too thin for Rethgar to see.

The blows continued, but in his fury, Rethgar hadn't noticed.

Davian had gained control of the chains.

He tightened his mental grip over them, and *pulled.*

The black chains were suddenly winding around Rethgar's body, faster than the other man could react. He cried out in shock, clearly losing his ability to grip kan; the shield around

Davian vanished and he gasped as Essence flooded back into him, flowing immediately to the damaged areas of his body. Which were everywhere.

Rethgar howled as he struggled against the chains, trying to wrest back control, but Davian had him now. Slowly, inch by inch, he dragged the chains toward him. Loosening them around his own body. Forcing Rethgar another step closer.

Finally they stood together at the edge of the gray river, Rethgar's eyes bulging with rage and disbelief.

Davian leaned forward, gritting his teeth. He gripped the escherii with his Essence-enhanced right arm, lifting him up and swiveling so that he was halfway into the gray void.

Escherii or not, Rethgar had a source. He could no more withstand the rift than anyone else.

"For Caladel," he whispered hoarsely in Rethgar's ear.

He let go.

Rethgar screamed; for a moment he locked eyes with Davian, pure panic in his expression as the gray current dragged him in.

Then he was gone.

The chains vanished, melting back into the steel floor, and Davian sucked in Essence hungrily as the void to the side finally faded away. His panic subsided as bones began to knit together again, his breath coming easier, his head clearer.

Finally he shakily stood, examining the spot where Rethgar had disappeared. A feeling of emptiness washed over him now that it was done.

He made for the door, still stumbling a little as he did so. He had taken careful note of the route, knew his way back to the safe room Nethgalla had shown him.

It took twenty minutes, all told—twenty minutes of creeping, using his invisibility Vessel to avoid notice, stumbling along and doing everything he could to stay focused. But he made it first to the darkstone passageway, and then to the hole in the wall Nethgalla had told him about. It was less than a foot high and perhaps three wide; he had to lie flat on his stomach and worm his way inside, praying that the tiny tunnel didn't get any smaller. After a minute of fumbling his way along, he risked sending a sliver of

Essence ahead of him to light the way. It was hard to do with all the darkstone around, but eventually he managed a steady light.

A few minutes later, he was emerging into the windowless, doorless, featureless cave.

He collapsed against the wall and let his light go out again, just breathing as the darkness enveloped him, the emotions of everything that had happened finally hitting home.

He stayed that way, head in his hands, for a long time.

Chapter 41

Caeden slammed his elbow hard into the Desrielite soldier's shoulder and then issued a more careful strike to the back of the head, ignoring the frozen rictus on the man's face as he moved smoothly forward and on to the next enemy.

The forest surrounding the small clearing—and Caeden's opposition—barely moved as he worked, scything through the small detachment of soldiers, breaking bones and knocking men unconscious with each clinical motion. Shadows inched along the ground as what was presumably a stiff breeze shook the branches above, and the clean noonday sun dappled through leaves, glistening where it hit red spurting in slow motion from smashed noses and mouths vomiting teeth.

He took a moment to glance back at the bright, frozen tableau of pain he was creating. This took so much more focus than simply killing. He had to be paying attention to the strength of each hit, always assessing just how hard he could strike from within the time bubble, measuring blows against the speed of motion outside. Sweat beaded on his brow and trickled into his eyes, as much from concentration as from physical exertion.

But it felt...*good*. Not good that he was hurting people, but good that he was choosing not to do worse. He hadn't fought like this in...how long? Death had been such a constant companion that for centuries he had just accepted its inevitable presence, turned off the piece of his mind that was sickened by his bringing it.

Refusing to kill now—now, when it would be easier, when it would be considered by many to be justified—was freeing. As if he was in some small way breaking the shackles of his past self, reaffirming that life did matter. *All* life, not just the lives of the people he liked or needed.

The last man in his immediate area fell and Caeden let his time bubble drop, gasping, grateful for the mental respite. The sounds of the clearing flooded in on him: birds and animals had abandoned the area, only the soft breeze sighing through the trees and the distant rumble of battles elsewhere. He glanced behind him, assessing each of the dozen forms on the ground. Injured, some of them badly. But all still breathing.

He put his hands on his knees, catching his breath. Fire and wind roared somewhere down the hill, where he had left the Shadows to take care of the Desrielites without Traps. A short way off to his left there were shining lights among the trees, men and women shouting in alarm; he winced as he saw one man appear briefly in midair, hurtling through branches with a thick tendril of Essence wrapped around him before slamming hard into the trunk of a tree. His shouting, along with the others', quickly went silent.

A second later Asha soared through the air and into the clearing, landing a few feet in front of him and skidding smoothly to a stop, her Essence armor pulsing blindingly bright. She examined the area before turning to him.

"They're dealt with," she said, sounding as dazed as Caeden felt. She glanced down the hill, where the Shadows were trudging up toward them, apparently having won their battle, too. "That went well."

Caeden nodded, once again eyeing Asha's armor with more than a hint of respect. Making that required not just a large amount of Essence, but significant skill. The girl truly had put her time in the dok'en to good use. "There will be more," he said soberly.

The message Wirr had sent him via Asha had given them some warning, but he had still dared to hope that things might not have progressed this far. They had been set upon almost immediately after passing through the Gate into the forest, though, stumbling across a large contingent of enemy soldiers almost before they'd had the chance to organize themselves.

And Gil'shar on this side of the Devliss meant that Wirr and his people hadn't been enough.

He straightened as Shana and another dozen Shadows jogged up, each one holding a Vessel. The woman's face was hard as she scanned the clearing behind Caeden.

"You're leaving them alive?" she asked abruptly.

"They're not going anywhere. They don't need to die," replied Caeden.

Shana was silent for a few seconds. "So you're leaving them to fight again later," she finally said flatly. "Despite us being at war."

"They won't be able to fight. They're all quite thoroughly injured. They will be nothing but a strain on the Gil'shar's resources," said Caeden firmly.

He looked Shana in the eye, recognizing what he saw there. This wasn't about the attack. The Gil'shar had been the group trying to kill her all her life. In both her time as a Gifted student and as a Shadow, Desriel's Hunters—the country's very way of life, in fact—were probably among the most unsettling, threatening concepts she'd known.

Now that she had a chance to respond, mercy wasn't something toward which she was inclined.

"Killing in war is sometimes necessary. That doesn't mean that war necessitates killing," said Caeden, raising his voice slightly so that the other Shadows could hear.

He caught sight of Asha's expression and grimaced, turning away. She was the only one of the group who knew who he'd been, knew about his past.

The Shadows, almost as one, turned to Asha and looked askance at her, to Caeden's vague irritation. To Asha's, too, apparently.

"He's right. Of course he's right," Asha said in exasperation, her Essence armor pulsing. "You don't need to take chances with your lives, but the goal isn't to kill Desrielites. It's to stop what they're trying to do here."

There were a few mutters from the Shadows, but in the end they nodded reluctantly.

Shana opened her mouth to say something. Then her eyes went wide, and she pointed down the hill.

"What about them?" she asked.

Caeden followed her gesture, spotting the half dozen dar'gaithin advancing on their position, pursuing a small group of men and women. Andarrans, Caeden was relieved to see. They weren't all dead yet.

Caeden grunted.

"Them, we can just kill," he said grimly.

The Shadows hurriedly arrayed themselves, but the fleeing Andarrans were in their path.

Caeden stepped outside of time and burst into motion.

He dashed forward past the Andarrans, infusing his legs with Essence, staying clear of the creatures' tails as his blade speared first one in the eye and then the next in the mouth. He twisted away from the group, cautious of the fact that the dar'gaithin were aware of him now and were not moving as slowly as he would have liked. He'd been concentrating fiercely for hours now—first building the Gate here, then immediately leaping into this battle. His time bubble was nowhere near as effective as he knew it was capable of being.

He attacked again; his next two strikes landed perfectly, difficult though they were as the creatures thrashed wildly at where they thought he was going to be.

The third strike sheared across the dar'gaithin's black plating, throwing his motion off.

He stumbled slightly, losing track of one of the creatures' movements—just for a moment, but it was enough. Its tail clipped him on the foot, breached his time bubble.

And then everything was back to normal speed.

Caeden dodged to the side as tails and claws whirled around him in a tornado of death. The hardened kan in the Bane's armor had disrupted his hastily made kan structure, collapsing the entire thing. He could get it back up again if he could just get a second to focus.

A blow caught him across the back.

There was a sickening crunch, followed quickly by a second blow to the ribs, this one shattering bone. He crumpled to the ground, mind blank as fiery, blinding pain ripped through him. Essence began to stream first toward the shattered ribs, then filled in his lung and allowed him to draw a rasping breath.

He tried to move. His legs weren't working.

His vision cleared just in time for him to see the dar'gaithin leering down, its tail on his chest.

A burning streak, and the creature vanished.

Caeden funneled Essence desperately into his broken back as the other dar'gaithin nearby slithered in his direction. By the time the first had arrived to swing down at him, he was able to roll to the side, the strike missing his head by inches and thudding into the dirt.

Another streak of light and then Ashalia was there again; the final dar'gaithin flew from Caeden's vision, its neck snapped by the boulder Asha had used to club it away.

Caeden struggled up onto an elbow as she appeared over him, holding out a hand to help him up.

Caeden groaned. "Closest I've come to dying in a while," he muttered.

"I thought you couldn't die," said Asha.

Caeden allowed himself to be pulled to his feet. "Being beheaded would have been inconvenient," he assured her, testing his legs cautiously. Still healing—injuries like that couldn't just be ignored—but good enough for him to walk again. He waved away her look. "I'll explain when I'm not so tired. Just...yes. If you think my head's going to be cut off, please do stop it."

Asha snorted in what he thought was a laugh. "I'll do my best."

Caeden looked around dazedly as strength returned to his limbs, eyebrows rising as he spotted the mangled remains of a dar'gaithin tangled in branches, halfway up an enormous oak. "How?"

"I used the ground under their feet, and just..." She shrugged, making a throwing motion.

Caeden shook his head, nonplussed. "You were *fast*, though."

"I told you. I've been practicing." Asha spoke absently, her gaze raking the forest for any further threats. When she didn't spot anything, she glanced back at the Andarrans they had just saved, who were talking animatedly with the Shadows.

"Let's go and see just how bad things are," she said heavily.

It was an hour later when they at last stumbled their way into the encampment, and Caeden could immediately see that the Andarran troops had taken heavy losses.

Off to the side, exhausted-looking Gifted worked intently on injuries as others clustered in small groups, talking worriedly. A sense of heavy inevitability hung over the camp; though there were far more people still alive than Caeden had dared hope after hearing what had happened, the sight still brought home the reality of their plight.

Someone emerged from a tent on the far side of the clearing, and in moments everyone had paused what they were doing, consciously or otherwise looking across at the figure.

Wirr strode across the campsite purposefully, oblivious to Caeden and Asha, his focus on a group of soldiers who looked as if they were waiting for him. He spoke quickly to one, who spun and barked an order to the rest of the men. Wirr watched them march off, and Caeden immediately knew that his determined expression was masking a host of emotions that he wanted to hide from those under him.

From the way everyone else was looking at him, it was working, too. It felt strange to see the young man he had sat around campfires with just a couple of years ago—and who, Caeden knew, had dealt with so much hatred simply because of who he was—be looked to with such hope. There were Gifted and Administrators giving him those looks, too, not just the soldiers.

These past few days had changed a lot of people's opinions of him, that much was clear.

"Wirr!" Asha was jogging forward and waving, an enormous smile lighting her face.

Wirr didn't react, as if not recognizing the name as his own. Then he frowned slightly and turned, eyes going wide as he saw who was calling to him.

"*Ash?*" He broke off his conversation, stoic facade briefly giving way to pure emotion as he took in the sight of his friend. There was joy on his face, but Caeden also saw the worry, exhaustion, and grief battling there before they were gone again, the mask reasserting itself.

The two friends embraced fiercely, Asha half sobbing, half laughing as Wirr picked her up off the ground in his enthusiasm. "Fates, Ash! It's really you?" His gaze slid past her, coming to rest on Caeden, who gave him a tired smile and nod. Wirr nodded back, a gesture of appreciation and respect. "He really got you out," he finished in delighted disbelief.

"I got your message," said Asha, some of the joy seeping from her face as she remembered their surroundings. "And we spoke to Administrator Terris and his team." She motioned back to the group they had rescued. "They told us a little of the situation."

"Only the good parts, I hope?" said Wirr lightly, though the effort at levity faded immediately. He gestured for them to follow him. "We don't have much time, but I need to get a better view. We can talk on the way." He glanced at the Shadows, who were watching uncertainly. "They have Vessels?" When Asha confirmed, he beckoned over a nearby soldier. "Vashan, assign Administrator Kestig to the Shadows." He turned back to Asha. "Can you tell them that I'll be issuing orders through Kestig, and that they need to follow them to the letter?"

Asha watched as Vashan hurried away. "They won't be happy about taking instructions from an Administrator."

"They'll get over it, or they can fend for themselves." Wirr gave her an apologetic smile to soften the words. "The Administrators and the Gifted aren't soldiers either, but they're doing what they have to. There's no room for grudges anymore."

Caeden watched silently as Asha conceded the point and hurried over to the Shadows, beginning a short but spirited discussion with Shana.

"Is she all right?" asked Wirr, quietly enough that only Caeden could hear, not taking his eyes from Asha.

"Better than she has any right to be," admitted Caeden. "Still incredibly strong, too, even with the Boundary draining her Reserve. You don't need to worry about her, if that's what you're asking."

Wirr just nodded, but Caeden could see his stance change, could feel the relief radiating from him. He'd been concerned for her, though he hadn't been willing to show it. Neither of them had known how Asha would react to returning to the real world; Caeden had hoped that her living in the dok'en would ease the transition, but even then he'd had to accept that it might not go smoothly. Asha's resilience spoke as much to her character as it did to anything else.

Asha soon rejoined them, along with Taeris, who had apparently just heard of their arrival. The scarred man embraced both Asha and Caeden delightedly, and Caeden gripped him happily, relieved to see the Elder still alive and well. Taeris had been one of Caeden's staunchest early allies, and seemed to have taken finding out about his past in stride. Even with his memories back, Caeden found the man's familiar, steady presence a comfort.

Wirr marshaled the group and they set off immediately, hurrying northward into the forest.

They walked swiftly as Wirr explained calmly and concisely what had happened since his arrival—from the discovery of the invisibility shield, down to the desperate attack and its consequences. Ishelle dead. Erran and Scyner gone, either captured or dead too. More than half of their people killed.

And the Columns still intact, and on this side of the river.

"You've performed a minor miracle here, Wirr," said Caeden after his friend fell silent, clearly having nothing more to add. He wasn't exaggerating. If the numbers Wirr had described were even remotely accurate, his holding the Gil'shar to their current position was truly remarkable.

"Give me a way to make it matter, and I'll be happy," replied Wirr. He wasn't being dismissive or grim, particularly, but rather just seemed too tired and too focused to respond with fake sentiment. He was driving himself forward despite his exhaustion. Caeden recognized the signs all too well.

In a better world, he'd tell him to rest.

They walked for a while; after a few minutes Caeden found himself in stride with Taeris, slightly apart from the other two. Taeris glanced across at him.

"Now you have your memories back...I have to know," he said softly, looking vaguely uncomfortable. "Are you...the one who brought Davian to me? When he was a child?"

Caeden stared blankly at Taeris, so surprised that he missed a root in his path and almost tripped.

"What? No." He shook his head firmly at Taeris's questioning look. "No. I would remember something like that. I knew that he would be at Caladel, and did everything I could to make sure that the Venerate didn't look around there. But I've never known where he came from before that."

Taeris nodded heavily. "Worth asking," he said ruefully. "I never even saw who left him. He just...appeared. I always assumed that he must have been given to my care because of Jakarris's memories. Because of anyone alive, I knew Alchesh's visions the best—knew that Davian had been Seen by him and by other Augurs throughout the years, and was destined to be someone special. Someone who needed protecting. It was the only logical explanation, because children have never been..." He rubbed his face, and the weight of his decisions was evident in the motion.

Caeden said nothing for a few seconds. Alchesh had written so much about Davian, because that was why he'd become an Augur in the first place. Caeden had pressed and pressed, held off and held off on using that Sever, all in order to try and find out more about him. He'd known that Alchesh was losing control, and still he'd pushed.

"I don't know why he was left with you," he said eventually, "but I'm quite sure that he was meant to be left with you. Maybe because of your knowledge, or maybe just because...someone knew that you were the right person. You're at least part of the reason Davian grew up to be the man he is." He clapped Taeris on the shoulder. "I know you made mistakes, but...I don't think that *you* were the mistake."

Taeris thought for a moment, then gave Caeden a small smile.

"Thank you." The smile widened slightly. "And if you do ever happen to remember dropping off a small child..."

Caeden chuckled as they climbed the final part of the trail and emerged onto the cliff top. "You'll be the first to know."

They joined Wirr and Asha at the edge, and Caeden's smile vanished as he gazed down on the scene in horror.

Wirr's assessments had been almost perfectly correct, but part of Caeden had still hoped that the young man's inexperience might have been exaggerating the desperation of the situation. There was no doubting him now, though. The three bridges burned bright even in the clear morning sun, soldiers still crossing, though it was just a trickle of men, some even going back the other way as they ran messages or returned to haul more supplies. If the bridges were cut now, it would be an inconvenience for the Gil'shar, but not much more.

The camp spread out below, centered around the massive Darecian ruin, which swarmed with soldiers and what appeared to be the remaining dar'gaithin. There were hundreds of tents pitched and thousands of soldiers moving purposefully around the camp, which itself looked ordered. Comfortably established.

In the middle of it all, right near the castle, were the Columns.

Caeden felt a wave of nausea as he gazed at them. Was it his imagination, or could he sense the death and darkness emanating from them even from this distance? The Desrielites would be sacrificing men every time they were moved, the soldiers who carried them drained of their Essence by mere contact. And that was while they were *inactive*.

He shuddered, flashes of Dareci filling his mind. How could the others have done this? After all they had been through, all they had seen, how could they have countenanced building this weapon again? Even Gassandrid, for all the man's flaws and zealotry, surely hadn't advised it. Hadn't planned this.

He swallowed against the nausea. "If I hadn't used Knowing on Alaris, they would have just...walked in here. Destroyed the Cyrarium before anyone even knew what was happening."

Beside him Asha shifted, glancing over at Wirr and Taeris. "They have Traps?"

Taeris nodded emphatically. "A lot of them."

"And you won't be able to use Essence around the Columns, either," said Caeden heavily. "They do much the same thing."

His heart sank as he stared down silently, not really listening as Taeris, Asha, and Wirr began discussing how they could possibly get to the Columns. He didn't need to. There was no way to do it by force, not realistically.

That left one option, though he didn't like it at all.

"I need to go down there and talk to them," he said abruptly.

The other three stopped dead, staring at him as if they thought they hadn't heard correctly. "What?" asked Asha, confused. "Why would that help?"

"Because they're doing all of this at the behest of their gods," said Caeden. "And I'm one of them." He gestured, making the wolf's head symbol glow briefly in the air in front of him. "I know what to say. I can convince them that I am Talkanor."

Taeris acceded thoughtfully, though neither Asha's nor Wirr's expression changed.

"You really think that will work?" asked Wirr, doubt thick in his voice. "If the Venerate went to all the trouble of making those Columns, hiding them from you all this time..."

"I know. They've probably anticipated my interfering," agreed Caeden bleakly. "But Alaris was supposed to be here, fighting with them, guiding them. I could never have convinced them if that had been the case. But now?" He pulled in a breath. "No Alaris. The eletai turning on them. Resistance when they thought that there would be nothing here but a glorious march to victory. I can use that."

He hesitated. "And I have to try," he finished softly. "Even if we could get Licanius and seal the rift before Shammaeloth makes it to Deilannis, we're talking about thousands of lives."

"If he can convince the Gil'shar of who he is, they *will* listen to him," Taeris agreed quietly to Wirr.

Wirr nodded slowly, hope sparking in his eyes. "So what are you going to tell them?"

"Whatever I think will work." Caeden shrugged. "There are tests in place to measure whether I am who I am—that will go a long way toward convincing them. After that, I'll just have to see."

There was silence for a few seconds.

"If they hid all of this from you, why did the other Venerate include you in the pantheon?" asked Asha curiously.

"I was still very much on their side back then. They would have seen keeping this from me as a kindness, not some hedge against my loyalty," Caeden said simply. "Easy enough for them to do, too. I wasn't involved with establishing Desriel—it was initially a resistance against the Darecians, and Gassandrid was the one who militarized that discontent." He shrugged at their looks. "The Darecians were the invaders here first, you know. When we came it was generations later, but plenty of Andarrans still felt as though they were living in an occupied land when we arrived—and their occupiers were defined by their ability to use Essence.

So Gassandrid gave those Andarrans anti-Essence weapons and suggested that they base themselves in the west, in what's now Desriel. Turned them from a rabble into a force. And with us invading from the north, the Darecians simply didn't have time to deal with it."

"So the Desrielites broke away and just…accepted that you were gods?"

Caeden snorted. "No. It took generations for that to happen, and it wasn't really our doing. Gassandrid made us known as heralds of the one true god—he didn't mention El, as that was too closely associated with the Darecians—and established the rules against using Essence. In retrospect, I think that might have been influenced by Shammaeloth's instructions, too," he added grimly. "But after the Boundary went up, the Gil'shar declared independence from the remaining Darecians, splitting Andarra. And out of all that, over the years, rituals and new laws were made surrounding what Gassandrid had said. His words got twisted or misinterpreted and other, outside stories about the Venerate made their way into the canon, too. People started adding to his rules, expanding upon them. Usually to further their own positions of power.

"None of us—even me—really cared. If anything, it meant that when the Boundary came down, they could be more easily used as a distraction." He shrugged awkwardly. "But apparently the others had much more in mind for them. This must have been part of what they were doing, this past year, once they knew it was safe to leave Talan Gol. Organizing the Gil'shar. Teaching them how to order the Banes, use the Columns."

He shook his head ruefully. "But enough of that. I'll sneak in—it will be much more effective if I just appear in their midst. And there's no time to waste, I suppose," he concluded cheerlessly.

"Now?" Wirr ran his hands through his hair.

"I'll build a Gate first, once I find somewhere secure a little farther down," said Caeden. "Regardless of whether this succeeds, I need to get to Ilshan Gathdel Teth as quickly as possible afterward. Davian will be getting out of Zvaelar very soon."

He paused, a thread of guilt worming through his gut. Even thirty years on, he was still deeply ashamed of what he'd done

there, at the end.

"But after that, yes—immediately. And I'll go alone," he added, anticipating the next question. "Gods don't need support, and there's no need to risk anyone else, anyway. Instead, position your Gifted at a safe distance around the outside of the camp. Everyone you can." He held Wirr's gaze. "I'll be back by nightfall if I'm successful. If you don't hear from me by then, wait until you see me signal, and then fire some Essence at them." He squinted back at the camp, thinking. "With a spyglass, you should be able to pick me out from up here. Attack in the right places, and the distraction might just allow me to get out again."

"I'll go, too. You can manage to sneak in one more person." Asha scowled at him as he made to protest. "If the Gil'shar capture you, then that's it—we lose. I'll hide somewhere while you try to convince them, and if it doesn't work, I can be there to help you escape." She looked at him resolutely. "From what Wirr says, they have a lot of new weapons down there. It's not smart to do this alone."

Caeden wavered, seeing the determination in Asha's eyes.

"If there's a fight, you won't even be able to rely on that armor of yours. You'll only have whatever extra strength and reflexes Essence gives you."

"The armor's anchored to my skin. It's basically internal," replied Asha firmly. "Traps won't affect it. I'll be fine."

Caeden sighed, but eventually nodded. He didn't like the idea of risking both himself and Asha—they were, arguably, the Andarrans' most powerful weapons now—but Asha was right. One other person could easily sneak in with him, and having such a formidable ally inside could make all the difference.

Wirr chewed his lip, sighing but not protesting as he realized that Caeden had conceded to Asha. "Nightfall?"

"Nightfall," confirmed Caeden. "If you've heard nothing by then, keep an eye out for some sort of signal. You'll know it if you see it."

"We'll be watching," Wirr promised, Taeris adding his agreement.

Caeden gave him a tight smile of acknowledgment, then beckoned to Asha.

They started down the hill.

Chapter 42

Caeden studied the Gil'shar soldiers from the cover of the trees, then focused and stepped outside of time.

He moved calmly but swiftly once his surroundings slowed to near motionless, pulling Asha with him, navigating past the guards and into the outer ring of the Gil'shar camp. Kan was already a little unstable here from their proximity to the Columns, and while he wasn't worried just yet, he had to acknowledge that he wasn't going to be able to do this for long periods. Particularly as he got closer to the castle.

"We need to find clothes," he said softly.

They sized up the area, beginning to check inside some of the more isolated tents. Soon enough they had collected two uniforms, and Caeden politely turned his back as they both swiftly changed into Desrielite attire.

As soon as they were done, Caeden glanced around to make sure no one would see, and let his time bubble drop.

No one stopped them or even looked twice as they walked down the makeshift street between the tents, heading directly for the castle. The sounds of the camp washed over Caeden as he made his way along. Soldiers laughed, cursed, gambled. Officers barked orders in irritable tones. Men and women moaned to each other about the drudgery of their tasks as they pitched tents or dug lavatories, or tried to show bravado by talking of what they would do when they finally got to face the Andarrans properly.

On the whole, then, it was the same as most military encampments Caeden had seen. Just a collection of people. Misled, and some of them—as with any army—undoubtedly here for selfish reasons. But far from evil.

He gave Asha's arm a warning squeeze and shifted them outside of time again at the next checkpoint—perhaps a few hundred feet from the castle—cognizant of how the time bubble shivered around him this time. He didn't dare let it drop here, though; this was clearly a more secure area of the camp, with everyone in sight bearing the markings of an officer.

They stepped quickly toward the crumbling structure, Caeden wincing at flickers of faster movement outside the time bubble. The Columns, in their inactive state, made kan much harder to grasp, but seemed to interfere with existing kan structures slightly less. He just needed to maintain his manipulation of time until they were in position.

The castle itself was in better condition than it had appeared from afar. Though the upper edges of the gray stone walls were crumbling, the courtyard and inner buildings remained solidly intact, and the soldiers on watch up above moved comfortably, with no fear of the stone giving way beneath their feet.

It was a massive fortress, capable of housing at least a thousand soldiers, though that number was undoubtedly lessened by some of the damage from age. The Darecians must have spent years building it, though to what purpose, out in this abandoned section of the world, Caeden had no idea.

Once through the gates, he located a tower with a good view out over the encampment, one of its sides crumbling. Though a path between two sections of the castle ran through it, the connecting hallway didn't appear to be well-traveled. As good a spot as any for Asha to wait.

It only took a few minutes to find their way there; once satisfied that it would be appropriate, Caeden guided Asha into one of the corners of a small side room. A position where she would be able to see out the window, as well as through the missing wall on the opposite side.

"You can't go anywhere once this is done," he murmured as he started on her invisibility shield. "It's anchored to the wall. You take more than a step out, and they'll be able to see you."

"I know." Asha looked pensive as she watched Caeden finish his work, but she sounded calm enough. They had gone over the plan several times already, simple though it was.

Caeden finally stepped back, Asha vanishing from view as the invisibility shield took hold. He gave a brief nod of satisfaction.

"El with you," he murmured.

"You too," whispered Asha's voice in response.

Caeden reduced his time bubble to encompass only himself, and then moved on.

It took him almost ten minutes—focus close to breaking point—to find the Gil'shar. They had, unsurprisingly, taken the massive main hall to use for their discussions. He slipped past the guards at the door and noted several men present inside, their ages ranging from twenty through to at least eighty. Each of them bore the golden knot that indicated their rank, though.

Chief priests. Desriel's equivalent of the Assembly.

Relief flooded through him. Wirr had told him that they were present—information uncovered from the soldier Erran had Read—and Caeden had assumed that at least most of them would be gathered together, planning out their next move. But there had been no guarantees.

He walked onto the dais, raised above where the men were talking, and carefully tapped Essence to form his own symbol— the wolf's head—large on the two side walls and the one behind him. Then he slammed the double doors to the room and sealed them with more Essence, locking out the guards.

He burned away the disguise that he had been wearing, leaving him naked—nothing man-made touching his skin; that was important—and let the time bubble drop.

"Priests." He let Essence shine out from him, a blinding wave of light. The men down below leaped as if physically attacked as Caeden's voice boomed unnaturally loud around the hall; as he let it fade he funneled more Essence to the symbols on the wall, drawing the men's attention to them. "Kneel."

The men knelt with alacrity. Eight of them, Caeden realized. One was missing. Unfortunate—it would have been best if all of them were present for this—but these should easily be enough.

"Command us, O Talkanor," called the man at the front. He was older, with graying hair and a face that spoke of restraint and severity. His knot indicated that he was High Priest of Alar.

Something was bothering Caeden about the scene, but he couldn't place it.

"No." He made his gaze hard. "Have you forgotten the signs required by law before divinity is accepted?"

The youngest man's voice shook as he spoke up. "The secret signs which you have already shown us, O Talkanor. And... the divine marks written upon your flesh." He faltered, clearly unwilling to push the point.

"Good. Then fetch your weapon," growled Caeden, his voice rolling around the room. "Let me prove to you who I am, and *then* you will listen."

The words hadn't yet faded to silence before one of the priests was scurrying to a large chest at the side of the room. Caeden had been expecting as much: the sacred artifacts used in rituals were rarely far from the high priests, and weapons were unfortunately all too often needed in Gil'shar rituals.

The man's trembling hands finally emerged clutching a spear, long and sleek. Caeden gave it a dismissive glance and then refused to look at it further, though he was not looking forward to the next part.

"You know what to do," he said.

"O-of course, O Talkanor," said the man, his head bowed. "For the glory of the Last God."

Caeden stretched his hands out to the sides, slightly above his shoulders, keeping his face calm. This *was* going to hurt: the spear would pierce his heart and he would leave it there, letting the blood flow from the wound, guiding it around his body to form the symbols of each of the Venerate. A disgusting ritual, but a convincing one.

"Strike," he said calmly, the word thundering off every corner of the hall.

The spear went through his heart, and Caeden immediately knew that something was wrong.

His jaw clenched and he looked down at the tip sprouting from his chest, dark blood already spilling down his skin toward his bare stomach. The tip of the spear was black, not metal. That was wrong.

He started funneling the blood into his own wolf symbol but halfway through had to pause, pain getting in the way; he tapped his Essence Reserve, quickly flooding some of it to the wound in order to ease the pressure.

The Essence dissipated.

Caeden felt a chill of panic, his mind suddenly hazy. He looked up at the priests for the first time, finally spotting what he should have seen earlier. Fear, but something else, too.

Excitement.

With a groan Caeden stumbled, going to his knees, trying to grip the spear and pull it out but unable to do so.

"Alar warned us that you would come. A man with the temerity to call himself divine. A false god," said the older man. "Had you not wondered where your own chief priest was?" He walked up to Caeden, evidently growing in confidence, and crouched down in front of him. "Didn't you hear his cries? Or those of half your followers? They have carried the Great Weapon as penance, you know. Some willingly, others not. But they have suffered and died and where have you been, O God of Balance?"

Caeden wheezed in reply, unable to do anything more than watch as the massive symbols on the wall faded into nothing. The spear was a Vessel. It was blocking his ability to stave off the effects of the wound. He wasn't going to die from this, but he couldn't do much else until the thing was pulled out of his body.

Alaris had anticipated this. Or Gassandrid, or Diara. One of them had equipped the Gil'shar with this spear for this very purpose. All such weapons were supposed to have been destroyed, but apparently the other Venerate had done many things of which he was unaware.

"You are...making a mistake," he gasped, knowing the facade of his godhood was done with now. "Alar is the one who...has betrayed you."

Should he have done this differently? Would it have made a difference if he had been honest and simply shown them the memory of Dareci's fall from the start, the millions dying in the life-draining shadow of the Columns? He'd been intending to do it eventually, but he'd thought it needed to come from Talkanor, not from him.

It probably wouldn't have changed anything. Still, he reached out, trying desperately to feed them the images, to change their minds.

It was far too late.

Everything faded.

Caeden tried to moan, but no sound came out.

He sluggishly fuzzed back to awareness, the breeze sweeping down from the mountains icy against his cheek, distracting against the surreal absence of any other feeling. It took a brief, disoriented moment to remember what had happened.

His heart started to drum as his eyes rolled down and he saw the spear, jutting a good foot out in front of him.

It had been moved. It was through his neck now.

His spine was severed, he realized dimly. He could tell that someone had clothed him again but he couldn't feel the fabric, or anything else, below the wound.

The spear had to be one of Andrael's weapons, given his body's inability to adjust. He hadn't recognized it—it wasn't one of the five Blades, at least—but this must have been an earlier attempt. Something else created during Andrael's hundreds of years experimenting with ways to end the Venerate.

He closed his eyes, cursing himself for his overconfidence. Alaris, as usual, had thought ahead. That he had poisoned the Gil'shar against Caeden was no surprise; Caeden had been prepared for that, had thought of plenty of ways that he might work to overcome whatever lies had been told. But he hadn't foreseen the weapon. Alaris must have guessed that he would try to use his 'godhood' to talk down the Desrielites, and planned accordingly.

He shifted his head slightly, relieved to find he could do so, even if the pain was exquisite. The injury must be toward the base of his throat. He closed his eyes again, reaching out for kan.

There was nothing there.

He frowned, searching apprehensively for the dark energy. He
could understand the spear blocking him, but this...

His heart sank as he realized what was wrong.

"That looks uncomfortable."

Caeden opened his eyes again at the voice, rolling his eyes to the left and then managing a wan smile as he saw who had spoken. He opened his mouth to reply, but all that came out was a gargle.

Erran smiled back through a mask of dried blood, which coated the left side of his face. The head wound he'd sustained was clearly a little higher, with much of his hair matted, caked with sticky brown. He wasn't bound.

"Sorry I can't pull it out. They don't like it much when I try," he said apologetically, gesturing to the blood on his face. He glanced upward, then quickly turned away at an angle, no longer looking at Caeden. "Try not to move. They'll probably make me go elsewhere if they realize you're awake."

Caeden grunted in response, doing his best to look around without moving his head. From what he could see, along with Erran, there were about a half dozen men and women in the courtyard. The others were all huddled together over at the far side, talking softly and occasionally glancing anxiously toward Caeden and Erran, though none of them appeared to realize that he was conscious.

The space in which they were imprisoned was at least a hundred feet long and perhaps a third as wide. Grass grew tangled and wild through the cobblestones, but otherwise it was in good repair, with sturdy-looking gates barring the only two entrances. Walls rose sharply on each side, fifteen feet to the top at least. As Caeden's gaze traveled upward, he spotted heavily armored, attentive-looking guards glaring down, crossbows readied.

Erran followed his gaze. "Not the best accommodations," he agreed quietly. "The Columns are on just the other side of that wall, unless I got completely turned around when they brought me in. I assume that they're the fates-cursed reason we can't use either kan or Essence."

Caeden grunted again in acknowledgment, still assessing the area. A lone figure lay prone on the ground nearby, and the longer Caeden stared at it, the more certain he was that it wasn't breathing.

The body was facedown, but Caeden could see black veins in the neck beneath the dark hair, knew the man well enough to realize who it was. He felt a slight, hollow twinge at the recognition. He hadn't liked the man, but he'd been an ally.

And it was strange, too. If the Venerate had taken the precautions they obviously had, then they surely would have warned the Desrielites to keep any Augurs alive.

He flicked his eyes questioningly at Erran.

There was silence, warring emotions flitting across the young man's face as he realized what Caeden was asking. He shifted awkwardly.

"They knew he was an Augur," he said softly. "I was too close to the Columns when they got me, and I asked the others to keep quiet, so they still think I'm Gifted"—he touched the red Mark on his left arm lightly—"but Scyner *wanted* them to know about him. He was going to let them take him back to Desriel. Risk everything, on the chance that he could escape and use that medallion." He saw Caeden shift slightly, and nodded. "Yes. He told me what it was for—it was a confession of sorts, I think. He wanted to explain why he was doing it." He shook his head. "That was right before he tried to kill me."

Caeden closed his eyes, feeling Erran's pain. Scyner had been intending to use Alchesh's medallion to sever his link with the Forge, to stop being an Augur rather than sacrificing himself. So when confronted with execution, he'd done the only thing he could to see himself saved—while making sure that the other remaining Augur was dead.

"I am assuming that the others will be coming for you—they can't exactly get Licanius back without you," said Erran, after a few long seconds. He sounded weary. Sad.

Caeden opened his eyes again and tried to speak, to tell Erran that Asha was coming at nightfall, but the spear through his throat left him with only a harsh rasping. Erran shifted uneasily, eyeing the guards up above.

"Don't try to speak. The fact is, it doesn't matter for me. I know this place. I know what happens here."

A concerned shout came from above; Caeden rolled his eyes to see one of the guards pointing at him, gesturing urgently.

Caeden gritted his teeth. He needed to tell Erran to hold on until the evening. That Asha was here somewhere. That someone would be coming for him soon.

He gargled desperately at Erran, but all it did was elicit more shouting from above.

Erran looked around, paling, then abruptly strode over and embraced Caeden as more guards appeared in the courtyard, rushing toward them. Caeden felt something heavy drop around his neck.

"Use it on Ishelle," Erran whispered, mouth right next to Caeden's ear. "Save one of us, at least."

Caeden shouted but it all just came out in a rasping hiss, tears of frustration rolling down his cheeks as Erran stepped back just before the guards arrived. The Augur gave Caeden a slight nod and cheerfully brave grin before he was dragged roughly away.

The other Gifted were being ushered out of the courtyard, too, and even Scyner's body was being carted away. But it was the look of brazen confidence on the young man's face that broke Caeden's heart. Erran had left him with a request that he could never fulfill.

He'd been the last of the Augurs who might have been saved, and now—from what he had said, the way he had said it—he was going to his death.

Caeden rolled his eyes skyward, the ache in his chest only deepening as he noted the light remaining. He couldn't see the sun, but it wasn't close to dusk.

Erran passed from view through the far doorway, walking with head held high despite the shoves of the guards. Caeden squeezed his eyes shut, breathing, doing his best to press down the pain.

What was done was done.

All he could do now was wait.

Chapter 43

Asha held her breath as another group of soldiers marched past the open room, though none of them even looked in her direction.

Like most of the men inside the castle walls, they appeared relaxed but purposeful, talking among themselves quietly as they walked from one section of the castle to another. They were organized and never lingered, but there was purpose rather than urgency to their movements as they passed through this ruined section. They all assumed—rightly, to be fair—that they were safe here.

Asha allowed herself to breathe again once they were past, forced to trust Caeden's makeshift Vessel yet again. She understood the theory behind it well enough—kan to mask and protect the Essence, as well as to create the illusion of invisibility—but the problem was that she had no way of knowing whether it was actually working, beyond the fact that no one thus far had raised the alarm.

She glanced restlessly out the nearby window. The sun had been creeping inexorably downward for some time now, and was close to touching the distant, snowcapped mountains on Desriel's side of the Devliss.

That was troubling. Even allowing time for the High Priests to be gathered, Caeden should have been finished with his trial by now—should have either convinced them to listen to him, or escaped. Both options would have involved his coming back to find her.

She stared out the window for a few more minutes, heart sinking faster than the sun. She'd suspected an hour earlier that there was a problem, but this was fairly close to certain. She itched to move; though it would be far more dangerous, she had seen plenty of individuals moving freely about the castle during the past few hours. There was nothing about her that looked more Andarran than Desrielite, particularly with the uniform. If she acted confident and looked like she knew where she was going when she came across other people, she didn't think that there would be a problem.

Still. That wasn't the plan—not for another hour. She knew better than to act too early. If Caeden was delayed for some legitimate reason, her being found sneaking around could ruin everything.

Time passed at a painfully slow crawl, Asha swinging between racking nervousness whenever someone passed by, to anxiety mixed with grinding boredom otherwise. She watched the shadows lengthen outside, though she couldn't see much beyond the ruined towers unless she moved closer to the window, which she had no intention of risking.

Finally, though, the last rays of the sun vanished as it dipped behind the mountains, and Asha began cautiously stretching out her stiff muscles.

Something had gone wrong, and now she had to find out exactly what.

She took a breath, and stepped out from behind the invisibility shield.

Apprehension gnawed at her as she walked out of the small side room in the tower, heading away from the stairs via which she and Caeden had arrived. The Columns were being kept on the western side of the castle, guarded by hundreds of soldiers, some of whom were atop the castle's thick outer wall. Caeden had said that any prison they put him in would likely be close by: the Columns were by far the most effective Trap for both Essence and kan.

Asha doubted that they would keep him out in the open, though. That meant a cell somewhere along the western wall, or near it. That was the part of the castle in the best repair; if there was anywhere secure nearby, it would be in that section.

It was, unfortunately, also the area that held the most soldiers.

Asha's heart skipped a beat and her mind went blank as three appeared at the end of the corridor, walking toward her. She forced herself to keep calm, to keep moving just as she had been.

She gazed steadily at the men as they approached, affecting interested nonchalance even as her heart pounded, doing her best to act exactly as Breshada would have. She didn't know enough about the Desrielite army to pretend that she was part of it, but she *could* be a Hunter. As she had all day, she ran through how a Hunter—a 'Seeker'—would behave. Their status, the gods they would be likely to reference, everything she knew from weeks of training and talking with Breshada.

The men passed her by without a glance.

She almost stumbled with surprise, but kept going and refused to look back or increase her pace, despite her instincts. Everyone here had something to do, somewhere to be; this castle was nothing more than a stopover, a convenient bastion against the initial Andarran attacks. No one had time to take note of every unfamiliar face—particularly when the army here numbered in the thousands, and this was its protected center.

She made her way through a maze of hallways, making certain to keep moving westward. She passed four more groups of soldiers over the next few minutes, none of whom batted an eyelid at her presence. It seemed that as long as she looked like she was going somewhere with a purpose, she wouldn't be stopped.

Soon enough she felt the change of pressure in the air, everything suddenly heavy and uncomfortable, cloying. She glanced around to check that she was alone, then cautiously tried to light a spark of Essence at the tip of her finger.

Nothing happened.

She grimaced. She was getting closer.

She was also in much more danger, now.

Asha soon found herself making her way along a narrow gallery overlooking a large courtyard below—this one well lit, ringed by torches. It was clearly in use, the surrounding gray stone walls looking more solid than elsewhere, supplies and weapons stashed off to the side.

Asha balked as a line of figures caught the edge of her vision, her racing pulse only easing a little when she realized that they were swaying slightly in the breeze, hanging from a gallows below. She swallowed, moving to hurry past the grisly spectacle. Caeden wouldn't be among the dead, even within range of the Columns.

A gust of wind made the torches flicker and flare, and Asha paused. Some of those people were wearing tattered red cloaks.

She slowed to a halt, squinting at the bodies, which were mostly hidden in the gloom. Her stomach twisted as she recognized Tiala, a Gifted from Tol Athian who had often visited the library back when Asha had been a Shadow. Her distinctive white hair concealed half of her face, but Asha knew straight away that it was she.

She scanned down the gallows and froze, heart stopping as her gaze settled on the last in line. The face was deep in shadow as it twisted gently in the breeze, but she knew the clothes, the form.

She spotted the way down, moving automatically. She had to check. Had to be certain.

Asha scrambled down the stairs and hurried across the silent courtyard, gaze transfixed, disbelief turning gradually to understanding and then trembling, gasping grief as Erran's bloated face resolved from the darkness. Torchlight reflected off his lifeless eyes, his head at an unnatural angle where his neck had been broken by the abrupt fall and short stop.

Asha reached up a shaking hand and gently touched his foot, for a desperate, vain moment wondering if she might be able to revive him. His body twisted slightly in response; she closed her eyes and let her arm fall back to her side, doing everything she could to hold back her tears. Not here. Not yet. She had to remember where she was.

But Erran...Erran had been her friend. Not to mention an Augur, one of the most dangerous people in the entire world. And now he was just...gone.

Fear seeped in, under her skin, into her bones. She felt a nauseating wave of dizziness.

"You. What are you doing there?"

Asha started, her light-headedness threatening to overcome her.

Then she exhaled, forced everything out. The aching sorrow, the fear.

She couldn't afford to break now.

She turned, staring calmly at the half dozen soldiers marching toward her. The man at the front was older, and from the crispness of his uniform and his attitude, he was someone important.

"Just admiring the gaa'vesh," said Asha cheerfully, inwardly thankful that her voice didn't crack. "Meldier knows I wasn't told that there was going to be any entertainment today." She eyed the man in what she hoped was a vaguely disdainful fashion. "Who do I speak to about keeping informed?"

The man gave her a perplexed look. "This area is off-limits. Even had you known, you would not have been allowed to watch." He squinted at her. "You are young."

Asha arched an eyebrow. Breshada had been a Seeker at sixteen; Asha was old enough to pass. "You do...realize who I am?" She sighed as the man shook his head, making a small sign with her hand. A dismissive gesture, something Breshada—Nethgalla— had done often to indicate irritation. "I swear by Alar that my terogesh was right. We Seekers are getting less respect than we deserve." She glared at him challengingly, resting a hand lightly on the blade strapped to her side.

It was a risk, being so aggressive—but Breshada had acted this way, and from both her stories and Wirr's and Davian's, it was clear this was simply how most Seekers were. They were considered the elite of the Gil'shar, divinely chosen, blessed with talent beyond even the highest-ranking soldier. Though they were not officially of a higher rank than anyone in the army—they were not ranked at all, in fact—she was certain that they were generally considered above everyone else.

The man eyed her, and everyone was silent.

Then he chuckled, echoed uneasily by the group behind him.

"Of course, of course. I am Saresh. My apologies..."

"Edesha."

"Edesha," repeated the soldier as he gave a slight bow, though Asha could tell it galled him to do so. "In the rush of war, sometimes hospitality is forgotten."

Asha sniffed, motioning with her head that she accepted the apology. Saresh straightened, and the group looked to move on.

Asha didn't think. Didn't hesitate.

"Is this all there is? I would be disappointed if there were not more," she said loudly.

She saw the almost imperceptible glower on the soldier's face. She was pushing her luck, but she needed information.

"These were the only prisoners for today," said Saresh.

"What about the other one?" It was a younger man stepping forward, his eager look shriveling beneath his leader's glared response. "I just...thought the Seeker might be interested," he finished, flashing Asha a warm smile.

Asha nodded back to him, then looked at Saresh. "Well?"

Saresh gave his underling another glare, but gestured. "I fear that we must continue upon our task, but Garis would be honored to show you the way. It will be something you have never seen, Seeker Edesha. Something you will likely never see again," he promised her, a brief spark of excitement in his eyes.

Asha's stomach churned at the words.

"Now *that* sounds like it is worth my time." She put as much upbeat enthusiasm into her voice as she could manage. "Lead the way."

Garis didn't need a second invitation, guiding her swiftly away from the gallows, which Asha left in their wake only too willingly. A minute later—the young soldier chattering brightly the entire way about the prisoner who refused to die—they turned a corner onto the beginning of a raised walkway, and Garis fell silent, gesturing downward and coming to a halt.

Asha tried to look fascinated rather than horrified as she peered down into the narrow courtyard.

"And you say he is still alive?" she asked, the disbelief in her voice not entirely feigned. Caeden was pinned to the wall by a spear through his throat, motionless, eyes shut. Even knowing what he was, he looked like a corpse.

"That's what they say. I haven't seen him move, but others have." Garis was standing too close to Asha for her liking, but she stayed in character, ignoring him completely rather than moving

away.

Asha snorted. "No man can survive that."

"The rumors say that he is not a man." Garis spoke in the breathless whisper of someone telling a secret he was certain the other person would find enthralling. "He went before the High Priests themselves to prove himself a god. And failed," he finished triumphantly, eyes alight with excitement.

Asha cocked her head to the side, pretending to be reluctantly impressed even as her mind raced. So Caeden had convinced the High Priests to administer the trial, but then failed? How?

"I wish to take a closer look."

Garis turned to her, wide-eyed. "We cannot," he said in a panicked whisper. "This far is allowed, but the guards are under strict orders. If we were to distract them from their duty…"

Asha glanced contemptuously at the young man. "You promised me something interesting. Not a dead body seen from a distance and half-baked rumors about why it is there."

Garis's face fell, and Asha thought he was going to give up.

"All right," he said finally, his voice low. "But we have to be quick. If we cause trouble…"

"If we cause trouble, I will deal with it." They were in the corner of the courtyard on the raised, covered walkway; Asha could see the guards standing in archways on the opposite side, but her view of the ones on this side was blocked by stone. She needed to know how many men were keeping watch.

She walked at a casual stroll, hands behind her back, Garis trailing a little behind as she stared down at Caeden as if in curiosity. One of the guards gave them a questioning, half-irritated glance, but Asha acknowledged him briefly and then proceeded to ignore him. The man shook his head and went back to watching the courtyard.

Within a minute they had reached the far end of the walkway, Caeden close enough now that she could see the slight rise and fall of his chest.

She steeled herself. Six guards. Six guards—all with crossbows—plus Garis. And Caeden incapacitated. She'd known that it would be difficult, but this…

She'd seen the determination in the guards' eyes, seen the way their gazes roved the courtyard below warily, despite the apparent lack of danger. These men wouldn't leave Caeden unattended, no matter what story she came up with, no matter what distraction she tried to cause.

She and Garis left the walkway, walking out the far door and into a new, completely empty corridor.

"So," said Garis, turning to her with a smile that looked eager now that they hadn't been reprimanded. "What did you think?"

Asha injected her arm with Essence and hit him squarely on the jaw. The blow was powerful enough to send him flying back against the stone wall; he hit hard and slumped to the floor, unconscious.

She slung Garis's arm over one shoulder and flooded her body with Essence, giving her a rush of strength, increasing her perception. Then she hauled the young man back through the door onto the walkway.

The two guards closest spun as they saw Garis, crossbows leveled at her.

"Meldier take it, get over here," she gasped, wide-eyed, stumbling and putting Garis gently against the wall. She feigned a wince as she did so.

"What happened?" Weapons wavered and then lowered as the men hurried over, out of sight of the others on guard.

"I punched him in the face," said Asha as she let Essence weave just beneath and over her skin. There was a moment—just a moment—where the Essence strained against the decay in the air, and she feared that even with the energy sitting as it should just within her body, the Columns' effect would be too powerful.

Then her golden armor was blazing to life around her.

She moved too quickly for the shocked soldiers to cry out, grabbing both of them and slamming them together with Essence-enhanced strength. Both men fell limply to the ground.

Four left, and no alarm so far. But the other guards would already have noticed the two missing from the edge of the walkway, even if they couldn't see where they were. And this area, while clearly closed off, wouldn't be free of traffic forever.

She sprinted down the walkway toward the third guard on her side.

There was a half-confused call from the other side of the courtyard, her blinding light easily spotted through the archways, but it was far too late for the hapless man with the crossbow. He was unconscious before he could even turn.

The three guards on the other side were aware of the threat now, though.

She flinched as a crossbow bolt sheared along her arm, grazing along the topmost layers of skin. She ignored the stinging pain, backing up as far from the courtyard as she possibly could, then bracing herself and sprinting forward.

She jumped.

Essence-enhanced legs gave her more than enough lift to cover the thirty feet of open air between the two walkways. The guard she had aimed for froze in shock at the sight of the blazing figure hurtling toward him; Asha crashed into the man, the force of the impact with her armor cracking his bones and sending him crashing backward. Asha rolled—she was well practiced in moving at speed from her time in the dok'en—and landed a solid kick to the soldier's head as she came to her feet beside him. He stayed down, unmoving.

She flinched as two more bolts slammed into her armor in quick succession, sending her staggering back, the impact far more noticeable than it would normally have been. They would leave welts, but nothing was seriously injured. The decaying effect of the Columns was clearly reducing her armor's efficacy.

She growled, and charged the final two guards.

Both men tossed their crossbows aside as they recognized the futility of trying to reload, and drew blades instead.

Then the one farthest from her and closest to the door ran for the exit, yelling.

Asha's own sword hissed from its sheath, her training both with Nethgalla's version of Breshada and over the past year in the dok'en giving her plenty of confidence. She knew that she wasn't a master swordsman and probably never would be, but with her Essence-enhanced speed, two soldiers were no match for her.

She attacked hard, slipping smoothly past the first Desrielite's strike and letting her blade slide along the man's stomach, the sharp steel slicing open a vicious wound. She ignored his cry of pain and burst after the second man; he half turned at the last moment as if realizing that he couldn't make the door, but it was too late. Asha's blow sent him reeling over the edge of the walkway and into the courtyard below, a dull crunch indicating a heavy landing.

Asha hurried back to the last man, who was moaning in fear and desperation, blood pooling on the stones near his stomach. Not a wound from which he would recover.

She vacillated, then shook her head to herself. Knelt.

"Shut up and hold still," she growled, grabbing his head and cracking it hard against the ground. The guard's eyes rolled into the back of his head.

Then she pressed her hands against the hot, gushing wound—firmly, despite the unpleasant sensation—and poured Essence into the man.

She could sense that even with the direct contact, a great deal of the energy was decaying; fortunately, with her enormous Reserve, it simply didn't matter. Within a few seconds the soldier was breathing more easily, the wound no longer bleeding.

Asha scrambled to her feet again and leaped down into the courtyard, landing in front of Caeden, a small puff of dust spurting up where her feet touched the dirt. She studied him worriedly as she crouched and wiped the blood from her hands on an abandoned cloak lying nearby.

His eyes rolled toward her and he gasped, clearly trying to say something.

Asha jumped—it wasn't far removed from seeing a corpse stir—and then shook her head at him. "I'm assuming that if I remove this thing, you'll be able to heal. And if you can't...well. We'll worry about that if it happens."

"What in Diaria's name?"

The alarmed utterance came from above, audible only thanks to the hush of the courtyard; Asha spun to see another soldier—only just arrived, apparently, and fortunately alone—watching her in horror. They both froze, and then the man was reaching for one of the dead guards' crossbows.

Asha didn't hesitate. She flooded her right arm with Essence, grasped the spear firmly and pulled with all her strength. The weapon came away from the wall with a shiver, Caeden sliding unpleasantly off it, neck trickling gore.

Asha ignored him, spinning and hurling the spear as the crossbow was leveled at her.

The weapon took the man through the chest, throwing him backward, the bolt from his shot pushed wide and missing her head by inches. She poured Essence into her legs and leaped up to the walkway, but the man was already dead.

Asha ignored the sick feeling in her stomach and didn't pause, jumping back down to Caeden, who—much to her relief—was staggering to his feet. She landed in front of him, examining him critically. The hole in his throat had already closed up. "Can you follow me?"

Caeden swayed and then steadied. "Think so," he rasped. He waved his hand urgently as Asha turned. "Erran," he gasped, worry in his eyes.

"Dead." Asha said the word as dispassionately as possible, not allowing herself to think about it.

Caeden's face crumpled, but he said nothing more, gesturing sadly for her to lead.

Asha hesitated, then wrapped one arm around Caeden, looking up at the walkway and fortifying her body with Essence once again. "Try to hold on."

She jumped.

The wall was only fifteen feet high but Caeden's weight dragged her down, and she barely managed to grasp the ledge with her free hand, hanging precariously before summoning every bit of strength she could and tossing Caeden up onto the pathway. The redheaded man was already showing signs of recovery, able to scramble the rest of the way himself, rolling to safety.

Asha dropped back down to the courtyard, taking a quick moment to recover her breath before leaping again. This time she made the jump comfortably, barely having to grab the ledge at all before hauling herself up to join Caeden on the walkway.

She paused, then hurried over to Garis's unconscious form, stripping the uniform from him—the only one without blood on it, she suspected—and tossing items of clothing to Caeden, who dressed quickly. Fortunately, the two men were alike enough in size.

The next few minutes passed remarkably well. Evening meant that many of those inside the castle were sleeping, and the few people who were around they spotted early and avoided easily enough. Asha breathed a sigh of relief as she felt the oppressive presence of the Columns finally disappear, and beside her she could see Caeden's shoulders relax just a little as he sensed the same.

"I still can't use kan," he said, a flash of pain flickering across his face. "That spear was a type of Vessel that…" He trailed off, as if realizing the pointlessness of going into detail. "I won't be able to use kan for a while. An hour or two, probably."

As he finished speaking, somewhere distantly behind them, the shouting began.

Asha and Caeden picked up the pace.

They jogged for a minute, and Asha was just beginning to think that they might be able to make it out of the castle unseen when there was movement up ahead. A half dozen soldiers appeared at a run, directly in their path.

Asha tapped Essence but Caeden was already leaping forward, blade flashing; he was suddenly a blur, moving smoothly between the opposing soldiers, dancing away from their thrusts and delivering his own with deadly precision. Asha watched in astonishment. If he wasn't using kan to slow time, then he had to at least be using Essence to enhance his reflexes.

Within ten seconds there were six bodies on the floor, none of them moving.

Caeden breathed deeply, sheathing his blade as Asha hurried over. "Much better," he muttered as he rolled his right shoulder experimentally, voice no longer hoarse. "Let's keep moving."

Asha swallowed, but nodded.

The shouts around them began to spread, angry and panicked in equal measure as torches—a distinctive white, not the usual orange—started flaring to life along the castle walls.

Asha and Caeden finally reached a gap in the rubble that opened to the outside of the castle, thirty feet above the ground.

Caeden brought Asha to a halt, hesitating.

"This is probably our best way out," he said, indicating the darkened ground below. "It might be time to signal Wirr."

Asha agreed, heart in her throat. She extended her arm to the night sky.

A blindingly bright bolt of Essence erupted from her fingertip, streaking to the heavens.

"That should do it," murmured Caeden as the shouting around the castle immediately increased in both volume and urgency. "Shall we?"

They leaped.

Asha hit the ground smoothly, quickly reaching out and steadying Caeden as he stumbled. He flexed his leg quickly before nodding and pushing upright.

Asha scanned the camp ahead, trying to see a potential path through. The shouting was spreading as more and more soldiers appeared, torches now illuminating the area Asha and Caeden needed to cross.

"Caeden. Asha. I see you," Asha said suddenly. "There's a patrol around the corner, coming from the east. Move."

Asha worked her mouth in surprise as she and Caeden both reacted at the same time, ducking behind a pile of stone and flattening themselves against the ground. A few seconds later a light appeared and three soldiers jogged around the edge of the castle, looking alert as they scanned the area but not noticing the two prone forms.

"Good. We have a minute now," said Asha as the soldiers passed out of earshot, the discomfort of speaking against her will unsettling. "This isn't going to be easy. The camp is like an anthill at the moment. If this is going to work, Caeden you're going to need to stay close and copy what Asha's doing exactly; I won't have time to give you instructions like this. Stand up if you understand and are ready."

Caeden ran a hand through his hair, looking at Asha. "I guess it's up to Wirr now," he whispered to her.

They both stood.

She dashed forward abruptly, sliding behind a half-erected tent as a group of soldiers passed nearby before leaping to her feet again, walking this time with a confident stride as if she belonged there, heading westward through the maze of tents. Caeden mimicked her exactly, silent, the tension on his face indicating his focus.

A couple of soldiers glanced in their direction; one began to rise but suddenly there was a roar of Essence elsewhere in the camp, a distance behind them. The men both leaped to their feet and sprinted away toward it.

Asha's heart pounded almost painfully in her chest. Many patches of the camp were still dark; thousands of soldiers meant that it covered too much space to have torches lit in every small area. Wirr guided them mostly toward these pockets, sometimes sprinting through shadows, sometimes walking, and sometimes hiding in one place for minutes at a time. More Essence attacks came at opportune moments to distract soldiers blocking their path, though Wirr was clearly spacing them out across the entire camp, not risking indicating any particular pattern to the Gil'shar.

Still, the Desrielites were getting more organized now, the margin for error when Asha and Caeden moved getting tighter and tighter, the two of them each time seeming to disappear behind a tent or into shadows just as soldiers would have spotted them. Sometimes they needed to move obliquely, even backward, but the edge of the camp crept gradually closer. Several times Asha could feel the weight of Traps bearing down on her, and she could see their effect in the blasts of Essence that dissipated into the ether overhead.

Fortunately, the bulk of the search remained focused back around the castle, the Desrielites seemingly convinced that there was no way anyone could have sneaked away from it. Asha felt a flicker of hope as they dashed forward once again, finally skidding to a stop in a relatively safe spot among some tents, coming within sight of the very edge of the camp.

That small flame immediately died.

"I don't think I can do anything about this part," she whispered, once again speaking without meaning to. "They only just got organized, but they're all the way around, and they seem to have Traps." There was a pause. "I'll fire some Essence around where you are in a minute or two—I don't think you should wait longer than that. I'll do my best to distract them, but that's all I can do. Sorry." Another pause. "Fates with both of you."

Caeden studied the line in front of them bleakly. Crossbow-wielding soldiers stood shoulder to shoulder with dar'gaithin; the Banes assembled here must be all that remained in the entire army. There were no gaps, not as far as the eye could see, and even with Essence enhancing their strength, there was no way that Asha and Caeden could just punch a hole through. "Thoughts?"

Asha pulled in a nervous breath, barely trusting herself to speak.

"We rush them," she said. "No fighting. Just jump over them, run into the forest. We're faster than they are."

Caeden sucked in air through his teeth. "Jump? They have crossbows. A *lot* of crossbows."

"Then let's not get hit in the head," said Asha grimly. "My armor will still work through the Traps, so I should be able to recover as long as I don't get knocked out. And from what I've seen, you can heal from pretty much anything."

Caeden exhaled. "All right," he said slowly. "But strengthen yourself as much as you can internally, too, and be ready to go *fast*. If one of those bolts gets you in the leg, or the back, you have to make sure you don't do much more than stumble. If you're not ready they'll toss you around, and you have to be able to recover, because those dar'gaithin will *swarm* us." He chewed his lip. "How high can you jump, at speed? Essence will help, of course, but there are physical limits no matter how much of it you have. The dar'gaithin can reach up to twice their height, easily, if they're quick enough to react."

Asha swallowed. That was twenty feet, directly up, to clear them. She'd done it before—more than that, even—but only in the dok'en, and even then only barely.

"I can do it," she said, with more confidence than she felt. There was no choice here, no chance to sit down and think of a better plan. If they stayed in the camp, it was only a matter of time before they were caught, even with Wirr's help.

"Good enough," said Caeden. "Once we—"

The forest behind the soldiers and dar'gaithin exploded in fire.

Many of the men and Banes spun instinctively at the noise and light, soldiers shielding their eyes against the blinding Essence flashing among the trees. Neither Asha nor Caeden hesitated, scrambling up and sprinting forward, Asha flooding her body with Essence and activating her armor again.

Time seemed to slow, the space between them and the line of enemies taking an eternity to cross. Screams of warning flew across the field as soldiers spotted them, crossbows rising, dar'gaithin darting forward with inhuman speed.

Asha waited until she was twenty feet from the closest Bane, and *jumped*.

Her stomach lurched as she rose sharply, the dar'gaithin hissing as it lashed out, barely missing her ankle. She caught a glimpse of soldiers watching slack-jawed as she and Caeden soared above them.

Then she shouted in pain as a crossbow bolt caught her in the shoulder, and another in her side, spinning her around before she landed. She rolled as she hit the ground, well clear of the nearest Desrielite, and scrambled to her feet before sprinting for the blazing forest.

Had Caeden made it? She risked a glance back, heart lurching. Caeden was close behind her, but beyond him a wall of men were taking aim.

The heaviness in the air disappeared, and Asha tapped Essence as she ran.

A thick barrier sprang into existence between them and the Desrielites; a moment later it flashed in a hundred different places as bolts ricocheted off the protective shield. Asha didn't stop, though she saw Caeden give her a grateful look. The man's shirt and trousers now looked as if they were made of blood; there was no telling how many times he'd been struck, but he seemed capable of continuing.

Without speaking they sprinted into the burning forest, leaving the furious howls of the Desrielites behind them.

Asha, Wirr, and Caeden sat silently, the thrill of their successful escape fading beneath the reality that now lay before them.

Erran was dead. A lump rose in Asha's throat and tears threatened to leak from her eyes; the raw emotion of his death, their failure to stop the Desrielites, her exhaustion...it was almost too much. Wirr looked hollow, and even Caeden no longer had the spark of determination that she'd seen in him since he had entered the dok'en. Essence trickled back into her Reserve—the part that she was able to use—but even the feeling of extra energy barely made a difference.

"We cannot win here," said Caeden into the hush. "The Gil'shar have too many weapons, too many soldiers."

Wirr nodded, eyes red with tiredness and grief. Erran's death had hit him hard, too. "You did what you could, Caeden."

There was silence again, Asha resisting the urge to lash out. She didn't agree. She blamed Caeden for not realizing that the other Venerate could use Desriel like this. She blamed him for starting this war. She blamed him for Davian's death.

But none of that was productive. She was tired, she was grieving, but she would *not* lose control.

If she did, she wasn't sure that she would ever get it back again.

"So the Boundary will fall," Caeden continued hollowly. "Northern Andarra will be lost." He reluctantly looked up at Wirr. "But...we might still stop the rest."

"I know." Wirr rubbed his face, exhaling heavily, then locked eyes with Asha. "And you two are the ones who have to do it. You have to go and get it."

Through the fog of tiredness and sorrow, it took a few moments for Asha to understand what he was saying.

"What? *No.*" Asha put iron into her tone. "If we're going to get Licanius, you're coming too. And if you're not, then I am staying to help you fight."

"Whoever stays is here to delay the inevitable," said Wirr quietly. "Caeden needs as much time as he can get to finish this, but you are too valuable an asset to waste." He said the words dispassionately.

"Don't be ridiculous." Asha could hear the desperation in her tone, but she didn't care. She couldn't countenance this, not so soon after Erran. "You're not thinking clearly. You can't just sacrifice yourself. The country *needs* you. Not to mention that your ability is far too valuable."

"Not without anyone to command, it isn't." Wirr gave her a gentle smile. "And the country won't be worth much if we simply let the Desrielites through. Our being here could delay them a day or two, maybe even a few. We know exactly where they're heading. We're not without advantages." His tone was light, but Asha could see in his eyes that he was deadly serious about this. "So go and find Licanius. Save Davian. Do what needs to be done."

Asha stared at him, and this time the tears in her eyes came unbidden. She felt like screaming at him, telling him that he was being stupid, that all he had to do to save himself was leave with them.

But she knew, just as he and Caeden did, that this was their best course of action. Perhaps their only remaining choice.

So she stepped forward and enveloped him in a long, tight hug, her tears making a damp patch on his shoulder. He held her silently; when her sobs stopped she took a deep breath and stepped away, dabbing her eyes.

"Dav is going to be livid if you get yourself killed," she said, her voice breaking.

Wirr choked out a laugh. He was fighting back emotion, too. "Same goes for you."

He kissed her on the cheek, then stepped away and stuck out his hand toward Caeden.

"No matter what you've done in the past, you *are* my friend," he said.

Caeden paused, then gave him a small smile and clasped his hand warmly.

"That's all I can ask for," he said softly. He dug into a pocket, then pressed something into Wirr's hand. "I've charged these again. If you get the chance, use it."

Asha caught a glimpse of the white Travel Stone as Wirr slipped it into his pocket.

Caeden clapped Wirr on the back. "Time for you to get back to the others—they need you. Just...do what you can. We'll make sure that it's not in vain."

Wirr nodded grimly, hesitating for just a moment.

Then he turned, starting back toward the trees.

Asha watched him as he walked away. Even in his ragged clothing, even tired as he was, he looked…*noble*. Nobody seeing him, even for the first time, would mistake him for anything but the leader he was.

He glanced over his shoulder, locking eyes with her and giving her one final smile.

Then he was gone.

She swallowed, then turned to watch as Caeden began opening the Gate into the heart of Ilshan Gathdel Teth.

Chapter 44

Davian watched as Nethgalla slowly turned the steel band over in her hands in the Essence-light he was providing, examining the incredibly fine, detailed kan structures that he had so carefully set into the metal.

"What do you think?" he asked when he could take the silence no longer.

Nethgalla continued to study the band, which was now bent into a shape closer to that of a torc since they had sliced through one part of the metal, allowing for an easier activation method without using Essence.

"It looks . . . right," she conceded, a note of vague surprise in her voice as it echoed slightly around the small cave. "I cannot see any reason why this one won't work."

Davian breathed out, shoulders sagging, finally allowing himself to feel the exhaustion of the past few days' work. He took a celebratory bite of the rock-hard bread that Nethgalla had brought him, chewing for several seconds before swallowing, even that tasting good in the glow of his success. This was his eighth attempt to make this Vessel: the more recent tries had been close, but each time Nethgalla had been able to point to a fault that Davian had been forced to agree was problematic. The level of precision required was far beyond what any normal Vessel would need.

That had resulted in his Reserve steadily draining again as he fought against sleep in this small, black cave, keeping his focus Vessel activated almost continuously. He knew that his time here was short, regardless of the fact that he would return to Zvaelar at the exact moment when he had left. Nethgalla had warned him that Gassandrid was furious at his escape and Rethgar's death, but was also confident that Davian hadn't yet made his way out of the complex. His description had been circulated, and people were alert to concerns that there might be a traitor in their midst; Nethgalla had been able to smuggle him small amounts of food and water so far, but that couldn't last forever. His hiding place wouldn't stay tenable for much longer.

Nethgalla was still peering at the steel band. "All right," she said slowly. "Time to see if it works."

She turned and looked at Davian expectantly.

"You...want me to use it?" asked Davian, the bottom suddenly dropping out of his stomach. "Now?"

Nethgalla sighed impatiently. "Yes. Now." She tapped her foot impatiently at his expression. "Just follow the logic through. If you test it, it must work, because we both know that you don't die here. Whereas if you *don't* test it here, it could very well *not* work, and your other friends in Zvaelar will die as a result."

Davian licked his lips. "What happens if it *half* works?"

Nethgalla held his gaze calmly. "Normally I would say death. Horrible, painful death." She cocked her head to the side. "In your case, though, I suppose it must just be horrible, painful injury."

Davian scowled at her. "You could pretend to care."

"I could." Nethgalla shrugged at him, then gestured. Davian focused to see a thin line of kan flowing out from her fingertips, gently settling just inside the walls. He frowned.

"You're Silencing the room?"

"Horrible, painful injury," repeated Nethgalla.

Davian glared, then gritted his teeth and took the Vessel from her, unable to help but push through kan and examine it again. The lines were almost invisible, the actual structure a mess of complicated components that he was still struggling to fully understand. If their situation here had not been so dire, Davian would have suspected Nethgalla of trying to fool him into making something else entirely. But she insisted that the majority of the mechanisms were to deal with the change of form—not just slight physical changes, but entire pieces of anatomy morphing.

It would, she had cheerfully assured him, be excruciating even if successful.

"You should probably take off your clothes, too." Nethgalla rolled her eyes at his expression. "I went to considerable effort to get you something to replace those rags you were wearing, so don't expect me to do it again because you were feeling shy. And no, before you ask," she added. "I'm not going to look away."

Davian snorted irritably, but began stripping. Nethgalla was right—dar'gaithin were much bigger than people. Keeping his clothes on would only ruin them.

He finished and glanced over at her again, surprised when she gave him the slightest nod of encouragement. Trying not to look as self-conscious as he felt, he picked up the Vessel, settled it around his neck, and—muscles straining—bent the two points of the cut steel band until they reconnected.

There was a small flash of light as the Vessel activated and began drawing a tiny amount of Essence from him, energy pulsing to life around Davian's throat as the cool steel pressed against his skin.

For a moment nothing happened, and Davian felt a selfish flicker of hope that perhaps this wouldn't work after all. Perhaps he'd done all he could, but it simply wasn't possible and they would need to find another way.

Pain ripped through him.

This wasn't like when he'd shape-shifted in Deilannis, deeply unpleasant though that had been. This felt as if everything were being torn apart piece by piece. His blood felt like fire, burning away at the inside of his veins. He fell to the floor, a bubbling scream ripping from his throat, which was suddenly clogged with hot, salty liquid; through the haze of red he saw his arms start to stretch, then ooze blood as sharp black slivers began crawling up through his skin. His squeezed his eyes shut as even those began to boil agonizingly in their sockets.

Then, after an age, it was over.

He opened his eyes cautiously, and panic immediately set in. It wasn't that he couldn't see, but everything seemed... bright. No color, just lines of light everywhere, forming images and outlines.

He twisted to look down at himself.

There was nothing there.

"Did...it work?" His gaze turned toward Nethgalla; his strange vision didn't allow him to see finer features, but it was her. His words came out harsh and he flinched at the sound, almost choking off the last word in surprise.

Nethgalla stirred from her reclining position in the corner, though he could see that she had been tense. "It appears that it did." There was a mixture of trepidation and fascination in her tone. "How do you feel?"

"How do I feel?" Davian felt a surge of anger and he tried to get to his feet as he hissed the words, only to fall back again when he discovered that he had none. "How do you *think* I feel, you stupid..."

He trailed off, forcing down the flash of fury. "Sorry."

Nethgalla hadn't moved, but he sensed something from her. Caution.

It annoyed him.

"You know who you are? You remember what you're doing?" Nethgalla asked after a moment.

"Yes," he snapped.

Nethgalla nodded slowly. "But you are affected in other ways."

Davian swallowed an irritated reply. "Everything you say makes me angry," he agreed as calmly as he could.

"I hear that all the time." Nethgalla smiled to show she was joking, but she swallowed the expression quickly when she saw no trace of amusement from Davian. "It must be the physiology. Your mind gives you more control than they have, but the instincts will remain as long as you are in that body."

Davian acknowledged the statement curtly and tried to rise, but immediately flailed to the ground again, landing awkwardly on his back and thrashing around furiously for several enraged seconds before forcing himself to calm. Everything felt wrong, from the scales stabbing into his flesh everywhere, to the strange vision, to the fact that he no longer had any legs. It was all so *disorienting*, and that made it even harder not to lose his temper.

"How do I stand up?" he snarled.

Nethgalla made no move to help him. "Your muscles are different from a human's. They will be strong enough—you will have inherited that from the body—but you are going to need to learn to use them correctly." She gestured, looking vaguely helpless. "Imagine the way a dar'gaithin moves, and try to replicate it. That is how I adapt to a new body quickly—I try to move in the same way as the Imprint did. It's the only advice I can give you for this particular problem."

"I don't remember any of them ever having to get up off the floor," Davian spat. Still, he stopped moving and closed his eyes. He had interacted with Isstharis and Theshesseth, and seen other dar'gaithin in the distance plenty of times now. He knew the creatures well enough to picture their movements.

Awkwardly, carefully, he pushed himself up, levering his body with surprisingly strong arms until he managed to curl his tail—he shuddered a little at the thought—beneath him. To his surprise, once it was in position, balance seemed to come naturally. It was only when he began to think about it that he found himself wobbling again, forced to brace himself against a nearby wall.

He twisted to see Nethgalla watching him silently. It was hard to tell what she was thinking as he couldn't properly make out her features, but eventually she shook her head.

"You look just like one of them," she said faintly. "I do not know whether to be relieved or horrified that this is possible, but..." She gestured. "Now we know."

Davian grunted. "So I can change back?" The thought of undergoing the pain of the transformation again filled him with dread, but not more than the thought of staying like this. Every moment he remained in this form felt *wrong*.

"Not yet." Nethgalla sounded almost apologetic, but mostly fascinated. "You need to walk...slither...around a bit. See how accustomed you can become to the body. Stay like this for a time, to determine whether there are any slow-acting negative effects. And to mimic what the others will likely need to go through," she added.

Davian let out a hiss of irritation, causing Nethgalla to take a wary step back, but acceded with a jerk of his head.

The next hour passed in stomach-churning discomfort. Davian followed suggestions from Nethgalla, learning to move, adapting to the strengths and weaknesses of the dar'gaithin body. His physical control improved dramatically, but none of it made him feel any better. There was a constant fury bubbling inside him, irrational and barely suppressed. He hated every second of it.

There were other things of note, too. Touching kan was immensely difficult, though whether because of his state of mind or because the black scales were interfering, he couldn't quite decide. The Vessels built into his arms were gone, too; Nethgalla postulated that they were akin to physical alterations to his body, like tattoos, and so would disappear and reappear as he changed forms. That was an interesting thought, though not something of which he could make immediate use.

Finally, Nethgalla gave a reluctant nod.

"That should be enough," she conceded. "You can tell Tal that an hour in this form is safe. Anything beyond that, though, is an unknown."

Davian didn't bother to point out that Tal was the only one he *wasn't* worried about. He carefully reached up and pulled the two points of the metal band around his neck apart.

Nothing happened.

Davian's heart began to pound wildly as the seconds dragged by. "I'm not changing back," he growled in horror.

"You will." Nethgalla's voice was soothing. "You just need to wait."

"Easy for you to say," snarled Davian, feeling his tail whip about wildly in anger.

Then there was something. A shift in his tail, pain ricocheting up his spine. A ripple of stabbing sensations as scales began to retract.

The next few minutes passed in a terrible red blur.

Afterward, Davian just lay there for a while with his eyes closed, breathing, gingerly moving his arms and legs. Barely daring to believe that the nightmare was over.

"Do I look...all right?" he asked, opening his eyes.

Nethgalla's arms were crossed. "That's subjective," she said, "but yes. You are back to the way you were before."

Davian drew a shuddering breath, pushing through kan, relieved to find it childishly easy to touch again. He examined the Reserve in his body and the Vessels in his arms. They seemed intact.

"Nothing was damaged," he said, too relieved to feel self-conscious this time as he retrieved his clothes and began to dress again. "The Vessels have re-formed. I even seem to have the same level of Essence in my Reserve."

Nethgalla nodded thoughtfully. "Just like any other physical attributes. Interesting." She sighed. "That alone is a year's worth of experimentation I would love to pursue."

Davian glowered at her as he slipped on his shirt. "No thank you."

Nethgalla smiled. "I know." The expression faded as she studied him. "How do you feel? Emotionally, I mean?"

Davian paused, considering.

"Better," he conceded. "Certainly less like I want to attack anything that moves."

"Good. A purely physical effect, then." Nethgalla stepped over to the metal band that Davian had placed on the ground once he had changed back, picking it up and running a finger along it in what looked disturbingly like a caress. "You have created something unique here, Davian. Truly a thing of great beauty."

Davian watched, not responding. Not really knowing whether he agreed, either. Nethgalla had been right about one thing—shape-shifting was unlike anything else that used kan. It dealt far less in hard angles and neat lines; as he'd built the mechanisms they had created complex forms, but they were unique, gave the impression of disorganization even as they were carefully positioned. The result was a haphazard maze of complexity. If he had not put it together himself—didn't understand how precise the positioning had to be—he would have said it looked more like a child's drawing than a work of art.

"It's certainly different from anything else I've seen," he conceded. "If you couldn't see the endpoints, I'm not sure that it could even be identified as a Vessel."

"You're right. The other forms of kan are all recognizably related, even if we can distinguish them. Like buildings. One may be a house, another a church, another a shop and yet another a stable—but they are all structures. They all follow certain rules, whether we think of them that way or not." Nethgalla gestured at Davian's creation. "That...looks like no other Vessel I have ever seen. It's not just an unrecognizable structure, it's unrecognizable *as* a structure. Even if one of the Venerate came across it, I cannot say whether they would be able to determine what it was unless they activated it."

Davian nodded slowly. "And you're sure that my providing the one Imprint will work for all of them? They won't need to have been the ones to kill the dar'gaithin?" Niha and Tal wouldn't have been an issue in that scenario, but he had no idea whether Raeleth had ever actually slain one of the creatures.

"I'm sure. If it works once, it will work for all." The woman stood, stretching. "I do not know how you intend to make something this delicate twice more in the time that you have, but I would start as soon as you can. People have begun to notice my absences. You have a couple of days at most to finish up."

Davian hesitated. "You're sure there would be no chance of me getting back in here, if I just—"

"No." Nethgalla said the word with simple, calm confidence. "Gassandrid knows that Tal is coming, Davian. The protections that the Venerate have around this complex are immense; I myself would never have been able to get through if I hadn't used the identity of someone who was already allowed in. If you want to go back to Zvaelar, then this is your one and only chance."

She waited to check that Davian understood, then reluctantly tossed the working metal band to him. "Use this as a reference. If something is even slightly off..."

"I know." Davian was already preparing to activate his focus Vessel. It would be difficult to get this done under such time pressure, but his control had improved enormously, and he had confidence from having a working prototype now. He thought he could do it.

If he didn't, his friends in Zvaelar were going to be stuck there.

He turned his attention to the next of the bands, letting more Essence flow into his fingertips as he prepared to make the incision in the metal.

There was still plenty of work left to do.

Davian studied the original steel band's kan structure, then carefully added another line—identical, whisper thin—to the third and final one.

He exhaled after it was done, comparing the results with a critical eye. This last section of the Vessel wasn't dependent on orientation, so it didn't matter where he placed it relative to the main mechanism, though he'd tried to keep everything consistent.

He nodded to himself. The copy was near flawless, at least at first glance; he felt a flush of pride, though he pushed it down quickly enough. A day and a half straight of work without sleep, and he was almost done.

He breathed out, then began the laborious process of checking the metal band against the original again. Every comparison was painstaking; sometimes he still decided to shorten or lengthen a line of kan slightly, or straighten another, but otherwise it was good. As close as he could get, given the circumstances and the speed at which he'd needed to make it.

The question, of course, was whether it would still work.

Remembering Nethgalla's logic, he had already undertaken the task of testing the second band. The process had been as deeply unpleasant as the first time, but it had worked without issue. Now—after a second fastidious recheck in which he changed nothing—it was finally time to try the third.

The sound of scrambling through the narrow, low tunnel to the cave made him flinch, and his heart leaped to his throat before he saw Nethgalla's now-familiar form emerging from the hole in the wall.

"You're early," he said accusingly, heart slowing to its regular beat.

Nethgalla waved away his statement, her face flushed with excitement. "A Gate just opened in the city."

"What?" Davian stared at her. "You mean..."

"It's Tal. It has to be. Gassandrid wouldn't need to open one here, and no one else has the ability to create them." Her eyes were alight with anticipation. "Get ready. Gassandrid will have felt it as well. We need to get out of here, find Tal, and help him."

Davian frowned. "No. That's not the plan," he said firmly. "I have to go back."

"That doesn't matter anymore," said Nethgalla impatiently. "He's *here*, Davian! It's happening *now*! You can't help him retrieve Licanius if you're in Zvaelar." She gestured, evidently thinking that there would be no argument. "Come on. There's no point in me concealing my identity now. I'm going to find him, and so are you."

Davian wavered, looking at the tunnel. It was tempting. He still had no idea whether this would work, and Nethgalla was right about one thing—if Caeden was here, then he was here to get Licanius. Not to mention maybe to try and rescue Davian.

Nethgalla plainly wasn't going to wait for him, either. This was probably his one chance to escape with someone who actually knew their way around.

But the moment passed quickly. Tal would get out of Zvaelar somehow—that much was a given, regardless of whether he went back. But Raeleth and Niha? They would be trapped. Without Davian, without what he had just created, there was *no chance* for them.

A little over eight months, he'd known them—but it felt like so much longer. It felt like a lifetime.

"No," he said softly.

Nethgalla stared at him blankly, as if not comprehending what he was saying.

"No?" she repeated, her voice low and dangerous.

"I have to go back." Davian met her gaze determinedly. "It's not just Tal. I have friends back there. They need my help. I *promised them* my help."

"They would understand!" exclaimed Nethgalla in disbelief. Her expression darkened further as she studied him. "Listen to yourself, Davian. *You* want to go and protect *your* friends—over the fate of the world. We all have to make sacrifices. Stop being so selfish." She nodded to the tunnel and waited expectantly, as if that were the end of the conversation.

Davian shook his head.

"I'm not like him. Like Tal," he said. "I'll sacrifice myself if I need to—I'm prepared for that—but I won't sacrifice other people. Even if I thought it was all right. Even if it wasn't possible to save them—*which it is*," he added firmly, forestalling Nethgalla as she opened her mouth. "Tal—Caeden—is my friend. I understand why he's done what he's done. But . . ." He gestured tiredly.

"He's always been an *effective* man, Nethgalla. A man who wins. But I think he knew that wasn't enough."

Nethgalla considered him. "What's the point if everyone dies? Morals are all well and good, Davian, but this is *reality*. We need people who will actually *fight* for what's right."

Davian shook his head again, something Raeleth had said coming to mind.

"It's not enough to fight for the right side. You have to figure out how to fight the right *way*, too. If winning is truly all that matters, then we've lost sight of what's actually right and wrong in the first place."

Nethgalla stared at him silently, her expression unreadable.

"Make certain to conceal those around your arm the same way as you brought them in," she said eventually, motioning to the three steel bands. "If you're caught, at least you might be able to get away again without them being seen. You shouldn't have too much difficulty, though. Everyone's still acting as if nothing's wrong, despite that fact that the entire place should be in an uproar by now." She shook her head worriedly at that last part.

Davian looked at her in surprise. "That's it?"

"I am not going to try and force you to escape," said Nethgalla drily. "I think you're foolish—possibly a liability. But my debt to you is paid, so I will not wait for you. If you wish to get out of Talan Gol, you will need to either catch up to Tal and me, or find your own way."

"Understood." Davian slid the bands under his sleeve. "How will you find him? This is a big city, and I doubt he's going to make his whereabouts obvious."

"I have a Trace," Nethgalla assured him. She paused for another moment, as if waiting for him to admit that he'd changed his mind.

Then with another sigh and a sharp nod, she disappeared back into the tunnel.

Davian stared at the darkened hole, a bud of panic threatening to bloom before he took a steadying breath. What he'd said to Nethgalla was true: he couldn't be like them. They—Tal included, possibly—would disagree with the choice. Call it weakness.

653

As would Gassandrid and the other Venerate.

And *that* was the point. Asha, Wirr—even *Caeden*, he thought—would consider it strength. Raeleth had been right: that he should fight was unquestioned, but *how* he fought mattered just as much as the result of the conflict.

Tal's entire history was testament to that.

It was decided, anyway. There was no benefit to second-guessing himself now.

He crawled out of the cave that had been his home for the past week, and headed back into the glimmering steel passageways.

Chapter 45

Davian moved silently along the newest of the shining passageways he'd opened, every sense straining for any sign of danger.

Nethgalla hadn't been wrong about the lack of reaction to Tal's apparent arrival: the main hallways had been close to empty, certainly no busier than they had been a week ago. Those who traveled them had looked calm, too, in a vaguely disinterested sort of way—simply going about their daily business. It was, just as she had said, as if nothing were wrong.

Even so, Davian had been forced to duck down passageways and stray from his path to the portal several times: though his invisibility Vessel might allow him to simply walk past most people, some of the ways were narrow, and there was too good a chance of an accidental collision giving him away. At one point he'd actually had to retreat to avoid a group of men in Telesthaesia who were taking up the entire breadth of the hallway, making it impossible to get by. They'd had their unsettling helmets on, too, moving in an organized band and accompanied by a single soldier at the rear whose vision was unimpaired. That had to have been the commander Tal had explained was necessary for these squads, the mental link of the armor providing coordination and sight to the whole team.

It hadn't been long after that he'd finally found his way into the passageways hidden away behind the steel walls, which Nethgalla had known about and suggested he use. They were expansive, a maze of metal corridors sealed off from the others, able to be completely reconfigured at will. It took only a quick application of Essence to the correct endpoints to open and close their entrances.

He paused and pressed through kan again, assessing his progress. It had been impractical to try and remember his way back to the portal, but the portal itself emitted a distinctive, pulsing kan signature that was impossible to miss, even with the myriad other Vessels blocking the way in between. All he had to do was keep angling toward the point from which that energy was emanating.

He kept his own kan at the ready, constantly checking for anyone coming up ahead, not willing to trust purely in the security of his invisibility Vessel. Nobody had appeared thus far, though.

Minutes passed in silence as he hurried forward. A couple of times he was forced to open ways around areas that were apparently tuned only to a specific person's Essence, the steel plates in front of him immovable. One was a room in which, after pushing through kan to look inside, he spotted several Vessels—easily visible due to their time-locked metal—including a sword that seemed to almost writhe with dark energy. In another there was a sleeping woman with kan threads branching off her everywhere, though he was too far away to determine the threads' purpose.

He hurried past. He could easily sense the portal now, could almost see the metal around him—this giant Vessel the Venerate had constructed—holding back the corruption of time. He still shivered at the concept. Whether that was due to the idea of Zvaelar's corruption reaching through to the real world, or the fact that the Venerate had been both knowledgeable and powerful enough to hold it back, he wasn't sure.

The flashing and quivering of the plate to his left was the only warning he had.

He dove forward as the steel snapped against the opposite wall with a crackling crash, blue energy spitting where the two met. He rolled smoothly to his feet, quickly checking his surroundings, but kan revealed no sign of an attacker. He tried to activate his time Vessel.

Nothing happened. He was too close to the distorting effect of the portal, now.

"I am impressed that you managed to hide for so long, Davian," came a female voice through the newly made opening in the wall.

Davian's heart lurched.

He knew immediately that it wasn't her as she walked into view; even from here he could spot the dead eyes, could tell from the unnatural way she spoke. Scars covered her entire body where she had been mauled, entire chunks of flesh missing.

She came to a stop, staring at the exact spot where he was standing.

"Fessi," he whispered, a chill of indecision and shock running down his spine.

"I was saddened by her death," said Gassandrid, the words grotesque coming from Fessi's mouth. "And I know that she was your friend, so I have truly done my best not to flaunt this body in front of you."

Anger flared at that, hot and dark. "But you're happy to use her corpse, of course," spat Davian. He took an unconscious half step forward before clenching his fists tightly to his sides, wrenching his emotions back under control. Gassandrid was undoubtedly trying to rattle him here, hoping to goad him into rash action.

He dropped his invisibility shield. The Venerate would easily and accurately be able to track his movements using kan, and presumably already was, so it was only a drain on his Essence now.

"I am not one to refuse the gifts El gives me, Davian, and ultimately our bodies are merely Vessels. I only use this one because she was once bound to the Forge, and there are benefits. It does not decay the way the others do, my connection is far stronger, and kan is…" Gassandrid trailed off, sighing, Fessi's empty blue eyes locked on Davian's. "But I do not expect you to understand."

Davian kept his breathing steady this time, watching in his peripheral vision for any shifting of the surrounding plates. Silently, he activated his strength and focus Vessels. Gassandrid was likely intending to throw him back into Zvaelar, but if Davian was captured, the Vessels he had hidden around his arm would undoubtedly be found and stripped from him first. He couldn't allow that.

"You're right," he said grimly. "I don't think I'll ever understand."

He twisted and leaped with Essence-enhanced legs along the corridor, moving at blinding speed away from Fessi's unsettling gaze and toward where he knew the portal to Zvaelar waited.

Behind him he heard a furious, surprised shout; Gassandrid

had probably expected him to face him head-on, to fight. He'd gained a precious few seconds doing this.

It would have to be enough.

The next minute was madness, an utter confusion of shifting, glittering steel and crackling Essence. The corridor became a blur of movement as plates everywhere began to tremble and spin, slamming together, a confusion of motion as they rushed to crush him, to block his way.

He knew how to manipulate them too, though.

He sprinted with everything he had, leaping over some plates and sliding under others as they moved, kicking off shifting walls to evade blasts of Essence thundering past him from behind. His focus Vessel kept him calm, let him calculate each step a second before he had to execute it. Every time he used his momentum to push off the steel, he sent Essence into endpoints and reversed or halted the upcoming plates' motion, continuing to open up the path in front of him.

Gassandrid clearly had the upper hand in experience, though: the way ahead became narrower and narrower, the furious activity of the plates increasingly hard to dodge. Finally he caught a glimpse of the black void of the portal, a steel plate ahead lowering into position to block him from it. It was already halfway to the floor.

He forced Essence into an endpoint—just enough to slow the plate's movement—and with a last, desperate dive he threw himself bodily beneath the shifting steel. The descending metal edge barely missed his face.

It did catch his arm, though. There was a pulling sensation, and then a clattering behind him.

Dismay stabbed at him as he clutched at where the metal band had been. The Vessel had been ripped off by the impact, possible only because of its new, open-ended shape.

He recovered swiftly, rolling and scrambling back, but it was too late and the band was too far away. The steel plate sealed to the ground with a crackle of blue energy, hiding the Vessel from view.

He stopped, mind racing, his panting breath audible over the furious buzzing of plates all around him. The portal was right here. He still had two Vessels. Perhaps he could make another while in Zvaelar. Perhaps if he gave one to Niha and the other to Raeleth, Tal would find another way out...

But no. Neither would work. The first he'd already discounted; there was nowhere near enough time and the delicacy required of the work made it impossible anyway, no matter how much he leaned on his focus Vessel. And the other...the other just wouldn't happen. Tal clearly ended up with one of the Vessels. There was no miraculous solution waiting to reveal itself.

He pushed his palm against the violently vibrating floor, activating an endpoint and commanding the steel plate to rise again.

Fessi—Gassandrid—stood patiently on the other side, examining the metal with intense curiosity. A plate slammed into place in the tunnel behind, sealing him and Davian inside the room with the portal.

"What *is* this?" asked Gassandrid as he held the steel aloft, the expression on Fessi's face one almost of distaste.

"Why don't you activate it and find out?" Davian assessed his options as he spoke. Gassandrid was better at manipulating the plates, but he'd also be cautious of being dragged into Zvaelar. That was something Davian could use to his advantage.

Gassandrid opened his mouth to retort, and Davian attacked.

He leaped straight at Gassandrid, crashing through the Disruption shield that he'd known would be there, the wave of dizziness and nausea that accompanied it hitting him hard. His focus and pain Vessels quickly corrected the sensation, though; Davian knew that it was going to be deeply unpleasant when he turned those off again—perhaps even dangerous—but right now, he didn't care.

He tackled Gassandrid to the ground and elbowed him hard in the face, doing everything he could to remember that the body he was attacking was no longer his friend. Gassandrid cried out in shock, no doubt stunned at both the directness and the effectiveness of the move. Disruption shields were made specifically to negate this sort of brute physical assault, and everyone who used kan knew as a rule not to bother with them.

Davian struck again, then wrenched the Vessel from Gassandrid's hand and rolled to the side, slamming his palm into the plate below him.

Gassandrid, dazed as he was, realized what he was doing too late.

He screamed as steel crashed down on his legs, accompanied by a horrendous cracking, squelching sound. Davian leaped to his feet and backed away, heart pounding.

Gassandrid was somehow still conscious, Fessi's face a mask of pain as her form dragged itself along the steel, bloodied stumps smearing red behind her.

"You are better... than I expected, Davian... but there is... still no escape." Gassandrid smiled coldly through evident agony, the expression heartbreaking to see on Fessi's face. "You cannot... help Tal'kamar now."

Davian locked eyes with the Gassandrid proxy, then placed his hand against the wall, locating the endpoint.

"That's not when I'm trying to do it," he said grimly.

Gassandrid's eyes went wide; Fessi's hand stretched out as if to try and stop him, but it was far too late.

The plate slammed down unthinkably hard, crushing the proxy to a red smear.

Davian closed his eyes, breathing hard, pausing and allowing himself to feel now that it was over. Sharp, deep grief, though he knew Fessi had been dead for a year. Horror at what he'd just witnessed, what he'd been forced to do.

His stomach finally settled, and he steeled himself, carefully pushing the metal back over his arm. Right now, he had to focus on those he could still help.

He turned and stepped into the black portal once more.

Davian stumbled to his knees as he burst into the dull crimson light of Zvaelar, everything trembling as the ground shook and the familiar rumbling, cracking sound filled the air.

He immediately checked his arm, giving a sigh of relief as he felt the three bands there. His pain and focus Vessels had remained active, thankfully; he was still nauseous and dizzy from crashing through Gassandrid's Disruption shield, which meant that without his Vessels, he'd probably be unable to move right now.

He sucked in a lungful of air, shaking his head for clarity. He
needed to get back to the tower, get to the others. *Fast.*

Where was he, exactly? He scanned the shadowed, broken city stretching away in front of him, several buildings still crashing to the ground as the latest tremor proved a final stress on their foundations. The areas he had come to know well as a scavenger would have changed a lot recently, given the increasing ferocity of all these shocks. In fact, he could already tell that since he'd joined Tal and the others in the crater, the taller buildings he'd once used as landmarks must have universally fallen. That made his months-old memory of the landscape here all but irrelevant.

Except for the positioning of the Breach, that was. That still threw virulent yellow into the sky, easily spotted against the red and black of the eternal Zvaelar night.

He traced a path along it, searching for the bridge, but it appeared that too was gone now. He grimaced and gazed around, then closed his eyes. He was on a forested rise overlooking the city. North of the Breach, thankfully, judging by the position of the moon. There were a few such rises, but if this was the one he was thinking of...

There. He spotted the gap, the complete absence of buildings that marked the crater.

He activated his strength Vessel, and ran.

Tremors caused the ground to shudder every minute or so now, the city more rubble than structures as he darted and swerved his way through it, buildings and walkways collapsing around him in constant, violent motion. He avoided tunnels entirely, choosing instead to scramble and leap over piles of rubble where he could, moving as fast as he dared and still keeping one eye open for any al'goriat. There were none, though, not even any sign of them. That was strange.

He reached the edge of the crater faster than he'd dared hope, a strange, rumbling chorus greeting his ears just as he crested the short rise.

He paled as he saw the source of the sound.

For a moment Davian thought that all was lost; there were hundreds of al'goriat below—every single one snarling, pushing desperately toward the center of the crater, a thick mass of arms and legs and red-tinged teeth. They pressed hard up against the invisible barrier created by the remnants of the metal tower, which

Davian finally spotted was still standing, though there was only a matter of feet between its edge and the closest of the ravening Banes.

His heart unclenched a little as he spotted the three figures pressed back against the steel, occasional flashes of Essence firing off in a vain attempt to thin the creatures. Al'goriat went down before the blasts but they were immediately replaced by others, trampling over their fellow Banes' corpses to get just a bit closer, their eyeless gazes transfixed by the metal tower.

Davian froze, considering, the focus Vessel keeping his mind on the task at hand rather than letting it slide into panic. Could he get through? The creatures wouldn't be able to see him, but he would still have to clear a path. Even with his strength Vessel, there were too many to simply barrel through or leap over. He had Essence, but far from enough to do anything useful with it.

"Well, I can't die," he muttered to himself. There was no time for anything else. No clever plan.

He fired off a quick Essence flare into the dead sky to let the others know he was coming, and then leaped down into the crater, strengthened legs absorbing the impact.

He started running.

He didn't stop to think, concerned that if he did, he would hesitate. There simply wasn't time for vacillating. He sprinted out into the open area and began heading for the back of the slavering, moaning crowd of al'goriat.

He swallowed as he approached, slowing despite himself. Getting by without touching them would be impossible: they were too closely packed, almost shoulder to shoulder.

He walked the last few steps and, heart in his mouth, reached out and tried to push between the first two. Their skin was damp and clammy against his hands, impossibly cold for something living. He took careful note of his position relative to the crimson moon; every single one of the creatures was taller than him by at least a head, and once he was in this crowd, there was a serious danger that he would otherwise be unable to tell if he was even heading in the right direction.

The al'goriat he touched turned their eyeless gazes down and

662

toward him. They bared their teeth, and their snarls changed timbre into something even more aggressive and feral.

"Davian!" It was Niha's voice, faint, but managing to pierce the chorus of growls. "If you're out there, get down and get ready!"

Davian went to his stomach.

A moment later, an enormous crowd of al'goriat exploded outward and away from the metal dome, just to the right of where he was, blown by a tremendously powerful blast of wind.

Davian didn't hesitate, scrambling up and sprinting with everything he had into the newly created gap, even as al'goriat began blinking into existence in front of him, filling the space in their eagerness to be close to the portal. He dodged and weaved and spun, vaguely aware of a few startled shrieks as he brushed against some of the creatures but not daring to look over his shoulder, even for a second.

Finally, he broke into the space between the tower and the al'goriat that was still clear. Ten feet, now, if that.

"Dav!" Tal staggered over to him, still providing the metal tower with Essence—just a trickle now, though—as Davian put his hands on his knees, arms shaking, gasping from both exertion and the release of tension. Niha and Raeleth were close behind him.

Davian gave them a grin as he straightened again, receiving a relieved clap on the back from Raeleth. "Thanks for the opening."

"Thank El I saved enough for one last blast," said Niha, adjusting the silver band on her ring finger.

"I can't sustain even this for much longer," said Tal bluntly, the words a grim warning to hurry. He watched with hope in his eyes as Davian removed the three steel bands from his arm. "Did you succeed?"

Davian coughed. "Not...exactly," he admitted.

It didn't take long for him to explain: it was far from a complex plan, after all, and Tal in particular immediately grasped the logic of what Davian was trying to achieve. Even if he seemed dazed and not entirely pleased at the prospect.

"This is madness," he muttered, gazing at the bands as if they were hot coals he was being asked to step on. Or maybe eat. "To even build a Vessel *capable* of this is madness. But to change us into one of them... this truly works?"

"It does. I tested it myself. It's safe for at least an hour." Davian made a face despite himself. "It's not *pleasant*, but it will turn you into a dar'gaithin, and turn you back again on the other side. Your mind will stay yours in between, though. Enough that you won't get lost in the time stream like they do." He said the last part with conviction and no one protested, though they all knew that there was no way to be sure it was truly the case.

Davian gestured to the two endpoints, pressing on quickly. "Just force these two edges together to begin the process. Then pry them apart once you're clear on the other side. It will draw the Essence it needs from the environment."

"What about Raeleth?" asked Niha apprehensively.

Davian shook his head. "I don't know," he said simply, addressing the statement to Raeleth. "The dar'gaithin form won't be infected by Dark, but when you turn back..." He shrugged, glancing at Tal.

"Dark is specific to Zvaelar—there's a chance that it will have no place in the real world. That the healthy time stream will simply exorcise it. But," Tal conceded softly, "if it does not..."

Raeleth took a breath, nodding.

"If I am still infected, I will come back," he said simply. He almost absently clasped Niha's hand; she squeezed it and gazed at him with a mixture of anxiety and pride, but didn't gainsay him. "I am certainly not going to stay a dar'gaithin just to survive, and I cannot risk letting this... *stuff* out into the real world. I won't loose it," he finished to Tal, the words a promise.

"But if you can find some Gifted..." Davian began.

"Where?" Raeleth said the word gently, strangely sounding like he was trying to comfort Davian. "I will still be trapped behind the ilshara, and those who can wield Essence in my time are placed in the Cyrarium. And while I have apparently started a rebellion, it's one that I have no idea how to contact." He looked him in the eye. "If El wishes it, I'll be all right. And if it is my time, then it is my time."

Davian bowed his head. It was Raeleth's decision, and there was no time to argue.

"We only have a few more minutes. We should let these two say their good-byes," said Tal as if reading his thoughts, putting a hand on Davian's shoulder. "And I need to hear what's going on in your era."

Davian swallowed, assenting as Raeleth gave Tal a grateful look; he and Niha walked a short distance away, hand in hand. Tal settled onto the ground with his back to the crimson-lit metal dome, gazing out over the slavering al'goriat, a trickle of Essence still flowing into the massive Vessel behind him.

"So," he said quietly. "What do I need to know?"

Davian quickly explained everything he had gleaned from his time back in the real world. Nethgalla's revelation about the location of Licanius, the time difference, Rethgar and his death, Davian's message to Asha. Neither of them knew whether Tal would have his memories back by the time it came to retrieving Licanius from Ilshan Gathdel Teth, but it seemed smart to arm him with as much knowledge as possible. And—as Tal had apologetically pointed out a few times—if he remembered, it could explain why he'd waited to save Davian. Knowing that he would come here, knowing that there was no point in trying to save him until after he left Zvaelar.

For his part, Tal took the news about where Licanius was being kept with resigned stoicism, though Davian couldn't help but notice the tension in his stance, nor avoid seeing the flicker of fear in the other man's eyes. He'd guessed that it was a possibility, clearly—and had desperately hoped against it.

Tal quickly recovered himself, though, immediately launching into a description of Shammaeloth's sanctuary and how to get to it from Seclusion. After a few moments, Davian hurriedly activated his focus Vessel and began setting several thin lines of kan into his left arm, creating a makeshift map of the path that he would need to take. If Nethgalla was right and Tal was already in Ilshan Gathdel Teth, then this would be where he was headed—and by this stage he might also know, hopefully, that Davian would try to meet him there.

Niha and Raeleth finally broke apart just as Tal finished talking; there were tears on Raeleth's cheeks, and even stoic Niha's eyes glistened. Davian felt a pang in his chest as they hurried back toward him and Tal, hands still clasped. Once they left, they would be separated by two millennia.

Finally Niha reluctantly disentangled herself from Raeleth's grasp, hugging Davian fiercely.

"You will never be forgotten," she told him, Davian's ribs creaking at the embrace.

Davian grinned, squeezing back. "Nor you."

Raeleth had moved in front of Tal, and there was an odd silence as the two men stared at each other.

Then Raeleth extended his hand to Tal, clasping the other man's firmly when he took it.

"Remember that your past does not define you—no matter the consequences," he said gently. "Choice is meaningless without consequences, and a privilege we do not deserve if we will not face them. You are facing them, Tal'kamar. You have changed." He hesitated. "I can speak only for myself," he added, emotion choking his voice. "But I want you to know—because I do not believe I have ever said it out loud. I do forgive you. I will always hate what you did. But I *do forgive you*." He smiled at Tal's suddenly emotional expression. "Just remember that I am not the one whose forgiveness is important."

Tal coughed; though he was trying to hide it, it was obvious he was moved.

"It's important to me," he muttered eventually, looking vaguely abashed. "More than you know."

Raeleth smiled and nodded. Davian watched, and once again couldn't help but admire the man's strength. In his position, even if he had managed to accept Tal's change of heart, Davian didn't know if he could ever have reacted with the kind of grace that Raeleth was showing.

Raeleth turned to him, his smile sad now as another rumble—the most violent one yet—rocked the ground.

"Niha is right. You will never be forgotten," he said softly after it had passed. "You've given us so much."

"That goes both ways," said Davian sincerely. His throat tightened with emotion. "I just wish we could have sent you both back to the same time."

Raeleth glanced over at Niha, looking lost for words. He scrubbed away a tear.

"Nothing can ever take away the time we had here. Besides— we will see each other again," he added. "One day."

He turned back to Davian, grasping him on the shoulder. "And I hope we shall as well," he said seriously. He held Davian's gaze. "I know you are still searching, still considering—but we both know what's coming. So don't put those questions off for another day." He took a deep breath. "El with you, Davian. Always."

Davian swallowed a lump in his throat. "And you."

Niha was finishing saying something to Tal; the two embraced, and then Niha and Raeleth were once again back in each other's arms. Their kiss was fierce, as desperate as it was lingering.

Tal stepped forward, carefully pressing a Vessel into each of Raeleth and Niha's hands. "It's time."

Raeleth and Niha looked at each other and then placed the Vessels around their necks. They carefully pushed the two points together.

Raeleth fell to the ground, shaking, a shout of pain ripping from him.

Niha watched in horror, even as she touched the two ends of the metal band together again, and again.

Nothing happened.

"No," muttered Davian, panic rising in his chest. He'd tested these. They *worked*. Even now, Raeleth was sprouting black scales, his legs gradually deforming and stretching into a single, long tail.

"Take mine," said Tal quickly, stepping forward. The woman faltered but Tal thrust the band at her; she acceded and removed the first band from around her neck, quickly replacing it with the steel she took from Tal and pressing the two points together.

Raeleth's screams lifted above the al'goriat's growling as his clothes began shredding away from his expanding body, but Niha still just stood there, looking bewildered and increasingly terrified.

"I tested them," Davian said desperately.

To his side, Tal hesitated. Something flickered in his eyes, gone in a moment.

"Hold still." He stepped forward, then placed one hand on Niha's head, the other on her stomach, closing his eyes. Niha flinched, her face going pale.

"What was that?"

"Just try again," said Tal urgently.

Niha frowned, but obediently pushed the two points of the steel band around her neck together.

There was a flash of Essence, and she crumpled to the ground, the transformation beginning.

"What did you do?" asked Davian in bemusement, breathing again now that the bands appeared to be working.

"I saved her." Tal gestured dismissively at his questioning look. "It's not important."

A flash of pain echoed through Davian's head at the lie; he considered questioning Tal further, but the fact was, his friends were going to get out. That was all that mattered right now.

He turned away as the final stages of the process began for Raeleth, instead choosing to eye the al'goriat as the closest ones managed another step forward. Only eight feet away, now. He could see the individual drops of saliva on their needle-like teeth.

When he turned back, two dar'gaithin stood before him.

"No time to adjust," Tal said briskly as the two moved drunkenly to the side, clutching each other for support. "Stay close to the tower."

He pressed his hand against the steel.

One of the plates in the dome slid aside; Davian flinched as there was a surge from all around them, a wave of al'goriat taking an ominous stride closer before they were stopped again.

Four feet, this time. The creatures could almost have reached out and touched them.

Davian unconsciously leaned away, toward the portal that somehow still stood in the darkened interior, the gray void swirling past.

"The time stream should send you back...what? Five or six weeks after you left?" Tal glanced at Davian, who nodded; the math made sense. "The portal won't be manned; we always assumed that either the dar'gaithin would report to us, or that they would be insane and their arrival would be apparent soon enough. Use the Vessel to change back again as soon as you're away from Seclusion, somewhere you can get clothes. Then hide," Tal continued seriously. "Change your names. Don't let the Venerate realize that anyone has escaped from here, or they will hunt you down." He looked at them both, something pained in his eyes. "Just...move on from this place. Live your lives."

"We will," hissed Niha—Davian thought it was Niha; it was hard to tell—and Raeleth indicated the same.

They held hands—a surreal sight to see two dar'gaithin acting that way—and vanished into the gray stream together.

Davian stared at the gray nothingness, then turned to Tal. "Your turn."

The words died on his lips. The other man's eyes glistened, his expression racked with guilt.

"Of course," Tal muttered after a moment, irritably scrubbing away the moisture that was leaking down his cheeks.

"You don't look happy," Davian said quietly.

Tal hung his head.

"Raeleth was wrong. I haven't changed." There was self-loathing in his tone now, though Davian couldn't fathom why. "I want to. I have all this information about El, and I believe that He is real. But I do not believe *in* Him." Frustration threaded through his voice. "How can I? How can I put my faith in a power that makes me..." He choked off, another tear running unchecked down his face. "Raeleth says that it's about so much more than just acceptance. It's about honoring, about truly trusting His plan, about *love*. But how can I feel those things when these are the terrible choices He keeps forcing me to make? I only feel anger, or *nothing*."

Davian's heart lurched. "Why...why are you saying all of this, Tal? Did they get out?"

Tal waved the question away, bringing himself back under control.

"To the best of my knowledge," he said softly. "Yes. You saved them, Davian. That's what matters."

Davian frowned, but there simply wasn't time; another rumble shook the metal dome, everything screeching and trembling, threatening to collapse at any moment. Great crashing cracks thundered over the city outside the crater, audible over the al'goriat's urgent growls.

"So I'm coming for Licanius. In your time," said Tal, recovering enough to move on from whatever was troubling him. When Davian nodded he breathed out, shaking his head dazedly.

"Then this is it," he said, barely loud enough to hear over the rumbling and snarling. "It seems that your training is at an end."

"This is it," repeated Davian.

Tal pulled in a steadying breath, then fitted the final Vessel to himself.

The transition was painful to watch but over quickly; soon enough Davian was face-to-face with another dar'gaithin. Pure, cathartic relief flooded through him at the sight. All three had worked.

Tal stretched out his hand, the appendage at the end of a disturbingly short and muscular arm. Davian considered it for a long moment.

He grasped it. "I'll see you soon."

Tal inclined his head, and slithered through the portal.

Davian took one last glance around at the red-tinted sea of slavering creatures, and stepped into the gray river once again, leaving Zvaelar behind for the last time.

Chapter 46

Wirr crashed through the shadowy, moonlit forest, beating a retreat alongside Taeris and Shana.

Trees passed in a blur through his blood-flecked vision, branches and dry leaves scratching at his arms and face as behind him he could hear the unsettling, slithering sound of pursuit. A half dozen dar'gaithin this time—the first he'd seen in a while. The Desrielites must have been keeping some of them back.

The three of them leaped a shallow gully and crested a steep rise; with a sharp motion Wirr flicked a twisted line of Essence behind him at the dry, dead undergrowth. Flames immediately sprang up, and with the stiff breeze the fire quickly spread.

It was a dangerous ploy, but it was also the most effective one they had left. Fire seemed to do a decent job of confusing the dar'gaithin, if not outright blinding them—something to do with the way their vision worked, he assumed. Not to mention that the Desrielites had been slowed as they fought to prevent blazes like this from spreading. The massive Columns they were transporting often minimized the damage, sucking the fire's energy away more effectively than fighting the flames with water ever could have—but the Columns themselves were cumbersome, far from maneuverable if a blaze got out of hand. The mere threat had helped.

It just hadn't been enough.

They were a half day from the position that Caeden had indicated on the map, now. Half a day from the Columns reaching the Cyrarium, and the Boundary falling. The Desrielites had broken camp and begun their march only hours after Caeden and Asha had left. Wirr's efforts to slow them—the fires, as well as swift strikes coordinated among the Shadows, Gifted, Administrators and soldiers, slashing at the army and pulling away again—had been for naught. The enemy's losses had been exponentially more than their own, but in the end they'd needed to do more. They needed more *time*.

And he was so, *so* tired. How long since he'd slept? More than two days, he felt certain. His Reserve could only sustain him for so long before he needed rest—and he was the one person who couldn't afford to rest, not even for a few minutes. He was the only way their forces could effectively communicate. If he fell asleep, people lost their lives.

The thought steeled him, forced him past his exhaustion and brought the world back into focus.

"Taeris, stay low, go left, and get ready to attack," he gasped, feeling the Oathstone against his chest. The Gifted wouldn't be able to hear him above the sudden, explosive roar of the flames, but he would obey. Wirr quickly signaled to Shana, who nodded her understanding and dashed off to the right.

He spun and dove to his stomach behind a bush, ignoring the sharp tang of smoke as it reached his nostrils. It made him uneasy—he had almost been caught in the fires twice, now—but the wind was blowing westward, away from him and back toward the oncoming army. There was no need to panic.

His body tensed as the group of pursuing dar'gaithin burst through the wall of flame.

The fire whispered out wherever it touched the Banes' scales; the creatures slowed, serpentine heads swinging wildly from side to side as they searched for their prey. He held his breath. Wirr's people no longer had the luxury of scouting, their numbers having dwindled too far. If they'd known the Desrielites were sending dar'gaithin ahead of their main force, they would have been more cautious.

Too late for regret now, though.

"Taeris, spear the one closest to you."

Wirr flicked his blade up in the air as he spoke, catching it with Essence and hurling it forcefully into the first dar'gaithin's eye as an Essence-carried spear took another of the creatures through the mouth from the left.

A moment later—even as three of the remaining four creatures snarled, searching for the source of the attack—the fourth stumbled, eyes bulging, unnoticed by its companions. Wirr pulled on the Essence to tug his blade free from the dar'gaithin's falling body and then sliced at the next in line. The creature was wary now, though, moving too fast, and the steel slid off its facial scales. Wirr scowled, swiftly drawing the blade back to himself, seeing Taeris doing the same with his spear.

The dar'gaithin that had been choking finally collapsed, its falling accompanied by a hiss of dismay from its companions. Shana's Vessel was one of the more useful that the Shadows had brought, allowing her to completely suck the air from a small area. Originally, Taeris believed, its purpose had been to remove the air from the walls of a room, a more primitive version of Silencing. The dar'gaithin needed to breathe just as people did, though. It was one of the few weapons that had proven effective against them.

Three remaining.

The dar'gaithin were splitting up now, slithering at blinding speeds away from each other, silhouetted dramatically by the flaming trees beyond as they began searching the surrounding brush.

"Taeris. Ground the one to your right. On my mark." The other two were headed in Shana's direction, but her Vessel was far more effective than Taeris and Wirr's Essence, even combined. She could handle herself. "Now."

The earth beneath the dar'gaithin exploded upward, sending the creature flailing and thrashing into the air. It half flipped before crunching back to the ground, its head taking most of the impact.

Wirr flicked his blade out again, and this time the dar'gaithin was too dazed to react. The steel caught it cleanly through the eye.

It twitched once, then lay still.

Wirr scrambled from his place of concealment, sharing a tight smile with Taeris as the scarred man emerged too, tinged red by flaming trees that were close enough for Wirr to feel their heat. Wirr's Essence was almost depleted—again—but the Gil'shar couldn't have many Banes left at their disposal. Taking out this many of the creatures was a good result.

A scream cut through the night, and Wirr's heart stopped as he and Taeris spun in the direction Shana had gone.

They sprinted as one, angling slightly away from the blazing forest toward the sound. Wirr was faster, though, bursting ahead through a tangle of leaves and branches, emerging into a small clearing and immediately having to vault the dar'gaithin that lay dead on the ground.

The other one had Shana.

The young Shadow was beating feebly at the massive snake's fist around her throat, feet swinging as it held her a clear foot off the ground. Shana's Vessel—a stone rod—was visible on the grass behind her.

Wirr put everything he had into his charge, but he knew it was too late. The creature threw Shana against the tree with a sickening crack of bone even as Wirr leaped forward, screaming in defiance and tiredness and fury.

His blade, miraculously, took the snake in its mouth. It thrashed, ripping the steel from Wirr's hand and wrenching his shoulder; he scrambled away with a shout of pain as its tail whipped around wildly.

Then it collapsed to the ground, twitching for several more seconds until it finally lay still.

Taeris burst into the clearing somewhere behind him as Wirr dashed over to Shana's crumpled form. The woman was still alive, though her breaths were coming in ragged gasps, tears trickling down her cheeks as she scrabbled desperately to raise herself up.

"I can't move my legs," she whispered, terror in her eyes. Her breathing was getting shallower and shallower.

Wirr swallowed. "Hang on," he told her gently, checking his Reserve. Barely anything left. Not nearly enough to heal a broken back—if he could even do that at full strength—not to mention whatever other damage had been done.

He tried anyway, letting Essence pour out of him and into Shana's chest. For a moment he thought it was working as her struggling eased.

674   Then he realized that her chest had gone still.

He kept trying, willing her to breathe again. A hand rested on his good shoulder.

"We need to keep moving, Torin," said Taeris. He crouched, gently taking the stone rod from the ground. "The others will be waiting."

Wirr forced a deep breath. Steadied himself. Stood.

The edge of the forest wasn't far; the spreading fire would buy them time, but not much. He clutched the Oathstone around his neck.

"Garron. Denn. Get your squads back to camp," he said quietly, sending the message to the only two groups remaining. He turned to Taeris.

"We've done all we can do here," he said grimly. "It's time to head to the Cyrarium."

Wirr gazed at the ragged group in front of him, each one looking as exhausted as he felt.

A hundred people. A hundred remaining against an army of thousands. Some of each squad he'd put together had survived, but each had also taken heavy losses in this last assault, their final desperate attempt to make the Desrielites think that they were stronger than they truly were. They had started off with seven hundred willing soldiers. This was all that was left.

He closed his eyes, trying to block out the soft moans of the injured who had made it back. A few had burns from having been caught between army and fire; more had gashes from skirmishes, though they had all been told to keep full-blown conflicts to a minimum. Hit hard with Essence and withdraw, wait and then repeat. Set fires for larger groups, annoy and distract the smaller ones. He'd coordinated as best he could, and he knew that his ability had made their stand last for far longer than it should have.

But it was over now. This was it. Their only option was to try and hold this relatively innocuous plateau against the Desrielites. Retreating was pointless, as once the Columns were placed here, all of them—everything and everyone within several hundred miles—would be dead anyway.

Part of him still hoped for a miracle. Hoped that Caeden and

Asha and Davian would somehow appear, Caeden with Licanius in hand, just as he'd done in Ilin Illan two years ago. He kept that tiny, flickering light to himself, though. He knew it was too much to ask, knew that even if Caeden and Asha had succeeded, their next step was to kill the remaining Venerate. They'd left knowing that this defense was nothing more than a stalling tactic. Coming back—even if Caeden knew to make a Gate directly here—would, at best, be a waste of time that they couldn't afford.

He breathed out and opened his eyes, surveying the area. The slope evened out to almost level here for almost five hundred feet, a mixture of grass and barren stone, before rising sharply again toward the peak of the mountain far above. Nothing to indicate anything special, anything different about this particular section of the Menaath Mountains. If Caeden hadn't described it so perfectly, marked it so precisely on his map, Wirr would have doubted that they were even in the right spot.

After a moment he started making his way toward where the ground sloped upward again, doing everything he could to keep his head up, to look confident and energized. People made way in front of him, letting him through, nodding respectfully. He couldn't tell whether they believed his act or not, but the small acknowledgments—from Gifted, from Administrators, from soldiers and Shadows alike—helped. Strengthened him just a little.

Eventually he made it to the base of the sharply rising slope, climbing atop a large boulder that allowed him to see across the entire group. Everyone went quiet, watching him.

"This is it," he whispered, acknowledging the fact to himself as he gazed over the expectant faces. They looked...hopeful, even now. He didn't know whether to laugh or cry at that.

He straightened. Lifted his face to the crowd.

"This is it," he repeated loudly. "I know it doesn't look like anything special, but this is where we stand. If we fall here, if we take even one step back, we let the Gil'shar unleash destruction the likes of which none of us can imagine." He knew that it was the Venerate even more than the Gil'shar who were responsible, but these men and women didn't need that information right now. They needed an enemy. A purpose. "Ilin Illan is gone, but we are still here. We are *still here*."

He paused. There was absolute silence below, every eye on him. "I am not going to lie to you. I am asking everything of you now. There's no retreat. Anyone who remains under my command here, is here until we win or we die." He kept his voice firm, steady. "So this is your last chance. Our odds are slim. Our purpose is to buy time—that is all. We are the delay. We are the sacrifice."

He swallowed. "If you stay, I will be *commanding* each of you not to retreat. Not to surrender. To fight until your last breath. If you are not prepared to do that, leave now and there will be no judgment. I have a Vessel that will create a portal out of here, out of range of the Gil'shar's weapon—though I cannot promise that where you'd be going will be any better." He smiled tightly, fiercely. "But if you do stay, I promise you one thing. The Gil'shar will not forget us."

He fell silent, hoping that those who were listening truly understood that he meant it when he said there was no judgment for anyone who chose to leave. It was one thing to ask people to fight, even to die. But this was something else. Even soldiers could break. Even the bravest among them could let the instinct for self-preservation force them to take a step back, and then another, and then another.

He couldn't let that happen. Not today, not in the middle of battle; he'd already learned that it took only one man to lose heart for everyone else around him to do the same.

But he wouldn't deny them a choice in the matter, either.

He kept his gaze steadily on the group, a lump forming in his throat. No one moved.

"We're with you, Prince Torin," shouted someone at the back.

A ragged cheer went up—more an enthusiastic mutter of agreement, really, but Wirr still took a moment, bowing his head, emotion suddenly choking his ability to speak. There was fear on the faces of those below, but a fierce determination, too.

The cheer petered out, and he smiled, hoping desperately that it did something to convey how heartfelt his appreciation was.

"Then fates with us all," he said, giving the Andarran salute to the people below.

The next couple of hours passed all too quickly.

Wirr spent time with each man and woman who bore a Mark,

learning their names, giving each of them the same command. Not to retreat or surrender. Not to break. To be focused throughout, never giving in to fear. To be organized.

And to not fear death when it came.

After them he spoke with everyone else, using his Oathstone to bind them as new Administrators. The soldiers. The Shadows. Each submitted readily, even if their discomfort was obvious. He issued the same commands to them, all the while hating having to do so.

He didn't show any of that to his people, though. He smiled, encouraged, exhorted. He did everything he could to be the leader they needed.

Before he knew it, the last man was walking away to join the larger group.

Wirr gave a soft sigh of relief, then pushed back his weariness once again and hurried to the vantage point that overlooked the gentle but thickly wooded slope leading up to the plateau. They had set the forest ablaze to buy themselves time, but already the flames were guttering out, leaving only great clouds of smoke and blackened, wizened trees in their wake.

The highest ranking of his remaining soldiers had already begun arranging people to best take advantage of the terrain, but the process went significantly faster once Wirr got involved. It was infinitely easier, now that everyone was in sight and directly under his control, though it still felt odd to be issuing orders to soldiers and Shadows—some of whom he had just met.

Under his breath, in rare spare moments, he continued to command those whom he was most worried about in the south to uphold the rule of law, too—to respect and protect the lives of those in charge. In particular, he targeted the Gifted and Administrators he thought unscrupulous enough to organize against Karaliene and Deldri, once he was gone. He resisted the temptation to outright demand their loyalty to the crown—his cousin and even his sister were already more than capable of handling the politics—but if Andarra survived this, there would be chaos for years to come, and there were plenty of men and women who were not beyond assassination attempts in that sort of climate.

He would go into this fight more easily knowing that he'd done everything he could to keep his remaining family safe.

It was less than a half hour later that the first of the Desrielite army began to emerge from among the scorched trees.

Even though he'd already known the extent of the forces opposing them, he could feel his heart steadily sinking as more and more soldiers streamed from the blackened forest, marching deliberately, arranging themselves just out of range of Wirr's forces. He saw fury, hatred, a few expressions of disbelief on many faces as they stared up at them.

That last was likely because they hadn't realized just how few the Andarrans truly were. He felt a rush of pride at that.

But it didn't matter. There were more, and more, and *more* emerging from among the charred trees. The first of the Columns appeared, black and glistening as drained-looking men and women strained to haul it up the hill.

The two groups watched each other for a while; the Desrielites probably thought that they were being intimidating, not knowing that every single one of Wirr's people was currently incapable of giving in to fear. Wirr stayed where he was, too, content to wait. Every minute that they bought here was an extra minute for Caeden, Asha, and Davian.

Finally a sole figure pushed its way forward, hands raised to indicate that they were unarmed, walking up the slope toward the group.

Wirr hesitated. A messenger, someone wanting to talk. He couldn't risk himself, though—his coordination was too important, and leaving his position would be foolhardy.

"Taeris, meet him halfway," he said. The messenger didn't appear to be carrying a Trap, and looked to be out of range of the Column's influence. That was something.

A moment later, Taeris's form appeared below, walking unhurriedly out toward the man. Wirr tapped Essence, sending a sliver at the scarred man, attaching it to his shoulder. Taeris glanced at the strand of Essence, then nodded approvingly, though he wisely didn't turn to look up at Wirr's position.

It was easy enough to eavesdrop using Essence. This was the

best way for Wirr to conduct a negotiation—though he doubted that there would be much to negotiate.

"That's High Priest Koresh," Taeris murmured as he drew closer, too softly for the other man to hear. "He's the Gil'shar representative for Meldier."

Wirr shifted. He didn't know anything about the man himself, but his position made him one of the most important people in Desriel. "Ask him what he wants."

"What do you want?" asked Taeris as he came within speaking range.

"There is only one thing about which I would like to talk, gaa'vesh. Surrender." The Gil'shar leader's eyes glittered as he took in Taeris, his ragged appearance, the small force behind him.

"Oh. Good," said Taeris, not needing any prompting from Wirr. "The first thing we'll need to do is get you to move that Column back. Then if you could tell your men to disarm and line up, we can—"

"*Your* surrender," snarled the high priest. "Lay down your arms and we will provide you with a swift execution."

Wirr shifted. "Try to explain what they're doing."

Taeris shook his head. "Tempting," he told the Desrielite drily. "You do understand what you're doing by activating those Columns, don't you? Killing every single one of your troops? Playing into the hands of—"

Koresh spun and walked away, sneering.

Wirr sighed. He'd known that there was no point—it wasn't as if the Gil'shar were suddenly going to back down, having come this far—but he'd had to try.

"Fighting it is," he muttered to himself. "Taeris, back to your position."

To his relief he saw only a few dar'gaithin among the Desrielites; as he'd suspected, the creatures' ranks had been severely thinned by the eletai. Still, the reality was that it didn't really matter now. Even with their relatively defensible position here, there were simply too many bodies opposing them. They might hold out for a few minutes, ten or fifteen at most. Hoping for more than that was pure optimism.

Another few minutes passed as the Gil'shar forces began to

methodically arrange themselves. Wirr watched closely, making sure he wasn't missing something, but he didn't spot anything unexpected. He was as ready as he could be.

The air was heavy with anticipation as someone down below began shouting words of exhortation to their men.

And then the Desrielites charged.

Wirr immediately began issuing orders, quietly and calmly, one squad providing a shield from the initial attack and one going on the offensive, tearing rock from higher up the slope and raining it down upon the Desrielites. Screams filled the air as stones shattered bones and skulls, soldiers dropping and being hauled back to safety, only to be replaced by the next wave. And the next. And the next.

Wirr helped where he could, one moment strengthening the shield, the next assisting in the assault where he saw an opening that no one else had spotted. But it was only minutes before his Reserve—already low to begin with—started to fail, and he could already see some of the other Gifted with blades in hand, staring out with hollow eyes at the oncoming force, no longer able to contribute Essence either.

It was just as Wirr had known it would be: there were simply too many of the enemy to overcome. They would stand here to the last—but they would be cut down.

Slowly but surely the fighting seeped closer, moving rapidly toward Wirr's position until finally he was in the midst of it all, his blade out as he defended desperately, using what little energy he had left to protect himself from the flashing steel of multiple opponents. Cuts opened up on his arms and legs, one on his chest dangerously close to his throat. The Essence in his Reserve was almost gone, his arms numb, his breathing labored as he backed away, step by reluctant step.

It was over. He felt…empty, inside. He'd done everything he could, but it hadn't been enough.

The Boundary would fall. They had lost.

And he was about to die.

Instinctive, animal fear clutched at his insides as a dar'gaithin appeared, carving a swathe through Wirr's allies, its gaze fixed on him. Wirr stumbled back, and his exhaustion didn't let him catch his footing. He fell clumsily, dragging his blade into position but knowing that there was no chance it would matter.

The creature lunged for him.

Its eye sprouted an arrow.

The dar'gaithin rocked back, hissing and thrashing wildly, hands scrabbling at the shaft and wrenching it free. Black blood spurted from the open wound; a moment later the creature was crumpling to the ground, and the Desrielite soldiers around it—charging at full speed a second earlier—were faltering to a halt, staring wide-eyed behind Wirr.

He turned his head from his prone position on the ground, catching sight of who was standing a short distance behind him.

He knew he'd lost too much blood; this had to be a mirage. Something for which his mind was grasping, an image that he wanted to see more than anything else. A last illusion before death.

Then there were hands grabbing him under his arms. Dragging him away. He struggled briefly, tried to speak, to scream at them that they had to stand, that falling back would kill them all.

It was no good.

Everything faded to black.

Chapter 47

Caeden beckoned to Asha and then slipped through the Gate into a darkened, empty street, the jagged black architecture around him unsettlingly, heartbreakingly familiar.

He came to a stop, pausing as he scanned the surroundings for any sign of movement, breathing in the familiar, stifling air of Ilshan Gathdel Teth. A strange sense of comfort settled in amid the tension that came from knowing what they were about to do. Despite its ugliness and no matter how else he tried to think of it, this was the place he had lived for half of his life.

Even with what he was about to face, it was hard not to feel as if he was coming home.

Asha joined him and he stepped to the side, turning slightly and slashing at the mechanism of the Gate with kan, watching as the portal vanished. Then he motioned silently to the left, down a narrow alley; Asha half jogged to catch up to him as he strode into the shadows. Though there was little doubt that Shammaeloth wanted him here, that didn't exclude an outright attack, and Gassandrid would still have detected his entry to the city. It was vital that they not linger.

They walked for a few minutes in silence, Caeden steering them clear of late-evening hubs like Anvil and Graveyard; though it was past midnight, those places would still be attracting crowds. Instead he guided her through deserted marketplaces and across streets lit only faintly by distant lamps, voices occasionally reaching their ears but never coming close.

That wasn't unusual, for Ilshan Gathdel Teth. A population

of only twenty thousand in a city designed for ten times that made for plenty of space. They didn't have to worry about being accosted by footpads mistaking them for easy targets, either. Criminality in the home of the Venerate was an unhealthily risky venture. Very few bothered.

"Where are we going?" whispered Asha eventually, her need for information finally overcoming the intimidating nature of the situation.

Caeden glanced up at the Citadel on their left to orient himself. "Underground. Shammaeloth's... refuge, I suppose you'd call it."

"You're sure that's where Licanius is?"

"Yes. Trust me."

Caeden jerked to a stop as Asha grasped his arm firmly.

"Then won't it be guarded?" she asked seriously, holding his gaze. "How many do you think we'll have to fight? Will Gassandrid be there? What should I expect when we're down there? I *am* trusting you, Caeden—but if I'm going to help, then I need to know more than you've told me."

Caeden grimaced. He'd been deliberately vague, mostly because enlightening her properly—going into enough detail that she would truly understand what they were about to face—could take hours. Days, even, if she was as inquisitive as he suspected. Millennia of myth and skepticism had mingled with half-truths surrounding Shammaeloth, making untangling his true nature such an involved task that Caeden himself wasn't sure he had yet fully completed it.

That, after all, was one of their enemy's greatest strengths.

"This... this is what Shammaeloth wants, Asha," he said. "There won't be guards, because he wants me to face him. He will not kill me without first trying to *own* me."

Asha frowned. "But why would he actually keep Licanius—"

"Because it is the only thing I need from him, now," said Caeden simply. "It is the only thing that guarantees I go to him. That doesn't mean that he will *give it up* without a fight—but our passage inside will almost certainly be unobstructed." He gently lifted her hand from his arm, gesturing. "I can answer your other questions as we walk."

Asha bit her lip, but assented and fell into step with him once again.

They moved swiftly along the deserted streets, and Caeden did his best to paint a picture of what they were about to face. Shammaeloth was unable to physically affect the world; explaining that, but also convincing Asha that he was still the most immediate and dangerous threat—not whatever other forces might be arrayed against them—was, as he'd already known it would be, beyond difficult.

That wasn't Asha's fault. For someone who had yet to experience Shammaeloth's presence, it was impossible not to think of the enemy's true weapons as merely words, something familiar that should easily be overcome. No one could imagine what it was like to have his focused attention, to have everything he said seep into the very pores of your mind, color every subsequent thought you had. Every subsequent thought you *would ever have.* Having Shammaeloth speak to you in his full power was nothing like listening to another human. He was older and smarter and more deeply powerful than anyone in this world could hope to properly conceive of without experiencing it for themselves.

Which was exactly why he needed Asha with him.

"So... you believe Essence weakens him. Lessens his influence," said Asha quietly as they paused at another corner, Caeden quickly checking the street ahead before waving them on. She scrunched up her face, looking unconvinced. "That's why I'm here? You need all that Essence so that Shammaeloth will be... less convincing?"

"And for the inevitable attack when I don't give in to him." Caeden said the words confidently, though they didn't reflect what he was feeling. "But yes. Essentially."

His heart sank a little as they turned another corner and came within sight of the Orb, the pulsing blue cracks in the massive sphere lighting the empty square around it. No Davian. He'd hoped, was still confident his friend would reach them in due course. But there simply wasn't time to wait for him.

Asha hesitated as she spotted the vaguely menacing glow of the Orb.

"What is that?"

"A doorway." Caeden strode over to the monument, placing his hands on it and allowing a trickle of his Essence to drain

685

away into the Vessel. The cracks of blue—where the light from the glowing steel underneath shone through—flared briefly in response, a low, grinding hum suddenly sounding as the sphere began to roll aside, revealing the stairwell vanishing deep into the black of Ilshan Gathdel Teth's belly.

He started onto the first step.

"Tal!"

The voice echoed across the square, low and urgent, a mix of excited and nervous. Caeden and Asha both spun at the sound.

A young woman hurried toward them, deep-brown eyes locked on Caeden. He'd never seen her before, and yet—from her expression, the light in her eyes, the way she swept back her long blonde hair as she looked at him—he knew immediately who it was.

"Nethgalla," he murmured to Asha, who stiffened at the name.

The shape-shifter drew closer, finally registering Caeden's companion.

"*Ashalia?*" Nethgalla's face drained of blood, even as her voice rose sharply in panic.

"The ilshara still stands." Caeden kept his voice quiet and cold. "What do you want, Nethgalla?"

Nethgalla flinched as if struck. "I want to help you retrieve Licanius."

Caeden glanced meaningfully at the stairway. "That's where I'm going now. And it's the one place I'm certain that you are not going to want to follow."

Nethgalla stared at him, and Caeden dipped his head slightly as terrified comprehension gradually spread across her face.

"You're going in yourself?" she whispered in disbelief.

"I have no choice," said Caeden softly. "Even if I thought that there was a way to get it from him otherwise, the ilshara *will* fall, and soon. They used Isiliar's Tributary to trace their way back to the Cyrarium—I'm not sure how—and they armed the Desrielites with Columns, like in Dareci. We couldn't stop them." He nodded at her horrified look. "Nothing to be done about it now, so we need Licanius *before* the ilshara goes down. Before he has a chance to reach Deilannis."

"So this is why the alarm wasn't raised," said Nethgalla heavily.

Caeden gave a short nod, doing his best not to show his unease. As much as he despised her, Nethgalla understood what he was about to do as well as anyone. "Where is Davian?"

To the side, Asha—who had remained icily silent throughout the exchange—shifted slightly, unable to hide her sudden anticipation.

Nethgalla scowled. "He went back to Zvaelar."

Caeden exhaled, placing the sequence of events, shame worming at his gut as he thought back to those last moments there. "He...won't be long. If you want to help, wait for him to come back. Let him know what's happening."

Nethgalla's reluctance to let Caeden start his descent was obvious. "Assuming that you get Licanius," she said. "What then?"

"We find Diara and Gassandrid, and kill them."

"How? Diara has hidden herself away for weeks, and Gassandrid is still working through proxies."

"Let me worry about that," said Caeden firmly. He beckoned to Asha, who was still watching Nethgalla coldly. "We'll see you soon."

"Tal." Something in Nethgalla's voice made him pause. The pretty young woman—a copy of some unfortunate resident of Ilshan Gathdel Teth, presumably—stared back at him earnestly. "I am coming with you. You need someone else who can use kan. We can face him together."

Caeden gazed back, then gave the slightest of shrugs.

He turned and started down the stairwell, into the darkness.

He didn't look back as he heard Asha and Nethgalla following him, tapping his Reserve and letting a small ball of Essence flare to life. The light flickered and waned, as any exposed Essence tended to do so close to darkstone, but it was enough to ensure that they didn't tumble headfirst down the narrow stone stairs.

Behind them the Orb ground shut again. The small pieces of time-locked metal inside it were what actually drove the Vessel now, though once the Vessel had been set into the stone itself, a creation of the Darecians. Corrupted within months of the ilshara's being raised, of course.

"Why build a hidden entrance in the middle of a public square?" asked Asha as they descended.

"It wasn't always a public square. The city's changed a lot over two thousand years," Caeden assured her.

"So he's been here since the Boundary was raised?"

"Almost entirely." He rubbed his face, thinking of that night on Taag's Peak. In all his years here, it remained the only time that he was certain Shammaeloth had emerged. "Coming out near the ilshara seems to . . . diminish him."

"It pains him. The more Essence there is nearby, the weaker his influence becomes." It was Nethgalla, speaking up for the first time, albeit quietly—almost to herself. "If he has appeared elsewhere, it would only have been a . . . projection, of sorts. An illusion. The only reason he would truly leave this place would be to march on Deilannis."

Caeden snorted. "*Now* you're willing to talk of him?"

Nethgalla looked away, but not before Caeden saw the glimmer of fear in her eyes.

"You know all that you need to," she said. "And I should not speak any further while we are down here, unless it is absolutely necessary. His influence will be . . ." She sighed. "I am not certain that I will be able to trust my own tongue."

Caeden eyed Nethgalla, and reluctantly conceded the point.

Nobody talked for a while as they kept moving downward, a thoughtful look on Asha's face. To the young woman's credit she seemed to be taking everything being said in stride, though Caeden supposed she had little choice in the matter at this stage.

After a while, she touched the stone wall. "Did you—the Venerate, I mean—create this place for him?"

"It was already here. At least . . ." Caeden hated having to dredge up these old memories, but ignoring them wasn't going to help anyone. "The Orb was, and this hidden stairwell—it joins a series of passageways that I think were built alongside the city. But where we're going, specifically . . . none of us were ever really sure. Shammaeloth cannot have made it himself, but he abided in a very similar place before we came to Andarra. If I had to guess, I would say that he arranged for it to be made, somehow."

"So it's special, in some way?"

"Yes. Kan doesn't seem to exist in there, at least for us. It's not
just blocked off. It completely vanishes," Caeden said quietly.

"We all used to think that was simply more proof of his power, to be honest. But when I went to Zvaelar, I realized that I was having exactly the same experience there—and that his refuge here probably sits fairly close to its portal, and all the machinery we set up to hold back the corruption seeping out of it."

He glanced across at Nethgalla for any hint of a confirmation of his theory, but the woman was forging ahead grimly, her face giving no indication as to her thoughts. He shook his head ruefully. "It's still only a guess, but if he has been harnessing Zvaelar's time corruption somehow, it would probably also explain the other strange thing about his sanctuary—that you can *lose* time in there, sometimes. Hours. Days. That's the opposite of a normal manipulation of the time stream, and it's not consistent, either, so I don't believe it's simply some hidden use of kan." He eyed her. "Regardless of whether I'm right about its nature, though, it's certainly one of the more secure places they could be keeping Licanius."

They reached the bottom of the stairs, and suddenly Asha's stride faltered. Caeden turned to her, nodding bleakly as he recognized the strange look coming over her face. "You're starting to feel his presence."

"No. No, it's not that," said Asha gently, a small smile playing around her lips. "I'm actually feeling...wonderful. Calm, like... everything's going to be all right." She gave a soft, disbelieving laugh. "Better than I've felt in a long time."

Caeden rolled his shoulders uncomfortably. Off to the side, Nethgalla frowned, though she stayed true to her word and said nothing.

"It's him. I warned you—that's part of how he works, Asha," Caeden said eventually, motioning for her to keep moving, down the long, dark corridor now stretching ahead of them. He wasn't feeling anything yet, but he knew he would soon enough, and part of him—that selfish, primal part that was always there—strained to. "It isn't real."

Asha accepted the statement reluctantly. They started walking again.

"How can you be so *sure?*" she asked abruptly. She waved a hand at his expression. "I do believe you, but this reassurance is so...deep. Why would *Shammaeloth* want anyone to feel this way?"

Caeden rubbed his face. "Because the things we crave are wonderful blindfolds," he said. "When they start to slip, we want nothing more than for him to pull them up again."

Asha stared at him, then nodded slowly, swallowing.

"What is it for you?" she asked after a while.

Caeden was silent for a long moment.

"Peace," he said softly.

They walked on; to his right, Nethgalla's steps had begun to drag, while to his left he could see Asha's eyes burning bright as she stared ahead with unconscious eagerness. He wasn't overly worried about Asha—he'd seen enough of her now to know that she would resist Shammaeloth's pull as well as anyone could, when the time came—but he still couldn't help but feel a flash of unease at the two very different reactions. It was another reminder of what they were about to face.

"Tap your Reserve, and keep Essence flowing through your body," he said to Asha. "It won't feel good, but it will sharpen your senses. Make it easier to focus."

Asha did as he suggested, and he could see the light in her eyes dimming as Shammaeloth's influence began to fade.

They kept on for several minutes, Caeden unerring as he navigated several branches of the tunnels. They finally came to the familiar, plain steel door and he hesitated. Beside him, Nethgalla—wearing her fear on her face, now, but still holding to her aim of not speaking—indicated her readiness determinedly.

"Remember. As soon as we're in position, create a barrier between us and him," he reiterated to Asha. "You need to light this place up with Essence. Don't hold back."

He paused to make sure she understood, then placed his hand against the metal.

There was a flash, and the door swung open.

They stepped out onto the semicircular platform, which ended abruptly less than a hundred feet away; after that there was only darkness, the light of Caeden's flickering ball of Essence swallowed by the vast emptiness. A soft, chill wind pressed against his cheek as he studied the ledge carefully, but as always it was completely bare. Just flat darkstone, the space beyond the edge a seemingly bottomless pit, and smooth, sheer walls that disappeared into the black on either side.

He placed a cautioning hand on Asha's shoulder as she made to move forward, toward the edge. "You don't want to get too close." He shut the door behind him, resisting the urge to kneel, as was custom. Then he briefly reached for kan, stopping as soon as he confirmed its unsettling absence. "Time for that shield, please."

Essence sprang to life around them, a dome burning thick and bright, though its light didn't seem to illuminate much more of the massive space than his small ball of Essence had. Caeden examined the barrier briefly, impressed. Darkstone had to be absorbing a lot of the energy, which meant that the consistency of the shield was quite difficult to maintain; Asha, though, didn't even appear to be exerting herself.

He took a single step forward.

The light burned everything, pain in his eyes making him stagger. Behind him, he heard what he thought was a gasp from Asha and a low moan of terror from Nethgalla.

Tal'kamar.

The voice was everything. Calm and yet crushing. Gentle and yet a roar. The feeling of peace that had hovered near the edge of his mind for the past few minutes was suddenly there, intense, enveloping him.

Gritting his teeth, he pushed it back.

"Shammaeloth," he gasped, the mere name making him feel as if there were blood pouring from his mouth. "You have something I want."

The sensation pressing against him changed to something... sadder. A deep, lonely, sorrowful ache.

Then you shall have it.

There was silence following the pronouncement, and Caeden struggled to breathe. Was Asha's barrier still up? There was no way to tell, no chance that he could open his eyes to look.

"At what price?"

Your attention, Tal'kamar. I would speak to you and have you truly hear me, one last time. A pause. **Then you will choose.**

Choose the fate of the world and all who are in it. But it will be your choice, not mine.

Off to his left, he heard Asha breathing heavily. He forced his head to the side and pried his eyes open to a squint, catching a stark glimpse of her on her knees, face to the floor as she tried to shield her eyes. He crawled over to her, putting a hand on her back and leaning in close.

"I thought you said he hated Essence," whispered Asha.

"It is an illusion," replied Caeden, his own words strained. "Make the shield larger, if you can. Flood this place with more Essence."

There was a sense of motion in the light and suddenly the pain in Caeden's eyes eased, just a little.

He squeezed Asha's shoulder and then struggled to his feet, facing the blinding brightness, accepting the pain. "Then speak," he snarled.

If you use Licanius as Andrael intended, then you will be making a choice. A more important choice may never have been made. The voice was gentle. **And our choices are nothing if they are not informed, Tal'kamar. They become something far less.**

"I am informed," spat Caeden. "I remember your true form and your true nature. You cannot deceive me anymore. I remember *everything*."

Not everything. Only the things you have allowed yourself.

Caeden's heart skipped a beat as he caught Shammaeloth's meaning. "I didn't relive the other memories because I was ashamed. Ashamed of the things I did for you," he said eventually.

You avoided them because they made you feel uncertain. They caused you doubt. The presence felt... pitying. **You could not take the uncertainty of whether you had chosen the right side, Tal'kamar. So you succumbed.** A pause. **I ask you: If you are so certain that you are right, why would you fear knowledge?**

It was hard to think. He tried to glance across at Asha again, but he couldn't see her expression. "I don't fear knowledge. I don't fear the memories, and having them would not change my mind," he rasped, as much for her as for him.

Then let me restore them. Prove to me that *you* are making the choice.

That is my price for Licanius.

The overpowering light abruptly winked out; the pressure against his eyes eased, and he tentatively opened them.

There was no sign of Shammaeloth, now, though his heavy presence still hovered in the darkness beyond. Caeden's gaze, though, was immediately drawn toward the edge of the platform.

The blade that lay on the ground, just outside the barrier, bent the light of Asha's shield. Twisted it.

He walked slowly forward, as if in a dream. His footsteps echoed against the stone, though he could barely hear them over the thundering of blood in his ears.

"Ashalia," he said. "Extend the shield a little further."

"Don't." It was Nethgalla, panic in her voice. "Ashalia, do not listen to him."

Nothing happened; Caeden turned, seeing Asha looking at him. Silently, he gave her a single, reassuring nod.

The bubble of energy expanded. Just enough to allow the sword inside.

Caeden felt a tear trickling down his cheek. Whether it was from fear or regret, he didn't know.

He bent down. Picked up Licanius.

The memories came.

One after another after another they hit him, with almost no pauses in between, each segueing into the next. These weren't the largely dulled, informational recollections that he'd had trickle back to him over the past year. They were vivid and bright, intense and emotional.

He lived a thousand moments, a thousand decisions, all over again. Some were weeks at a time and numbing in scale, like the War of Theria, or the wiping out of the Jereth, or the destruction of Li Teroth. Others lasted only minutes and were intensely personal, manipulations and lies and ugly losses of temper. The time his bitterness had led to him sneering at young Elina Devries, publicly lecturing her to tears after she had worked up the courage to ask him to dance. The lies he'd told to convince Damon Rel, who had all but worshipped Caeden, to send his son to prison. The four words he had used to rip apart Siara Calethi's marriage, all because of a perceived slight.

Shouting at Ell after choosing to escalate an argument, leaving her white and trembling and close to tears. And then walking away.

A thousand moments, a thousand decisions—and each one a dagger. Each one was disgrace and regret, deep and twisting and wretched.

And yet, he knew that these were not even all the terrible things he'd done.

They were only the worst.

At some point there was a longer pause, a few seconds for him to catch his breath, the cavern back in view. He turned dazedly, to his horror seeing tears streaming down both Asha's and Nethgalla's faces.

"What are you showing them?" he gasped.

Exactly what I am showing you.

"No," he whispered, humiliation warring with panic as he watched Asha's eyes, which were full of grief and despair.

He had time only to take in her distress before the beginnings of yet another memory wiped her from view.

He lost track of time, of where he was, of why this was happening. Shame ate at him, wormed inside his gut, seeped into his very core. This wasn't a deception, some mental trick devised by Shammaeloth to turn him or break him. This was *him*. This was *who he was*. It was a dream. A nightmare. He could see only pain, and he was responsible for all of it.

And then, finally, after moments and years, it was over.

He was on his knees now. This was worse than just remembering, worse than simple knowledge. He felt...stained.

He knelt there for what seemed like an eternity, lost to his surroundings.

"The past is the past," he whispered, finally reaching up to wipe the tears from his face with his left hand. Licanius was still in his right, his grasp on the hilt white-knuckled. "The past is the past." He needed to believe it. "The past is the past, and you cannot break me with it. It has no hold over me anymore."

The words were to himself, but Shammaeloth answered anyway.

Is that what you believe?

"It is the truth," choked Caeden. It was, wasn't it? "I have left it behind."

You chose to leave it behind. But in the world for which you fight, Tal'kamar, that means very little. In your world, the past is something from which you can never be free.

The cavern faded again. Became memory one last time.

But this... this one wasn't his.

The palace hallways. Anger burned in his stomach, ugly and hot and heavy, as he carried a tray of food. Knocked at a door.

Karaliene answered, let him in.

She was talking cheerfully but he wasn't listening; her voice grated on his nerves and her saccharine smile only stoked his anger. Her? He just didn't see it. He put the tray down and shut the door behind him, shielding from Karaliene the fact that he was locking it, too.

The princess had turned away. Two steps. A hand snaking over her mouth. She struggled, bucked against his grip, but her movements quickly became weak as Essence drained from her and into him. He held her steady as her skin began to pale and wither and crack. Her head lolled back and he watched with that familiar, strange combination of satisfaction and shame as her eyes glazed and then shriveled.

He lowered the corpse to the floor, continuing to drain it until there was nothing but fine gray powder.

He dusted off his hands and then focused, picturing the princess. Let kan flow and embraced the delicate agony of the change.

Bones broke and reformed, skin writhed, muscles tore—and then it was done. He stood, quickly practicing a few of those annoying, girlish smiles and mannerisms in front of the mirror before touching the Vessel by the door that would summon someone from the servants' quarters.

There was some cleaning up to be done.

Caeden's limbs trembled as he found himself kneeling on the cold stone once again.

The memory hadn't been as smooth as his own, events and emotions conveyed in violent flashes of moving image—but it had been enough.

"You're lying," he rasped. The words were hollow; he felt completely wrung out, unable to put any passion even into this denial. "You always lie. She's not dead. You *always lie*."

I have shown you nothing false, Tal'kamar. You know this.

Caeden knelt there, head bowed, grief and fury and shame mixing into a red haze.

He stumbled to his feet. Turned to Nethgalla.

He only had to see her eyes to know the truth.

"When?" he asked, voice cracking.

Nethgalla struggled for a moment to find an answer, her fearful expression lit by Asha's shield.

"A month after the siege of the city, when you killed Mash'aan and his men. I had to. I had to get close so that I could take a Trace for the Vessel I'd made—Isiliar was coming for you, and amplifying your Essence signature was the only way I could mask your real one for a while," she said tentatively. She paused for a long second, watching him pensively. "It saved your life, Tal. And... even if it hadn't, I think you know that what you had with her wasn't real. She was too young to..."

She cut off, eyes widening. Caeden was stalking toward her, though he didn't remember instructing his legs to move.

"Tal." She started scrambling backward. "*Tal*."

Her skin writhed and her bones cracked; before he could reach her, it was Ell staring back at him in open fear.

Everything was a blur through tears and agony. His grief wasn't just for Karaliene. It was for everyone whose life had been touched by him. It was for himself.

He flooded his arm with Essence and grasped Nethgalla. The image of his wife screamed at him, beat him with her fists, begged him to stop, professed her love for him. The blows were powerful, but they didn't make him flinch. He was beyond the physical pain now.

He choked down bile and more tears and dragged her to the edge of the shield. The Essence parted for him; whether he'd sliced it open with Licanius or whether Asha had created the gap for him, he wasn't entirely sure.

He gathered all his strength, all his fury.

He threw Nethgalla out into the darkness.

The Essence shield closed around him again as he stood there, panting, listening to the Ath's shrieks as they faded into the abyss. Every limb trembled; his mind was a jumble of stark, raw emotion at both what he had learned, and what he had just done.

Tal'kamar. The voice was gentle. **I feel your pain, and I am sorry for it—but it was the only way left to reach you. You know, deep down, that the fault is not yours to own. Not for any of it. Not while you are imprisoned by fate.**

Caeden glanced across at Asha. He knew, somehow, that she couldn't hear what was being said now.

The look of raw shock and disgust on her face as she met his gaze was too much.

He didn't blame her—how could he? He felt the same. Everything was shame, deep and dark and red.

The things he had done. The things he had *done*.

"I *am* responsible," whispered Caeden. He knew it, despite the overwhelming desire to say otherwise. "Everything you showed me, some part of me knew that it was wrong. There are no justifications—only excuses. I *chose*." Knifing shame tore at his chest, and he couldn't even look at Asha now. "You have not changed my mind, Shammaeloth."

Your needless suffering breaks my heart, Tal'kamar, but I will not deny you your choice. The voice held echoes of grief. **I will continue to hope for your heart to change, for no matter your choices, my love for you endures. My deepest wish is that I may still fulfill my promise to you—to send you back. To give you another chance.**

Licanius trembled in Caeden's hand. His deeds crashed around in his head. He saw the expression on Karaliene's face as she died. On Alchesh's. Isiliar's. Davian's.

Shammaeloth was right. He couldn't escape who he was; these memories proved that.

So how could he possibly trust himself to finish this, the way it needed to be?

Shammaeloth was trying to plant a seed in his mind, trying to make him believe that he could undo all of this. Make him stumble at the last hurdle.

And deep down, he knew that there was a possibility it would work.

His presence was a risk. It was better if Asha took Licanius, found Davian, and they dealt with the other Venerate. They were strong, capable. *Good.* They would follow through to the very end.

He had delayed, and delayed, and delayed. But perhaps the time for waiting, the time for patience, was done.

"Caeden," said Asha, a warning note of concern in her voice. "What are you doing?"

Caeden stared at the blade in his right hand. The edge hovered just above his left wrist.

"What is necessary," he said softly.

"We still need you." Asha stepped forward, but cautiously, as if worried that any sudden movement could set him off.

Listen to her, Tal'kamar.

"Be silent!" shouted Asha furiously at the void, her Essence shield flaring as she poured more energy into it. She shook her head, holding out a hand gently toward Caeden. "Ignore him. *We need you.*"

Caeden's muscles tensed, the sword trembling.

"She's right, Tal."

Asha and Caeden both started at the voice coming from the entrance. Neither had heard the great steel door open again.

Davian stood in the entrance, grim expression illuminated by golden Essence.

Caeden straightened, the blade in his hand dropping slightly, though he still held it at the ready. Davian looked...old. Weary beyond measure. New scars covered his face and body, though that body was now leaner and more muscular. His movements were smooth and confident as he walked forward onto the platform.

He was just as Caeden remembered him from Zvaelar.

The joy in Davian's eyes as he gazed at Asha was unmistakable. A flash of...something ran through Caeden. Relief. Happiness for his friend.

"Tal." Davian's smile for Asha turned to Caeden, and that expression—that joy—didn't disappear, as Caeden had expected it to. As it should have. "You have Licanius. Let's go."

Davian. You are brave, to work with the man who killed you.

Caeden's hand shook as the memories threatened to overwhelm him again. He forced them back.

"I am glad you're here, Dav." Caeden forced a smile through the pain. "But...it's time. If I do not do this now..." He gestured, exhaling shakily. "There will always be reasons to not. Always be something more that I believe I could do."

"Just think. He is deception," said Davian calmly. "He is lies—you told me this yourself. This is what he wants, Tal."

"Karaliene is dead." Caeden bowed his head, the words sticking in his throat. He heard a soft gasp of horror from Asha, but he plowed on. "Nethgalla killed her. She killed her because I *exist*, Dav. No matter what I do, no matter how I change, I *cannot* outrun my past. Its dangers. Its consequences. So the longer I am here, the worse things will be for you and everyone you love. Everyone *I* love. And I cannot abide that."

Davian was silent for a second.

"Do you remember what Raeleth said to you, at the end?" he asked quietly. "About consequences?"

Caeden closed his eyes, blade still hovering above his wrist.

"How do you know?" he whispered.

"Because I know you." Davian's voice was sure. "Because you are my friend. Because I and those of us who love you *will* accept those consequences. This darkness in you, telling you that we are better off with you gone—it's him. It's *him*, Tal. *This* is the trap."

Caeden took a slow, shaky breath.

Nodded slowly.

"Thank you," he said faintly, lowering the blade. The shame was still there, overwhelming, but...that smothering curtain of darkness was gradually pulling back. He breathed again, some small measure of clarity returning.

I am sorry that it had to end this way, Tal'kamar.

"Tal!" Davian moved and Asha flinched toward him, both focused on something behind him.

He tried to turn but was caught in an impossibly strong grip. Everything happened so fast; he flooded his arms with Essence but the hand holding Licanius was being forced around by his attacker and Caeden had no time to react, no time to stop it.

The steel plunged into his stomach.

Caeden twisted as he fell, hot pain knifing through him. An al'goriat loomed over him, slavering mouth wide as its needle-like teeth descended on his arm; a massive bolt of Essence slid through the air but the creature was already gone, reappearing a moment later with claws swiping at his face.

Then Davian was there, his blade buried in its chest. He yanked the steel out again and kicked hard, forcing the body back until it slumped to the ground. Beyond him there was more motion, the shadowed walls suddenly crawling with movement just beyond the light of Asha's Essence.

Davian ignored the unsettling sight, skidding to his knees beside Caeden. Caeden looked at him blearily.

"Fates, Tal." Davian tore a strip of his shirt, pressing it desperately against the wound even as he poured Essence into it.

"Al'goriat," gasped Caeden. The creature must have slipped inside the Essence shield when he'd killed Nethgalla, staying hidden outside the flow of time until Shammaeloth had needed it.

"I noticed." Davian's expression was determined. "I was watching for the time corruption when I came in—it's nowhere near as strong as in Zvaelar, and it's only in here. The rest of them won't be able to go past that door. So right now, we just need to get you patched up and out of here."

"Leave me." Despite Davian's efforts, he could tell his wound wasn't healing.

Davian scowled. "Tal, if you give up, we are dead."

"It's too late." Caeden closed his eyes, a quick check confirming what he already knew by instinct. "Licanius did exactly what it was meant to. My source is gone. This...this is it." He said the words dazedly, faintly, not quite believing them. After all this time.

Davian stooped. Picked up Licanius.

"Ash, you need to save him. I don't think even your barrier will stop these things for long, but I can hold them off."

Asha hesitated, and Caeden could see the conflict within her. Then she nodded.

Davian turned as al'goriat—crawling on all fours, claws somehow finding purchase in the smooth darkstone as they scuttled along the walls—flooded into the light.

Caeden's breathing was labored, but his heart still managed to constrict at the sight. There were *hundreds*.

Davian squared his shoulders. Vanished.

The barrier of Essence flickered, and then the al'goriat began dying.

It happened so quickly, and Caeden was still so hazy, that he could barely credit what he was seeing. The creatures hissed and screeched and shrieked as limbs and heads were cleaved in quick succession, an invisible wave of death that rippled outward, an explosion of black blood and rent flesh. Even al'goriat that had stepped outside of time were suddenly reappearing, mortally wounded, some of them flailing and screeching as unseen, powerful blows sent them careening into others and over the edge of the platform.

Asha watched for a moment, wide-eyed, then turned back to Caeden. He could see the reluctance in her eyes before she closed them. He was too weak now to tell her not to bother.

He felt the Essence pouring into him, being eaten by the wound from Licanius. His body reached hungrily for the life-giving energy but something stopped it from healing, stopped it from knitting together as it should.

He blinked blearily. He was so tired. He could see Asha's face straining as she forced more and more energy into his body; Essence flooded him, sank into every pore. Was the wound healing? It was hard to tell. He wasn't sure that he could feel anything anymore.

Vaguely, he was aware that the al'goriat continued to emerge but that Davian, somehow, impossibly, was still scything through them. A blaze of death that was holding each and every one of them back. Caeden's head lolled to the side, and he saw that Asha's shield had thinned, weakening and shrinking as she put everything she had into reviving him.

And then—full of more Essence than he had thought was even possible—Caeden saw past it, into the darkness of the abyss.

An immense, heaving mass towered over the platform, impossibly tall, formless and writhing and slick with wet darkness. Tendrils covered in black pustules whipped around and slithered along the cavern walls; some of the boils throbbed and burst into dripping shadow as it seemed to lean in eagerly, excitedly, drinking in what it was witnessing below.

Asha was watching him, and he tried to point, to give voice to what he was seeing, but it was too late. He was too far gone. Licanius had done its job.

The cavern faded.

Chapter 48

Asha's breath came in short, sharp gasps as she plumbed the depths of her Reserve, pouring everything she could into Caeden.

A nightmare surrounded her. Beyond her Essence shield she could feel Shammaeloth's presence in the darkness, and long gone was the joy she had felt when she had first come here. Now she sensed only menace, looming and heavy with anticipation.

And then there were the Banes.

She risked a glance up, her concentration almost failing her as she saw more bodies flying through the air. The darkness crawled with motion as the monsters scuttled with clawed hands and feet, their bloodied, needle-like teeth bared, eyeless gazes fixed upon her and Caeden. Al'goriat. She'd fought them, but never outside the safety of the dok'en.

As fast as the al'goriat were moving, Davian was faster.

She couldn't see him but she knew what was happening, could follow the line of creatures being scattered back into the abyss. Black blood sprayed liberally, glittering in the clean white light of Essence, as Davian somehow managed to keep a tiny pocket of calm surrounding her and Caeden.

But the flood of creatures showed no sign of stopping. Even using Licanius, how long would Davian be able to keep this up?

She turned her focus back to Caeden, desperation and fear tearing at her chest as she examined the wound. She was *pouring* Essence into it—everything she could handle—but it was healing so *slowly*. As if the injury were sucking in the Essence, devouring it.

Still, the flesh *was* gradually, lethargically knitting back together.

"Can we move him?"

Asha started as Davian appeared in a crouch beside them, tension straining his voice. He glanced up and vanished again before she could reply, more bodies flying away in a wave of gore and limbs, animal snarls cut short.

He reappeared, and Asha nodded. "Won't they follow us?"

"No." Davian sounded certain.

"Then let's go."

She strengthened her arms with Essence and scooped Caeden's limp form off the ground, trying to be both swift and gentle, even as she continued to pour life into him.

She let the shield drop—it was too difficult to maintain now—and broke into a sprint as Davian carved a path in front of her, somehow *still* outside of time and showing no signs of weakening. The steel door flung open as she approached and she dashed through, flinching as a claw raked the air desperately close to her face, snarl turning to a bloody gargle as Davian took care of the attacker.

She risked a glance over her shoulder, heart dropping. Now the Essence shield was gone, the platform was barely lit, crawling with al'goriat that blurred toward the door in a mass of dripping teeth and snarls and outstretched claws.

Then the door was closed and Davian was there, hands on his knees and breathing hard as the sound of heavy, raging blows came from the other side. He stayed like that for a second, then looked up, giving Asha a weary smile.

"Well, that was close."

Asha stared dazedly, gaze flicking between him and the door. "Won't they just—"

"Even if they break through, they can't survive out here." Davian straightened. "That cavern has a sort of time corruption—they live off it. Depend on it," he explained quickly. "How is he?"

Asha shook her head. "I don't know." She crouched, trusting Davian's judgment, and lay Caeden on the ground. His chest rose and fell, but his breathing was shallow. "The wound isn't closed yet," she said, pressing her blood-soaked hand against the former

Venerate's stomach and redoubling her efforts to force Essence into the damaged area. "It's not healing the way it should."

"Could be that it's just the darkstone interfering," Davian said, though he didn't bother to conceal the doubt in his voice. He knelt by Caeden, putting a hand on the other man's shoulder. "Come on, Tal," he muttered, staring at Caeden as if willing him to wake up. "We need you."

Asha swallowed. Caeden's skin was waxy, and his breathing was unsettlingly shallow now.

"It was Licanius," said Asha worriedly as she worked. "What if we just can't..."

"We have to." Davian's tone indicated that he shared her fear, though.

The next few minutes passed as if they were hours. The furious banging on the steel door never stopped, but though Asha couldn't help occasionally eyeing it nervously, the door itself never budged.

Caeden's wound sluggishly, inexorably closed. His breathing deepened, steadied. Color began to return to his cheeks.

"He's looking better," noted Davian.

"He is." Asha didn't keep her uncertainty from the words, though. The wound itself had disappeared, but the Essence she was pouring into Caeden still seemed to be vanishing. That definitely wasn't normal.

Gradually, carefully, she eased off the flow, watching closely. Nothing happened. Frowning, she cut off the flow completely.

Caeden twitched, and then began to shake violently.

Asha quickly resumed tapping Essence; as soon as it began flowing into Caeden again, the shaking stopped, his breathing almost immediately calming.

"Fates," muttered Davian, seeing what was happening. He closed his eyes, placing a hand briefly against Caeden's chest.

"What is it?" asked Asha.

"He was right. His source is gone. *And* his Reserve." Davian's voice was hollow. "He...he's like me, Ash." He ran his hands through his hair. "Except that he doesn't take Essence by instinct."

"What do we do?"

"We keep feeding him Essence until he wakes up. There's nothing more we can do until that happens. And it *will* happen," he emphasized determinedly.

"I believe you." Asha's shoulders slumped as she finally took a moment, letting down her guard and leaning against the wall, even as she made certain the flow into Caeden remained steady. She gave Davian a small, exhausted smile. "Nice to see you, Dav, by the way."

The next thing she knew Davian was there, his arms—considerably stronger than they had once been—wrapped around her in a firm but gentle embrace. She gripped him back tightly, reveling in the familiar smell of him, giving a half sob, half laugh into his shoulder. She wasn't sure herself whether it was from happiness, relief, grief, or a mixture of all three.

They stood like that for a while and then Davian shifted slightly, putting his forehead against hers and locking gazes with her. Tears shone in his eyes, too.

"Nice to see you too, Ash," he said with a grin, and for the first time since he'd appeared, she saw the boy from Caladel in his expression again.

He kissed her, deeply and passionately, and Asha sank into an embrace that even now—after everything they'd been through, all this time wondering if she would ever see him again—she could barely dare to believe was truly happening.

She clung to him fiercely, and she felt his arms tighten reassuringly around her in response.

They eventually parted, eyes still locked, some of the tension of what they had just been through seeping away beneath the comfort of each other's presence and their shared delight in seeing one another again. Davian gestured and they sat against the cold darkstone wall, shoulder to shoulder. They both stared at Caeden's prone form as Asha continued to feed Essence into him.

"Dav," she said uneasily. "There's something that you should know about him. Something he did to you in the past. Will do."

Davian glanced down at her with a tight, rueful smile. "He kills me. I know."

Asha opened her mouth, then closed it and just pressed herself more closely against him.

"How did you do all of that, back there?" she asked. "It was... incredible."

"Vessels. Built into my body," Davian replied almost absently, his gaze on Caeden. He chewed his lip. "Now his source is gone, we might be able to do the same for him. But I'm not sure that there's time."

Asha blinked. A hundred new questions came to her mind, but she didn't ask them. This was enough for now.

"Wirr?" Davian asked quietly.

Asha swallowed against a wrench of pain. "Still alive, when I last saw him. Though..."

She shook her head miserably, and Davian's face fell.

They talked for a while, Asha updating Davian on everything important that had happened during his imprisonment, speaking as dispassionately as she could and not trying to lessen the desperation of their situation. For his part, Davian listened calmly, a deep sadness in his eyes as she listed the casualties they'd suffered. The friends they had lost. She saw the quiet grief stirring in him at every name, but he just acknowledged each one with a silent, accepting sorrow, letting her speak.

Finally, she had finished relating everything she thought he needed to know. They spoke for a time longer after that, heads bowed close. There was no urgency to the conversation now, no sense that they needed to impart vital information. Just a desire to understand what each other had been through. A commiseration of sorts.

A rasping cough finally interrupted them, and they both turned to see Caeden stirring, levering himself up onto one elbow. Asha immediately checked the flow of Essence. Still steady.

"I'm alive," said Caeden woozily, disbelievingly, his gaze sliding to the blade hanging at Davian's side.

"Well," said Davian, forcing a grin as he got to his feet, offering a hand to help Asha do the same. "Not *exactly*."

Caeden's eyes widened as he took in Davian's meaning. He swallowed and steadied himself against the wall, breathing suddenly shallow again.

"My source." His gaze fixed on Asha. "You're keeping me alive."

Asha gave him a brief nod, a response more to the gratitude in Caeden's eyes than to the statement. It hurt her to admit it to herself, but in that cavern, with Shammaeloth's presence pressing down on her, with all those awful memories flashing in front of her eyes...she'd considered it. Just leaving him. For more than a brief second, she'd wondered whether she and Davian might be able to figure out the rest on their own.

Part of her felt a deep shame at that.

Another part still saw all that Caeden had done, and wondered whether she had made the wrong decision.

"Can you take over?" she asked Caeden, not letting on to her internal conflict. "Can you draw Essence from me, rather than me having to maintain the flow?"

Caeden indicated he could, and Asha let the connection drop. A moment later, a thin trickle of Essence started drifting away from her. Barely anything compared to her Reserve, but it still made her...uncomfortable.

"I can get it from other sources once we're outside. But I won't be able to do this while I'm asleep," said Caeden worriedly, groaning as he forced himself to his feet.

"We can sleep in shifts, if we need to." Asha and Davian had already discussed this.

Caeden dipped his head in acknowledgment, glancing at Davian. "Not as though it needs to be for long, I suppose," he said bleakly. He looked back at the steel door. "There's no telling how long passed while we were in there. We should get out as quickly as we can."

The three of them started back down the long passageway toward the city, Asha and Davian modifying their pace to allow for Caeden's weakened state. Asha kept an eye on the Essence flowing from her Reserve, but didn't complain as Caeden modulated the amount here and there, generally increasing it. She knew they needed him healthy rather than just alive.

None of them spoke for a while, and then Caeden coughed awkwardly.

"I'm sorry," he said softly. The words were directed more at Davian than at Asha. "I let him get to me. I knew what was coming, I had so much time to prepare myself, and I still..." He shook his head, frustration and shame warring on his face. "He knew that I was willing to die, and he used it."

Davian said nothing. He looked like he wanted to be understanding, but couldn't quite hide that he wasn't impressed by the explanation.

"You can't imagine what it was like, Dav," Asha added. Her stomach threatened to empty itself at the memory.

Davian's frown didn't dissipate, but he nodded slowly.

"It shouldn't have mattered." Caeden stared straight ahead, his expression determined. "Ashalia's right, but that's not an excuse. It wasn't Control. We still make our own choices."

There was silence for a few seconds.

"And you did." Davian's voice was firm, his expression finally relaxing into something approaching sympathy. "You were tempted, but you made the right decision in the end. That's what matters."

"Only because of you."

"Your choices, Tal. Always your choices. Influences don't get blame or credit."

Caeden grinned suddenly, the conversation evidently straying into territory familiar to both men. Then he stopped, putting a hand on Davian's shoulder to halt him as well.

"Caeden," he said firmly, taking a deep breath. "Caeden has always been the best version of me. Tal... Tal died in there."

Davian gave him a lopsided smile, clapping him gently on the back. "Caeden."

They kept walking.

"Did you ever find out whether Raeleth and Niha were all right?" asked Davian suddenly. There was a tinge of nervousness to his tone; Asha didn't recognize the names, but it was clearly something that had been plaguing him.

Caeden shook his head regretfully. "No. I searched for any word about Raeleth for the longest time, but... there was no record of him. No trace. Which is what we told him to do," he reminded Davian quickly.

Davian rubbed his forehead. "And Niha?"

"Niha would have escaped not long after everything started in Andarra. The rebellion, the appearance of Shadows and the sha'teth...there was too much happening, and too many eyes on me. I couldn't seek her out, no matter how much I wanted to. And she never approached me. Which—again—was exactly what we told her to do," he added firmly. "It is not cause to believe that either of them didn't make it."

Davian conceded the point, though Asha could see that he wasn't entirely happy with the answer.

"Is your Finder ready?" asked Caeden.

Davian nodded. "Right hand. Just need a Trace."

There was something about the way they strode together, the easy way they spoke, the familiarity in their unconscious gestures. They had the feel of two men who were perfectly in sync, who had worked together so often that there was no chance of miscommunication, no hesitation or doubt over how their relationship worked.

She studied Davian. He was older, harder. Even more thoughtful in his responses than he used to be.

But it was still him. The way he twisted his face when he was thinking about something that worried him. The way he tried to cover over that concern, smiling absently at her as he noticed her silent observation.

They soon ascended the stairwell and came to the entrance, Caeden indicating to Davian where he should place his hand to make the Orb roll aside, clearly not wanting to use more Essence than he absolutely had to. The stone ground away, revealing the night sky of Talan Gol and the silent, empty square beneath it.

Asha slowed as they cautiously emerged, the other two not noticing her hesitation, deep in quiet conversation even as they both continued to scan their surrounds for any sign of movement. What was different? Everything seemed normal, and yet...

The air felt fresher. Cleaner.

She stared up at the sky again, and swallowed.

"Dav. Caeden."

The other two stuttered to a stop, looking back at her. "What's wrong?" Davian asked.

Asha shivered.

"Look up," she whispered.

Both men raised their eyes to the heavens, not reacting for a long moment.

Thousands of stars sparkled in the cloudless sky, sharp against the black night.

"El take it," said Caeden heavily, his shoulders slumping. He glanced at Asha. "I thought, maybe, when we went in and it was still up..."

Asha nodded silently, a lump in her throat. She looked at Davian, who was standing very still, his jaw clenched. She'd explained what had happened with the Gil'shar, how they had had to leave Wirr to come here. Davian knew as well as she did what the Boundary falling meant.

Davian ripped his gaze away from the sky. "Let's get moving," he said, his voice rough.

Asha agreed, forcing down her own emotions. There was no time for grief. Briefly, she hoped that if Wirr hadn't somehow escaped, Deldri was at least safe somewhere in the south. With Karaliene dead, there were no other heirs to the throne—and without one, she knew that the struggle for power would get bloody, even if they did manage to avoid the end of the world.

The three of them set off into the darkened city, Caeden leading the way and navigating with unconscious ease. They were heading for Seclusion now, where he had apparently hidden Traces for all the Venerate after his escape from Zvaelar, preparing for this very moment.

They specifically needed Gassandrid's and Diara's, though Caeden wasn't certain that Gassandrid's would be of any help. Diara's, though, he'd assured them would be useful: she would be drenching her body in Essence to stay alive without eating while in the dok'en, and she'd had no reason to try and shield her Essence signature. With the Vessel built into Davian's hand at their disposal, it should be easy enough for them to locate her.

Their path remained mostly unobstructed, though they made certain to keep to the shadows, their tattered and blood-soaked clothing too obvious to hide even in the darkness. It seemed that despite the hour, crowds had gathered in some areas, their shouts echoing around the surrounding streets. The cries were a mixture of joy and confusion, shock and delight. It clearly hadn't been too long since the Boundary had actually come down.

Caeden guided them skillfully around the hubbub until finally, a massive black gate loomed up ahead, and Caeden and Davian both faltered.

Asha's heart skipped a beat when she saw their expressions. "That's the entrance to Seclusion?" They had told her about it, about how dangerous it was. Davian had said it was where Gassandrid claimed Fessi had died.

Asha had known it was the truth as soon as he'd described it. She'd read Fessi's visions, and Davian's description of the place had been too similar for it to be a coincidence. From what he'd explained, Fessi must have recognized her surroundings while they were in prison, panicked, and run.

Directly into Seclusion. Directly to her death.

Another twinge of sadness threatened Asha's focus but she shook her head to herself, not letting it take root. That was getting easier and easier, in a way. There was so much for which she wanted to grieve, one more thing barely seemed to make a difference at the moment.

The gate swung open at Caeden's touch and they slipped inside, Caeden making certain to close it again before beckoning them silently on. The streets here were physically no different from those in the main part of the city, but there was a true sense of abandonment here. A menacing stillness that was heavier and darker than elsewhere in Ilshan Gathdel Teth.

Twice they had to take shelter in nearby buildings and cloak themselves using a mixture of kan and Essence, watching silently as strange, terrifying-looking wolves stalked past, almost as big as horses, their eyes eerily intelligent as they scanned from side to side. An ugly black rot covered them in patches, and through it Asha could see raw flesh and white ribs peeking through.

Caeden didn't know what the creatures were, exactly, but there was no doubting they were dangerous.

They pressed on, Caeden leading them to a house, outwardly no different from any of the surrounding ones. Once inside he walked directly into a small side room and stooped, hands pressing against the wall.

Stone shifted, and a metal box glimmered beyond.

Caeden removed it, glancing at Davian.

"I hated using this," he told him.

"I know," said Davian quietly. He caught Asha's confused glance and smiled at her, though the expression held sadness. "Any Vessels you see in this place were paid for in blood," he said softly. "The blood of people we knew."

Asha laid a hand on his arm, squeezing gently.

Caeden trickled Essence into the top of the box; the edges glowed blue and the top slid aside, revealing several hourglass-like containers. Two swirled with the yellow glow of Essence, and a third throbbed with the energy as well, though dully in comparison. Asha studied the three signatures intently, the differences among them—the rates at which they pulsed, the slight variations in color and intensity—obvious to her now.

The other containers appeared to be empty. Caeden froze as he took in the sight.

"That...cannot be right," he muttered.

"What is it?" asked Asha.

"Cyr." Caeden pointed to one of the dark vials. "This should be glowing, too."

"Could he be shielding himself from it, somehow?" Davian asked.

"No. Essence..." Caeden shook his head. "Essence *is* life; it is inextricably linked to the one from whom it came until it decays. Shielding, or shape-shifting, or going through the Chamber, could all prevent it from being used to find him. But this..." He stared at the vial in disbelief, shaking it slightly as if that would somehow force the Essence to reawaken. "This says he is dead."

"Isn't that what we want?"

"Yes, but..." Caeden shook his head dazedly. "It's not possible. He hasn't been anywhere *near* Licanius."

There was silence, and then Caeden grimaced. "Nothing to be done about it," he observed, replacing the vial and then pocketing the one that glowed dully. He handed the two that were brightly lit to Davian. "Diara, and Gassandrid. But start with Diara. We need to get to her before Garadis's ward wears off."

Davian nodded, carefully unstopping the vial. Tiny cracks ran along the glass as Essence abruptly broke free, swirling around Davian's hand, darting between his fingers, pulsing and straining as if trying to escape his grasp. Asha watched in fascination. The Essence should be swiftly decaying, but the Vessel within Davian was clearly preventing that, using it instead to lead him toward its source.

"She's close," said Davian after a moment, surprise in his tone. "Here in Seclusion."

Caeden thought, then grunted.

"Of course," he sighed. "I think I know where we need to go. Don't let that Essence decay. We're going to need it."

They set off again through the deserted streets. Twice more they had to conceal themselves from the massive, rotting wolves; one appeared to have spotted them but Davian briefly encapsulated them in a time bubble, and they were soon several streets over, with no sign of pursuit.

Caeden eventually guided them to another stairwell leading down into the earth; from Davian's expression, he recognized this one. They descended silently, every muscle tense. The others didn't have to say anything for her to understand that they might encounter resistance at any moment, now.

They reached the bottom, and Asha's step stuttered as she took in the passageway of Essence-lit, shining steel that stretched out in front of them.

"Each plate is a Vessel," explained Davian as they started forward. "It can be moved and reconfigured individually, but it's also part of a much larger whole—one designed to hold back the effects of the time distortion coming from Zvaelar." Asha could hear the begrudging note of respect in his tone. "If it hadn't cost thousands of lives, I'd probably say it was quite brilliant."

They came to a seemingly arbitrary point in the hallway and Davian eased to a stop, staring down at his hand. "She's close now. Somewhere that way." He gestured at the wall to their left.

Caeden acknowledged the statement and placed his hand against the steel plate. "I'm going to take a little extra Essence from you," he warned Asha.

The steel flashed blue, and the hallway... transformed.

Asha watched in astonishment as steel snapped away and

together again, plates moving at blinding, terrifying speeds as they shifted smoothly in a balletic, kaleidoscopic dance of motion and crackling blue light. Within seconds, a new hallway stretched out before them.

"This way," said Caeden, striding forward.

Asha exchanged a glance with Davian, who shrugged and followed.

They walked the newly formed corridor for another minute before more glimmering metal up ahead signaled a dead end. Caeden paused at the blockage, nodding to Davian's hand.

"You need to release that into the steel," he said.

Davian grunted, recognition in his eyes as he pressed his hand against the door. "This was one of the rooms blocking my way earlier. I thought they might be keyed to an Essence signature." The power swirling around his fingers dissipated, sucked into the metal.

Nothing happened for a long moment, and then the steel slid smoothly aside.

The three of them entered the room beyond warily, though there was no sign of any resistance from within. Asha was surprised to find the space warmly decorated. Homey, even. Rugs covered the steel on the floor; one plate on the wall pulsed bright with Essence, apparently providing heat for the room as well as the warm, fire-like light. Well-read books lined the shelves.

The large, comfortable-looking bed in the corner was occupied, and Asha didn't have to look closely to recognize Diara's form. The woman breathed regularly, her expression peaceful. Only the telltale glow of Essence flowing from a nearby plate into her body gave away the fact that she wasn't simply taking a nap.

Caeden didn't hesitate. He walked over to the bed, drew Licanius, and pushed it carefully—almost gently—through Diara's heart.

Asha looked away, skin crawling. No matter the necessity of what they were doing—no matter what Diara had done—there was no getting away from the quiet ugliness of the act. Davian, she noticed, continued to watch, a profound sorrow in his expression.

"Don't feel too sad for her, Dav," Asha murmured.

Davian shook his head. "It's not for her."

Asha turned back, falling silent as she watched Caeden leaning forward, resting against the hilt of the blade, head bowed over the corpse. His body shook with silent sobs.

Finally he murmured something before straightening, gently drawing Licanius out of Diara's chest, wiping the blade solemnly before sheathing it again.

"It's done." Caeden looked at them tiredly, and Asha could see the toll that simple act had taken on him. He picked up Diara's limp hand, displaying a ring on her index finger. "This was Isiliar's dok'en key. Diara must have modified it to access mine. She always was brilliant," he finished softly.

He was about to move back toward the entrance when he paused, spotting something sitting on the desk to the side. He walked over, shaking his head slightly, and reached down, wordlessly displaying what he'd picked up to Asha and Davian.

Asha stared, nonplussed, as she recognized the silver ring— the one she had given to Davian so long ago. To her side, Davian smiled ruefully. "They took it off me the day I was taken prisoner," he explained. He held out his hand.

Caeden hesitated, then shook his head and pocketed the Vessel instead. "I'll hang on to it for now." He shrugged at Davian's expression. "You don't go back until you have it, so..."

Davian grunted. "Good point."

Asha watched the exchange mutely, heart wrenching as it always did when she was reminded of what was coming. Caeden had taken the ring from Davian's corpse—she had seen it herself. So if Davian didn't have it, it meant he couldn't go back in time just yet.

That was entirely fine by her.

"We need to find Gassandrid now," said Caeden. He drew out another vial of Essence—the dull, lifeless one—and handed it to Davian. "See what you can do."

Davian opened the vial, letting the energy dance around his fingers once again. This time, though, the Essence seemed...sluggish. Lethargic.

Nobody spoke as Davian closed his eyes, focusing.

"They are..." He gestured vaguely. "Everywhere. Scattered.

A couple of pulses nearby, but others...I can barely feel them. They're not in Talan Gol, of that much I'm certain." He paused. "Though...there *is* a group of them still together. Somewhere to the south."

Caeden rubbed his face. "He's gone to Deilannis, then," he said, sounding unsurprised.

"You thought this would happen?" asked Asha.

"Yes. Once the Boundary fell, it's what I expected," Caeden admitted morosely. "So we go to Deilannis. We're going to need to go there anyway, to stop Shammaeloth from getting in. And to..."

He gave Davian an apologetic look.

Asha's breath caught, and she gripped Davian's hand almost on instinct. He squeezed back, the gesture both a reassurance and a search for comfort.

"It's likely that Shammaeloth will have found a way to tell him that Licanius is a threat again, too, even if they're assuming I'm dead," Caeden continued. "Gassandrid will be heading for Deilannis regardless—he believes that he's getting sent back, and that can't happen from anywhere else. But if he spots us coming, he won't stay there for long."

Davian nodded slowly. "I'll let you make the Gate," he said, the small smile shared between the two men speaking of an inside joke.

"We'll have to detour past the Tributary, too," Caeden added, almost as an afterthought.

Asha frowned. "Why?"

"We can take that linking Vessel from Tenvar, use it to maintain the flow of Essence between us instead. If you have no objections," Caeden added. He shrugged at her expression. "We'll leave Tenvar himself with the Shadows; he'll be no worse off than he was at the Tol. But we are going to need to separate eventually, and Deilannis is one place where I cannot afford to run out of Essence. If it comes down to a fight, I'm going to need strength, not just kan. And you," he said significantly, "are going to need everything extra you can get to maintain an ilshara around all of Deilannis. That's the only way left to keep Shammaeloth out, now."

Asha stared at him blankly. "What?" She shook her head. "I . . . I don't know how to do that."

"I've seen what you can do, Ashalia." Caeden spoke almost cheerfully, his words full of confidence. "Don't worry. You're more than capable of this."

Davian touched a hand to her arm. "I'll be there to help where I can, too," he assured her.

The responsibility settled heavy on Asha's shoulders, but she nodded. There weren't any other options left to them now, anyway.

"So we sneak in. Kill Gassandrid. I create this ilshara over the entire city to hold back Shammaeloth," she repeated faintly. "What then?"

Caeden slipped his hand into his pocket, pulling out the last vial. He stared for a long moment at the dancing energy within.

"Then we end this," he said softly.

Chapter 49

Wirr groaned, every part of his body feeling as though it were on fire as he groggily came awake.

What had happened to him? His mind struggled to catch up. They had been fighting the Desrielites for days. They had been losing. That desperate, futile last stand, knowing he was going to die.

And then...

His eyes snapped open, his breathing shallow and panicked. The Columns.

"Be easy," murmured a deep, unfamiliar voice to his right.

He twisted to find a stranger sitting across the campfire from his prone position on the ground, perched atop a log and watching him intently. It was night, stars glittering through the haze of wood smoke, though Wirr thought he could see the last vestiges of dusk still fading in the west. They seemed to be high up; Wirr could hear the sounds of other people somewhere farther below, but the edge of the campsite's small plateau blocked his view downward.

The crackling fire lit the stranger's face a ruddy red. His skin was pale, nose sharp, hair braided in an unusual pattern. Wirr struggled to place it for a moment.

Then he tensed. "You're Neskian?" he croaked.

"I am Neskian," replied the stranger calmly. His grasp of the Andarran language—shared by all countries north of the Mountains of Alai—was surprisingly good, with very little of the thick, slurring accent that Wirr had come to expect from someone

719

native to Nesk. "And you are Andarran. But today, at least, I will not hold that against you."

The man spoke lightly; Wirr's eyes narrowed, feeling certain that the Neskian was making sport of him. He blinked, trying to clear his head. "Who are you? Where are we?" His heart pounded almost as hard as his head. "How long have I been unconscious?"

The man raised a hand in a warding gesture, a small smile on his lips. "I am called Ankalat. We are not far from where we found you, but you have been asleep for nearly a day. You were very badly injured, *dhan*. Do not try to move."

Shock made Wirr struggle to sit, despite Ankalat's warning. "The Desrielites," he gasped.

"Have stopped their advance. We are holding them."

"You're not holding them," Wirr said desperately. "They are exactly where they want to be."

Ankalat looked at him as if he thought Wirr wasn't fully conscious yet, but he was stopped from saying anything more by a feminine voice behind him.

"Wirr?"

Wirr's heart beat faster. He turned slowly, fearful to find that his ears had deceived him.

Dezia stood at the edge of the fire, looking at him with light in her eyes.

He stared openmouthed as she grinned at him; suddenly she was on her knees by his side, embracing him so tightly that only the fact that it was her stopped him from flinching away as his already-sore ribs creaked. He held her dazedly.

"What...how?" he whispered.

Dezia laughed, though it was choked off by what sounded like a small sob. "It's a long story."

She kissed him and he returned it eagerly, ignoring Ankalat's presence. Eventually he heard a half-awkward, half-annoyed cough from over Dezia's shoulder, and he reluctantly pulled away again. At some point Ankalat had left, and another figure—this one familiar—had taken his place.

"Aelric?" Wirr felt another grin split his features as he recognized the young man standing across the fire. He looked older by much more than the year or so since Wirr had seen him, body leaner and harder than it had been. He was clothed in unusual-looking black sleeves and gloves. "Fates! It's good to see you!" Wirr had long regretted his decision to let Aelric leave, to not tell Dezia about it until it was too late. Seeing him here, alive and apparently well, was a genuine moment of joy and relief.

Aelric hesitated, then smiled back.

"Good to see you as well, Torin," he said, though the strange tension in his stance didn't ease. "You look like you're recovering." He cast a wry eye at his sister, who blushed.

Wirr tested his limbs one by one, stretching stiff muscles and probing at bruises. "I can fight." A jolt of concern ran through him; he scrambled to his feet, ignoring the pain. "What about everyone else?"

Aelric shook his head. "You, Taeris, and a few others were the only lucky ones."

"Taeris made it?"

"He hasn't woken up yet, but the healers say he'll pull through."

Wirr closed his eyes, exhaling. He'd already known that casualties would be high, but Taeris's surviving was wonderful news. "The Desrielites. What's happening?"

Aelric shrugged. "We withdrew a little way, decided to get our bearings before starting anything. Why in fates were you fighting back there? Why didn't you retreat?"

"Do you have eyes on them?" Wirr asked, not bothering to hide the tension in his tone.

"Yes. Of course," Aelric said slowly. "Scouts are rotating out every hour, but so far none have reported any signs of them advancing. If anything, they seem entirely content to stay where they are. They've even set up some sort of structure in the middle of their camp."

Wirr felt a chill. "Black columns?"

"Yes." Aelric's gaze turned sharp as he saw Wirr's expression. "What are they?"

"Vessels. And if they activate them, everyone and everything for several hundred miles will be dead within a day." Wirr rubbed his face, ignoring Dezia's and Aelric's shocked expressions, trying to get his bearings. He desperately wanted to ask Dezia where she'd been, whether she was well, how circumstances had brought her here—but there simply wasn't time. "These people you're with—Neskians? Are you in charge?"

Aelric coughed. "Not exactly."

"We have Warlord Amar's ear," added Dezia quickly, "but they're sort of...allies, I suppose?" She looked to Aelric for help, but he just shrugged ruefully.

Wirr frowned. "Warlord? There's a Neskian *Warlord* here?" There were only four of those in all of Nesk—it was the highest position in their country. Wirr watched the others' faces, then turned and walked toward the edge of the small plateau, heart sinking.

"Wait!" Aelric held a hand out as if to stop him with the motion, wincing as he did so.

Wirr reached the edge, staring in disbelief at the scene below.

"There have to be a thousand troops down there," he whispered, blood turning cold. Campfires stretched away deep into the approaching valley, each one surrounded by men in distinctive red-and-black uniforms. "A thousand *Neskian* troops."

"Surprise," said Dezia weakly.

"How? Why?" Wirr ran a hand through his hair, calculating. "Wait—*this* was the invasion force we kept getting reports about? How did you know to come *here*, of all places? How did you get here so fast?"

"Cyr," said Aelric. "He's one of the Venerate."

"Was," corrected Dezia, sadness flickering briefly across her features.

"And we are able to move our troops swiftly. That is all you need to know."

The new voice cut through the air behind Dezia and Aelric; Wirr turned to see Ankalat standing at the edge of the fire, having apparently materialized from nowhere. The handsome young man was watching Wirr intently, and Wirr got the distinct impression that his gaze was a disapproving one.

A moment later Ankalat's gaze switched to Dezia, and Wirr suddenly thought he knew why. He resisted the irrational, jealous feeling of insecurity that stirred in his chest.

"We will pose no threat to your country, and my father has agreed to help turn back the Desrielite invasion," continued

Ankalat. "So long as you can guarantee the peaceful transfer of ownership of Lord Aelric's land, now that he is a citizen of Nesk."

"*What?*" Wirr shook his head in confusion, glancing across at Aelric. "A Neskian citizen?"

"Believe me, that's not the strangest thing that's happened," Dezia assured Wirr, laying a hand gently on his arm. "As I said. Long story. We're still with you," she added softly, quietly enough that the other two couldn't hear the words.

Wirr gestured in frustration. "I can't just cede Andarran land to Nesk. I don't have that kind of authority." Not only was there no time for nonsense like this, but Aelric didn't officially *have* any land yet, even if the paperwork was technically underway.

"As second in line to the throne, your word will be enough for my father," Ankalat assured him calmly. "The rest is detail."

Wirr felt a pang of grief as he thought of his uncle. "Heir, actually."

"What?" Dezia and Aelric both spoke at once and Wirr met their gazes, shaking his head.

"Uncle didn't make it out of Ilin Illan," he explained heavily, watching as shock and sadness crept over their expressions. Kevran had been like a father to them.

"What...what about Karaliene?" asked Dezia, voice threatening to crack.

"I don't know," admitted Wirr. "She was in the north when the city was attacked. Hopefully, by now, she's had the sense to head to Prythe."

There was silence, and then Dezia and Aelric both nodded, a fresh, cheerless resolve pasted on their faces. Wirr nodded back. He knew that look.

Grieve later.

Wirr turned to Ankalat. "When can I speak with Warlord Amar? If he wants this deal, then it needs to be *now.*" This was the least terrible of his terrible options, and there was simply no time to argue or negotiate. He needed the Neskian army, and he needed it immediately.

As if on cue, Ankalat produced a document and pen with a flourish, laying them flat against the smooth surface of a nearby shield and gesturing expansively. "No need. Sign, and our men are yours to command until the Desrielites have been defeated."

Wirr restrained a scowl—he was quickly coming to the conclusion that he didn't like the man—and strode over, scanning the paper quickly. It was in the Andarran language and seemed to all be in order, though he knew it didn't really matter. Right now, he would have agreed to a treaty handing over half of Andarra if it meant stopping the Desrielites.

Exhaling heavily, he signed, then handed the document back to Ankalat.

"Are we done?" he asked coldly.

"We are done," Ankalat assured him.

"Then get your people ready. We don't have much time." Wirr stumbled a little as he made to move.

Dezia gave him an appraising look. "Are you up to this?"

Wirr grunted. "Well, we could ask the Desrielites to wait a few days and let me recover, but..."

Dezia held up her hands as Aelric gave him a slight grin. "All right." She moved over next to him, offering him her shoulder to lean on. He took it gratefully.

"Let's go and help our new friends figure out how close we all are to dying," he said grimly.

Wirr crept along the heavily treed ridge, every tired muscle tense, dried leaves crunching faintly underfoot as he made certain to follow exactly where the Neskian scout ahead of him trod.

They were far enough from the Desrielite camp that they didn't expect to be spotted, but the Gil'shar had set up an array of traps along their perimeter. Another gift from the Venerate, apparently: the devices dissolved anyone who stepped on them in a burning flash of Essence, which also served to reliably indicate the position of anyone accompanying the unfortunate victim. The Neskians had swiftly learned to watch for the Vessels, but the devices were usually half-buried, often covered over with leaves and brush. It would be easy enough for even the most skilled scout to miss one.

That level of preparedness didn't bode well for their chances of
a counterattack, no matter how many soldiers Dezia had brought.

The scout who had been chosen to accompany them—a slight man with two fingers missing on his left hand—motioned them forward. The thick, prickly foliage of the mountainside scratched at Wirr as he pushed his way cautiously through, the sounds of soldiers' voices echoing up to him now. He came to a halt beside Dezia as they reached a protruding section of the ridge that would give them a clear view of the encampment below.

He wormed forward the final few feet so as to not reveal himself to any guards, paling as he finally got a good look at the Desrielites.

The Columns were arranged in a ring, and all upright.

His breath caught. Though the ground looked uneven where the massive black pillars stood, they appeared stable, surrounding something on the ground that Wirr was certain hadn't been there before. A circle of obsidian, he thought, deep lines cut into it to form some sort of image. It must have been covered over by dirt and grass before, and the Desrielites had cleared it all away.

Wirr squinted, then felt a chill as he realized that he was looking at it upside down.

It was a wolf's head. Caeden's symbol. The symbol of the Boundary.

"That has to be the Cyrarium," he whispered urgently to Dezia. He'd already explained the Columns' purpose during their short journey here. "And it looks to me as if they're ready to destroy it. We need to attack. *Now.*"

Dezia glanced at him, and he could see the hesitation in her eyes. He couldn't blame her. He was asking her to throw men and women at certain death.

She finally gave a short nod. "Ankalat will have them ready to move by now. Stay here—you'll just slow us down," she murmured. There was no judgment to the words, just simple truth. He was far too weak to move swiftly. "Ten minutes."

She motioned to the scout, and the two of them hurried off.

Wirr watched them vanish into the forest and then turned back to the scene at the bottom of the long, steep incline, heart in his throat. The Desrielites moved like ants below, swarming around the Columns, a fascinated audience as well as defense. Even from here, Wirr could feel their anticipation.

He tensed as he spotted the crowd making way for several men, who were striding confidently toward the center of the ring. Once there, they turned to face the assembled soldiers; after a few moments Wirr could hear projected voices floating up to him, though he couldn't make out the words.

A speech of some kind. That didn't bode well.

He glanced in the direction from which he knew the Neskians would need to attack, willing them to appear even though Dezia had been gone for only a couple of minutes. He stared longingly for a few seconds before his gaze was dragged back to the Columns.

Something was happening.

A crimson light was creeping from one pillar to the next along the edge of the obsidian circle, almost invisible at first but thickening, like a rivulet of bloodred lava. A cheer—a thousand voices raised in joyous celebration—echoed up to him.

The Columns were being activated.

"No," he whispered, scrambling to his feet, suddenly not caring if he was seen. "No, no, *no*."

The red light continued to crawl along the ground, spreading outward from the first Column, inexorably encircling the wolf's head. Shouts of anticipation made their way to his ears, as if the onlooking Desrielites were at a race and urging the light onward toward the finish line. Wirr felt his breath getting short as a low, unsettling thrum began to emanate from the black pillars, the sound increasing each time one was touched by the red energy.

The process had taken only minutes so far; Wirr shifted, again looking back in the direction of the Neskian camp, willing soldiers to appear. He knew it was a vain hope: Dezia would barely have reached the camp at a dead sprint, let alone been able to mobilize a large force so quickly.

He steeled himself and stood, gathering all the Essence he had left in his Reserve. Focused on the Gil'shar leaders standing triumphantly among the Columns, bathed in the eerie red glow. He knew this wouldn't do much—it was a token at best—but perhaps, somehow, it would delay what was happening.

He unleashed.

His bolt of Essence sped downward, a blinding, twisting, molten beam of light.

A hundred feet from the closest Column, it vanished.

Wirr sank to the ground, the strength gone from his limbs. Many of the soldiers looked up at the flash, spotted him. A few pointed and laughed.

None seemed worried enough about him to even try to climb the slope.

Wirr struggled to his feet again, the ache of his previous injuries suddenly feeling far worse now that he was drained of Essence. What else could he do? He took one staggering step, then another, down the hill. The soldiers who had initially noticed him had already turned back to the spectacle in front of them, ignoring him as they joined their voices to the roar of approval.

A nightmarishly long minute passed as he stumbled downward, but his body simply hadn't had enough time to recover; what was left of his Reserve was going to simply keep him from collapsing. He was running a race against that cursed, creeping red light now, but he had known from the beginning that it was one that he would lose.

Before he was even halfway down, the red line joined back to the first Column, the circle complete.

There was a screaming sound, like metal being torn apart by some great force. A thunderous crack as the obsidian wolf's head began to fracture, then break apart.

A white pillar of Essence like nothing Wirr had ever seen screamed into the sky.

He gasped, rolling away and collapsing against the hillside, pain tearing at his eyes as the afterimage left him blind for several seconds. As the initial shock passed he cupped his hand over his eyes, shielding them as he peered down below at the starkly lit Desrielites; most were on the ground and clutching at their faces, apparently having anticipated the explosion of energy as little as Wirr.

The intensity of the light was already fading as the Columns seemed to suck in the glow, the low thrumming pressing hard against Wirr's ears and twisting his stomach into a knot. The pillar of energy bled gradually from white to a deep, ugly crimson.

The chanting and cheering of the Desrielites had petered out into a stunned hush. Wirr couldn't see what had happened to the Gil'shar leaders who had been standing in the middle of the Columns. He hoped fervently that they hadn't moved.

Suddenly there was shouting, panicked yells echoing up to Wirr. He rolled into a seated position, squinting down as a starkly lit flood of bodies crashed out of the forest, a wave that smashed into the dazed Desrielites.

The Neskians had arrived.

They threw themselves into battle with a ferocity and willingness that shocked Wirr. The Desrielites, still stunned by the light, didn't counter well. Not with any sense of organization, certainly.

But with the light at their backs—a significant advantage, given how bright it was—they did enough to hold, resisting the initial Neskian surge toward the Columns. The entire scene was bathed in garish red now, matching the color spraying upward from combatants' bodies as blades and spears slashed wildly into flesh.

Wirr dragged himself to his feet once again and scrambled down the steep hillside as fast as he could, blade out; he would barely make an impact, but he was also painfully aware that it was the best option available to him. The Cyrarium was emptying rapidly, and Caeden had explained exactly what would happen after the Columns had drained it. They *had* to stop that device.

He was almost to the fighting when he saw the Neskian soldier.

He was wearing Telesthaesia, but it was unlike any set of the armor Wirr had seen before. The scales that made up its plates looked distinctly red, not black, as they glittered against the bloody, dying light of the broken Cyrarium. The helmet had a slit for eyes, and a different symbol from the Blind's was inscribed across it. Wirr couldn't quite make it out, but it wasn't the wavy lines within a circle, of that much he was certain.

The Neskians quickly ducked aside as the warrior strode forward, an enormous blade—red, too, Wirr thought, though it was hard to tell in the crimson light—held aloft in his hand. It looked like a broadsword, far too big for one-handed use, and yet as the soldier reached the front lines he swung smoothly.

Wherever he made contact, the enemy just...disintegrated.

Wirr watched in mute shock as the swordsman crashed through

his opponents; the Desrielites surged against him but he simply plowed on, every motion fluid and every deadly strike flowing gracefully on to the next. He danced between them and through them, a glimmering light among a flickering sea of raging enemies, moving ever closer to the nearest of the Columns. The red Essence had dimmed to a dull glow now, making it hard to follow exactly what was happening.

Wirr stuttered to a stop, watching, barely daring to hope.

Behind him, filling the space cleared by the soldier in red, a group of Neskian soldiers flowed, their blades flashing in a dance almost as balletic as their champion's, carving a protective space around the man in Telesthaesia.

And then suddenly, impossibly, the soldier was there—alone, in the tiniest of pockets with one of the Columns. The Desrielite army saw him, raged and surged and attacked with red-tinged fury, and somehow the Neskians protecting their warrior held.

The soldier in red drew back his fist, and punched the Column.

There was an odd sound, a whining echo, as if the thrumming had been disrupted for just a moment. But the Column didn't move.

The red light was almost gone now, fading so that everything was left in murk barely tinged with crimson. Only the initial red ring linking the Columns remained bright.

The screams began.

Wirr's blood froze at the sound as almost everyone on the battlefield faltered. He stared in horror.

Those immediately next to the Columns were...disintegrating. Just like the Blind had in Ilin Illan, when Caeden had used Licanius. They tore desperately at their skin, but it shredded off, the sight somehow more horrific in the disturbing light. The soldier in red still stood, somehow, but everyone else around him was falling. Dying.

Wirr's blood turned to ice as the whispering began. A susurrus that swept across the battlefield, mingling with the screams of the dying, wordless and menacing and hungry.

Formless dark shapes, somehow darker than the shadows, began to emerge from the Columns. Hands reached out and began grasping greedily at the dying, caressing, pulling at skin 729 and bone as it fell away. A ripple of stillness swept outward as the fighting faltered to a stop, combatants from both sides watching in uncontained horror.

And then only the soldier in red still stood in the space around the Columns, dark forms drifting and whispering all around him.

He drew back his fist and punched again; again the strange disharmony in the thrum, but again nothing changed. He punched again. Again. Again, as the effect of the Columns began to spread, more soldiers from both sides falling, the whispering getting louder. People started backing away. Then fleeing, a sudden flood away from the oncoming wall of death. Some fell and were trampled as the fear and desperation reached a crescendo.

Another punch, and a chip of black stone—visible even from this distance—flew away from the pillar.

Wirr just stood there, too tired to run, fortunately still in an elevated position and out of path most were taking. He knew that there was no outrunning what was coming. So instead he watched, the tiniest flicker of hope in his chest.

With a scream the lone soldier punched again, and again, and one more time. Wirr watched in shock as the red armor on his arm shattered on the last blow, falling away.

There was nothing underneath. No flesh.

The soldier stumbled backward, falling to the ground, clearly spent. Wirr's heart sank.

There was a creaking, cracking sound.

The Column trembled.

A shrieking sound filled the air as the whispering shadows that had been emerging wailed.

The pillar began to crumble around the base, right at the point at which the soldier had been striking. Wirr watched wide-eyed as it leaned and then slowly, impossibly, toppled, snapping with a crack that echoed around the hills before thundering to the ground in a cloud of crimson-tinged dust.

The glowing red ring on the ground winked out.

The thrum increased for a brief second into a harsh, dissonant, screeching note, and then vanished, leaving only the echoes of crashing stone as chunks of the Column tumbled away. Wirr just stood and watched, not daring to believe what he was witnessing, breath coming in short gasps as the sound rumbled away into the surrounding hills.

And then there was silence.

Dawn was brightening the horizon when Wirr finally found Dezia again.

Something eased in his chest as he spotted her, deep in discussion with two soldiers outside one of the Neskian tents. He'd had no reason to believe that she had put herself on the front lines of the assault on the Columns—but knowing her, it also wouldn't have surprised him.

He hurried toward her, rewarded with a smile of joy and relief as Dezia spotted him.

"Wirr!" She flung her arms around him, pulling him close for several seconds. He held her back slightly and kissed her, eliciting a couple of whistles from the surrounding men. They both ignored them.

Finally they broke apart, Dezia still grinning. "You need to stop making me think you're dead," she said, a little giddily.

Wirr laughed. "Let's both try to do better on that front." He glanced around. The camp appeared fairly orderly, all things considered. "How many did they lose?"

"Enough." Dezia's smile faded. "Not as many as the Gil'shar, but those Vessels..." She trailed off, shivering.

"You were there? You saw?"

Dezia nodded. "I saw," she repeated softly. "So the Boundary..."

"Will be gone." Wirr's stomach twisted as he said the words, as if admitting it finally made it real. "And if what Caeden says is true, Shammaeloth himself will be marching on Deilannis now."

Dezia shuddered. "Once, I would have laughed at anyone who told me that. But after last night...I can believe it."

They remained silent, and then Dezia beckoned to Wirr. "We should discuss what happens next. Ankalat will be waiting."

Wirr followed Dezia as she confidently navigated the camp, impressed with how at ease she seemed to be here, among what were ostensibly enemy soldiers. For himself, Wirr couldn't help but eye every armed man who walked past warily. "Is Aelric all right?" he eventually asked pensively.

"He's alive." Dezia's expression betrayed her concern. "Badly injured, though. Taeris is doing what he can for him, as are some of Warlord Amar's best physicians. He'll be gloating about how he saved us all in no time," she concluded, though Wirr wasn't sure whether she was confident or just trying to convince herself.

He frowned. "What do you mean, 'saved us all'?"

"Well. You saw what he did. Destroying that Column," said Dezia, glancing across in surprise.

Wirr's mind went blank.

"The soldier in red," he said slowly. "That was Aelric. *Aelric.* Your brother Aelric," he clarified, somewhat unnecessarily.

Dezia smiled slightly as she ushered him toward a tent that was slightly larger than those around it. "I told you. Long story."

Their conversation came to a halt as they approached the two men standing at attention in front of the entrance. The guards stepped aside respectfully when they spotted Dezia, though neither man bothered to hide his glare as Wirr ducked inside with her, still reeling as he processed the new information.

The inside of the tent was spacious; several desks were set up along the side, and soldiers were poring over a map on another one in the center. Ankalat was slouched tiredly on a chair nearby, an older man in the process of binding a wound to his shoulder. He used his free hand to lazily wave Wirr and Dezia over when he spotted them.

"Prince Torin," he said, his gaze assessing. "I am glad to see that you survived. Now that Nesk's side of the bargain has been fulfilled, it will be much better to have your word to back up your signature."

Wirr felt his expression harden.

"The Desrielites are far from finished," he said firmly. "They are broken, without leadership—but they could still do an untold amount of harm if they are allowed to run unchecked in Andarra. And if we survive all of this, there will be war with Desriel—*if* they still have an army. So we need to go after them."

"You mean my men need to go after them," said Ankalat

smoothly. "Which was not in our agreement. We promised to turn back the Desrielite army, and that we have delivered."

"You won a battle." Wirr was glad that he was too tired to show his emotions right now. He knew Ankalat was right—the document he had signed was, technically, fulfilled—but he couldn't see another option. "I am grateful, but that wasn't the spirit in which I took the deal."

"Are you suggesting that you will not honor it?"

There was an immediate, noticeable tension in the stance of everyone nearby at the words, and Wirr could see that the group of soldiers by the desk had stopped what they were doing, watching intently. He quickly calculated. Four men, plus two at the door and a wounded Ankalat. If Dezia helped, they could probably take out—

"You will do as he says, Ankalat."

There was a surprised silence as the stern voice came from the entrance to the tent.

Wirr turned to see Aelric propping himself up against a tired-looking Taeris, who sported an ugly new scar across his cheek but otherwise appeared healthy. Aelric, though, was deathly pale, his eyes frighteningly hollow.

Wirr swallowed as Dezia scrambled to assist Taeris in helping her brother inside. His gaze went to Aelric's arm—or the place where it should have been, anyway. The long sleeve just hung there now.

Ankalat scowled, looking thrown by the interruption. "My father—"

"Your father will do whatever it takes to secure that land legally. He knows that taking it, or any other Andarran land, by force would contravene the Claim. And he's no fool. The south still has an army." Aelric nodded gratefully to his sister as she eased him into a seated position on the floor. "But most of all, you'll do it because it is the right thing to do. And if you're not willing to accept that, then you and I will be parting ways."

Wirr exchanged a silent look with Taeris, whose tiny shrug indicated he knew as little about this conversation as Wirr.

Ankalat's eyes darted between Wirr and Aelric, concern warring with his evident desire to push the issue.

Finally, though, he exhaled.

"Of course, of course." He stood, offering his hand to Wirr. "We will hunt down the Gil'shar and end them. For the good of our countries' ongoing relations."

Wirr tried not to show his surprise as he grasped Ankalat's hand. Neskians were not known for negotiating on...*anything*, really.

"But," added Ankalat, his eyes glittering as he refused to let go, "I want your word. This is the last...*reinterpretation* of the agreement. On your honor," he added seriously.

"On my honor," agreed Wirr.

Ankalat studied Wirr, seemingly satisfied with what he saw in Wirr's expression. Then he glanced across at Aelric.

"The men will be glad to see you awake," he said roughly.

He stood and left without another word.

Wirr watched the abrupt departure, thrown, before turning and grinning at Taeris. The two embraced.

"Fates, Sire," said Taeris with a laugh. "Between you and Davian, I will never again assume that anyone is actually dead. Ever."

Wirr chuckled, then paused as he caught Taeris's meaning. Taeris's smile widened at his expression.

"The lad's still alive," he said, gesturing to the scar on his cheek, not hiding the relief and joy that simple statement clearly brought him. "I can sense him again. Somewhere to the north."

"Talan Gol?"

"Closer." Taeris hesitated. "Deilannis, maybe."

Wirr closed his eyes, reluctantly acknowledging the suggestion. Assuming that Davian was with Caeden, that made sense. Whether to protect the city or to help Caeden close the rift, it was always going to be their next destination.

From what Asha had said, it was also very likely Davian's last.

"Then that's where we need to be," he said heavily. "We should leave straight away."

"You cannot get there in time to be useful," observed Aelric gently. "Not from here."

"I have this. Caeden has the other," said Wirr, holding up the white Travel Stone, which had miraculously stayed safe on his person throughout the past few days. He toyed with it, then turned to Dezia. "I know Ankalat doesn't like me overly much, but if we explained—"

"He won't lend you any troops. Not even if you tell him that the world depends on it," said Dezia. "Be glad that you got what you did. I've never seen him bend that much before."

Wirr raised an eyebrow. "That was bending?"

"You have no idea."

Wirr sighed. "Regular soldiers probably wouldn't be of much use, anyway," he mused. He eyed Aelric. "You, on the other hand—well. Let's just say I'm looking forward to understanding exactly how you were able to save us all last night. Thanks for that, by the way." He gave the other man a slight grin, which was quickly returned. "We should leave soon, but if you need care first—"

"We won't be coming with you, Wirr," interrupted Dezia gently.

Wirr blinked at her. "Why not?" he said, bemused. "I assumed..."

"It's complicated. But the bottom line is, Ankalat will not lend you *any* soldiers. And that includes us."

"But you're not..." Wirr trailed off, understanding. "The Neskian citizen thing."

"The Neskian citizen thing." Dezia leaned forward, taking his hand. "Wirr, you know I would come with you if I could," she said seriously, looking into his eyes. "But if I go—if Aelric goes—then Ankalat will consider your agreement with him broken."

Wirr didn't respond for a second, mind racing as he tried to think of a way to get around the situation. He didn't want to leave her again—not now, not so soon after they had somehow, miraculously been brought back together.

"Are you in trouble?" he asked. "In danger if you stay? I won't—"

"We're not." It was Aelric, his tone confident despite his weakened state. "They're here because of us, Torin. They like us. Believe me—we're probably safer with them than we would be where you're about to go."

"And we will be allowed to leave, after the deal has been completed," added Dezia. She held his gaze. "Once you're done helping Davian and Caeden, come and find me."

735

Wirr felt a pang in his chest as he looked at her. "Of course." He stared down at the white stone in his hand, then reluctantly handed it to Taeris, who looked in a significantly better state to use Essence. "We can't delay," he added softly.

He pulled in a breath, then drew the Oathstone from around his neck, clutching it tightly.

"Ash," he said, picturing his friend. "I'm alive. If you're able to do so safely, tell the others that I'm coming via the Travel Stone in a few minutes." If they were close to Deilannis—or really anywhere in the north—there was a chance that they were near Banes. He didn't want his arrival to surprise them at an inopportune time.

He tucked the Oathstone away again, ignoring the confused expressions of both Dezia and Aelric, and then wrapped Dezia in a fierce embrace.

"I have so many questions," he whispered.

"You're not the only one," said Dezia, holding him tight. "So fates know you're required to be around to answer them once all of this is over."

She brushed her lips against his and stepped back, giving him a tight smile to cover the tears glistening in her eyes.

Wirr smiled back as Taeris began pouring Essence into the Travel Stone. Aelric struggled to his feet and slung his arm around Dezia, though whether it was to comfort her or for his own support, Wirr couldn't tell. From their expressions, though, it was obvious that they both desperately wanted to go with him—even with Aelric barely able to stand.

He turned, watching as the disc of light emerging from the Travel Stone spun and expanded until the portal was completely open, showing a vista of open, rolling green hills on the other side.

And Caeden, Asha, and Davian, all staring through at him with expressions of dazed delight.

Taeris and Wirr beamed back at them, then Taeris nodded his farewell to Dezia and Aelric, tossing the white stone to Wirr and quickly stepping through.

Wirr caught the Vessel neatly, steeling himself to depart.

"Oh, and Torin?" Aelric spoke quietly, a small smile suddenly on his lips, the playful expression out of place on his deathly pale face. "Tell Davian that his stances need some work." He shrugged cheerfully at Wirr's puzzled expression, then turned and gave Davian a casual salute through the portal. Davian grinned back, though it was more with bemused happiness than anything else.

Wirr glanced once again at Dezia, taking a quick last mental image of the woman he loved. Her eyes drank him in as she smiled.

He turned and stepped through the hole in the air. The portal winked shut behind him.

And then he was being wrapped in a fierce embrace by his friends.

Chapter 50

Davian fidgeted as he, Asha, and Caeden gazed at the black Travel Stone expectantly.

The rolling plains at the base of the Menaath Mountains were silent, calm, bathed in early-morning sunshine. It had been only a minute since Asha had abruptly spoken, though it already seemed like forever.

Davian drew a breath, opened his mouth to speak.

The stone began to glow.

His heart skipped a beat and he leaned forward instead, anticipation and nervousness growing in equal measure as a circle of light formed in the air, spinning and smoothing and widening.

And then he could see through it to Wirr's battered, grinning face.

There was a stunned moment in which no one reacted; then he and Asha were both yelling and laughing delightedly at the sight, even Caeden giving an unexpected whoop of excitement. To Davian's dazed surprise he could see more familiar faces through the opening—Dezia and Aelric standing with Wirr, and Taeris just off to the side.

Taeris was first through, receiving immediate embraces from both Asha and Caeden; Davian grinned as he spotted Aelric giving him a nod and a cheerful salute, then hesitated for just a moment before walking over and clapping Taeris on the shoulder as the other two pulled away.

"Good to see that you're all right," he said, giving the scarred man a small smile.

"You too," Taeris said sincerely.

They were interrupted by a blur of motion to the side as Asha all but sprinted to meet Wirr, who had finally joined them. Davian turned, Taeris forgotten for the moment, as Asha wrapped Wirr in a fierce hug.

"Fates, Wirr." A lump formed in his throat as he hurried forward, he and Caeden both joining the embrace. "You scared us."

"About time it was my turn," gasped Wirr, exaggerating his inability to breathe due to his friends' grips.

Davian snorted, thumping the blond-haired man firmly on the back as Caeden and Asha both laughed. Wirr was really here. Really still alive. Suddenly, for the first time in as long as he could remember, he found himself unable to stop smiling.

Once the initial joy of the reunion subsided, Caeden accepted the white stone from Wirr, then walked over and picked up the black stone from the ground again, pocketing it. "Why didn't Dezia and Aelric come?"

"They wanted to, but...it's a long story. Most of which I don't know." Wirr looked around, clearly not wanting to go into the details. "Where are we?"

"About a half hour from Deilannis. Which is lucky, because much closer and we'd have risked Gassandrid sensing the portal," said Caeden, adjusting the torc around his neck that he'd taken from Ilseth Tenvar a few hours earlier. "We need to find him before he knows we're coming."

"You think he'd run?" asked Taeris in surprise.

Caeden held up Licanius, the morning light bending oddly around the blade. "He'll run," he said confidently. "It's the smart thing to do. He's stayed patiently behind the ilshara for two thousand years, all because the risk of being struck down with Licanius was too great. He'll be willing to wait a little longer, if that's what it takes." He sheathed Licanius again, nodding to the west. "We don't have that luxury—we should get moving. We'll talk on the way."

A jolt of unease shot through Davian at the words, though he ignored it as best he could. According to Caeden's assessment, Shammaeloth and the Banes from Talan Gol could be less than a day away from reaching Deilannis. Asha's immense power might buy them some time, but ultimately, they had to close the rift before then.

Less than a day before he had to go back for the last time.

He fell into step with the others, seeing Asha's concerned glance in his direction but pretending that he hadn't. None of them could afford to dwell on this. He knew that if he did, at least, there was a very real chance that he would change his mind. Turn around and head in the opposite direction.

He accepted that it had to happen, but he didn't want to die.

Despite his efforts to ignore what was coming he found himself distracted, only half listening as Wirr and Taeris explained what had happened during the stand against the Desrielites, the mysterious and miraculous appearance of the Neskian army. He didn't contribute much as the flow of information switched, either, with Asha and Caeden largely relating the trip into Ilshan Gathdel Teth and the retrieval of Licanius. Davian did give a brief description of his imprisonment, of course, but kept it only to the relevant details. Wirr and Taeris, perhaps sensing his mood, didn't press.

He was grateful for that. So much had happened already since his time in Zvaelar, but it had been only hours since he'd said good-bye to his friends there. Had they made it? Caeden didn't know, so there was no way to tell now. Raeleth, at least, would have lived and died thousands of years ago regardless.

The thought was of little comfort.

It was Caeden who broke the news of Karaliene's fate to Wirr; though he had told Davian and Asha of it earlier, the subdued ache in his voice showed that explaining it again was by no means any easier. Still, he kept nothing back, quietly laying out the painful truth of just how long Nethgalla had been impersonating the princess—as well as his conclusion that Scyner must have covered for Nethgalla during her infiltration of Ilshan Gathdel Teth. Forged reports were one thing, but too many trustworthy people had claimed to have seen the princess safe and well on her supposed sojourn north. Only an Augur could have made that happen.

Wirr took the revelation and the others' condolences stoically, simply bowing his head as he continued to walk before finally nodding heavily, straightening once again, expression resolute even as his eyes glistened. He quickly moved the conversation on to other matters. His cousin's death—and what it meant for Wirr's position—was a weight that he had clearly decided to try and set aside for now.

After a while Davian found himself walking alongside Taeris, apart from the others as they talked. He glanced across at the scarred man, who looked pensive, as if composing his thoughts.

There was a brief, awkward silence.

"I...owe you an apology," said Taeris softly. "And an explanation."

Davian said nothing, though inwardly his chest tightened with a sudden, expectant tension. He knew that this was unimportant right now, but he'd wondered about it for so long. His entire life, in fact.

It would be nice to know how it had all begun before it ended.

"What Driscin told you about me, back when you met him. It's...true," Taeris continued slowly, the words clearly difficult. "All of it."

"So you're the one who left me at Caladel." Davian's heart pounded. He looked across at the Gifted, suddenly unable to keep the quiet, longing plea from his tone. "Who were my parents, Taeris?"

Taeris met his gaze, eyes full of sympathetic sorrow.

"I don't know. I swear by all fate to you, Davian—I would have told you long ago if I knew that." Taeris's voice was earnest, imploring Davian to understand. "I knew of you from Augurs' visions and Alchesh's writings, and I *had* been searching for you. I believed that we might be at that point in history. But...I didn't find you. You found me."

Davian's expression twisted, confusion mixing with abrupt, creeping disappointment. "What?"

"I'm sorry. I know it's not what you want to hear, but..." Taeris looked wretched at not being able to give him more. "It wasn't long after the Treaty had been signed, and the schools had been reestablished. I was in the process of organizing to set out to look for you, but we had to finalize some of the details of the Tenets. I was staying at the palace for the negotiations. And you...you just appeared in my rooms, one evening. A note with your name, telling me to take care of you. And a Vessel that was worth a small fortune under the new laws, which I had to give to the guards to convince them not to ask questions."

Davian's shoulders slumped. "That's it? That's...everything?" He shook his head, part of him refusing to believe that there weren't more answers to be found here. "How did you even know that Davian was really my name?"

"I didn't. In fact, for most of that evening, I assumed that it was all some sort of elaborate prank. The other Elders already thought I obsessed too much over Alchesh, and..." He shrugged awkwardly. "But children that young don't exactly go missing without someone noticing. I made all the inquiries I could, and when no one was looking for you, I had to take it all seriously. I had more information about you than anyone alive, at least to the best of my knowledge. And I knew that you would be in danger, that the forces on the other side of the Boundary would be afraid of you, if you really were...*you*." He stared at the ground as he spoke, the words tumbling out of him now. "So I volunteered to inspect the schools in the borderlands, and took you to Caladel."

Davian hung his head, his last flicker of hope fading. Despite himself he'd been focusing, and no black smoke had escaped from Taeris's mouth. There hadn't been even a hint of an ache in Davian's forehead, either.

"You chose such an out-of-the-way school," he realized heavily. "In case someone was searching for me."

"The exact same reason Wirr got sent there," agreed Taeris. "Though that was nothing to do with me."

Davian took a slow, shaky breath, touching the oldest of his scars absently. "And the attack?"

Shame clouded Taeris's expression. "I knew what was happening with the Boundary, and no one was listening to me," he said softly. "And you...I had no way to tell. I was never certain but every year that passed, I doubted more and more whether you were the one of whom Alchesh had spoken, and I needed to know. I needed to start looking elsewhere if it wasn't really you. That doesn't excuse what I did, but...it's why."

There was silence after that, Davian feeling empty.

"I remember what happened that day, now. What I did," he   743 admitted after a while. He looked over at Taeris tentatively, taking in the terrible mass of lines on his face. At least one of them looked angry, fresh. "Your scars. Are they my fault?"

"They are my fault," said Taeris firmly. "But yes, the connection you made that day did...linger. It has caused me some pain, but it is also what allowed me to find you in Desriel. It's what let me be sure you were still alive, when I would have had no other way of knowing. So there have been benefits. And the cost...the cost is something I deserved."

"Still. I could try and stop—"

"We have more important things to worry about." Taeris smiled as he shook his head, softening the words. "Besides. If we get separated, there's a chance that knowing where you are could still help."

Davian reflected for a while longer, then inclined his head. There was another silence but this one was easier, somehow. A little sadder, perhaps, but less fraught.

He might not have found the answers he'd wanted, but for the first time, it felt like the air had been cleared between them.

"Why not simply tell me?" Davian asked eventually. There was no judgment in his tone now, just genuine curiosity.

Taeris sighed.

"Pride. Embarrassment. Worry that my admitting to my mistakes would set you against me, no matter how much I wanted to help. Though in hindsight, trying to cover them up was a worse move by far." He gestured. "I always thought...you had been left to my care, and when you came to Desriel, I thought it was fate. I thought it was my responsibility to guide you, to make sure that you fulfilled Alchesh's visions." He smiled tiredly. "Sometimes it's hard to see the extent of your vanity until it's too late."

Davian accepted the explanation reluctantly. "And that's all there is? Everything you can tell me?"

"Yes."

Davian said nothing for a few moments, then took a deep breath, giving Taeris a small smile. "Thank you anyway," he said quietly. "I'm glad I heard that before..."

He trailed off, gazing westward toward Deilannis.

Taeris studied him.

"It's my pleasure to finally give you the truth. I'm sorry it took so long," he said sincerely. "Asha told us about... about what might be coming. About you going back in time again. Are you certain—"

"I've seen it myself." Pained, pent-up heat leaked into Davian's voice as he cut Taeris off, despite his best efforts. He didn't want to discuss this, didn't want to have to think about it. "Caeden remembers it, and the rift won't close with me around, anyway. Besides, it fits—it fits with what you and Nihim and Laiman have thought all along. I'm the one who Alchesh foresaw. I'm the one who stops Aarkein Devaed. This is just how I have to do it," he finished bleakly.

He didn't mention how unfair it felt. He didn't add how Caeden's memory haunted him, and how even the briefest thought of it turned his blood to ice, tempted him to turn and run with every step closer they came to Deilannis.

He didn't tell Taeris how desperately he wanted to live.

Taeris considered for a moment and then gave a single, solemn nod. There was respect in the motion—but a heartfelt sorrow, too.

"Have you ever actually read any of Alchesh's writings?" he asked, shifting the subject.

Davian shook his head. He'd never even heard of Alchesh until he'd met Taeris, and there had been nothing of the first Augur's writings in Tol Shen's library. Unsurprising, given their connection—however weak—to the Old Religion.

"His visions are funny things," Taeris said as they walked, the clean heat of the morning beating down on their backs. "The ones from before his madness are very specific, detail oriented—like the ones you might find in the modern Augurs' Journal. But those ones all clearly came to pass within a hundred years of his Seeing them." He scratched his head. "The rest read like fever dreams. They are vague and violent and given to strange flights of... poetry, almost. Strange, unsettling imagery. Their interpretation is difficult enough that even amongst those of us who believe that they hold important information, there is plenty of argument as to which of them might point to events that have happened between his time and ours. Only one thing *is* clear, really, based on the language—and that is that they all refer to events that were in Alchesh's future."

"So you're saying that you might have been wrong, now?"

"No," said Taeris patiently. "I'm saying that Alchesh didn't go mad until after he helped raise the Boundary—and unless my history is off, that was after Deilannis was destroyed. He foresaw you stopping Aarkein Devaed *after* you died, Davian." He glanced over at Caeden, who was deep in conversation with the other two. "To my mind, that part of the visions has already been fulfilled. Even with his memories back, I see more of you in him than ever. Your death might be the spark, but it's *you*—your friendship with him—that has made the difference in him."

Davian chewed his lip, but nodded. He didn't know whether Taeris was right—but the concept made him feel a little better, at least.

The older man didn't press further, and eventually they rejoined the others, Caeden in the midst of explaining to Asha the intricacies of creating an ilshara. Davian listened with interest, nodding along as Caeden registered his presence and started making note of ways he might be able to help, to use kan to protect the barrier against the draining effect of the Banes' armor. It was mostly going to be an exercise in concentration for Asha, though. And she wouldn't be able to falter for a single second, no matter how tired she became.

He ignored the occasional, worried glances from the others, ignored the steadily increasing sense of dread that grew in his stomach no matter how hard he tried to focus elsewhere.

It felt all too soon when the distant roaring of Lantarche began to press on his ears, and they found themselves climbing a short rise to one of the high ridges that overlooked Deilannis.

"Down," whispered Caeden, dropping to the ground himself. Davian and the others followed suit, lying flat against the long grass and crawling forward cautiously to peer over the steep drop to the familiar mists below.

The thundering of Lantarche was at once louder, more immediate. Familiar. In other circumstances, Davian might even have found it comforting. Through the twisted foliage that blocked much of their view, Davian could see the long, smooth, rail-less white bridge that spanned the chasm, vanishing into the dense fog, only the vague outlines of buildings farther in indicating that it went anywhere.

Or he could see parts of the bridge, anyway. A large section of it was clogged by Banes.

Davian's heart sank as he studied the mixture of dar'gaithin and, from Asha and Caeden's description of them, what he assumed must be tek'ryl. They were mostly still, only occasionally shifting, almost as if they were asleep. Clearly alert, though; as he watched, a dozen more dar'gaithin abruptly slithered out of the mists, and the waiting Banes turned as one toward them. Though he was too far away, Davian imagined that he could hear the heavy grinding of scales against stone.

The new group said something to their counterparts standing guard at the near end of the bridge; some split off, leaving to patrol west, while others headed toward Deilannis, vanishing swiftly into the murk.

Davian grimaced. He didn't fear the dar'gaithin as he once had—he'd been too long in Zvaelar for that—but he still had a healthy respect for their strength and speed.

His gaze traveled to the side, and he shivered as he watched the other black forms scuttling around. Tek'ryl. The scorpion-like creatures were three times the size of dar'gaithin, albeit without their intelligence or the completeness of their armor. Still undoubtedly dangerous, though, especially in the numbers he was seeing below.

"This is a problem," Caeden observed with dour understatement, the plain-looking torc around his neck glinting in the sunlight. "They're too close together. Even slowing time with Licanius or making ourselves invisible, there's no way we can get through all of them unnoticed."

"I thought you said that the Banes would arrive with Shammaeloth," Davian said pensively.

Caeden nodded. "They can't use Gates, but Shammaeloth is obviously not here, so these must be the remainder of those that made it through a year ago. They must have been hiding somewhere around here. Waiting." He glanced restlessly northward, though there was nothing to see. "Which means that there will still be many more on the way. Shammaeloth will be using them to carve a path for himself."

Davian acknowledged the statement bleakly. Caeden had already explained that Shammaeloth would be driving the Banes in front of him, using them to wipe out as much as possible between Talan Gol and here. Removing as much Essence from his path as he could.

"Do you really think that he can get here so quickly, if they have to destroy everything in their way?" asked Taeris.

"I've seen those creatures whipped into a frenzy. Believe me. We have less than a day." Caeden said the words with grim certainty. "We need to have Gassandrid dead and an ilshara up before then."

"We don't even know if he's here yet," observed Asha worriedly.

"He's here—the Banes wouldn't guard the city like this otherwise. He's using them to get advance warning of any attack." He sucked in a breath, thinking. "He'll be at the Jha'vett. He probably thinks I'm dead, but he knows that Davian and Asha have Licanius—if he gets even a hint that there's danger, he'll vanish." He clenched his fist in frustration. "He's cautious. He'll know straight away if Banes start dying."

Davian hesitated, glancing at Caeden. "I could shape-shift. Go in by myself."

"No." Caeden clearly knew immediately what Davian was referring to, but shook his head. "That gets you in, but not Licanius. Even the Banes would recognize that it's not a normal sword."

Davian nodded slowly, vaguely relieved, then waved away the curious looks of the other three. "Another time," he said drily.

"That's all right. I know how we can all get in, anyway." Asha said the words confidently as she peered down at the mists.

Davian and Caeden both glanced at her in surprise. "How?" asked Caeden, dubiousness in his tone. Davian understood his doubt. Caeden knew Deilannis better than anyone.

Asha smiled slightly. "It's not...the *easiest* way," she conceded. She gestured to the west, away from the masses of Banes on the bridge, down toward the chasm containing Lantarche.

"Follow me."

The five of them stood at the edge of the chasm, gazing down at the thundering white water hundreds of feet below.

"No," said Wirr, his eyes wide as he gazed into the churning mass. "Fates, no."

"It'll be fine," said Davian, mostly to cover his own nervousness.

"Trust us," added Asha.

"Nothing to worry about," chimed in Caeden.

They were a mile or so away from the Northern Bridge, their position concealed by boulders and thick scrub. Banes patrolled the area, but their movements seemed to be regular, predictable enough. They had a few minutes before being spotted.

Wirr glowered. "Easy for you lot to say," he grumbled.

Caeden glanced across at him. "We'll make sure you're safe. We're all painfully aware that you're the weakest one here."

"It's a little awkward," concurred Asha.

"Lucky you're a prince, really," continued Davian absently, peering over the edge into the raging white water. "You wouldn't have a whole lot going for you if you didn't have—"

"All right," growled Wirr.

Davian shared a grin with Asha, for the briefest of moments the banter making him feel like they were all back in Caladel.

"Tek'ryl will be coming this way soon," said Caeden, reluctantly interrupting. "If we're doing this, we need to go now." Off to the side, Taeris shuffled his feet and peered with some discomfort into the churning depths. He hadn't said anything, but he clearly wasn't enamored of what they were about to do, either.

Davian looked at Asha seriously. "Ash, you're *sure* that you can handle us all?"

Asha shrugged. "I guess we'll find out." Davian glowered at her, and Asha shot an innocent smile back at him before glancing around. "Everyone ready?"

The others nodded reluctantly, and Davian was about to as well when the sky to the north caught his eye.

"What is that?" he asked, pointing.

The clean light of morning continued to shine down on their

position by the chasm, but the northern sky to the right of Deilannis was...*fading*. Not the black of an oncoming storm, but more like the light was bleeding from the entire world. Shadows snaked across the sky, tendrils of smokelike darkness shading out the blue, leeching it of its color and luminescence.

Davian's heart stopped as he recognized the sight, albeit on far greater a scale than he had ever seen it before.

It was the same shadowy-black smoke that appeared whenever he saw someone lie.

"It's him. We have...hours. If that," confirmed Caeden heavily. He motioned to the others. "Time to go."

Taeris sidled over to Asha, looking at her worriedly. "You're completely certain about this?"

Asha rolled her eyes, and shoved him over the edge.

Taeris's shout of alarm never eventuated as Asha's tendril of Essence snaked out, catching him before he dropped and covering his mouth, then spinning him to face the rest of them. The scarred man glared at her with a mixture of fury and terror, eyes bulging, as he hung in midair.

Asha shrugged at the others' looks, lines of Essence flashing out and wrapping around each of them. Davian felt his feet lift slightly off the ground.

Asha took two steps back, then sprinted at the edge of the chasm and leaped.

Davian's stomach lurched as the feeling of hurtling downward took hold; he swallowed a scream and gritted his teeth, concentrating on staying the right way up and getting ready to activate his healing Vessel. The white, churning mist of Lantarche rushed up to meet him, more quickly than he could have anticipated.

There was a flash of white and then, suddenly, he was floating gently downward. He gasped as he hit icy cold water, the energy that had held him up finally vanishing.

He felt his skin going numb as he flailed, the freezing water buffeting him; he was sucked under and for several seconds lost his sense of direction, a seed of panic growing as he quickly flooded his body with Essence of his own, allowing him to fight the powerful current.

Finally his head broke the surface, and he struggled toward a low-sitting cave, recognizing that it was where Asha had intended them to go. He hauled himself up out of the water, accepting Taeris's helping hand to drag himself the last small part of the way.

"We all here?" he gasped, shivering.

Asha and Caeden, much to his irritation, looked barely fazed by the fall. Wirr was already dry, grinning at him.

"Not a word," muttered Davian as Asha used Essence to dry his clothes, heating his body rapidly back to an acceptable temperature.

They soon set off into the narrow network of openings that stretched deeper beneath Deilannis, following Asha. Caeden murmured in appreciation as he studied the design of the tunnels. From his idle, out-loud observations, he seemed to think that it was some sort of heat dissipation mechanism, though from the way he talked, it was also a design that he hadn't encountered before.

Before long they began climbing a stairwell that had been carved into the bedrock, and soon after that Davian found himself wiping beads of sweat from his brow.

It was getting hotter.

The stairs finally flattened out, emerging onto a smooth stone platform.

He stuttered to a halt, gazing in wonder.

Glistening, black, diamond-shaped Vessels of stone swirled around a column of Essence that split the center of the massive sphere, yellow-white energy crackling and snapping between them, the glowing pillar and the walls. Davian squinted against the blinding light, turning away slightly but unable to stop watching. It was mesmerizing.

"So this is a Cyrarium?" he wondered aloud, raising his voice above the noise. He flinched as a bolt of jagged energy crashed toward them, only to be blocked by some sort of invisible shield.

Caeden was standing closest to the edge of the platform, arms crossed, studying the scene.

"It *was* a Cyrarium," he replied. "This is...a shell. Almost empty."

Davian stared at Caeden in disbelief, then turned his gaze back to the insides of the sphere, reassessing. He couldn't begin to conceive of what it must have been like when it was full.

Asha beckoned them toward a second set of stairs—looking less impressed than the others—and they moved on, climbing higher, the heat of the Cyrarium gradually fading. They were mostly silent now, every step laden with a steadily increasing tension. They all knew what waited for them once they reached the top.

Davian's pulse quickened as the stairs narrowed out into a long passageway, a single stone door set into its end. Caeden grunted as they approached it, staring with a vexed expression.

"El take it. I searched for months and had no idea that this was here," he said ruefully, keeping his voice low. "It must be concealed, even from kan. I knew roughly where the Cyrarium was hidden, but if I'd known that there was such easy access…" He shrugged with a sigh. "It probably wouldn't have made a difference."

There was a pause, a moment of silence as Caeden rested his hand against the door. The redheaded man turned to the others.

"Once we go through here, there is no turning back," he said seriously. "If Gassandrid escapes, we lose. If we don't kill him, we lose. If we don't raise a new ilshara before Shammaeloth gets here, we lose."

"Huzzah," murmured Wirr.

Caeden gave him a wry grin. "Not my best motivational speech," he admitted, "but…this is it. If there's anything you want to say to each other, now is the time."

He looked at Davian, his meaning clear.

Davian's heart pounded, the fear he had been holding at bay for so long momentarily threatening to overcome him. The Jha'vett and the rift lay just beyond.

A hand clasped his, and he turned to see Asha looking up at him, her eyes shining.

"I love you," she whispered, pulling his head down to lean his forehead against hers. "And I'm not ready to lose you. So don't you dare leave me in there."

Davian gave her a soft smile, bludgeoning his panic into receding once again. He had to put on a brave face for the sake of his friends, if nothing else. "I love you, too, Ash." He took a shaky breath, then held her by her shoulders and gazed into her eyes seriously. "And I will *never* be ready to lose you, either. But we both know what's coming. If it's now…" He cupped her cheek in his hand. "Just know that I have no regrets. Not when it comes to you."

Asha kissed him then, and he could taste tears. He didn't know whether they were hers or his.

They finally broke apart, and then Wirr was embracing him.

"Be careful in there, Dav," he said, thumping him on the back harder than usual. Davian thought he saw him swallow a lump in his throat.

"You too," said Davian roughly, giving his friend the ghost of a grin, then acknowledging Taeris too as the scarred man clapped him awkwardly on the shoulder, unable to keep the melancholy from his scarred features.

Mustering a semblance of calm, he turned. Caeden had been watching the farewells—they were farewells, no matter what the others pretended—silently, an inscrutable look on his face.

"El with us," he eventually said grimly, giving Davian a meaningful nod.

He drew Licanius, and opened the door.

The last time Davian had been in the Jha'vett, the massive chamber had been dark and empty and silent, only a single beam of light illuminating a space at the very center that held an altar-like table.

Now, that space was a whirlwind of twisted light and shrieking chaos.

Davian came to a stuttering, jarring halt as he tried to take it in. Each of the columns in the massive room burned with almost imperceptibly thin lines of Essence, though some of them still had parts that remained dark. Men and women worked feverishly on those sections, and after a few seconds Davian recognized them as Gassandrid's proxies, spotting several from their last meeting. They were entirely focused, no one noticing the newcomers. Lines stretched between the pillars, too, though these were smudged, like white flames being sucked toward the nightmare at the center of the room.

Davian's head spun as he identified the space where the altar had once been. It was a contained tornado of gray time-smoke, furious and thundering against invisible walls, dizzying to the eye. Flashes of figures and faces raced through its wisps, a confusion of terrified expressions that were just real and solid enough for Davian to be sure that he wasn't imagining them.

Worse, though, was the sound. A mélange of shrieks and screams and moans and whispers and cries, each one cut off in a moment and also echoing far too long, lingering on the ear unsettlingly, the mind trying to trace the sound against all the others but always failing.

It was immediately painful, an assault on the senses that none of them—not even Caeden, from the look on his face—had been prepared for. They all stood motionless, horrified.

Then Caeden broke the spell. He turned back to them, gesturing to a figure on the far side of the room. He'd found Gassandrid.

Davian nodded along with the others, every muscle taut as he activated the Vessel in his arm that allowed him to step outside of time.

Nothing happened.

He paled, flicking the Initiation endpoint again but to no avail. He glanced across at Caeden, who was looking frustrated, too. The other man shook his head silently. They were too close to the open rift.

Caeden squared his shoulders and drew Licanius, the blade bending the lines of Essence toward itself. He strode forward.

The frenzied work of the Gassandrid proxies halted as one.

To his side, light flared; Davian turned to see Asha blazing with Essence, the energy wrapping swiftly around her in a thick, protective layer. Wisps of power pulled away from her, sucked toward the void in the center of the room, but the armor still looked effective.

He blinked, startled at the sight before realizing what Asha already must have: that this place was shielded from the draining effect in place everywhere else in Deilannis. Before he could move she was streaking forward, a blade of Essence springing to life in her hands as she met the first of Gassandrid's proxies in a spectacular shower of light.

"Here we go," muttered Davian, heart constricting in his chest.

He activated the Vessel in his arm that tapped his Reserve for strength, drew his own blade, and charged after Caeden.

Essence flashed and roared everywhere around him as he dashed between the columns, the Gassandrids—nine of them here, he thought—leaping to intercept. Bolts sizzled against his kan shield as he sprinted to catch up to Caeden, only vaguely aware of the others as they met their opposition with blades and white energy. He could tell from the violent, searing flashes that Asha was likely doing the bulk of the work, but he didn't dare look around to see.

He focused ahead, on the man for whom Caeden was heading. Gassandrid was a hulking figure, muscular and tall, jet-black hair hanging loose around his shoulders. A fierce light burned in his gaze as he spun in response to the sounds of fighting, though he was clearly unarmed.

He faltered when he saw Caeden walking toward him.

"Tal." Gassandrid studied Caeden and though his voice was calm, barely audible over the din, the shock in his eyes was unmistakable. He started backing away, circling around toward the shrieking gray insanity in the center of the room.

"Gass." Caeden continued to stride forward. "Nowhere to run."

"You're dead," said Gassandrid.

"True." Caeden didn't stop moving, stalking toward the other man. Behind them the furious flashes of Essence had stopped, the battle evidently already over; Davian risked a quick glance over his shoulder, relieved to see the other three still standing.

"It's not too late, Tal. Look!" Gassandrid had backpedaled until he found himself with his back to the rift; he gestured urgently behind him at the whirling mass of horror. "He showed me how to fix it. To correct their mistakes. I opened the doorway!" He finally stopped retreating, instead staring defiantly at Caeden. "You can go back now. All you need to do is wait, and you can go back and save her. Save Elliavia. Save *everyone*!"

Caeden finally slowed, then stopped a few feet from Gassandrid, as if the man's words were a physical obstacle. Davian glanced across at his friend, suddenly uneasy. Caeden stayed motionless, saying nothing as his gaze flicked between Gassandrid and the open rift, betraying nothing of whatever was going on in his head.

"No," he said eventually.

He stepped forward and batted away the other man's attempt to ward him off, plunging Licanius deep into Gassandrid's stomach.

The unarmed man gasped as the blade bit into his flesh, his eyes going wide, red-coated steel protruding from the other side of his body.

Then he straightened.

Caeden frowned as he tried to pull Licanius out again but Gassandrid had gripped Caeden's hands with his own, holding them firm. The whispers and shrieks from the rift suddenly intensified; from out of the gray behind Gassandrid, Davian could see dark shapes taking form, hands reaching out. Reaching *into* Gassandrid's body. Steadying him and giving him strength when he should have had none.

Gassandrid painstakingly raised his head again and bared his teeth at Caeden, eyes burning, their faces inches apart.

"There only needs to be one of us for Him to succeed," he said between gritted teeth. "And I know you, Tal'kamar. I know that you have not left me until last."

He took a step back, toward the tornado, somehow forcing a straining Caeden to take a reluctant step forward with him.

"Dav!" Caeden roared his name desperately. "Asha!"

They rushed forward, Davian strengthening his body with Essence and gripping Gassandrid's arm. From behind him a blinding coil of Essence snapped out, trying to encircle the massive man, but it evaporated as soon as it touched him.

Davian pulled with all his strength, but more black, shining hands appeared, claws sinking deep into Gassandrid's shoulders, blood seeping where they touched. Wirr and Taeris joined him, muscles straining, but it didn't feel as if it even made a difference.

Gassandrid took another step back, the motion inexorable. Another. He half laughed, half snarled as Davian drew his blade and slashed at the limbs protruding from the rift; ethereal shrieks resonated around the room as some of the hands withdrew.

Gassandrid took another step back, half of his body in the gray smoke now. Blood poured from the gaping wounds in his side and back, dozens of clawed hands embedded in him. His crazed smile was a rictus of triumph.

He twisted. Somehow, impossibly, leaned back and raised his foot.

Kicked Caeden in the stomach.

Caeden's grip slipped, and Gassandrid used the opening to punch him squarely in the face.

There was an audible crack as Caeden stumbled back; Davian dove, snatching desperately at Licanius's hilt with his right hand, his strength Vessel flooding every bit of Essence it could to his arm and legs as he caught it and braced. Gassandrid's expression, half-obscured by the gray smoke now, faltered.

Then he snarled. Took another step back, dragging Davian forward as the glistening black claws hauled the Venerate deeper.

Davian heard panicked shouts from behind him; he thought he could hear Asha begging him to let go but the gray smoke was in his eyes and ears now, shrieking and wailing and whispering and filling his senses. Still he gripped the hilt of Licanius with everything he could, his Essence draining away, sucked in hungrily by the beckoning gray river.

It was just him, now. The others couldn't haul him back, couldn't afford to touch the rift in the way he could. They would die. He wouldn't.

He couldn't let go. If they lost Licanius, they lost.

He roared against the raging smoke; he was still on the horizon of the rift, could still feel his body. Agony snarled up his arms as some of the black claws reached him, elongated fingers digging deep into his flesh, melting through skin and scraping delicately along bone.

Somewhere in the gray smoke, Licanius came free.

Davian swiveled, using the last of his strength to twist and fling the blade back, part of his mind registering relief as he heard the metal ring against stone.

He went slack. He had done everything he could.

He closed his eyes and surrendered to the gray mists.

A hand gripped his.

For a moment he didn't register that it was different from the claws raking at him, didn't understand what was happening in the midst of the maelstrom. He opened his eyes again, confused.

There was an instant of balance; he felt suspended, an equal force tugging him in either direction.

"Dav!" It was Asha's voice, fear and pleading and desperation in it. "Pull!"

He pulled.

Claws ripped his skin—but, somehow, he still had skin.

And then he was falling hard onto the stone ground, four other forms around him tumbling back as he finally, abruptly came free.

He groaned as blood gushed freely from his arms and neck, only dimly aware of Asha crawling across to him and putting a hand on his chest, flooding him with Essence. Life burst back inside of him, his Reserve leeching from the torrential flow to fill again even as his wounds closed and the pain, miraculously, began to recede.

"What…" Davian's voice was little more than a rasp. "How?" He looked up at Asha, who was staring down at him with a strange mix of relief and sorrow.

Her gaze slid to the side, and Davian twisted, following it to the figure on the ground a few feet away.

"Fates. Taeris!" He scrambled despite Asha's attempt to stop him, crawling across to the scarred man and preparing to use Essence himself, though he was in no state to do so.

Only Taeris's ashen, withered features and empty eyes stopped him.

A hand rested gently on his shoulder. He looked up to see Wirr crouching beside him.

"He was the one who was holding you. He wouldn't let go," he said, emotion thick in his voice.

Davian gazed at the motionless form, then let his shoulders slump. He seated himself next to Taeris's head and gently drew his eyes shut.

"Why?" he whispered. Taeris had known he had to go back. He could have let it happen, and lived.

The howls of the rift were his only answer.

Over near one of the far columns, Caeden had staggered dazedly to his feet. Blood was smeared across his mouth from where his nose had been broken, though it had already healed.

He slowly walked over to where Licanius lay on the ground. Picked it up and sheathed it, every motion heavy.

Davian took a deep, shaky breath, forcing down his grief at Taeris's death as the four of them huddled together, close enough that they wouldn't have to shout over the cacophony. "What now?"

"Now, you three need to get outside of the city as quickly as you can, and raise that ilshara. The Banes in here will come for you, but you need to keep it up for as long as you can hold out. Shammaeloth won't be far away." Caeden's look included all of them but settled on Asha, who dipped her head in assent, though she looked understandably tense at the prospect.

He took a deep breath. "And I'm going to finish this," he concluded softly.

Chapter 51

Asha burst through the thick mists with an Essence-enhanced leap, a tek'ryl claw swiping perilously close to her head as she brought her steel blade down hard against the face of the dar'gaithin in front of her.

The creature hissed, the blow hard enough to snap its head back, though the metal scraped across its scales without doing any real damage. The strike had done enough, though; Davian was suddenly there, his weapon spearing the creature through its gaping mouth. Even as it slumped to the ground he was blinking away again, moving on to the next.

Before Asha could focus on her next target she found herself abruptly diving to the left, not of her own accord; a moment later a massive tek'ryl stinger arrowed down, spearing the stone where she had been standing with a resounding crack. The scorpion-like creature screeched as she regained her footing and leaped high in response, slicing hard at the exposed area of its neck. Black blood hissed as the creature went stiff, then toppled with a crash of armor to the ground.

Asha exhaled as she saw Davian dispatching the last of the two dozen or so Banes that had been guarding this side of the Andarran bridge; she glanced over her shoulder back at Wirr, giving him a grateful nod. Of the three of them, Wirr was least equipped to deal with these creatures, but he had saved her from serious injury more than once since they'd left the Jha'vett.

She put her hands on her knees, catching her breath. They'd managed to avoid most of the Banes in their dash to get out of the city, Davian's ability to create a time bubble invaluable in their doing so. He was still comparatively weak from his encounter with Gassandrid, though, and the Vessel in his body only altered his own passage through time. This group guarding the bridge had been too large and too alert for him to simply sneak them past.

It was done now, though. The way back to Andarra was open.

"Everyone all right?" Davian appeared in front of them, breathing hard. The strain of what he'd been doing was beginning to show.

"Alive," said Wirr.

"Alive," agreed Asha.

Without anything further, they made their way up the stairs and onto the smooth white stone of the Andarran bridge.

They proceeded at a cautious jog, Caeden's dire warnings about how little time they had pressing constantly on Asha's mind. She kept a sharp eye on the thick, swirling mists ahead, though part of her continued to run through the instructions the former Venerate had given her. Creating an ilshara shouldn't be overly difficult; at its core it was simply an Essence shield, completely encapsulating an area.

Only this was her first attempt, the area was an entire city that would drain any Essence that veered too close to it, and getting anything wrong would result in the end of the world.

The bridge—somewhat miraculously, given the press of Banes they had had to navigate inside the city—was empty as they hurried through the fog, though Asha's every muscle remained tense. She couldn't help but recall the last time she'd been here.

Then, abruptly, they were breaking through the edge of the mists.

Asha stuttered to a horrified halt, joined swiftly by the other two.

It had to be late morning, perhaps marginally after noon now, with the sun almost directly overhead. Its clean warmth pressed against Asha's skin, a welcome feeling after the clammy, grasping tendrils of fog.

And yet as she gazed northward, the sharp blue of the sky just... vanished.

Part of her wanted to dismiss what she was seeing as a thick, fast-approaching storm, simply an unusual weather pattern of black cloud covering the sky. The longer she stared, though, the more impossible the sight became. There were no clouds at all. No gray, no suggestion of height or depth or end. It was just shadow, roiling and churning, twisting the eye and blotting out everything beyond. A wall of darkness that stretched to the heavens, raging, sending a crawling unease through her like nothing she had ever felt before.

And as she watched, she could tell that it was creeping closer.

"Fates," whispered Davian.

"That's not our only problem. We need to move. Now." Wirr's voice cut through Asha's and Davian's daze.

Asha's gaze fixed ahead. The bridge wasn't completely empty; a half dozen dar'gaithin stood between them and its end, tails lashing wildly in anticipation as they spotted the three humans.

Beyond—perhaps a thousand feet farther back—the hillside leading down to the bridge crawled with charging Banes.

Beside her, Davian gritted his teeth and started running.

Asha dashed after him, hurtling along the length of the bridge with blindingly quick bounds; a few seconds before they reached the first of the creatures Davian vanished, only to reappear in front of the farthest one, his blade embedded in its right eye. Asha leaped to engage the closest two, keeping them occupied as three more snakes abruptly launched over the edge of the bridge with steadily fading shrieks as they fell, Davian's Essence-enhanced kicks made even more powerful due to his time bubble.

Asha evaded the final two Banes' attacks smoothly, darting back again. She could probably have dealt with them herself if need be, but here in Deilannis, where Essence decayed the moment it touched the air, Davian's abilities were far more effective.

She focused on the hills past the bridge as Davian appeared and reappeared again, both times drawing his black-smeared blade from a dar'gaithin mouth. The final two creatures slumped to the cold stone in unison as Asha took in the horde of Banes flooding toward them.

At least fifty within a few hundred feet, now, and hundreds more a little way behind them.

With even more appearing along the rise every second.

Wirr caught up to them and they dashed to the end of the

bridge, Asha exhaling as they finally stepped onto Andarran soil. She put a hand on Davian's shoulder as he tensed, as if ready to try and take on the entire oncoming army by himself. He turned to her, and she shook her head.

"You've had your fun," she said with a tight smile. "My turn."

She steeled herself. Tapped her Reserve.

The ground began to tremble.

She heard Davian and Wirr both gasp as some of the creatures spilling down toward them began to stumble, the line of oncoming nightmares shivering uncertainly as the hill beneath their feet suddenly began to break apart.

A massive split tore along the ground between the three humans and the Banes, immediately filled with a steadily rising, golden wall of Essence. Rock rent with a screeching sound and turned red where Essence cut through it, melting away to slag. The earth shuddered again as raw power sliced downward, anchoring itself; a moment later a wall twenty feet thick began rising into the air, rippling and pulsing with blinding yellow light. All along the Andarran side of Lantarche the wall crept upward, stretching out until it was lost from view, slowly but surely encircling the entire city.

That menacing, all-encompassing darkness was closer than ever now, blotting out the blue sky as far as she could see to the north, the boiling shadows chasing on the heels of the Banes. Asha trembled as she focused and poured everything she had into the shield, using Deilannis as a guide for the wall, letting Essence creep ever closer to it and then adjusting away again when she sensed the drain of the city beginning to affect the ilshara.

"Fates," whispered Davian next to her as he stared upward at the shining barrier, pure awe in his voice.

The golden wall crept higher still as Asha closed her eyes, letting more and more Essence flow through her. Dimly, she could sense the Banes beginning to throw themselves at the barrier. They made little headway, but each effort—particularly given their Essence-absorbing armor—stole a tiny amount of her energy, even if she barely noticed it. A tiny cut, but too many would bleed her dry as effectively as a slit throat.

"Dav." She said his name softly, distractedly. "I need you to protect the ilshara however you can with kan. The Banes will absorb too much if it stays unprotected."

Davian nodded; a tiny hole—almost imperceptible—opened up in the shield, and Asha immediately felt the tiny pressures against the barrier begin to ease. A few seconds later and the hole was filling in again, the kan that had been threaded through vanishing.

"I can patch hardened kan here and there. Especially around the ground, where I can anchor it properly," said Davian grimly, "but it's unstable at best. It won't last."

"It will have to do." Asha's words were clipped as she tried to concentrate. All of Caeden's advice, all of her training in the dok'en, hadn't come close to preparing her for manipulating and maintaining something so unthinkably *immense*.

She strained, willing yet more Essence into the flow as she saw the raging wall of shadow rushing over the hill, swallowing up her vision of the Banes that still rushed to join the attack. It was almost here.

With a last burst of effort, the golden dome sealed high above Deilannis.

Moments later, the darkness hit the barrier with a primal howl of fury.

Asha was braced for the impact to drain the ilshara, but instead—to her vague, relieved surprise—nothing happened. The wall of writhing shadow was right there, completely covering the dome now, but it seemed to be hovering inches above the glowing Essence. It sucked in the light outside the dome, but either would or could not attack the barrier itself.

The sound, however, was another matter.

As the darkness wrapped itself around the city's protection in a smothering cloud, howls and shrieks began to pierce the air. A chorus of haunted, agonized voices that filled every open space like a physical presence, separate and yet melding into one horrendous cacophony. The noise assaulted Asha's concentration, started to worm inside her head.

"Wirr," she said through gritted teeth, her voice cracking. "Tell me to focus."

Wirr, who along with Davian was looking at the threatening shadow in open horror, didn't hesitate. He placed his hand on his chest, where Asha knew the Oathstone was hanging. "Asha, stay focused. Stay strong. Ignore that sound and do everything you can to keep that barrier in place," he said urgently, loud enough for her to hear, even if she didn't strictly need to.

Immediately the pressure on her mind seemed to ease and she steadied, quickly adjusting a section of the barrier that had been trembling. She breathed out.

She could do this.

The three of them stood there, Asha keeping her breathing steady, straining to hold the massive sphere still and tight around the edges of the city. Even with Wirr's instructions echoing around her head it was a struggle; she could feel the darkness probing, oozing over the barrier, searching for any cracks. The noise railed at her, and a dim part of her was aware that it would quickly become unbearable if she paid it any attention.

"What now?" shouted Wirr, his eyes glued to the frenzied attacks of the creatures only a hundred feet away, barely visible against the raging darkness that hovered over all. Her ilshara was all that provided light within the dome now, casting everything in a soft yellow.

Davian answered by pointing back toward Deilannis. Asha's stomach wrenched as she saw the Banes boiling out of the gold-tinged mists and hurtling toward them.

Caeden had been right. The immense energy required by the ilshara had drawn them like flies.

Davian turned back to her, putting his hand on her shoulder and looking deep into her eyes. He didn't say anything, but understanding passed between them. She forced a smile at him, and he nodded.

He turned to Wirr, tossing the black Travel Stone on the ground next to Asha.

"Now we hold," he shouted, determination in his voice.

He and Wirr walked calmly away and took up positions on the bridge, waiting for the flood of creatures to reach them.

The variegated veins of Mor Aruil rippled with color and light as
Caeden walked the lonely tunnels, Licanius gripped tightly.

He'd stepped outside of time the moment he had arrived, a process made all the easier with Licanius in hand, but he still moved as quickly as he dared. He couldn't afford to be too casual, to let down his guard and miss an ambush from Alaris. But with Shammaeloth bearing down—with Davian and Asha and Wirr undoubtedly having to hold off a horde of Banes—every second he spent here could potentially be one too long, too.

His path took him toward Asar's old rooms; that was where he had found Alaris last time, and though the other man had all but destroyed the place, it remained one of the only vaguely livable areas in the Wells. Varying hues seeped from the jagged lines around him, Licanius sucking at the energy and light, bending it wherever he passed.

The door to Asar's rooms, which had been broken last time, was now mended and slightly ajar. Caeden tensed as he spotted the gradually pulsing light of Essence coming from within.

He nudged the door open with his foot, blade at the ready.

Alaris was sitting at the far end of the room, reclining with his eyes closed; he'd tidied, cleaned, even repaired the chair in which he now sat. Caeden frowned. Alaris would have known that he was here from the instant the Gate had opened. He'd expected fierce opposition, not this.

He scanned the room suspiciously, both for kan traps and—though he knew it was impossible—anyone else lying in wait.

But there was nothing, and no one.

"Alaris," he said, stepping inside, allowing his time bubble to drop. He stayed tense, though, prepared to raise it again in an instant if necessary.

Alaris exhaled, not opening his eyes.

"I am tired of fighting, Tal," he said, his tone heavy with the sound of defeat. "You have nothing to fear from me."

Caeden remained alert despite the words, despite sensing that Alaris was telling the truth. He didn't lower Licanius, either.

Alaris finally opened his eyes, taking in the sword.

"So. You are winning," he said bleakly. "You're here to kill me?"

Caeden hesitated, then shook his head.

"Not necessarily, my friend."

Keeping Licanius in his right hand—and a Disruption shield spinning furiously—he reached into his pocket, locating the amulet Erran had given him. He held it up for Alaris to see.

Alaris's eyes widened as he took it in. He knew exactly what it was. All the Venerate did.

There were several seconds of silence.

"No," said Alaris quietly.

Caeden felt his heart sink. "Why not?" he whispered.

"Because I will not make it that easy for you." Anger finally flashed across Alaris's features, though it was gone in an instant. "And because I am tired of living in a world where I can never be in control of my own actions."

Caeden scowled, despite doing his best to push down his own frustration and ire. "So you're choosing to die," he said bitterly.

"I am fated to die. Just like your friend. Just like Davian." Alaris studied Caeden darkly. "He is the perfect example of why I fought, you know. You keep saying that our future decisions are our own, regardless of whether they are immutable. And yet his life is going to end thanks to your petulance, and you're not even *trying* to save it. There is nothing *he* can do to save it, either. Is that what he wants? Would he have chosen that path unless he believed that there was no other way? No," concluded Alaris in disgust, answering his own question. "Not unless he had already accepted it to be inevitable—the planned outcome of this unseen, indifferent god whom you are both so quick to serve."

Caeden swallowed, the observation hitting closer to home than he would have liked.

"Davian *has* chosen. Time and time again, even knowing what is coming," he said. "Sometimes the choice is doing something that we believe is important, *despite.*"

He unconsciously gripped Licanius a little tighter.

Alaris eyed the blade.

"You are so certain of your El?" he said softly.

"No," admitted Caeden. "But I do know that the creature *you* call El is...intimidating. Persuasive. Smarter than all of us put together." Caeden gazed at his friend, willing him to listen, though they had had variations of this conversation too many times to believe that he would. "And I am certain that he is no god."

He walked forward. "Let me show you," he added, pressing two fingers against Alaris's head.

His friend flinched back in surprise but it was too late; the memories were draining into him. Caeden watched as Shammaeloth slithered along Taag's Peak, the creature's illusions failing as it made a desperate last attempt to stop him from leaving Talan Gol. He watched as Asha's Essence burned bright in the space beneath Ilshan Gathdel Teth, revealing the true filth and ugliness of the creature they had both followed for so long. Paring back even the concealing darkness and showing Shammaeloth for the sickness he truly was.

It was done in a moment; Caeden stepped back, feeling almost as emotionally drained as he had when he'd actually experienced those events. Alaris's face was white and he was silent, breathing heavily.

Then the other man's brow creased. He shook his head, slowly at first but with increasing anger.

"I didn't think that you would stoop to these levels, Tal'kamar." His voice was low and cold. Furious.

Caeden looked at him blankly. "What?"

"Fabricating something like this." Alaris shook his head again, this time in disbelief. "To go to such lengths...it is *disgusting*, Tal. Even with everything else that has happened, I expected better from you."

Caeden blinked, a sickening shock running through him.

"El take it, Alaris," he said, desperation seeping into his tone. "This...this isn't a trick. This is *exactly* what happened. You *know* it's a memory!"

Alaris glared. "So you see darkness where everyone else sees light? That speaks to your issues more than mine. I already know your *perspective*, Tal. You need *proof*."

Caeden gave a disbelieving laugh despite himself. "Proof? *Proof?*" He raked a hand through his hair as he finally understood.

Even Alaris—even his amazing, intelligent, thoughtful friend—couldn't see it. *Wouldn't* see it.

"So you will not accept my offer?" Caeden already knew the answer, but he had to ask. One last time.

"No," whispered Alaris. He stood in front of Caeden, arms outstretched, looking at him determinedly. "So choose, Tal'kamar, if you truly think that is what you are doing. Your friend, or your belief."

Caeden felt a tear roll down his cheek.

He stepped forward, and plunged Licanius into Alaris's chest.

The sword slipped between the ribs smoothly; Alaris gasped as it went in, eyes wide, as if he hadn't really thought that Caeden would do it.

Caeden clasped Alaris close, hugging him, forehead against his friend's. Alaris didn't struggle, didn't try to fight as Gassandrid had.

Alaris's breathing gradually slowed, then stilled. He slumped to the ground.

Caeden went with him, cradling Alaris's head in his lap.

He wept.

He wept for his friend. He wept at the unfairness of it all. Alaris had been right in so many ways: it *was* wrong that he'd been forced to do this, wrong that events were unfolding as they were. This, all of this, felt like a nightmare from which he desperately wanted to wake.

Eventually he closed Alaris's eyes; Mor Aruil would be his tomb. In better circumstances Caeden would have buried him, but there was no time; even if Asha was somehow holding her ilshara around the entire city, every Bane that had been in Deilannis would be coming straight for her.

He stood, gently laying Alaris's head on the ground.

Then he activated the white Travel Stone, and stepped through into the screaming maelstrom that was Deilannis.

Chapter 52

Wirr grunted as a tek'ryl limb smashed into his shoulder, sending him spinning back away from where the smooth, white Andarran bridge met the ground.

He struggled to his feet, stumbling over to regain his blade before turning to face the creature again. It was badly injured, several of its limbs incapacitated, but it still tried to drag itself onward to Asha's position.

Wirr hurried over, evading the powerful, sweeping swipe this time and ending the tek'ryl's life with a swift thrust to its scorpion-like face.

He staggered, fresh pain wrenching at his shoulder from the creature's blow, joining the ache of the countless other injuries he had sustained over the past ten minutes. He took a moment to recover, even as he watched for any other Banes that threatened to make it past the whirlwind of death that was Davian.

They had fallen into a rhythm of sorts since the first wave of creatures had boiled out of the mists: Davian held the bridge with his abilities, and Wirr stayed back near Asha—warning Davian via his own ability of any creatures that looked like they were slipping past, and providing a last-ditch defense against any of the not-completely-dead ones that Davian didn't have time to finish off.

It was working, even if it wouldn't for much longer. Bodies highlighted by the golden Essence of the ilshara continued to topple off the bridge as more Banes pushed their way through and over the dead, some of the falling figures flailing as still-living creatures were shoved off in the frenzy to reach the source of the massive Essence shield. Davian himself blinked constantly from one spot on the bridge to another, steel flashing wherever he appeared, dispatching monster after monster after monster.

But even with the Vessels built into his body, Wirr knew that he had to be getting tired.

"Stop the tek'ryl going underneath," he said suddenly, stiffening as he saw another of the creatures trying to sneak past. Their spiderlike legs allowed them to latch on to the sides and crawl upside down, almost entirely *underneath* the bridge, leaving only a few of their feet showing on either side up above. Not invisible to Davian, but much easier for him to miss amid the chaos.

The Oathstone went warm against his chest and then the creature was falling, the legs it had been using to grip the left side of the bridge separated from its body. Wirr hadn't even seen Davian's strike, that time.

He scanned the next pack of rabid creatures, every nerve taut, blood rushing in his ears as he willed each Bane that charged from the mists to be the last. From the mania of their attacks, all mindless fury as they threw themselves into the churning maelstrom of death, it was clear that they were being driven.

Wirr risked an uneasy glance to the side, the scene still too surreal to properly comprehend.

It wasn't hard to guess what was doing the driving.

The world outside Asha's golden ilshara had been swallowed by raging darkness, a swirling vortex that howled and slithered and smashed itself again and again and again against the dome surrounding Deilannis. The shield flashed with a constant, alarming intensity everywhere Wirr could see along the ground as more slavering Banes threw themselves at it, pushed themselves up against it, hammered at it. As Wirr looked, he could see bodies smeared up against its edge where the creatures behind had pressed so hard that they had killed those in front.

Wirr couldn't begin to imagine how much raw Essence Asha was using to maintain the barrier under that sort of pressure.

"Keep it up, Ash," he murmured under his breath, again feeling the heat of the Oathstone against his skin. "Focus on keeping that ilshara whole, and don't worry about the rest. Be sure that

Davian and I will do our jobs." He glanced across at the young woman, hoping that he was helping his friend.

Asha, for her part, had barely moved since the ilshara had sprung to life. Beads of sweat glinted gold on her forehead in the ethereal light, but she showed no other signs of strain. Banes had almost reached her twice, now, Wirr striking the last one down only a heartbeat before it had attacked. She'd seemed not to notice, either too focused or simply unable to react. It wouldn't surprise him if it was the latter.

He turned his attention back to the battle on the bridge, doing his best not to be distracted by the massive wall of Essence that stretched above and over them, slicing through the ground only a hundred feet away.

"Stop the tek'ryl jumping on your right," he said quickly, spotting the creature making a scuttling, blindingly fast run at the edge. Davian was holding his position but it was temptingly close to the Andarran side of the bridge for the tek'ryl, who were infinitely more agile than the dar'gaithin.

The tek'ryl leaped and Wirr's heart went to his throat as it soared through the air, describing an arc that would see it land safely.

At the peak of its jump a dar'gaithin's flailing body hurtled from Davian's position and slammed into it, knocking it violently sideways and sending them both down into the roaring white waters of Lantarche far below.

"Fates," murmured Wirr appreciatively.

Davian appeared for a brief second on the bridge and yelled something indistinguishable to him; Wirr spotted the two more tek'ryl that had slung themselves under the bridge and were now scuttling toward him and Asha at an alarming speed.

He stepped forward in response, blood pounding in his ears.

"Stay on the bridge, Dav," he said softly, bringing his blade up. If Davian gave any more ground, he would lose their only advantage to the position. Wirr was going to have to deal with these ones himself.

He tried to force down the fear that was suddenly gnawing at his chest. He had so little Essence to spare, and these creatures... they were enormous.

He heard Davian give a shout of frustration but there was no time to pay him any attention; he charged the massive scorpion-like Banes, every nerve taut as he watched for the first attack.

The tek'ryl scuttled with astonishing speed at him, massive black stingers poised above their backs, dripping black liquid that glistened in the Essence-light. The first one struck and Wirr dove to the side as the thick needle speared the ground where he had been standing, then rolled as the second tek'ryl's attack followed immediately after, barely missing his head.

Wirr maintained the momentum of his roll and lashed out with his blade, aiming for one of the small, unarmored weak points that each of the creatures had around its knees. He missed, his steel bouncing off hard shell and sending a shock down his arm instead.

He scrambled back to his feet in dismay, backing away slightly. He was a perfectly capable swordsman, but this...this was beyond him.

A massive blast of Essence swept the creatures to the edge of the chasm and then into it, their limbs flailing as they tumbled down and into the icy waters of Lantarche.

Wirr stood frozen in shock, then turned, half expecting to see that Asha had noticed his predicament and had somehow diverted precious Essence to help.

Instead he saw Caeden already striding toward the bridge, Licanius bending the light, portal winking out behind him.

Hope suddenly surged within him and he stumbled to his feet again, quickly assessing the fight on the bridge. Davian was still standing, still blinking between Banes, a flood of the creatures dying and falling and screaming. But though Wirr had been distracted for only seconds, he could see fresh cuts on Davian's face, could tell that his movements were heavier. He'd been weak after his encounter with Gassandrid. His Reserve was probably running out by now.

Then Caeden was there.

Licanius blurred in his hands and a wave of the creatures broke, scattering off the sides of the bridge. Caeden's expression was calm as he took up a position by Davian, but there was something in the way he moved now. A barely concealed anger that

Wirr had never seen in him before. A simmering fury that he was looking for somewhere to direct.

And as the Banes started their attack again, it quickly became apparent where he intended that outlet to be.

Where Davian had been a whirlwind of last-moment defense, Caeden was...*aggressive*. As Wirr gaped he actually took a step forward, farther onto the bridge. Then another. Then *another*. Davian moved up beside him, though Wirr's friend was clearly drained by this point.

The howling from above increased as if in fury at Caeden's success, but that only seemed to spur the former Venerate onward. Licanius sliced through the Banes' armor as if it didn't exist, and Caeden often bodily grabbed creatures and tossed them off the side, sending them flying away a shocking distance before they finally began to fall.

The tempest of violence continued for what seemed like hours, though Wirr knew it had to be only minutes. Banes broke from the boiling mists and streamed across the expanse of white stone, only to be met with steel and fury time and time again. Wirr did his best to direct Davian, this time aiming to shift him to best support Caeden, though Wirr wasn't sure it was even necessary.

The stream slowed—almost imperceptibly at first. Banes still rushed from the white of Deilannis, but they were no longer shoulder to shoulder, no longer jostling for position and threatening to knock one another off the edge.

Then the creatures appearing thinned more. Three abreast. Two. A few individuals sprinting from the mists.

And then finally—miraculously—nothing but the empty howling of the darkness above, and the glistening gold of the ilshara that held it back.

Wirr breathed heavily, eyes wide, barely able to fathom what he was seeing. The white of the bridge was almost entirely gone, covered in black ooze and bodies. Caeden and Davian stood alone in its center, facing the mists, chests rising and falling and every inch of their bodies tensed, as if they too couldn't believe that there were no more to come.

Then they turned. Started picking their way back to the Andarran edge.

Wirr watched for a moment longer and then jogged to meet them, casting a cautious glance across at Asha and then at the raging hordes still throwing themselves at her ilshara from the outside. The Banes in here had been defeated, but that would be moot if they had to face the thousands more waiting to rip them apart out there. Still, his shoulders loosened just a little and a thrill of excitement ran through him as he headed toward his friends, the beginnings of a smile on his face as he considered what they'd just achieved.

Then he saw Davian and Caeden's faces illuminated by the stark gold of the barrier, and his heart twisted, the joy of their victory short-lived.

Of course.

He slowed to a halt, waiting for the two men as they walked purposefully, grimly toward him. Neither of them spoke.

They joined him at the edge of the bridge, neither one stepping off onto Andarran soil.

"Not bad, Wirr," said Davian over the muted shrieking of the darkness, mustering a forced, exhausted grin at his friend. "You saved my life... what? Three times?"

"At least five," replied Wirr immediately, though his smile was half-hearted. He glanced back at Asha, whose face glistened with sweat now, plainly straining to keep the ilshara whole.

Caeden saw his look and nodded. "We cannot delay. What she has done..." He shook his head, admiration in the motion. "I didn't think it was possible to control so much for so long. But she won't be able to sustain that level of focus, not even with the power at her disposal. No one could. If we don't close that rift before Shammaeloth gets through, this is all pointless."

Davian glanced across at him. "Is Alaris..."

"Yes." Caeden stared at the ground, emotion thick in his voice. "It's just us, now."

Davian said nothing for a long moment, and then abruptly stepped forward.

Wrapped Wirr in a tight embrace.

"It's been my honor to be your friend," he said softly, barely audible above the howls. "I know that whatever happens next, the best person for the job is in charge. I couldn't ask for more than that."

Wirr blinked away the beginnings of tears, a lump in his throat. He wanted to tell Davian to stay, that there was a way out of this.

"Fates. I'll miss you," he whispered fiercely instead. "I hope you know you'll *never* be forgotten." He pulled away, wiping his face in mild embarrassment.

Davian gave him a sad, tight smile, his gaze drifting past Wirr to fix on Asha. She couldn't see him, Wirr knew.

"Tell her I love her, Wirr," he said simply. "Make sure she's happy."

He turned away quickly, facing Deilannis. Took a step back onto the bridge.

Caeden, who had been watching, closed his eyes.

"Wait."

"What?" Davian looked across at him, then up at the golden light. "Caeden, we don't have time for anything else."

"Alaris was right." There was anger and frustration in Caeden's voice. "If we don't have a choice, then what's the point?"

"We've both made our choices."

"I have. But you never did. Not really."

He drew something from his pocket. A small amulet.

"You already explained what that is," said Davian immediately. "I'll die if I use it."

Caeden reached up and took off his torc, then walked over to Davian and, before he could protest, fastened it around his neck.

"And now?"

Davian's eyes had gone wide as he adjusted to the sudden influx of Essence. After a moment, he shook his head dazedly. "It doesn't matter. We both know what happens. We already know how this ends." He frowned at Caeden as realization hit. "*You* need to use it, Tal, if Asha is willing. You can survive." He reached up to take the torc off again.

Caeden vanished, blinking into existence behind Davian.

He pressed the amulet to the base of Davian's skull, and began feeding Essence into it.

Davian's eyes went wide and he gasped, dropping to his knees; outside the ilshara the darkness seemed to react, its screeches increasing in volume and intensity, clouds of black beating at the golden light high above. Wirr took a hesitant, confused step forward.

"What are you *doing*?" he shouted above the shrieking.

"Saving him," Caeden yelled back, face a mask of grim determination.

Wirr stuttered to a halt. Davian was clearly in pain, his expression twisting, mouth wide as he tried to catch his breath. Dark tendrils of smoke began to rise from him.

He screamed.

Wirr stepped forward again, heart pounding as he tapped Essence. "Stop it!"

"It's necessary!" Caeden glanced up at Wirr, pleading in his expression now as they locked gazes. He saw Wirr's temptation to intervene, but he didn't stop funneling Essence into the amulet. "It will stop him from being an Augur without killing him, Wirr. You have to trust me!"

Wirr closed his eyes, Davian's pained screams digging at his soul.

He slowly, carefully forced his fists to unclench. Nodded.

"I do," he shouted to Caeden.

Caeden glanced up again, and Wirr saw the depth of his gratitude in the look.

Wirr stood, unable to do anything but watch, stomach churning as the strands of oily smoke rising from Davian twisted together, gradually coalescing into a glistening black ball that flexed and pulsed wetly in the air. The last of the darkness drifted into it, sucked inside. It shimmered for a heartbeat.

There was a cracking sound, thunderously loud even above the howling, and Davian slumped as the ball exploded into a puff of white mist that immediately faded into the atmosphere.

Wirr hurried over as Caeden caught Davian and lowered him gently to the ground. Davian was still breathing, much to Wirr's relief, though his face was pale and his eyes shut.

Caeden's hand came away from Davian's neck, and he brushed a fine grit from it. The amulet was gone, Wirr realized. Disintegrated.

"It's done," shouted Caeden. He sounded stunned, as if he hadn't truly believed it would work. "Don't let him take off that torc. And don't let him come after me unless…" He grimaced, his expression turning to determination. "Don't let him come after me," he finished firmly.

He waited for Wirr's dazed acknowledgment, then spun toward the gold-tinged bridge.

"Caeden!"

Caeden wavered, then turned back to Wirr.

Wirr strode over to his friend and embraced him.

"El with you," he said, putting all of his sincerity and emotion into the words.

Caeden smiled, and Wirr could see him swallowing a lump in his throat. "And with you, Wirr." He glanced back at Davian and Asha. "Look after them. I've been around a while, and people like them don't come along often. Ever, really," he finished softly.

He gave Wirr a final nod, and started across the bridge.

A few moments later, Davian began to stir.

Wirr dropped to his knees beside his friend, who looked up at him dazedly. "Wirr? What happened?" His voice was barely audible above the screaming all around them; his eyes suddenly widened and he sat upright, hands going to the torc around his neck.

"Fates." He looked around wildly. "I…I can't feel it. I can't sense kan. It's gone."

He made as if to take off the torc but Wirr quickly pushed his arms down again, shaking his head. "It's keeping you alive."

"But…" Davian scrambled to his feet, turning toward Deilannis. Caeden was still visible, almost at the mists now.

"Caeden!" Davian yelled.

Caeden paused, somehow having heard the shout through the shrieking all around them. Glanced back.

Grinned and gave them a cheerful salute farewell.

Then he turned and walked into the mists, vanishing from view.

Davian and Wirr were silent for several seconds, stunned, just watching the spot where he'd disappeared.

Davian made to rise. "I need to go after him," he said in frustration. "My fate's sealed, but he could actually survive this."

"Not anymore. That amulet's gone. He's made his choice." 779

Wirr pushed him back down firmly. "I don't understand how it's possible, but he seems certain that your being alive won't keep the rift open now. So fates take me if you're not staying here."

Davian struggled but finally subsided, his brow creased, confusion the foremost of a jumble of emotions flitting across his face. He glanced around, back at Asha and beyond, to the ravening hordes of Banes railing against the ilshara.

"So what do we do now?" he asked faintly.

Wirr hesitated, then sat, settling down beside his friend.

"Now we wait," he said quietly.

Asha kept her breathing steady, and the ilshara whole.

Every heartbeat was...impossible. A struggle against the desire of Essence to break free from the form she was forcing it to take, to escape into the ether and dissipate. A constant cycle of realizing that part of the barrier was weakening and flooding more Essence to it, shifting energy around even as it constantly decayed, reinforcing sections as quickly as the Banes could throw themselves against them, time and time again. The howling darkness all around beat at her barrier furiously, physically ineffectual but mentally draining, its shrieks daring her to pay attention for a moment. Just a moment.

She kept her breathing steady, and the ilshara whole.

Caeden had been right about doing this without any guiding Vessels or kan to help. She knew how to manipulate Essence beyond her immediate vision—most Gifted could do that—but this...this was barely comparable to anything for which she had trained. Keeping the structure steady in her mind, not allowing it to shrink or expand, making sure that each section had just enough energy to maintain its form. The power needed was exponentially more than the Tributary had ever taken, too; without a Vessel to make her use of Essence economical, this was draining her Reserve. Not quickly—she still had time—but enough to be a problem.

In her field of vision now, though she couldn't afford to focus on them, were Davian and Wirr. Miraculously still alive. Keeping her company. Watching over her. Caeden had disappeared into Deilannis...hours ago? Minutes? Time felt meaningless.

But Davian was *still here*. She knew that much, recognized that much. She couldn't lose focus to think about what that meant, why he was here, why he was just waiting. Couldn't afford the sliver of hope that the realization brought.

She kept her breathing steady, and the ilshara whole.

Suddenly there was movement and she saw Davian and Wirr scrambling to their feet, bodies tensed. At first she couldn't see what they had spotted.

Then the ground trembled beneath her.

Across the chasm, the gold-tinged mists of Deilannis... *shifted*.

The shrieking darkness overhead rose to a crescendo as, without warning, the top of one of the tallest buildings in the city suddenly vanished from view, disintegrating into the swirling fog. Asha felt the ilshara tremble; she quickly refocused, breathing steadily.

More buildings shuddered. Disappeared.

Wirr and Davian were shouting excitedly now, pointing, though she couldn't give them enough attention to process what they were saying. The mists seemed to be retreating, creeping inward, more of the bridge across steadily revealed. After a few seconds, with a sort of absent shock, Asha realized that she could see the end. She could see the edge of Deilannis.

And the entire city was collapsing.

Buildings were crumbling to the ground, stones cracking and loosening and crashing together as they tumbled. The entire island was moving; Asha could see fissures beginning to form in the sheer stone cliff beneath the streets, small at first but rapidly widening.

Pieces of rubble began to slide into the chasm, splashing with a roar into Lantarche far below. Then more.

Then a whole section of Deilannis, impossibly, began to shudder and move ponderously to the side.

Asha watched in detached disbelief as at least a third of the city emerged from the steadily shrinking mists, architecture collapsing in on itself as the grumbling of stone against stone turned to a deafening roar, matching and then exceeding the shrieks from above. There was a violent flash of gold as what Asha thought was the Cyrarium was briefly exposed, beams of energy stabbing upward. The mists writhed and contracted.

A cracking sound broke through everything else, earsplitting and abrupt. A wave of... *something* washed over them, a blast of dark energy.

The ilshara shattered. Vanished.

The howling stopped just as abruptly, replaced only with the thundering of falling debris and the crashing of water from far below.

Otherwise, all was dark. Silent.

Asha gasped, fumbling to grasp Essence again but she was mentally spent, her concentration finally broken, completely blinded after focusing so long on Essence. Fear ripped at her chest and she scrambled as she imagined the Banes that she had been holding back rushing at the three of them, ready to tear them apart.

She stumbled, but a hand caught her. Held her up.

"Ash!" It was Davian; after a moment Asha realized she could see his outline, her eyes slowly adjusting to the lack of Essence-light. "Ash! Are you all right?"

"The Banes," rasped Asha, gripping Davian's arm tightly as she warded off outright panic. She straightened, trying again to take hold of Essence.

"Ash," said Davian gently, relief and joy in his voice. "Look. Just look."

Asha followed the silhouette of his arm pointing to the east. Dawn was close to breaking.

And as her eyes adjusted to the steadily brightening light, she saw the bodies.

They littered the ground, dark mounds that stretched as far as the eye could see, forming a perfect, unbroken line where her ilshara had been. The corpses glistened in the light and through the stunned, disbelieving hope that suddenly blossomed in her chest, Asha realized that the creatures' armor seemed to be just... gone. Disintegrated to dust.

"How?" she whispered.

782   "The rift is closed." Davian sounded as though he barely

believed what he was saying. "Caeden said that the Banes wouldn't be able to survive without a connection to the Dark-lands. That has to be it. The rift is *closed*."

Asha swallowed, her hands trembling as she sat abruptly, relief warring with concern that she was still missing something. That it couldn't possibly be over. "Then Shammaeloth..."

"I don't know. Gone, I suppose," said Davian, scanning the sky pensively as he said it. Asha followed his gaze, marveling at the clear, deep emerging blue that was swiftly banishing the last of the stars.

"You don't think he's dead?" asked Wirr, though his tone indi-cated that he knew the answer already.

"No. I...I don't think that's even possible," said Davian qui-etly, and Asha silently nodded her agreement. Nobody who had truly experienced...*whatever* that thing had been would think it could be killed. Not completely.

"How is *this* even possible?" asked Asha, still unable to bring herself to trust what she was seeing. She turned her attention back to Deilannis—or where it had been.

The mists had dissipated to nothing more than a light haze, now, revealing...nothing. The entire city of Deilannis, as well as the looming island it had perched atop, had collapsed into the raging waters below and apparently sunk beneath the earth. The river that had once split itself around the island was now forming a new, vast lake, the dark-brown sludge and debris from the col-lapse already washing away, though a low-hanging cloud of dust remained. In the distance, she could even see the cliff that marked the beginning of Desriel's territory.

"Dav...if the rift is closed, then you can't go back. Right?" Asha continued softly. She knew it was the case but she feared that she was forgetting something, missing some way that Davian could still end up at the end of Caeden's blade. It was supposed to be inevitable. It was supposed to have *already happened.*

"If the rift is truly closed, then no one can go back," Davian confirmed, sounding just as dazed.

"Well I think it is," observed Wirr, peering down into the newly formed lake. "I really think it is." He turned to them, a slow grin splitting his features.

Asha grinned back, then turned to Davian, who was watching her and touching the steel torc around his neck.

"Ash, I...I can't take this off, now. Not permanently, anyway," he said, looking embarrassed. "I would have asked, but—"

Asha snorted as she threw her arms around him. "Don't be a fool," she murmured in his ear, then kissed him, deep and long.

Eventually they collapsed to the soft grass, the tension of the past few hours draining away to utter weariness. Wirr joined them and they sat shoulder to shoulder, watching in exhausted silence as the first bright rays of the sun peeked above the horizon.

Suddenly there were tears in her eyes and she was sobbing. Crying into Davian's shoulder, gripping Wirr's hand so tightly that it probably hurt, but she found she couldn't stop. From the shaking of their bodies as they returned her embrace, they were feeling the same thing.

There was no exultation, no sense of triumph. Just mourning for those they had lost, and...relief. Pure, blessed relief, the release of a tension that had been with them all for far, far too long.

"It's over." Davian whispered the words in her ear; whether they were for her or for him she didn't know, but they were a comfort nonetheless. "It's over."

"It's over," she repeated, holding him tight. There was more to do, she knew. More to face in the coming days, probably the coming years.

But now—right now—all she cared about was that he was there with her. He was *safe*.

She huddled with the other two, weeping with joy and grief and that overwhelming sense of utter, utter relief. The bright dawn settled warm against her shoulders, bathing the three of them in its clean light, rays shearing through the space where the city of Deilannis had once been.

It was over.

Davian sat beside Asha and Wirr at the edge of the chasm overlooking Lantarche, still staggered by what he was seeing.

Sunlight glittered off the fast-flowing water far below. The mists had completely vanished with the full coming of the dawn, revealing a smooth, newly made lake that stretched seamlessly to the Desrielite cliffs, not even a vestige of the fallen city that had once obscured the view remaining. The distant green of Desriel looked vibrant in the early-morning light. Everything was calm, quiet. Peaceful.

It was the most beautiful thing he had ever seen.

Absently he searched for kan again, repressing an instinctive shiver at its complete and utter absence. Not being able to even sense it, after so long, after depending on it for his entire life...'unsettling' didn't do the sensation justice. He could feel Essence trickling into him through the torc, could feel that if he used energy from his Reserve, it would quickly be refilled by the power streaming in from Asha.

He suspected that the Vessels in his body would still be there, too—the torc worked, after all—but he could no longer see them. The ones that drew on kan wouldn't do anything, but others might still be useful. He would try them, in due course—see which, if any, he could still use.

But right now, with Asha's head nestled against his shoulder and his arm around her, bathed in the morning's warm, clean light, that all felt so...irrelevant.

"How is this possible?" he murmured, not taking his eyes from the magnificent sight in front of them. He shook his head, not for the first time trying to wrap his head around it. "Did we...did we actually *change fate*?"

"Honestly? I don't care," said Asha, looking up at him with a smile, her eyes shining. "As long as you're here, I don't care."

"My thoughts exactly," added Wirr, shifting slightly to clap him on the back.

Davian gave them an appreciative smile, heart lighter than it had been in...he didn't know how long. "No way to know, now, I suppose," he observed. "Not for us. Not for anyone." Wirr raised an eyebrow at him, and he shrugged. "No more visions. No more knowledge of what's going to happen." He stretched. "Something may have changed, but there's just no way to tell anymore."

Wirr lay back on the grass, staring up at the cloudless blue sky. "Might be for the best."

Davian and Asha joined him, murmuring their heartfelt agreement.

"So what now?" asked Asha quietly as they lay there.

None of them spoke for a moment, and then Wirr was the first to respond. "As insignificant as it seems to me right now? I'll need to go and find whatever's left of our government. There's a lot of work to do, I'm afraid," he said reluctantly.

"Straight away?" asked Davian.

"Straight away," affirmed Wirr. "We have an army from Nesk and an army from Desriel inside our borders, *and* maybe an army from Talan Gol coming. Even if Caeden was right and they're willing to negotiate once they realize that the Venerate are dead and their special armor doesn't work anymore, I need to be involved." He shifted, a flash of sadness crossing his face at the mention of their lost friend. "Besides. The Assembly's a political mess right now, and Tol Shen are still in prime position to take advantage. I think we all know how likely they are to look out for the country's best interests. Someone needs to keep them in check."

Davian gazed out over the lake. "Personally, I hope you tear them and their petty Tol to the ground, Wirr," he said softly. "But whatever you decide to do, you can handle them."

Wirr patted his Oathstone. "Fates yes, I can."

Davian grinned, and he heard Asha chuckle next to him.

"I imagine your first priority will be the Neskians, though?" asked Asha abruptly, a slyness to her tone.

Wirr glanced over at her, a half smile on his lips. "Definitely."

"Good." Asha lay back with a satisfied expression.

Wirr rolled onto his side, looking across at them. "What about you two? Will you come with me?" He cleared his throat. "Not to make too big a deal of the situation, but you're probably the two most powerful people in the world, now."

Davian stretched, looking at Asha. "Sounds like we can probably demand some time off, then."

"It does sound that way," agreed Asha solemnly. She hesitated, glancing at Davian. "We...may have to figure out some things with the Lyth at some point, too. That's a discussion for later, though," she added firmly to his questioning look.

Davian nodded his acceptance, sharing in Asha's determination to just enjoy the moment. He turned back to his friend. "Fair?"

Wirr laughed, waving his hand. "Given what you two have been through these past couple of years, I won't begrudge you a little time to yourselves." He gave them a mock-stern look. "But then you're back to work. For me. That's an order."

"Well, I suppose you need *someone* around who will listen to you," Asha said with a dramatic sigh.

"Don't worry, Wirr. We're not going to abandon you to do it all alone," agreed Davian lazily. He closed his eyes, soaking in the sun.

There was silence for a while and then, as if at some unseen signal, they started talking about the people they had lost. Began remembering the friends who had fallen. Asha laughed tearfully as she recounted how Erran and Fessi and Kol had first treated her. Wirr talked of Taeris, and his father, and his uncle and Karaliene.

Davian talked about Raeleth and Niha, about Ishelle. Mistress Alita and the others from Caladel. All of them so important to their journey. All of them gone forever.

Lastly, as if by unspoken agreement, they talked about Caeden, and as they recounted stories—Wirr and Davian in particular, given how much better they'd known the man—Davian couldn't help but wonder. Wonder whether their friend *had* somehow changed fate.

He lingered on the thought, letting the others' conversation wash over him. What would that even mean? Caeden had believed that their choices were always theirs, regardless of whether they were fated. So had Raeleth.

Did Davian believe that, too? He thought he did.

Finally, though, he shook his head. It was a question that he wanted to answer, but now wasn't the time.

Now was a time for grieving, and reflection, and rest.

Finally, as the sun crawled upward, they fell silent. An unspoken acknowledgment passed between them that it was time, that there were still things to be done.

Wirr was the first to rise, stretching and giving the other two a slight nod before wandering away from the chasm. Davian got to his feet and helped Asha to hers before standing for a long moment at the edge of the cliff, staring down into the glittering lake. Marveling.

Asha took his arm gently, pulling him away to join Wirr.

The three of them walked back into the forests of Andarra together.

Epilogue

Caeden took a long last look at his friends, and turned.

Strode determinedly into the swirling mists of Deilannis.

The white tendrils sucked at his skin, caressed him, the fog thicker and more active than he had ever seen it as he made his way across the smooth white bridge. The howling from outside was muted in here but still audible, fumbling its way eerily through the dense atmosphere until it arrived murkily at his ears, jumbled and somehow even more unsettling.

He reached the edge of the bridge and jogged down the stairs, heading along the central street toward the Inner City. His footsteps were automatic, certain, even with visibility low enough that he could barely see the facades of the buildings to either side. He knew this city—had studied it, explored and memorized every inch of it over the years in an attempt to better understand the Jha'vett. He didn't need to see the way ahead to know where he was going.

He felt his pulse race as he walked, still not quite believing that any of this was actually happening. Gassandrid was dead. Alaris was dead. Davian was no longer an Augur.

He was the *last one*.

And he was dying.

He could feel it, feel the Essence leaving him as it leaked from his makeshift Reserve with every step. No longer linked to Asha and without a source of his own, he didn't have long to do what he was intending.

Not that it was going to work.

Caeden's expression blackened as he walked, the solitude and space finally giving him the chance to think. The latent anger that had been building up inside him abruptly came bubbling to the fore.

Davian didn't have to die—the rift should close without him, now—but it wouldn't. *Couldn't.* That wasn't how this worked, and Caeden knew it.

"This isn't fair." He snarled the word at the mists, because he didn't know where else to address it. "I deserve what's coming, but he doesn't." He glared into the white, raising his gaze toward where he knew the heavens would be, releasing his frustration and pain into the words. "Why not show yourself? Intervene? If you truly exist and Shammaeloth is your enemy, then *why do you hide?*"

His words were devoured by the muting mists, vanishing swiftly to nothing.

Did he believe that El cared? Even here at the end, he wasn't sure. He was certain that Shammaeloth was evil, certain that this was the right thing to do—that didn't worry him. But the rest of it...

Raeleth would have told him that there was no decision without doubt. He would say that all of this, all of the suffering and death and madness, was just a consequence of the world's separation from El. A consequence, in a way, of choice.

"You want me to believe that we all choose?" he muttered grimly. "Then you'll let me go back. You'll let me stop him from walking out of that building and talking to me. I've had my time a hundred times over, but he... he hasn't even had a chance to live. You have to let me change things, send him back here so that he can *live.*"

Nothing happened. No response, no sign. Just as he'd expected.

There were no answers to be had here.

Caeden shook his head tiredly, set his jaw, and increased his pace, angling for the Arbiterium.

The streets of Deilannis were dead as always, even his footsteps swallowed by the encroaching mists as he found himself navigating patches of dark bodies where Davian, Asha, and Wirr had evidently been forced to fight their way through. He eyed the corpses uneasily—he could still use kan, but without sources of Essence to draw on, he didn't particularly want to have to fight any Banes—but none of them stirred.

He exhaled as he walked into the Inner City, the mists still thick but easing somewhat. He soon found himself passing the house in which he and Davian had lived while they'd trained. That had been only... a century ago? It seemed like so much longer.

He sent a hopeful thread of kan into the mist, but for the first time, there was no response. What had happened to Orkoth? He very likely would have attacked Gassandrid as soon as the Venerate had arrived here, despite its being a battle that he was always going to lose. Orkoth's mind was too far gone, and Gassandrid probably hadn't even realized what Orkoth was before killing him.

Perhaps now, finally, he was at rest.

It didn't take long before he came within sight of the Arbiterium.

He stuttered to a brief halt as he took it in. No mist touched the building that housed the Jha'vett, each stone in its structure glowing a dark, pulsing red. Caeden had never seen it this way before.

Gassandrid had claimed he'd fixed it. Perhaps he truly had.

Bracing himself, Caeden approached, pulled open the doors, and walked inside.

The chaos of the inner workings of the Jha'vett struck him like a blow, even though he'd been expecting it. The thousands of lines of Essence blurred as they were drawn toward that storm of gray smoke, which impossibly was still contained, roaring and shrieking and beating at its restraints like a wild animal that had been chained.

He stumbled to halt, staring, the surreal import of the moment finally sinking in.

He was about to die.

Stepping into the torrent would suck away the last of his remaining Essence, killing him once and for all. What would happen to the rift, though? Would it still close if Davian had yet to go back?

He squared his shoulders.

Going back to save Davian wasn't possible, he knew that. But he could still choose to try.

He stepped forward, into the long corridor that led to the Jha'vett itself.

The ground rumbled beneath his feet warningly, the tremor causing him to stumble hard against the nearby wall before he regained his balance. The howling mass of gray smoke up ahead seemed to shriek louder in response, more furiously than it had a moment ago.

Caeden frowned. He took another step, and a thunderous cracking sound cut ominously through the shrieking of the rift.

His heart leaped to his throat as he looked up. Saw the fissure as it began to make its way along the heavy stone roof, accompanied by dark, jagged splits that ran down the walls everywhere. Farther ahead, he could see fractures opening in the columns of the main room, small chunks of stone beginning to slide off them onto the floor.

The Jha'vett—the Arbiterium, maybe Deilannis itself—was collapsing.

Caeden ran.

The floor began to buckle and break beneath his feet but Caeden risked pushing a little Essence to his legs, leaping over large, broken shards of stone that jutted up in front of him and landing relatively smoothly, managing to keep his balance despite the shaking. He sprinted forward, twice having to dodge chunks of ceiling as it collapsed, then skidding over a column that had fallen across his path.

The gray whirlwind was fluctuating now, thrashing one moment and then completely still the next. The inner columns— the ones keeping it contained—were somehow still intact, but Caeden could see that they were about to go.

He dashed forward, heart pounding.

Leaped into the maelstrom.

The slithering tendrils of the gray river immediately tore at his mind, sinking in and ripping at his thoughts, at his understanding of reality. For a second, he was sure he was dead. He tumbled wildly as the stream dragged him and battered him and tossed him from one unidentifiable place to the next; he had no body here, but the sense of chaotic motion filled him, overpowering everything else. He shouted in panic but nothing came out, no sound, the empty void of twisting gray swirling through him. Ripping him apart over seconds. Minutes. Eons.

And then somehow—in the briefest instant between one act of churning violence and the next—he focused.

Kan gushed through him like a wave, dark and cold, flooding every pore.

The thrashing abruptly eased; he was still being swept along at a dizzying speed but now the motion was more logical, as if he had finally managed to break the surface of the river after flailing about underwater. The crash of sensations lessened enough for him to get his bearings, and part of him was tempted to pause, to marvel at where he was.

This wasn't like escaping from Zvaelar, which had been akin to falling down a waterfall. This was like swimming in a vast ocean of eddying currents, millions of them, each one trying to take him in a different direction. Each one a different possibility. A different time and place.

He knew that he couldn't survive here for long, though, so he pictured Davian. Homed in on his desire to save his friend. Things and events of personal importance, according to the Darecian theories, could act as a kind of beacon in the time stream. There was no telling how close to correct they had been, but the ring had worked for Davian. It was his best chance.

A lighter patch of gray in the distance.

Caeden had no physical body here but he willed himself toward it, reaching out almost by instinct toward the light.

Something *shifted*.

He stumbled to his knees as everything spun; torches around him winked out as he drained them of their Essence, taking a few gasping, gulping breaths of air as his vision cleared enough for him to take in his surroundings.

His heart sank.

It was night and the narrow alley was deserted, but the jagged architecture of the darkstone buildings around him was too distinctive, too familiar.

Why was he here? *When* was he? He dragged himself to his feet, anxiety sucking at the pit of his stomach as he realized just how little Essence he had left. He stumbled to the mouth of the alley, orienting himself against the towering outline of the Citadel. He was somewhere in the eastern district of the city—which did contain some people, but there had always been a lot of empty buildings out this way, too. The population of Ilshan Gathdel Teth had never been large enough to fill the city's accommodations.

That was bad news, because sources of Essence here were rare even where there *were* people around.

He propped himself up against the nearest wall, breathing hard, then flinched as he felt something...*pulling* at him. He looked down on instinct, but there was nothing there.

The sensation came again, insistent and strong, real enough to throw him off balance. He braced himself against the wall and then pushed through kan, trying to see what was going on.

His blood went cold.

Ethereal gray tendrils crawled over his arms, his legs, his torso. Sinking into his skin, latching on and straining. He couldn't see where they were trying to haul him to, but he could feel the gray river just beyond his sight, reaching out greedily.

He resisted. Focused. The wisps of gray relented, though nothing he did—no use of kan, no amount of concentrating or physical movement—seemed able to shake them off entirely.

Time was already trying to take him back.

He finally accepted that he'd done all he could, releasing kan and stumbling back down the alley, light-headed, as Essence leaked steadily from his body. Where to from here? A flicker of light off to his left caught his eye—a lamp still burning inside a nearby house, maybe a fire. A moment later he heard the muted sound of a baby's cries coming from within. A mother still awake, then, probably nursing her child.

There was nowhere else to go: he needed more Essence, even if it was just from the flames. He fumbled at the handle to the door, surprised and relieved to find it unlocked.

The woman inside was already on her feet, eyes flashing, when he stumbled through.

He stared at her, mouth agape, not sure he could trust his own eyes.

"Who are you?" snarled Niha, brandishing a knife with one

hand even as she held a shrieking infant with the other. The child looked pale as it cried, thin and sickly, while Niha's own features had been made haggard by stress and tiredness. She looked considerably thinner and weaker than in Zvaelar, but her eyes burned with such familiar fire that despite himself, despite the situation, Caeden couldn't help but smile.

"Niha, it's me." Caeden coughed, the flames in the fireplace dimming as he drew some Essence. "It's Tal."

It was Niha's turn to stare, the only sound the child's wailing.

"*Tal?*" The olive-skinned woman gazed at him with equal astonishment. "What…*how*? You said that we shouldn't have any contact. How did you even…?"

She trailed off, eyes suddenly narrowed. "Prove it. The last time we saw each other…"

Caeden gripped the frame of the door to steady himself. "You were significantly uglier."

Niha snorted, but Caeden saw a small, disbelieving smile touch her lips as she lowered the blade. She placed the weapon on the table beside her, careful not to put it within the child's reach. "There would have been trouble if you hadn't said 'significantly.'"

"I know you too well to risk anything less," said Caeden with a tired grin.

Niha tarried, then swallowed and walked over, one arm encircling him tightly as the other held the baby, who finally seemed to have settled. She pressed her forehead briefly, joyfully against his shoulder.

Caeden almost fell into the embrace.

"Tal!" Niha grunted, straining with one arm as she helped him into a chair, then snatching a clean cloak from nearby and wrapping it around his bloodstained shoulders. "Are you hurt?"

"Dying, actually." Caeden rubbed his eyes blearily, waving away her shocked expression. "The other Venerate are dead. I came through the rift in Deilannis, believe it or not. If you're here then this is…nearly twenty years ago, for me."

Niha immediately pressed her hand against his chest. "So we won?"

"I think so." Caeden gave an unconscious sigh as Essence began flowing into him, his head finally clearing, strength returning to his shaky limbs. The time stream still tugged insistently at him, but he steeled himself more easily now, resisted its pull more firmly.

"Thank El," Niha breathed. She removed her hand, looking vaguely embarrassed as Caeden gave her a grateful nod. "That's all I have to spare right now," she added.

Caeden looked at her, puzzled. He was thankful for her help and didn't need more straight away, but that should have been only a fraction of Niha's Reserve.

"Something to do with the transition between dar'gaithin and human, I think," explained Niha ruefully. "Or maybe the trip back here through the time stream. But I haven't had close to my full strength, this past year." She shrugged, absently stroking the child's hair. The little boy seemed to have run out of energy, his eyes closed.

Tal's thoughts finally clicked into place, and he stared at the child, mesmerized.

"Niha," he said softly, barely daring to hope. "You said it's only been a year since you got out?"

"Perhaps a little more." Niha followed his gaze, beaming proudly.

Caeden swallowed, dazed. It shouldn't have been possible, and yet...

He laughed, smiling, a blaze of relief and joy loosening his chest. Niha hadn't been able to shape-shift because of the second source inside her; he'd guessed it the moment both shape-shifting Vessels had failed to work. She hadn't even known at the time, he was certain.

So he had done the only thing he could think to do, even as it had shamed him as deeply as any of the other deaths he'd caused. But he'd known that she would never have agreed to it, would have stayed and died rather than made that choice—and that even if she had not, she would never have been able to live with herself afterward. So he'd made the decision, and prayed that she would never realize what he had taken from her.

And yet here she was, smiling in mild bemusement at his reaction, her and Raeleth's little boy sleeping soundly in her arms.

"May I?" asked Caeden dazedly, still smiling, holding out his arms.

Niha assented, carefully transferring the boy. The child squirmed, but his eyes remained closed.

Caeden studied the child, trying to look happy for Niha, but he couldn't ignore the sense of unease washing over him. His first impressions had been accurate. The boy's skin had an unnaturally pallid hue to it, almost gray, and he wheezed as he breathed, each lungful sounding like a struggle.

Caeden swallowed, then almost stumbled as a momentary wave of dizziness washed over him. He frowned. His Essence shouldn't be running out that fast.

He focused, examining the energy remaining within him. Still some, but not nearly enough after what Niha had just given him. Was being in Talan Gol somehow draining him faster?

He pressed through kan, trying to see what was going on.

To begin with he couldn't see anything unusual, and he almost let kan go again, ready to move on to more important things... and then he saw the strands. Three of the tiniest, thinnest lines of Essence he'd ever seen. Impossible to even glimpse unless you were looking for them. Stretching from him to the child in his arms.

And Caeden hadn't created them.

His heart beginning to pound, Caeden kept his grip on kan and carefully examined the little boy, absently allowing him to wrap an entire hand around his forefinger. It took only a second to find what he had been looking for.

The child had no source.

Caeden's mind went blank.

Niha saw his expression, concern immediately flooding her features. "Is something wrong with him?"

"No. No, it's..." Caeden took a steadying breath as a chill ran down his spine. "Is he ill very often?"

Niha hesitated.

"Almost always," she said, a slight tremor to her voice. "Sometimes...sometimes he seems like he's barely breathing, but I can't take him to a proper healer. I'd be assigned to the Cyrarium, and then he'd..."

Her eyes glistened, and he saw exhaustion. Frustration. Fear for her child.

She quickly recovered herself. "He hates being alone, but being around him I always feel..."

"Weaker," finished Caeden, a heavy pain in his chest.

So this was why he'd been drawn here—and remarkable though it was, it only confirmed that he couldn't save Davian. Not when it mattered.

Because surely, this proved that nothing could be changed.

He closed his eyes as the heartache settled deep, weariness already beginning to eat at his concentration again, at his ability to resist the time stream. Niha's son had been draining her Essence because here in Ilshan Gathdel Teth, there was nothing else. And when Niha wasn't near, he suffered. It was an untenable situation.

"What's his name?" asked Caeden in a low voice, holding out the sleeping boy back to his mother. Wondering if, on some level, she might already know who he was.

Niha took him gently, gazing down at his face. "I..." To Caeden's shock, he saw tears trickling down her cheeks this time. "I haven't been able to decide. I want to choose something I know he'd have wanted, and..." She gave a half sob, half laugh as she gazed at the boy's sleeping form. "It's been months. It's stupid."

"No. It's not," said Caeden quietly.

He closed his eyes. Came to a decision.

He had to tell her.

"What I did to you, to make the shape-shifting Vessel work," he said, not knowing how to broach the subject better, even if he'd had time. "It hurt him. He doesn't have a source anymore." He held her gaze firmly. "He...he died because of what I did, Niha. But it seems that he's an Augur, and you're Gifted, and some instinct has allowed him to survive by taking Essence from you instead."

Niha blanched. "But you..." She trailed off, eyes wide with pain and broken trust as she looked at him. Lost for words.

Caeden hung his head.

"I'm sorry. You wouldn't have left otherwise." He looked up again, accepting the betrayed shock in Niha's gaze. "I wish that I had more time to beg for your forgiveness, but there's something else you need to know. There's only one other person I have ever met who was able to survive like this, and your son...he's the right age."

Niha stared at Caeden blankly, hot anger and confusion warring on her face, before suddenly her eyes went wide.

"*Davian?*" she breathed, looking at the boy in disbelief, her fury melting away in an instant.

Caeden smiled at her reaction. "I believe so."

Niha's brow creased, and another tear trickled down her cheek as panic slowly replaced amazement. "You want me to give him up," she breathed. "To let you take him to that school in Andarra."

"I want you to save him," said Caeden gently. "He cannot survive here. I think you already know that."

"But you will ultimately kill him." Niha's voice shook. "He travels back in time, and you kill him. *Again.*"

Caeden squeezed his eyes shut tight.

"Yes," he whispered. He wanted to say something different but he couldn't lie anymore, not to her.

There was silence, long and cold, and Caeden could almost physically feel Niha struggling with what he'd just revealed. Despite the gray stream scrabbling at the edge of his mind, he gave her the time she needed. He owed her that, and far more besides.

Eventually, Niha spoke again.

"I don't want to give him to you," she said, voice cracking. "But Raeleth would say that we had to. He would say that we should be proud of the man he becomes, and for the part El has chosen him to play." She sobbed. "He would tell me that he will grow to be brave and intelligent and important and good and happy and *loved*. That faith in El's plan was pointless if we were shown it so clearly, told of its *success* and still tried to change it. Still made the choice to reject it." The tears flowed freely now, sliding down her cheeks and nose; she nestled the still-sleeping boy on her lap and bowed her head, weeping into her hands.

Caeden drew a shaky breath. He wanted to go over and comfort her, but he knew that wasn't the right move. "In twenty years the ilshara will fall, Niha. The ilshara will fall and the rift will close." He silently prayed that would happen. "When it does... 799 you should go south. Find a girl named Ashalia Chaedris. You'll want to meet her, and I think that she will want to meet you." He smiled slightly as Niha looked up, recognition in her eyes. Of course Davian had talked about her. "Because you're right—he is loved, deeply. By others. And by me," he finished softly.

Niha's tears continued to fall as she cradled her son, stroking his cheek gently.

"Davian," she whispered, giving a tearful smile to the sleeping boy. "How long do I have?"

"An hour, maybe. I need to make a Gate, but I cannot delay any further." Caeden gritted his teeth as the time stream tugged at him again.

Niha just nodded, her eyes never leaving Davian.

Caeden stood. "Is this place important to you in any way?"

Niha shook her head. "It was just the best place to hide with him. Not many people around." She swallowed, the reality of what was ahead causing pain to flit across her features. "But if it's just me, I'll find the resistance."

"Good. As soon as I'm through the Gate, you need to go," Caeden told her quietly. "The Venerate will sense it opening, though they won't have a clue as to who activated it. They'll be here within minutes. If you're not gone, they'll find you. Put you in the Cyrarium again."

Niha's expression clouded, but she took a deep breath and acknowledged the warning.

Caeden got to work.

He had built enough Gates recently that this one was done in under an hour, Niha occasionally, reluctantly giving him a boost of Essence when he started to falter. He could see her the entire time, couldn't help but admire her resolve as she would gaze at her son, waver, and then steel herself once again.

Davian—Caeden had to remind himself of that reality more than once—slept peacefully in his mother's arms, thankfully. It was hard enough to stay focused without his plaintive cries, but Caeden wouldn't have dared suggest that Niha wait elsewhere even if he'd woken. If he let the two of them out of his sight, he wasn't convinced that he'd ever see them again, no matter Niha's

remarkable strength.

Finally, somehow—despite the time stream's constant pull, despite his tiredness—he was done.

He leaned back against the nearest wall, going over the kan mechanisms wearily before looking up at Niha, nodding apologetically to the dread in her eyes. "It's time."

Niha took a shaky breath.

"I was always a little jealous of his relationship with you," she murmured, gazing at Davian. "Seeing how easily he got through to you, when you were always so aloof with the rest of us. Seeing how much you admired him." She gave a tremulous smile, then bent down, kissing Davian gently on the forehead. "I am so proud of you, my boy," she whispered.

The infant stirred, but didn't wake. Niha eventually tore her gaze from her son, looking up at Caeden, who nodded once and gently took the boy from her grasp. She clung to him instinctively but finally, reluctantly, let go.

Caeden turned to activate the Gate.

"Wait," said Niha suddenly, voice shaking as she hurriedly fumbled with something on a cord around her neck. "It was too risky to wear this—it would draw attention, here—but..."

She took the loop off her head, and placed the silver ring on the end into Caeden's hand.

"I want him to have it," she finished softly. "A piece of his parents."

Caeden froze, his mind not processing what he was seeing. He could feel the ring—the *older* ring—still sitting securely in his right pocket, from when he'd taken it off Diara's desk.

"It will mean a lot to him," he promised her, recovering and slipping it into his left pocket. Cradling Davian carefully, he triggered the Initiation endpoint.

The Gate flickered to life.

Niha watched, her gaze fixed on Davian's sleeping form as Caeden started toward the portal.

"I love you. Both of your parents do," she called to the child, fresh tears in her eyes, her voice cracking.

Caeden didn't stop, despite the hard lump in his throat.

He stepped through the Gate. Turned.

Niha was watching with eyes full of anguish, hand covering

her mouth, looking like she was doing everything she could not to follow. Her gaze was fixed on her son, drinking in the sight of him. He forced a sad smile to her and she raised her hand, though he knew it was to Davian more than to him.

Heart breaking, he sliced through the Gate's mechanisms.

Niha vanished from view.

Caeden breathed out shakily, letting the emotion of the moment pass before proceeding. The infant in his arms—it was still hard to think of him as Davian—continued to sleep, though Caeden could tell that he was still drawing Essence from him. Too much longer, and that would become a problem.

Fortunately, Davian was about to get all the Essence he needed.

The lights of Ilin Illan below seemed brighter than ever as he moved cautiously to the edge of the balcony, though stars still sparkled keenly in the deep, moonless night sky. Surreal, staring down on the peaceful beauty that he would eventually destroy.

He turned, gazing briefly through the window. Empty.

Another pang of regret and deep sorrow shivered through his chest.

Moving carefully so as not to wake Davian—he had already spotted guards patrolling the grounds below—he descended the spiral staircase and hurried cautiously from shadow to shadow through the grounds, several times using some light Control to send guards in another direction. He knew the palace well enough to guess where Taeris and any Gifted with him would have been accommodated.

He breathed out in relief as he came in sight of the east wing, and sure enough, several guards stood at the entrance. The Treaty was barely in place; the Gifted were no longer prisoners, but they were hardly honored guests right now.

Caeden adjusted his grip on Davian, who was becoming increasingly heavy in his arms. His heart skipped a beat as the boy squirmed and shifted in response, but in the end he settled back down with a soft sigh.

"All right," Caeden whispered to him, feeling sweat beading on his brow now despite the cold night air. He'd drawn patches of Essence from his surroundings, but he was already running low again. "Let's see how this goes."

He grasped kan, and stepped outside of time.

The time stream screamed at him in response, scrabbling angrily at him, almost causing him to lose his grip on kan immediately. He took a moment to focus, then slipped between the guards and hurried inside.

It didn't take long to spot the only room with light filtering out from underneath the door. Caeden opened it—relieved to find that it wasn't locked—and stepped inside.

Despite the cacophony in his head, he almost chuckled when he saw the man sitting at the desk, head bowed over some paperwork. Taeris was actually...handsome. *Young.*

Caeden carefully lay Davian on the bed and then half stumbled over to the desk, snatching up a piece of paper and pen. His vision swam as he scribbled the note.

This is Davian. Watch over him.

He couldn't manage more than that, but he didn't need to; he already knew that Taeris knew Alchesh's prophecies, would take Davian to the school in Caladel. He placed the note next to the sleeping boy, and the silver ring from his left pocket on top of the paper. The ring would go to Administration, sooner or later—but that knowledge stung much less, knowing that one day Davian would get it back.

He gave the infant a small smile.

"El with you," he murmured.

He left, closing the door carefully behind him and finally, exhaustedly letting the time bubble drop. He stood outside the door, panting, then winced as a plaintive cry from inside the room indicated that Davian had finally woken.

"What in *fates?*" came Taeris's bemused voice.

Caeden allowed himself a small smile. He wanted to keep listening, to see what happened next—maybe even talk to Taeris—but the pull of the time stream was too much. His Essence was waning again, and he knew how this ended.

He stumbled and slumped against the wall, his head pounding. Everything faded.

How long had he been here?

He tried to focus but the torrent ripped him from place to place, his mind shattering and reforming and shattering again as he struggled to orient himself in the shifting, swirling mass of liquid smoke.

He cried out, though no words formed; instead they were ripped away before he had a chance to voice them, devoured by the void. Fear surged through him—true fear, one that clawed at his chest, sent him to the edge of panic. He couldn't let this end yet. He still had to fix things, to *change* things. A primal dread that he had all but forgotten settled inside him, deep and violent.

He might die here. After being given so much time, he might actually *die* before doing the things he needed to. The thought was absurd, so much so that he almost let out a terrified laugh. Almost.

How long had he been like this? He could feel himself being battered by the time stream, the river tossing him violently from one place to another, one era to the next and then back again with no respite, no rest. As if it were offended by the presence of one who had hated it with such passion, who had worked against it for so long. Since the moment Ell had died.

A light. A patch of gray that seemed...meaningful.

Caeden struggled weakly toward it, his focus failing.

And then he was lying in bright light, sun-warmed stone at his back.

He rolled instinctively to the side, holding up his hands to shield his eyes. The initial exposure had seared his vision, rendering his surroundings bright white, though the pain felt wonderful compared to the bodiless nightmare of the rift. He gasped like a landed fish, staying still with eyes squeezed shut even as he reached out with kan. He immediately found a source of Essence, allowing the energy to trickle into his body. Extending his life for just a little longer.

The roaring in his ears faded, and he heard the gentle tinkling of water everywhere around him.

He opened his eyes. His heart began to pound.

Fountains of artfully crafted white stone, spouting sparkling water in joyful, coordinated bursts. Perfectly manicured lawns stretching down the hill to the gently shifting forest below.

And atop the hill, a shining palace made of crystal.

For a brief, stunned moment he thought that he'd somehow found his way back into the dok'en, but the differences were easy to spot. Walls, smooth and tall and white, encircling the palace and grounds to keep the general populace—which had been him, for a long time—out. Small scuffs and marks on the stone, some stray dead leaves on the lawns, a heat that was immediately warmer than was strictly comfortable. The tiny imperfections a dok'en couldn't properly replicate, the ones that made up life and made this place somehow even more remarkable than the replica he had built in his mind.

He stood, then immediately ducked down again behind the low white wall of a fountain as movement caught his eye. Guards. They hadn't seen him yet, but there were several patrolling the grounds.

His mind raced and his heart drummed painfully as he slumped there, stunned, slowly understanding. Ell would be here somewhere. *Ell.*

Everything else seemed suddenly unimportant.

He closed his eyes, resolve flooding his limbs with renewed energy. If he wanted to speak to Ell, for her to actually have a conversation with him, he'd need to look as he once had.

That would take care of the guards, too. He *was* allowed in here, after all.

Trembling, he grasped kan, letting the dark energy flow into him. Settle into muscle and bone. Shape-shifting had never been a strength but he'd practiced so much and today, right now, he *would* make it happen quickly. There was no room for failure, no time to do anything else. Already he could feel the insistent tug of the time stream, wrenching at his limbs, threatening to drag him back again.

Bracing himself against the pull, he pictured himself. His original body.

Pain, sharp and bright.

When it was over there was hot blood in his mouth from where he had bitten down hard on his tongue, forcing himself to stay silent through the transition. He spat red onto the white stone ground and then lay there, panting, before hauling himself up and peering over the edge of the fountain, into the rippling pool.

The man staring back at him was someone he hadn't seen in more than four thousand years. A face he had refused to go back to for so long that it looked like that of a stranger.

Tal'kamar Deshrel.

He quickly splashed the worst of the grime and blood from his skin and clothes, fastening the cloak Niha had given him over the top. He was hardly presentable, but he at least wouldn't look as though he was dying now. Weariness washed over him, and he sank back to rest against the low wall of the fountain, drawing more Essence as he did so. He was tired after that. *So* tired. He just needed to close his eyes.

He wasn't sure how long had passed before a body was sliding in beside him, shoulder nestling against his.

"Are we...hiding?"

He froze. Opened his eyes and turned, heart beating out of his chest.

Ell's deep-blue eyes sparkled as she looked at him.

"You *do* know that the men won't try and arrest you anymore, correct?" she continued in amusement, pausing to peek out girlishly from their position at the patrolling guards. "No matter what Revan would like?"

Caeden gaped, tongue like lead. Ell's long dark hair was simply bound, stray strands drifting across her face as she grinned at him. She was wearing a summery dress that brought out the azure in her eyes, the light cloth rippling in the breeze.

For a moment an irrational suspicion gnawed at him as he wondered how she had found him, but then he looked into her eyes. Those *eyes*. The light behind them. The barely contained joy and happiness and sheer vivaciousness as she looked at him.

It was her. Not Nethgalla. *Her.*

"Of course, it *is* much more romantic to find you lying in wait on my morning walk like you used to. Even if you did apparently fall asleep in the process." She leaned forward and kissed him lightly, then peered at him. "And have become mute, apparently?"

Caeden coughed and shook his head, finally finding his voice. "I'd forgotten how beautiful you are," he said softly.

Ell flushed slightly, a smile curling her lips upward. "Well. If you're going to say sensible things like that, I may just keep you around." She shook her head in half-embarrassment and half-amusement, twisting in her seated position to study him, those ocean-deep blue eyes gazing into his. "I thought that you were leaving for Dianlys last night—I didn't think I'd see you again for weeks." Her eyebrow rose slightly as she noted his attire. "More... *disagreements* changed your plans, I assume?"

Caeden glanced down at his tattered and bloodied shirt and trousers. The shadows and his seated position disguised some of the damage, and he'd cleaned away the worst of it, but there was no hiding that he'd been in a fight. "Something like that."

"But you're all right?" When Caeden nodded, Ell relaxed slightly, sighing. "I won't ask. But you really need to stop letting them provoke you, Tal. *I* know why you're with me. And Mayden and her men will say what they say, no matter what you do."

Caeden's mind raced as he gazed at her, barely hearing the words. He was supposed to be heading to Dianlys, several hundred miles to the east. The Tal'kamar of this time *was* heading there. This was... a year and a half before their wedding, then? Almost two? He and Ell were very much in love by this stage, but it was still a while before he even proposed.

"I know. And as long as you know, too, that's all I truly care about," he said eventually, rewarded with a smile from Ell that stole his breath. He forced himself to continue. "I don't have long before I do have to go," he added, feeling the unrelenting pull of the time stream tighten, "but I wanted to see you again first. Just for a few minutes."

He finally began to calm, began to accept that this was really happening. He'd envisaged coming back to see Ell a thousand times, but it had always taken place at his wedding. Always been with the intention of preventing that one event—stopping her from leaving the main hall, or dealing with the priest outside before she left, or making a scene to force everyone to go home, or... a hundred other ways he might have changed what had happened.

For just a moment, despite everything, he considered whether it was still possible. How could he convince her, here and now, in only a few short minutes? Scenarios started racing through his head, each one less likely to work than the last. He could hardly tell her that he was from the future and had come back to save her from dying at their wedding—he was going to sound utterly insane if he tried. He could try and break things off with her, end the relationship to save her, but he immediately knew that the Tal of this time would do everything in his power to undo such a move. Or perhaps it didn't need to be that dramatic. Perhaps...

His train of thought faltered, his most recent conversation with Niha finally pushing its way insistently into his head.

Reluctantly he let it in, his heart aching as the realization finally, truly sank in deep.

No matter what he said or did here...this wouldn't change anything. Couldn't. This was past, had already happened. His actions here were an already-written history.

Which meant that he could spend his last minutes with his wife burdening her with the knowledge of what was to come—maybe even *cause* what had happened, somehow.

Or he could finally say good-bye.

"Well, there are certainly more comfortable places to sit around here," observed Ell, oblivious to his thoughts. "And I'm late to see Faris. Walk with me?" She made as if to rise.

Caeden held out a hand, gently holding her back.

"I really do have to go. Soon," he said seriously. If he tried to make it to the palace, he wasn't sure that he wouldn't collapse on the way, or become too weak to resist being dragged back into the time stream. "Would it be all right if we just...sit here? Just for a minute longer?"

Ell gave him a half-amused, half-concerned look. She sank back against the wall next to him.

"You're sure you're all right?" she asked quietly, squinting at him. "You look tired."

Caeden smiled weakly. "I am." His body was also a couple of years older than the one Ell knew—not enough for her to specifically notice, sitting here in the shadows, but enough for her to register that something was different. "I'm...struggling with something. A kind of crisis of faith, I suppose. I thought maybe you could help."

Ell blinked. "Of course," she said, sobering to seriousness immediately.

Caeden exhaled. "I know this is going to sound morbid, but... what would you do if I died?"

Ell's brow furrowed.

"If you died?" she repeated softly. "If you died, Tal, I would grieve for the rest of my life." Ell said the words simply, with an honest, quiet sadness at the thought.

Caeden nodded slowly. "I'd be the same if I lost you, too," he assured her, a deep, sharp pain in his chest at the words. "But what do you think it would mean for your faith in El? In His Grand Design? I've been trying to come to grips with that question, and..." Caeden rubbed his forehead. "I don't doubt His existence, but how could I continue to love, worship, even just *accept* a god whose plan involved something so precious to me being ripped away?"

Ell was silent for a few moments, thinking.

"As much as I'd like to think that it wouldn't shake my faith...I'd be angry, too. So angry," she admitted, an ache to her voice. "But I also hope that my grief and pain would eventually fade enough to remember that He gave us each other in the first place." She smiled slightly and cupped his cheek in her hand, holding his gaze. "I know that's easy to say, though, while living it would be infinitely more complicated. So as much as I would love to ease your mind here and now, Tal, I just...don't think that there are any easy answers. It could take a lifetime to come to grips with something like that."

"Maybe more," agreed Caeden softly. He took her hand in his, squeezing it, his heart a stone in his chest. "I worry about the man I'd be without you, Ell. I'd fight El Himself, break His plan and burn the world if I thought that it could bring you back."

Ell smiled slightly. "No, you wouldn't. You aspire to be better than that," she said, brushing back a strand of his hair affectionately. "Besides. You'd know it's not what I'd want."

Caeden looked away, emotion choking him.

" 'Be the man I aspire to be,' " he murmured eventually. "A friend of mine said that to me, once."

Ell leaned in, putting her head against his. "Terrible advice for most people, but for you?" She kissed him gently. "Be that man, and I will never stop loving you."

Caeden looked up again, into her eyes. That genuineness. That light and happiness as she gazed at him.

A lump formed in his throat.

"I'll do everything I can, then," he promised.

Ell grinned back at him, giving him a cheerful kiss on the head as she used his shoulder to push herself to her feet. "I know you will." She gazed at him, caught between affection and mild concern. "Faris is waiting, but I can stay for a little longer if you need to—"

"Go," he said, forcing a reassuring smile through the ache in his chest. "I'm just glad I got to see you again before I leave."

"Me too. Stay safe in Dianlys, and we can talk more when you get back." She kissed him. "I love you."

"I love you, too," said Caeden, voice almost a whisper as he memorized her smile. He watched as she started to walk away, willing himself not to call her back. Willing himself to finally let her go.

"And Tal?"

Caeden's heart felt as if it would wrench from his chest. The sunlight caught Ell's hair as she looked over her shoulder at him.

"If you died, I *would* trust that I would see you again one day," she called, strands shining in the reflected morning sun from the Crystalline Palace. "In a better world than this one."

With a final, brilliant smile, she was gone.

He sat there for a while longer, the time stream tugging harder and harder at him, his emotions a jumble, replaying the conversation again and again. He wiped at his cheek, vaguely surprised to find tears leaking down his face.

Ell had been wrong about him then, but he could prove her right now.

" 'Be the man I aspire to be,' " he murmured to himself.

Then he froze. Thought for a long moment, barely daring to breathe.

He shook his head dazedly and gave a soft, disbelieving laugh. Asar would have found it funny, too.

Caeden finally knew what he had to do. Knew how this had to end.

"Thank you," he whispered.

He closed his eyes, relishing the warmth of the sun against his skin.

Let his defenses drop.

Let the gray stream take him, one last time.

Caeden wrenched himself free from the grasping tendrils of the river, crumpling to the stone underfoot and snatching at the thin strands of Essence that now flowed wildly around him.

The last echoes of the explosion faded as the shattered lines of power pulsed gold, red, and blue in a chaotic web, the dizzying colors of kan-modified Essence twisting and melting into one another, then diminishing as they decayed in the broken feedback loop of the Jha'vett. Red with flecks of yellow pulsed everywhere in the stone, the ground rumbling ominously beneath him.

Caeden gritted his teeth as his awareness sharpened, life flowing back into his limbs. The time stream was pulling at him fiercely here, so close to the rift. He dragged himself away from the center, every movement an effort both physical and mental, past the inner ring of columns.

The pressure on him eased, and he collapsed against one of the pillars, panting. He'd made it. Impossibly, he was here.

But there wasn't much time.

He closed his eyes, heart drumming in his chest. Focused. Kan was simplicity itself to grasp here, only feet from the rift, but with the chaos around him and the insistent pull of time, it was still difficult to concentrate.

For a long few moments nothing happened, and Caeden's apprehension began to grow. He took a deep, measured breath. Tried again.

Pain arced through him.

This was harder than his transformation into his original self. His body protested, resisted. Everything snapped and tore in violent argument, but he kept going, the sliver of consciousness that he was able to maintain focused only on pushing back the time stream, keeping him here and now.

His arms thickened and tightened, everything in his body suddenly leaner and harder than it had been before. A small, detached part of his mind noted the pull of the old scar on his face as agony twisted his expression.

And then, as abruptly as it had begun, it was over.

Caeden lay there, trembling, before draining more Essence—the last of the fading power in the room—and crawling to his feet.

Step by aching step, he made his way along the corridor and, with a final burst of energy, pushed open the doors of the Arbiterium.

He blinked in the garish red light for a second, looking around dazedly. After a moment he spotted whom he was looking for. A man staring in disbelief at him.

Himself.

Caeden walked forward slowly, each step an effort, though he tried not to show it. The Essence from the Jha'vett was almost gone now. It didn't matter. All that mattered now was what was left to say.

"Tal'kamar. Aarkein Devaed," Caeden said calmly as he reached the stunned-looking version of his past self.

"Yes."

Caeden let out a long breath. He'd seen this so many times. He'd played the words over and over.

And yet right now, his focus gone in a haze of exhausted emotion, that memory was just a blur. All he knew was that he had to finish this, convince himself. Set himself along the right path once and for all.

"My name is Davian. I have used the Jha'vett to come here, now, to deliver you a message." He swallowed. Davian *would* have said this to him, given the chance, but Caeden...Caeden *knew* it was the truth. Felt it more deeply than anything he'd ever felt.

Perhaps, ultimately, that was why it had worked.

"It is...something that you need to hear," he continued softly. "Something which only a friend can tell you."

Tal'kamar glared at him skeptically.

"The Jha'vett is broken. What you see are the consequences of it breaking." He shook his head, a frustrating arrogance to the motion despite the consequences of what he had just wrought surrounding them. "But let's say I humor you, stranger. What message does my friend bring that requires him to travel through time itself?"

"That you have been deceived," said Caeden, calm certainty in his tone. "That no matter how much it hurts, you need to recognize that El is not who He says He is. You need to accept that you are on the wrong side of this fight...and that you always have been."

"Is...that all? Is that the best that you have to offer? 'Change sides'? Just like that?" Tal'kamar gave a cynical laugh. "I fear that you have come a long way for no reward."

"That is not all," Caeden assured him. "You also need to accept that it is your fault. It is your fault, and there is no undoing it."

"You'll have to do better than—"

"You alone." Caeden cut him off before he could speak further, a spark of anger suddenly igniting at his former self's attitude. His myopic, deliberate ignorance. "You killed your friends and loved ones. You destroyed a civilization and sent the scant few survivors on a path that led to yet more destruction. None of this can be undone. None of the lives that were lost can ever be brought back."

"Enough," snarled Tal'kamar, looking rattled.

"You slaughtered innocents. You hid behind the names Aarkein Devaed and El, but it was always Tal'kamar—always you," said Caeden insistently. "You lie to yourself about what you truly believe, and you do it over and over and *over* every single day because you are afraid of admitting to what the alternative means."

"Enough." It was a clear warning this time.

Caeden kept going.

"You need to accept that your wife is dead and that she cannot be brought back. That Elliavia is dead and that you will never see her again." The words tore at his chest but he pushed through the emotion, willing himself to get it all out. "You need to do this, because your selfishness has already cost the lives of more good men than there are stars in the sky. Your *selfishness*, Tal'kamar. Not your blindness, nor your arrogance, nor your good intentions. Your utter contempt for *anyone but yourself.*" Caeden said the words loudly now, furiously, begging his past self to listen even as his body's remaining Essence began to fade. He needed to hear this. He needed to accept it.

"That's not—"

"Listen to me, Tal'kamar!" snarled Caeden, putting every ounce of urgency and emotion and energy he had left into the words. "You are at fault! You and you alone! You shield yourself from what you've done, you justify and justify and justify but you know deep down that it is NOT ENOUGH! For all that you've been given, you are fearful and weak and cowardly! For all you have lost, you have not learned! It's not fate and it's not love and it was never, ever because you thought that you were doing the right thing! You know this! You know this better than—"

"ENOUGH!" Tal'kamar screamed, and as Caeden felt the last of his Essence trickle away he could see that the man before him was lost to his anger now. Blinded by a red haze of enraged denial.

It didn't matter. Eventually, he knew, that man would change.

Licanius was out of its sheath. Tal'kamar raised it high.

Caeden smiled.

Acknowledgments

This trilogy has been an immense undertaking, and as it comes to a close, I find myself owing a huge debt of gratitude to the people who have made its completion and success possible.

First and foremost, thanks go once again to my wife, Sonja. A lot's changed in our lives since I started writing this series, but one thing that hasn't is her practical and emotional support—first of a dream I wanted to pursue, and then of a job that can at times be all-consuming. Her contribution to the success of this trilogy truly cannot be overstated, and I am thankful for her and her involvement every day.

Next, to my editors at Orbit, Priyanka and James, who have helped hone this book (and the series in general) so much. Priyanka has had the unenviable task of jumping into this series at the end of what is quite a complex story, but her insights have proven immensely valuable, and I've been delighted that her suggestions have meshed so well with my own vision for the book.

As always, a huge thanks to my awesome agent, Paul Lucas, who continues to be utterly invaluable in navigating the business side of this industry. I have absolutely no doubt that I would be in a far inferior position in my career right now without his hard work and advice.

Thank you as well to all my beta readers from throughout the series. These are big, complex books, and reading the earliest versions of them—trying to decide what's working and what's not, picking up inconsistencies, and constantly having to separate time-travel twists from stupid mistakes—I suspect can end up being more chore than fun. It's hard to express just how much I appreciate everyone who was willing to contribute to that process.

Last but certainly not least, a massive thank you to all of you who have taken the time to read the Licanius Trilogy. I know that starting a big series like this, especially from a first-time author, is a risk: you're committing a huge chunk of your entertainment time to what's basically an unknown quantity. That so many of you have done so—showing so much enthusiasm and support along the way—has genuinely, measurably changed my life for the better. I will be forever grateful.

Author's Note
Aelric and Dezia

To answer a common question that arose during beta reading: yes, there is more of their story to come! I should firstly emphasize that this **won't** be my next project—I'm excited to move on to writing something in a new world for a while, now—but it's definitely going to happen at some point, and probably not *too* far down the track. For the curious, here's some background on why I decided to shift it to a standalone book...

Years ago, Aelric and Dezia's story line was planned to fit within this trilogy. When I started outlining *The Light of All That Falls*, though, I pretty quickly realized that the size and scope of what I wanted to do meant that something of a rethink was needed.

The first, and probably most practical, reason for this was sheer word count. My (probably conservative) estimate puts the Aelric/Dezia narrative at around 100k–150k words; *Light*, for reference, is around 280k. Combine those numbers and you get something impractically large, especially for print... which means that if I had gone ahead and included it, the trilogy would almost certainly have ended up extending to four books.

Which, of course, would have just forced everyone to wait another year or two for the conclusion you've (presumably) just read.

While I think that would have been unfortunate (and possibly unpopular!), I'd have happily made the call to do it, *if* I'd thought that it was going to result in a better overall reading experience...

but there were some important artistic reasons for the decision, too. Introducing new points of view midway through a story sort of dampens the pace by default; time has to be spent getting comfortable with a character's internal dialogue, and as a reader, you generally aren't as invested in them for a while—if ever—compared to more familiar faces. On top of that, the main setting (Nesk) in this instance is an entirely different country and culture, and the extra world-building needed to do that justice would almost certainly have affected the pacing even further.

All of this, I think, could have caused frustration for a lot of readers. Slowing down the narrative like that—especially toward the end of the overarching story—may have ended up *feeling* like filler, even if it wasn't.

Aside from that, the last relatively minor (but still important) consideration was that Aelric and Dezia's narrative is one that I think will work quite well as a standalone. The consequences of their time in Nesk are obviously significant, but their story just isn't as intimately tied to the larger plot as it is for the main four characters. So giving the Shainwieres a separate book (and thus some breathing room from needing to drive the larger Licanius Trilogy narrative relentlessly forward) will, I'm confident, allow it to become a much more fully realized tale.

Anyway, I hope that provides a little insight into the thought process surrounding this part of the story—and, of course, that you'll be interested in the finished product when it's eventually written. As always, thanks for reading!

—James

Glossary of Characters

Aarkein Devaed (ARE-kine deh-VADE): A powerful Gifted whose invasion of northern Andarra two thousand years ago resulted in the creation of the Boundary. Considered by the Old Religion to be a figure of great evil, strongly associated with Shammaeloth himself. Also see *Caeden.*

Aelric Shainwiere (AIL-rick SHAYN-weer): Ward of the king, brother to Dezia. A talented swordsman who, for political reasons, deliberately lost the most recent final of the Song of Swords held in Desriel. Left Ilin Illan to deal with his disgruntled financial backers.

Aelrith (AIL-rith)/The Watcher: One of the sha'teth, who was once commonly seen by Shadows in the Sanctuary. Now deceased.

Alaris (al-ARE-iss)/Alarais (al-are-ACE)/Alarius (al-ARE-ee-us): One of the Venerate, and former king of the Shining Lands. Considers himself Tal'kamar's friend.

Alchesh Mel'tac (AL-chesh MEL-tack): The first Augur. In legend, driven mad after seeing too much of the future. Soon after the creation of the Boundary, he warned of its eventual collapse and Aarkein Devaed's return. Though his visions were initially considered reliable, after several hundred years without apparent threat from Talan Gol, his writings were dismissed by the priests of the Old Religion and struck from the canon.

Alita (ah-LEET-ah): The head cook at the school at Caladel, who largely took responsibility for raising Davian when he was left at the Tol. Now deceased.

Ana (AHN-ah): A member of the scavenging team in Zvaelar to which Davian belongs.

Andrael (AN-dree-el)/Andral (AN-drahl): One of the Venerate. A talented inventor. Creator of the five Named swords, which were forged for the purpose of killing the other Venerate. His deal with the Lyth forced Tal'kamar to erase his own memories in order to reclaim Licanius.

Andras (AN-drass): The royal line of Andarra.

Aniria (ah-NEER-ee-ah): One of the identities Nethgalla takes in Ilshan Gathdel Teth.

Asar Shenelac (AY-sarr SHEN-eh-lack)/Tae'shadon (TAY-shah-don)/The Keeper: One of the Venerate. Meets Caeden in the Wells of Mor Aruil in order to help restore Caeden's memories. Now deceased.

Asha (ASH-uh)/Ashalia (ash-AH-lee-uh): Main character. Formerly a Shadow, now immensely powerful thanks to her connection to the Siphon. Childhood friend of Davian and Wirr, having grown up with them in the Gifted school in Caladel. Turned into a Shadow by Ilseth Tenvar in the aftermath of the attack on the school. Made Representative for Tol Athian by Elocien Andras, who also had her secretly take on the role of Scribe for the Augurs Erran, Fessi, and Kol. Willingly entered a Tributary in order to restore the Boundary.

Ath (ATH [rhymes with *math*]), The/Nethgalla (neth-GULL-uh): A creature of legend, known for her ability to take the form of others. Largely responsible for the rebellion that overthrew the Augurs a generation ago.

Breshada (bresh-AH-duh): A Hunter who mysteriously saved Davian and Wirr from two other Hunters in Talmiel. Wielded Whisper, one of the Named swords. Killed and her identity stolen by Nethgalla.

Caeden (CAY-den)/Tal'kamar (TAL-cam-are): Main character. After waking with no memories in Desriel, Caeden eventually discovered that he had deliberately erased them, primarily in order to fulfil Andrael's bargain with the Lyth and obtain the sword Licanius. After traveling to the Wells of Mor Aruil and meeting with Asar Shenelac, he remembers that he once called himself Aarkein Devaed.

Calder (KAL-der): A general in the Andarran army.

Ched (CHED): The leader of the scavenger team in Zvaelar to which Davian belongs.

Celise (sell-EESE): the current Scribe for the Augurs in Ilin Illan.

Cyr (SEAR): One of the Venerate. Assisted Aarkein Devaed in the destruction of the city of Silence.

Dav (DAV [rhymes with *have*])/Davian (DAY-vee-en [rhymes with *avian*]): Main character. Grew up an orphan in the Gifted school at Caladel, where he became childhood friends with Asha and Wirr. An Augur.

Deldri Andras (DELL-dree AN-drass): Younger sister of Wirr, daughter of Elocien and Geladra.

Deonidius (dee-on-ID-ee-us): One of the sha'teth.

Dezia Shainwiere (DET-zee-uh SHAYN-weer): Ward of the king, sister to Aelric. Talented archer whose romantic relationship with Wirr must be kept secret, due to her lack of an official title. Departed south to find her brother.

Diara (dee-ARE-ah)/Diarys (dee-ARE-iss): One of the Venerate.

Diriana Traleth (deer-ee-AHN-a trah-LETH): Scribe to the last generation of Augurs before the rebellion. Leaked information regarding the
Augurs' visions to Lyrus Dain. Now deceased.

Dras Lothlar (drass LOTH-lar): The former Representative for Tol Shen.
Suspected by Taeris and Laiman to have had a hand in the king's
strange illness during the attack by the Blind.

Driscin Throll (DRISS-kin THROLL): An Elder at Tol Shen. Mentor to
Ishelle. Formerly part of the sig'nari, and attempting to locate and
train the newest generation of Augurs.

El (ELL): The benevolent deity of the Old Religion.

Elliavia (ell-ee-AH-vee-uh)/**Ell** (ELL): The murdered wife of Tal'kamar. Her
name is sometimes shortened to Ell, pronounced the same as El.

Elocien Andras (el-OH-see-en AN-drass): The former duke and Northwarden.
Father to Wirr and Deldri, husband to Geladra, brother to King Andras.
Killed by an Echo during the battle for Ilin Illan against the Blind.

Erran (EH-rin [sounds like "Erin"]): An Augur who worked in secret at the
palace for Elocien Andras. Later revealed to have been Controlling
Elocien for the past two years.

Esdin (EZ-din): The Shalis from whom the dar'gaithin were created.

Ethemiel (eh-THEEM-ee-el): The name given to Davian by Gassandrid for
his fight in the Arena. Known in Ilshan Gathdel Teth as "destroyer of
false idols."

Fessi (FESS-ee [rhymes with *messy*])/**Fessiricia** (fess-eh-REE-sha): An Augur
who worked in secret at the palace for Elocien Andras, alongside Erran
and Kol. Panicked and fled after she and Davian were captured and
imprisoned in Talan Gol.

Garadis ru Dagen (GA-ruh-diss ["GA" as in *gash*] rue DAY-gen): The leader
of the Lyth. Struck a deal with Andrael in which he agreed that the
Lyth would guard the sword Licanius in exchange for the promise of
eventual freedom from Res Kartha.

Gassandrid (gass-AN-drid)/**Gasharrid** (gash-AR-id): Considered the founder
of the Venerate. The first to reveal to Tal'kamar the inevitability of the
future, and suggest to him the reasons behind it.

Geladra Andras (gell-ADD-ra AN-drass): Wirr and Deldri's mother. Elocien's widow. A former Administrator who despises the Gifted. Now
deceased.

Gellen (GELL-en): The "Voice of the Protector" in Ilshan Gathdel Teth.

Ilseth Tenvar (ILL-seth TEN-var): Gifted who deceives Davian into leaving
the school at Caladel and turns Asha into a Shadow. Now catatonic
after Davian forcibly broke into his Lockbox while trying to Read him.

Isaire (iss-SAIR): Davian's guard prior to fighting in the Arena.

Ishelle (ish-ELL [rhymes with *Michelle*]): An Augur originally met by Davian
on the road to Ilin Illan prior to the Blind's attack on the city. Has been

under the tutelage of Elder Driscin Throll, with the full knowledge of Tol Shen's Council, for the past two years.

Isiliar (iss-ILL-ee-are): One of the Venerate. Driven insane after she was imprisoned in a Tributary by Tal'kamar. Now deceased.

Isstharis (iss-THAR-iss): A dar'gaithin from Zvaelar.

Ithar (EETH-are): An Adminstrator with prior military experience.

Jakarris Si'Irthidian (jah-KARR-iss see-er-THID-ee-an)/Scyner (SIGH-ner): An Augur from before the rebellion, now a Shadow. Killed the other twelve Augurs at the beginning of the rebellion twenty years ago. More recently posed as the Shadraehin to the Shadows in the Sanctuary. Killed Kol after attempting to blackmail him, Fessi, and Erran into helping him. Killed Rohin and stole the amulet that prevents an Augur from using kan.

Karaliene Andras (KA-rah-leen ["KA" as in *carry*] AN-drass): Princess of Andarra. Daughter of King Andras, cousin of Wirr and Deldri.

Kevran Andras (KEV-ran AN-drass): King of Andarra. Brother of Elocien, father of Karaliene, uncle of Wirr and Deldri.

Kol (COLE [rhymes with *pole*]): An Augur who worked in secret at the palace for Elocien Andras, alongside Erran and Fessi. Killed by Scyner.

Laiman Kardai (LAY-men CAR-dye)/Thell Taranor (thell TAR-ah-nore): Chief adviser to King Andras. Former Gifted who was responsible for the creation of the sha'teth. Along with Taeris and Nihim, was a memory proxy for Jakarris.

Lyrus Dain (LIE-russ DANE): An Elder at Tol Shen and the leader of the Council there. Killed by Rohin.

Malshash (MAL-shash): The name Tal'kamar gave to Davian during Davian's training in Deilannis.

Maresh (MA-resh): Prisoner in Zvaelar whose team attempts to extort scavenged metal from other teams.

Marut Jha Talkanor (MAHR-ut JAH TAL-can-or): The Desrielite God of Balance.

Mash'aan (mahsh-AHN): The leader of the initial attack on Ilin Illan by the Blind. Now deceased.

Meldier (MELL-deer): One of the Venerate. Imprisoned in a Tributary by Tal'kamar.

Metaniel (meh-TAN-yel): The swordsman Davian faces during his fight in the Arena.

Nashrel Eilinar (NASH-rell EYE-lin-are): Head of the Council for Tol Athian.

Nethgalla (neth-GULL-uh): See *Ath*.

Niha (NIGH-ah): Gifted. Assisting Tal'kamar in Zvaelar.

Nihim Sethi (NIGH-im SETH-eye): The priest who accompanied Taeris, Davian, and Wirr to Deilannis. Killed by Orkoth.

Olin (OLE-in): Head Elder at the school in Caladel. Now deceased.

Ordan (ORE-dan): The Shalis who trained Tal'kamar to use Essence.

Orkoth (ORE-koth): The creature from Deilannis that slew Nihim. Has been instructed not to harm Davian.

Raeleth (RAY-leth): A member of the scavenging team in Zvaelar to which Davian belongs. Infected by Dark.

Rohin (ROE-in): An Augur who arrived at Tol Shen after the Augur Amnesty was announced, Controlled everyone there using his innate ability, and was subsequently subdued with an amulet from the Tol Shen vault. Now deceased.

Rethgar Tel'An (RETH-gar tell-AN): The first Gifted whom Thell Taranor attempted to turn into a sha'teth.

Sarrin (SAH-rin): Leader of the Shalis.

Scyner (SIGH-ner): See *Jakarris si'Irthidian*.

Sekariel (seh-KAR-ee-el): One of the sha'teth.

Shadat (SHAD-at): The false name Davian uses in Zvaelar.

Shadraehin (SHAH-druh-eh-heen): The leader of the "rebel" Shadows who once lived in the Sanctuary and are now on the hidden island to the north that houses the Tributary. Originally thought to be Scyner, later revealed to be Nethgalla.

Shammaeloth (shah-MAY-loth): The malevolent deity of the Old Religion.

Shana (SHAH-na): A Shadow, originally from the Sanctuary, who in the absence of the Shadraehin now effectively leads the group of Shadows living near the Tributary.

Tae'shadon (TAY-shah-don): See *Asar Shenelac*.

Taeris Sarr (TAY-riss SARR): A Gifted. Face heavily scarred. Currently the Representative for Tol Athian despite a contentious relationship with Tol Athian's Council. Accompanied Caeden, Davian, and Wirr during their escape from Desriel via Deilannis. Present three years ago at Caladel when Davian, as a child, was attacked. Has been researching the degradation of the Boundary for many years.

Tal'kamar Deshrel (TAL-cam-are DESH-rel): See *Caeden*.

Talean (TAY-lee-en): The Administrator for the school at Caladel. Now deceased.

Tarav (TAH-rav): The leader of Tol Shen before the rebellion. Murdered by Lyrus Dain.

Thell Taranor (thell TAR-ah-nore): See *Laiman Kardai*.

Theshesseth (THESH-ess-eth): A dar'gaithin.

Torin Wirrander Andras (TORE-en weer-AN-der AN-drass): See *Wirr*.

Tysis (TIE-sis): One of the Venerate. Killed by Andrael during the destruction of the city of Silence.

Unguin (UN-gew-in): The swordmaster at the palace in Ilin Illan and Aelric's former mentor.

Vardin Shal (VAR-din SHALL): The leader of the Loyalist forces during the rebellion to overthrow the Augurs.

Vhalire (vah-LEER): One of the sha'teth. Killed by Asha with the sword Knowing.

Vis (VISS): A general in the Andarran army.

Wereth (WHERE-eth)/Werek (WHERE-ek): One of the Venerate. Creator of the Siphon. Now deceased.

Wirr (WEER [rhymes with *beer*])/Torin Wirrander Andras (TORE-en weer-AN-der AN-drass): Main character. Gifted. Northwarden. Prince of Andarra. Brother of Deldri, son of Geladra and Elocien, cousin to Karaliene, nephew to Kevran. Secretly sent to the Gifted school in Caladel by his father, where he met and became friends with Davian and Asha. Due to his lineage and ability to use Essence, he was able to change the Tenets by himself.

Glossary

Absorption endpoint: A common element of kan machinery that absorbs Essence.

Administration: An Andarran organization dedicated to upholding the terms of the Treaty with the Gifted. Led by the Northwarden, members are bound to the Tenets via Oathstones, by which they receive a red Administrator's Mark on their forearm.

Administrator: A member of Administration.

Adviser: A Vessel in the Great Library in Deilannis, used to locate texts about specific subjects.

al'goriat (al-GORE-ee-at): One of the five types of Banes led by Aarkein Devaed during his invasion of Andarra.

Alkathronen (al-KATH-ron-en): The last city of the Builders. Also connects each of the Builders' various wonders via portals.

Aloia Elena (al-OY-ah EL-en-ah): Also known as the Serpent's Head. Where the Shalis keep their Forges of Rebirth.

Andarra (an-DARR-uh): The country in which Davian, Wirr, and Asha reside. Originally spanned the entire continent north of the Menaath Mountains before Devaed's invasion two thousand years ago. Now bordered by Talan Gol to the north and Desriel and Narut to the west.

Arbiterium (arr-bit-EER-ee-um): A structure in Deilannis in which the Jha'vett is housed.

Assembly: The Andarran legislature.

Augur (AWE-ger): A person who has the ability to use kan to Read and Control minds, manipulate time, and see into an inevitable future.

Augur Amnesty: An amnesty passed by the Assembly in response to the attack by the Blind, removing the death penalty for any Augurs who are willing to undertake the task of sealing the Boundary.

Banes: In Andarran legend, warriors led by Aarkein Devaed during his invasion that were mixtures of men and animals, and all but impossible to kill.

Blades, five: See *Named swords.*

bleeder: A derogatory term used by the Andarran populace to refer to the Gifted.

Blind: The invasion force from beyond the Boundary that attacked Ilin Illan. Known for their unusual helmets, which completely cover their eyes.

Boundary: The enormous wall of Essence to the north of Andarra, which encapsulates all of Talan Gol.

Builders: The mysterious race that constructed Ilin Illan, Alkathronen, and many other wonders.

Breach: The massive chasm that splits Zvaelar in two.

Breachlight: A piece of glowing stone hewn from the Breach in Zvaelar.

Caer Lyordas (care lee-OR-das): Castle from Caeden's homeland.

Caladel (CAL-ah-dell): Town on the southwest coast of Andarra where Davian grew up. Formerly home to one of the Gifted schools run by Tol Athian.

Conduit: The enormous cylinder of constantly flowing Essence in the Sanctuary.

Cyrariel (sear-AIR-ee-el): See *Conduit.*

Cyrarium (sear-AIR-ee-um): A massive storage container for Essence.

Cyrrings (SEAR-rings): Vessels created by Cyr to enable Control of another person.

dar'gaithin (dar-GAY-thun): One of the five types of Banes led by Aarkein Devaed during his invasion of Andarra.

Dareci (DA-reh-kai): The enormous capital of the Darecian Empire. Destroyed by Aarkein Devaed. Now known as the Plains of Decay.

Darecian (dah-REE-see-en): Refers to the long-vanished race that came to Andarra a thousand years prior to Devaed's attack. Extraordinarily advanced and powerful Gifted.

Daren Tel (DAH-ren TELL): The area in which the Tel'Andras family estate is located.

Dark: A mysterious liquid-like substance found only in Zvaelar, usually deadly to the touch.

Darklands/Markaathan (mar-KAH-thahn): The realm beyond the rift in Deilannis, from which kan is drawn.

darkstone: The kan-absorbing black rock found in Ilshan Gathdel Teth.

Deilannis (dye-LAN-iss): Long-abandoned, mist-covered Darecian city straddling the border of Andarra, Desriel, and Narut.

Desriel (DES-ree-el): Hostile country to the west of Andarra. Governed by a theocracy that believes Essence is not for mortal use.

Devliss (DEV-liss): The river that separates Andarra and Desriel.

Disruption shield: A complicated shield of kan designed to protect an Augur from both physical and mental attack by other Augurs.

dok'en (dock-EN): A device used to create the illusion of a physical area within someone's mind, which can then also be accessed by others.

Door of Iladriel (ih-LAD-ree-uhl): Archway in Deilannis, the official entrance to the Inner City.

Echo: A being originating from the Darklands that uses a dead person's body and memories.

eletai (ELL-eh-tie): One of the five types of Banes led by Aarkein Devaed during his invasion of Andarra.

endpoints: Common mechanisms within kan machinery that serve pre-defined purposes.

Eryth Mmorg (EHR-ith MAWG): Also known as the Waters of Renewal. Located in Talan Gol.

escherii (ESH-er-eye): A sha'teth whose host remains self-aware, willingly sharing their body. Able to use a connection to the Forge to access kan, making them significantly more powerful than other sha'teth.

Essence: Energy, the life force of all things. Used by both the Gifted and Augurs.

Fate: See *Licanius*.

Fedris Idri (FED-riss ID-ree): The sole pass into Ilin Illan. Cut from the heart of the mountain Ilin Tora by the Builders, with three defensive walls known as the Shields.

Finder: A Vessel that detects the use of Essence.

gaa'vesh (gah-VESH): The derogatory Desrielite word used to describe the Gifted.

Gate: A construct of kan and Essence that allows instantaneous travel between two physically distant points.

Gifted: People who have the ability to wield Essence, their own life force.

Gil'shar (gill-SHAR): The governing body that controls all aspects of life in Desriel. Members are considered to have been appointed by divine selection.

heatstone: A type of Vessel in Alkathronen that provides warmth.

Ilin Illan (ill-INN ill-AHN): Capital of Andarra. Accessible only via the difficult-to-navigate Naminar River or through Fedris Idri.

Ilshan Gathdel Teth (ILL-shahn GATH-del TETH): A city in Talan Gol. Home to the remaining Venerate.

Ilshan Tereth Kal (ILL-shahn TEAR-eth KAL): The Shalis's fortress, now destroyed.

ilshara (ill-SHAH-rah): A type of shield, used to protect individuals against being drained of Essence when working with a Cyrarium. Thanks to similarities in their design, the term is now commonly used by the Venerate and others to refer to the Boundary.

Initiation endpoint: A common element of kan machinery that allows a device to be triggered.

Ishai (ISH-eye): Nesk's capital.

Ironsail: A type of ship used by the Darecians.

Jha'vett (jah-VET): Device in the center of Deilannis that draws Essence from every part of the city. Designed by the Darecians to allow time travel.

kan (KAHN): The power used by the Augurs. Drawn from the Darklands.

Knowing: One of the five Named swords. Stored by Tal'kamar in the Tributary with Isiliar. Used, and subsequently hidden, by Asha in the catacombs beneath Ilin Illan.

Lantarche (lan-TAR-ka): The massive river that flows around Deilannis and forms much of the border between Andarra and Desriel.

Licanius (lie-CAN-ee-us): One of the five Named swords, also known as Fate. The only weapon that can kill one of the Venerate.

Lockroom: A room that is specially shielded to prevent all kinds of eavesdropping, even by Gifted or Augurs.

Lyth (LITH [rhymes with *myth*]): Powerful beings composed almost entirely of Essence. Originally the High Darecians in Deilannis. Freed from Res Kartha by Caeden, but now tied to the Siphon.

Mark: A symbol—a man, woman, and child enclosed in a circle—that signifies being bound by the Tenets. For the Gifted, this symbol appears in black on their left forearm when they first use Essence. For Administrators, it appears in red on their right forearm when they are bound to the Tenets using an Oathstone.

Mor Aruil (more ah-RUE-ell): A network of underground tunnels, once used by the Darecians as conduits to draw Essence to the surface. Inaccessible except via a Gate.

Named swords: The five swords created by Andrael in his attempts to find a way to kill members of the Venerate. Also known as the five Blades in Desrielite religion. Individually the swords are known as Whisper, Thief, Knowing, Sight, and Fate.

Narut (NAH-rut): Small country to the north of Desriel and northwest of Andarra.

Nesk (NESK [rhymes with *desk*]): Hostile country to the south of Andarra.

Northwarden: The head of Administration. An inherited position, currently held by Wirr.

Oathstones: Vessels used by Administration to bind new Administrators to the Tenets.

Portal Box: The small bronze cube that originally led Davian to Caeden. Created by the Lyth, it enables a portal to be opened to any of six preset destinations—one for each face of the cube.

Prefects: See *sig'nari*.

Prythe (PRITHE [rhymes with *tithe*]): City in the south of Andarra near Tol Shen.

Res Kartha (rez CAR-thuh): The home of the Lyth. The only place in which they can currently survive, due to their susceptibility to kan.

Scribe: The person responsible for reading through each Augur's visions of the future, then determining if there are any that corroborate each other.

sha'teth (shah-TETH): Creatures originally used by Tol Athian to hunt down and kill Gifted criminals. No longer under the Tol's control. Created by Thell Taranor, with help from Taeris Sarr.

Shackle: A Vessel that, when worn by a Gifted, prevents them from using Essence.

Shadow: A Gifted who has been stripped of their ability to use Essence. Signified by dark veins marring the face.

Shalis (SHALL-iss): Serpentine race that trained Caeden to use Essence. Now extinct.

shar'kath (shar-KATH): One of the five types of Banes led by Aarkein Devaed during his invasion of Andarra.

sig'nari (sig-NAR-ee): The name given to the Gifted who served directly under the Augurs before the rebellion. Also known as Prefects.

Sight: One of the five Named swords.

Talmiel (TAL-me-el): Town on the Andarran side of the bridge that crosses the Devliss River. Talmiel's bridge is the only official inland crossing between Andarra and Desriel.

tek'ryl (TEK-rill): One of the five types of Banes led by Aarkein Devaed during his invasion of Andarra.

Tel'Tarthen Prison (tel-TARTH-in): The primary prison of Ilshan Gathdel Teth.

Telesthaesia (tel-es-THAY-see-ah): The Essence-absorbing armor worn by the Blind. Telesthaesia helmets completely block the wearer's vision.

terogesh (TEHR-oh-gesh): A Desrielite Seeker's mentor.

Thief: One of the five Named swords.

Thrindar (THRIN-dar): Capital of Desriel.

Time endpoint: An element of a kan-powered device that deals with the manipulation of time.

Tol Athian (toll ATH-ee-en): One of the two remaining major outposts of the Gifted. Located in Ilin Illan.

Tol Shen (toll SHEN [rhymes with *pen*]): One of the two remaining major outposts of the Gifted. Located next to the city of Prythe.

Trace: A sample of a person's Essence, potentially allowing them to be tracked.

Treaty: The agreement signed between the besieged Gifted and the rebellion fifteen years ago, resulting in the end of the war but the submission of the Gifted to the Tenets.

Tributary: A device designed to hold one of the Venerate. It uses needles to cause persistent injuries to its occupant's body in order to generate a constant and uninterruptable flow of Essence.

Venerate: An immortal group of Augurs, originally brought together by Gassandrid with the aim of freeing the world from fate.

Vessel: A device that stores and/or uses Essence for a particular purpose.

Wells: see *Mor Aruil*.

Whisper: One of the five Named swords.

Zvael (zeh-VAY-el): The name of the people from whom Gassandrid is descended.

Zvaelar (zeh-VAY-lar): The desert capital that was once Gassandrid's home.